THE PIONEERS

Novels of the American Frontier

THE PIONEERS

Novels of the
American Frontier

Selected and condensed by the editors of
Reader's Digest Condensed Books

The Reader's Digest Association, Inc.
Pleasantville, New York
Cape Town, Hong Kong, London, Montreal, Sydney

READER'S DIGEST CONDENSED BOOKS

Editor-in-Chief: Barbara J. Morgan
Executive Editor: Tanis H. Erdmann

Senior Managing Editor: Marjorie Palmer
Managing Editors: Jean E. Aptakin, Anne H. Atwater,
Thomas Froncek
Senior Staff Editors: Angela H. Plowden-Wardlaw,
Virginia Rice (Rights), Ray Sipherd
Senior Editors: M. Tracy Brigden, Linn Carl,
Joseph P. McGrath, James J. Menick, Margery D. Thorndike
Associate Editors: Thomas S. Clemmons, Emily Easton, Catharine L. Edmonds,
Alice Jones-Miller, Maureen A. Mackey
Senior Copy Editors: Claire A. Bedolis, Jeane Garment, Jane F. Neighbors
Senior Associate Copy Editors: Maxine Bartow, Rosalind H. Campbell, Jean S. Friedman
Associate Copy Editors: Ainslie Gilligan, Jeanette Gingold, Marilyn J. Knowlton
Art Director: William Gregory
Executive Art Editors: Soren Noring, Angelo Perrone
Associate Art Editors, Research: George Calas, Jr., Katherine Kelleher

CB PROJECTS
Executive Editor: Herbert H. Lieberman
Senior Editors: Dana Adkins, Catherine T. Brown, John R. Roberson

CB INTERNATIONAL EDITIONS
Executive Editor: Francis Schell
Senior Editor: Gary Q. Arpin
Associate Editors: Eva C. Jaunzems, Antonius L. Koster

The credits and acknowledgments that appear on page 639
are hereby made a part of this copyright page.

Library of Congress Cataloging in Publication Data
Main entry under title: The Pioneers: novels of the American frontier
Contents: Young pioneers/by Rose Wilder Lane — Miss Morissa/by Mari Sandoz —
Giants in the earth/by O. E. Rölvaag — [etc.]
1. Frontier and pioneer life — Fiction. 2. Western stories. 3. American
fiction — 20th century. I. Reader's digest condensed books.
PS648.F74P5 1988   813'.0874;08   85-23236
ISBN 0-89577-229-9

Printed in the United States of America

CONTENTS

YOUNG PIONEERS

A CONDENSATION OF THE NOVEL BY

Rose Wilder Lane

ILLUSTRATED BY DENNIS LYALL

The pioneers of the American West lived
out one of the great stories of all time—a story
that has attracted scores of writers ever since.
Young Pioneers tells how David, 18,
and Molly, 16, headed west in the 1870s to the
plentiful land of the Dakota Territory.
How they staked a claim to a choice "quarter
section"—a quarter of a square mile of prairie. And
how that land put all their strength,
determination and love to terrible tests.

Rose Wilder Lane had pioneering in her blood.
Her own family's experiences formed the
basis for her novels, as well as for the
beloved *Little House on the Prairie* series
of her mother, Laura Ingalls Wilder.

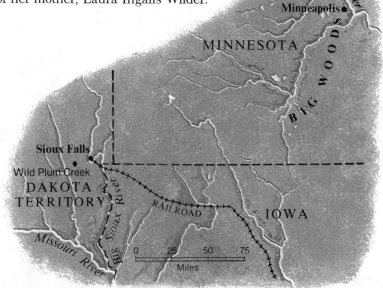

Chapter 1

WHILE THEY WERE children playing together, they said they would be married as soon as they were old enough, and when they were old enough they married. David liked to remind her that he had never really asked her to marry him; he liked to see her smile sedately, as she always smiled at his teasing.

She was a quiet person. When she was a little girl she was often asked if the cat had got her tongue. Even with David she had a way of saying nothing in words. Her eyes, which could not lie, told what she felt. Before she smiled, a shadowy dimple quivered in one cheek. Her face was quiet under smooth wings of hair, and all her movements were gentle and deft. In her heart she never quite lost the wonder that she, so quiet and shy, had won such a man as David. He was laughing and bold, a daring hunter, a dancer, fiddler and fighter.

She thought of him always as he was on summer Sunday afternoons when his family was spending the day with hers. Perhaps some other neighbors were there too.

The old men sat on the bench against the shady side of the log house, talking slowly, with chuckles and long pauses. Children ran about, climbing the rail fence, raiding the wild blackberry thickets. The babies slept on a faded quilt in the shade of the oak, and near them the women rested on benches brought from the house. Everything in the clearing was drowsy till David sat down on a stump and tuned his fiddle.

His favorite hymn always lifted him to his feet. His chin left the fiddle; he shook back his thick brown hair. His voice rang out above all the

9

other voices; it led the defiant, triumphant song that surged across the stumpy fields and echoed into the vast, unconquered forest:

> *"Let the hurricane roar!*
> *It will the sooner be o'er!*
> *We'll weather the blast, and land at last,*
> *On Canaan's happy shore!"*

Many settlers had come to the settlement in the Big Woods while David and Molly were growing up. When they married there was little good land left. Farther west, the country was not yet settled and the land was said to be rich and level, and without forests. So they went west.

David was not yet nineteen. His labor belonged to his father until he was twenty-one. But his father gave him his time—a gift of more than two years. To cap this, for good measure, he gave David the team and wagon he would have earned by working till he was twenty-one.

Molly's parents gave her two blankets, two wild-goose-feather pillows, a cooking pot and pan and skillet. They gave her a ham, two molds of maple sugar, and Tennyson's *Poems* beautifully bound in green and gilt. She had the patchwork quilts she had pieced. David had his fiddle and his gun. Their families together sent East to buy them a Bible, and the circuit rider wrote their marriage certificate on the page included for it. So, well provided for, they set out to the West.

At first Molly was sad because she was leaving her family forever. But her memories soon ceased to hurt her, in her happiness with David.

They could never decide which was best—the fresh mornings, when the first rays of the sun found David whistling while he hitched up the team; or the varied days of traveling west on unknown roads; or the evenings by the camp fires, talking about how they would file a claim for land, and about the home they would have.

Every day David shot game. When they needed flour and tea and sugar, they camped at some settlement while he worked for supplies. Whenever he had money, he brought her a present: once a little box covered with tiny shells, and once fifteen yards of calico for a dress she didn't really need. She scolded him, for she was thrifty, but she never cured him of bringing her presents. He liked to see the shining in her eyes.

Late that summer they reached the western prairie. They were going to have a baby, and David wanted to earn money. The homestead would have to wait, he said. The railroad was being pushed west. Scores of men and teams were working on the long embankment, raising a low smoke of dust under the enormous sky, and David joined them.

The railroad camp was small—a bunkhouse, cookhouse, the company store and a shanty for the contractor's family. David built a sod shanty to live in. He cut the strips of tough earth, and Molly helped him lay up the walls and stretch the canvas wagon top over them. A thatch of prairie grass kept out the heat of the sun. In two days the house was done.

David was hauling supplies to a new camp, twenty miles west. Every second night he was away from her, and she was lonely. On such nights she lay awake a long time. A distant wolf howled. A coyote prowled softly around the shanty. The company store was noisy with the rough voices of men drinking and gambling. A lonely voice went by, singing:

> *"I've been working on the railroad,*
> *All the livelong day. . . ."*

David had given her a gun and she was never afraid. But the loneliness was hard to endure.

Her hands and face were brown as an Indian's from the prairie sun. When she unpinned her collar, it was odd to see the brown face on the milk-white neck. David teased her. "Your baby's going to be a papoose!"

In September the winds were edged with cold, and all day long the gray sky resounded to the signal calls of wild birds flying south. The construction camps were closing; there would be no more work till next year. But David had earned money enough for winter supplies and for tools and seed, and he had found a homestead. His blue eyes sparkled when he told Molly. There was already a dugout and barn, and fifty acres of the sod were broken. Another man had taken the land and done all that work, yet he was giving up, he was going back East. He said he could not stand another winter of loneliness.

David asked, "Would it be too lonesome for you, Molly? There wouldn't be another human being within forty miles."

"You wouldn't have to go away?"

"No, I'd be there, but—"

"No, I won't be lonesome," she said.

In the middle of the night David started the thirty miles to the Land Office, to get that homestead before anyone else. He was the head of a family, so he need not wait till he was twenty-one to file a claim. Molly listened to the jolting of his wagon, going away in the dark.

Three days went by. The sun had set and the sky was a pale, cold yellow when Molly heard the rattle of the wagon, far away. David was jubilantly singing. She knew he had the papers.

In the chill wind Molly helped David pack supplies and take the canvas wagon top from the sod shanty. They slept in the wagon that night, and next morning David hitched up the horses and they started west in the dark.

When the sunshine came across the prairie, they were both light-hearted. All day the horizon maintained its unvarying circle around them. On the immense plain there was nothing but miles of wild grass blowing in the wind. Twice David pointed out a buffalo wallow, and once they saw a wolf loping by. In the afternoon they passed a solitary cotton-wood, a landmark for all that country, and David drove out of his way to get some seeds from it.

Just before sunset they drove by a sod barn. Suddenly the level-looking prairie split apart; the horses stopped at the edge of a chasm.

"Here we are!" David said.

Molly's eyes were round. He helped her down from the wagon, and together they stood looking at water in the creek bed below. David laughed aloud in joy. He had kept this creek a secret, to surprise her. They would not have to dig a well.

"I thought we'd name it Wild Plum Creek," David said. Two little wild plum trees, bare of leaves and distorted by the winds, stood by the water. "They're alive," he said. "They'll blossom in the spring."

He could hardly wait to show her the dugout. It was under their feet. The prairie sod was smooth over it and the grass hid the top of the stove-pipe. A path went slanting down the steep creek bank to the doorway.

The ledge of earth before the door was narrow and could easily be kept clear of snow. The door opened into a room large enough to hold all their supplies. It was clean and neat. The floor was pounded smooth and hard. There was a bunk, a table, a bench and an iron cookstove. David had bought them from the man who abandoned the place. Sunshine came through the doorway, which looked across the low western bank of the creek to the endless prairie and the sky. There was even a small window hole covered with oiled paper; it would let in daylight during the winters.

"Like it?" David asked unnecessarily.

"Yes," she said. He smiled deep into her eyes and almost crushed her in his joyous hug.

Nothing could have been more cozy for wintertime, cooler in the summers. And all this comfort, the good sod barn, the quarter section of treeless land, the creek, the plum trees—all this was theirs! There was even a bit of a slough, or bog, where the creek spread and vanished in the soil, keeping it damp through the summer drought. The slough grass would provide hay for the horses and hay to twist into firm sticks to burn in the cookstove. They need only live here and work the land, and in five years they would have the title.

Everything was snug before the blizzards came. The horses were warm in the barn, with slough hay and oats to feed them till spring. David had cut all the slough grass and the stacks stood high beside the barn.

On clear days David went out with his gun and came back with meat and furs. Molly scrubbed and baked and ironed and cooked. When the snows finally came shrieking from the northwest, David groped his way only to the barn and back. He had stretched a rope to the barn door, so he would not lose his way in the blinding storms, but Molly was uneasy until he came back safe.

Yet those days were best of all. David cleaned his gun, oiled his boots, twisted hay for the fire. From two packing boxes he made a cradle. On the headboard he carved two birds and a nest. Molly saved her mending and sewing for these stormy days. She worked quietly, smiling to herself. The lamplight was cheerful, the stove gave out its heat and the good smell of cooking. Then David took his fiddle from its box; he played and sang, keeping time with a patting foot. Those were festive days.

On Sundays they did not work, and David played only hymns. It was splendid to see and hear him, roaring out his favorite to the wind that howled in the stovepipe. Then Molly read to him. She read the Bible, and she read Tennyson. That winter she read the green-and-gilt book from cover to cover.

February was clear; the cold was so intense that the air seemed glittering ice, and the silent world was buried in snow. Molly was heavy now, and clumsy, and her breath was short. Though the weather was good for hunting, David went only to the barn and back; he would not leave her long alone.

Molly tried to remember all she had heard about childbirth; it was very little. She did not let David guess how much she wanted her mother.

The pain began early one afternoon. She had set a batch of bread out to rise; she moved the pan nearer the stove so that the dough would rise more quickly. David must have food while she was unable to cook. He was twisting hay for fuel, whistling. She was able to knead the bread and mold it into loaves before he saw her face.

She had known the pain would be bad and was resolved to make no outcry. That night was very long. She lay in the bunk and smiled at David whenever she could. Desperately she clung to him, glad and a little proud that she had not screamed. David wiped the sweat from her face. Several times she asked in surprise, "Isn't it morning yet?"

Then everything became confused. Daylight and darkness were mixed. She heard shrieks and knew they were hers; she could not stop them. Even David was gone. There was nothing anywhere but unbearable agony. She herself was ebbing, going—a last little atom fighting, failing. . . .

The baby was born in the morning of the second day.

For a long time she lay under eyelids too heavy to lift. She lifted them at last and saw David's face. Tears came into her eyes. Her voice had no sound. He bent lower, and she whispered, "How—is—the—papoose?"

She wanted to make him smile. When he cried, she thought the baby was dead. The tears ran from her eyes. But David sobbed, "He's all right. Oh, Molly, Molly—"

The baby had been born on her seventeenth birthday, like a present. They named him David John. He was a fat, healthy baby, and almost never cried. David teased him, tickled him, rumpled and tossed him. Molly washed his clothes every day and bathed him in snow water heated on the stove. When she sat holding him while he nursed, her happiness almost frightened her; it seemed too great to keep.

The snows went out with a rush that spring; the creek roared to the door ledge. Then overnight the prairies were gay with wild flowers. The air was scented with violets, the plum trees bloomed. All day long the door stood open, and in the afternoons Molly took the baby and walked to the field where David was plowing.

The whole land was exuberant with change and promise. Again the sky was clamorous with wild geese and ducks, but now they did not stay to feed in the sloughs, for they saw the covered wagons and heard hammers and saws. That year the railroad tracks would be laid within ten miles of the homestead. At the newest town site frame buildings were going up. Everywhere men were taking homesteads. Six miles, four miles, three miles away, there were dots of sod shanties on the prairie. Molly and David were glad they had come first and got the best homestead. Now David sowed the fifty acres with wheat. They would have the first wheat in that country.

South of the town site a man was killed by claim jumpers who had taken his homestead while he was wintering in the East. The territory was not yet organized; there was no law. A posse pursued the claim jumpers, but they fled westward and got away.

One morning in May, when the wheat field was green and David was planting potatoes in newly broken sod, a covered wagon drawn by oxen came slowly nearer across the prairie. That evening David showed Molly a camp fire half a mile away, just beyond the head of their creek, and next morning the strangers were building a sod shanty.

"We're going to have neighbors," David said, pleased.

He walked the half mile to welcome the newcomers. He came back bringing disappointment; they could hardly speak English. They were Swedes, and their name was Svenson.

At noontime a few weeks later, Mr. Svenson appeared in the doorway. David sprang up and asked him in, but he shook his head. He stood on the threshold, a big man in dusty clothes with calloused, helpless hands and a sorrowful, broad face. He stretched out his arm to the vast prairie and held up two fingers; one, he showed them, was himself, the other he left standing up alone. His wife. He held out his hands to Molly imploringly. His wife was lonely.

That afternoon Molly put on her best dress and bonnet, and taking the baby in her arms, she walked across the prairie. It was an adventure to go so far alone. There was no sound but the sound of the wind in the wild grasses. Beyond the Svensons' sod shanty a wisp of dust followed Mr. Svenson along a furrow. With the slow ox team, he was breaking sod.

Molly stood by the blanket that covered the shanty's doorway and shyly called, "Mrs. Svenson?"

A yellow-haired woman, no older than Molly, lifted the blanket and cried out. Trembling with excitement, she led Molly by the hand into the shanty. The only chair was the seat taken from the wagon. Mrs. Svenson, eagerly smiling and gesturing, urged Molly to sit upon it. Then, she put coffee and water in a pot and to Molly's surprise, hurried out to set it over a fire in the open air. She had no stove.

The canvas wagon top lay folded on the floor, and on it a fat feather bed was neatly made up with fat pillows and counterpane. Barrels and boxes were neatly arranged in a corner. There were two large painted chests, and on the sod wall hung a picture in a gold frame of a cliff jutting into the sea.

Mrs. Svenson opened the chests and showed Molly her Swedish Bible and a Swedish-American grammar. She spread out a strange, outlandish dress, which Molly knew was her wedding dress because she pointed to her ring. She covered one of the boxes with an embroidered cloth and set on it two cups and saucers, then brought in the coffee. Molly had never imagined such delicately thin cups. Mrs. Svenson was anxious to please, and little pleading looks darted from her eyes between her smiles.

"Cup and saucer," Molly said, pointing. Mrs. Svenson repeated, "Cup—and—" She laughed, shaking her head. Her blue eyes squeezed to twinkles and her strong white teeth showed. Molly liked her.

"Saucer," Molly said. "Saucer," Mrs. Svenson said eagerly. Then she began pointing to other things. It was like a game. They were having a good time, laughing together.

"Ba-bee," Mrs. Svenson repeated many times, and Molly let her hold him. He laughed and kicked in her arms; he seemed to like her too.

When Molly was leaving, Mrs. Svenson took her out by the sod barn to show her two hives of bees. Molly taught her "bees," and "honey," and went home excited by so many things to tell David.

Sometimes twice a week, after that, Molly and Mrs. Svenson spent an afternoon together. They were company for each other. There were only men in the other sod shanties, and the town site was ten miles away. The horses worked too hard in the fields to be driven for pleasure.

There was really nothing more to wish for. The crops were thriving; there would be potatoes, turnips, carrots and flour for next winter, and money enough for other supplies. Next year, if all went well, they would have a cow. The year after that, a calf. In less than five years, now, David would get the title to the land, and then they would build a frame house.

They had planted the seeds from the lone cottonwood tree in a double row around the place they had chosen for the house. Every day now when her other work was done, Molly lugged dozens of pails of water from the creek to the seedlings. Someday they would be a tall windbreak around her home. When she bent over the tiny leaves and saw the water sinking into the thirsty earth, she felt a deep contentment.

One morning late in June she was startled at the washtub by a sudden darkening of the room. David was on the threshold. "Come," he said. "I want to show you something." His voice shook with excitement.

She stripped the suds from her arms and dried her hands. David picked up the baby and went up the path so quickly that Molly almost ran to keep up. He went with long strides toward the slough.

The coarse slough grass, taller than she, rustled harshly along the narrow path. An earthy smell came from its damp roots. She followed David out of the slough, and stood amazed. The wheat field's green stalks rose before her.

"Look. Molly, look!" David said, quivering.

It looked like a good crop, and she was glad.

"If it don't run forty bushels to the acre, I'll eat my hat!" he shouted.

"That's nice," she said.

"Nice! You know what wheat's worth out here now? A dollar a bushel! This crop's worth two—thousand—dollars!"

The baby screamed. David let her take him. She stood dazed, hushing the baby. Two thousand dollars—it was a sum outside reality. She couldn't imagine it. David had saved one hundred and six dollars, working on the railroad; they had been rich with all that money. Two thousand . . .

She said, awed, "Could we—we could have the cow."

"A cow!" David shouted. "A herd of cows! We'll fence the land. We'll build the house. I'm going to buy you a silk dress!" He seized her up in his arms and swung her around dizzily, prancing, whooping. "We're rich! Rich!"

"Goodness, David! Careful—the baby! David! Stop!"

He held her and the screeching baby still enclosed in his exuberant hug. His laughing, panting delight went all through her while they looked at the wheat. The wheat was real.

David had always been so much quicker than she. Slowly she came to share his feeling of liberation. They had always been happy and comfortable, and the future had been bright. Yet now it was as if, chilled to the bone, they had come into a warm place.

Every evening they went to look at the wheat. They were silent, listening to the myriad stalks in the wind. They gazed at the ripples of darker and lighter green passing over multitudes of bending heads.

Day by day the wheat was growing. The time of frosts was past. It needed no more rain. Under the beneficent blaze of the sky the thin heads were growing plumper, the milky kernels swelling.

17

Inside the rows of tiny cottonwood seedlings David began to dig the cellar of the new house. He would have it built before the snows came. "We won't spend another winter in this hole in the ground!" he said. He despised the dugout now. Molly did not despise it; she forgot it in thinking of the new house.

In the evenings David figured the lumber he would need, while she pored over the lines he had drawn on paper. Here would be the kitchen, the pantry, the dining room, there the two bedrooms—two bedrooms!—and a parlor! She had been born in a log cabin, but David could remember a white-painted house far in the East; this house was to be like that.

David's mind leaped into the future. "Next year, with the whole quarter section in wheat, we'll clear around five thousand dollars. By George, we're growing up with the greatest country on earth! Five years from now we'll be riding high, wide and handsome!"

He thought that the homestead was not enough. "I ought to file on a tree claim."

"We'd have to set out a hundred trees and cultivate them five years," she said. "Haven't you got your hands full now?"

He laughed at her. "You little goose, what's money for? I'll hire help."

How simple! She hadn't thought of that. David was always opening wider vistas to her. He was right; they needed more land.

Before sunrise he was riding away in the wagon. A Land Office was at the town site now; he could drive the ten miles each way and be home that night. Molly stood on the prairie above the dugout, holding the baby and watching until the wagon went out of sight in the tall slough grass. On the low rise of ground beyond the wheat field, David turned and waved his hat to her.

The wind tugged at Molly's skirts. Already insects were shrilling to the sun's heat and grasshoppers leaped in the parching grass. The baby began to fret. His screwed-up little face and the thrashing of his weak fists set the dimple quivering in her cheek. She held him close.

"There, there, Mother's little man! Poor baby, he shall have a bath, he shall!" She carried water to the dugout for bathing and washing clothes.

The day's work was only a shell filled by a future more real to her than the present. At the new house there would be a well, with a pump; she would not carry water up the creek bank anymore. The baby would have new clothes. . . . And suddenly she stopped, David's patched, faded shirt twisted between her hands, and her eyes widened at the thought, We'll have so many clothes that I'll do the washing only once a week!

A fiercer note in the sound of the wind alarmed her. The dugout was safe from a cyclone, but the wheat field . . . From the doorway she could not see a cloud. The sky was a colorless vibration of heat, and the wind scorched her face. These hot winds, endlessly blowing, were ripening the wheat.

That afternoon when she carried water to the seedling cottonwoods, Molly looked at the raw hole in the earth that would be the cellar. She thought of the white house, sheltered by its windbreak of tall trees, surrounded by fields pouring forth a wealth of wheat. Their home. The baby would never know any other. He would grow to boyhood and then manhood in the big white house; he would work in the wheat fields and in the large barns; he would ride his own horse over the prairies. He would have no memory of a life in a dugout.

It was dark when she heard the wagon and went to meet David at the barn with a lantern. The light fell on packages piled on the seat beside him, and on a load of lumber. Behind the wagon was a new red mowing machine, its steel parts glittering.

David jumped over the wheel and seized her in a hug. "Guess what I got for you!"

"But David—oh, you didn't go in debt?"

"Why not? We're good for it, aren't we? Say, you ought to hear 'em talking, in town, about our wheat! I filed a claim on the quarter section across the creek. We've got the best half section in this country!"

She shared his excitement, admiring while he showed her the marvelous mowing machine, with its levers that raised and lowered the sharp knives, and its iron seat on which a man could ride at ease while he was working. She patted the lumber and caught her breath when David showed her four window sashes with panes of real glass. Then he heaped her arms with packages, and she exclaimed, "Oh, David, you shouldn't!"

There had never been such a supper, such an evening. David had brought a beefsteak. He had brought candy and raisins, and even a pound of butter. He had brought a rattle for the baby, and a tin horn, and a pair of little boots much too large for him now. And a soft package disclosed yards of shimmering brown silk. Molly gasped, incredulous. But it really was silk. She touched it reverently.

David put his arm around her and stroked her hair. "I guess maybe I forgot to mention it, but I'm kind of glad I've got you." He tried to speak lightly, but a cry burst from his heart. "Thank God, I'm going to be able to take care of you and the baby the—the way I ought to."

She had never doubted that. She hadn't guessed that under his jovial confidence he had sometimes been frightened. Now he wasn't ashamed to let her know it, because the fear was gone. He had proved what he could do in the West.

After supper was eaten, the baby nursed and put to sleep, they sat together in the doorway and looked at the stars. They were closer together, more married, than they had ever been.

Next morning they went to look at the wheat. It was almost ripe. The long heads drooped with the weight of grain. David examined the kernels in his palm and said reluctantly, "We better give it another two weeks—maybe ten days. If this heat keeps up . . ."

There was no wind, the sky was growing pale before the terrible sun. Already the air began to waver in glassy sheets.

In midmorning David came from the field where he was breaking sod. "Whew!" he said. "Today's a scorcher! The horses couldn't stand it. I had to put 'em in the barn where there's shade. If this keeps up, I'll be cutting the wheat end of next week." He sat down to play with the baby.

Molly was putting the noon meal on the table when they heard the scream. It came again and again—a woman's frantic screaming.

"You stay here," David said. He seized his gun and was gone. The baby kept on gurgling and kicking. Molly put on her sunbonnet and went out into the dizzying heat. She went no farther from the baby than the top of the path.

Mrs. Svenson was coming, running, and David was running toward her. Mrs. Svenson cried out, panting, some word of warning and terror. She clutched her side, turned, and pointed upward.

A cloud was coming from the northwest, moving swiftly over the sun. It was a cloud like none that Molly had ever seen. It was ineffably beautiful, soft and iridescent as the sun shone through it gently. It moved above the windless prairie with the speed of wind.

Mrs. Svenson fell on her knees, sobbing, her apron over her head. Then she jumped up and ran back toward her sod shanty. David took his gaze from the cloud to glance after her, and shook his head, puzzled.

Molly thought there was a pattering like rain on the grass around her, but she could see only rustling blades and springing grasshoppers. David called to her, "Molly, what do you make of—"

She saw him stand as if frozen. He cried out, "Good—God—almighty!"

Grasshoppers were coming out of the sky, out of that cloud. They were dropping by hundreds. The air twinkled with their shining wings. The cloud was grasshoppers.

David ran toward the barn, shouting, "The wheat! Fill the tub, soak blankets! Fire—maybe fire'll save it!"

Chapter 2

THE DESCENT of the grasshoppers was, mercifully, unbelievable. It was a horror, but some saving resistance in David and Molly refused to believe that they would not save the wheat.

The windless day encouraged them. They could control the fires they lighted. Surely the grasshoppers, with hundreds of miles of prairie before them, would avoid flames. Before the winged creatures had ceased to fall from the sky, David had driven the snorting, trembling horses thrice around the wheat field. Three furrows of upturned earth protected the wheat from the fire he set in the wild grass.

It was Molly's part to follow the fire along the strip of plowed ground, to keep the flames from leaping into the wheat. David had the harder task of fighting the fire in the grass. If it escaped him, the whole country would be burned over; nothing, then, could keep the grasshoppers out of the field.

The fire ran merrily crackling, sending up waves of fiercer heat into the heat of the sun. Back and forth Molly ran, gasping, beating at wisps of burning grass, stamping them into the earth. The smoke came in gusts, stinging her eyes. With its smell there was another, oilier smell; grasshoppers, caught by the licking heat, fell wingless into the fire.

It seemed that this madness of fighting would never end. Yet it ended. And as the last clump of burning grass smoldered on blackened ground, David came striding to her. He was grimy with smoke, and the hair was scorched from his arms.

"They don't seem to be eating anything," he said huskily, and coughed. "Maybe it was a false alarm."

The wheat stood as before, golden-green and beautiful, with a whir-ring of grasshoppers over it.

"You go in and rest," he said. "I'm going to keep up a good thick smudge. That'll do the trick!"

Molly walked through grasshoppers thick as spray around her knees. They crunched sickeningly under her feet; she could not avoid stepping on them. Grasshoppers were in her hair, in her sleeves, in her skirts. Her ears tried to shut out the whirring of their wings.

Mechanically she cared for the baby. At the usual time she cooked supper. David was cutting slough grass and piling it on the burned strip around the field. Thick smoke rose and spread in the motionless air.

Molly kept supper warm for a long time. Then she let it grow cold, and she lay down and slept a little. David came in at last, too tired and restless to eat. He was angry when she urged him to rest.

She went with him back to the wheat field. In the starlight they stirred the heaps of smoldering grass, buried the flames under masses of dampened stalks, kept the heavy smoke pouring into the air.

Dawn came murky through the smoke. When the sun's first rays struck across the prairie, a sound rose—a small, vast sound of innumerable tiny jaws nibbling. A trembling began in the wheat field. Tall stalks shivered; here and there one moved and leaned crookedly against its fellows.

David shouted hoarsely and plunged into the field. They had never walked into the wheat, unwilling to break down one of the precious stalks. Now David trampled them, tore them up by armfuls, shouting, "Molly, quick! Come help!"

Smudges placed thickly through the field might save some of it. David raved, "Fool! Fool! Why didn't I do this sooner?"

It was like tearing their own flesh, to pull up the roots of the wheat, to pile up heaps of the ripening grain and set fire to it. Through the smoke, David shouted, "Molly, get back to the dugout."

"No, David, I—"

Coughing in the smoke, he croaked, "Get out, I tell you! What're we thinking of? You're nursing the baby!" Tears from his reddened eyes smeared the grime on his cheeks.

At the edge of the field she heard again that sound of nibbling. She stood and looked at the wheat. Scores of stalks were moving jerkily, as if they were struggling. The nibbling sound came from the whole prairie.

The Svensons were burning smudges around their poor little field of sod potatoes and turnips.

Outside the door of the dugout Molly took off her shoes. In the door-way she took off her dress and petticoat and shook the grasshoppers out of them. The baby lay wailing in his cradle. She talked and sang to him while she bathed in the washbasin, then took him in her arms and lay down to rest. When she was cooler she fetched water from the creek and mixed a generous drink of vinegar, molasses and water to take to David.

He drank gratefully, draining the last drop from the little pail. Looking into his bloodshot eyes, she found courage to say, "David, you might as well rest. It's no—"

He shouted, "I'll save it or die trying! I'm not licked yet, not by a damn sight!" He dashed the pail on the ground and left her.

Every hour she carried a cool drink to him. She took him food, but he would not stop to eat. His wild look frightened her. She could not persuade him to leave the field. That evening she did the chores and went to the field again, determined to make him rest. He would not listen.

Next morning Molly took tea and bread to David. He drank thirstily and choked down a few mouthfuls of bread.

"We'll save some of it," he said, looking at the ravaged field. "Not much, but some. I figure near a tenth of it's still standing. They can't take all of it, you know. It isn't possible. Some of it's bound to be left. Enough for flour and seed. If we just have seed—"

Molly felt a little hope. If even a few stalks were left, she and David could gather each one carefully. They could live that winter on game and the sod potatoes, and put in another crop in the spring.

That afternoon the grass was no longer standing on the prairie. It lay as if mowed. Bringing a pail of water from the creek, Molly halted and stared at the little plum trees. Not a leaf was left. She went into the dugout and set about mixing David's drink. The doorway behind her darkened. She was still an instant, then turned.

David's eyes were red in his sooty face. He straightened his shoulders and tried to speak robustly through a raw throat. "Well, Molly, the jig's up. I—" His mouth twisted and he said brutally, "The wheat's gone. Every spear." He dropped heavily onto the bench.

Molly had known this could happen; she had known it when the first wheat stalk fell. But now something within her cried out that it could not be true.

"Why don't you say something?" David raged at her. And covered his face with his hands.

She turned away. "I guess if there isn't any wheat, we'll get along without it," she said. "You've got along all right without it so far."

But they had never been in debt before.

She measured the molasses, poured the vinegar, stirred the mixture. "You'd better wash up and drink this while it's nice and cool."

To her surprise she began to cry. Her mouth writhed uncontrollably and tears ran from her eyes. She went on stirring till she heard David at the washbasin, then she dried her face.

David wiped his blistered arms gingerly, ran the comb through his wet hair, and drained the cup she handed him. Tears brimmed his raw lids. He drew her against him where he sat on the bench. She felt the sob shake his body when he turned his face against her shoulder, and she knew that he was clinging to her in a misery too great to bear alone.

24

"There, there," she said. "It's all right. I was afraid you'd get sunstroke. We're going to be all right."

"Oh, Molly, if I hadn't been such a fool! Those debts I ran up—almost two hundred dollars. Not even flour for this winter; not even seed."

"Never mind now. You'll manage all right. You're worn out. You'll feel better when you've had some sleep."

He slept heavily. Next morning his face was creased and his eyes swollen. After he had done the chores and eaten breakfast, she persuaded him to lie down again. He fell asleep at once, and Molly sat quietly in order not to disturb him. Her head was heavy and she let it sink against her arm on the table. Dozing, she was all the time aware of David in the bunk, of the baby on the floor. Her eyes opened and she saw the baby absorbed in his own pink feet.

Suddenly Molly noticed a new sound—a rasping, scratching sound. She started to her feet, and saw the top of the doorjamb rippling like a snake. She snatched up the baby, covered him with her arms. Then she saw the thing clearly. The grasshoppers were coming into the dugout. The ridged long backs jostled one another. Hundreds of hard, triangular heads, knobbed with eyes, were coming downward, turning, moving inward over the doorjamb.

She screamed.

The door stood open against the creek bank. She seized the latch. In an instant she saw the whole earth crawling—path, creek banks, prairie, scaly and crawling. The door closed horribly, crunching grasshoppers. "David!"

He seized her. "Molly, what—"

"Kill them!" she screamed. "Kill them!" In the darkened room she could hear them crawling.

David lighted the lamp. She stood trembling while he brushed grasshoppers from ceiling and walls, crushed them with his boots, and hunted them out of the hay box and the stove. He looked into the water pail.

"Throw it out!" she cried.

"I don't know— You want me to get more?"

"No, no, don't open the door! I'll boil it!"

He skimmed the creatures out of the water with the dipper.

She was ashamed to be behaving so, and with an effort she relaxed her clenched jaws. Then the baby screamed, a sharp yell of pain. From his soft armpit a grasshopper leaped to her cheek. She struck it away and began to cry loudly, like a child. For a time she could not stop crying, even in David's arms. When she was quiet, they heard the grasshoppers crawling on the paper windowpane. A mottled shadow moved steadily downward across it, and by that they knew that the whole earth was still crawling in the sunlight outside.

All that night the creatures crawled, and all the next day. David slipped out to take care of the horses. Then they sat in the dugout behind the closed door.

"The railroad's still left," David said. "I'll go back to work on it for a while. Oh, we're not licked yet by a long ways!"

She knew how he hated to go back to work on the railroad. It had been different when they were starting out. Now for a year he had had his own land. It would be hard to go back to obeying other men's orders for wages. But it couldn't be helped.

Later that afternoon the oiled paper windowpane shone clear. David opened the door. As mysteriously as they had come, the grasshoppers were going. A translucent cloud, colored like mother-of-pearl, swept northwestward across the sun.

Dust blew in the evening breeze. A faint stench rose from the creek. The water was solidly filled with drowned grasshoppers. No more clean water remained in all that country.

"I didn't want to worry you," David said, "but the horses haven't had water since yesterday. Creek was full of grasshoppers."

Long after sunset he worked, digging a hole in the slough. Mr. Svenson came, carrying a shovel and a pail and leading his oxen. They worked together, digging. When the hole was deep enough, they had to wait for water to seep into it. At midnight the horses and the oxen drank, and Mr. Svenson started home with the pail full of water. Molly was lying awake when David came in, mudstained and cheerful. She sat up eagerly to drink from the brimming dipper he gave her.

"Thank God the horses are all right," he said. "I'll be sure to get a job on the railroad with the teams."

He drove away next morning before daylight. The nearest railroad camp was twenty miles away and he said that he'd waste no time getting there. "If I get a job right away," he said, "I'll stay with it. I'll try to find a rider coming this way and send you word, but don't be worried if I don't get home tomorrow night."

"No," she said.

26

"Svenson'll kind of look out for you. He told me he'd be glad to."

"Yes," she said.

He held her close for a minute, by the wagon. Then he kissed her. She held up the baby, and David tickled a gurgle from him. "Be good, little shaver. Take care of your mother." He climbed to the wagon seat, and drove away.

In a little while she heard a whistled tune growing fainter across the dark prairie. She knew he was whistling to cheer her.

IN THE DAYLIGHT she saw the devastated country more clearly. There was nothing but bare earth to the rim of the sky. Earth, and a little litter of old, dead weed stalks. The grasshoppers had not eaten the stacks of slough hay left from last year. They and the barn stood gaunt above their shadows.

She fetched water from the hole in the slough to bathe the baby and wash his clothes and hers. The stench from the creek grew stronger in the heat. Everything she touched was gritty with dust. At sunset she carried the baby up on the prairie to escape the smell of the creek. The seedling cottonwoods were dead, of course; they had been tender twigs and leaves; the grasshoppers had eaten them.

On the second night David did not come. She told herself that she had been sure he would get a job. Now they could pay something on the debts and buy supplies. He would need the mowing machine, and some day no doubt they would use the lumber and the windows. Only the brown silk had been a serious mistake, but she could not really regret that David had bought it for her.

Late that night she fell asleep in a great sense of safety. In the morning she felt rested and strong. The days since the grasshoppers came had been a delirium; now it was gone. Grass would grow again in the spring. She told herself that the loss of the wheat was not a real loss; they had never harvested the grain, they had never had the new house, the pump. None of these had been real. Yet when she struggled with the broken lid on the old stove, she felt defrauded of her new stove. And the thought of the cow was a poisoned stab.

"David has a job," she said to herself. "We will have a cow next year." She need not be afraid; little David John would have milk.

"Yes, he shall; so he shall," she crooned to him, glad because his wandering fist tugged sharply at her smooth hair. But the angry sense of

27

injustice welled up again. She hated the dugout—"hole in the ground" as David had said—she hated the broken stove, the heat, the wind that rasped her nerves, the stripped, ugly prairie. Her whole life seemed poor and mean. Bitterly she pitied her defrauded baby. She pitied David. They did not deserve this suffering. They had trusted, and been betrayed. Her cry was "It isn't right! It isn't fair!"

She laid the sleeping baby on the floor, and barricading the doorway with the bench, she went through the hot and dusty winds to the field where David had planted potatoes. The potato tops were gone, but part of a crop remained buried in the parched earth. Carefully she dug and sifted the earth with her fingers, so as to lose not the smallest potato.

Late that afternoon she wearily bathed. She fed the baby, and carrying him against her shoulder, she walked to the Svensons'. She felt that talking with her friend would ease her bitterness.

In the shanty, Mrs. Svenson eagerly described their fight against the grasshoppers. With gestures and halting words, she told how the bees had poured from their hives to attack the crawling hordes. She lamented the garden, but some turnips and carrots remained, and the potatoes.

"Iss no goot! Iss bad, bad! So! Ve make out, yes?" She patted Molly's hand.

Molly thought the Svensons had not lost a great deal. They had their sod potatoes, turnips and carrots, and their bees. They wouldn't have had much more if the grasshoppers had not come. And they were together; they were not separated. They were not in debt. Molly's sense of her own loss did not grow less bitter.

Suddenly she was tired, exhausted. She wanted David. Nothing was right without him, and her longing was more than she could bear. Tears came into the corners of her eyes; she turned her head and winked them away. Mrs. Svenson's hand took hers, and Molly clung to it.

When Mr. Svenson, going for water, stopped the ox team by the door, Molly gave her friend the baby to hold while she climbed into the wagon. The two women leaned toward each other and for the first time they kissed. "Yes, yes," Mrs. Svenson said, nodding her bright head. "You coom. I coom, ve— Like this, we make out!"

The oxen drew the wagon slowly across the prairie. Behind the seat the empty pail and tub jangled together. The sunset had never been so gorgeous. Great banners of crimson unfurled to the zenith. Their reflections colored the air and land, and the putrid water in the creek glowed like jewels. Molly thought of David, far away. She tried not to think of all the empty days she must endure till winter, when he could come home.

He came five nights later. Molly was nursing the baby when she heard the wagon. She laid him on the bunk, took the lantern and went outdoors. David was hunched on the wagon seat. "Here I am," he said bitterly.

"You must be tired out." Her voice caressed him. "I'll help unhitch."

"I can't get a job."

She had known that when she heard the wagon. She said, "Well, you're here!"

He climbed stiffly down over the wheel. Dust slid out of the folds of his sleeve when she laid her hand on his arm. She held up her face, and he kissed her briefly and turned away to unfasten the traces.

Molly knew what he felt: that a man had no right to a wife he couldn't take care of. She was frightened; she didn't know how to reach him. Nothing else mattered, if only she and David were close together. He was there, he had kissed her, and he hadn't come back to her.

"You run along!" David said brusquely. "I guess I'm not so beat out that I can't unhitch my own team!" He was on the edge of collapse.

"All right," she said quickly. "I'll go put the teakettle on."

She tried not to feel so forlorn. There was new bread for supper; she had baked a loaf that day. The small potatoes would boil quickly in their skins. A cup of strong tea would make David feel better.

The tea was boiling and the potatoes steaming dry when he came in. His mouth and jaw had a new, hard look, and he seemed older. Molly was surprised by the thought, Why, he's only twenty years old.

They did not talk much while he ate. She spoke of the potato crop and the Svensons, and refilled his cup. All the time she was crying to him silently, "David, David, come back to me! Don't stay so far away!"

He pushed back the teacup and plate, and folded his arms on the edge of the table. His mouth hardened. "There isn't a job in the whole country."

Molly did not say anything. She knew if there had been a job, David would have got it.

"They're turning away men at all the camps," he went on. She saw his brown hands grip hard on his arms. "Everybody's looking for work. Half the folks at the town site are quitting, getting out. They're shutting up the stores. At the railroad camps it's— They're— Molly, they're begging! Men with families, begging at the cook shanties."

"Why don't they live on jackrabbits?" Molly asked sharply.

"There aren't any. The jackrabbits have left the country. All the way east, sixty miles, or some say a hundred, the grasshoppers took everything. Molly, you don't understand."

"We aren't going to beg," she said.

"Oh, aren't we?" The words were cruel. "I'll let you and the baby starve, will I? Of course I'd beg! What do you think I'm made of?"

She steadied herself and said quietly, "David, it's not that bad. There's slough hay for the horses, and we have potatoes, and you can hunt."

"Stay here, you mean? We'd have to have flour, and salt, and—oh, my God, and you nursing the baby!" He struck the table with his fist. "And I can't hunt! I haven't the powder and shot, and my credit's no good!" He pressed his fists to his temples. "No. We've got to give up the homestead and get out—if we can. Maybe I can get work if we can get far enough east."

"Give up the— Oh, no!"

"Yes!" He turned on her savagely. Molly knew he was not angry with her. "And I'll be lucky if I can steal—that's what I said, steal!—steal my horses to get out with. Oh, you got a fine husband when you married me!"

"David, don't—"

"It's my fault. It's those damn debts. I tell you I'm licked. I'm— I tried everything. All the camps. Coming back, Loftus, the lumberman, stopped me at the town site. Said I had to pay him for that lumber. I tried to get him to take it back; he wouldn't. He said if I tried to skip out without paying, he'd attach the team and wagon."

"He can't!" Molly cried. "He couldn't! Why, it's murder—leaving a man on foot—"

"Oh, yes, he can. Yes, he will. There's law at the town site now. And I— He as good as called me a thief, and I didn't do anything."

Molly was afraid to speak and afraid to let him hear his own breath shaking in the silence. If he broke down, he'd hate himself. If his pride went completely, there would be nothing left.

Suddenly she was almost happy, because she understood why he hadn't come to her for comfort. It was his pride—his pride in taking care of her and the baby. She would love him just as much if he couldn't take care of her. But she wouldn't love him at all without that pride; he wouldn't be David without it. That was why he had to save it; that was why he fought for it even against her.

She knew they must not give up the homestead. Only a defeated man traveled eastward, homeless, with a wife and little baby. All the way David would know, and every man he met would know, that he hadn't been strong enough for the West.

"Why don't you just go east till winter?" she said. "Don't give up the homestead. Loftus will give us time on the debts if we hold on to the homestead."

"How can we make a trip like that and get back inside five months?" he answered dully. "We'll have to travel slow with the baby, and we've got to live. Somebody'll jump the place as soon as we're gone, anyhow. A fine place like this—all the plowed land—"

He had not even thought of going east without her. "Nobody'll jump it while I'm here," she said stoutly.

He understood then, looking up quickly, looking into her eyes. "Molly, you don't mean you'd—"

"I'd be just as lonesome, no matter if you were working on the railroad or in the East." She would not let her voice tremble. Hurriedly she ended, "I'll be all right. The Svensons are here."

He came swiftly and gathered her up in his arms. "Molly, sweetheart! My poor dear. Did you miss me so much?"

"Yes," she said. He was trembling and tears came into his eyes.

"I won't leave you," he said. "I won't ever leave you anymore. We'll stick together, no matter what happens. That's all that matters."

"Of course," she said. But she knew he must go.

That night they lay talking while the baby slept cozily between them, and she was able to make him see that it was quite simple; he could be working in the East instead of on the railroad. That was all.

THEY HAD TWO DAYS together before he went away. She helped him dig the rest of the potatoes and the turnips. He deepened the well in the slough and set a windlass above it, so that she could draw a full pail of clear water. The second evening they spent at the Svensons', and walked homeward together in the moonlight, the baby asleep on his shoulder.

Next morning, with the lumber and window frames on the wagon, David drove to the town site. That night he came back triumphant, with flour, salt, molasses, kerosene, and even a piece of salt pork and two pounds of tea. He had traded the lumber and the windows for these supplies—enough to provide for Molly till he came back in the fall.

31

"And, Molly, you'd never guess!" he said, grinning. "Loftus attached the team!"

"Oh, David—"

"Wait till you hear. Just as I was pulling out of town, here came the sheriff with the paper. He said he hated like the devil to take a man's team, but he'd have to do it unless I squared the bill with Loftus. Well, I told him how it is, and that sheriff's a good fellow. Had to take the team, he said, but the attachment didn't apply to my load, and he couldn't let me dump it in the street—that being against city ordinance. He said I'd better haul those supplies wherever they were going, and come back with the team. Kind of winked when he said it. He thinks he's giving us a chance to get out. He's going to be a surprised man tomorrow morning. And so's Loftus.

"Because, Molly, think. Loftus has to take the team, and he can't get rid of 'em as a gift, the price that feed is now. He'll feed them till fall, and when I come back he'll be facing feeding them all winter. Why, I bet I get 'em back for cost of the feed he's put into them. How's that for a joke?"

He hugged her jubilantly. They laughed a great deal that evening, trying to forget that David was leaving tomorrow. When they spoke of that, they spoke cheerfully. David would travel fast when he reached railroad trains. Crops were said to be good in the East; he would easily get work in the harvest. In the fall he would come back with plenty of money. They would have another cozy winter together, and then there would be a spring again, a new year, a new crop.

To the very last they were cheerful. Their smiles were shaky, but they smiled. David turned to wave his hat from the rise beyond the field, and Molly held up the baby and flopped his little fist. She listened till silence closed down behind the wagon.

Day after day the sun rose and declined in the burning copper sky. Whirlpools of dust appeared and scurried and vanished. Thunderstorms moved across the prairie, dropping gray curtains of rain. Where they had passed, the unconquerable sod sent up its green blades.

At night Molly dreamed horrible dreams. She had not told David how she feared trains. When she slept she saw the monstrous, inhuman things of steam and iron, swiftly coming, roaring, staring with the headlights like eyes. She saw David spring forward, confident, valiant for her and the baby. She saw the trains killing him.

In the daytime she would not think of trains. She was waiting.

She had three spools of thread and her small steel knitting needles. When everything in the dugout was washed, scoured, patched and polished, when she could find nothing more to do, she knitted. She knitted up all the thread and unraveled the lace so she could knit it again. Often Mrs. Svenson was with her, but Molly was always waiting.

Poor little David John was cutting teeth. His gums were swollen and hot, and nothing could help him. He lay whimpering, turning from side to side, till he wailed because he could find no escape from misery.

Molly watched for riders on the prairie. All the shanties but the Svensons' had been deserted since the grasshoppers came, and few riders passed that way. When she saw one loping toward the south, she would call and run to him. Panting, one hand against her side, the other shading her eyes, she would look up and say, "Are you going to the town site? If you are coming back this way, would you ask if there's a letter at the post office for me?"

A man with narrow eyes in wrinkled eyelids, a scar across a leathery cheek, two guns on his thighs; a frank boy, smiling with a white flash of teeth; a black-eyed Indian, riding a barebacked pony—they all said, "Why, yes, ma'am, be glad to." But they did not come back.

Molly was sure there must be a letter at the post office—if nothing had happened to David.

Finally one afternoon she heard a horse's hoofs on the dugout; she heard a call. The scarred man sat on his horse beside the chimney. He had a letter.

Afterward Molly hoped she had properly thanked him. She remembered that he had wheeled his horse and galloped away to the southeast; he must have come miles out of his way.

The letter was from Iowa.

Dear Wife:
  I take my pen in hand to let you know that I am well and hope you are the same. How are you and the little shaver? I have a job working at Roslyn Feed Mill, $30 a month and food and lodging. Roslyn treats me fine. Write me at this address. I will be home in Oct. I hope everything is all right there. Let me know.

                                                                    Your Loving Husband
XXXXXXXX for you and the little chap

Molly wore the paper limp with reading it. Long after, the words would repeat themselves to her. They eased a little the strain of waiting for October.

Mr. Svenson walked to town to mail her reply. He was so kind that Molly felt she could never repay him. She decided to let him cut the slough hay for her on shares. She could have cut it herself, little by little. But he needed the hay for his oxen, and she and David would have enough with the two stacks left from last year and half the new crop.

All one week Mr. Svenson was cutting, raking and stacking the hay. Mrs. Svenson came with him every morning, always bringing some part of the dinner, and all three ate together at noon in the shady dugout. That week would have been a pleasure but for Mr. Svenson's gloom. The hay, with some of his turnips, would winter the oxen through, yet still he shook his head and muttered.

Molly thought at first that he was poor spirited. But when he attacked the whole country, the West, she was angry.

"Ta tam country," he said. "No tam goot."

"The country's all right, Mr. Svenson," Molly said.

Mr. Svenson lifted his big fist and pointed with his knife to the vista beyond the doorway. The prairie was lost in heat; there was no horizon. Undulating air poured upward from all the wavering land. Dust devils were whirling, scurrying, leaping.

"Ta tam country, she feed nobody," Mr. Svenson said bitterly. "She iss devils, ta country."

In September the summer heat was gone. The prairie stretched firm again to the sky's rim. Overhead the first long lines of wild birds were flying south. Molly was counting the weeks till October.

One morning Mr. Svenson came and stood in the door of the dugout. He spread out his calloused hands and let them fall lax. "Ve go."

"Go?" Molly asked. But she knew. The Svensons were giving up; they were going east.

Mr. Svenson struggled for words. Tears came into his eyes. "Ta bee— little, little bee—big bee kill. Dead, all dead."

His bees were killing their broods because they could not feed them through the winter. The grasshoppers had killed all the plants; the bees could find no blossoms from which to make honey. Passionately Mr. Svenson said that he would not stay in a country where not even a bee could live. "Vork, vork, all time work! No goot, no eat! Ve go!"

Molly was a little frightened when Mr. Svenson had gone on to water his oxen at the well. She had not realized how much a part of her life the Svensons had become. Their going made her feel insecure.

She left her washing in the tub and hurriedly dressed little David John, thinking how David would grin to see the wave of hair on top of his head and the triumphant tooth in his moist smile. She put on her sunbonnet and walked across the prairie to see Mrs. Svenson.

Mrs. Svenson talked cheerfully about the East. She had a brother in Minnesota; they would go to him. That winter there would be wood for the fires, and wood ashes for making soap; there would be milk and cream and butter. People would come and go; there would be gossip, jokes. Mrs. Svenson talked of all these things and was very busy getting ready to go.

Only once, without meaning to, her eyes confessed the truth, and quickly Molly looked away. Mrs. Svenson knew that her husband was giving up, that he would be only a hired man in the East. But she smiled and said, "Ve coom back! Iss plenty land, yes?"

Mr. Svenson began hauling his potatoes and turnips and his share of the slough hay to the town site to trade for supplies. Even his plow went for powder and shot and grain to feed the oxen. Finally he set out on his last trip to town. When he returned, they would be all ready to leave as soon as David came.

The next evening at sunset, Molly heard Mr. Svenson call. She ran up the path. He was leading the oxen to the well to drink. He fumbled in his blouse, took out a letter. His broad face beamed with pleasure in Molly's joy. The letter would say when David was coming.

Quickly she slit the envelope with a hairpin and took out the folded sheet. Two limp bank notes lay in it. Her heart stopped, and started with a jerk. She could hardly hold the paper still.

Dear Wife:

I take my pen in hand to let you know do not worry. I have met with an accident but am getting along fine. Molly I cannot get home in Oct. My leg is broke but the doc says I am mending fast. I have your dear letter and am glad you are well and the little shaver fat and sassy. Molly you better make arrangements to stay with Svensons. I do not know when I can travel and it is liable to be a bad winter there. Game will be scarce. Wolves and outlaws will be moving back to settled country. Stay with Svensons and he will take care of you. I send what money I can for supplies. Now do not worry about me. I will come as soon as I can. Try not to miss me the way I miss you. I am never going to leave you again as long as we live. Write to me.

Your Loving Husband

Mr. Svenson returned from watering the oxen and looked expectantly at Molly. He and his wife were waiting only until David came. Every day was precious, for they must reach Minnesota before the heavy snows fell. His pleased expectancy changed to dismay when he saw Molly's face.

"He isn't coming," she said. "He's been hurt." Only a little part of her was alive. She was numb. She must decide what to do. Her eyes were looking at the bank notes. Two ten-dollar bills.

She realized all the responsibility was now hers. A corner of one bill was turned down. She straightened it and carefully smoothed out the creases. "I must take the baby and go to the town site," she said.

Chapter 3

AFTERWARD MOLLY remembered the day at the town site as though it had happened to someone else.

She was ready to go when the Svensons came. There had been a great deal to do. She did not seem to need sleep that night; it was as though she slept while she worked. She washed clothes and bedding, and hung them out to dry by starlight. Then she cleaned the stove and rubbed it and the stovepipe with kerosene to keep them from rusting. Her clothes and the baby's she made into two bundles, and in a box she packed the Bible, Tennyson's *Poems*, her sewing things and knitting needles, the brown silk and the shell box David had given her. The pistol and its box of cartridges fitted neatly into a corner.

The baby was limp in sleep when she dressed him. When the Svensons came, she had only to put on her bonnet and padlock the door. Mr. Svenson carried the box and bundles up the path; she snapped the padlock shut and followed with the baby. Molly felt neither asleep nor awake while the jogging wagon took her away from the snug dugout.

Dawn came, and sleepily Molly and Mrs. Svenson got down from the wagon and walked. The load was heavy for the oxen. At noon they stopped and made a little fire with buffalo chips, and Molly boiled tea. In the shadow of the wagon they drank it and ate cold boiled potatoes with salt, bread and molasses, and good raw turnips.

Almost all the afternoon they could see the town ahead. The railroad embankment and the buildings detached themselves from the horizon and came nearer with every mile. By dusk the buildings rose tall and square against the sky, and Molly nerved herself to approach this populous place.

Half a dozen glass windows shed light on high porches where knots of men stood talking. A burst of shouts and laughter came from the saloon. Its door opened and two men swung onto horses and rode clattering away.

Two little boys came out of the dark and stood watching while Mr. Svenson unyoked and fed the oxen and Mrs. Svenson made the camp fire. Molly sliced the rest of the potatoes into a skillet.

"Is he your husband?" one of the boys asked her.

"No." Molly nodded toward Mrs. Svenson.

"Is that their baby?"

"No, he's my baby." She straightened up and smiled.

"Then where's your husband?"

The innocent question pierced through her numbness. She felt a pain, an anguish screaming for David.

"Well, I guess you got a husband, haven't you?" the little boy said.

Molly gasped. She turned upon him, trying to speak. He stumbled backward, and words rose harshly in her throat. "Yes, I have a husband! He's in the East."

The boys were silent, and after a moment they went away.

Molly crawled into the wagon, the baby gathered into her arms, and rested against the bedding piled there. The baby nuzzled and gurgled at her breast, and a tear ran down her cheek. She brushed it quickly away; tears are bad for babies.

As soon as she had helped to wash the dishes and make the bed in the wagon, she took off her shoes and dress and lay down. Her busy mind held her between sleep and waking. She was aware of the baby and Mrs. Svenson with her in the feather bed. The thin arch of canvas did not shut out the strangeness of noises made by human beings in the night. Even when the last horse galloped away and the last door slammed, the town was still there, a disturbing sense that other people were near.

In daylight the town was less intimidating than it had been by night. Surely, Molly thought, among so many people, under so many roofs, she could find shelter for the baby and herself.

After breakfast she took the baby in her arms and set out. Mrs. Svenson, sympathetic and anxious, went with her. The Svensons had come out of their way to bring Molly to the town site; they had given her a day and were giving her another. Molly was burdened by this kindness. She would not take more; today she would find winter shelter in the town.

There was the lumberyard—a stack of boards and a hill of coal glinting black in the sunlight. There was a barber shop; they passed it quickly, averting their eyes. Next was the saloon. They hurried, turning their heads and looking at the dusty street and the gaunt depot. The steel rails were laid, but trains would not be running till spring.

There was the store. Molly drew a deep breath and shifted the baby on her shoulder. He was wide awake, squirming, and his soft fist fumbled at her neck. Once, in the springtime, David had brought her to the town site; she had seen the owners, Mr. and Mrs. Henderson, and spoken to them. But it took all her resolution to go into the store. She had always been shy.

Mr. Henderson propped a broom against a nail keg. He was lean and a little stooped. "Good morning, ladies. What can I do for you this fine large morning?"

He did not recognize Molly at first, and she was ashamed that she had not come to buy anything. She told Mr. Henderson she wanted to stay in town till David came back. "I thought you might know where baby and I could stay. If I could work, perhaps, to help pay our way— David sent me some money, but—"

Mr. Henderson tugged his beard. "Tell the truth, there's not many womenfolks left in town. Men with families mostly cleared out after the grasshoppers hit us. Mrs. Henderson, now—we're kind of crowded, but you might ask her. Anything suits her, suits me." He opened the door into the back room and called, "Ma! Here's a couple ladies to see you! Go right in."

Mrs. Henderson was getting breakfast. Two pigtailed little girls were setting the table, and through a door, in the lean-to, a little boy splashed at the washbasin. A bed, a trundle bed and a pallet were visible through another door. Mrs. Henderson was small, quick and voluble. She asked Molly and Mrs. Svenson to sit down as she went on with her work.

"Well, of course you can't stay by yourself on a claim, and winter coming on! There's not many men'll do it. Let's see. I'd be glad to take you in myself—goodness knows a little board money'd help out—but you see how it is: just the one bedroom for the five of us, and when it's our turn to board the schoolteacher I'll have to make a bed for her here in the kitchen. One mercy: the cookstove'll keep us warm. . . . Well, let's see. Now there's Mrs. Decker, the saloon keeper's wife, but a good pious woman. She has only the one room, but it's good-sized. She could put up a curtain. Then there's Mrs. Insull—her husband's going to be the station agent. I don't know if she'd take a boarder—she's high-toned and they've got his salary—but no harm trying."

Breakfast was on the table and Mrs. Henderson urged them to take potluck. But Molly said no, thank you, they had already had breakfast.

Mrs. Henderson went into the street with them, to point out Mrs. Decker's shanty. "If you don't find what you're looking for, you come right back here. My land, you've got to have someplace. I guess we'll manage to squeeze you in somehow."

39

Molly and Mrs. Svenson walked down the dusty road to Mrs. Decker's. The shanty had a glass window, with curtains. A thin, sallow woman with bright black eyes and sun-dried hair pulled tightly back from her forehead stood in the doorway. She looked sharply at Molly, the baby, and Molly's wedding ring.

"Your husband's in the East, you say? Whereabouts in the East?"

"Iowa."

"Why's he staying in Iowa? Why isn't he here taking care of you?"

"He went east to work," Molly repeated. "He's coming back as soon as he can." Her arms were tired and the baby jiggled up and down.

"Well, I'd have to ask my husband. I guess it's all right, but I'd have to ask him. What would you be willing to pay?"

"I want to pay what it's worth. But I—"

"Well, come in," said Mrs. Decker.

The shanty was large and nicely furnished. There was a bedstead, a table and benches, the cookstove and a rocking chair. The bed was covered with a spotless sheet; there were pillow shams at its head embroidered in red thread: "Good Night" and "Sweet Dreams."

"I hope the baby wouldn't make much trouble," Mrs. Decker said.

"No. He hardly ever cries," Molly said. Mrs. Svenson began eagerly to praise the good baby.

Mrs. Decker interrupted. "Well, I only hope he don't cry in the mornings. Mr. Decker has to get his rest. . . . We could put your bed behind a curtain in that corner. Have you a bedstead?"

"No. I have bedding."

"Well, I wasn't brought up to have beds on the floor. But I guess it can't be helped. Could you pay four dollars a week?"

Molly was stunned. She looked wide-eyed at Mrs. Decker.

"You're eating for two, and everything's high. I don't see how I could do it for less. There's coal to buy too. You can't expect to be warm all winter for nothing."

There was not enough work in the place for two women. And Mrs. Decker was a woman who would do all her own work, because nobody else could do it to suit her.

"Of course, if you can't pay—" Mrs. Decker said. "I wouldn't turn even a dog from my door that hadn't any other place to go."

Molly said with dignity, "It's a little more than I wanted to pay, but I will think about it. Good morning, Mrs. Decker."

In the doorway Mrs. Decker seemed about to say something more, but shut her lips together and didn't. Mrs. Svenson took the baby.

It seemed unreal to Molly that she was walking on the dusty road, in this strange town, homeless. Two black horses came dashing past the lumberyard, drawing behind them a buggy and a swirl of dust. In front of the store the buggy stopped. A young man wrapped the lines around the whip and jumped down. Face to face with Molly, he swept off his hat.

"Good morning, ma'am! Get your letter all right?" He was the young rider she had stopped on the prairie and asked to bring her the letter from David.

"Good morning," she said. "Yes, thank you."

"Second time I asked for it, they told me Two Gun Pete got it."

"Thank you just the same."

"Don't mention it, ma'am."

It was all a dream. People come and go like that in dreams, without reason or purpose. In a dream one has this heavy burden on the heart, a sense of loss and woe. In a dream Mrs. Svenson plods beside you, dumb with sympathy and concern, and Mr. Svenson sits by his covered wagon patiently waiting. Molly knew she must do something.

Mrs. Insull lived above the depot. The rough stairs went up from the waiting room, where Mr. Insull and another man were storing tools.

"Go right up and knock," Mr. Insull said.

Molly summoned all her resolution. She went up the stairs, rapped upon the door. Mrs. Insull was cleaning house. She had been working with fury and she was in a temper. A towel was around her head, a mop in her hand, and a swirl of soapy water lay behind her.

The room revealed such luxury as Molly had never seen. The walls were covered with a flowery paper. Shiny furniture was pushed back against them.

"Good morning. I'm looking for work," Molly said.

"Well, there's plenty of it here! But if you think I can afford a hired girl, you're mistaken!" Mrs. Insull replied tartly.

"I'd work for my keep," Molly said.

"You're with the campers down the street, aren't you?"

"No. Yes. That is, this is my friend Mrs. Svenson; I came to the town site with them, but—"

"Well, take my advice and keep right on going east with them. This country's gone to the dogs. The sooner you get out of it the better for you.

I can't ask you in, I'm busy; but it wouldn't be any use. We've got three growing boys to feed and not enough left over to keep a cat. So, if you'll excuse me—" She was shutting the door.

"Good morning," said Molly. She turned and took the baby from Mrs. Svenson. Holding him to her fiercely, she marched down the stairs and out of that place. Mrs. Svenson hurried beside her.

"I'm going home," Molly said. She felt she should never have budged from the homestead. David's wife, David's baby, being offered charity, having doors closed in their faces! While David, far away, was hurt and helpless. David had made a home for her and she would stay in it. If she had to face loneliness, cold, wolves, outlaws, she'd face them. She'd be right there when David came back.

She couldn't let the Svensons lose another day, taking her home. But she was going. The young man was coming out of the store. Awkwardly he tried to balance packages and reach his hat.

"Is that your team and rig?" Molly asked him.

"You bet!" he answered proudly.

"You know where I live. Would you take me out there for a dollar?"

"You bet I would!"

Mr. Svenson tried to use his masculine authority, saying he was responsible to David for her safety. Mrs. Svenson pleaded, almost crying. If there was no place for her at the town site, they would take her with them to Minnesota. But Molly wouldn't even consider it.

Prudently, carefully, she bought supplies for the winter. She thanked the Svensons with all her heart. She would never see them again, her only friends, and she kissed Mrs. Svenson as she had kissed her sisters when she left them forever to come west.

Then she was speeding over the prairie behind the swift black team. Their flashing hoofs, their manes and tails blowing in the wind, and this stranger beside her were the last fantasy of that incredible day. She rested in a kind of stupor, waiting for this dream to end.

After a few remarks, the young man too was silent. His name was Dan Gray. The skyline did not change, but within it the prairie whirled past in inconceivable rapidity. In the distance Molly could see the dots that were the haystacks and the sod barn. Absently the young man began to sing; he stopped at once, shocked by his impoliteness. Molly said, "Do sing. I like it."

The sun was sinking in a chill apricot glow, the baby slept on her tired

arm, and she was carried onward smoothly and swiftly while the young
man buoyantly sang the jolly song:

> "Oh, when I left my eastern home, so happy and so gay,
>   To try to win my way to wealth and fame,
>   I little thought that I'd come down to burning twisted hay,
>   In a little old sod shanty on a claim!
>
> "Oh, the hinges are of leather, the windows have no glass,
>   And the roof it lets the howling blizzards in.
>   And I hear the hungry coyote as he sneaks up through the grass,
>   'Round my little old sod shanty on the claim!"

"I like that song," Molly said. "Have you a sod shanty?"

"You bet! My claim's four miles west of the town site. Grasshoppers
cleaned me out, but I can winter the team through and buy seed."

"You're doing well."

"Yes, I'm in pretty good shape." He paused. "I got a girl too."

"That's nice." Molly smiled. She liked Mr. Gray.

"She's about your age. I'd like to bring her out to see you folks some
Sunday. We go driving on Sundays. This team'll cover forty miles and
come in as fresh as daisies."

The Svensons were gone, Molly thought, but here were other friends
already. Neighbors were not so far away when a driving team could go
forty miles on Sunday.

There was the well in the slough, the haystacks, the barn, all strangely
unchanged. Mr. Gray carried her bundles, and held the baby while she
turned the key in the padlock. The dugout was bleak with its packed
stores and bare bunk, but it was home.

"You got a snug place here," Mr. Gray said. He fetched a pail of water
from the well and asked if he could do anything else. When Molly
thanked him and gave him the dollar, he took it as if he didn't like to.

"Kind of hate to leave you out here alone, but I guess it's safe enough for
a while, with this good weather. When's your husband coming back?"

"I don't know exactly."

"You got a gun and know how to use it?"

"Yes."

"Likely you won't have any trouble, but it's just as well . . . Ada and I'll
be driving out this way next Sunday if the weather's fine. Well, so long!"

He was gone. Molly got the pistol from the box and loaded it. She could hardly keep awake. She spread the bedding on the bunk, undressed in a daze and lay down with the baby. Well, little David John, here we are, she thought, and she fell sound asleep. She slept sixteen hours.

Next day the familiar objects about her gave her a sense of security. She felt that she would get through the winter all right. Now and then a man stuck it out on a lonely homestead; why shouldn't she?

That week she wrote David a long letter, which she meant to ask Mr. Gray to take to the post office in town. She would not worry David by telling him that the Svensons had gone. With a pen she was more articulate than with spoken words; she wrote him that she loved him. She wrote about the baby's tooth and Mr. Svenson's cutting the hay on shares. And carefully, in her delicate writing, she wrote:

> We are having hard times now, but we should think of the future. It has never been easy to build up a country, but how much easier it is for us, with kerosene, cookstoves, and even railroads and fast posts, than it was for our forefathers. I trust that, like our own parents, we may live to see times more prosperous than they have ever been, and we will then reflect with satisfaction that these hard times were not in vain.

This letter, carefully sealed and addressed, was never mailed. It lay all winter between the pages of the Bible, for the weather changed suddenly. Saturday morning was mild as May; Saturday afternoon a dark cloud rose from the northwest. Then, like a solid white wall, the blizzard advanced.

Chapter 4

THREE DAYS AND NIGHTS the winds did not cease to howl, and when Molly opened the door she could not see the door ledge through the swirling snow. How cold it was she could not guess. At sight of the cloud she had hurriedly begun cramming every spare inch of the dugout with hay. Twisted hard, it burned in the cookstove with a brief, hot flame. Her palms were soon raw from handling the sharp, harsh stuff.

In the long dark hours—for she was frugal with kerosene and only a wavering light came from the drafts and the broken lid of the stove—she began to fight a vague and monstrous dread. It lay beneath her thoughts. From time to time it flung up questions.

What if the baby gets sick?

"He won't be sick!" she retorted. "He's a strong, healthy baby. If he's sick, I'll take care of him. I would anyway; there's no doctor in town."

Suppose something happens to David? Suppose he never comes back?

"Be still! I won't listen."

Wolves?

"Nonsense, I have the gun. And how could a wolf get through the door? Why am I scaring myself? Nothing like that will happen."

The wind howled. Gray darkness pressed against the paper pane, and a little snow, dry as sand, was forced through the crack beneath the door.

On the fourth morning Molly was awakened by a profound silence. The frosty air stung her nostrils; the blanket was edged with rime from her breath. Snug in the hollow of her body the baby slept cozily. She got up, lighted the lamp and started a fire in the cold stove.

She was not perturbed until she tried to open the door. Something outside held it against her confident push. And suddenly wild terror possessed her. She felt a Thing outside, pressed against the door.

It was only snow, she said to herself. There was no danger; the ledge was narrow. She flung all her strength and weight against the door. The stout planks quivered, and from top to bottom ran a sound like a scratch of claws. Then snow fell down the abrupt slope below the ledge, and sunlight pierced Molly's eyes.

Taking the shovel, she forced her body through the narrow aperture she had gained. Then she saw the immensity of whiteness and dazzling blue. Under the immeasurably vast sky, a limitless expanse of snow refracted the cold glitter of the sun. Nothing stirred, nothing breathed. Air and sun and snow were the whole visible world.

When Molly first came out of the dugout after the October blizzard, it was a moment of inexpressible terror, courage and pride. She felt that she was alive, and that God was with life. She thought, The gates of hell shall not prevail against me. She could feel what David felt, singing: "*Let the hurricane roar! . . . We'll weather the blast.*"

She drew a deep breath, and with her shovel she attacked the snow. The winds had packed it hard as ice against the door and the creek bank. The path was buried under a slanting drift. Inch by inch, digging, scraping, lifting, she made a way on which she could safely walk.

A blizzard of such severity so early in October seemed to predict an unusually hard winter. Her first care was fuel. She dug into the snow-

45

covered stacks by the barn, and tying a rope around big bundles of hay, she dragged them one by one down the path and into the dugout.

When she threw out the water in which she washed her hands, she noticed that its drops froze in the air. Startled, she looked into the mirror. Her nose and ears were white, frozen. They thawed painfully.

Then for three weeks the weather was mild, the snow was melting. There were days when the door stood open and the air was like spring. From above the dugout she could see the town; she could, indeed, see fifty miles beyond it. But her letter remained unmailed. The nice Mr. Gray and his Ada did not come; perhaps they dared not venture so far from shelter lest another blizzard catch them.

In early November the winter settled down. Blizzard followed blizzard out of the northwest. Sometimes there was a clear day between them, sometimes only a few hours. As soon as the winds ceased their howling and the snow thinned, she went out with the shovel.

On the dark days of the blizzards she twisted hay; she lighted the lamp for cleaning and cooking. And she played with the baby.

He was older now; he watched the firelight and clapped his hands, his soft little palms hardly ever missing each other. His blue eyes looked into Molly's. He could sit up and he could crawl. Kicking and crowing, he burbled sounds almost like words. "Mama," she could hear him say.

"Papa," she urged him. "Say it, baby dumpling! Say 'papa.' "

"Blablub!" he replied triumphantly, giving her a roguish glance that melted her heart. Playing with him, she was almost gay.

But there was always the ache of incompleteness without David. The shapeless dread might at any moment stab her with a question. But day by day the baby and she survived, and in the dugout the winds, the cold and snow and dark could not touch them. Her gaiety was a defiance.

Then came the seven days' blizzard. Molly had enough hay for three days. She had never known a blizzard to last longer. On the third day she burned the hay sparingly, but she was not alarmed. On the fourth day she broke up and burned a box, keeping the stove barely warm. On the fifth day she burned the remaining box. The heavy benches and table were left, which she could not break up with her hands, and the cradle. She had left the axe in the barn.

She sat wrapped in blankets on the edge of the bunk. When the fire went out there was no light at all. The window was obscurely gray, a dim square eye, looking in upon her. The stout door shook to the pounding

46

winds. She did not know whether this was day or night. The tiny pocket of still air in the dugout was increasingly cold.

During the seventh day she smashed and frugally burned the cradle. She boiled tea and potatoes. She mashed a potato in a little hot water and fed it with a spoon to the baby. Then she lay down with him under all the bedding and fell asleep.

A change in the sound of the wind awakened her. When she forced the door open, the storm had diminished so that she could see vaguely into it. She cleared the path, and when she reached its top she could see dim shapes of barn and haystacks. She filled the dugout with hay, and stretched a rope from the barn, as David had done, so that she could fetch fuel, if necessary, during a blizzard.

On the opposite bank of the creek she saw a dark patch. It troubled her, for she could not imagine what it might be; perhaps an illusion caused by her eyes' weeping in the wind, perhaps some danger. She shut the door against it hurriedly and gave herself up to the marvel of warmth.

In the morning, in the dazzling glitter of sun on snow, she saw across the creek a herd of cattle. Huddled together, heads toward the south, they stood patiently enduring the cold. In terror she thought of the haystacks. The creek bank hid them from the cattle now, but if the herd moved and saw that food, what would prevent them from turning back and destroying her fuel?

She put on her wraps and took the pistol. The cattle did not move. It came to her, while she watched, that for a long time they had not moved. Were they dead—frozen? No; breath came white from their nostrils.

The thought that they might be dead had brought a vision of meat.

Her courage quailed. But, jaw clenched against the cold, she went, knee-deep in drifts, down the bank and across the frozen creek. Was this too great a risk? Leaving the baby in the dugout and venturing into she knew not what? Still the cattle did not move. She went within ten yards of them, five, two. They did not even lift their heads.

Over their eyes—thick over their eyes and hollowed temples—she saw cakes of ice. She understood. Their own breath, steaming upward as they plodded before the storm, had frozen and blinded them.

In a rage of pity, she plunged through the snow to the nearest patiently dying creature; she wrenched the ice from its eyes. The steer snorted; he flung up his head in terror and ran, staggering, a few yards away.

Molly knew what she must do. She thought of the baby. She held all

47

thought, all feeling, firmly to the baby, and walking to the nearest young steer, she put the pistol to his temple, shut her eyes and fired. The report crashed through her.

She felt the shudder of all the beasts. When she opened her eyes they had not moved. The steer lay dead, only a little blood trickling, freezing, from the wound. And perhaps it had been merciful to kill him.

Then, like an inspiration, a revival of hope, she thought of a cow. Why not? In the herd there were many cows. Alas, they belonged to somebody. They were branded. She could not steal. Yet, if she did not take one of these cows, would it not die? The whole blinded herd was helpless.

She thought that perhaps there was a yearling that was not branded.

In her excitement she was almost laughing. Clumsy in boots and coat and shawls, she pushed into the harmless herd. The heifers, she knew, would be in the center. The old bull grumbled in his throat, shaking his blind head, but he did not move. There was a young red heifer, unbranded, almost plump. Molly marked it for her own. What a triumph, what a joke—to take a cow from the blizzard! And to have a cow, after so many calamities—this was a vindication of all confidence and hope.

She struggled through the drifts back to the dugout. She fed the stove with hay; she wrapped the baby warmly in blankets like a cocoon. Then she went to the barn for a rope.

The short winter day gave her little time. The sun was overhead before she had succeeded in prodding and tugging the terrified heifer out of the herd. And she had still to get it across the creek.

It was near sunset when she got the heifer into the barn. She put hay into the manger and tore the ice from the beast's eyes. With the rope and axe she went back to the herd. She cut the best parts of meat from the carcass of the steer, tied the pieces together and left all but one outside the dugout door to freeze. Then, trembling in her weariness, she went from animal to animal, tearing off the blinding ice. The old bull bellowed weakly, and slowly the herd drifted before the wind.

In the dark they would not see her hay. The wind was blowing toward the town; let the townspeople deal with the survivors who reached it. She had given the cattle a chance to live; she felt she had earned her cow.

The blizzard that came that night lasted only a day. Molly lay cozily in bed. The baby gurgled and kicked in exuberance of spirits; a great beef stew simmered on the stove, filling the air with its fragrance. If only David could know that they had a cow! But now she was confident

that David would come home strong and well; this winter would end, they would be together in the spring. How good to be warm and to rest. She felt she had never been thankful enough for all her blessings.

Late the next day she dug the path again. The heifer snorted and plunged when she brought in hay and set two pails of snow within its reach. She spoke to it soothingly, but did not touch it. In time it would learn her kindness and be gentle. It had all the marks of a good milk cow.

She closed the barn door. Afterward she always said she did not know what made her stop and turn. By the barn stood a wolf.

If you went out— If a wolf sprang— What would become of the baby alone in the dugout? It's come, her frozen heart knew.

She had only the shovel.

It was a gaunt, big timber wolf. His eyes shone green in the half light. She dared not turn lest he spring.

He shifted a paw. Molly did not move. Swiftly he turned and vanished, a shadow in the falling snow.

When she reached the ledge of the dugout a long wolf howl rose from the ceiling above her. Another answered it from the frozen creek below. She slammed the door behind her.

She knew the wolves were hungry; they must have been following the cattle, and the steer she had killed had kept them near. After that she often heard wolves howling, and found their tracks in the snow. She never left the dugout without the pistol.

The reality of the wolves constantly reminded her of David's warning. Wolves, he had written—and outlaws. When she stirred the fire she thought of the smoke ascending the chimney. For miles around it could be seen. Claim jumpers would probably not come. But outlaws?

She felt within herself a certainty that at any human threat of danger she would kill. She said to herself that no stranger should enter that dugout—not under any circumstances, not with any fair words.

Blizzard followed blizzard. She had lost reckoning of time and was not quite sure whether December had ended and January begun. But each day brought nearer the end of winter, David's return. The baby was healthy, the heifer was safe in the barn. She had only to hold on.

February had come, though she did not know it. Three clear days of terrible cold were ending, near nightfall, in the rising of the blizzard winds. That day Molly had filled half the barn with hay; the heifer was now provided for if this storm lasted a week. The baby slept. There was twisted hay for the stove, the supper dishes were washed, and by the faint light of the dying fire Molly combed her hair for the night.

All at once the howling of the wind, racing and circling overhead, seemed like unearthly, inhuman screams and a wild halloo. Molly thought how like demon riders it sounded. She shook her hair back and put her hands to braid it, and in the gleam of light from the broken stove lid she saw a joint of the stovepipe suddenly bend. A crack opened between the two ends of pipe. Petrified, she heard a human cry.

A man was on top of the dugout. Blind in the storm, he had stumbled against the chimney. No honest man, no lost homesteader. All afternoon the blizzard had been threatening; no honest man would have gone far from shelter. Only a rider out of the northwest might have fled before the storm. Out of the northwestern refuges of the outlaws.

He had struck the chimney on the eastern side; he was going toward the creek. Only a few steps and he would fall down the creek bank, down into the deep drifts below. He would be buried. Keep still! she said to herself. It isn't your business. Don't let him in. Who knows who he is. Think of the baby. *What are you doing?*

Her mouth close to the stovepipe, she shouted, "Stand still! Don't move!" Soot from the open joint of the pipe fell on her face.

A vague shout replied. He seemed to have wandered a step or two toward the creek. She knew how the winds were swirling, beating and tugging at him from every side. She saw him blinded, deafened, lost. An outlaw, but human, fighting the storm.

"Lie down! Crawl!" she shouted. "Creek bank ahead! There is a path! Path to the left! Find a rope! *You hear?*"

If he shouted again, she did not hear him. She twisted her hair and thrust pins into it, buttoned her wrap and lighted the lamp. She got her pistol and made sure it was loaded. Some instinct made her lift David John, wrap him in a blanket and lay him on the bunk. She felt better with the baby behind her. Then she lifted the bar on the door, and retreating behind the table, she waited.

She had time to regret what she had done, and to know that she could not have done otherwise.

The wind suddenly tore open the door. Snow whirled in, and cold. The lamp flared smokily, and as she started forward, the man appeared in the white blizzard. He was tall and shapeless in fur coat and cap; he was muffled to reddened slits of eyes and snow-matted eyebrows; it was an instant before she knew him and screamed. Then his arms closed around her, hard and cold as ice.

"Oh, how—how did you get here?" she gasped after a while, unable still to believe it. Her hands kept clutching the snowy fur, frantic to make sure this was David.

"Gosh, I'm freezing you to death! I got to shut the door," he said. And at these homely words, she burst into tears.

"H-h-have you—had any supper?" she wept.

"Hang supper!" he sang out joyously.

Later he teased her a little. "What's so surprising? Didn't I tell you I'd get here quick as I could?" Then he scolded her seriously. "Molly, God only knows what I went through when they told me in town that you were out here alone. Don't ever do another fool trick like that. Do you suppose I care for anything in the world compared to you?"

51

He asked, "How's the little shaver?" and she said, "Oh, David, he's wonderful! He's got two teeth! Just—" But then he hugged her, and there was so much to ask, to tell.

"And we've got a cow!" she told him.

"A—not our own cow?"

"Well, a heifer. A good, red heifer. She'll make a fine milker."

"But how did you ever— Look," he said, "I've got forty dollars."

"Oh, David, how's your leg?"

"Well, I have to favor it a little—you notice I've got you on the other knee. But it stood the walk pretty well; it'll be fine as ever for spring plowing."

"And you walked ten miles! Oh, David!"

"What did you think I'd do, and you out here?"

"David, the whole country's overrun with wolves."

"Fine. I'll get some good skins."

It didn't matter, really, what they said. They were together; everything was all right. She heard the clamor of the storm, all the demons shrieking; simply a blizzard, simply the winter weather on their farm.

A little sound made her turn; the baby! There was little David John, wide-awake, lifting himself up with his tiny fingers on the edge of the bunk. And then, clearly, triumphantly, he spoke.

"Blablub!" he said. A dimple quivered in his cheek; then his mouth spread in David's wide grin, and there were the two white teeth.

"Look, David, look! Oh, did you hear him call you papa?"

Somehow, without quite thinking it, she felt that a light from the future was shining in the baby's face. The big white house was waiting for him, and the acres of wheat fields, fast-driving teams and swift buggies. If he remembered at all this life in the dugout, he would think of it only as a brief prelude to more spacious times.

MISS MORISSA
Doctor of the Gold Trail

MISS MORISSA:
Doctor
of the Gold Trail

A CONDENSATION OF THE NOVEL BY
Mari Sandoz

ILLUSTRATED BY BOB CROFUT

Western Nebraska in 1876
was cow country still, where cowboys
and ranchers grazed their herds on
the open range. But the railroad now linked
the lawless region to the eastern states,
bringing fortune hunters and
outlaws on their way to the rich gold strike
at Deadwood Gulch, just north in Dakota.
It brought homesteaders also,
who planned to fence the range and raise
crops. Into this explosive situation came
a much-needed physician—twenty-four years
old, and a woman. Dr. Morissa Kirk.

Mari Sandoz was born in Nebraska in 1901.
Her many novels of the West, among
them *Cheyenne Autumn*, draw on the vivid
memories of an earlier generation to
achieve their remarkable realism.

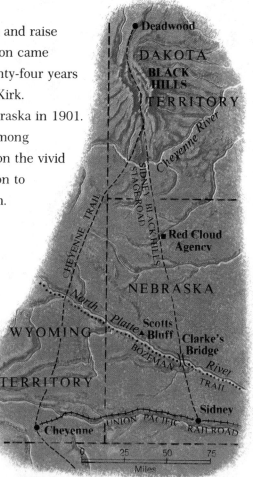

Chapter 1

THE WHEELS OF THE STAGECOACH stirred up a long trail of dust, to sift away eastward like a plume of smoke sprouting from the wide spring prairie. All except one of the passengers were content to be closed in by the heavy side curtains, even the sunburned rancher and the naked-faced youth with small dark freckles thick across his cheeks. But the young city woman pulled back the stiff canvas and thrust her head out. She did it with a practicality and foresight that belied the feathered little hat tipped toward her nose. She had asked to change seats so she could look out on the windy side, away from most of the dust. But the wind was strong. The feathers on her hat struggled like agitated yellow birds, and her fashionable bangs that had seemed so duskily black in the shadow were shot with gleaming copper light where the sun ran over them.

With her white skin unprotected by powdering or veil, Morissa Kirk leaned far out to look at the guard carrying a Winchester across his knee, and to watch the driver swing his six fast horses out around the slower travelers. They passed gold seekers, mule freight outfits, and files of wagons drawn by long teams of bulls. As the coach jounced and jolted, a little round-topped trunk tied on top jounced, too. It was a new pressed-metal trunk that was to have accompanied Morissa Kirk on her wedding journey to Scotland, and was still filled with her trousseau, although her hand was bare of rings. Beside the small trunk was a doctor's black bag and a chest of surgical instruments, while inside, cradled on Morissa's lap, was a case of vials and bottles and other physician's supplies.

The coach swung down toward a rugged range of buttes that tapered

57

off to Courthouse and Jail Rocks, standing out together and alone. At their feet the trail turned northwestward, upon the broad North Platte valley of Nebraska, the spreading bottoms grazed so bare that no stock was nearer than the far blue slopes. But as the swift coach approached the river, Morissa saw at least thirty great circle corrals of covered freight wagons and a far spreading of other vehicles, with tents and bedrolls scattered among them, and knots of men—all jammed together closer and closer toward the new bridge. The crowd was thick as a close-corralled herd, and as restless. All were waiting for the bridge that Henry Clarke was building to be finished, to carry them over the roily, flooded stream, release them to hurry toward the Black Hills of Dakota where gold lay thick at the grass roots. They had seen the shining proof of it in the tiny bottles of yellow dust set to catch the eye in the windows of every depot across the nation.

It was this rush to the new Eldorado of Deadwood Gulch that had gathered the great wagon trains of mine machinery and equipment here, trains of whiskey, too, and mahogany bars and roulette tables, guns and ammunition, and finery for the fancy-houses.

While still far off the driver of the stagecoach called out his loud "Yip, yip, yip; yi, yi, yi!"—the signal to get the change of horses ready for the ride to Deadwood if the bridge was opened, otherwise for the return trip to Sidney. And as they neared the river the passengers heard the dull thump of the pile driver and knew that no one would cross this afternoon unless he swam, or took a chance on old Joe Lenway, who had his handwritten sign in all the outfitting places back down at Sidney:

I HAUL YOU OVER NORTH RIVER SAFE
$2.00 DOLLAR A WAGON.

Horsebackers had met the coach a mile out to make a flying wedge for it through the crowd to the stage station beside the river. The galloping escort stopped with snort and clatter of harness, and the passengers stretched stiffly and one after the other stooped out and down into the curious crowd.

"Hey, a lady-woman, an' a good looker!" a tipsyish youth shouted as Morissa was helped off the high step by a station hand. Then she stood alone in her feathered hat and dark green traveling suit, with sun-darkened faces turned toward her from all around.

After Morissa, the freckled young man came out. He jumped down and slipped away into the crowd, a man or two speaking of him as he went, "Fly Speck, Fly Speck Billy." A weary crinkle came to Morissa's hazel eyes. Of course—the dark freckles. But she remembered something else now: this must be the highwayman from Dakota Territory, a "road agent" as Robin, her stepfather, called him. That smooth boy-face hid a thief, a cold-blooded murderer. And yet, well recognized, he walked unchallenged through this public place.

Uneasily Morissa glanced around the rough crowd. There were few women beyond those from the saloons, and most of the men had guns in their holsters. She managed to push through to her belongings, wondering how she could ever find Robin in all this throng. And as she stood there, with nowhere to go, she finally had to doubt the wisdom of her impulsive, unannounced journey into this wilderness.

When the crowd began to drift back to watch the thumping pile driver, Morissa Kirk found the station keeper.

"Yeh," he admitted, replenishing his cud. "Yeh, I know Robin Thomas." But Robin was off across the river there, boss of the graders refilling the new approach to the bridge. Washed out yesterday. Water came roaring down the old Platte. The keeper pointed off over his shoulder to the bridge that stood like some long, low, many-legged creature.

As Morissa looked, a shouting came from the riverbank, and a wagon broke from the mass of people waiting on the far side of the wide rolling Platte. It swung around and then headed in toward the river, turned expertly a little upstream, coming at a good pace—the momentum to carry it through the quarter mile of flood and quicksand.

At the shouting the bridge workers all stopped to look. "It's old Joe Lenway!" voices called. "Hold the Sidney coach. Lenway's bringin' a sick man over!"

A murmuring of uneasiness and protest stirred around Morissa. The river was too high, after the sudden thaw in the western mountains; but Joe Lenway would try anything for two dollars.

Morissa was being carried along toward the river by the push of the crowd. She could see the moving wagon and a man whipping his team into the gray stream. The horses tried to rear sideways at the flood edge, but under the fury of old Joe's lashes they settled to the pull, the current boiling up around their bellies, then at their breasts. They began floundering and tried to rear above it, leap its pull. The team and the wagon lurched forward together once more and went off into deep water as over a bank, sunk clear under. Joe grabbed the tail of a swimming horse. Behind him a bedroll—no, a man—was washed up on the flood. For a moment the appalled crowd watched a feeble splashing and then the man was gone.

"Save him!" Morissa Kirk cried out, commanding them as though none could see that this must be done.

Two riders broke from the watchers at the far side and sent their horses into the water where the current swept in toward the bank. When the man reappeared, their ropes shot out and the man stopped, swung in an arc against the angry water, and then one of the horses was struggling back, drawing him in like a bawling calf to the branding fire. At the bank the cowboys carried him out, laid him on dry ground, and stood around him, helpless.

Now Morissa Kirk could not restrain herself. Grabbing up her wide skirts she pushed back to the stage station and with her little doctor's bag hanging from her arm she swung herself up on one of the horses at the hitchracks. With a knee crooked around the horn like the knob of a lady's sidesaddle, she was off on the rearing, fighting, white-stockinged black, through the crowd and then over the bank into the cold snow water in one splashing leap, the shouts of anger and warning lost behind her.

The horse snorted and began to plunge as he felt the sand moving and alive under his feet, but a sharp cut of the saddle quirt sent him forward, an experienced, well-trained animal. He swam the current strongly, and finally they were out on the other side, the crowd pressing close around.

Morissa was soaked, even her yellow feathers hanging wet, but the doctor's bag was still on her arm and as someone grabbed the horse's bit she slipped off and ran for the man on the ground, the watchers parting for her. She stooped over him, felt for his heart under the wet clothing and laid an ear to his breast, but there was no beat. Quickly she drew the tongue free, and showed a cowboy how to turn the man over, grasp him about the middle and lift up, bringing a gush of dirty water bursting from his mouth and nose. Then, with the man's head turned up sideways on her arm, Morissa knelt over him, lifting, pressing, forcing herself to calm her breath to the slow rhythm as someone brought a buffalo robe and started a little fire. When she tired she shook back the hair stringing over her face and gave her place to one of the men.

A man came pushing through the crowd, elbowing his way. The young woman did not notice him or his exclamation when he saw her, but the one word "Morissa!" from Robin Thomas started a wave of low voices. Morissa? Then this must be his stepdaughter, who was a lady doc.

While the young woman fingered her vials and powders, she glanced anxiously at the man on the ground and the cowboy bending up and down over him. Still no color came, and she was less confident now, more fearful that in her hurry and her inexperience she might have forgotten something, something that could have been done. The man had no signs of any living that she could see, and so without hope she took over from the cowboy again.

The young doctor worked until her arms ached to breaking. But when it seemed that she must give up, a change came, an almost imperceptible change, yet she knew they were winning. Against the excitement of this, she held herself to the steady pressures, and finally a tiny bubble rose to the man's gray lips. Tears stung the young woman's eyes but she shook them away, and when there was breathing, shallow and weak, but breathing, she turned the man onto his back and groped for her bag. Somebody pushed a bottle of Old Crow into her hand. Without glancing around she licked a test drop spilled on the back of her hand and nodded. Carefully she gave the man a little swallow and then another, and finally she got him out of his wet clothing and rolled into the warmed buffalo robe beside the fire.

"I been sick couple weeks, I guess, bad sick," the man murmured to the doctor's questions. "I been havin' a gnawin' a long time, inside the belly there, like it had a hole. . . ."

That, and his name, Tom Reeder, was all Morissa discovered before his voice trailed off into exhaustion and sleep. So she had him carried away toward a tent, and when she had time to thank the man who offered the shelter, she realized that it was Robin. He let her sob out her relief against his bearded cheek.

But in a moment Morissa remembered her patient and gathered up her awkward, bedraggled skirts to run after him, barely seeing a man who had stopped his horse in her path. The fine bay he was riding was wet to the mane, the rider soaked, too, from a Platte crossing—a tall, stern, sunburned man, his gray eyes very angry.

"Don't ever do that again, ma'am," he warned. "That Cimarron horse isn't broke for ladies. A wonder you weren't killed."

At first Morissa was angry, too, but her manners came back swiftly enough. "Did I take your horse? I'm sorry, but I don't think I've hurt him, Mr.—"

"Polk. Tris Polk."

"Thank you, Mr. Polk. You have a good right to be proud of that splendid animal, so ready for an emergency."

But the man still stood his stirrups, his palms on the saddle horn. "Well, let me tell you something, ma'am," he said. "In these parts taking the poorest crowbait without the owner's permission's a hanging matter."

"Oh, really?" Morissa inquired, her anger back. "I am sure in these parts, as in all others, letting a man die without attempting succor would be a matter of murder to an enlightened conscience, Mr. Polk."

With this she went around him and his horse, leaving the man free to look after this soft-voiced girl who could muster such fire to go with her courage, and poise too—bedraggled as she was, with a hat as silly as any that the women of the Black Hills dance halls might be wearing.

BY NIGHT MORISSA KIRK was settled in Robin's one-room sod-house, set beside his wagon corral south of the river. Undismayed by the bare earthen walls or the dirt floor and the nail-keg chairs, she had changed her suit and brought out her diploma and arranged her medical books and essentials in a big box, pegged up on the sod wall. She hung her clothing and the white hospital jacket behind a blanket above the cot; she unpacked a few of her pretty things from the trunk, too, and set her silver toilet articles on the bare windowsill, making a steady fussing of it all, giving herself no free moment to think of what lay shut away under the thin ice of her energy.

Robin Thomas asked no questions of Morissa, just washed the dust from his long graying hair and beard, buckled on his gun, and took down the lantern. Then, with Morissa neat in a Scotch-plaid walking suit and a sailor hat tilted over her bangs, he took her to see the camp. They walked from Clarke's supply and whiskey store at one end to the road ranch of Ettier, the Canadian Frenchman, at the other—Etty's place a string of weathered sod and log shacks. "Old Etty's been around here, on and off, more than twenty years. Stood off outlaw gangs and a few Sioux bucks full of whiskey, too, although he's married to a woman who's part Sioux—a nice woman," Robin said.

Inside, the smoke hung thick around the kerosene wall lamps, the low rooms packed, particularly around the bar and the fiddlers. In one of the rooms Morissa stared at stacks of gold coin glinting in the smoky light.

Between Etty's place and Clarke's were shacks, tents, and open-front shelters with counters rough-sawed of pine from the Wild Cat Mountains. There were even covered wagons offering the evening's entertainment and necessities, the price a little less because it was three steps up, with the need to duck the head under the wagon bows.

All were busy tonight, particularly where there was gambling, now that a belt of gold nuggets had been found on Tom Reeder after he was pulled out of the water, and more yellow dust in the little box chained tight to the wagon bed, when Joe Lenway got the wagon out half a mile down the river. Morissa saw the leather pouches of gold it contained— enough to keep the man for life, it seemed. Because the box was carried into the stage station by two men with armed guards riding alongside, all the camp knew what it must contain, and that it was a great deal. Tomorrow the planking of Clarke's bridge would surely thunder to thousands of impatient hoofs, and so for this one night many spent as though fortune already weighted down their jeans.

The girl held the hem of her skirts out of the dust as Robin Thomas guided her past the lurching drunks and the urgently woman-hungry. Several times he stopped to introduce Morissa. "My daughter, Doctor Kirk"—saying it proudly to the handsome, bearded, and warm-eyed Henry Clarke of the bridge, and to some army officers.

"Yes, we're heading for Red Cloud Agency up the trail there," the young lieutenant said. "Reports are that the Sioux warriors have been slipping away north to Chief Crazy Horse—gathering against our troops headed into the Yellowstone country."

"Plenty of them red devils're workin' up around the Black Hills," a driver of a freight wagon standing nearby complained. He had some mules driven off on his last trip to Deadwood, and had bullet holes in his wagons to prove the attack. "There's thousands of them hungry bucks no more than a day's ride from here. Claim the bridge's on their land. Probably be burning it some cloudy night."

Robin offered no softening words to all of this. Instead he showed Morissa her first ranch foreman, a man working for Bosler, a rancher and beef contractor charged with defrauding the Indians on government beef deliveries. Bosler had one of the biggest cattle outfits of the West. Claimed a hundred fifty miles of water here, and had the guns to hold it. "But that's the north bank, across the river."

Morissa glanced over that way in the pale moonlight, but there was no time to consider these things tonight. She met several owners of the big freight outfits and an advance man for an English troupe of singers. They planned to put on some Gilbert and Sullivan for the miners at Deadwood Gulch, if a hall could be found.

Tris Polk came up, too, courteous this time, impersonally complimenting Morissa's riding and her skill with the sick. "I hear the man is sleeping for the first time in days," he said.

"But it may not mean much. We can only hope," Morissa replied, matching the man's impersonality.

There were only a few women out tonight, mostly around the dances, particularly Etty's big one where the fiddlers sawed and stomped. Huff Johnson had a handsome Junoesque blonde standing beside him at the faro table. She couldn't be lured away even by Tris Polk, it seemed. "But Huff'll have trouble keeping Gilda Ross if Polk really wants her," Robin predicted.

He pointed out a dozen men who were known as outlaws: holdup men, road agents, murderers. Fly Speck Billy was still there, but when the young man lifted his hat gravely to Morissa, so recently his fellow traveler, Robin looked at the girl in surprised concern.

She managed to laugh a little. "Oh, water finds its own level very quickly. Or, as you recall Mother saying, 'Short grace for hungry folk.' "

"Or 'Rubbin' your nose in a hog trough don't even make friends of the hogs,' " Robin answered sourly. Fly Speck was just out of the Ogallala jail because everybody was afraid to testify against a cold-blooded killer. "I got my fill of his kind years ago, but Jackie's excited as a kid by them," he added with concern. "I try to keep him up with my horse herd, away from the show-offs around the bridge here."

"Oh, Jackie's only sixteen," Morissa started to comfort. "He'll be all right—he's of your good stock—" but she caught herself, always having to stop her stupid tongue. Robin seemed not to notice her confusion.

They stopped at the grading corral to look in on Tom Reeder in one of the bowed wagons, sleeping heavily although his small dose of morphia should have done no more than quiet him. As Morissa replenished the fire in the little wagon heater, she wondered how much of this was disease and how much exhaustion and anxiety from guarding his treasure through the long dangers of Deadwood Gulch and the trail.

In the little sod-house beside the corral gate Robin settled down on a nail keg for his evening pipe. Morissa sat hunched forward on the cot, worn and pale now for all her sunburn, her hat still on, staring straight ahead. For a moment Robin thought of a grouse or a dove, wounded and huddled close as possible to the ground. But this girl, who had pulled herself up from her days as a woods colt on a poor farm, was no dove or even a grouse, no matter what the wounding.

"Morissa," Robin said softly, "Morissa, do you want to tell me why you came? Last I knew the wedding was next week. . . ."

For a long time the girl made no reply, so still the old cot did not creak. "No—I guess there's nothing to tell," she said at last.

"It wasn't just a lovers' quarrel?"

Morissa shook her head, her eyes bleak in the lantern light. "He asked for his ring back," she said. "Couldn't take me into the family, not after what his sister found out. . . ." The girl stopped, her full soft lips quivering for the first time.

"Found out—about your mother? Oh, I could kill the fool!" Robin exploded, his voice loud as though shouting against a northwest blizzard wind. "No," he added more moderately, "that wouldn't help. But you know you are welcome here with me, Morissa, to all these poor accommodations. Now get a little sleep. We'll need you tomorrow. There will be man and animal hurt in the tearing hurry across the bridge."

He started out, but turned at the door and slowly unbuckled his gun. "I better leave this with you. There's no law here for anybody, you know, except what you make."

Reluctantly the girl reached out and took the heavy cartridge belt, holding it away from her as she laid it on the end of the cot.

Chapter 2

MORISSA AWOKE into the emptiness of a great sorrow and loss. She kept her eyes closed and held herself quiet, waiting for what seemed a nightmare to pass. But the sense of it remained, and finally she had to acknowledge that she was not asleep. So, while still hiding in her own darkness, Morissa swung her long, gown-covered legs over the side of the cot. Her sleep-blurred eyes opened to the sod walls and the early sun stretched over the packed dirt floor. Horsebackers were riding by on the trail, the campers beyond it out and shouting, rattling harness, getting under way.

She dressed quickly, slipping into her gray street alpaca with the mustard-colored trim. Then, with her hair still in the thick braid down her back, she went out, stopping to look under her palm toward the sun just up over the long, low bridge that waited in silence now, the last of the pilings set.

But a very sick patient was waiting, so the young doctor hurried across the dewy ground. The man was awake, attempting to sit up, his gaunt, gray-stubbled face bleak with fear at the approach. When he saw who it was he let himself back, yet still uneasy, alarmed.

"My outfit—was it all lost?" he whispered.

"Oh, no, Mr. Reeder, only one of the horses. Your box is safe at the stage station, your gold belt too," Morissa assured him cheerfully. She smiled down into the whitened, suspicious eyes and nodded in approval that his tin cup of soup was empty. Then she took the man's temperature and pulse, washed his gaunt face, and prepared him for examination. Yesterday he was a man to be kept alive; today he was one to be cured.

After a while he began to talk, weakly at first, but with urgent snatches about some trouble last night. "All that yellin' an' shootin'," he complained in a vague, futile anger. "They hung a man," he said.

"Well, at least your dreams aren't dull," the doctor soothed as she started to go over the man methodically, particularly the hollow belly and the bony chest. "It's there, the hole that's gnawin'," he said as she probed below the ribs for a possible growth or sign of infection.

Suddenly Tom Reeder grabbed for the buffalo robe. "I ain't gonna be shamed this way by no she-doc!" he shouted hoarsely, sweat popping out milky on his face.

Morissa tucked in the corners of her mouth and wiped the man's forehead. "Would you object to your nakedness if I was a prostitute?"

That brought a swift flush. "No," the man admitted; and at the matter-of-factness of the young woman, Tom Reeder became silent, although his wasted muscles were tense, ungiving as ropes of chicken wire. So Morissa turned the talk to his dream again. "Maybe it was after you awoke this morning, and then dozed off. That's when you remember the dreams so clearly."

"No, I hearn him, yellin'. . . ."

"Who?"

"I don' know—some poor bastard," he said, closing his eyes. He did not see the pain his words brought to the young face bent above him. Quickly the doctor spread the buffalo robe over the man and went out. From the step of the wagon, Morissa looked toward the bridge. The queue of those waiting to cross reached far back along the trail, as far as Courthouse Rock. Shielding her eyes from the sun, Morissa noticed that something hung from the railing, something that resembled a suspended man. She went over that way, and one of the group called to her. "That's number one on this bridge, Doc, an' room for a lot more!"

The form was unmistakably a man, a man with a tortured tilt to the head, his chin turned up and a little to the side, as though in pained disdain of the noose about his neck, the horror only in the staring eyes, the hands turned palm out in pitiful supplication. To Morissa it seemed a sacrilege upon the most beautifully balanced and artistic instrument, the human body; a defilement upon the noblest creation, the mind of man.

In a cold fury the young doctor gathered up her skirts and hurried over to the bridge owner's office. Henry Clarke was not there, but she saw him on his star-faced bay at the toll shack. She pushed past the men who would hold her back and stopped before Clarke, forgetting that he was her father's employer, knowing only that he was in command here.

"It seems to me you might have the humanity to take down that terrible thing hanging at the bridge," she burst out, speaking overloud to cover the weakness caused by her emotion.

The bridge builder turned to look down upon her, his long gauntleted hands settling to the saddle horn, his reddish beard glowing in the sun. After a long time of silent, remote appraisal he spoke. "I am sorry that I must deny a beautiful woman anything, but this is a humane act, keeping the owls away by nailing up a dead owl as an example."

"But this is sinful, or, if sin has no meaning here, let us say unlawful."

"Yes, unlawful, Miss Morissa. But have you heard of the murder of the Metz family, up the trail in the Hills?"

"What pertinency could that have here—that massacre by Indians?"

"By Indians for gold dust? That's all that was taken, Miss Morissa. No clothing, no food, not even the gun they had or the cartridges. Persimmon Bill's gang of road agents have already made their brags about it. Even the arrows and moccasin tracks they left are old tricks."

For a moment Morissa was nonplussed. "I still don't see what that has to do with this—" she objected finally.

"My child, there were at least twenty thousand people around here within five, ten miles last night. Fortunes in money on this side, and in gold dust on the other, all without a sheriff or police or court. No law for the protection of property or of life, and perhaps a hundred Persimmon Bills among us, ready for murder. That's why the man is hanging there— because we have no law except the gun and the rope."

"But what did this man do?" Morissa still persisted.

"That, my dear, cannot be put into words today, but you might notice that there is not one known outlaw left here this morning. Now if you will excuse me, I hope to get the bridge opened by noon."

Angry and humiliated, Morissa pushed through the crowd to the stage station. There she bought space on the coach that would start back to Sidney in two, three hours. Then she hurried as fast as she could back to the little sod-house so gray and sad beside Robin's wagons.

Inside, she began to throw her belongings into the pressed-metal trunk. It did not matter that she had no plans. Certainly she could not return to the practice she gave up so gaily for her wedding. No, it must be somewhere new, still in the West, but not so far beyond the law next time.

And in her horror and anger she forgot her patient in the wagon. Before she thought of him there was a sound of hoofs, a shouting, "Hey! Lady Doc! Hey!" and of horses stopped in midrun, a man off, pounding urgently at the jamb of the open door.

Morissa wiped the wet from her cheeks and went out into the sunlight.

"I'm from Polk's beef herd downriver a couple miles. Man with a party of gold seekers near us been knifed," the sunburned cowboy said, motioning to the extra horse he led. "Bleeding bad, about gone . . ."

Morissa snatched up her black bag and swung into the saddle, knee about the horn, holding on as she followed the man spurring ahead. When they neared the party a knot of men in black came from the wagons to meet the doctor and then drew together, their bearded faces darkening at her approach. "No—not a woman doctoress!" one shouted, with the accent of the Pennsylvania Dutch. "This we want not."

"But at least let me look at the man," Morissa pleaded with them. "Perhaps I can tell you what to do—"

"No! No!" they said sternly, gathering in a dark wall around the fire where the man apparently lay.

"You damn fools! Doc saved a life here yesterday," the cowboy said angrily. But the dusty group only drew nearer to each other, seeming even more determined and afraid.

"Ignorant bigots!" Morissa wanted to cry against them, but she held herself to an inner raging. Plainly there was no use waiting, so she turned back to her horse and mounted. She let him start off in a shying run, leaning forward in the saddle, her braid snapping out behind her.

"I had no idea, Doc," the cowboy apologized when he caught up. "I'm from over in Wyoming myself. We don't see things that way. Women got the vote there years ago."

Back at Robin's house the young doctor sank down in the duskiness of her sun-blinded eyes, still shaking with anger. Not that she hadn't met this attitude before, but here it was not just a preference for a male doctor but a preference of none at all to a woman, even of letting a man die.

As she sat despondently on the cot, Morissa recalled the words of a slight, earnest young army surgeon named Walter Reed. He had given up a good position in New York and stopped on his way to an Arizona post to speak to a group of young doctors. "I suggest that you go to the frontier," he had told them. "Your patients will be the young, with the ills of youth and a new country. Epidemics, appalling accidents and violence. Too often there are only the grieving to watch the sick tonight, and many are dying entirely alone."

Yet just now, she, Dr. Morissa Kirk, had been ready to sit beside such a one with the little that her hands could offer. And what would it matter to the man, dead or alive, that the doctor had been a woman?

But the stage taking her back to Sidney would soon be leaving. She must dress, try to eat something. Wearily she combed her long hair in the doorway, the sun running like fire over its moving darkness. With the hair pinned up, her bangs smooth, she looked through the covered tin cans back of Robin's little two-holed stove: flour for flapjacks, tea, smoked side meat, dried peaches, apples, and white beans.

Almost as soon as the smoke curled up around the stovepipe oven and out into the sun there was a tap at the door. A hairy, gray little man in a dusty frock coat and bare feet stood there, with a lidded old pail in one hand and a willow withe strung with four dressed fish in the other.

"Good morning, fair one!" he announced. "I am the laughing cavalier!" Setting his pail down he slapped his chest as he bowed, and with a slender, scar-twisted hand held up the big trout. "May I offer these piscatorial prizes to milady?"

"Fresh?" Morissa asked, having to laugh in spite of her mood.

"Very fresh. Caught and dressed this morning by Wilmer D.Q.—for DeQuincey—Jones. May I suggest a genteel barter? Two of these most excellent fish for bread or the wherewith to accompany the other two."

Morissa had to be amused at this foolishness. She added a little more flour to the biscuits and got out Robin's big spider to fry the trout. In the meantime the little man sat talking with his back against the doorjamb, the tails of his coat turned up out of the dust.

When Morissa was ready for the trout, he interrupted himself. "Ah, miss, honor me by discarding not one head of these beautiful fish. The cheek of the noble trout is a tidbit fit for the immortals."

Morissa nodded her appreciation, grateful for this diversion. A wee bush is indeed better than nae hiding at all, she told herself. And when the man reached to take the tin plate of trout and brown biscuits from her, she asked about the peculiar gnarl of flesh on both the back and palm of his right hand. "How did you get that scar?"

"Indian arrow," the man said modestly. "A lovely Sioux maiden fled her irate father with me. We were overtaken. An arrow clove my hand, felled me, and she, thinking me dead, threw herself over a cliff."

"Oh, nonsense, Mr. DeQuincey Jones!" Morissa started to protest, but the lope of a horse interrupted her. It was Robin, shouting, "Fish Head! You son of a gun! It didn't take you long to smell out a meal!"

So the little man licked the last bit of meat from a fish skeleton, slipped the four fried fish heads into his pocket, and shuffled away.

Robin looked around the bare house, with the girl's pretties all packed away, her diploma gone. He grieved for the young doctor whose mother he had married long ago, and he yearned to ease the misery and anger he saw lying deep within her now. "The bridge will open around twelve or one," he announced grandly, "and a man's gone up to the horse herd for Jackie. I thought he'd better come to visit with his sister before your fame spreads so's you won't have time for us." He laughed as he nodded in the direction Fish Head had gone.

"Ah, Robbie, you sing a mighty pretty song to catch a crow!" the girl replied.

"Aye, it is true nothing can enter the closed fist, my girl," the man said. Fish Head had come all of twenty miles to see her. He was a man of parts, with a silk hat in that old axle-grease pail, ready for the most formal occasion. He had been a flashy figure, a railroad cardsharp. But when he tried to clean out a lot of Mexicans one of them flipped a knife through his hand, and when they got the blade loose from the table underneath, there was an ace of spades, split and bloody, under his palm. The tendons were cut, left the nimble fingers stiff as sticks.

Morissa nodded without looking up, and so Robin had to drop it. He finally left, for Morissa seemed to have nothing to tell him.

After Robin was gone, she went to her patient and rolled up the canvas to let in a little May sun. The man looked gray as death in the sharp light, his heart only a furtive, reluctant little beat for all the digitalis the young doctor dared administer. "I am leaving orders you must go down to Sidney tomorrow," she said as she counted the pulse.

Tom Reeder lifted himself in protest. "I'll be robbed and throwed out the window," he exclaimed hoarsely.

A wagon hurrying up outside saved her from arguing with the sick man. It was two men from the Pennsylvania Dutch party. They had come to ask about medicines to be bought for bleeding and the easing of pain.

Morissa felt the anger come up in her throat again. "You are inhuman men," she said to them. "You are letting a fellow creature suffer for a bigoted whim!"

But in a moment she was ashamed. Bustling her bag together she climbed into the wagon unasked and motioned them to hurry. When they got her back to the man, he was already white as death, the eyes glazed. She laid her head to his bloody breast, felt for the pulse that was gone, and folded the limp hands.

"Who did this? Who stabbed him?" she asked, and as she had expected, she was not told.

IT WAS VERY LATE when she could start back, too late, unless the Sidney coach was long delayed. Afoot she headed straight for Robin's house, almost two miles away. Suddenly a small black bird with white on the wings rose into the air, singing all the way, a trilling so clear and sweet it stopped the heart. And as he slanted down, still singing, another arose, and then a third almost at her feet, and when they were gone into the light spring wind, Morissa Kirk stood still and for the second time that day she had a wetness on her cheek.

Then, as with sudden resolution she hurried on, she heard the rattle of impatient harness and a call from the stage office for "Morissa Kirk! Dr.

Morissa Kirk!" until they probably let someone else have her place. At the driver's whoop the coach hurried away toward Sidney behind the escort of horsebackers. The dust of it spread over the long line waiting for the bridge to open and over Robin Thomas, come to stand where he could see who got on the stage, and then slip away.

Morissa pushed in at Clarke's big store and saloon and then out again, elbowing her way with her black bag. Finally at Etty's she found a little cache of Indian trade goods in a lean-to off the gambling rooms. There was not much for her in the place, crowded with trail wares—barrels of hardtack and twist tobacco and stacks of shovels and gold pans. But there was a bolt of red calico under a lot of Indian goods, dusty and pushed aside because very few Indians traveled the route since the buffalo herds vanished.

"Not that we're looking for Indians in particular, with most of the bucks on the prod," a clerk called Eddie said when Morissa got him diverted from his brags about the gold he would dig as soon as he raised a grub stake.

While he talked she looked the material over, turkey-red with a small black and yellow figure. She pulled a couple of threads from the cut edge and chewed them to test the color. Over the acrid taste of the dye she noticed the man, only a boy, perhaps not twenty, with hair as fair as a child's, his innocent long-fringed eyes all over her, bold as a road agent.

She bought sixteen yards, enough to curtain a dressing corner and a closet nook for her wardrobe. With a smooth two-foot board from a packing box, she went back to the sod-house, carefully turning her face from the bridge and the lonely figure still hanging there. Yet all the anger and sorrow swept back over her and she wanted to fling herself on Robin's cot and lose it all in sleep.

Contemptuously Morissa Kirk reminded herself that it was the young colt, the wind, and the unbedded maid who run this way and that. The wind and the colt she could not control but the unbedded maid she could certainly put to work. But before she could start there was a hoarse shout outside and a boot kick at her door. A man stood in the sunlight, blood all down his pants, the right hand bound up in a blood-soaked shirttail. "Got it caught under some shifting mine machinery when a wagon started to go over."

It must have been very painful, but the man refused morphine or even a drink of whiskey. "Just fix 'er up anyway, Doc," he said, and when

Morissa still hesitated, he shouted, "Damn it, woman, fix 'er up so's I'll have something left to pull a trigger with!"

Morissa soaked away the blood in a pan of warm water with carbolic acid, lanced the accumulated clottings pocketed through the crushed flesh, and trimmed away the dead tissue. Then she set the broken bones as well as she could. The man never made a sound, and when the bones were lightly splinted, the fingers wrapped separately in vaseline-soaked gauze, she comforted him. "You certainly are one man who is fitted to this raw country!"

But she had to warn him that there was still blood poisoning, gangrene, and lockjaw to think about. "You better get close to a hospital," Morissa started to say, but the man suddenly turned green under his stubbled beard and she got the washpan to him just in time.

"I didn't go to puke before a lady," he stammered miserably.

When the man was gone the doctor thought about the effect of courage on the beholder. After the man's fortitude she could sit here in fair contentment and run up the curtains, although she knew she was busying her hands with these little tasks to shut out the picture of a man hanging at the bridge, and of an ivory-white satin wedding gown that she would never wear.

She ran a string through the curtain and hung it along the wall. Then she penciled the letters DR. KIRK on the board she got at the store, blackened them in solid with shoe polish, and tacked the sign up on the door outside.

Standing before her sign Morissa realized that for the second time in two days she had committed herself to a life here, where the gun on the nail in reach of her cot was to be her sole protection—that and such wit as she might have inherited from her Grandmother Kirk. But it would be a long, long life without the man she was to have married Wednesday.

Suddenly Morissa was crying, overwhelmed in it as in the waters of the Platte flood. Yet even this could not be a thing of privacy here, not with the sound of more hoofs already at her doorstep—a rider leading a horse with a sidesaddle, a handsome white-stockinged black.

Morissa wiped her face like a rueful child and rose slowly to go to the door. It was Tris Polk, slicked up as for a dance, his hat in his hand, the sun bright on his thick black hair.

"Come see the bridge opening, Dr. Kirk," he called. "I brought you Cimarron to ride since you seem to like him so well."

Chapter 3

AT CLARKE'S SUGGESTION, Morissa and Tris Polk crossed the bridge afoot before the official opening, following their horses led over by a station hand. They made a fine tall pair for the idle watchers, the young doctor elegant in a riding habit of her favorite green, the long skirt held off the rough planks as she walked beside the rancher, smooth-shaven and browned, handsome in his black flannel shirt with tan Stetson hat and chaps, his spurred heels loud on the bridge.

"Looks like the lady doc's gonna give that Gilda over to Johnson's a run fer Polk there," one of the loafers told the rest.

On the rise north of the river Morissa and the rancher sat their horses to watch the great run up the trail. The bridge stood empty under the windy May sky, empty and ready, a saw-toothed railing along the sides to prevent the incompetent from ending up in the river.

Finally Clarke rode through the crowd at the south entrance and fired one pistol shot into the air. The toll arm flew up, and before the gunsmoke began to drift away, his pony express rider was thundering over the bridge and on northward, carrying government mail for the troops at the Sioux agency posts, and illegally on through Indian country, where no white man had a right to be, to Custer City and Deadwood Gulch more than two hundred miles away.

With the westerner's reluctance to ask questions, Tris Polk made no inquiries of Morissa but kept up a little talk about the last weeks here, while he waited to cross with his beef herd, overdue for meat at Deadwood. He spoke quietly, and with long silences, for he was apparently no banterer but more like someone older than his twenty-six or -seven years—a man who had accepted responsibility when very young. The two watched as the throb of the bridge rose from a rumble to a pounding roar, until Morissa's horse began to prance his elegant white feet, eager, it seemed, to join this rush to the Hills.

As the afternoon lengthened the noise increased and the exuberant whooping and pistol shots, too, particularly when Madame Volanda, one of Denver's vice queens, came through. She had chartered a big street omnibus and had it modeled into a beautiful boudoir. Through the many

lace-touched windows, all could see Volanda and four, five handsome sporting men sitting elegantly inside as they passed. Behind her came ten gaudy wagons carrying her girls with all their finery.

The bridge opening was a fine show and apparently a paying one. Five dollars for the earlier places per wagon with driver and team, two dollars for the later places, and always fifty cents for each extra animal or man. The money went right to the toll shack, into the padlocked steel box that was forged to the bridge bolts. No outlaw gang could rush it away with less than dynamite, even if they got past the Winchester-armed guards, doubled since the hanging.

"Who was he—the dead man?" Morissa managed to ask, her voice tight and small, so intense that her horse began to grow edgy.

"Let's say nobody knows his name," Tris said, putting out a hand to Cimarron's tossing black neck, the touch so gentle it seemed almost a caress for the girl in the sidesaddle. "You must not grieve yourself."

The man, Tris told the young doctor, was one of the outlaws from Robbers Roost over in Wyoming, on the trail from Cheyenne to the Black Hills. They worked the stages hard; maybe they wanted to keep the gold coming through their wild country by blasting the bridge of the Sidney gold trail here. The Sidney route to the Hills would be tough competition for Cheyenne, with a shorter rail haul, the trail itself shorter, easier, and safer from both outlaws and blizzard snows. But last night the man with the dynamite dropped it and got away.

"Then this man here isn't even the one with the dynamite?" Morissa demanded, color rising in her face.

"No, just the man standing guard for him," the rancher admitted. But that didn't matter. Where there was no law there could be no common bedding ground for outlaws and honest men. " 'You run with horse thieves you hang for a horse thief' is an old rule on the frontier."

"I think it's savagery, and you're siding with the savages!" the girl retorted angrily.

"Maybe, but this is still wild country, Dr. Kirk, and on the trails danger makes jobs for the gunmen riding protection."

Morissa turned her head from the rancher, her soft bangs tossing a little on the wind. She did not trust her voice or its certain betrayal of her anger, and so she occupied herself with the hypnotic movement of the people funneling slowly over the bridge and then whipping away up the trail as though the gold were just over the first rise. She thought of the other hopeful trails that had led through this valley. The Mormons had fled persecution up the north bank here. On the other side of the river was the rutted trail of the Overlanders, those who were tolled west by earlier dreams of gold, and the homeseekers on the way to Oregon and the rolling western seas.

One of Tris's cowboys came from the beef camp with a can of coffee, tin cups, and a hot raisin pie in a Dutch oven he carried in a gunnysack. They spread their slickers and made a little picnic there on the knoll beside a patch of wild yellow sweet peas, their fragrance so heavy that the butterflies clung dizzily to the glowing spikes of bloom.

"I guess I let my mind fly off for a while. . . ." Morissa apologized. "I was thinking about the emigrants who used to come up the trails along the river."

"You certainly can quit the country without moving an inch," the rancher said ruefully. "Do you like what you see around here?"

"Oh, I do!" Morissa replied, speaking with the sudden identity of the homeseeker in a new region. "Look at the crops that will grow here."

"Crops! A city young lady like you thinking about crops! Even the grass burns up clear to the bogs here in July. Not enough rain."

"Not enough rain with all the water running past? Irrigate!"

But this the rancher beside her seemed not to hear. Instead he watched the curve of her brows that were like the wings of a river swallow, and talked about getting up a big picnic. "You can't leave us here without seeing the valley from the top of Scotts Bluff. A representative from a British financial syndicate's around, looking for a ranch. He brought his new wife, a London actress, and a whole spread of housemen and maids. I'd like to get up a picnic for them on the bluff, if you'll come."

"It sounds fine," Morissa said, "but you know there's always a chance I'll be called away. A doctor can't be too definite in her promises. . . ."

"A doctor? How about the woman?" Tris Polk asked, his eyes searching the girl's flushed face until she wanted to cry out the pain and hurt she had endured for being a woman, but she was silent.

IT WAS WELL MORISSA had her little black bag tied to her saddle. First it was a broken tooth to be pulled, and then injuries and dosings, one after another, until she was so weary she was relieved when Robin signaled to them. Their horses prancing side by side, Morissa and Tris Polk fell in behind the stagecoach coming in from Deadwood, a couple of arrows still sticking in the side.

Toward sundown Jackie rode in from the horse herds, full of excitement over his sister's visit and over the live young antelope he brought rolled in a gunnysack and tied across the back of his saddle. The soft brown eyes were glazed with terror but the trembling nose reached out to sniff at Morissa's hand, the tongue eagerly sucking at her little finger.

"Oh dear, starving! But what will we feed it, with no milk cow?"

"Mare's milk's better, the men tell me," Jackie said matter-of-factly as he slid his long length from the saddle. Morissa saw with joy how much he looked like their slight, earnest-faced mother, almost as though she lived again in the bearding youth, and yet how much like Robin he was in the strength of his body and in his quiet manner.

Avoiding the kiss Morissa might have given him, he grinned, untied the antelope, and set it down; it staggered stiffly around them, the shy, lovely head reaching out, the tongue searching. Then he rode off for one of the wet mares in the grader herd. He milked enough for one of the nippled bottles from Morissa's emergency case, and together they taught the baby antelope to drink.

That night the little creature slept inside because there was lightning in the west and it would surely get wet in the rain, although Jack laughed aloud at the idea. "Oh, Sis! They always stay out."

"But he might wander off. With those dogs around Etty's, and still so much commotion around . . ." That was true. Although thousands had passed over the bridge, the planks rumbled with hoof and wheel far into the moonlight. Some said that Clarke took in twenty thousand dollars this one afternoon. Morissa believed it.

By now the side of the bridge was clear, the man hanging there finally gone, buried beside the one from the Pennsylvania party, who had died with his boots on too—both at peace. Alone in the house Morrisa took down Robin's gun belt from the peg and looked at it a long, long time in her lap, touching the pistol grip cautiously, drawing the gun from the holster out upon her knee. She was sitting like that when Robin and Jackie passed on their way to their bunks.

"That's a fine new Peacemaker you got there," the boy said, and together they showed Morissa something of the gun's working. "Yes," Robin said. "Tomorrow Jack'll show you the fine points of pistoleering."

Now for the first time the girl looked up, surprised that a sixteen-year-old should know anything about the gunman's craft. Seen this way, Robin's concern that Jack was being drawn to the professional killer did not seem absurd at all.

But the target shooting had to be put off, for later in the night it began to sprinkle. Slowly, grayly, the rain fell, on and off, for almost a week. Morissa was glad to have her family together this little time. She tried to get reacquainted with the young stranger who was her half brother, but usually he was over talking to his friend Eddie Ellis, the boyish youth she had met at Etty's, now clerking at the bridge. One day she sloshed along the bottoms in gum boots with Jackie, taking up willow and cottonwood seedlings to plant around Robin's sod-house.

"Temporarylike?" the boy asked slyly.

"Well, if I'm temporary, I hope the trees will last," Morissa replied, as she selected another new-leafed whip of cottonwood for Jackie's spade.

Back at the house they met Robin riding in from the stage station with a roll of mail, mostly the Sidney and Omaha papers. "Here's something for you!" he said, and threw a patent-medicine circular over to Morissa. Only when he had said it, and saw her look, like a sun's ray striking Chimney Rock and gone as swiftly, did he realize what he had done.

THE FIRST DAY OF RAIN three Indian families came through on their way down to their relatives in Indian Territory, where they hoped there might be more to eat than at Red Cloud Agency up the trail a way. One of the children was very sick and old Etty came riding over with the father, a tall, silent Indian, to ask the doctor to come quickly. "He say it is the disease of the little red spots and the son will die like his mother if you will not come. But there is nothing for pay."

Morissa hurried her essentials together and rode out, the rain loud on her slicker as the squeegeeing hoofs of the horses splattered mud. She stooped under the tepee flap into the duskiness around a handful of red coals, the boy on a ragged blanket beside the fire, unmoving, burning with fever. Morissa had never been closer to an Indian than at a circus, and with the darkness and the brown skin, it was only the smell and the degree of collapse that told her the father's diagnosis was correct—a severe case of measles, with, from the chest indications, serious complications.

There was little that Morissa could do except work on the fever and hope to get a little strength into the small boy. She administered a febrifuge, oiled the poor withered skin, sponged the child with cool water and then rolled him in a moist towel. Now and then she tried to get the boy to swallow a little warm mare's milk taken from the antelope's ration, or a little venison broth.

And while she watched and worked, sitting awkwardly on the ground, an old Indian woman was squatting on the other side of the fire hole, wailing her mournful medicine songs, the black eyes hot and angry upon the white doctor, the firelight flashing on the long butcher knife at her waist as she swayed.

It was a hard, long night, but toward morning the child seemed a little easier. Morissa went home, but returned several times during the day and for most of the next night. By the second morning the boy slept, and two days later he was hungry.

Before the sky cleared, the Indians moved, their tepee poles dragging the mud behind the horses. But the boy's father stayed back, gazing after them, and then he and Etty rode over to visit Morissa. Slowly the Indian dismounted and tied his oddly spotted gray horse to the corral fence. There, through old Etty, he made a little talk. "The white man has taken our land, our homes, our buffalo, and given us only hunger and the sicknesses to kill our people. But you are not like these others. You are a healing woman. You have given me back my son."

Then he drew his blanket from the horse, and with it folded over his arm, he strode away in spite of Morissa's protests.

Before an hour passed, a dozen men had ridden over to look at the doctor's new horse, with the spotted hindquarters that were like a light brocaded drapery thrown over him, the tail thin, the eyes light, and the head magnificent as from an old Grecian frieze.

"An Appaloosa, and a damn good one," they said.

"That horse is one of the finest of the breed developed by the Nez Percés up north," Robin agreed. "He will carry you a hundred miles day after day and stand up to graze afterward. But we'll have to teach him to let you mount on the white man's side, not the side of the Indian with a bow in the hand. And to stand with the reins down, so you won't be left if there's no hitchin' post."

Tris Polk rode in through the rain and was as complimentary. "A fine-looking twosome you'll make when you get that horse fed up and curried a little," he said, as he looked at the tall, straight girl in Jackie's slicker, her suntanning skin tawny and glowing. "I have a silver-mounted side-saddle back in Texas, ordered as a gift for Empress Carlotta of Mexico from a Texas saddler. It was never delivered because the revolution came and she never got back. Ride it for me on the Appaloosa in the Walker horse show they're planning. With your green habit and that horse—Carlotta's court could have seen nothing finer."

The young doctor smiled at this, thanking the man for his pretty words, but drawing away within herself. Robin moved his hands uneasily as he watched, and if he thought of Allston Hoyt and the unworn wedding dress he gave no notice of it.

As soon as Robin Thomas finished the work up the trail, he would take his grading outfit east to a new railroad line heading toward the Black Hills, but still many years away. "We'll be living in tents and shacks, far ahead of settlements," he told Morissa; "nothing much for doctoring, unless you find a place you like and settle to wait for it to grow."

"Oh, I guess right here is as good as any," Morissa said as she mulled up a little ointment in the mortar in her lap.

"But Jack and I will both be gone. . . ."

Yes, she understood that, but she would stay as long as she could, or as a doctor was needed. She had decided she would file on a piece of land on the north side of the bridge, just right for a garden patch.

"Oh, I couldn't advise that, Morissa," her father said soberly, pretending to be concerned with his pipe. "There'll be trouble if you grow vegetables here for the homeseekers to see, even a shirttail patch. The ranchers have killers on the payroll, to keep the range clear. One of the men working for the government surveyor sent over north of the river to put down section corners was hung by the Boslers, just for a hint."

But Morissa was not listening. "Maybe I'll take up a tree claim, too, north and west of the homestead for winter shelter," she added.

"Oh, Daughter!" Robin protested. "I can understand your shrinking back, hiding yourself, particularly just now, with not even a letter, but your plan here is suicidal."

"Suicidal—" Morissa repeated, but as though facing the word for the first time, her arms gone slack in her lap, her face suddenly blighted. Once more Robin thought of the day he stood behind her mother as she told the twelve-year-old girl that her poor-farm days were done forever. There had been no joy in the young face, only a frozen standing away from them both, as though she could not choose the good, as though it could not be for her, was somehow not fitting.

81

Chapter 4

AND THEN THE LETTER CAME. Morissa received it from the hand of young Eddie Ellis, coming to bring it to her from the stage station. She accepted it as for a stranger and then went slowly along the weeding bottoms to the shade of her sod-house. There she sat on her nail-keg stool among the flourishing young willows and cottonwoods, with the portulacas blooming about her feet. She laid the letter on her knee, the rectangle creamy white against the dark blue of her skirt, the address bold in black broadstroke.

At last she had to open it. There was one paragraph:

My Dearest:
    I was pained and grieved by your inconsiderate disappearance, and it took me some days to discover your probable hiding place, which I abstracted from the Omaha offices of Henry Clarke, Esq. Come back, Morissa, my child. I assure you that the unhappy circumstance of the gap between our stations need be no obstacle to our love.

As ever, ob'd'tly,
Allston

Her eyes ran over it again, selecting the words she would see: "no obstacle to our love," and she could not hold back the tears. She would fly to her trunk, pack it swiftly, perhaps in time to catch the coach for Sidney today. But then she had to consider the sentence more carefully, all of it, the part that spoke of bridging "the gap between our stations" too. So there was a gap to be bridged. And nowhere was there any mention of marriage or a return of his mother's ring to her hand.

Slowly Morissa looked back over the life that had made the gap, back to her earliest recollection of waiting for her young mother to return from her work as a hired girl, worn out, white-faced. Later, when the mother sickened, five-year-old Morissa was put out with a dozen other children at an unhappy sort of poor farm. And at the little Missouri crossroads school the shameful term "woods colt" was spoken openly before Issy, Morissa, the meaning of the phrase eagerly explained to her in words from which the girl could only flee into work. At school she learned envy, too, particularly of one pupil who was never called by anything less than her whole name: Martha Jane. It was said that her mother was not one to soil her white hands with work. Instead she rode the region on a fine Kentucky mare and spent the money her husband's family sent willingly so long as he kept his wife far away, out of sight of God-fearing people. But even if this was true, and Mrs. Canary really had come from a waterfront dive in Cincinnati, she was legally married, and so her Martha Jane could speak out Morissa's shame boldly before all the school, skipping her red-handled rope to the beat of a song. Shaking back the curls from her pert, pretty face, and smoothing the wine-colored velvet of her dress she sang the words:

"*Issy over the ocean,*
Issy over the sea,
Issy's a bastard kid,
She can't catch me."

But as soon as Martha Jane's breasts began to push at her velvet bodice she followed her mother to the gay young soldiers. On the shady hotel piazza the mother and her precocious twelve-year-old flirted with drummers and spies, anyone with flash and gold.

All this time Morissa was at the poor farm. She helped milk, churn, slop the hogs and then plodded to school barefoot, with a chunk of cornbread and sorghum wrapped in newspaper.

Then the pale, sick Lorna Kirk married Robin Thomas, a road worker, a grader. He bedded her down comfortably in his covered wagon and took her west. Four hens rode beneath the wagon, and a milk cow followed at the tailboard. In this way they would have the eggs and milk Robin believed his wife must have to live. But it was a precarious venture, with little hope of work, and Morissa had to be left behind. During this lonesome, deserted time she withdrew deeper into work. In the late evenings that were her own she lost herself in her schoolbooks and in dreaming over the letters that came, telling of a lovely wild country, and later of the worrisome time before a brother was born. In time they told of the slow gathering of strength, until one day they were back, her own mother there beside her, with the quiet, bearded Robin, and the four-year-old Jackie clinging to his trouser leg. At first Morissa dared not trust their words, feeling unfit for the new family, but after a few days she put on the new shoes they brought her and went with them, slowly believing the kindness that could lie in the calloused hands of this sunburned man as he cared for his ailing wife, and the prideful look that could live in his eyes as he considered his family.

"You must get some schooling," he had told the girl. "Good steel rusts a lot faster than old stove iron if it ain't used."

But he couldn't help much with her mother's illness. Morissa managed to pass the teacher's examination and at fifteen she was teaching at a nearby school, with boys who towered over her using Martha Jane's taunts against her. Hurt and proud, she turned her back on her first beau without explanation or more than secret tears. She studied, and saved every penny because she must learn all she could about this consumption that had gnawed at her mother's breast so many years. But Lorna Kirk could not wait, and after the funeral Robin helped her serious, big-eyed daughter get to Philadelphia. There she won her medical degree and then went back farther west to set up a little practice out near Omaha, leaving the words of Martha Jane behind her.

Morissa met Allston Hoyt by answering an emergency call. She found him on the ground beside his broken buggy, apparently dying from a runaway of his flashy team, and she kept him alive until his coachman came with the ambulance. Afterward, at the big white house high above the river, she directed the nursing and told him that he must now always be careful. It was a heart attack that had brought on the runaway, she thought; his own failing hand on the lines over his fiery matched blacks.

After he went back to his office he kept sending the carriage for Morissa. He was still a young man, barely forty in spite of the silvery touches at his temples. He must be taught how to live, he argued. He kept calling her to him at the pillared house on the rise above the Missouri until it became a joke between them. Then one afternoon he led her out upon the terrace overlooking the river. He talked a long time, going back, back. Immediately after college he had had to take over the family's investment firm because his father, too, suffered from a heart condition. He had built up the business in spite of war and the crash of Black Friday. Then this illness struck at him on a side road. And now in his first leisure, no, idleness, he had fallen in love, wholly in love with his doctor.

"Come with me. I'll take you to Scotland on our honeymoon. We'll look up your grandmother's people and perhaps locate some of mine," he urged, his eyes dark against the pallor of his sudden emotion.

It was then that Morissa should have spoken, but she was suddenly like a spring hillside in sun-shot rain, with such a softness, such a glistening

84

happiness that she could know nothing else. When she left, the fine old diamond that had belonged to Allston Hoyt's mother was on her finger.

The plans went well all the winter, although Morissa would not give up her practice and still made the rounds of the river-bottom shacks. Then suddenly Allston's sister had sent the coach for her. The fragile, elegant woman poured her a cup of tea in her handsome green parlor, with the long, white-dressed windows and the pale gold upholstery. Speaking calmly, Alicia Hoyt asked Morissa her father's name, and when the girl replied that it was Robin Ralston Thomas, the woman shook her head gently. "My dear, I mean your own father," she said.

Now Morissa had to remember all she had hoped was forgotten.

"My hobby is genealogy," the woman explained. "Allston wanted to make you a gift of your family tree to carry along to Scotland. Despite much careful search I can find only one use of the name Kirk by your mother—*Miss* Lorna Kirk—up to her marriage to Robin Thomas."

So it was done, swift as a surgeon's knife, and given such circumstances it was the kindest way, Morissa realized. She could have said that Robin Thomas knew all this and yet married her mother, and made a beloved daughter of the bastard child. But a railroad grader, no matter how fine and good, was not an Allston or a Hoyt.

As she rose to go Alicia offered her smelling salts. "I shall not offend you with my expressions of sympathy. Dear Allston is prostrated, and thought this would be kinder, coming from one of your own sex—"

Morissa thanked her and went away, dismissing the coachman outside the grounds. She walked five miles toward the city along the bluffs of the Missouri, and saw nothing at all about her, not the swift spring that ran in new grass along the rutted road, or the pale cloudy green of the wooded river valley below. She saw nothing at all until suddenly a broken-backed bullsnake struggled to drag its useless length out of the rut at her feet. Morissa looked down at the injured creature and with a swift blow of a rock she flattened the head, and then with two sticks she rolled the twisting length off into the grass, where the dumb writhing could wear out its necessity in the good way, alone.

Afterward she stopped at her office only long enough to pick up her pill bag and then went down through the river-bottom shacks, seeing to their needs for one last time. In two days she was on her way west to Robin and Jackie and the North Platte valley, where no one asked a man's origins or his past, no more than "What name you travelin' under?"

85

And now there was this letter from Allston Hoyt, thick creamy paper lying on her knee. But almost as though from her memory of the crippled creature in the road that day, a call of "Snake! Snake bite!" brought Morissa out of herself. A man was spurring up to the house and shouting this over and over until he slid from his lathered horse. "They's bringing a kid what's been rattlesnake bit!"

Morissa ran around to the door, the letter left to blow forgotten where it slipped from her lap. A heavy work mare was galloping ponderously in from the bridge, a man riding her bareback carrying something, a child in a pink dress. Close behind him came a woman astride another old mare, bareback, too, whipping the man's horse along ahead of her and then her own, riding bent forward and whipping, whipping.

The young doctor was already inside, reaching for boiled scalpel and knife. She flipped open the handiest book, her *Hartshorne,* to "snake bite" and slapped a pane of glass over it, angry that she was so inexperienced. She had never even seen a case of rattlesnake bite, and already the child was being carried through her low doorway. The little girl was about six, curiously stiff and awkward, stuporous with the smell of raw alcohol about her. Morissa had her laid on the cot and made a swift examination. One of the legs was hugely swollen below a handkerchief tourniquet twisted with a wagon bolt, tight enough for gangrene. Above the ankle a big cud of chewing tobacco was tied over the wound, hacked but ragged and shallow. That and a drink of corn likker was all they knew, the gaunt woman sobbed.

"How much corn liquor?" Morissa asked. Even *Hartshorne* seemed doubtful about whiskey, but he had nothing much to offer, particularly this long after the biting.

"All the corn we had, about half a cup. . . ."

The doctor's lips tightened. "Make coffee," she ordered the woman, and tried to give the child a small tablet. But she could not swallow, so Morissa loosened the tourniquet a little and slashed into the wound, squeezing it. Only black clots and a yellow oozing came, and the doctor ran her slender steel up along the vein as along a fish's belly, and down into the foot, too, clearing out the thickened blood both ways until a weak bleeding started. Then she stood back, brushing the hair from her cheeks with her sleeve. There should be something more to do but Morissa Kirk, M.D., did not know what or where to look.

"How big was the snake?" she finally asked.

"It was big as my wrist," the woman cried, holding up a work-gnarled arm. But the gesture and her anger were both turned against her husband. "Bringin' a woman and a child to such a country!"

In the morning, while blackbirds sang along the marshy ground, Morissa helped bury the small girl. Most of the night the child had lain quiet and remote, never conscious, and the doctor couldn't be certain when the pulse finally died whether it was from alcohol or venom. She brought out a white cashmere shawl and wrapped the child in it. The mother stood dry-eyed with her back against the window. "She ain't even got no doll baby to be buried with!" she cried when one of Etty's men drove up with a little pine coffin hammered together like a feed box.

Quickly Morissa rolled up a finger towel, tied it tight for the neck and sewed on two shoe buttons for eyes, red yarn for lips. Then she tucked it into the child's arm and folded the corner of the white shawl down over the quiet face. Lorette, old Etty's wife, heavy with child, joined Morissa and the parents as they followed the coffin to the knoll beside the new mounds of the Pennsylvanian and the hanged man. Morissa read a little from her white wedding prayer book. Old Fish Head was there too, with his tall hat held elegantly over his heart, water running from his rheumy eyes. The curious little antelope had followed very close at first, but now he stood off a way, big ears erect, with animal instinct remaining aloof from death.

Then they went back down, silent, the anger between the parents something cold and dead, the link that had perhaps bound them broken. Morissa hurried to her neglected patient, fed him, gathered up her laundry whipping in the wind behind the sod-house since yesterday, and lay down to catch a little belated sleep after the night's long vigil.

Not until the antelope came to waken her toward evening, nuzzling the screen of the open window, did Morissa recall the letter from Allston Hoyt. Tear-blinded, she looked all through the little house for it, and tucked up her skirts and ran all around outside, the antelope at her heels, bumping her every time she stopped to look. Finally when the late darkness came, Morissa went with the lantern to ask at the station if a letter had been picked up. But no one had seen it.

She returned to the sod-house, stopping at the lighted window to look at the sign: DR. KIRK. Even if she kept on letting children die in her arms, it was plain that there was nothing else ahead for her. Gently she pushed the little antelope away from the door and went inside.

87

There was a tremendous electric storm that night, the sky an angry violet-rose, shot with blazing, jagged bolts, the earth shaking with the roar and crash that knocked bits of sod from between the roof boards to the cot and the floor. Around one o'clock, when it seemed that the rain must begin at last, there was a running outside and a shout at the door. It was one of the men from a big beef herd that came up out of Texas a week ago. The steers had been held up north in the sandhills since then, to fatten a little. Tonight they went crazy in the electric storm. Sid Martin, the owner, helped try to turn the stampeding herd. His horse stepped in a badger hole and it looked like Martin's neck was broken.

"But he's alive?"

"Yeh—was when I left."

"Oh, I hope nobody tries to move him! Go get my Appaloosa. . . ."

"I brong you a horse—them 'Poolusas is nervous in storms. And I fetched you a pair of chaps to hold off the rain, 'n' spurs. This ain't the night for no lady sidesaddlin'."

So with Morissa's medical bag rolled in an oilskin behind the saddle and her slicker buckled high, they started into the rain. It was lucky that she rode astride, for a hundred times the horses plunged over banks, slipped, or side-jumped as some wild thing flushed before them. Then it began to hail, the horses plunging and rearing like wild creatures as they fought to turn their backs to the storm, and now Morissa discovered one purpose of the spurs and cruel bit that so often brought blood from the cowboy's horse. But she thought of the man with his neck broken, and spurred on, too, trying to keep the bay ahead within sight.

It was clearing for dawn when they came out on a broad flat, the hail white over everything in the morning light. As they neared the trail wagons, a wrangler came to meet them. "Yeh," he said, taking the horses, "he's alive. We pulled the wagons up on both sides of him and spread a tarp to keep off the hail, but it's been damn cold for a hurt man."

Morissa stooped under the canvas to look down at Sid Martin in the light of the morning lantern. He was conscious, turning only his pain-filled eyes to the young woman, his gaunt face gray. Without moving him, she seated herself behind the man's head and slid her fingers gently along under his neck until she found a displacement, what seemed an appalling displacement, so she gave him a stiff dose of morphine. "You've been amazingly courageous not to move all this time, but maybe I'll have to hurt you, and even the slightest jerk . . ."

From the man's eyes she knew he understood, had known from the first, and she blessed the knowledge of anatomy these men of the out-doors learned. When he seemed to doze, she went to work, very carefully, remembering how tender the spinal cord was, recalling the pulpiness of the gray-white mass even in autopsies—much of it soft as a custard. A thousand times she wished that she were old in experience, double her twenty-four years. Every second she feared for the stopped heart that would mean she had crushed or broken the cord. And every bit of gain must be held with her numbing hands until she gathered control and force enough to apply the next gentle, steady little pull on the head, always toward her—not the tiniest fraction of an inch to one side or the other—until there could be space enough to clear the cord, realign the vertebrae.

Once the cook touched her shoulder and held a tin cup of hot coffee to her lips with his hairy hands. She shook the sweat from her face and looked about, amazed to see the sun high as her head. She swallowed the coffee gratefully, awkwardly, and nodded the watching men to her. "Get me some heavy leather, any stiff, heavy leather. Maybe saddle skirts . . ."

They brought leather skirts and an empty flour sack to make a pattern. Their boss must have a proper cast to hold the break in place, if he wasn't to die. So, while she held the head and the man slept, they cut the skirts to fit the pattern two cowboys had made around her hands. They joined the pieces with copper rivets and made a lacing up the side with rawhide strings. By the time Sid Martin woke he was laced into a neck-and-shoulder boot, to prevent turning the head.

He tried to move and was held down by an arm across his chest. As he grasped the extent of the leather brace, he grinned. "Think you got me trapped fer sure, don't you, Doc, Miss Doc Morissa. . . ."

Morissa settled to a late dinner of fried beef and canned peaches, wondering how long she dared remain here, with Tom Reeder alone and unfed at the bridge. She needed a nurse and a little hospital, even if only two rooms.

"You pull me out of this, Doc, and you sign your own ticket," Sid Martin said, cautiously trying to ease the stiffness from his legs.

"I think the doc here needs her a good team and buggy," the cow-puncher who had come for Morissa suggested.

She laughed at the absurd fee and sat awhile, warm and happy in the silence of the lean, sunburned men who had no itching need to talk. Suddenly she remembered that she hadn't thought of Allston Hoyt or the lost letter since a cowboy rode shouting out of the storm last night.

Chapter 5

MORISSA HAD NEVER SEEN so flowery a region, or one so fragrant. First there were the Easter daisies, bright soon after the snow, and then came the sweetness of the sand lilies, the golden banner, purple sweet peas, and the wild plums and chokecherries. Great patches of violets stretched along the bottoms, followed by a scattering of blue tulip gentians, and higher up, tangles of wild roses. Later the gravelly knolls were covered in the purple, white, and cerise of loco peas, and the ridges beyond carried the waxy white spikes of yuccas and the yellow of cactus bloom.

The willows Morissa had set out were shooting up fast and the little cottonwoods rustled over the morning carpet of portulacas. A month before, Etty's Lorette had beckoned the young doctor into her garden plot. There she thrust her spade into the russet patch of last year's bed of moss roses, lifting a sod of them for Morissa. "You can pull 'part," the heavy-bodied young woman had suggested. Now the seedlings had spread into a mat of color under the long morning shadows.

By now the cowboys had taken to stopping in. "Could I trouble you for the borry of a match?" one might say, and Morissa would offer the box, smiling at the man's sheepish grin. "I thought you all kept to chewing tobacco on the range, with the fire hazard."

"Yes, ma'am, but when I comes off it, I likes to roll me a prairie burner." Then perhaps the man would squat on his heels at the door awhile, his horse standing with patient reins dragging. Sometimes he might say as many as five words to the antelope nosing along the yard fence while Morissa kneaded bread or folded powders. Finally the man would reseat his old Stetson, swing into the saddle, and lope away.

Sometimes Lorette came, moving ponderously across the bottoms from Etty's stockade, to throw her Sioux blanket back from her neat braids and sit awhile with Morissa. Her French father had sent her east to a Sisters' school for a few years and she could read and write and embroider, too, Morissa discovered, her silken work lovely as delicate paint strokes. But now she was heavy with child, her fifth, only two having survived diphtheria. Lorette asked in her soft Indian way about a good school for her girls when they grew older. "Their father he say they must be same like white. . . ." she murmured with the sadness of a woman whose husband would have his daughters depart from her ways and her station for his; doubly humiliating, Morissa knew, to the Sioux in Lorette, since in the tribe a man customarily left his people for his wife's.

Then one day while Lorette was there, Etty rode in with a deer across his saddle. The woman sprang up so fast she dropped a teacup and fled for the stockade. The next day she held her blanket close about her head when Morissa came for some string to train her morning glories. She turned her eyes down, without greeting, but it was plain that her face was bruised and swollen.

Two evenings later Etty came riding over and Morissa went uneasily to the door, expecting some complaint. But his wife's time had come. "I think maybe the baby she come backward, like the colt sometime. . . ."

That night Morissa learned how silent a woman of Indian blood could be in pain. But Lorette was strong and patient and young. By morning Etty had a son, his first, and Morissa went home to drop to her cot without undressing. She still did not know why the Frenchman had beaten his wife, whether because she was visiting the doctor when he came home or for some more private reason. But Morissa realized now that she must move cautiously here.

Before nine in the morning a man from Sid Martin stopped by. "The boss was rarin' to get on a horse couple days after you was up, but he's been gettin' yellow since. Outta his head all last night."

Morissa rubbed her eyes wearily, trying to wake up. "Any pain, maybe under the ribs somewhere?"

"No, guess not, but his head's a-bustin', he says." And the cowboy rode on toward Sidney.

So the doctor put her saddlebags on the Appaloosa and started out, her first trip alone into the vast, undifferentiated country of the sandhills. Sid Martin did look bad inside his worn leather neck brace—gaunt, yellow, with a slow pulse, whether from an injury in his fall or from gallstones or infective jaundice she couldn't decide in a moment. She gave him a mild liver dose and a diuretic and had the cook make up a blancmange flavored with the vanilla she brought. The patient seemed improved by the time she had to start back. "Feed him like a sick man, not fried beef and beans," she ordered, and wrote out a diet and dosing list.

She felt so worn that she could scarcely climb into the sidesaddle. Yet she had to hurry to get out of the hills before dark. Several times she caught herself dozing in the hot afternoon sun. She pulled herself up firm and erect for a while, yet it seemed only a moment before she was nodding again. Her head drooped, sagged lower and lower, until suddenly she felt a great jerk and semed to be flying through the air. When she came down she hit headfirst, so hard it seemed her skull crushed in like a hollow pumpkin.

A long time afterward Morissa Kirk began to come out of a deep darkness, her stomach retching. With bursting head she held herself together as well as she could and gradually her eyes cleared. But when she tried to sit up everything spun around and she was sick again.

Afterward she tried to think. The throbbing head and periodic vomiting meant concussion. She had been thrown by her horse out in the open sandhills, far from any trail. Only Martin's men knew where she had been and they wouldn't discover that she was missing for a long, long time. Miserably she wondered once more what she was doing in such a wilderness, when people needed doctors everywhere.

When she could, she tried to plan what must be done. Slowly she lifted herself to an elbow, holding her reeling head when she must. There was something nearby and when her eyes focused she saw it was the Appaloosa, quietly grazing. He was waiting as Robin had trained him, and suddenly she understood the affection of the cowman for his horse.

But night was coming and she did not dare go near the Appaloosa yet, the retching sure to frighten him, send him off into the hills out of her reach. So she drew herself together upon her quivering stomach as an ailing child would. With her hair loose to spread about her, and the denim riding skirt drawn up around her shoulders against the chill, she managed to sleep a little between the intervals of sickness. When dawn finally came she was shaking with cold, her throat raw and dry, a lump like a rounded plateau on the left side of her aching head.

Weak and stiff, she tried to sit up and finally she stood, bent over yet on her feet. The Appaloosa was nowhere in sight. The morning hills seemed empty, bare except for a prairie chicken calling to her young, at least a dozen of them, all standing innocent and open, staring at the woman on the hillside. Morissa called "Appaloosa!" At the first sound the young chickens were gone, the prairie hen fluttering along the grass tops to toll danger away. But there was no sign of the horse.

Finally, when Morissa thought to try a loud Indian whoop, a head lifted from a low place, a gray head, ears erect. Morissa started toward him, stumbling and crawling. The Appaloosa snorted a little as she approached, but he only drew back a step or two and waited as her hand crept toward the reins at his feet. Then he came to rub his nose against the girl's stooping shoulder, nickering softly.

She pulled herself up with the stirrup, making herself speak quietly, steadily. "Whoa, 'Paloosa, whoa, boy." She went up along the stirrup leather, choking back the nausea, until at last she was mounted.

It was old Etty, out for a little fresh meat, who saw the Appaloosa coming slowly down a long slope toward the Platte and brought Morissa in, leading the horse, people running out across the bridge to see, the antelope along behind, all recognizing the Appaloosa from far off.

By morning Morissa felt better, still weak, with a headache, but probably without permanent damage. Beside her sat Lorette, silent.

"You should be home and in bed!" the doctor scolded.

"It is now the third day," Lorette said cheerfully, and went to make a cup of tea.

So Morissa drank her tea and turned her face to the wall to sleep. But first she should write a note to be sent to Robin: "Your training showed up well. Appaloosa did not leave me."

EARLY SUNDAY MORNING Tris Polk tied his horse to a yard post and walked up between the flower beds, come to take Morissa to watch Bill Tillow, the wild horse catcher, handle some of his stock. He spoke of her accident. "We've been worried about you. I heard clear up at Deadwood that you were left hurt out on the prairie," he said quietly as he walked beside the girl to the Appaloosa, not looking at her.

They met Robin and Jackie coming down the trail. In their western way they made no fuss, but Robin saw the yellowish stain left at the girl's temple, and a pallor that remained from her fall. "A day in the sun will be good for all of us," he said heartily, and was caught up in the absurdity of his words by the laughter in the sunburned faces.

They had brought Eddie Ellis along. After the bridge rush he was now working at Red Cloud Agency. Even in the dust of the trail, Ed's blue eyes looked like those of a long-lashed child smiling through tears, but a child with full, aggressive lips barely shadowed by beard.

Together the little party headed eastward, Robin riding a little ahead, with Jackie and Ed; Morissa and Tris following close behind. Morissa looked at the man riding beside her, the fine ease of the long body in the saddle, the narrow hips, the lean face. As usual, except when working cattle, Tris wore a yellow silk muffler knotted at the nape of his neck. It went well with Morissa's yellow shirtwaist that pointed up the hazel of her eyes. Against Tris's dark skin the yellow made his eyes darker, gave them a hint of fire somewhere behind the deep smoke. But always the eyes were aloof, and for just a moment Morissa caught herself wondering what passion would bring to them, and had to turn her burning face away, feeling the man's presence beside her as though his hand were cupped on her yielding shoulder. Angrily she reminded herself of what she was, how one man had received it. So her eyes found refuge in the three riding ahead, Eddie on a fast horse, a step out in front of the others.

"He seems to know where the corral is located," she said.

"Oh, Ellis would know," Tris replied, almost angrily. "The horse-thief trail from the Indian herds crosses there."

Morissa nodded, but then grew uneasy as she realized the man's apparent meaning, with Jackie a close friend of Eddie's.

Finally Eddie led them around the side of a bluff overlooking the narrow neck of a rocky, brushy box canyon filled with dust. The wild horses, about fifty, had been driven inside the long arms of a trap corral, the lower opening closed by a pole and brush wall and gate, built high enough so the mustangs couldn't get a nose over or they would be climbing them like cats. They were circling away from bowlegged Bill Tillow in the center of the corral. He spread his loop this way and that, the horses trying to keep their heads back behind others, all of them trying to hide except one bold mare, bright as a red fox, taking the lone, unprotected front as the roper waited his chance.

Suddenly they got the scent of newcomers and stopped, heads lifted. The powerful necks were raised high, the manes falling thick and long, their tails reaching the ground. At a switch of the rope they ran again. This time the loop snaked out and an iron gray was suddenly left behind as the rest broke from him. Bill threw a hitch around the snubbing post in the center of the corral; the gray hit the end of the rope and went over.

Morissa gasped. "Oh, he'll break every bone!" she cried.

"You'll get used to seeing them do that," Tris said, laughing gently. The gray was up immediately and already knew how he could ease his choking breath. At the first little pull of the rope he took a step toward the man and, because the slack was gone immediately, he took another, and again another, his whitish eyes enraged, but his feet obedient.

95

"Sure looks like he's gone against a rope before," Tris said to the men at the gate. They nodded, their eyes sneaking shy looks at the young woman and her Appaloosa.

Slowly Bill worked the horse in, until the gray made a great lunge to escape the nearing smell of man and the cutting rope, and as he went down again, the dappled body rocking in the dust, a man named Hank dropped from the fence and was on the neck with a knee. Bill threw a breaker W loop on his legs, so even a child's jerk on the rope could bring the horse to his knees.

Hank grabbed the W string and let the horse up, and now slowly Bill began his soft, coaxing horse talk as he started down the rope, his voice quiet but firm. "Whoa there, whoa"—moving his hands very slowly along the rope. "Whoa"—until finally he turned his back and, drawing on the rope, walked slowly away, the gray following—the horse from the wild herd leading almost as well as a work mare.

"Why, it's amazing—what that man can do with a horse!" Morissa exclaimed.

Tris lifted his hat and shook his thick hair into the wind. "Yes. Probably won't be another in the whole lot learn to lead like that and not make at least one good try to get away."

At noon they had beans with sowbelly thick in them, Dutch oven biscuits and coffee, followed by a sack of raisin bunches from Tris's saddlebags for a little sweetening.

Afterward Tris and Morissa went to sit on a high rocky bank far above the corral wall and watched Bill settle the next rope on the fine fox-sorrel mare, around five or six, well fleshed, alert, powerful. She hit the end of the rope going away and somersaulted, shaking the ground. She was up immediately, her eyes red, her lips drawn back, and fast as a cat she charged upon Bill, her forehoofs flailing out for him. He jerked the rope to take up the slack at the hitch, but it had got crossed against the pull, and the loop that Hank snapped out for a foot missed too. Bill fled for the gate and rolled under it just as the mare was upon him, hitting the solid poles a thunderous crack that echoed in the canyon. Then the mustang turned on Hank, her teeth bared like a snarling wolf's, and he ran, too, the men at the gate flapping their hats to draw the angry mare's attention.

"Whew, a born outlaw!" Tris exclaimed.

But the young doctor thought she saw something else in the mare, something wild and incorruptible that brought a smarting to her eyes.

The men came from all sides upon the fox mare now and got the rope solid to the snubbing post once more, only this time she would not go against it. Instead she fought the rope, struck at it for the enemy it was, fought panting and foam-flecked, her hoofs like lightning in the dusty heat. And when Hank finally snagged a hind leg and she felt the pull there, too, she made one final attempt to break free. She reared, going up into the air, up in a great flying, pawing leap, and then came down forward on her head, her neck folded under, and lay still, the spurts of dust spreading in the air and settling slowly about her.

"Oh, no!" Morissa cried out, the tautness in her arms painful.

"She could have been gentled with a bucket of oats, and a patient, affectionate hand," Tris said quietly.

But Morissa wanted to cry out against this also. Such brightness, such wild spirit was not to be betrayed. She turned her face away as the men dragged the dusty carcass out with their horses.

"We better ride for home," Robin said.

Mounted, the visitors swung off down the mouth of the canyon and out upon open prairie. The lanterns were already lit on the bridge ends when they reached the valley of the Platte.

At the sod-house Tris helped Morissa off the Appaloosa and for a second it seemed he would kiss her, but he gave her the opportunity to turn her face away without seeming to, with no words needed, no notice of it at all. "All day I've thought about you hurt up in those hills alone," he said gruffly, and swung into his saddle.

Morissa went to the wagon to see her patient, but she stopped outside to look into the darkness after Tris. She thought about the wild horses, and about the dead mare, red as a fox.

THE BIG PICNIC for the visiting Britisher, Harry McApp, had to be put off because he broke his foot in a runaway, Tris told Morissa, but the Walkers were giving a reception at Sidney, for him and some financial and packinghouse representatives from Chicago. "It won't be as much fun for you as the picnic, but a better chance to see you look pretty."

When Tris came for her at the hotel in Sidney, Morissa did indeed look pretty. Her gold-shot, gray-green gown of summer taffeta brought out the golden flecks in her eyes, and the shining glint in her dark bangs.

"Marry me—" Tris Polk said softly. "Marry me tonight at the post here."

Morissa tried to laugh. "Why, of course, darling, but shall we look in on the Walker reception first?" turning it aside as lightly as she could. And when Tris started to protest his seriousness, she put her hand through his arm. "Choose a Sunday maid and ye'll hae a Sunday wife," she warned him. "You better see me in a kitchen apron sometime."

The evening was a gay one—the whole occasion planned, Morissa suspected, to sell ranches or ranch shares to the syndicate represented by Harry McApp. She thought about her plans to take up a homestead, become a despised settler, and then recalled a few half-heard words McApp had said to Clarke, with Forson, the meat packer, beside him. "Slaughterhouses near the herds, that's the best way. If you had a railroad at your bridge . . ."

So, if Clarke had the railroad, there might be a packinghouse at the bridge, Morissa thought.

The dancing was a lovely sight. Cantwell Walker led the grand march with the tiny blue-gowned actress Grace Enders, McApp's wife. But many eyes followed the tall pair that was the Texas cowman Tris Polk and the handsome, even elegant young woman who claimed to be a doctor and had come so mysteriously to bury herself in the wilds. There were half a dozen men for every woman here tonight and it was the first fun she had had since before that afternoon with Alicia Hoyt, the afternoon that sent her here.

When Tris came with her velvet wrap to take her away, it was late, even for Sidney, but the saloons and the dance halls were still open. Tris and Morissa moved through the milling street slowly, like two sightseers, Morissa holding her skirts above the rough planking. "It's been a lovely evening," she said afterward, speaking a little sadly into the silence between them, but when Tris drew her gently toward him, it was her cheek she turned to him.

The next day Morissa took the train east to the land office and filed on the homestead and timber claim—altogether four hundred and eighty acres of her own. Suicidal, Robin had called it, and yet perhaps that was what she sought; certainly it was suicide for her career, so well launched only a month ago. Even now she could return to Omaha, where she had been invited to join the rising medical group—the first woman so honored. What if she was a woman rejected, did life stop for that?

Or was this suicide what she really wanted—and to make the guilty knowledge of his part in it an eternal accusation to Allston Hoyt? Was it, too, at the bottom of her attitude toward Tris Polk? That she was drawn to him as a man much more than to Allston would have been clear to any doctor with a patient named Morissa Kirk, yet she was choosing a lone homestead in the wilderness instead of a good life as Mrs. Polk.

Chapter 6

ON HER RETURN from the land office Morissa found Sidney stirred by something besides gold rumors. General George Crook had met the hostile Sioux under Crazy Horse up in Montana and whipped them.

"Yeah, the report says he whipped 'em, but I see he's withdrawed to his camp. That don't look like no victory to me," Morissa heard one of the old Indian fighters tell the crowd at the stage station. They listened attentively, for they were waiting on the coach from the Hills, already long overdue. Not only did the gold trail pass within whooping distance of Red Cloud Agency, but the entire region from south of there to Canada, including all the Black Hills, was legally Indian country, where no white man had the legal right to go. Those wilder northern Indians under Crazy Horse claimed the land clear to the Platte and the bridge and planned to hold it. Morissa said nothing of her homestead north of the river.

When the coach finally came in, the passengers from Red Cloud said that the Indians had kept them awake with their victory dances the last two nights. They claimed Crazy Horse whipped the pants off General Crook. Yes, and this morning the last of the young warriors vanished from the agency like fog before the sun. One party followed the stagecoach halfway to the Platte bridge and then cut in ahead, blocking the trail. But the driver was an old friend of Chief Red Cloud's and so the Indians parted, the angry warriors sitting their horses on both sides of the trail as the coach galloped through. The escape still had some of the passengers feeling their scalps uneasily.

"You better settle in Sidney awhile," the station manager advised Morissa. "You're the only white woman for two hundred miles along the Platte. Be bad when the Indians strike."

For a moment she felt afraid, with only the Peacemaker on the sod wall against the silent moccasin in the night, the tomahawk, the knife, and the bark of the rifle. "No," she answered slowly. "I'm the only doctor for those two hundred miles," and handed her valises up.

Guards were shifted from the gold coach to ride the regular north stage, empty today except for two ranchers hurrying to their beef herds, and Morissa Kirk. The other spaces had all been canceled. With Crook's large army defeated, the hungry agency Sioux, still something like ten thousand, were buzzing like angry hornets only eighty miles from the hated Clarke bridge that brought so many gold-hungry whites running into the Indian's Black Hills. With the help of the northern hostiles they might certainly feel powerful enough to throw all the whites out of the region, including those of Deadwood itself, all the ten, fifteen thousand people, women and children, too.

Henry Clarke had wired Washington for troops to protect the bridge, although he was an old friend of the Sioux and usually more worried about white outlaws. Two days later a small, dusty guard of troops came to pitch their tents at the north approach. The government had three armies up north and was pushing the beef contractors to hurry their deficient deliveries to the hungry agencies, particularly Bosler, already under investigation for fraud.

The next day, a prairie scorcher with the temperature above one hundred degrees, Morissa had to go up the trail to set a broken leg and help get the man down. She strapped on her Colt and as a special precaution she rode awhile beside a wagon train going to Red Cloud, and was almost overcome by the stink of it.

"Salt pork fer them Sioux," the whackers called to her. "An' you better keep your gun oiled up, ma'am. That there braid o' yourn'd look mighty good hangin' to some buck's belt."

Two DETACHMENTS of army officers out to inspect the situation at Red Cloud Agency came through, and young Lt. Wilbert Larman from the bridge was ordered to join their mounted escort. Robin decided this looked like a good opportunity to get past the Sioux for a Fourth of July excursion to Deadwood. It might be the last if the mines were actually played out or, as seemed likely, the hostile Indians eluded the troops up north and struck toward the settlements. Clarke was going up to strengthen the defenses of his stage stations and get his pony express established to the Black Hills mining camps. He took Gwinn, his bookkeeper, along to ride the back of the special coach while a guard sat beside the driver, rifle across his knees. Jack and Robin would be on horseback, and Tris too.

On Independence Day in Deadwood there would be a celebration of the nation's Centennial. Tris was bringing his Chicago guests along, the packer Hurley Forson, his vivacious daughter, Yvette, and her chaperon, her Aunt Clara, a fiery old feminist. While it didn't look like the time for a tenderfoot outing, Morissa knew it must be important to the men—a matter of large Eastern and British investments if the Indian scare could be discounted. So she hired Charley Adams from the bridge guard, who had been a field nurse in the Civil War, to look after her patients.

Clarke's coach, with the horsebackers following, rumbled over the bridge soon after sunrise, close behind the two military vehicles carrying the officers with their escort of bluecoats riding in double file ahead and behind. They swung off northward on the empty trail, with the meadow-larks still singing in the morning cool. But soon the heat drove the birds to pant in the shade of weeds or brush on the yellowed prairie. That night they stopped, halfway to Deadwood, near Red Cloud Agency. Even Aunt Clara, worn to silence by the heat and the long rough road, was ready for her bed when supper was done.

In the morning Lieutenant Larman came galloping up from the agency on a fresh horse, eager as a hungry man drawn to a coffee cooking. He had a nice six-day leave and could go all the way to Deadwood, and his young face flushed with pleasure as Yvette Forson cried, "Oh, Lieutenant, then you can keep us safe!"

As the sun climbed hot and clear, Yvette kept up a mild flirtation with the lieutenant riding alongside, and with Gwinnie up behind and Jack and Tris, too, giving Morissa an occasional sweet and tolerant glance. She did not notice the strange badland formations that lay on both sides of the trail. From a distance the naked reaches of earth looked like the palms of mammoth dying hands, cupped, yellowish, and withered. Upon approach the witherings became gullied canyons, bluffs, and buttes, with hundreds of little pinnacles and toadstool formations that rose stark from the water-torn slopes.

Finally they were out upon the high table with a ridge rising dark in the northwest, so blue-dark that Morissa knew it was the Black Hills. Inside the jolting coach the weary newcomers began to doze, their heads pillowed against each other in the heat and dust. Clarke settled back, too, smiling companionably to Morissa as he closed his eyes for a little rest until the next change of teams.

But suddenly half a dozen horsebackers rose up behind a low ridge to the left, moving parallel to the coach, little more than their heads showing—hatted heads, not Indians, unless they were disguised. The guard leaned down toward the window and spoke quietly, pointing. Clarke peered out beside the curtain. Morissa looked, too, and gripped her hands tight, for already Robin and the lieutenant were turning down along a dry creek bed between the men and the coach. Tris came hurrying up, held his horse as close as he could beside the flying wheels, and silently handed his belt, holster and pistol in to Morissa. Their hands touched a moment, their eyes met.

"Be careful. . . ." the young doctor whispered, her throat tight. But in a moment she calmed, and moving softly so none would be awakened, she drew the cartridge belt about her narrow waist and set the pistol ready under her hand. Outside, Tris balanced his rifle across the saddle and fell back to plan with Jackie, who was riding without apparent concern over the coming attack.

By now the driver was easing his six horses into a clattering run, but the men on the ridge were spurring up, too, rising higher into sight, sending a couple of bullets into the trail before the coach, and apparently heading for a place where the ridge dipped toward a creek and met the trail at a twisting, brushy crossing. The violent jolt and lurch of the coach had jerked Aunt Clara awake. She stared around with frightened eyes and grabbed at her brother and the others, all bracing themselves as they could. Then she took Yvette's hand to comfort the girl.

Robin and Lieutenant Larman sent the riders a few shots while Tris and Jack cut in past the rocking coach for the creek. Then suddenly a rider rose out of a gully and charged for the crossing. There was a quick movement in the brush before the coach. Morissa saw Tris stop, lift his rifle and shoot, then spur ahead to Jackie's shout. She closed her eyes a second for courage and then drew the heavy Colt and steadied it against the edge of the swaying window, waiting for the first highwayman to step out into the road. As she braced herself for this killing, the driver sent the coach plunging down toward the creek close upon Tris and Jack. The top-heavy vehicle swayed dangerously as it took the turn and dip into the broad muddy crossing. Yvette sobbed in fright against Clarke's shoulder and Aunt Clara prayed aloud as dirty water splashed in over them and bullets whistled past.

Feet braced, the driver cut right and left with his whip, skillfully holding his galloping horses together. Then the coach was up on the far bank with a lurch, and the horses settled into a lathered panting trot, in plain sight of a big freight outfit barely half a mile ahead.

Behind them the pursuing riders had stopped and were bunched together, apparently discouraged. They headed into the creek bed and up toward the dark canyons of the Hills. Morissa looked after them, recalling something familiar in the way one of them rode. Then she remembered that Jack had asked last week if Eddie Ellis could come along, so Ed must have known about this special coach, and through him perhaps Fly Speck or any of half a dozen other road agents hiding out among Red Cloud's Indians. Robin came up and asked a quiet question of Clarke: "You think they were a little easy to drive off?" looking under his palm all around the prairie and back toward the Sioux agency.

Uneasy, Morissa settled herself to quiet the aunt. She poured a little camphor into a handkerchief and cooled the woman's brow. Yvette needed no easing. With her veil thrown back she leaned out the coach to thank the lieutenant. Oh, he was so *splendid*, so *brave*.

THEY PULLED INTO the packed and noisy gulch of Deadwood as the last sun left the timbered peaks. The gold town was in deep shadow, lights glowing suddenly here and there from the log and slab and canvas structures jammed along both sides of the little Main Street.

The gulch walls climbed steeply from the town, shacks leaning one over the other far up on each side. Robin had arranged for a two-room log house many rough steps above the noise of the street. The girls and Aunt Clara had the larger room, with a stove to take off the mountain chill and to heat bath water for the tub that was a whiskey barrel sawed in half and set behind a sheet hung across a corner.

Next morning all of Clarke's party was out in time for the Centennial Independence Day celebration, with whipping banners and rifle salutes, the orchestra from the Golden Belle, Deadwood's popular log theater and dance hall. The blond-bearded General Samuel Dawson, an old acquaintance of Clarke's, read the Declaration of Independence and electioneered a little for Rutherford B. Hayes. But nobody could vote here in the Indian country anyway, and so the general read a memorialization to Congress: "We petition that august body for speedy action in extinguishing the Indian title to the country we are occupying and improving. . . ."

Morissa watched the crowd line up to sign the petition, mostly young men. "We won't need that petition," a loudmouth offered easily. "Custer'll wipe out them red devils up north and they won't be givin' us no more hot powder."

As the crowd moved off to wet their gullets, Tris led his party over to see the new Black Hills jewelry store. The clerk helped everybody get a souvenir of Deadwood, and when Morissa shook her head to Tris, he urged her gently. "Just a remembrance of a pleasant outing." He said it sadly, with something autumnal in his voice, something final, and the girl wondered if he might be joining Forson's packing firm, or taking up with Gilda Ross for good.

So she selected a ring: a greenish vine to circle the little finger, with a bunch of reddish grapes and a handsome green gold leaf. Afterward Robin took the lieutenant and Yvette and Jackie to see the gold bricks in the bank window and then to pan a little gold dust for themselves at a friend's diggings. The rest went with Tris along Main Street, Morissa beside him in a white dress, carrying a ruffled rose-and-gold parasol. At Number 10 Saloon a woman in a bedraggled dress leaning against the wall stopped them as they tried to push past. "Well, if it ain't Trish Polk, you old son of a gun!" she shouted thickly. "How's about buyin' a lady a drink?" So, to the amusement of the Chicago packer and the increasing delicacy of Aunt Clara's thin lips, Tris introduced the woman.

"The famous Calamity Jane," he told them, "well known around Sidney, Cheyenne, and Deadwood Gulch. . . ."

But when he spoke Morissa's name, Calamity, with the occasional acuteness of the drunk, recalled something from long ago. "Kirk? You say Morisha Kirk?" she cried, and held out a small, dirty hand. "Why, you growed up real nice, you little bastard!"

Once more the hated word was like a slap across the face to the young doctor, her angry flush plain to everyone in the bright mountain sunlight. Calamity Jane began a childhood chant. "*You* remember it, Issy Kirk, jumping rope, don't you?" she demanded of Morissa, and began again: "Ish-Issy over the ocean, Issy over the sea . . ."

"You met Dr. Kirk before?" Tris interrupted, trying to draw the woman aside, to relieve Morissa's mortification and ease his guests away.

Calamity stopped. "Doc? Did he say *doc*?" she shouted. "So you're a-dealin' in corn plasters an' snake oil 'stead teachin' school like you was plannin' back in Missouri?"

Now it was up to Morissa. "Yes, sometimes I can cure corns," she managed to say pleasantly enough, "although I haven't had much practice handling the snakes. . . ." and was immediately ashamed of the poor joke, the unprofessional taunt.

But the crowd roared. "Calamity knows about them there snakes all right!" someone yelled, and Jane joined in the laughing, happy to be part of it on any terms.

Tris slipped Calamity a gold piece and moved his friends away, and later, on a grassy spot up the turbid little creek, Morissa thought about the pert, pretty Martha Jane in the red velvet bodices she had envied so much. Now Martha Jane was this sodden, unfortunate creature in an ugly little gulch town—a broken, miserable woman at twenty-six.

Once the young doctor wanted to jump up and run to find her, tell her that there were cures for this illness, and she, a genuine doctor, would care for her. But instead she sat demure amid her white ruffles and listened to Tris tell his guests the newspaper tales about Calamity sneaking in among Crook's soldiers and scouting for him, when she was really found drunk among his mule skinners and sent right back.

It was an excellent occasion for Aunt Clara's stern little lectures on the new Women's Christian Temperance Union and the need for women's suffrage, but her words were not at their most effective from a seat beside a creek in Deadwood Gulch, the elocutionist's nose peeling from sunburn. Tris exchanged a grin with the packer and Morissa.

"Clara's been a good mother to Yvette since my wife died," Hurley Forson told the young doctor afterward, "but she does coddle her notions."

Morissa smiled in preoccupation. Everybody coddled a notion or two, an illusion, good or bad, but today one that had tinged all her values since childhood had been shaken, brought down. Somehow the fall of Martha Jane Canary left an ugly place, like an oak's fall that suddenly exposed all the sad, stunted growth within its shadow.

It was Gwinnie hurrying out with a carriage to fetch them that broke up the outing. The young man managed a word with Tris, and later the rancher came, serious-faced, to speak low to Morissa.

Trouble, he said. A rider from the Red Cloud stage station came to warn Clarke that the Indians claimed Custer's whole regiment was wiped out up in the Yellowstone country.

"Wiped out?" Morissa whispered. "You mean killed?"

"Yes, claim every man was killed by the Sioux. We better try to get back down while we can. No telling when the Indians may decide to strike our bridge and cut the trail running right past their noses."

They started back at dawn the next morning. The dusty, rutted little main street of Deadwood Gulch was almost empty. Here and there a drunk was sleeping in the gray dust, and two who would never awaken were laid out beside a saloon. But in an hour or a day the Custer news would explode like the mine dynamite hidden around the gulch.

THE CUSTER ANNIHILATION had already affected the North Platte valley, Morissa discovered when their coach rolled to a stop at Clarke's. Tom Reeder had quit the place. As soon as he heard about the Custer fight he bought another horse from Etty, got his gold at the stage station, and with old Fish Head to drive, he started for Sidney and the railroad. He had left a package for the doc, and a note written with a lead bullet on a paper sack: IM TAKEN MY STUFF AN PULLEN OUT AND IM TAKEN THE ANTLOP SO I WON BE LONSOM TOM REEDER.

The package was a little rawhide bag. Morissa poured the contents into her palm—gold nuggets, looking curiously like shining beans, mostly with the same bent shape only a great deal heavier. "Oh, he'll get killed for his gold, sure," Morissa exclaimed.

But it was wise for him to go. Now he could get the care that might keep him alive a while longer. She would miss the antelope, although he had grown large enough to jump the fence into the yard and the flowers.

Before Morissa could get to bed, a cowboy rode up, speaking apologetically. A man was took sick with typhoid down at Redington's on Pumpkin Seed Creek, south of the Wild Cat range.

"Oh, I just can't go now," Morissa protested wearily. "Not without some sleep. We've come straight through from Deadwood."

"He's took pretty bad, ma'am, mebby dyin'," the cowboy said slowly. "Them Sidney docs won't come; got typhoid down there too. We borried us a wagon from Clarke's, got it ready with a bedroll spread in it. Mebby you could catch you a little sleep on the road."

So Morissa tried to shake the pall of weariness from her. "Give me half an hour to clean up and get my pill sack together."

Two DAYS LATER Morissa had the man in her sod-house, working to lower the fever and keep a little soft but nourishing food in him. She tried the less drastic of the new remedies for disinfecting the intestinal tract.

While Charley Adams sat beside the sick man, Morissa went over the bridge and with a map in her hand that she unrolled here and there, she sought out the almost obliterated government corners of her land. Then she decided on the site of her new home, on the second bottom, well out of reach of floods. There she set the stakes for the house, in the V made by the river and the trail—two streams that crossed, the stream of water and the stream of man. Here she would put down her roots and, she hoped, grow like the occasional towering cottonwood of the region.

The next morning Robin set his breaking plow into the virgin earth for the home of the first settler north of the river. As his plow turned the dark strips, smooth and shining, blackbirds followed close, gobbling up bugs and worms. His men cut the sod into manageable lengths with their spades, stacked the slabs carefully on the wagon, and then laid them like long dark bricks on a foundation of stone.

In two days the door casings of Morissa's house stood up stark as play entrances to an imaginary dwelling. Wide double-window spaces were set in, with deep ledges for sunny winter seats, and for pots of flowers. Long, straight pines were hauled in on wagons for the ridgepoles, and for the stable and the windmill tower later. She moved in before the place was half finished.

Long before the last rattlesnake seemed gone from the gentle slope, and the walls were high as a branding corral, visitors showed up, to hunch with forearms crossed on their saddle horns. Sometimes a cow-puncher would get out his makin's, sift the tobacco into the pinched paper, and lick it thoughtfully. "Plannin' on runnin' cattle?"

"Yes, some," the girl usually said to this query. She had ten cows and planned to get more, since cattle were easier for patients to come by here than money. But she would need all this space to care for the sick.

When the visitors spurred away, they usually left a hazy sense of unfriendliness behind. Morissa realized that this unfriendliness would grow when the ten acres were broken out for her tree claim next spring, and her little irrigation ditch was started.

Then the new Centennial Model Winchester rifle came. Robin opened the box casually. "Guess maybe I better leave this here with you," he said, as though the gun hadn't been ordered for Morissa.

He settled his hat on his shaggy gray hair and went to lay out a target, clearing a square yard of sand on the slope of a ridge where the heavy .45-70 bullets could bury themselves. Then he showed Morissa how to use the new rifle and got Jackie to challenge her every few days. At first the gun left her shaken, not the recoil against her shoulder, but the thought that she was practicing for murder. Yet she would soon be alone here, with helpless patients in her sole care, and so she kept on. Although the target was only two hundred yards at first, men came from the saloons to watch this young city woman kick up the sand every shot. Then they hurried back to throw down a few fast drinks.

MORISSA HAD A TEAM and top buggy now, sent up by Sid Martin. He was no longer yellow as a Chinese, he wrote, but still fighting the saddle skirts around his neck instead of riding them. Otherwise he was doing all right for a man who ought to be dead.

A ranch hand brought the shining new buggy to the doctor's yard gate, the bays standing with their ears up as Morissa came out, and shying a little from her blowing calico skirts. But the mare reached out a soft, inquiring nose to the low words Morissa made for her.

"This is ridiculous overpayment," she said to the man, but he made it clear he wasn't sent for conversation and set his spurs.

Nellie and Kiowa were four-year-olds, the gelding a little too flighty, but Morissa found him an amusing horse. And it was as well that he was an engrossment, for Morissa needed something to laugh at.

She missed Robin and Jackie very much. Robin was gone to look over his new job before moving down, but what disturbed Morissa was word that Jackie and Eddie Ellis were seen with the outlaws hiding around the Red Cloud Agency.

Perhaps Morissa was alone too much. Tris Polk had not stopped in since she moved to the north side of the river. But Lt. Wilbert Larman was turning his young eyes in all their blue seriousness toward her now that Yvette Forson and Tris both seemed gone. Saturday nights he and Morissa usually looked in at Etty's roadhouse for a while, enjoying the square dances, the reels, and the polkas. Once Morissa danced with Eddie Ellis there, his baby-lashed eyes searching out hers, until she wondered in exasperation how she got herself into such a situation, with boys like Wilbert and twenty-year-old Eddie hanging around when there were so many men in the country, not only Tris Polk, but dozens of others. She wondered if she was being quarantined, and how much of Tris Polk's avoidance grew out of Calamity Jane and her "You little bastard."

Then one afternoon a stagecoach left the road to the bridge and came thundering to her door, swaying crazily. As Morissa ran out, the driver toppled toward her from the box. She caught him, eased him to the grass, her hands slick and sticky from the bleeding under an arm. Inside, four of the five passengers were wounded, and Owen, the guard on their Black Hills outing, too, with a thigh shattered. The stage had been held up by a gang of masked men, but the driver refused to stop. While Owen, riding guard up in front, winged one of the road agents and picked off three of their horses, the driver was shot. Owen was left clinging to the high seat, his broken leg pounding helplessly against the side of the thundering coach until they could stop to get him inside.

Morissa called for Charley Adams from the bridge troops to help her work with the patients. Together they got the driver's bleeding stopped, and started after the bullet and the bone fragments in Owen's thigh. Although the splintered femur had punched out through a jagged hole big as two fists, the artery was untouched or there would have been a dead man inside when the coach reached the valley. So, with the grizzled old army nurse handling the ether, the doctor gently probed the welling wound. Finally they cleansed it with carbolic acid solution, drew the leg out straight and long as the other, and packed and stitched the wound, leaving it deep-tubed and open at the two ends. Because this would need constant observation, Morissa had Clarke's blacksmith make a sort of iron frame over a temporary open cast, fastened the leg securely against slip or shift, and slung it up with a pulley and sandbag.

The wounds of the others were all comparatively minor. A little morphia would get all but Owen and the driver to Sidney, and so the bullet-pocked coach went on.

Several times that bad first week the guard's fever went very high, and angry red streaks began to move along the blood vessels. Morissa thought seriously of amputating the leg, but she clung to it as desperately as the patient now, in a land where the cripple was indeed a misfit. Somehow they kept Owen alive through the next weeks. Then suddenly he began to take notice. "Still got me in one piece, eh, Doc?" he asked weakly one day as Morissa examined the scant discharge from the tubes, sniffing it, testing it for grit between her fingers. Now the man began to eat, and the wound began to drain and stink. Finally the doctor put a solid cast inside the iron frame and got the patient ready for Sidney, nearer to his friends.

Henry Clarke stood beside Morissa as the wagon took the guard away. "I have been withholding my objections to your move across the river, my dear, hoping that you would get discouraged and leave for a more salutary location without my intercession," he said, speaking with stiff formality. "I am still certain there will be serious trouble if you remain. However, I must express my gratitude to you, not as to the daughter of a trusted employee but to an excellent physician."

Morissa felt herself blushing over the forced little speech and tried to thank the man as she looked after the wagon with misted eyes.

LIEUTENANT LARMAN took Morissa through the new blockhouse on the little built-up island joined to Clarke's bridge. Of native pine, it was erected as a warning and a protection against red men and white who would attack this crossing. The second story was set diagonally upon the first, giving the gun slits complete command of any approaching enemy. So the new Camp Clarke stood, like a sort of thick, shaggy head lifted to look both ways over the long bridge.

"At the first sign of danger you're to hurry in here, and bring your pill sack and instruments, in case we have to stand a siege," the young lieutenant said, laughing, but underneath there was a deep seriousness. Morissa knew that his orders were sound.

No one knew where Crazy Horse and his great force of hostile Sioux were, and this, with the rumors continuing that the mines were played out, kept down the travel past Morissa's place for weeks. Then suddenly there was a new gold strike in the Deadwood region, several, but in the more difficult business of hard-rock lodes. The richest one, the Homestake, was optimistically labeled the most promising gold mine in the world. The movement to Deadwood quickened once more, with the curious urgency of the gold-hungry, and many remembered uneasily that every dollar of gold taken from the earth up there was still the legal property of the Indians. So another conference for the purchase of the Black Hills was arranged.

It must turn out better than last year. There had been an hour or two then when none of the commission to buy the Hills, not even the generals, hoped to get out alive, so angry were the young warriors at this talk of selling their country. But this year the wild young Sioux were away north with Crazy Horse; and the conference would meet inside the agency stockade, with bayoneted troops all around, and cannon.

Morissa went up to the agency with Sid Martin, who had to see about beef contracts if he was to make anything out of his cattle. With this horse collar that she kept on him, he felt safer with his doctor along. So Morissa took a wild ride in his top buggy behind a team of calico broncs that he managed by half standing at the dashboard, herding them along in the general direction with whip and line. Morissa's little velvet hat was over her nose one minute and flying back the next, but they got there.

"I did a better job on your neck than I realized," Morissa said ruefully, as she took Martin's hand to step from the buggy.

There was a post dance that night, and the next day she went down to the Sioux conference with the men. The stockade was full, mostly with whites, for no Indians except the chiefs and headmen were permitted inside. The commissioners talked a long time, and then one blanketed Sioux after another rose from their council circle on the floor. They talked but they would not sign for the sale, and so the third day all visitors were sent out and the gates of the stockade bolted. There the chiefs must remain until they did sign, and their families outside would get no flour or meat, nothing at all until the pen was touched. It was a difficult time for Chief Red Cloud. Only ten years ago he had been powerful enough to force the army out of the Bozeman trail forts that were set up in country promised to his people so long as grass shall grow and water flow.

But his people were trapped in the shadow of the soldier cannon and the hunger the white man brought. With his face like the eternal granite of the Hills the chief arose, drew his blanket about him, and led the row of silent men to the table where the white paper lay, and that night the keening of women along White River was as for a great man dead.

Chapter 7

ONE NIGHT MORISSA'S gray cat came scratching at the door and crawled with frosted whiskers under the cover at her breast. In the morning there was a white rime over all the river valley. But it was a fine golden fall, the upland tawny and red-clumped where the prairie rosebushes sat close to the earth, the deer leaping from the berry patches to stand off against the hillside and look as Morissa rode by.

One day Tris Polk came, driving a handsome yellow-wheeled buggy with white-stockinged blacks, the kind of horses he liked. "Same stock as Cimarron, fine and showy," he said, "but you know the old saying, 'Four white feet, feed 'em to the crows.' "

Morissa laughed as easily as she could with the hurt of the man's absence, and her own undeniable joy at seeing him again, even if the buggy was purchased for Gilda Ross. They looked the new team over together, and talked about what was going on around Sidney and about the sights that Tris had hoped to take in while he was in Chicago with the Forsons. Then there was the Presidential campaign too—anything except Morissa's move north of the river to what looked like a pretty permanent settler layout plunk in the middle of the cattle country.

"I hear you patched up Owen's shattered leg fine, and have Sid Martin planning to ride in the fall roundup."

Morissa raised her hands in despair. "You western men! Sid will probably get his head snapped off again, and live through that too. Next time I'll wire him together—"

So they talked, a little awkwardly, and in the afternoon they drove out to the Wild Cat range. Through Tris's spyglass they saw a bighorn sheep far up on the gray bluffs with her young standing behind her, and farther off two rams, their great curling horns a vague darkness over their heads.

"Proud, noble creatures, aren't they?" Morissa said, a choke in her throat as the rams turned and leaped over a crevasse. "My, I love this country," she exclaimed, holding out her arms.

"But your doctoring'll fall off to nothing in the winter, when the travel slows down."

"The country will still be here."

"With thirty-five below zero, and a blizzard wind . . ."

They returned through the evening sunlight that lay orange along the far ridges of the northeast. Two antelope grazed beside the trail, tamer than all summer, and soon the sky would be full of geese going south.

At her place Tris stopped up beside her little creek dam. Morissa sat quiet, ready for the complaints against her, the protests and the anger. But the rancher looked down along the little ditch to the golden-leafed young cottonwoods of the yard, some already as tall as the low sod-house. "Water makes a lot of difference in this country," he said.

"Yes, all this wide valley could be fruitful as—"

"I know, fruitful as the Nile. But it would mean the end of cattle here, the finest business in the world."

And to this Morissa had no reply. It didn't matter, for today was like a homecoming, with Tris back.

THE WINTER was a mild one even to the easterners. The coaches ran on schedule and the bull trains kept the freight moving. There was a little St. Patrick's dance planned at Clarke's but Morissa missed it. She was far away, near the place where Sid Martin's herd stampeded last June. A note had come by stage saying a man was dying of pneumonia in a sod-house up there. Morissa was uneasy about starting out alone, with the morning sun so curiously white, but Charley Adams was off with a party scouting for some Indian herds reported stolen.

So she left a note asking him to keep an eye on her convalescents and drew on a heavy pair of woolen pants of Robin's and high overshoes. She put his old buffalo coat into the buggy and a sack of provisions. Then, with her rifle and her compass she settled the bays into their steady little trot up the worn trail, watching for the angle-off into the sandhills.

By the time Morissa left the trail the sun was gone and a thin rain had started. By two o'clock it had frozen to sleet and the sharpening wind veered toward the northwest. The sleet became fine sharp snow that searched out every crack of the buggy curtains and ran about the horses' hoofs. Gradually all the holes and little washouts were covered over and the buggy lurched and swayed in the rising blizzard. Twice the horses refused a drift and the doctor had to wallow out into the powdery snow and lead Nellie around gullies that would have swallowed buggy and team. Finally she had to stay at the heads of the horses to keep them moving at all, floundering breathlessly in the buffalo coat, hip deep.

When the whipping blizzard was so thick that she could hardly breathe standing still, she stopped at what seemed a sheltered little hollow and unhitched. She rolled the provisions and her rifle into the buggy robe, and fastened the bundle on Kiowa the best she could with the lines and tugs. Holding her pill bag and her lantern, and very bulky in her buffalo coat, she climbed on Nellie and started away into the roaring storm, leading Kiowa by his hitching rope tied to Nellie's harness. All Morissa could hope to do was hold the horses in the general direction of the wide flat that she had found once before, and somehow locate a new little sod-house, built near the seepage springs, with a sick man alone inside. If she missed it—but she wouldn't think about that now.

Then she remembered that her horses had been up at Sid Martin's cow camp, so she took the desperate chance that she must: she let Nellie have her head. The cold was very sharp now. Morissa's foot and all her leg on the windy side were numb when the white dusk of early evening began to settle. Soon she would have to admit that they had passed the flat and were lost. Twice the horses stopped and would hardly go on in spite of all her urgings. Suddenly Nellie's snow-caked head seemed to come up; together the horses turned and, side by side, plunged through a breast-deep drift. Then Kiowa whinnied and they both stopped, close up against a wall that seemed to be sod under the drifting snow.

Sobbing her relief, Morissa slid awkwardly into the snow and, dragging the horses, started to plow along the wall. It was a sod-house, and she pushed the door open into a dead chilliness and the smell of dreadful disease. Stiffly she tied the horses and went inside.

A man lay on a wall bunk, half conscious. A touch of her frozen fingers to the brow and the pulse, and the doctor could have cried again. Instead she asked about fuel. At the slow turn of the man's eyes she plunged out into the storm and found a snowy cow-chip pile against the house. With the fire going she tried to give the wasted man a little brandy with hands that ached as the blood returned. She was very clumsy, but he could not have swallowed at the best. The gray, opaque eyes held an apology, the apology of the dying, and so she arranged him more comfortably and then sat half the night beside his body.

Finally when the man was like a frozen creature, she decided to put him outside for the long wait before burial, in a sort of return to the cleansing elements from his house of disease. She rolled him in the old tarp from his bed.

When she went out to look after her team the man's two horses came to her, as though expecting a little grain. Cautiously she moved around the sod-house into the blinding storm, careful not to lose touch with the wall, until she found what she hoped—a wheel, a wagon up close, and under the covered bows a sack with a few ears of corn. She drew out eight and let the horses take them from her mittened hand.

Although still half frozen and shaking, she propped the door open a while to let the clean blizzard air sweep through the place. Then she dug the contaminated earth away under the wall bunk, filling the hole with clean, powdery gray ashes from the stove. She melted snow and boiled the tin cups, and then scrubbed the frying pan with earth until it gleamed. Afterward she fried a couple of strips of bacon and a little baking-powder bread. Finally she rolled up in her buffalo coat and slept.

On the fourth day the sun came out clear. The broad flat valley was the same pure glistening white as the first time she saw it, in hail, the day she tended Sid Martin's broken neck. She took the horses over to the wind-bared ridge to the south, hobbling Nellie and Kiowa and turning the others loose. She would have to leave the man's team behind, but not to die in the sod corral. The horses grazed hungrily with no urge to drift, her hobbled team pawing awkwardly.

That afternoon Morissa was bundling up to go out for the bays when a herd of horses appeared along the barer ridges to the northeast. At first she thought they were wild, but then she saw horsebackers close, closer than any wild mustang would permit. It was probably one of the stolen Indian herds the troopers were looking for.

As they came up even with the four horses grazing along the slope, one of the riders turned to wrangle them in. He whooped the unhobbled ones into a run toward the herd for all Morissa's angry shouting. Then he turned back for her bay team and started them up the ridge too. But their hobbled movement was so slow he stopped. He was surely going to cut them free, leave the doctor afoot here in the snowbound hills. Furious, Morissa ran for her rifle, steadied it against the doorjamb, and put a bullet into the snow at the man's feet. The man turned to look and the three driving the herd also stopped, one of them jerking a rifle from a scabbard. This was the showdown, Morissa knew, and she fired again, this time to strike among the close-running bunch of horses. Apparently it nicked one, for the herd exploded in a great burst of snow and scattered off southward, the horsebackers hard after them.

But the man on the slope showed fight. He spurred his gray horse through the drifts straight for the sod shack. Morissa had to make a quick decision. If she could put a bullet very close over his head, he might decide it wasn't worth the risk. She shot, but her hand was unsteady and the charge went wide. The man kept coming, with a red spurt from his pistol and a bullet that splintered the doorpost beside her.

Morissa realized this was like an emergency operation, with the stake a life—her life. And so she calmed to the task at once and aimed on the horse plunging straight for her. She shot. The horse pitched forward, but the man stayed with the saddle as the gray pawed himself up, reared and floundered, then recovered and ran crazily back toward the hill, plainly

dying. One of the riders driving the herd turned and spurred over the wind-blown slope to pick up the man. Together they whipped away on the one horse, but they emptied a warning revolver toward the sod-house, one bullet making a neat hole in the stovepipe.

When they were gone Morissa leaned against the door, trembling. It occurred to her that the men might return, come up from all sides, and so with a knife she dug gun slits through the sod near each corner, her hands shaking. The house grew very cold for she didn't dare go out for fuel, any more than for the horses. She could see Nellie moving with her hobbled jump, quieted, and after a while Kiowa was back beside her.

As soon as dusk moved out of the low hills Morissa tramped snow into the wool of her buffalo coat to whiten it; then with corn in her pocket and her rifle across her arm, she slipped out. The cold burned her nose; the drifts creaked under her feet. A dozen times she stopped, stooping low, but there was no shot, no sound in the white starlight except the noise of the hobbled horses, still feeding. Nellie nickered softly and came forward, smelling the ear of corn Morissa held out to her.

Cautiously, walking hidden between the two horses in the dusk, Morissa returned to the sod-house and brought the team inside, the protesting Nellie first, snorting at the smell of fire and death. After a while Kiowa followed his teammate through the open door.

The waiting depressed the weary doctor, with the poor man lying frozen beside the sod wall outside. This afternoon the drive to self-preservation had carried her even to a willingness to kill, but now that was gone and the doubt of her presence here settled down like some dark and sooty cloud, bringing mistrust of every action, even the impulse to come west at all. Nellie stirred from sleep and rattled her halter as she reached toward the woman. Morissa went to her, rubbed the soft nose and Kiowa's, too, then looked all around the empty night snow and hoped that the man who had brought up the stragglers of the horse herd today was not Eddie Ellis. It looked like him, a little. Morissa knew he had lost his job at the Indian agency.

Dawn came clear, with the sliver of late moon white as ice. It took a long time to get the dead man on Nellie, shying and fractious, but finally Morissa put the frozen body into empty corn sacks with the smell of grain still in them and tied it firmly across the mare's back. With her rifle handy, Morissa started away on Kiowa, leading the mare. She rode a saddle now. Just before dawn she had gone boldly out and got it from the robber's dead horse.

She angled along the barer ridges toward the nearest trail station. In a snow-filled canyon she saw what looked like a whole bull train drifted with the storm, a few heads and frozen backs showing, eagles and buzzards already circling against the pale spring blue.

When Morissa finally reached the little log station her throat was raw and swollen, and she was shaking. "The trail to the Platte isn't open?" she asked.

"No, not even a horsebacker over it yet."

So she took a dose of quinine for her cold, and slept.

TEN DAYS AFTER she left the north valley, Morissa came riding back on Nellie, leading Kiowa—the first traveler on the trail except Clarke's express riders. Everyone was out to meet her, soldiers and everybody from Fish Head up, even Clarke, who had come in from Sidney on horseback to count his losses. "Never go out on a long winter call alone again, my dear," he said, holding the worn, snow-burned girl in his arms a moment. "We can't have anything happen to our lady doc."

As he talked, mostly to cover his anxiety, Morissa looked around the emotional faces, the watery eyes of old Etty, and the tear on the quiet, reticent cheek of his wife.

"It's like coming home from a far, far journey," the doctor finally said, and kissed the brown cheek of Lorette's baby.

Chapter 8

ROBIN HADN'T MENTIONED Jackie in his last letter. Anxious about rumors placing him with Eddie Ellis, Morissa finally admitted that something must be done about her brother, and she sat down to write a note to Eddie. "There's always a slice of cake or something waiting for any of Jack's friends who come past my door," she told him.

Eddie came sooner than she expected. Barely a week later, he brought Jackie in, riding double, with his right arm tied up across his breast by a kerchief knotted around his neck. They had been running antelope, trying to rope one. Jack's horse stepped into a badger hole, snapped a leg, and threw Jack over his head, breaking the collarbone. They made a straight story of it, Eddie, around twenty-one by now, the leader in the telling, Jack nodding.

Eddie rode away before dawn, saying he must get back to work, although Morissa knew he had lost his job at the agency long ago. But it was fine to have Jackie around for the planting, handing her the roots as she set out a lot of rhubarb, enough for a supply of pleasant physicking syrup, and asparagus, so good for the kidneys.

About a week later the Bosler cowboys brought a small bunch of herd sires through. While the men wet their throats at Etty's, some of the bulls broke down Morissa's pasture fence and tolled away two of her young heifers. On the Appaloosa she went to look for them, riding northeast the way the bulls had gone, to some high ridges overlooking the sandhills.

It was somewhere off this way that the boys had chased the antelope, and when Morissa saw buzzards circling slowly, she went over and found the horse half gutted by wolves. It had Robin's RT brand all right, but no broken leg; instead there was a bullet through the heart.

As she stood looking, Morissa noticed old tracks leading down the slope that funneled off toward the Platte. She rode down that direction with her rifle ready across the saddle. In a washout the earth showed tracks of animals, attracted by another carcass, that of a man, poorly buried and now half uncovered where wolves had begun at his belly. Morissa scraped the earth back from a face that was bearded, with an old scar across the corner of the swollen, blackened mouth—surely the outlaw Cut Lip Johnson from Red Cloud. He had at least two bullets through him, and many would say he had them coming a long, long time.

With the big knife left in Cut Lip's sheath, Morissa dug sand and sod down upon him. Then she slipped her boots and socks off and tramped the earth with her bare feet for the human smell. When she was about a mile on her way home she turned the Appaloosa back to the dead horse and cut out Robin's brand, haggling it as though wolves had been gnawing there, looking over her shoulder several times, furious that she felt driven to such trickery.

Home without her heifers, she unsaddled and went in to talk to Jackie. He finally broke down and admitted that Eddie's story was a lie. They had hired out to help drive some horses down to the Platte, but a bunch of Sioux bucks came whooping after them, shooting as they rode. One got Jack's horse, but the Indians whipped right past him after the herd. The man who dropped back to stand off the Sioux was killed, the rest got away, letting the horses scatter. "Eddie came back for me when the Indians had whooped their horses off back north, and brought me in."

"Who buried Cut Lip?" Morissa demanded.

For a moment the boy looked at his sister, his young face naked in astonishment and fear. "I don't know," he finally admitted. "Eddie went down to help him, too, but he was dead. Eddie's very brave."

"Bravery is a relative thing. There's nothing brave about getting a seventeen-year-old boy in with horse thieves. You know what happens to them if they're caught. Strung up to the first tree. In a country without courts you're as guilty as the gang you run with."

The boy sat looking straight ahead, his bony young face drawn and afraid, and yet Morissa knew that her talking was futile. Jackie had understood these things long before she came to the valley.

"You know I have to report this," she added slowly.

"Turn in your own brother?" the boy said angrily, flushing under the thin bearding.

No, she couldn't do that, not the only blood kin she had, and so she wrote the sheriff in Sidney about finding the dead man while hunting stock, but nothing more. The next morning she rode out with Lieutenant Larman and two of his bluecoats to bring in the body. No one seemed to care how Cut Lip was killed; the sheriff didn't come, and so another grave was added to the knoll across the river.

The next week Eddie Ellis came back and took Jack out for a ride, away from Morissa; it was then that Charley Adams said that Cut Lip had been with Sam Bass in the Deadwood holdup. So she bought Jackie a ticket to his father, and packed him off on the first coach to Sidney.

WHEN MORISSA had come back from the blizzard and found her cattle fed, her plants saved by the daily fire somebody had troubled to build for her, she had known she must have a hired man. One did not impose on good neighbors like that. She needed a man with a wife or sister, or even a mother—preferably a woman who could tend the patients when Morissa was called away. She knew the couple she needed must be available, with much unemployment all over the east and wages going down again.

The week after Jackie left the problem seemed solved. Charley Adams said he was through soldiering after sixteen years. He wanted to file on a homestead in the valley and bring his wife up from Kansas. But his Ruth was uneasy; she knew about cattlemen warring against settlers.

"I suppose she's wise to weigh that possibility. There will be difficulties here someday, but if we stick together . . ." Morissa said thoughtfully. "You're a crack shot; you'd be very useful then too."

So Charley sent for his wife and built a bunk and a bureau and chairs for the little ell along the far side of Morissa's hospital room. Then he went down to file his claim and brought back a team, wagon, and plow, and a tent that he pitched beside Morissa's pond.

Ruth Adams turned out to be a plain woman with a bleakish face, perhaps from waiting sixteen years for her soldier husband to make a home for her. She looked at Morissa, tall, slender, and high-busted, her uncovered hair shining like a dark bay filly in the sun, and she went to live in the tent instead of in the house.

But two weeks out there cooled Ruth off a little, Charley whispered to Morissa when he came back from Sidney with a load of wire fencing. Maybe it was being alone through the cold rain of late April, or perhaps that Morissa's cat went up to rub his back against the woman's gray calico skirts. Who can say what little wind will veer the set of the mind?

Charley went to lay out the ten acres on Morissa's timber claim. His breaking rolled back smooth as satin bands, with blackbirds, gulls, even meadowlarks following at his heels, pecking in the new-turned earth. Morissa followed, too, working in a navy denim jumper suit and yellow sunbonnet, her hair in the thick braid hanging below her waist. She carried a sack of seedling cottonwood, box elder, and ash slung under one arm, and with the spade she set them out two swinging steps apart, driving the blade deep through the sod, working it back and forth to make a little bed for the rootlets. With her gloved hands she packed earth around them, stepped a firm foot on each side, and then went on to the next. The riders on the trail who stopped to slouch over their saddle horns were pointed in their disapproval, telling the city woman about the drought, the hail, and grasshoppers, and the range cattle running loose here.

"Oh, there's the state herd law to protect cultivation from straying stock," she reminded them easily.

"You mean you expect the courts 'way off at Sidney to make us keep our cows up, just for your little shirttail patches here?" one of Bosler's men asked in astonishment.

"Well, I have a legal claim to the land, and that's more than you cattlemen can say for your range," she said, her teeth white, the hazel eyes luminous with their remote glow, the lips humorous.

It was the foreman of the Cradle Six, setting up a new ranch in the Snake Creek country, who finally put it straight to Morissa. "You remember your first day here, ma'am," he said over the impatient stomp of his horse, "when Clarke nailed up the dead owl to warn the others off? Hanging the first man who threatened his bridge . . ."

Morissa scraped at a bit of earth clinging to her spade with a chip of flint. So he knew what Clarke had told her. They all worked together. "Are you threatening me?" she finally trusted herself to ask. "Because if you are, let me tell you I'm from a breed of owls that don't scare easy."

The man grinned, showing his strong brown teeth pleasantly, still wishing to seem gallant. But only for a moment. "Why don't you leave before your luck runs out? Be mighty easy to make a case against you here, you know. Shielding outlaws. People have been hung for less."

Morissa didn't overlook the threat that had been spoken so plainly. In the morning she took her rifle out to her tree planting. The next day a smooth-fingered man from Bosler's came to offer her five hundred dollars for her departure, "providing you don't file on another place in the country. . . ."

Morissa smiled. "I like it here—" and to this the man set his spurs.

ALL WINTER there had been news of Indian battles and now Crazy Horse and the last of his followers were finally driven to the reservations, not by guns so much as by the disappearance of the buffalo. With the surrender of the Sioux the troops began to leave, and the coaches from Cheyenne had to fight their way past Robbers Roost and other hideouts. Men like Jesse James and his gang, along with the regular road agents, were free to work in the open again. Stories of a woman riding with the outlaws sifted down to Clarke's bridge, and then late one night there was the quiet but firm tap of a gun butt against Morissa's door.

In the darkness she opened the middle window a little and looked out, a man vaguely visible in the diffused light of her sign. "You have the wrong place," she said, keeping her voice down from Ruth. "What you want is available over across the bridge."

"Ain't you the lady doc?"

"Yes, I am."

Then he had come to fetch her. Sick woman off west here a ways.

For the first time Morissa hesitated. "Who is sick, and who are you?"

Now the man made no pretense. With his gun he motioned the young doctor outside. "Get on that horse or I'll put a bullet through yeh. . . ."

"And then who'll care for your sick woman?" Morissa said scornfully.

"If you don't come you ain't gonna be feedin' nobody no more pills—"

That made sense, and so Morissa smiled a little. "If you are afraid to let me know who you are now, what proof is there that I'll live to tell what I might find out?"

"Oh, that's easy, sis. I'll take an' blindfold you, in 'n' out. Please hurry, ma'am, the woman's a-dyin'."

"Wounded?"

"No, don't know what's ailin' her. She's feverin', and talkin' wild, and goin' into fits. . . ."

Morissa couldn't get anything more out of him, so she said she wanted her own horse and would need Charley Adams, up at his tent tonight. He was a good nurse, good with ether, if it was necessary to operate.

"Operate—" the man said in sudden fear, but he was still adamant. "No, I ain't takin' nobody else."

"Then I don't come. You can blindfold him too."

So with the man slipping up to listen, Morissa woke Charley. "Need you on a call," she said. While he dressed she managed to leave an awkward little note written in the dark depths of the trunk where she pretended to dig for medicines: "Taken away with Charley to woman patient off west by threat of gun. Slight man with limp."

Saddled up, they rode through the darkness. Toward dawn the man stopped and ordered Morissa to blindfold Charley and then herself. Soon other horsebackers joined them, without a word. When the sun had boiled down hot for hours and the lagging hoofs struck rock, the man stopped at the sound of a murmuring creek. The Appaloosa drank deeply, and a tin cup was put into Morissa's hand, brimful of cold sweet water. Then they followed up this stream and dismounted. Morissa was led over a step into walls, a stinking shack, and told to remove her blind.

Although the door had been open, the stench of dead flesh roiled even the doctor's empty stomach. As her eyes adjusted themselves to the windowless place, she saw a woman on a bunk, only the white skull-face clear. Swiftly Morissa counted the failing pulse and verified her sudden fears. "The man should have told me what was wrong," she said, angry to be caught so unprepared.

The woman tried to speak. "They don't know . . ." she finally managed in a breathy whisper. "It was—before . . ." her voice stopped.

"I must know how long . . ." Morissa urged gently.

Four months, and took sick a week ago. She had done what a woman at Deadwood told her. "I—I was afraid, but when I come to—come here I couldn't have me a—a bastard."

Morissa felt herself grow unprofessionally angry. "Don't use that vile and dreadful word!" she commanded. "Abuse the father or yourself, but not the innocent." But the woman seemed unable to listen. Her sunken, fevered eyes sought the open doorway.

Morissa knew she must do what little she could immediately, with the

abdomen hard as from peritonitis. She called for the man, who came to stand behind her, his blue neckerchief drawn up across his face when she turned to give him a note. "Send this to my place if you won't go to a pharmacist. Get Mrs. Adams to send me what I want."

"No!"

"Yes! Even now it may be too late." For a moment she saw a look of misery come into the shadowed eyes, of fear and sorrow that made the woman in the doctor feel rejected and depressed. But she could give only a passing notice to her sudden envy of this affection, and a gladness for it too. She set out the carbolic acid and her instruments on a towel spread over a stump bench and began her task, the woman no more than a girl for all the gaunt and bloated skeleton, the doctor still hoping that the distended abdomen was not from a break into the pelvic cavity.

Twice Morissa stopped to give the girl a heart stimulant and finally it was necessary to call Charley, although the watcher outside stood against it. "I won't have no man in there!" he commanded.

"But Charley is like a doctor." And when he still resisted, Morissa told him the rest. "Perhaps it won't matter now anyway."

Slowly the man slid a hand down upon the grip of his pistol and then let it fall helplessly, his face convulsed. So Charley came into the silent shack and closed the door against the deep, choking sobs outside.

At last they could do no more; even the final irrigation and disinfection was completed. Morissa sat down, pinned her hair back, and hoped that she had done no more harm than good. After a while, when the girl seemed quieter, the man outside brought in a little beef stew with onions and potatoes in it. It was late afternoon now, a long time and a long ride since their last meal, and so Morissa and Charley ate heartily.

They took turns beside the girl in the low lantern light, and toward midnight the breathing became deeper, more regular, and Morissa's hand found the forehead cooler. At her first move, the man outside was peering through the crack of the door. She nodded reassuringly and awoke Charley to show him the change in the smoky light.

BY THE NEXT AFTERNOON it was plain that no one had been sent on Morissa's errand, but with the patient very much better, the two were blindfolded again and led away. The girl had cried softly as she clung to Morissa's hand, and the young doctor choked back the advice that rose in her: "Go home, wherever that is." For who could see the life of young Dr. Morissa Kirk of the gold trail this moment and not say to her also, "Go home, wherever that is."

Before they left, the man had laid five double eagles in her hand—heavy, glistening new gold. When Morissa objected to the amount, he said, "Interest comes correspondingly high as the risk increases."

"But you are an educated man!" Morissa exclaimed in surprise.

Immediately the outlaw returned to his surly, illiterate speech behind the blue cloth. Blindfolded again, they rode out. After a while more hoofs joined them, more clink of bridles until there were at least five men around them, silent. But after a long winding stretch Morissa sensed that the hoofbeats were lessening. Finally the outlaw spoke. "You kin jerk the blind, miss." Without another word he swung away into the darkness.

When they got home Ruth was at the stable to meet them, pretending not to cry that her Charley was back. Morissa saw a horse near the gate beyond, and Tris was waiting on the bench before the lighted doorway.

"We've been very uneasy about you, after a Wyoming outlaw was seen riding this way couple days ago, and Ruth found your note," he said sternly.

"Oh, nobody's going to hurt me," Morissa said as she stretched herself wearily on the low bench.

For a long time Tris was silent. "I ran into your heifers, up near where you left your buggy in the blizzard," he finally told her. "In with the Bosler herd. I had them brought back."

"Oh, you are kind, Tris." Morissa tried to make herself recall why she should have heifers astray but she was too worn out tonight.

The man did not seem to listen to even the little she said. "I can't have you going on like this, Morissa," he protested angrily. "Out nights, kidnapped by outlaws. Next month is the horse show at the Walker ranch, and you're going to marry me there."

Chapter 9

MORISSA WAS RETURNING from a call when she saw troopers riding south across the bridge two abreast. Behind them came a row of mounted Indians, a few wagons, and a long string of people walking, many bent to the bundles on their backs—men, women, and children.

She stopped and knew what it was—the first of a thousand Cheyennes starting on their transfer down to Indian Territory. Here they were, most of them afoot, to walk across Nebraska and Kansas and farther—all moving like dead ones, a beaten people driven into exile.

Suddenly the young doctor's face was scalded with tears and such a fury rose in her that she had to whip her horses, letting them out as they leaped ahead, jerking the buggy along in a lope until she got control of herself and was ashamed. But she knew it would be a long, long time before the guilt of this was washed from the grass where their moccasins had moved.

The Indians camped south of the river, and after the evening smoke one of the men came over the bridge to Morissa with a small boy at his side, the baby she had saved from measles last year.

By signs the man asked permission to see the Appaloosa. "Talk with horse," his signs conveyed to Morissa. She quickly nodded and he went to squat beside the animal. The Indian was silent, it seemed, for a long time before he touched him at all, and held the child up for the horse to smell. Impulsively Morissa ran out. "I give you—" she motioned.

The Indian smiled sadly and shook his head. "They take from me—white man take all horse—" he said, and then he touched Morissa's hand and guided it to the velvety place under the horse's jaw, moving her fingers up and down until the Appaloosa closed his eyes and stretched his head forward, like a cat rubbed on the back. But the Indian could not take the horse. It had been a trade, the horse traded for the life of his son, and he would never have that undone.

Morissa went back to the house and left the man there until the night darkened and the fireflies laced the riverbank.

TRIS POLK, like the other cattlemen, sent his roundup wagons to the Walker ranch for their summer horse show. He had an extra house tent for his pretty twin cousins and their mother, furnished with cots, wolf-skin rugs for the floor and a dressing table. With a little trouble he got the ranch cook into a white cap and willing to set flowers beside the breakfast biscuits. Then he drove over for Morissa Kirk. The Appaloosa was tied beside his buggy team, Morissa's green riding habit and her plumed hat in the valise under the buggy seat. "This is a proud day for me," the rancher said, and the young doctor smiled.

The show grounds lay on a little half-dry creek on the north Sidney table, the long scattering of log buildings and corrals among a few cottonwoods, with the shimmer of dust over it in the hot afternoon sun. Out a ways was a tent and wagon city of visitors, with cowboys riding here and there, their loping horses kicking up spurts of dust.

Morissa was welcomed almost as a betrothed by Auntie Mae and then by Li-Laurie and Li-Annie as Tris called the twins. They had gray eyes, too, but without the stormy darkness of their cousin's. The girls already had a following among the young men of the ranch country, one a reserved Englishman with sun-bleached hair and very good financial connections, Li-Laurie whispered to Morissa.

After the early supper they all moved across the slanting sunlight toward the big dance pavilion of new pine, where the fiddlers and a dulcimer player were tuning up. Morissa wondered once if Tris realized the story of her parentage, perhaps from Calamity Jane's remark, and thrust it from her mind as she swung from his arms to those of some young Englishman, to Colonel Walker, or to Sid Martin, whose neck turned easily enough to look after Tris's laughing Auntie Mae from Texas.

Morissa danced once with young Ellis too. He spoke intense, angry words into her ear. "If I was a few years older I'd trample that Tris Polk in the dust gettin' to you!"

Morissa laughed. "Ah-h, Eddie! That Texas sweet talk seems to be catching. Why don't you try it on one of the pretty southern girls?"

He seemed embarrassed and was silent, and afterward every time Morissa turned his way, she saw the pale, hurt eyes following her.

After the return to the tents, Aunt Mae took Morissa's arm and led her out into the moonlight for a little walk, and when they returned past the silent wagons, she sat down on one of the tongues, easy as any old gold trailer at eveningtime.

"I have been a boomer too," she reminisced. "I was scarcely more than a bride when we went down the Santa Fe trail, Illinois to Texas, sitting on the wagon tongues a spell every night before we crept into our beds for the early morning start."

"Well, you *are* a pioneer!"

"And so are you, in this new country and also in a new field for women. I am very happy about you for Tris."

The girl's face grew warm in embarrassment. "I—there's nothing settled. . . ." she had to say.

"I know, but you will marry. Tris is a fine man. He's had to give up, too, in his life. His father and my George were killed in the war. . . ." She paused a little, to steady her voice, and it was so much like Tris, this self-restraint, that a sudden warmth for him flooded over Morissa.

Then Aunt Mae's soft voice was firm again. "We die for our neighbors in their need, whether we know it or not. Tris, the only man left of our two families at sixteen, returned from his first-year study of engineering. He had to get into his chaps, round up our scattered stock, set the two ranches back on their feet. But with the war over, there was all this beef and so he started north to market with one of the first big herds. He was only a seventeen-year-old and new to fighting outlaws and Indians, but he learned. When he saw all the grass up here eight years ago he located the TeePee ranch for what is left of the family—we four. Now there's that new packinghouse he plans to go into with Forson from Chicago. Tris says it may make us all rich, very rich." She stopped and in the moonlight Morissa saw the pretty woman draw her wrap about her shoulders in satisfaction, as though it were already ermine.

"I'm glad to hear this good news for you and the girls," Morissa told her. "He hasn't said much about it to me."

"You don't need money as we do, my dear. The twins and I . . . But don't you think that handsome young English boy is drawn to Laurie? It would be so pleasant to have good connections in England. Tris says the boy is from a financial syndicate but only an employee—although he is the second son of an earl," she hastened to add.

THE CAMP STIRRED EARLY, the men setting the fires in the barbecue pits at daylight to get the coals ready for the meat. By ten the August sun was shimmering and little heat dances played along the west.

The horse show started gradually, with an easy western casualness. Colonel Walker and his redheaded daughter-in-law led out on Kentucky mares, followed by other ranchers from the region, Tris on Cimarron, between his pretty cousins in wine-colored habits on silver-maned buckskins. There were four visiting officers in army blue, followed by the racehorses, and then the bronc riders, a dozen, or so. Indians joined the parade, too, the men in paint, the women with their small children in skin sacks. Finally the real backbone of the cattle business came past: a thick crowding of cowboys and ranch hands with rope and gun and branding iron, followed by the cook and bed wagons, and a calf wagon, too, with a couple of bawling dogies looking out the slats.

The calf roping began, with a couple of bowlegged cowboys trying to keep a calf away from the fence for the roper, and Morissa laughed with the others as the little brindle dogie dove between this pair of barreled knees and that to escape the zinging loop. But finally the calves were all neatly footed and dragged to the branding fire.

Then the horse races were called, with a free-for-all-comers, and Bat's Blue, the blue roan belonging to Big Bat from Red Cloud Agency, was led out. Now the Indians became interested; one by one they got up, walked solemnly to their betting post and threw down beaded robes, shirts, pipe bags, and even knives and moccasins on the blue roan to win, matched by goods and tobacco and money on the other side of the post.

A pistol shot started the horses. The Kentucky stock drew out ahead, followed by the fast cow ponies and then the slower-starting Blue, with a dwarfed and twisted little Indian riding him bareback, with only a jaw rope, whooping every few jumps. He was the clown of the show, and everybody laughed and then looked to the leaders, but as the laps piled up, the Blue's tough distance blood began to show. Then suddenly the heels of the hunched little Indian went deep into the Blue's flanks as he lay close to the back. The horse lengthened out, too, his belly close to the ground. Running like a scared coyote, he shot past the others, and the whole band of Indians whooped to see it, as well as some of the whites.

Finished, the rider turned back to the judges to receive the applause and the ribbon that the Indian tied into the mane, one more ribbon to go with the dozen already feathering the show gear of Big Bat's wife.

The other races were less fun but more fitting to Colonel Walker and his special guests. There was the star-faced Neptune, a descendant of the all-time finest, the unbeatable Eclipse, besides half a dozen others of fine blood from the ranches toward Denver and Cheyenne.

"We better watch that fancy stock here for horse thieves," Sid Martin was telling Morissa from his horse when one of his cowboys came up, embarrassed at the need to interrupt. "A Seven U rider got a knee kicked, boss. Mebby . . ."

So Sid walked over with Morissa, leading his horse, the girl holding up the long side of her green habit, the feathers of her hat blowing. Then he loped off to the tent for her little black bag. But while Morissa was kneeling beside the horsebreaker, examining what seemed a cracked kneecap, a man in a dusty frock coat came pushing through. "I am Dr. Meddows," he said importantly, and elbowed Morissa aside.

"This here is Dr. Kirk," one of the cowhands said. Meddows looked up. "Ah, Dr. Kirk? A midwife, no doubt," he said, and fell to straightening out the leg. Morissa walked away and later Sid came riding by to apologize. "I hate that happening, ma'am. Meddows has hung up a shingle over one of those saloons in Sidney. Just a big blowhard, I hear."

"He's probably all right," Morissa said quietly, "but I was taught a different courtesy to a fellow physician."

They started back along the fence, and now the colonel led his guests out to watch the bronco busting. At the big pole corral the horses were roped and saddled. Then the gate was thrown open, the ropes were released, the blind snapped away, and the wild horse found himself on his feet and loaded with leather and man. Now it was a fight to the finish.

Once Morissa cried out within herself as a cowboy went off an end-switching bucker and sprawled into the dust, the horse still pitching on top of the man, trying to rid himself of the saddle right there, coming down again and again over the dark little bundle that was lying curled up motionless as a rabbit.

After what seemed a winter's age, Tris's rope got the horse, head down and hard to snag, and jerked him away, crashed him to the ground. Men hurried in from all directions to pick up the thrown rider. His clothing was in tatters but he was certainly the luckiest man alive, Morissa thought, for he was not even seriously cut.

Before long it was noon and the barbecue cooks were calling, "Come and get it!" Everybody trooped over to the long tables of planks laid on salt barrels with stacks of tin plates, cups, and cutlery laid out. Men with long gleaming knives sliced into barbecued halves of steers, brown and fragrant. Others piled hot Dutch-oven biscuits, pit-baked potatoes and beans on the tin plates, and ladled out canned tomatoes and coffee and cut the great pies of raisins and dried apples.

Afterward there was steer roping and tying, and then more races, including the wild, whooping, Indian pony free-for-all. There was the cook-wagon race too. The tailgate of the leader flew open in the wild swaying run; pots, pans, tin plates, and an open flour sack scattered out over the racetrack as the cook whipped his galloping horses to win.

Then there was the showing of handsome horses, and finally it was time for Morissa to ride. But instead of being with her horse she was up at the tent, talking to a gaunt-faced man who had ridden in on a lathered old crowbait that had no place on the Walker ranch today. At the repeated call to the show ring, she finally gathered up her skirts and ran, riding out alone on her Appaloosa with the shining silver-mounted saddle.

"Made for the Empress Carlotta of Mexico, but her whole outfit was driven out by the revolution before the saddler finished it," Aunt Mae told everyone around her. "Finest example of Texas saddlery in the world."

The Appaloosa was slowed to show his delicate Arabian head, his light eyes, the dark gray body with the lightish, elaborately spotted hindquarters. The ornate silver glistened on the black saddle leather, the young woman handsome in her dark green habit with the small gray and yellow ostrich tips on her tilted hat, her dark hair gleaming with the curious golden light against her brown skin and high coloring as she turned her dramatically beautiful horse. "Remarkable! Good seat and carriage too," one of Colonel Walker's British friends exclaimed.

At the corral Tris helped Morissa from her horse and held her in his arms an instant before all the grinning cowboys. "So it's settled you'll marry me at the dance tonight," he said lightly, making his voice matter-of-fact for the listeners. "There'll be two other hitchings, you know, with a cowboy preacher and all the trimmings."

Morissa looked up into the man's gray eyes, darkening like a summer storm, and for a moment he was a warm blur to the girl, everything a shimmer like sun on moving water. But she made herself stand away. "I can't," she said slowly, looking down so her feathers hid her eyes. "The man that's waiting at the tent came for me. Typhoid's hit the trail north, one man dead and five more bad cases. I have to start home right away—don't you see, Tris? A doctor would be no wife for you."

But as the man let her turn away, there was sadness in her, as though something fine was left here, finished, cut off. And at the tent there was another horsebacker to ride back up the trail with her—Eddie Ellis. She was glad to see him, to have his inconsequential talk to divert her thoughts from their foolish self-concern.

Chapter 10

THERE WAS MUCH TALK and rumoring about horse thieves in the neighborhood, professionals like Fly Speck Billy maybe, or Doc Middleton. Charley Adams took special precautions with Morissa's horses. "Hang a noose over the stable door an' see that the horse ain't inside, that's my motto," he said as he whistled the Appaloosa up for a can of oats and then took him over into his tent for the night. Ruth worked at it, too, feeding Etty's big white-faced dog Blaze in the evenings until he began to stay for the pan he got in the morning.

Morissa was busy every day with the typhoid that struck like buckshot scattered over the prairie. Yet the people living along the trail still argued that their wells were the sweetest in the world. How could they suddenly be poison? Most of the stage passengers were carrying jugs of cold tea now or keeping to something stronger. Fortunately Morissa had Charley and Ruth for her six bed patients, one with smallpox isolated in the lean-to she added on the north for a pesthouse.

Throughout the nation one out of every four typhoid patients was dying. Morissa refused to accept such mortality; she rode night and day, clinging to each man like a buffalo burr to a wooly pup, urging that all drinking water be boiled. "Carry a tin cup, make a grass fire." With so much driving, the doctor had another young team broken out from her growing herd, hired a driver, and tried to sleep between stops.

When Tris Polk returned from Chicago she was just coming into the yard from a night call to a Bosler camp, the despised settler welcome enough now that men were dying all around. She was so worn that Tris lifted her from the buggy seat like a child; she didn't remember to ask how his packinghouse deal was going, and barely remembered to appreciate the goodness of this man.

After Tris was gone Morissa wondered if she was taking the Texan's sweet talk too seriously. He was a determined man; perhaps he was just getting the one settler north of the river out, even if it took marriage to do it. Or did these questionings, these doubts, rise out of some deep urge to self-destruction lying within her?

Before the doctor could settle herself to sleep there was another hurried kick at the doorjamb and once more she started out, keeping herself awake with a jug of cold tea under the buggy seat. Her driver was already gone; drank water at one of the wells and was down too.

ONE MORNING A MAN came riding for the doctor, not by the bridge, but across the river far below and up through the hills. When Morissa's yard was empty he rode by and tossed a note over her fence. It was in a large, weak scrawl on wrapping paper: "Typhoid, come get me in wagon alone. Ed." There was a sketchy map, too, but Morissa didn't realize until later how much nearer he was to Sidney and the post hospital.

She found him alone in a dugout in a deep box canyon that broke toward Lodgepole Creek, with signs of many horses held behind a brushy gate. Eddie barely recognized her; he was much too weak to sit up and too heavy to lift into the wagon. With her shovel she sank the hind wheels almost to the hub, made a ramp with the door from the dugout, and drew Eddie up into the wagon on a blanket. Then she drove home, coming in late at night, and with Charley's help got him into bed, burning with fever, delirious, talking snatches of this and that, but little that could be followed.

They took turns keeping him in sheets wrung out in a tub of cold water and tried to feed him a little medication in scalded milk, a teaspoonful at a time. For three weeks Morissa was afraid to ask about him each time she returned.

By then two of the other patients were gone, one well enough to start home, the other hauled to the railroad in a box—one out of seven in her little hospital.

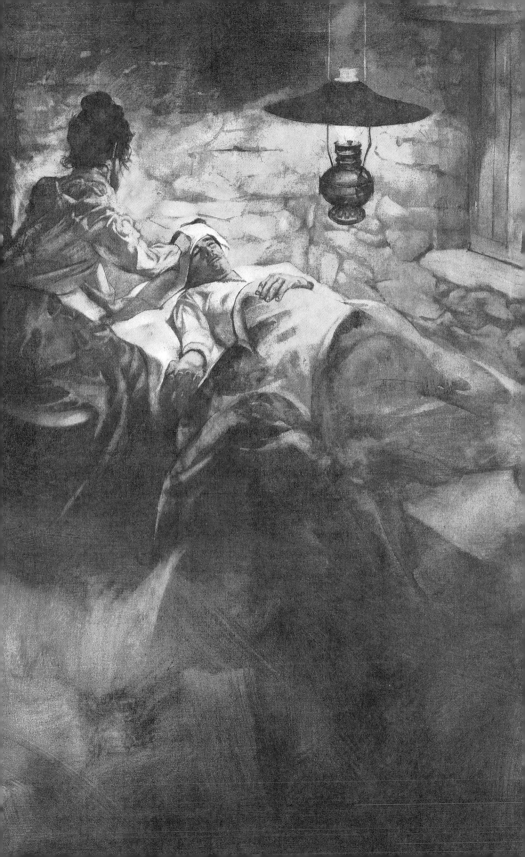

IN SEPTEMBER SAM BASS AND HIS GANG got between sixty and seventy-five thousand dollars in a Union Pacific holdup, east of Sidney, not very far from the hideout where Morissa found Eddie. She wondered if typhoid had kept him out of the holdup, still refusing to believe this, yet telling herself that a nod truly is as good as a wink to a blind mare. But the sheriff wouldn't be blind when he brought a charge of harboring criminals against her.

There was talk that the Bass gang had split up, with Sam going back to Texas and the rest heading north toward Clarke's bridge. Morissa found signs of a night camp at her dam in the little canyon, and an old piece of canvas half sunken in the mud of the shallow reservoir. She pulled it out, a heavy leather sack with a slide top and padlock, evidently a registered mailbag with the federal mark cut out. She sent this down to Sidney but all she ever heard was that several of the Bass gang traveling the Black Hills trail at night ran into some patrolling cavalry. There were seventeen thousand dollars of the Union Pacific loot under one of their saddles.

Three nights before this a man had come to Morissa's door to ask about Eddie Ellis. He came so quietly that Blaze never awoke. Morissa let the man in, and with his hat tipped to shadow his face to the bearded cheekbones, he looked down upon the gaunt skeleton on the cot. Suddenly Eddie opened his eyes. "Hello, Jim—" he said weakly, and then stopped when he saw that Morissa was there, too, holding the lamp.

The man left quickly. At the door he whispered, "He's a goner," and put a roll of bills into the doctor's hand. "Have him buried right."

Afterward she went in to look down on Eddie. "If I dared move you I'd send you straight to Sidney. I don't like harboring outlaws."

But there was still slyness in the sunken yellowed eyes. "You got no proof," he said, low and weak. "I—we made some friends up to Red Cloud, me and Jack. . . ."

"Well, plainly you did," Morissa replied and drew her hand from his clutching grasp. "I trust my brother is not involved with such men."

LATE ONE EVENING a man rode up from one of the saloons at the bridge. Doc was needed right away; a woman there had the screeches or fits, he couldn't rightly say which. Morissa found that it was Calamity Jane and screeching all right. Seems some fool tried to see how much whiskey the lady wildcat of Deadwood Gulch could hold. Four bits worth of Etty's snakehead whiskey about did it.

Morissa got Jane quieted and over to the sod-house. But Ruth banged her door at the sight of so dissolute a woman, and the doctor had to put the coffee on herself. Toward morning Morissa got her patient out of her ragged, stinking old rawhide suit, scrubbed and into a nightgown, perhaps the first Calamity had worn in years. Jane got to Eddie next day, talking to him about men whose names Morissa couldn't catch because Ed kept shushing the woman.

In two days Morissa had Jane's hair soft and fluffy from an egg shampoo and got her into one of her own dressing gowns, a rose-sprigged mull from the trousseau trunk. It restored a hint of Jane's winsome childhood as she came to sit in Morissa's window for a cup of tea. Yes, she felt much stronger, strong enough to roar for a drink, it seemed. Morissa poured her a little brandy and then tried to visit with her about the Canary family and discover what might be done for their Martha Jane. But already she was Calamity again, slyly drawing the bottle into the folds of her skirts. Morissa pretended not to see, and listened politely to her howl of laughter at their reversed positions.

"You sure been climbin' up, Issy, callin' yourself doc an' all. Remember when you was bein' passed 'round to do the dirty work, a poor-farm kid with no pa? Now you're in cahoots with them big horse thieves plain fer everybody to see, an' a-ridin' pretty as a picture book behint them spankin' bays. Who'd expect it of such a hombly little bastard!"

Morissa gripped her fingers on the teacup, surprised that the handle didn't crumple like a curl of white meringue. But soon Jane slipped into her crying jag and so the young doctor gave her a golden double eagle to warm her palm, brought out the rawhide suit, washed and neat, and took her out to a bull train heading back toward Deadwood.

NEW PATIENTS couldn't keep Morissa's mind from some of the things Calamity Jane had said, not even when Gwinnie came down with typhoid too. He asked for nothing, just lay like an emaciated young saint, his blue eyes burning in the skull holes of his face. But Eddie on the cot beside him was never quiet and kept Morissa reminded of his probable tie-up with outlaws. She decided that as soon as Ed was strong enough for the journey to Sidney she would take him to the hospital, the responsibility of his people, wealthy Ohioans, as she had discovered. But when she read the youth a paragraph from a letter from his father, he cried like a hysterical child. "You had no business . . ." he repeated over and over.

"A doctor must get in touch with a patient's relatives."

"When he's dying!" he finished for her. "Well, I rather die here with you. I hate my father and now he's got my mother sidin' with him, too, saying she wants me to come home, go to college, be a credit to him. I'll kill myself first," Eddie sobbed, tears running unnoticed into the pillow.

So Morissa soothed him and put the idea aside for a while.

TRIS WAS BACK from Omaha and had been up to the Dr. Kirk Sanitarium, as Morissa's new sign in the window announced—an absurd, squat little sod sanitarium standing alone, without city or settlement beyond the few houses of the bridge. The tall rancher was quiet the first time he saw the sign with the little vigil lights behind it in the darkness.

"What would you say to a practice in Omaha again?" he asked the next Sunday as they rode up the river toward Ted Sailor's British ranch.

"You aren't going to quit running cattle?" Morissa asked, dropping into the ranch expression in her concern.

"Oh, no, but with as good a foreman as I have—" he stopped, and busied himself switching the black mane of his horse all one way and then back. "The meat-packing business that's opening up in Omaha will make money for the first comers. . . ." It seemed somehow very serious, this that he was trying to say and yet did not. Morissa remembered his Auntie Mae and her twin daughters who needed money to make good marriages. There was a silence between them.

That night there was a fine ranch supper at Sailor's, and later a couple of fiddlers played for the stomp of boots, although there were only four women for around twenty-five men, including about everybody of the ranch except the bronc-crippled choreman. When they were ready to start back through the clouding night, a couple of shots down at the corrals started everybody looking out to see who had so much steam to let off.

But there was a yelling that sounded like the choreman, and so everybody pushed out the door together. There were three, four more shots, and then the running of a horse. When they reached the corrals everything was still, but as the light of a lantern swung through the gate, it fell on a man down in the dust. It was Sailor's new gun hand, Pete Shrone. Then the choreman came sidling out of a stable, still cautious.

"Man come ridin' in a little piece ago, askin' for Pete," the crippled old cowboy managed to say. "So I fetches him down to where Pete likes to set nights, seein's he don't have much truck with the bunkhouse—"

"Yeh, Pete's kind don't," someone volunteered readily enough, now that the gunman was dying.

So Tris and Morissa had to stay. After the man was dead the doctor cut out a bullet—a mushroomed gray lump just under the skin. The man had spoken no word, although he was conscious to the end.

Tris was quiet on the slow ride home in the dawn, and Morissa too. At the house Eddie was crying into his pillow because the doctor had been gone so long. Morissa found herself impatient with the sick youth as a mother might be impatient, and as contrite and loving, too, it seemed.

But before sleeping she wrote his father a little more urgently. "I really think your son Edward Ellis should be removed to a hospital where he can receive the very best treatment and care. His condition continues most serious, mentally as well as physically." Yet instead of relief Morissa felt a loss, a sad and empty loss, as though her patient were already gone. Something like the loss she felt when Tom Reeder left, only this went deeper, deep as a scalpel's blade.

MANY TIMES in her months here at the bridge, Morissa was out when Tris came, and slowly she admitted to herself what she had often said lightly to him—that the wife of Tris Polk should not be a doctor. Yet he had always waited, sometimes many hours, and when she put on the gold-shot gray-green gown or the pink brocade, lovely as the prairie roses of August in the evening sun, no trace of annoyance seemed to remain. Finally, the Sunday after the Sailor visit, he spoke of the new ranch house that was to be ready for them when they came back from Texas and Illinois. "Unless you prefer your home in Sidney, or in Omaha."

"Oh, the ranch, certainly the ranch," Morissa said, still trying to make it light, protecting herself, not clear just from whom; but when Tris kissed her she knew he took it as acceptance. She knew, too, that now she had dared to mean it, and was just a little saddened by what seemed a curious sort of desertion of Allston Hoyt and the memory of him.

The next week the stage brought up a great box of roses that Tris had sent from Omaha, with a June calendar sheet for next year enclosed and a ribboned bit of pencil that Lorette's young daughters would receive with joy. Morissa held the armful of roses up high for Gwinnie and the others to see, their sick eyes momentarily alight with pleasure at the flowers and her flushed face. But when Morissa looked over to Eddie he had turned toward the plastered wall, his thin shoulder racked with crying.

At first Morissa found herself resisting the June plans, perhaps because of that other spring date set two years earlier with Allston, and all the humiliation and unhappiness that grew out of it. But Tris was a man of different caliber. He knew Robin was her stepfather and that Morissa had been put out on a poor farm, and surely all that Calamity Jane could tell. For it turned out that Calamity had wandered back to hang around Clarke's and Etty's, until she was howling again, shouting out her damning words against their lady doc who would throw a sick woman into a bull wagon to get rid of her. Finally Clarke's man had her loaded on his train, to ride the bedrolls out of there, cold drunk.

Nothing of this was mentioned directly to Morissa, except that Tris seemed even more openly proud of the doctor's accomplishments, which warmed Morissa's cheeks to glowing. So she circled the twenty-sixth of June for him, and wrote her dressmaker for fashion plates of wedding attire. Perhaps it would be a silk suit this time, more fitting than a white dress here in the valley. Besides, a woman should have only one white wedding dress and hers was already in the bottom of a trunk, folded away carefully in blue tissue paper.

With this feminine planning started, she wrote a letter to Dr. Aiken of the medical school about her work here and her plans, asking him to recommend a substitute for the summer, perhaps permanently. Then there was a letter to Robin and Jackie, too, and finally one for Tris's Auntie Mae. "I am a happy betrothed. . . ."

Chapter 11

THE YEAR TURNING toward fall was the finest Morissa had ever seen, sweet and golden, fragrant as her muskmelons ripening in the sun. But she couldn't live in this mood long. Lieutenant Larman told her about Indian uprisings all over the West, particularly up north again. Lines of troops had marched over Clarke's bridge this summer, hurrying to go north against the Nez Percé. And now, with more troops drawn away from around Red Cloud Agency, it seemed Crazy Horse and the Sioux were ready to hit the warpath again, only one good ride from the bridge.

One night a courier galloped out of the darkness, warning all the trail and the bridge to prepare for a siege, a Sioux uprising. Morissa replied to his call and went back to bed, but several bluecoats came to take her to the darkened blockhouse.

"And what's to become of my bed patients, five with typhoid, two smallpox?" she asked.

So the troopers went back without her. Because Charley was off at Sidney, Ruth brought the dog Blaze into the hospital room, away from the silencing knife, the arrow and tomahawk. For the first time she consented to put her hand to the steel of a gun as Morissa showed her how to fire the Colt, the Peacemaker, the doctor very patient, remembering her own horror of its dark weight only a little over a year ago.

While they were seated at the kitchen table, the gun between them, there was a soft tap at the door, unannounced by the fat, overfed dog. Morissa looked into the frightened eyes of Ruth Adams. With a swift motion of her hand the doctor pushed the gun to Ruth and sent her into the darkened hospital room. Then, with her rifle across her arm, she swung the shielded wall lamp around so the light fell upon the door, leaving her in duskiness, and called, "Come in!"

A man stood in the opening doorway, a white man, young. "I came to see how Eddie Ellis is getting along," he said apologetically.

"Well, you picked a good time, in the middle of an Indian scare!"

Afterward Morissa discovered it was Doug Goodale, said to be an outlaw, too, but he visited pleasantly with them that night. When he left he thanked the doctor. "A very pleasant evening, Miss Morissa," he said, tipping his western hat as though on a city street.

"He's the son of a banker," Eddie said proudly, and Morissa was pleased in his pride, which seemed a good omen; perhaps this patient would yet become a well man.

Soon after dawn Charley was back. He had heard of the Indian alarm and drove his load straight through to get in, very uneasy after he heard the death keening of Etty's wife as he passed there.

Morissa knew of no one dying, but when the sun came out hot on a peaceful valley, the trail was stirred by the hurrying dust of an army ambulance in from the north—a bearded private of the infantry riding in lone and healthy importance inside. It seemed Crazy Horse had plotted the assassination of General Crook at the chief's camp outside of Red Cloud. Crazy Horse was captured and this soldier, William Gentles, bayoneted him through the kidney. Now the Sioux were up and so the man had to be hurried away and everyone must flee the country.

It was keening for the dead chief that Charley had heard at Etty's, but the stocky little Frenchman stood like a tree against any move. "I have the story from the relative come last night. He say no Indian is killing anybody up there." The government, according to his story, wanted to take the Sioux off their reservation, move them to a hungrier country, but Crazy Horse had been promised an agency up on the Yellowstone. He would make trouble. The soldiers arrested him to be taken south, to the stone prison of Florida. When they pushed him into the guardhouse, he jumped back and was jabbed with the bayonet.

So there were two versions of this, too, Morissa thought as she saw even the most land-hungry around the bridge have a moment of regret that this wild, free man must die, as though they knew that a little of themselves had died, too, no matter how treacherous they thought him.

THERE WERE TWO CHILDREN in the little sod hospital now, belonging to a gold seeker whose wife had died of typhoid in a wagon camped one day's drive up the trail. Morissa had been called at the last, when there was nothing to be done except take the two small ones, ill, too, away from the lame nursing of their grieving father. The girl was five, the boy three, and although weak and scrawny as birdlings, they wouldn't eat, only sobbed softly for their mother. Finally the small Alice forgot her fierce protectiveness of her younger brother long enough to go to sleep in Tris Polk's arms and let the doctor take the boy, Georgie. Over the children they talked about the plans Morissa had when she entered medical school: the alleviation of pain and sorrow for sick and lonely children, to help them be as happy and healthy as she planned her own should be someday. And now, with a woman's eye, Morissa Kirk appraised the man who was to be their father, and smiled within herself, a woman fulfilled.

Soon Fish Head discovered Alice and Georgie, and almost at once he was a child with them. Morissa saw it the first time she found them together, the gray little man sitting first on one cot and then the other, giving them their turns at the set of tiddlywinks the father had sent. Almost every day after that the Fish slipped up to the back door with the catch of his lines or more often cottontail or grouse, for a trade with Ruth, who saw that he never went hungry, and that his old black broadcloth suit was cleaned and set aside for the funerals he loved, and for Morissa's wedding next June.

THERE WAS A RUSH OF TALK against the government among the agency contractors and freight outfits around the bridge now, even from Clarke. With Crazy Horse killed before their eyes, the resistance of the Sioux was really broken and they must move, in spite of the local contractors who protested that this destroyed their business investments. The Indians complained too. There was no game on the new place over beyond the Bad Lands, no farm ground, only the whiskey that ruined their young men. But the luck of the Sioux was really done. In October their agencies were packed on wagons for the move. The traders were scattering from Red Cloud, and one started a little sod place facing the trail just north of the bridge, across from the new whiskey saloon going up there with Huff Johnson as faro dealer and general gunman, a fast hand at both.

These places on a homestead north of the river, together with the expulsion of the Indians, seemed a sort of bridge, too, a bridge from one era to another, and so Morissa decided to go up to see the Sioux taken away. Sid Martin had bought one of the road ranches on the White River and was pointing a herd of cows up there to winter in the canyons. He offered to bring back the three horses Morissa was to pick up from Etty's Indian relatives for medical fees. Tris came along, and two army couples from Camp Sidney, all invited to a dance at Fort Robinson. It lasted late and so it was almost noon the next day when they finally reached the Red Cloud Agency. The Indians were already on the move, two troops of cavalry in the lead, then Red Cloud and his chiefs riding their ponies abreast in a short line, and the many thousands of Sioux behind them.

Morissa and Tris watched the people go along the valley of the White, sad, silent, with no joyous noise of whoops and laughter in the usual way of a Sioux camp on the move. This time it was Tris Polk who could not bear to look, and for a moment Morissa caught the glint of tears in his gray eyes. Tris said nothing then but later he began to talk a little, standing his stirrups as the Texan he was, while the two horses, the stockinged black and the Appaloosa, jogged along abreast. Eight years ago when he first saw this White River valley on a hunt, it had been buffalo country. Then suddenly the herds were gone, and now the Indians, too, their tracks not yet cold before the cattleman was tromping them out, like Sid Martin with his cows and cowboys coming down the slope over there. And who could say how soon these too must go?

143

Morissa touched the man's arm comfortingly, and as he bent his head to hear her soft words above the call of the cowboys, she kissed his smooth brown cheek. "You are a serious man," she said.

"We are both serious people," he replied, a little embarrassed, as though caught out with a branding iron at midnight.

As Morissa and Tris came back from the deserted Red Cloud Agency into the North Platte valley, Morissa saw that Charley had started the sod-house on his homestead, the walls up waist high. Tris didn't stop his horse at the sight, but Morissa caught his surprise.

"Well, that makes four moved in north of the river," he finally said, "counting the new roadhouse and the saloon. But you and your trees were the first, like the first cow to slip from the roundup herd, tolling the rest to follow her for the canyons."

Yes, Morissa admitted, smiling a little and ignoring his bitterness, but she remembered that trail herders carried guns to bring such bunch-quitter cows down. Sobered, she wondered if this matter was to stand between them in the wall that sometimes grows up between man and wife, a wall that becomes rock, massive and high and cold.

But the next morning there was an early tap at her door. It was Tris, starting home. Taking Morissa's arm he hurried her out to her little pond. There a swan floated in the early fall stillness, his reflection motionless, a pure white swan with graceful bend of throat.

MORISSA WAS RETURNING from a call one graying afternoon when a rider came kicking a work mare toward her buggy, the swaybacked old horse jumping washouts and gullies to head her off. She reached for her rifle as every settler did these days, but the man held up his empty hands, shouting, "Doctor! Doctor!" It seemed that John Callwin, living up one of the box canyons, got hit on the head in a well. Although the man's story was jumbled and incoherent, Morissa dared not doubt it. She turned her team and followed him, whipping her horses into a run.

"I—let a plank s-s-slip!" the man kept saying over and over, "I—I—let it . . ." The two-by-four was one of those laid across the top of the well curbing to serve as a platform for the buckets of excavated earth, and the well was deep. Morissa took her bag and, tucking her skirts back out of the way, went down the ladder into the well. The man was there, crumpled under a slanted plank, jackknifed into the wet narrow bottom with a hole in the side of his skull almost as big as her palm. But he was still alive, and with a rope tied under his arms and run up through the windlass, the two got him out.

By now snowflakes were sifting like chaff from the gray sky, and the frightened settler had to go home to his wife, sick and alone with a blizzard upon them, and expecting her first baby. He helped Morissa get Callwin into his little dugout and left apologetically. In the light of the lantern Morissa built up a fire and set to work. She laid back the skin, lifted out the skull fragments, and cut away the damaged tissue. Somehow the man's heart kept beating, and over and over the young doctor thanked God for this strong country, these strong men. She would not, she must not lose this patient today, not when she had just helped bury a child taken right out of her hands by diphtheria.

Next there was the crushed and swollen scalp to consider. It seemed alive enough to repair itself but not over a naked brain, and there was no time to send to Sidney for anything. Then she remembered the silver half dollar in her pocket that the father of the dead child had put into her cloak as a token of his indebtedness.

Quickly she tied the scalp together by knotting the hair, and with the lantern she went into the thickening snow to scratch for a claw hammer among the tools left at the well. At last she found it, and at a wheel of the man's wagon she pounded the half dollar into an oblong silver plate, thin, and slightly curved from the shape of the iron tire. She roughened the plate carefully and punched a few smooth holes around the edges for tissue penetration, with a larger one toward each end for drainage tubes. Then she washed the plate carefully in strong carbolic solution, sewed it over the quivering brain, and drew the mangled, swollen scalp together. And still there was the marvel of the man's living.

Chapter 12

IT WAS A LONG NIGHT, this time of sitting in a little dugout beside a man with a broken head, and toward four Morissa caught herself up from a doze. Startled and afraid, she put her fingers to the man's pulse and found it almost gone. Quickly she administered the heart stimulant laid out ready, a light dose that would not overwork a weakened organ, hopeful that it would be enough.

145

The fall snow was gone from the south slopes before the doctor dared to think of leaving the man even long enough to get word to Charley Adams that she needed the wagon to move a patient. By then Charley had come looking for her, riding along the rocky crest of the Wild Cat range. She saw him stop here and there to search the far slopes both ways with field glasses, the sun glinting from them as he turned.

Two days later they had John Callwin in the little hospital. There was infection in the mangled scalp, although the fever was down and the drain tubes oozed only a little watery fluid. Still the man barely clung to consciousness and was very weak and pale, with curious insensate areas, and no real paralysis where it might be expected.

Morissa searched her medical bookcase and found no remedy except good nursing and time, so she turned to cool packs for the unwounded portions of the head and tried to shut her ears to the man's groaning.

WHEN LITTLE GEORGIE was too restless in the night, the shy-mouthed Gwinnie liked to have the boy brought to lie beside him awhile as though beside his father. But Ed was troublesome about the children, complaining over the attention they got, the noise they made. Ed's health was worse, too, with a persistent rectal bleeding, and vomiting. Morissa hadn't dared to ask what happened the six days she was away, but the young man's return to a babyishness beyond even small Georgie's worried her, his sobbing if she left the place for even an hour, and her own foolish tendency to humor his jealousy.

Now Ed's pale eyes burned feverishly toward John Callwin, because Morissa had to go over him repeatedly, mapping out the insensitive regions to discover what she might of his total injury, both for herself and for John's uncle, a doctor in Seattle. The uncle had written immediately upon receiving her telegram, wishing he could get away. "The brain cavity is one we cannot enter with impunity; not at all unless we must. That my nephew is still alive testifies to your skill and your courage." But even as she read this, with burning face, to John, there was the cry of "Bedpan! Bedpan!" from Eddie. And Ruth wouldn't do, or Charley.

The hospital patients were down to seven now, counting Alice and Georgie. John's head wound was some better, enough so that Morissa really hoped for a healing over her silver plate—his hand-hammered pot lid, as he called it. But now he began to worry about his homestead. If a man didn't live on his claim it was subject to contest, and while there was plenty of free land around, he had a dugout and a well with a good curbing down to water sand—a place of sorts for his wife in the spring. So Morissa drove him over to spend a night or so in the dugout, with Charley along as nurse and witness and to do a little winter work around the place, cover the well and stack the stovewood inside.

By now the story of the silver plate had spread. John Callwin's uncle wrote of it to Dr. Jacobs of Sidney, who took the stage out to see the patient. Afterward he sent a letter to the Sidney paper, telling of the fine piece of emergency surgical work. Next time Morissa went to Sidney she found herself described as the Silver Doc of the Gold Trail by the newspaper and on the street. Several times during the winter she was called into consultation, once as far away as the middle of the state. When she returned, John Callwin had a welcome for her. He moved his left arm easily, flexing his fingers to show his progress.

But Eddie was no better, and the letter from his father was no help:

> We are anxious to do what we can for our son but, frankly, we prefer that he remain in your care. A pretty and long-awaited baby, he was a great favorite with everyone and idolized by his mother. By way of gratitude he drove her into sorrowful seclusion. He was irresponsible, insolent and indolent as a boy; sly, thieving and vicious as a youth. He attempted to kill one of his friends and forged the signatures of a dozen relatives. Only his flight to the frontier saved us the embarrassment of a son who was a convicted felon or worse. He is like a changeling among us, or one possessed.
> I speak frankly; he has brought my beloved wife into invalidism.
> Your Obedient Servant,
> Culver Ellis

Slowly Morisssa unpinned the enclosed check, folded the letter, and put it away.

ALL THE AUTUMN road agents worked the Cheyenne trail like beavers piling up young cottonwood for a hard winter. Several times Morissa tried to get Eddie to talk about his associates. He still seemed very weak, yet sometimes it was hard to accept his sickness as real.

With no more Indian herds to run off and the trail stock guarded, horse thieves began to move south. Two of them tried to run off some horses down near Sidney. One was killed, the other shipped to Wyoming to face earlier charges.

As winter closed down many of the bad men deserted the region, gone south with the geese. Even so, Morissa was happy that Jack seemed safely away at school, and Ed in his hospital bed. She went to Sidney with Tris at Christmastime and came back loaded with presents and trimmings for a tree, a quiet one, with so many critically weak. Next year . . .

"Next year we'll bust the sky open!" Tris promised little Georgie.

"Shhh!" Morissa whispered, certain Eddie would be crying again.

"Send him to Sidney," Tris commanded, but Morissa laughed at his angry face and in a moment Ed seemed forgotten.

By late January Gwinnie could walk clear across the bridge and Alice and Georgie were strong enough to be out on sunny days. One afternoon Ruth took them to the river to see the ice break. It cracked like pistol shots under the film of water and then began to grind and tip up, throwing fans of spray.

When the children left the house they had waved to Morissa as for a long journey and Georgie ran back awkwardly in his heavy little coat for another good-bye kiss. Morissa watched them go with a catch in her throat. One of these days the father would return to take them away.

But soon it would be spring, and June. The geese came north a week before their time, as though they knew the river would be open. Then suddenly none were flying, only snowbirds flocking together. The next day a blizzard struck. It began with a warm day. Morissa was coming in from below the Wild Cat Mountains, her coat thrown open, the morning sun on her face. She had delivered a strong baby boy who would take the place of one who had died of black diphtheria last fall, and she hummed a little Scottish tune as she turned in for a look at John Callwin.

She found him cutting fence posts and it was a joy to watch him. When he saw who it was he came striding off the slope to sit on a rock, fill his pipe and talk. His wife and the baby he had never seen would arrive in May, and he wanted to fence the range cattle out of a small garden plot. Soberly he pulled his stocking cap away and bent his head to the doctor. She examined the thick scarring, the hair working in from the sides and starting in little tufts through the twisted red tissue.

"Sore?" she asked as she probed here and there with her strong fingers, testing the firmness of the plate.

"It's really fine. My uncle writes me it's a remarkable recovery and that he has a place for you in his hospital any time you want to leave us here—"

But Morissa shook her head. "I've not told even Charley but I'm marrying Tris Polk in June."

Oh, the settler hadn't known; none of them had any more than guessed that it would happen eventually. Thoughtfully he drew his knitted cap back over his dark hair. "We hoped you would stay here. My wife already thinks of you as a sister."

"Oh, thank you! I do plan to keep the hospital going. I'm making arrangements now for a doctor, a man who needs to live in a dry, sunny climate for his health, to take over while I'm away."

She tried to speak with lightness, to meet the man's dark eyes squarely, but somehow something had come into his brown-bearded face to close away the affection and respect she had seen there, replace it with a curious anger against her. So Morissa got into her buggy and was nearly home before she noticed that the sky had grayed out of the northwest.

Charley was away rounding up the cattle, his three cows and Morissa's little bunch, some of the bigger heifers old enough to be calving soon. He would throw them into the draw up the little creek, where the bluffs furnished protection and prevented drifting in any storm. He came in safely, but snow-caked and bent into the growing storm.

Tris had planned to come up that evening, and all night Morissa found herself rousing to every sound, hoping that he had not started into the storm. For four days not even Charley went farther than the well, and always with a guide rope tied around his waist to bring him back. Then it cleared and he walked over the great frozen drifts glistening in the morning sun, the shovel on his shoulder to tunnel down to the door of his sod-house. All the valley of the Platte was lost in the deep drifted snow, the bridge silent and white, only the center of the river a dark broken channel of angry water flowing.

Morissa saw two antelope sunning themselves inside a high swirl of drifts around her stable wall, reminding her of the young antelope that Tom Reeder had taken away. Soon it would be two years since she came fleeing here with the little round-topped trunk of her trousseau. And nothing from Allston Hoyt for a long time except a clipping last week announcing his engagement to a young woman of most irreproachable name, another May wedding, this one to be carried through.

Morissa was glad that she had stated her intention before that, even though it was not to Tris but to the settler John Callwin. She had said nothing of it here, not with two of her hospital patients homesteaders and

Charley Adams' yard fence cut several times this winter, his windows shot out. Fences were going up between people now, everybody having to pick his side. Already Charley and Ruth were polite as enemies to the rancher Tris Polk. Besides, any hint of Morissa's engagement would bring real hysteria to Eddie Ellis. He had been learning to walk again but still wept like a child at any disappointment, like a sick and forlorn child clinging to her hand and moving her in a way she knew was very foolish.

The next morning a rider brought her a note from Tris: "I regret that the severity of the storm kept me from my appointment—" as formal as the distant smoke-gray of his eyes. But Morissa knew the fire that could burn behind that grayness, and in her relief that he was safe she held the small sheet of paper between her flattened palms, and a vastness as of all the prairies filled her breast.

After the heavy snow and the rains that followed, even the driest table lay green and beckoning for the rush of settlers. With times hard all over the world, the Indians gone at last, and the pull of free homes almost as strong as gold and vastly more fundamental, the cattlemen saw they must work fast, cover all the watering places with filings if they would hold their free range.

But while the cattlemen tried to cover all the permanent waterways, most of the settlers came prepared for drylanding with spade and rope and bucket, perfectly willing to haul water for stock and for drinking and to do without for the rest until they could dig for it. They came by railroad, covered wagon, and afoot. They settled as close as possible to markets, or scattered out over the region below Sidney and up along Pumpkin Seed Creek toward the Wild Cats and anywhere that an earlier granger had a toehold. Then they moved out into the larger ranches, unaware of or in spite of the smooth-fingered range protectors.

Morissa Kirk felt herself a part of this stream, but most of the homesteaders, even John Callwin and Charley Adams at her own breakfast table, were increasingly distant, withdrawn. Only Gwinnie, who took up a homestead for Clarke south of the river, seemed the same, if one could tell from his customary silence as he came in for a cup of coffee and a piece of Ruth's sorghum gingerbread.

In early June Morissa was called to Sidney for the Pete Shrone murder trial. A man suspected of shooting him had been picked up in a saloon. Jim Hobert wouldn't talk except to say he knew nobody named Pete Shrone.

But a bullet from his revolver seemed to fit the markings on the one Morissa had cut out of Pete's shoulder. Law must be coming to the region if a man could be tried for a shooting scrape with a professional gunman. "Yeh, but makes a difference on whose payroll the pistoleer was working," a long, sunburned granger from over at the Wild Cats said to a whole roundup camp in at Clarke's one evening. Morissa saw him stand up to them all for a while, but when he got out he never returned.

Much against the urgings of Eddie's father, Morissa was taking the young man along to Sidney and sending him home for a three months' sea cruise with his mother, to restore him in strength and balance. But it was hard to send him away. She started off on the Sidney trail, waving good-bye to the children standing by the yellow roses around her door. Then she let the bays out, shining and handsome in their new fly nets.

In Sidney she dropped Eddie at the depot, the gaunt youth silent, angry-eyed. "I'll never go," he said dramatically. "You'll see. . . ."

But Morissa lifted her whip in farewell and drove away to the hotel. Tris met her there, his smoldering eyes lighting at the sight of the girl in her new linen suit, a yellow and green plaid that showed off her fine figure. "From our trousseau?" he whispered as he took her arm, and she nodded, smiling.

Together they went down the afternoon street, crowded for the court session. Feeling ran high over the drawn-out case that came up before the Shrone shooting—a homesteader being tried for killing a cowboy. Two ranch hands had gone to drag a homesteader's empty shack into a washout with their lariats because he was eating beef. But as the shack went over, the settler, unexpectedly home, shot from inside the toppling doorway and emptied one of the saddles. The other man released the rope from the horn and spurred away.

The settler, afraid the ranch hands around would gang up on him, walked to Camp Sidney in the night for protection. He was turned over to the sheriff, although he kicked and fought, certain that he would be dragged out of jail to a necktie party. He wasn't molested, perhaps because he went to the troops first, but there was a lot of mean talk around the jail. The sheriff promised a swift trial and now, three days later, the case was almost finished.

Morissa Kirk felt the anger along the street, the settlers gathered up solid around the courthouse—angry men, mostly with guns over their arms, or clubs. Inside, the judge from over in the middle of the state had his two revolvers out on the pine table before him. Because no local lawyer would go against the cattlemen, an eastern man out for a ranch foreclosure sale had hurriedly been retained for the defense by a group of settlers, John Callwin among them, all shut out of the courtroom.

The eastern attorney was summing up his defense before the antagonistic spectators when Tris and Morissa squeezed into the back of the hot, sweaty little courtroom and stood on a bench cleared for the ranch owner. The lawyer was working up through the record of ranch violence here, beginning with the government surveyor's helper hanged at Sidney several years ago by the Bosler men, ending with a neighbor of the defendant whose field fence was cut to pieces, his corn eaten up, and bullet holes put through his door barely missing his wife.

"All the settlers left that country before the next sunup, except the defendant here. So he must become an example to all would-be settlers in this ranchman's paradise, his home be dragged away into a canyon. The prosecution charges that the settler was stealing calves and eating ranch beef. Then why not try the defendant for theft? A man's homestead is his legal residence, his castle. He has the right, more, the obligation to defend it!" the eastern lawyer shouted—loud enough to be heard in all the murmuring courtroom and through the open windows over the growing noise outside.

Morissa felt herself caught in the trial as in the surging floodwaters of the Platte, but beside her was the hard shoulder of Tris Polk. The roaring outside was so great that the windows were shut against it, and immediately opened again by the crashing of one pane of glass after another. Morissa tugged at Tris's arm, to get out now while they could. But the judge was already up, a gun in each hand, his eyes cold and hard upon the leading cattlemen and upon the faces crowding the windows. To the immediate silence he sat down, motioning the attorney to proceed.

The outsider nodded his thanks. "All the evidence proves that the defendant shot to protect his property, his right by law and the Constitution. It was a shot fired in defense of his home, his very life, in the tumbling little house at the end of the cowboy lariats. And the reiteration that the neighboring ranches follow this custom does not serve to establish legality for what is patently a criminal act, even if those ranches are the powerful Scottish Glasgow Arrow and the Texas-owned TeePee!"

"The TeePee!" someone near Tris Polk whispered in astonishment at this daring. "By God, he spits it right out—the Arrow and the TeePee!"

Morissa stiffened. So people were supposed to be afraid even to mention these names! Stone-angry she turned her face from the undenying rancher standing beside her, and withdrew her hand from his arm. She saw how the case must end, with the jury made up of cattlemen or those who hung upon their favor and custom. Now she could only look upon the backs in this crowded room as upon stangers from a strange and violent land where a man who chose to live in a wilderness in order to have a home of his own was to be hanged or at the least imprisoned for life. In this strangeness Tris Polk was certainly like the others.

Suddenly she could bear no more. Ignoring the rancher and everyone around her she left the courtroom, elbowing her way out into the street. Tris Polk was right behind her, trying to take her arm as she hurried on. "Please, dear, please let's go somewhere to talk this over," he begged.

Without reply or even a turn of her head the young doctor sought an escape from the crowd, fleeing like some wild thing, almost like the fox-sorrel mustang mare of the horse catchers they had watched destroy herself at Bill Tillow's corral up in the sandhills. Morissa's feet took the pathway to the top of a bluff overlooking the town, Camp Sidney, and the wide, sweeping valley that lay green and shining in the lowered evening sun. And with the bright light upon her passionate face, Morissa Kirk finally turned to the man behind her.

"So it's true," she said, "all I have been hearing. Your cowboys are tearing down people's homes too."

Tris made a motion toward her but she stood firm and distant.

"Yes, I suppose you could say that," he admitted finally. "As I've told you, I have a good foreman; I pay him to run the ranch the best way he knows how, and I don't ask questions about his methods."

Now anger came up in the girl's face again. "Have you no sense of responsibility in this at all?" she demanded.

"Oh, Morissa, would you want me to hire a Pete Shrone? Give the grangers no warning beyond finding a neighbor face down in his plowing? I don't like it either, but we drifted into this protecting our range, our investment. It's Aunt Mae's even more than mine."

Morissa closed her eyes. There it was, a fine, strong gentlewoman like Auntie Mae, and a man like Tris.

"You must understand me, my dear," the rancher pleaded. "I would not do those things myself. You must see that."

But his words only lifted Morissa from her moment of sorrow and weakening. "I know you wouldn't do them, Tris," she said slowly, firmly, "but they are done for you, and that seems far worse to me. Now I am to marry a man who takes this power but delegates it, and feels he need ask no questions at all."

"Morissa!"

"No, it's no use now. I can't do it. I can't marry into such a circumstance," she cried. Before Tris could stop her the doctor had gathered up her skirts and was stumbling down the steep bluff. Once, after they reached the shadowing tracks and the warehouses, the man tried again. "Go to Aunt Mae's for a few weeks," he begged. "I can't bear to see you like this, going home to your place alone, with Robin and Jackie away. Go to Mae. She'll welcome you like a daughter, no matter what. . . ."

But Morissa couldn't even thank the man, no more than she could have thanked Allston Hoyt, only this time there seemed nowhere to go, certainly not to throw herself upon Robin again. No, nowhere. . . . She left the rancher standing and went up the plank steps of the little hotel, her feet wooden and awkward. Inside the door two men in railroad uniforms were holding Eddie Ellis, pale in the early lamplight, his suit dirty and torn, his cheek bleeding. He was sobbing, trying to pull away from the men, to run. Then he saw Morissa and clutched for her arm. "Oh, don't leave me—don't, don't!"

"Throwed himself in front of the engine," one of the men said.

"Yeh, Joe here yanks him back just in time. We brung him here, seein's he claims he's your patient."

So Morissa put an arm about the young man and guided him away through the crowd, trying to comfort him a little out of the bleakness of her own heart. "Yes, yes, you can stay with me," she was repeating over and over, dully. "You can stay with me forever. . . ."

In an hour they were returning from Camp Sidney, married.

Chapter 13

LOOKING BACK, MORISSA KIRK always thought of this time as the Year of the Eclipse. There was a total eclipse of the sun late in July, the strange darkness so convincing that the chickens sang a few sad and confused little evening songs and a rattlesnake crawled under the step of the back door. The snake was easily settled with the hoe, but the uneasiness of a rattler so close to the house was like all the unease of that summer.

They had come back in her buggy, Eddie wearing the new suit that she had paid for. He pushed the bays along in a lathering sweat. Anxious to get home, he said, to plan all the things he would do. Ed looked almost well again, curly-headed and very young with a faint line of mustache shadowing his soft lip. Everyone around the bridge told him that if a week was a fair sample, marriage was sure the range to put fat on his ribs. Then the eyes would move to Morissa, and if they had known they might have compared the jilted girl of two years ago with the one today and understood that there are far worse things than a public rejection from an Allston Hoyt. If anybody here had heard the news of Morissa's hasty departure from the trial with Tris Polk running after her, no one spoke of it. "Mebby our lady doc's still against killers," one of the freighters said before Morissa was out of earshot, "but she fetches that outlaw's hired hand to live right here 'mongst us!"

Ed planned to file on a homestead. Although not quite of age, he was entitled to one now as the head of a family. Perhaps he would take up a preemption, too, he said, but Morissa must promise to see that he had the money when the time came. "Oh, you'll have the two hundred dollars by then," she said confidently. "You're well enough to work. You should take up a timber claim, too, and we'll have the increase in value when the settlers and the railroad come in."

But Eddie met this with a pout. "You have to kiss me if I am to take orders from you," he said, and when Morissa treated such talk as a joke, his face clouded sullenly. It was over in a moment, but when he went to make his filing, the land he took up wasn't even in the Platte valley but in a deep, rugged canyon fifteen miles off, on the horse thief trail.

By then Charley Adams had come to stand before Morissa, his weathered face stubborn, his hands working over each other. "I got to know where we stand, Doc. Eddie give me my time."

"You mean he paid you off?" she demanded.

"No, he ain't paid me a cent, but he says I'm through workin' fer you, an' Ruth is too. Come end of July we're both through. . . ."

Morissa's face was flushed and angry. "I'm sorry, but Ed misunderstands the situation. I want you to stay."

"I don't know, Doc," Charley said slowly, moving his cud around in his stubbled cheek. "I don't like workin' fer two bosses. . . ."

"At least try it a while longer," Morissa asked, and was prepared to talk of this with Ed, but when he came home he brought her an armful of hothouse roses and a pretty white goatskin rug for the bedside. In addition he seemed content to work in the garden, leaning on the hoe now and then to watch the herds that splashed through the July river and bawled off northward.

Underneath, Morissa was uneasy. Soon Eddie was spending every evening at the whiskey saloons around the bridge. Once he brought back a piece cut from the Sidney paper, an interview with Doc Middleton, who claimed he wasn't the leader of any organized band of horse thieves. He did admit running off Indian ponies but he hadn't done any of that in six months, and never except to get money to live on.

"That's the motive of every thief, I suspect—getting money to live on," Morissa commented.

"Oh, Doc's all right," Ed replied casually. "He gave me this clipping. His outfit's camped off north a ways from my homestead. Talked about starting a ranch up there. He says he'll stake me if I go in with him."

"Into horse stealing?" Morissa demanded. "Horse thieves end up at the busy end of a rope."

She knew this was the wrong approach, but Eddie was so excited by the adventuresome talk that he must be settled down immediately. So that evening after supper she told him that he might be a father by spring.

Ed had been sprawled out on one of the benches under the cottonwoods, as Morissa busied herself arranging a bouquet. He sat up like a lazy young animal stretching, and grinned a little. "You can't bring me no squalling brat," he said, as to some worn-out joking threat. "*I'm* your curly-headed boy. Your time and love all belong to me." Then his young face changed a little. "Oh, I just about forgot. I wrote Ira Marker up in Deadwood to come get the two brats you already got here."

Morissa stopped, her hands full of pinks and nasturtiums. "You are getting to be a real tease!" she laughed. But she had to go look anxiously for the children, as though the father might have come to steal them away. They were with Fish Head, coming down along the bank of the cloud-reddened stream, helping him catch frogs with the little dip nets he had made for them.

"It's bedtime!" she called, to cover her anxiety. "Alice! Georgie! Bedtime!"

In a week Morissa had to tell Eddie that she was mistaken about the baby, but by then she knew he really had written to Ira Marker, for Ira drove his wagon down from the Hills. He stood helpless before his children, embarrassed that they had grown so much since he saw them, and looked so healthy; yet he was happy, too, that this was so.

"I know I been neglectful, Miss Doctor," he said, "but there wan't steady work 'round the mines. I—I guess I just got to send them to a orphanage someplace."

But this was like talk of violence to Morissa. "No! No orphanage!" she exclaimed. "We'll be glad to keep them until you can take them."

The father stayed overnight, but in the morning he was out very early, and without a word to the doctor he started down the trail with the children. Young Alice sat quietly beside her father, trying to comfort the small brother she held between her knees. Georgie had clung to Morissa's skirts and then to Ruth's, but his fingers were pried loose.

"There's the end of childhood for Alice," Morissa said as the wagon drew away south. Bleak and angry she walked past Charley and Ruth, and past Ed, too, knowing now that he had gone to the man in the night and ordered that he take the children away. Truly, as her grandmother wrote her once, a woman who makes a quick and bad marriage she gang to the de'il with a dishclout on her head. Aye, the dishclout of sorrow and humiliation. In furious self-contempt Morissa strode down the rows of her trees, some now fifteen, sixteen feet tall.

THREE DAYS LATER Eddie rode up with a new buggy and team, a long-barreled Kentucky racer trotting nervously alongside. The man with him stayed in the buggy while Eddie came out to look for Morissa. She was at the well, filling her jug with safe water to take out on a call to a new typhoid outbreak. He tried to kiss her boyishly, his hands as clumsy as his walk, his breath heavy with rotgut. "Bought me a running horse, Morissa, and a team and buggy. Come see."

"I can see all I want to know from here," she said.

"You gotta come, to pay the man."

"What gives you the impression I could pay for these things?"

"Oh, I got it all fixed. Just sign the little mortgages on the preemption and our cows and horses. . . ."

Morissa walked beside him to the new buggy, her step firm. "I think you should know that we have no funds for racehorses, and one buggy is all we need," she told the man.

Eddie began to bluster angrily, reaching for the buggy whip. "By God, I'll show you who's boss!" he shouted.

But Morissa took the whip from him as from the clutching hands of a child. Motioning the man toward the road, she went back to her task.

"I'll kill you!" Eddie shouted after her. "Damn bitch! I'll kill her!"

But Morissa was already the doctor again. Charley brought up her team and she took the lines, got in, tucked the dust robe over her knees, and let the bays have their heads. The next issue of the *Sidney Telegraph* carried a small, hastily composed advertisement that many noticed or were referred to when Morissa returned their bills:

> I will not be responsible for any debts incurred or any agreements or contracts entered into by my husband Edward Elton Ellis.
>
> Dr. Morissa Kirk Ellis.

That was the last time she intended to use the name of Ellis as long as she lived.

THE LADY DOC of the gold trail no longer stopped at Clarke's or Etty's for a little visiting when she passed. She was aware of the contempt she had brought upon herself. A good man can have a bad wife, but no wife is better than her spouse. John Callwin came and stayed a couple of hours one afternoon, to walk with her through the garden and the little grove on the timber claim.

"You sure did make a good start here. . . ." he said, letting his voice trail off into a sort of transparent regret. He said nothing of his silver plate, or his uncle in Seattle—so swiftly is good work destroyed. But a few people were unchanged. Gwinnie of Clarke's store brought the mail over to save her embarrassment at the station, and offered to drive her on late night trips, or in storms when Charley had to stay at the hospital.

Then there was Sid Martin. He overtook Morissa going up the trail to see about her typhoid patients, and rode beside the Appaloosa for a couple of miles. He made no pretense of good wishes either, nor spoke sour words of blame. "I think maybe you busted my chances with Aunt Mae down in Texas," he laughed ruefully. "You know I had half a mind to make me some business down there, after fall roundup."

"Oh, why not? She liked you, and I can recommend you as an excellent risk physically. A man who can come through a stampede and a broken neck . . ."

But few of her acquaintances were as natural. Then in the midst of this August time Robin was suddenly there, walking over from the stage station, and Morissa, for the second time in a little over two years, buried her miserable face against the shoulder of her stepfather.

"You never wrote me," he scolded softly.

"I couldn't, Robin. It seemed too shameful."

Slowly the man nodded, his face grieved for the girl. "Tris came to see me. Hunted me up on the job. He said you maybe needed me."

"Tris! Oh—" and now at last Morissa began to cry. Ruth, coming to greet the visitor, saw her and slipped away to leave the two together, Robin holding this daughter he had taken to his heart a long time ago.

DURING THE SUMMER the fever of lawlessness seemed as catching as measles.

Morissa, returning from a call, saw new horse droppings on the thieves' trail where she had shot at the man taking her team that first winter. The dugout where Eddie was struck by typhoid was down this trail too. Yet with this knowledge she had still married him. Perhaps Dr. Aiken was right; perhaps a woman needed the close rein of a man every moment of her years and should most certainly be kept out of the practice of medicine. Morissa had admitted a little of this to the doctor when she canceled her request for the young man to take over her practice. "A woman's foolish whim—" she wrote, ashamed.

Eddie hadn't been around the bridge since Robin came to visit those two days. Morissa suspected that he had warned Ed to keep away. But it didn't last. Eddie came, brought back by a bullet in his foot. "Gun went off this morning. Hurts bad," he said to Charley as he sank miserably down to the bench beside the door. The two men with him put spurs to their horses and headed north, leading his saddle horse, a good one.

Morissa came out to see, and was at once the doctor. She cut out the bullet, cleaned the wound of some bone fragments, set in a couple of tubes for drainage, and put a temporary cast on the foot. "You say that your gun went off this morning," she told Eddie when he was out of the ether. "This wound is at least two days old and the bullet came from some distance or it would have gone clear through. Besides, it entered from the heel, probably from behind you while in the saddle."

Eddie grinned up at her, his curly hair in a tangle, his thin face white from ether. "You're getting pretty again, like the day I married you—"

Morissa held her anger. "I've taken care of the foot well enough to get you to Sidney. Charley will see you meet the stage."

Then she went to make her report of the gun wound for the sheriff at Sidney. She sat over the report a long time. Two days ago the Cheyenne treasure coach had been held up at the Canyon Springs station in a narrow cut of the western foothills. The station keeper had been tied up, and as the driver jerked to a stop for the change of horses, the robbers began to shoot from the buildings and the brush. One of the five guards fell dead, another was seriously wounded, while a third ran for the timber to shoot from shelter. He brought down two road agents but the rest used the driver as a shield and ran him out of rifle range. Then they forced the coach and the treasure box and rode away loaded down with gold estimated at from forty to two hundred thousand dollars. Among the road agents was Doug Goodale, who had visited Eddie last winter.

Now THAT MORISSA had taken a public stand against Eddie and sent him away, the bridge community softened toward her, became more friendly. Even Etty's Lorette walked over for a cup of tea and a little visit. She was pregnant again but without the heavy dullness of the last time.

"You stay here with us. It be many peoples soon, my Ettier he say," the woman told Morissa, showing her white teeth in a shy smile. "Your Eddie man he bad. Ettier he see him with other woman. . . ."

Morissa brushed this aside with the crumbs she swept into her napkin. "I don't care if he is with a dozen. I've been wondering about your children. They'll soon be old enough for school."

"Aha, yes. He send . . ."

"Soon there will be enough children for a school somewhere near. Alice and Georgie may be given back to me. Yellow fever struck them all and the father isn't recovering well, nor Alice either. One of the settlers over near the Wild Cats has a sister coming who has taught. Maybe next fall we'll have a school."

Gradually, too, the freighters began to stop at Morissa's again with their small complaints. In a few weeks it was almost like before her marriage, except that it wasn't at all. She couldn't go anywhere that required an escort. In a region where women are very scarce, no husbandly claim, even of an absent one, could be ignored.

Then the sheriff finally came about Morissa's report on Eddie's foot. Seated beside the kitchen table, an elbow on it, he spoke of Eddie Ellis.

"You ain't made a home for your husband like a good wife should."

"You know the kind of man Eddie is."

"But as a patient o' yours all winter his character might have been known to you."

Yes, it was, and his father had written her of their difficulties with the boy: a truant, in bad company, a thief, a forger, and dangerously violent.

"Well, he's forged Henry Clarke's signature this time."

"Oh!" Morissa exclaimed. Her father's employer, her benefactor. "He's never done such a thing before, not out here so far as I know."

"His mother probably paid up, or it would have been the penitentiary faster than by holdup or murder."

"I won't pay this; I won't buy off a forger."

"You might try bein' a wife to Ellis."

No, that she couldn't do. She had nothing but contempt for him. She admitted she had little more than that when she married him, some compassion perhaps, and a curious and morbid attachment, but nothing more.

"Then you went into this thing for spite, an' him just a kid. Now you oughta try to make a marriage of it."

Morissa thought about this, made herself think about it. Perhaps she had used Ed as an instrument of spite, certainly of self-debasement.

"You better do like I say. It'd be mighty easy to make out a case against you here, harborin' criminals," the sheriff reminded the young woman, his eyes bold upon her helplessness.

For a moment Morissa stared at him, the badge shining on the dark flannel shirt, the cartridge belt sagging over his chaps, his hat brim drawn down upon his eyes. "All right," she said slowly. "If Ed will be content to live on his homestead I'll go there with him, give him a trial."

"Well, that's better. Mebby I can work out a parole to you," the sheriff replied, standing a moment to look down at Morissa, his thumb hooked into his cartridge belt, his eyes humid with contempt, and desire, too, desire to overcome this woman. Without a word he turned and went out of the door. Not until he was in the saddle did he speak. "I'll be holdin' you to your word!" he called out.

All that evening Morissa walked through the white frosty moonlight of November, knowing that the agreement would be the end of Dr. Morissa Kirk, that it was surely intended so. She couldn't decide if the sheriff was trying to drive her out of the country or destroy her here, whether for the cattlemen or for his own satisfaction.

The night was a bleak one—a long, chill night of trying to understand how one born a bastard could have been so stupidly unguarded, acted so irresponsibly, knowing the long pay-time one foolish moment could extract from a life. Perhaps the narrow moralists were right: Morissa Kirk, born in shame, could never hope to escape the shameful existence.

The next morning she rode out early on the Appaloosa to have one last day of freedom on the tawny fall prairie, riding him hard into the wind. At night they returned, worn out together, and as she unsaddled and rubbed the dried sweat from under the pad, she determined to find the man who gave her this horse, or his son, the boy she treated in infancy. She would return the Appaloosa. Such an animal belonged to the brave, to people like the man who left him here beside her fence.

Before Morissa went into the house she slipped up to a window. But she couldn't see Eddie Ellis. No one was at the open fire except Ruth and young Hilda Gray, an expectant mother come in early because her settler husband was away earning a little track-laying money.

Cautiously Morissa pushed the door open and stood blinking in the lamplight. A pile of mail was on the table. On top was a letter from a friend in the state medical association. Morissa's name was being put up for vice president at the winter meeting, and he hoped she could give them a talk on surgery along the gold trail, about the broken neck and particularly about the Callwin head injury.

Morissa saw Ruth and the young woman watching her, the sorrow, the concern over the letter plain on their faces, and suddenly the young doctor's throat filled with gratitude.

"Oh, darlings, it's all right! This is good news!" she cried. And then she started to laugh and the other two, not knowing just why, joined in.

Chapter 14

EDDIE DIDN'T COME, but finally the story of the sheriff's visit got out and the promise he extracted from Morissa: that she would leave, take her husband away. "You mean leave the valley?" the old station keeper asked, and fell silent over his slack cud.

"Leave the trail?" a bullwhacker asked. "Why, just seein' Doc's place with them flowers of a summer, an' knowin' there's geraniums bloomin' in there winter times, shortens up them long pulls to the Hills. . . ."

But several drifting cowboys were standing around the bar too. "This here country ain't no place fer a woman," one of them said, spreading tobacco along a cigarette paper with his thumb to roll it. "This country's fer cactus, rattlers, 'n' mebby cows, when it don't get too cold," he said after the paper was licked.

So for a little while the emphasis shifted from the place north of the river with its thriving ten acres of trees, the slope of vegetable garden, and the flower beds. The sly remarks now were still of Eddie but not as a weapon to remove Morissa, rather against him as a man and a husband, and without her notice these dropped off. Yet each time that she had to defend him in her mind she wondered if he might not write, let her know how his foot was, and he himself, for Ed was truly not a strong man. She was still paying off the first debts he made, and had had to write Henry Clarke in embarrassment to apologize for his forgery. "I am grieved that your favors have been so illy repaid."

Clarke answered in a quiet little note from Omaha. "The check, un-honored, is put away as an effective bit of evidence for some future time, when you may need it desperately." Morissa knew this was wise and still she wanted to beg that it be destroyed. Truly a woman's mind and the winter winds blow this way and that.

Yet Ed was in very bad company, and as his wife she was legally responsible in many things. Every time the sheriff or a deputy came as far as the bridge she wanted to gather up her skirts and run for the shelter of her thickened grove.

BANKS HAD BEEN FAILING all over the East, with trouble at Sidney too. The bank there had been shaky, Clarke told Morissa. Then new people took it over and put their new money in the window. But times must still be hard, for homeseekers kept coming. Some who came late in the summer or had their crops eaten up by range cattle lived on pretty thin soup this winter, with no jobs, more than half of the regular ranch hands laid off until spring with cattle prices so low.

Morissa got so she dug into her root cellar every time she started on a call, taking along perhaps cabbage, or turnips, or carrots and potatoes, setting the sack beside her hot footstone under the buffalo robe. Toward Christmas she sent word around that there would be a big dinner at the hospital, everybody welcome. Even Fish Head helped, gathering red rose hips wherever the snow blew off, to string for the tree. Ruth knitted late, her steel needles flying, making a dozen pairs of black mittens with small rosebuds on the backs for the girls, little yellow dogs for the boys.

"But if more come?" she asked anxiously.

"We'll have other things in reserve," Morissa promised. Her uneasiness was that there might be no one. A year ago she would have been gaily confident, with Tris beside her. But as the wife of the shadowed Eddie Ellis—the forsaken wife of Eddie . . .

Just before Christmas word of guests coming poured in, many wanting to help. One woman was bringing a jar of pickled ground cherries, another preserved prickly pears from the bull-tongue cactus. One from a ranch over on Pumpkin Seed Creek would make little dip candles for the tree, with chopped pine needles in the tallow for fragrance. John Callwin offered to run the barbecue pit and make the sauce, if there was room for his Nancy and the little boy overnight.

Christmas morning the thermometer was down below zero, but by ten o'clock black dots were moving into the bleak valley. Some came horseback and others afoot over the hard snow, but Hilda Gray and her Dick were not among them at all, and it was really for them that Morissa had planned the dinner. One of nature's dreadful accidents had happened to that gay and energetic young couple. Their child was born a lump, squat-bodied and brown, with a dull face and slanted eyes.

"It's the Indian scare what done it, marked the baby!" some said darkly, and Morissa tried to explain that mongolism could happen anywhere. She grieved with the parents and assured them that the next child would be fine. But they had put the baby into the wagon in silence.

And now the Grays didn't come, although it seemed almost everybody else was there. Tables were laid through the long sod hospital room, pleasant with the big blaze in the fireplace, the patients moved out into Ruth's quarters. But there was some uneasiness in the kitchen, and elsewhere too. "I hear Ed Ellis was in Sidney this week. I figger he'll come hornin' in here," one of the men said out at the barbecue pit.

"Never no pot boiled but a little scum didn't rise to the top," Clarke's old blacksmith agreed.

They had fat venison and a half of a young beef that Sid Martin sent, along with a barrel of apples, and a pail of hard candy from Owen, the coach guard. There were dishpans full of watercress salad with bits of smoked bacon in the vinegar dressing; potatoes baked in coals raked

from the barbecue pit; beans, mashed turnips; several kinds of pickles, wild plum preserves, wild grape and chokecherry jelly, and buffalo berry, too, quivering and shining orange-red in the light. There were pumpkin pies big as a woman's arms could circle, baked in tub and bucket lids.

Finally the people were gathered, at least five men to every woman. Morissa got them seated at the three long tables. Then she had her patients brought in for a little while, and planned to ask John Callwin to say grace, but Clarke's old blacksmith spoke up. "Miss Morissy, I want to get my ante in first. I'm throwing Fish Head in to ask the blessin'."

It was Christmas and no feelings must be hurt, so Morissa tried to stop it, to save the little man the jibes and laughing, but he was already on his feet, standing no taller than a twelve-year-old boy, just a shoe peg of a man. He smoothed his gray beard a little and moved his watery eyes benignly around the tables. Then quietly, earnestly, he started, and Morissa realized once more how well this man could use his voice, the quality of it, the rise and fall. And before he said two dozen words, an earnestness crept into the bent faces. "We are here in a sort of double thanksgiving, Dear Father, thankful for a Saviour born and for a new world created to our use. Around these laden tables are men and women who have come here seeking homes for themselves and their children, setting the plow to Your virgin prairie, turning their faces to a life as new as when You first gave Adam and Eve the earth and its promise for their toil, the promise of rain and sunshine, of seeding time and harvest. . . ."

As the man's words spread over them, Morissa found her face wet, and when he finished and gravely sat down, other eyes had to turn to their plates to hide from the glinting firelight.

"By golly, Fish, you'd oughta been a preacher," one of the freighters roared out, and from the sudden flush on the little man's bearded face

Morissa knew that somewhere, sometime, Fish Head had been a preacher.

Afterward was the children's time, fifteen of them here, counting the three infants Morissa had delivered and a fourteen-year-old boy. A closet door was opened and inside the duskiness stood a Christmas tree. Four men drew the tree carefully out into the big room, barely swaying its strings of popcorn and rose hips. Then, with the shades drawn, the fragrant little candles were lit. The big gilt star on the top glistened, and the gilded walnuts and the sugared boy and girl cookies, too, and the little sacks of candy and the presents for the children. The faces of the young ones were a joy to see. "I wish Alice and Georgie could have been here," Morissa whispered to Ruth and Lorette, and when her back was turned Lorette moved a finger across her throat in the typical Sioux gesture. "I like do so to this Eddie who send them away."

There was Sid's barrel of apples, too, a tub of popcorn balls, and a big gunnysack of roasted peanuts for everyone to dip into. Then a Pole from over in the hills, a stranger "with the few English" as he expressed it, set his bright red accordion on his knee and bent his head to it, crying a little as the others sang, for this was his first Christmas in a far country.

As the early gray of evening came, the teams and horsebackers started away. Morissa looked anxiously into the northwest sky, and hoped that the storm would hold off until everyone was home.

ALL THE NEXT WEEK Morissa planned. Then she rode the Appaloosa out through the frosted valley and the Wild Cats and pounded on Gray's dugout, the sod chimney smoking peacefully in a little nest of pines. When she was finally asked to come in she was not shown the baby at all, even when its peculiar cry arose and Dick moved his foot to sway the cradle. After a while Hilda listened to the request the doctor had come to make. To the plea in the man's sorrowful eyes, the wife finally nodded agreement, and so Morissa went back home and wrote a dozen copies of a letter offering three months of schooling at her place, to begin March first. Any child from six through fifteen would be welcomed by Hilda Gray, an experienced rural teacher from the state of Michigan. The children could board the five days of each week at the sanitarium, or the entire seven. "As pay I hope you will trade me one day's work, man and team, if you have it, for each week, payable next summer, when I hope to erect an extensive log addition to my hospital," Morissa wrote.

With the letters off, she went to the medical association meeting in

Omaha, her talk neatly written out. Robin had caught a train down from his work and was at the depot to meet her. The tall, neat-haired and red-cheeked youth beside him turned out to be Jackie, and Morissa flew at them both. She was very happy to see Robin, but Jackie—Jack now! She could barely take her eyes from him, so fine had he grown. He was poised, and talked of being a doctor too. "Oh!" She turned to Robin. "Why, that's wonderful!" she cried, her eyes a golden hazel in her joy.

Yes, he was taking the prep course now and planning on medical school next fall. They had kept it as a surprise for her. "I have permission to go sit in on the meetings tomorrow," he said boyishly.

It was very difficult for young Dr. Morissa Kirk to stand up before the roomful of bearded men. It was much more difficult than to get an unconscious settler out of a well and keep him alive while she extracted crushed bone and cleared away damaged tissue, hammered out the silver plate and sewed it into place. "But one does what one must."

Finally the paper was finished and she sat down with her knees still shaking, wondering if she had shamed young Jack, and if the applause was anything more than just good manners toward a weak female. Then the door opened and John Callwin was brought in, a little embarrassed.

"I had to go show my mother-in-law anyway," he apologized to Morissa. "Uncle Bob thought it would be nice if I stopped off here for a few hours today." But Morissa couldn't hear for the pounding of her heart.

Afterward there were three men waiting outside the door for Morissa, Tris standing tall between Robin and Jack. For a moment Morissa wanted to run because his face seemed almost the same as when she left him standing on the hotel steps in Sidney last June—with all the hurt and disbelief, the guilt, too, and the admiration. Yet now he stood here as though none of the things since had happened.

But they had happened, and now Morissa must greet him, passing off her flushed excitement as from the paper that she read and the election—vice president of the association. She touched the back of a hand to her cheek. "Feverish, decidedly feverish, I'd say," she laughed. "It's just been too much for this simple country girl."

Together they went along the street and once more Morissa found herself falling into easy step with this man, her hand tucked into the long-known crook of his arm.

They were together several times the next two days, talking over Tris's new plans. He was sending an engineer out to the North Platte valley toward spring. "What I want to know is how practical large-scale irrigation would be out there. Have you ever been up the river into Wyoming? There are several good sites for dams, although the best seems to be far up at the Narrows, where the river boils out through a deep rocky cut. There's the place for a dam and a great reservoir behind it." The man's face glowed as he talked, his gray eyes not smoky now, but like spring clouds, like April with sun spilling through.

"You're still the engineer!" Morissa exclaimed. "Your Aunt Mae said you were planning to be one when your father was killed in the war."

"You always remember the roots of everything, don't you? What a wife you would be for a scientist—or an engineer—" he said, carried along by embarrassment. But the sudden shadowing of Morissa's face made him stop. "I—I guess there's a lot of money in the packing business here," he added lamely, "but I can't make slaughtering my life work."

"You're a rancher too."

"No, I'm selling my interest in the ranches. Part of the money is going into the railroad that's to come through the valley. That won't bring much return for some time, but what I put into the packing business, that will pay. Anyway, I'm getting out of ranching."

"Oh, that's too bad. You belong out in that region," Morissa said, and felt ashamed of her part in this decision, ashamed that there was so much to separate them now.

EVEN WITH ALL THE SADNESS of seeing Tris so short a time, and the uncertainty about Eddie, the new year had promised to be a good one. But now she heard about the Cheyennes, scattered dead over the snow up around Fort Robinson. They had come north from Indian Territory, been ordered back, and refused to go. Food was cut off, then fuel, with the weather far below zero, and finally water, too, and so at night they strapped their children to their backs and poured out of the barrack windows into the guns of the troops, preferring to die in honor. The few men captured were ironed for the South; the widows and orphans were allowed to go to Red Cloud's Sioux. When the wagons of prisoners came slowly down to Clarke's bridge, Morissa hurried to the officer in charge. "The Indian children—are any alive up there?"

"Yes, some; mostly wounded."

"Is there anything I can do?"

"No, they were taken to Red Cloud."

The next morning, telling her errand to no one, Morissa rode up the North Platte alone, going to where she knew a few Indians had wintered in a hole in the badland slope of Scotts Bluff. She had been up that way twice before, leaving sacks with flour, coffee, and a little brown sugar, the first time with a drawing of two Indian children made by Lorette pinned to the outside. When Morissa had come back that way the sack was gone, and in its place was a little piece of rolled buckskin tied to a stake, a drawing of an Indian with his left hand up in friendly greeting to a long-skirted woman on an Appaloosa.

But now there were no horse tracks around, and when Morissa returned next day the new sack was untouched.

HILDA CAME the evening before school opened, carrying her poor helpless baby in a willow basket. Four children would be starting, with perhaps two more later. Morissa had schoolbooks, slates, and paper, and a folding blackboard that Charley had made. They went to bed late that night, Morissa happy that Hilda was already looking better.

For once she went to sleep without thinking about Eddie or wondering who was looking after him tonight. She heard that some of Doc Middleton's gang were captured at North Platte City but Doc had spurred off over the railroad bridge, a pistol in each hand, shooting both ways. So far Eddie Ellis was not among the captured.

With the spring rush of settlers into the cattle country, there was great excitement over the trial of the Olives, ranchers down in Custer County, for the hanging and burning of two settlers they claimed rustled their beef. This was to be an honest legal test between the settlers and the cattlemen. Sid Martin and even the Boslers called the Olives a gang of outlaws who gave the ranchers a bad name.

The stockmen had other worries too. Almost as soon as the winter snow cleared off the vast, unoccupied sandhills, prairie fires sprouted in the thick long grass, perhaps set by Indians still hidden up there. Morissa knew about these fires burning for weeks, driven this way and that in the wind until finally forced to feed upon their own ashes. So far she had seen only the rolling clouds of pearly smoke on the horizon.

Then one April day when the wind ran in waves over the dead grass of the upper Snake Creek region, a prairie fire was almost upon her, the bays suddenly shying before she even saw the smoke. She stood up in the buggy and whipped for a gravel slope where the grass was no more than ragged fuzz. Here she might hold her horses together in the face of the flames, only two, three miles away southeast now, the smoke rolling over her and splitting against the hill beyond.

But suddenly the wind shifted into the south and the smoke of the fire trailed straight toward a wide wet valley that Morissa knew, one with all the thick accumulation of grass since the buffalo herds disappeared. And there, in a tent out in the middle, lived a new settler, his ankle broken and not so much as a horse to carry him away.

Swiftly the doctor hitched up again and let her excited horses out, the buggy bouncing and swaying down the path of the rolling smoke that choked and blinded her and the team, galloping before the fire. They plunged into a hidden gully and were almost out the other side when a wheel caught and the harness separated from its fastenings. Morissa pulled the frightened team to a stop, and with her black bag pounding against her side, she rode Nellie, with Kiowa alongside, toward the man's tent.

But before she got to the settler she saw the Bosler fire crew race past in the smoke, first the two plows, each with a rider on the left horse of the double team, whipping them on while two men, their feet flying high, clung to the plow handles and tried to hold the breaker bottom in the rough sod, leaving a strip roughly forty feet wide between them. Behind them came a horsebacker dragging a long rope, the raveled end soaked in coal oil, burning, to set a line of guard fire between the two plowed furrows, close to the downwind side. At least fifty men were strung out behind to fight any little blaze that might jump the furrow.

Somebody saw Morissa. "The lady doc!" he yelled, swinging his hat to stop her, but she galloped her horses on. At the settler's tent she saw the man trying to escape through the smoke on his crutches. The fire topped a hill less than a mile off, the Bosler crew barely ahead of it now.

With the settler up on Kiowa, Morissa hurried back toward the comparative safety of the burnt fireguard. Beside the Bosler crew she slid off. Waving the man on, she grabbed a fire hoe, too, to chop and beat at the backfiring wherever the plow had jumped from the earth and left no turned furrow. Twice the wind swept the fire like an express train straight upon them, with only the narrow, half-burnt guard against it, driving them straggling back, their clothing full of smoldering holes.

But each time they edged a little closer into the wind-driven fire, tapering it more and more, until the last tongue was pinched together in some broken hills and finally headed by the plows and fighters. The burnt ground reached back southeast, a great rolling mass of blackened hills shouldering away to the horizon. The furrow-edged ribbon of the Bosler fireguard stood against it all the way from the Platte, over thirty miles of guard thrown up in the face of the wind-driven flames.

Now the men lay scattered over the prairie like old bundles of blackened rags, flat, played out. Somebody remembered the lady doc and rose stiffly to look for her. Morissa opened her eyes to the man's call and got to her feet, her lips blistered, her brows burned off, her bangs scorched. The cowboy laughed a little to see her, the blood seeping from his blistered lips bright in the sooty face. The crippled settler was coming back along the fireguard with Morissa's team, and now she remembered her buggy off in the gully. But it was gone, burned to the axle and hub.

Chapter 15

FOR THE FOURTH SPRINGTIME Morissa Kirk watched the wheels lurch heavily through the mud of the North Platte valley, drop dark earth on the bridge planks, and stop to rest a while. This year the colonization literature of the railroad really drew the landless. Homeseekers poured out of the emigrant cars, stiff and sooty, or came the cheaper and slower routes of horse or by foot. "Looks as hopeless as holdin' back the north wind with a wire fence," Sid Martin admitted. Besides, the trial of the notorious Olives for lynching had aroused the public. Ranchers began to drift their herds north into the sandhills or clear into Dakota; some, like Tris, sold out to combines of British or eastern money.

The spring was a busy one for Morissa, and later she was glad that Hilda Gray wanted to take her poor baby home after only two months of teaching, for the next week smallpox broke out at the bridge. There had been a winter-long scourge of it at Deadwood where Calamity Jane, it was said, nursed the pest shacks, and it was true she went anywhere if there was a jug of whiskey to keep her company. Morissa sent word around that she would be happy to vaccinate everyone who came.

Perhaps the winter of smallpox had been too hard for Calamity Jane. At least she was leaving. "Shaking the gold dust of the gulch from her feet," Owen told Morissa when he came in for something to relieve the rheumatism that pained his injured leg in damp weather. The next day

Calamity came down the trail with a couple of her kind, stopping at an invitation to wet their gullets at the roadhouse north of the bridge. She saw Morissa from the door and shouted greetings as the doctor passed.

"Hello, Issy! How're you, you little bastard!" she roared out for the bullwhackers passing. This time the word brought no blush, no anger to Morissa Kirk. Truly a bastard might seem as good as anyone else by a time, as her grandmother had written to her long ago.

THE CHILDREN HAD DONE so well at their books this spring that two school districts were being organized down near the railroad, with sod schoolhouses and at least a hope of teachers. Morissa planted more trees on her homestead, the new grove a hollow rectangle open toward the south. Inside the opening she planned a large log building, E-shaped, the back section a story and a half, or perhaps two.

Tris Polk wrote every few weeks now. He began with impersonal notes and the engineer's report on irrigation for the valley. These grew into friendly letters about the progress of the plans, or clippings about irrigation perhaps as far away as the Nile valley. A little doubt still gnawed at Morissa: How could she welcome this correspondence with a man she had so summarily rejected on imperative ethical grounds? How much of that had been a flight? But even so Morissa kept the letters in a sweet-grass box that Lorette gave her when her last baby was delivered.

ONE RAINY EVENING when Morissa came in, Gwinnie was waiting to bring her over to meet some surprise guests of Clarke's. They turned out to be the Walter Morton Company, an English theatrical troupe going to Deadwood to put on *H.M.S. Pinafore.* They seemed a gay and hardy lot, even Walter Morton himself, with his huge belly. An earlier troupe had been so successful—six weeks of *The Mikado* in Deadwood—they had to try it too.

Morissa missed the opening of *Pinafore*. She had two serious cases of what seemed mountain fever. She had never seen this spotted fever, and for all her bathing and dosing, one of the patients died the third day, dark-mottled and terrible. The other was a little better in a week. By then a man had come for his dead brother, getting off the stage at the bridge shouting, "Where's the she-doc what lets people die? Them women docs got no business hornin' in on what's a man's job!"

Some of the cowboys standing around nodded, perhaps because half a dozen settlers had taken up land alongside of Morissa this spring, making a solid five-mile barrier between the ranches and the river front. And still nothing had been done to drive them out except a shot or two through an empty window. So far no one had dared attack the hospital, the place where the sick were resting and ailing children slept.

The new hospital wasn't started but the cured logs were there, the last load just in when the doctor was called to a new little ranch down the south side of the river. But she wasn't allowed to see the patient, delirious with a high fever, only to treat him from beyond the door.

"Take the man to Sidney," Morissa told the men. As she let the bays out she looked back at the little log shack. The place seemed a hangout for rustlers and horse thieves more than a ranch, but the voice of the sick man hadn't seemed to be Eddie's.

As she waited in her new buggy at the bridge for the toll arm to go up, she found herself staring at a familiar figure coming across the dusty morning road. "Tris!" she cried, and then remembered to say the name softly the second time, with so many around to hear. It seemed he must kiss her, but instead he took the hand she barely remembered to give him, holding it between his, the gray eyes dark as a thunderstorm.

"Get in," Morissa said, trying to make it casual for the freighters. "We'll have a nice visit while Ruth gets us a late breakfast."

He had to see how the cottonwoods had grown, and the young planting of trees for the new building. They walked through the meadow, fenced for winter hay, thick and green, with tulip gentians holding dew in their blue cups. At the timber claim Tris looked up at the fine growth a long time, and the difference one watering a summer made.

"Well, this certainly is the place to sell irrigation to the valley someday," he said.

That morning they rode up the south side to Scotts Bluff, the great, bold yellowish wall that almost filled the west between the river and the arm of the Wild Cats. From the top of the northern point they looked far down over the sloping yellow-white patch of badlands that was eating into the foot of the bluff from the river. This bluff, the torn Wild Cat range, and Chimney and Courthouse Rocks were the last outposts standing stubbornly against the roaring North Platte of springtime, the river that today flowed so placidly out of the west, where July thunderheads rode the Wyoming horizon.

"Here you can see how water will be brought down to make all this region fruitful." Tris said. "The river carries a lot of water. Wide as it is, stories are told of an early steamboat making it up almost this far."

Morissa laughed at the apparent improbability. The broad flat river below them was choked with islands, and by September there might be no stream beyond a thread of tepid water.

But Tris, with the enthusiasm of the convert, could not be stopped. "It's water any time it runs, and generally a lot of it, enough for great reservoirs. Remember your first day here—when the man was swept from the wagon, and you stole my horse?"

"So I'm still a horse thief to you!" Morissa objected, but in a moment her laughter was gone, for Tris had dropped his concern with the future. "No, not a horse thief even that day," he said, without looking at Morissa, still Morissa Ellis. "Already you were the woman I loved."

EVEN WITH HER SADNESS that Tris must go away, there was the glow that came from the assurance of his affection. "You have the color of a prairie rose in your cheeks these days, dear lady, and the beguilement of a Sataness in your golden eyes," Fish Head said to her.

"Then I should think you'd be very much afraid," Morissa replied, "and run for your life."

The Fish took his hat out of his axle-grease can, wiped its black sides carefully with his sleeve, and put it back. "I cherish no ambitious succumbing to beguilement," he said sadly, "but I would appreciate a sprig of mignonette."

"You're a humbug, Wilmer DeQuincey Jones, and a punk actor, with a strong craving for fried cheek of trout or breast of grouse, garnished."

But most of the time Morissa was too busy for such banterings. John Callwin was laying the stone foundation for the new hospital and she hoped to get the logs up before the chinking mortar froze in the drying. She was also too busy to go to Clarke's for the news and rumors the stage brought of road agents and horse thieves working closer. Then one morning the Appaloosa was gone. Nellie was gone, too, from another pasture. Obviously the thief knew the doctor's favorite horses; Eddie Ellis, perhaps, or someone for him.

Morissa made the rounds of the bridge town, going in everywhere, watching the faces in the dark, bleak morning bars and out at the hitchracks. Nobody seemed to know anything, although it was plain that Eddie was suspected, Eddie or Doc Middleton. Morissa wrote out notices to post in all the public places up and down the trail and on the bridge. She also had a copy inserted in the Sidney paper:

STRAYED OR STOLEN
1 Appaloosa gelding. Seven-year-old saddler
with three diagonal Cheyenne tattoo marks inside left foreleg.
1 Bay driving mare, small K brand under mane on left side of neck.
REWARD for return or information leading thereto.

Dr. Morissa Kirk, Camp Clarke, Nebr.

Then she saddled Kiowa and headed for Eddie's homestead and the old thieves' trail, to examine every soft spot for the small and very narrow track of the Appaloosa. She was foolishly frantic, as though a child had been taken, but she had to return at night without news. Yes, there were tracks on the thieves' route, but none like the Appaloosa's.

Then Doc Middleton was caught. He was promised a pardon from the governor and a job with the federal marshals if he surrendered. He did, was ambushed, and wounded one of the officers in escaping. But he carried a bullet in his hip away from the fight and so was captured at last.

No one brought up the name of Eddie and there was no Appaloosa in the captured herds in Doc's hideouts. But news of Morissa's horse finally came. Fish Head had disappeared from the bridge some time ago. No one paid much attention, none beyond predicting that he'd come trotting back like a hungry hound dog to the smokehouse. The little man did return, but flat in a wagon bed, dead. Tied to the end gate behind him plodded Nellie, with the handsome Appaloosa nervous beside her.

It was an accident. A freighter from a station up the trail had shot him. Out hunting meat, he had seen a horsebacker leading the Appaloosa down a gully. At a yell to stop, the horsebacker put the horses into a run and as they dipped out of sight, the freighter fired. When he got up close there was poor Fish Head on the ground, the two horses shying off into the hills. He dropped a loop over the Appaloosa, and with the Fish tied over Nellie's bare back, returned to the station. By then word had come down that the two horses belonged to the girls at a road ranch near Chief Red Cloud's new agency. Seems they got the horses from a man called Eddie running with some of Fly Speck Billy's gang.

Fish Head looked like a patriarch, small size, in the coffin that Morissa ordered up from Sidney, and there were few who did not recall that the gentle, lost little man went to every funeral and always wept a little, with the rusty old silk hat held respectfully over his heart.

THE DROP IN BEEF prices had dumped many cattlemen into the hands of eastern loan sharks. Then the hard winter of 1878 cut the heart out of the herds. The new owners seemed a little less vigilant against settlers, at least at the start. But suddenly two settlers were left dead down below the Wild Cats. The next week Charley Adams found a noose hung on his doorknob. He kept it from Ruth as long as he could, certain she would pack her dish towels and drag him out of the country. But when she found out she sneaked the noose over to the bridge in her market basket and hung it up in the mail corner at Clarke's, beside the handbills offering rewards for outlaws. To the noose she had pinned a card saying, "Stray taken up on Charley Adams homestead. Will be surrendered on proof of ownership and payment of two match boxes well filled. Ruth Adams."

Of course the rope and card were taken down almost immediately, but she had selected the night the fall roundup gathered at the bridge; the room was packed and every ranch outfit in over fifty miles knew about it in a minute. Morissa laughed the next morning when the roundup passed her door, the men turning in the saddle to look after Ruth peacefully feeding her hens.

This fall typhoid hit the roundup as it had the trail in the late summer, and with greater force than ever before. It became a real scourge in Deadwood, where many thousands of people lived jammed close together, with no sewage or water system. Then late in September fire swept through the flimsy wooden structures of the gulch, and set off eight kegs of blasting powder in the supply store on the main drag, scattering the fire like seed on the wind. The best that could be done was get the people out. Ten thousand, the sick and the well, were without shelter.

Soon after the fire the Gilbert and Sullivan troupe returned to the bridge. The first Morissa knew of their coming was the man who galloped ahead to find her, so she could prepare for all this sickness that seemed to be more typhoid. Charley was away somewhere and Ruth up on their homestead, so the doctor ran out and fired her rifle three times fast into the air to signal them both in. Then she set the long hospital room in order and drew the center curtain across it. With a fire started in the laundry stove for the dry sterilizing heat of the pipe oven, she put on a boiler of water, too, and waited.

When the first coach drew up to the yard gate, the driver leaped from the box and carried in a young girl whom Morissa remembered as Lola, a vivacious little brunette. Now she drooped over the man's arm, pale as tallow. "She took sick up the road a piece, an' already she's limper'n a gunnysack—" he said in alarm.

They got the passengers into the house, two of them very ill, the others apparently coming down, too, or at least worn out by concern and fatigue. The second carriage was worse, and those in the slower wagon were unable to lift their heads, the great, loose-fleshed body of Walter Morton like a soft feather tick, his wife sitting beside him in the bouncing wagon, holding his head in her lap.

Morissa got everybody down on her temporary pallets of cottonwood leaves that were so easily burned and replaced, and by then Charley was in the doorway. She had him set up the cots with waterproof drawsheets, and put Ruth to scalding milk and whipping up eggnog with brandy to put a little strength and heart into these poor people. They worked straight through the next twenty-four hours, all three missing Fish Head running errands night and day, speaking his elaborate nonsense to those still able to listen.

With all the self-blame of the last year like a pall upon her, Morissa was increasingly unsure in that difficult medical decision she must make between the extremes in typhoid treatment. Should she accept the newer, radical procedures, disinfecting the bowel tract with mammoth doses of iodine or carbolic acid? She was afraid of the irritation, the toxic effect, and leaned toward bland diet and moderate medication, with cool baths and wet sheets against the fever. The expected mortality was still one out of every four in the large hospitals, which meant a probable two, even three, out of the troupe of eleven here. The doctor closed her eyes and made her decision for blandness, setting herself against even her Dr. Aiken.

Each day, when the sick were bathed, fed, and dosed, Morissa walked softly between the cots. Swiftly she went over the fever charts, with their consistent two-degree rise from morning to evening, the next day the same, but always beginning a degree higher, climbing. By the middle of the week two of her patients were no more than alive. The worst was Walter Morton, head of the troupe. His appearance had shocked Morissa when they carried him out of the wagon, the great belly of the man, like an old gray comforter, lying in folds on each side of him on the cot. His face looked small and bony, his eyes yellowed and burning with fever. This was his night of crisis, and Morissa hunched beside him all the long hours, Charley looking in now and then as he attended the others.

Toward morning the man seemed to rally a little, and once more Morissa found herself warm with affection for this sturdy showman and the fight he was making.

As the Morton troupe drew out of immediate danger, the well members went off to do skits. But two of them, Walter Morton and the one they called Deadeye Dick, still lay gaunt and yellow-eyed in Morissa's sod-house. It had been a hard winter.

It was a violent winter, too, with more shootings around Huff Johnson's roadhouse, one that ended in railroading a settler to the penitentiary. Once more the doctor shot target at a sandy spot, particularly when the freight trains passed. Word traveled here, and no man with sense went against a Winchester with a pistol.

Morissa expected more trouble with Ed, but not even Lorette knew it if he came to Clarke's. Later there was a rumor that he was with Fly Speck Billy up near Deadwood.

A voting precinct had been established at Clarke's, and cowboys from half a dozen other precincts came to vote—some several times, to keep the grangers out of office. The settlers talked about a new county centered here on the North Platte valley, with their own courts and sheriff. Morissa thought about the change in four years, from Tom Reeder and his gold belt dragged out of the flooded Platte and a man hanged from the bridge. In her rides now she rarely saw wild game larger than a jackrabbit, and it was amost two years since anyone had told of seeing a bighorn sheep in the Wild Cats.

Between the typhoid cases and the early winter there had been no time to get the new hospital up more than knee high, so Charley banked the foundation with manure and let it wait for spring. Along in January a mother of two children came to ask if there would be school again. Morissa let her look into the crowded hospital room. "Oh, no, you can't have children here, with all the sick," the woman agreed regretfully. "But ours'll sure grow up like wild Indians."

"Oh, you can get a school district organized for next year, if there's another family or two," Morissa said.

Doubtfully the settler's wife climbed up on her old plow mare between the sacks Morissa had filled in the cellar, and started away into the gray wind. The woman had asked for something else: a loan on their team for shoes for the children, and food. "We just haven't even a smidgin of flour. The range cattle ate up our corn and potatoes, plants and all. . . ."

Morissa gave her a little money, to be worked out in the spring, but she couldn't make the loans that the settlers needed to tide them over to a crop. That would mean bankruptcy for the hospital, for many would fail. It was hard to send women back empty-handed to their children.

WHEN MORISSA CAME HOME early one afternoon in April, Tris Polk was waiting there, sitting with his long legs stretched out before him, talking about Deadwood and Gilbert and Sullivan with the two patients. But whatever he came to say had to wait. Morissa had barely washed off the dust when a stagecoach rattled up to the gate and Lola and the rest tumbled out with all their normal gaiety and excitement. Before night there was a big blowout going over at Clarke's hotel, with the Britishers coming from as far as Sidney for the surprise farewell party that the troupers had been planning for weeks. It was both a happy and a lugubrious evening, with even the head of the troupe weeping a little as they left for the slow night trip to Sidney and their Pullmans east, everybody kissing Morissa, and Ruth, too, while those of the valley stood by in farewell.

Tris Polk had brought a big roll of maps, with contours and elevations and an entire irrigation plan for the valley. He was determined to show these to Morissa and so he stayed over after the party and rode out to the north ridge with her in the morning. They stopped here and there, letting the horses stand while they looked from the outspread maps to the valley, until Morissa was dizzy with the grandeur of the plan. Not a plan for today, Tris admitted, or even tomorrow, but in some rich, fruitful future when the valley bloomed.

But suddenly the man became quiet. "You will need to do something about Eddie," he said. "He's your legal spouse. You can't sell without him, or mortgage or commit your land to any large improvement plan. . . ."

Morissa looked down to the sheaf of maps Tris carried and she could neither speak nor even bow her serious head in hearing. Instead she pretended to struggle with the map she held, making an awkward task of it against the wind, until Tris took it from her and folded it swiftly.

"Li-Laurie's marrying the English boy she met at the Walker horse show," he said. "A second son of an earl with a ranch in Wyoming, to be theirs after the wedding. If you can't make up your mind about Ed—split the blanket as the bullwhackers call it—I'm giving her the Carlotta saddle."

Morissa looked up from her engrossment with these plans and with the man who held them. His sudden petulance was so reducing, somehow so human, that a little amusement came to the corners of her full lips, to her sun-shot hazel eyes. But today Tris Polk had no patience for any possible Scotticisms. Leaving her standing there he strode to his horse, jammed the maps into the saddlebags, and gathering up the reins, swung into the seat and was gone. Two weeks later Morissa saw an item in the Sidney paper saying Tris Polk, the prominent owner of the TeePee ranch, had taken the train west with Hurley Forson of Chicago. They planned to buy a large spread up the North Platte in Wyoming.

Chapter 16

SID MARTIN RODE UP to the rising walls of Morissa's hospital, his graying hair neat over his white sun-shielded forehead as he swept off his Stetson. "Looks like you was plannin' to run a orphanage," he said, motioning at the size of the place. But his squinted blue eyes were on the young woman working in her flower bed. She wore a blue denim skirt, a black and yellow calico shirtwaist with yellow rickrack, and a matching sunbonnet that was pushed back to rest against her heavy braid.

"No, no orphanage. I don't like them," she said, "but I wish I could have the place good for children, make it as full of promise as that little patch of corn coming through out there."

"Frost will take the corn before it's ripe."

"Oh, you cattlemen! Always belittling your country, when you're willing to shoot to keep it."

"Only followin' in your tracks, ma'am, you and your rifle out popping cans off the posts around your timber claim," Sid said, laughing. But plainly this lightness was only a preliminary to something else. "I hear tell," he finally said, "that you're thinking of goin' in with your brother on a practice off farther east somewhere."

Morissa scrubbed at the earth on her gloves with the trowel. "Well, news does travel! Just this week Jack decided he would like it. He's marrying, and the girl's father has to give up his practice. Maybe it would work out better—"

But she was interrupted by one of Sid's cowhands, spurring up and setting his horse back to its haunches in the dust. "One o' them red-eyed grangers back yonder's holdin' part of our herd fer damages he claims was done last night. Got a double-barrel loaded with buckshot."

Later Morissa saw the herd come trailing into the river valley, the longhorns running and bawling as they smelled water. She watched them from the empty window holes of the new building, and then went to see about her patients—a child with yellow jaundice still a little delirious, and a man with a hole in his cheek eaten out by the plasters of a cancer quack up in Deadwood, a hole bigger than a silver dollar through into the mouth. The whole side of the face had been swollen and purpled, the edges of the wound angry in proud flesh, saliva running out night and day. When Morissa first saw this she had been so angry she could hardly hold her hands steady to ease away the wet and bloody bandages. Truly man must endure a great deal from his healers.

Morissa knew something about the cancer man up in the Black Hills, her little hospital a sort of dressing station on what seemed suddenly a cancer trail; but Rem Smith's wound was the most pitiful of all. Apparently a well man otherwise, and not over thirty, he was left with this hole in his face, and not even certain that the small knot removed had been malignant at all. Perhaps she could clear up the wound, then draw the sides together. It would make a shocking, twisted cheek, but the man might yet have a face.

Finally the preliminary operation was done, the wound clean. Then the doctor drew the sides in close with pressure bandages to push the flesh together at the cheek to avoid strain on the stitches. So much depended now on the man's patience and fortitude to endure the packing that blocked off the entire cheek inside, and the saliva drain pipe that must remain at the far corner of his lip. Because this must always be the lower corner, the doctor tied the patient on his side with strips of canvas to keep him from turning in his sleep. She went in often those first three days to lay a hand on the man's shock of reddish hair, but remembering Dr. Aiken's teaching, she was determined not to disturb the healing by dressing or even inspection until she must.

She had to think about Jack and his offer now. If she went into practice with him, the hospital here must have a good doctor, someone who saw the valley as it could be someday, green and lush from the water that men like Tris Polk would bring. Curiously she never thought that this doctor might be a woman.

WITH SO MANY SETTLERS in the region, even though mostly single men, there were increasing sociabilities, and some fights. On the Fourth of July all the valley and many from farther away gathered at Morissa's grove, almost without her realization that anyone was coming. "A grove like that belongs to the community," John Callwin had once said, and so wagons, horsebackers, and people afoot came from all directions to spread their blankets and picnic baskets under her trees.

There was a little politicking, too, with candidates and speakers for candidates. Even Tris Polk came up for a short talk. Standing in the back of the wagon, he praised the progress of the valley since the first piling was driven for Clarke's bridge. Through Indian scares, dynamiting and outlawry, blizzards, prairie fires, falling beef prices and hard times, the North Platte region had settled down, become The Valley, a place that could gather so many here today, women and children too.

"Looks like mebby you're runnin' fer office, Tris," one of the old TeePee punchers shouted. "Wanta be dog catcher?"

"No!" Tris answered, cupping his hand to his mouth too. "I'm trying to round up votes for Governor Nance, but mostly I'm talking for The Valley and all the new regions of the state, for a cleanup of the rustlers and outlaws, for better brand control, and for railroads and irrigation."

Morissa was late in going over from her patients, and surprised to see Tris. She had received a couple of photographs of the Narrows that he sent from Wyoming, and a note that he might be in the valley soon. Now here he was in her grove, standing up tall in the tail end of a wagon finishing a speech and saying that he must leave immediately to make another talk at Sidney that evening. Morissa was happy to see him, the first time since he rode away with his bundle of maps, hurt by her apparent lightness. Fortunately, in this crowd there was no opportunity or need for explanation and apology. Yet somehow he didn't seem the Tris Polk that she knew—more like the man who crossed the river that first day to tell her that she had done a dangerous thing in flood time, and that taking a man's horse was a hanging matter. Many things had changed since then and yet the Tris of that day stood beside her, looking up at the magnificent growth of her trees. Some were big enough for the cowboys to make swings for the younger children, using their lariats in a wholly new way.

People were passing back and forth, smiling their greetings. One woman came up to Tris and Morissa, moving vaguely and alone, as

though to wander past. Then suddenly she stopped as at a discovery.

"The shade of a tree"—she murmured—"you know, the shade of a tree it lays over you like a cool and gladsome thing." She spoke as though to herself, seeming not to hear their friendly replies that followed her down between the thick, shaded rows.

Guardedly Morissa glanced at Tris and caught the softness, the understanding and compassion in his face as he watched the sad, bemused woman, and once more the young doctor had to admit the incredible and appalling realization that this was the man she did not marry.

BY LATE OCTOBER the windmill and reservoir up on the knoll north of Morissa's place were done, the running water ready when she moved into the new building. The hospital rooms were all plastered and white-washed, along with the adjoining pharmacy and the operating room. The rest of the building was left in log, the recreation and the convalescent rooms divided by a partial wall with a double stone fireplace, one face to each room. In the back of the building, with a solid wall between them and with independent outside doors, were the isolation rooms.

The wings of the big E-shaped building held large sunny windows bright with geraniums and five canary cages. The office in the center projection of the E had wall bookcases for the medical publications, with the framed diploma and the certificate of election as officer in the medical society hung over them.

Slowly the doctor let herself down in her desk chair the first day and tried to feel like the head of a real hospital, but to the Morissa Kirk of the poor farm it brought up such a flood of sadness, such dissatisfaction, that she had to laugh. Such self-dramatization was for the patient, not the doctor. She went out into the fall sunlight, to see the place as passersby saw it. The building of browned, sunburned logs seemed solid and strong. The sliding roof windows for tuberculars were already up. She thought of this as the Lorna Kirk division of her hospital; such a place, with good food and nursing, might have saved her mother's life.

But even here in the taming wilderness the log wings were already topped by the taller of the young trees behind them, particularly the cottonwoods with the evening song of the wind in their yellow fall leaves. Suddenly Morissa felt so good she went to Etty's store to round up Lorette and a couple of settler women trying to trade garden truck for jeans and calico. With Ruth and these tea guests, Morissa Kirk opened her new place. The next day she moved the patients in.

But Morissa's concern for the new settlers was growing. Many left after the first few weeks, or months, and some were hauled out, or buried here. There was Mrs. Thacker, the woman who had spoken of the shade that lay on her cool and gladsome, and moved Tris to such compassion. Somehow she got her hands on a bottle of strychnine, and died. "Seems she just couldn't go on," her husband told Morissa. She was buried in the valley cemetery, and afterward Morissa and Callwin balled a little pine from the Wild Cats and planted it on her grave so she need never be without the shade of a tree again.

ELECTION DAY the voters gathered to cast their first national ballot in the valley at Clarke's. Many wandered over for a taste of Ruth's coffee cake and a look at the new hospital. Tris Polk was among them.

"After all your electioneering, aren't you going to vote?" Morissa asked.

"Of course; this is my precinct now too. I filed on all the land the government permits me, a homestead and timber claim up above Scotts Bluff, along the line that our first ditches are to take."

"Oh, stay until it clears out here and celebrate!" Morissa urged. "Come see the whole place." They went through it all, and afterward Tris waited until the other visitors were gone and then sat in the pleasant west window of Morissa's parlor.

"I hear that the settlers lost some horses along the river last night," he said. "One of Clarke's men thinks he recognized Ed Ellis."

"Oh!" Morissa cried, "why doesn't the sheriff pick him up?" as though she had no more connection with this than any other citizen.

But Tris Polk couldn't let this evasion stand. "Didn't your Scottish grandmother ever tell you that a man should never marry a widow unless her former husband had been hanged?" He said it almost angrily, but wryly too, and Morissa had to accept the reminder without reply.

Soon after New Year there was a report that Fly Speck Billy was dead. A freighter on the Black Hills trail who didn't know the Speck gave him a ride, even loaned him his revolver, and then was shot with his own gun. The sheriff arrested Fly Speck, but a mob gathered and while a dozen men sat on the sheriff, the rest strung Speck up to a pine tree.

Morissa heard the story in relief. Even though hanging was a violent, a lawless act, and it had come to the freckled-face youth who rode the same coach that brought her to the river almost five years ago, she was relieved, perhaps because this would surely break up the gang Eddie seemed to be running with. If only Ed would go home before he slid into real violence.

Instead of rumors of a capture of Eddie Ellis, she began to hear hints of a big robbery, the biggest in the history of the Sidney gold route. This was a Fly Speck Billy holdup, it seemed, and that was why he was hanged so swiftly and silently, given no opportunity to run off at the mouth, some said.

After a while the story thinned out and was lost in the new excitement over the rise of gunmen in Sidney. They had been threatening to take the town over entirely, and at last local protest brought some action. Although the Sidney Regulators had strung a man up to a telegraph pole, the quieting effect hadn't lasted. In a few weeks three more were lynched and a long list of men, and some women, too, were given twenty-four hours to get out of town. They scattered, to Denver, Julesburg, or Cheyenne. Some came up the gold trail, mostly stopping at the growing cluster of roadhouses and saloons north of the bridge.

Morissa saw them loafing around there, their narrow, unblinking eyes upon her with a kind of arrogant admiration. Surely being the wife of Eddie Ellis didn't justify this. They made her feel very uneasy, and also uneasy about her place that was less than one good whoop from them, or a pistol shot.

Chapter 17

WITH THE FIRST SIGNS of spring the Sidney outlaws seemed to be moving home. At least those from the bridge were back at their old stands with card, roulette wheel, or holdup pistol, prepared for the seasonal roundup of fat stuff, including the more moneyed travelers to and from the Hills. By then water stood on the ice of the Platte and the snowbanks were shrinking along the darkened slopes, the gullies roaring. The mud of the worn trail was hub deep and the stage passengers had to get out and help lift the wheels.

The ironclad treasure coach overtook Morissa one day up on Sidney table, great balls of mud flying from the hoofs of the sweating horses as Owen and the others tipped up their Winchesters in greeting to the doctor as they passed. Morissa looked after the coach and pushed her young team along, too, for she was in a hurry today, going for a consultation on another head injury—man at the army post kicked by a mule. As she passed the railroad station the train came puffing in from the west, the treasure coach ready at the express office to unload its gold bricks. Morissa slowed a little, out of curiosity, but the guards waved her on. "No loitering, Doc!" Owen called as the agent came running out, shouting something to the driver.

So the doctor went on, but almost immediately a rattle and pound of hoofs made her look back. The coach, with its guards still riding, was swinging back toward the stage station. Morissa thought nothing of it until the next day. By then all the consultations and tests were over and it was decided not to operate on the unconscious man since there was no open wound as with John Callwin. Later perhaps, but not now.

The morning's bluster of spring snow was clearing off as Morissa stopped to buy her supplies. A great shouting and running went by, and she gathered up her skirts and ran toward the express office. Suddenly men with guns were everywhere and a crowd was pushing and milling on the board walks, all shouting, those who asked, "Was there a robbery?" getting the answer, "Three hundred thousand in gold bricks stole!"

Yesterday the express agent had refused to accept the gold because it came in a little late. So it was taken to the stage station and guarded all night. Today, a while before noon, the guards returned the gold to the express office and got a receipt for the three hundred thousand dollars.

Owen, the guard, saw Morissa and came over. "Damnedest thing you ever saw, Doc. The guards wanted to put the load into the big safe, but the agent gave them the receipts and said it was only an hour to train time, to leave it on the push truck. Then he locked the door and went out to eat. We got the town circled and there's no tracks on the fresh snow leavin', so the bricks're still here in Sidney."

The sheriff and the deputies were searching, Owen said, and Morissa knew that these included the former sheriff who made her promise to move in with Eddie at the homestead after his forgery, and give up her doctoring. Yet nothing was ever done to Ed about that and certainly a dozen other crimes, although he was openly in and out of town, bold as any other thief. Suddenly Morissa felt she must start for home at once.

At the edge of town two men with sawed-off shotguns demanded a look through her supplies. She laughed, but was angry too. "Perhaps you might look through my purse as well," she said sweetly. But one of the men did peer into the little satin-lined pockets of it, his big finger probing as though a gold brick might be there beside her lace handkerchief.

"We know you been shieldin' outlaws up there on the river. Could be sneakin' the bullion outta town," one of the men said, and to this Morissa had no reply.

Before she reached home a cowboy returning to Bosler's caught up. Hell yes, he said, the robbery was all cleaned up. They finally gave up searching people's rigs and went back to the express office and took another look in the cellar. There was just that little coal pile to look through—"and there they was, all them big gold bars!"

"All the big bars of the three hundred thousand?" Morissa asked.

"Well, seems it wasn't quite as much as that, ma'am. I hear it was more like eighty thousand."

So the Sidney robbery seemed solved, with probably nothing more than the express agent fired for it. Charley Adams snorted when he heard the story. But almost at once that other story was whispered around again, the story of a greater bullion haul right on their own trail, up north a ways. While this apparently happened some time back, before Fly Speck Billy was hanged, that was really a three hundred thousand dollar haul, and so far not one bar of all that gold had been discovered.

Three days after the Sidney theft of gold bricks, Morissa found Eddie Ellis at her door. He had ridden boldly up to the new hospital in midafternoon, and without a look around, as though he actually lived there, he turned the iron knob. He bothered with no preliminaries when Morissa faced him as the door opened, her hand reaching out to the jamb to hold him out—not so much as a hello for the woman who was still his wife.

"I come to get you in on that three hundred thousand dollars of gold stole some time ago," he said, speaking under the wide black hat tipped over his squinting eyes. "We'll be rich," he argued when Morissa made no reply. "I'll take you out of this stinking pus business, go see the world; Europe, Egypt—Scotland even," watching her slyly for pain at this reference to the past. "We'll go anywheres, a lifetime just layin' around. . . ."

"How can you expect anyone to believe such talk?" Morissa asked curiously, the first words she had spoken.

"I know," he said, swaggering his shoulders, and for a moment the bragging boy of five years ago was before her again, but now he turned wilier, more nervous. "I got to come in. People listen."

With both Ruth and Charley away, Morissa refused to take this man even into her kitchen, so she slammed the door behind her, and with her back against it listened to the agitated Eddie.

"I heard one o' the outfit spill the whole story before he got choked off," he insisted. "The man got caught ridin' one of the horses stole from the coach. They packed the gold off down the river from the wrecked coach, he said. Even offered to take us all to the place if we let him go," Eddie said, growing expansive.

"Who's this *he?*" Morissa asked, and to her plain disbelief Eddie answered, "Oh, I know where the gold is all right, the whole three hundred thousand!" rolling the sum like a bonbon on his tongue.

But the woman who was his legal wife only smiled a little and so he had to add details, make it stick. "I can show you! The gold's hid just below where the Niobrara cuts down into a canyon, and there's three pines standin' on the bluffs, and a little cave below," he continued, needing to talk faster and faster as a man must against an unreceptive woman. "Nobody's knowin' how to dispose of the stuff without gettin' caught. So they hid the whole kaboodle until things blow over."

"Who are these men that you can't name them?" Morissa demanded.

That made Eddie cautious again. "You ain't said if you'll help me."

"And I won't. I'm no thief. And even if I were, how would I know the gold is still there? Everybody knows the story—the robbers, the law, and the express company detectives. That's a lot of money."

"I know it ain't gone," Ed maintained doggedly. "You won't believe that we—that they got the gold?"

From that slip, plainly deliberate, Morissa realized Eddie Ellis had not been in this robbery either, only once more wished that he had been. She told him there was talk enough about such a robbery, and some ugly rumors of more shooting down at a place called Fly Speck Billy's cave, where she heard the haul was supposed to be hidden.

"Yeh, to fool the treasure hunters," Eddie said, easier again, his thumbs hooked in his cartridge belt. "The gold's still there and I got a good scheme to turn it into cash. You just start out with the buggy—"

"Me?"

"Yeh, start out like you was going on a call up past Snake Creek flats and keep going 'til you see Box Butte off northeast. I'll meet you there."

"And what is the rest of my contribution to this crazy scheme to be?"

"It ain't crazy. You can get some of the bricks out of the country in your buggy and smuggle them across the border into Mexico."

Morissa looked at Eddie Ellis in amazement. Why, this was a crazy man, really insane. "You have it all planned so I'm the one to get shot by the officers sure to be watching the border."

"They won't suspect you. People think you're honest, a doc goin' about her business."

"And who's to finance this long trip to Mexico?"

"You got the money, and can borrow what more we need."

So that was the scheme, Morissa thought, get her out alone in that empty country up there, with money, and her team and buggy to sell, even a husband's share in her property here.

But Eddie Ellis was too self-concerned to see the doctor's suspicions. "You meet me at Box Butte. I'll give you until two weeks from today to get everything set. Be there," he said, as though it were settled. As he left he stopped to look all around the neat new building, with its trees and shrubs already growing up so well. Then he walked to the bridge and across it, leading his horse, giving everyone plenty of time to see that he had come from Morissa's, from his wife's place.

191

At first the busy doctor tried to ignore Ed's presence around Huff Johnson's, but he rode over toward the hospital every day at dusk now, and past it, to some hideout—so late that no one could see he went on. Once more the people around the bridge began to stand away from Morissa Kirk, and a settler let a child die because he wouldn't call this doctor in league with outlaws.

Morissa did have one happy interlude during this time. One of Lorette's little girls came riding over, clinging to her barebacked Indian pony. A friend wanted to see Dr. Kirk at the bridge. Morissa went. It was Dr. Walter Reed, looking much as he had six years ago when he started west, his fine earnest eyes very alert. He was on the way to his new station at Fort Robinson. "I just remembered your letter from here some time ago, and the report of your head surgery in the medical journals."

So Morissa took him over the bridge to cook him an antelope steak while the horses of his troop escort were fed and rested.

He seemed pleased with her little hospital, and stopped a moment before the flower-trimmed sampler that Lorette had worked:

> If you want to be true physicians and learn to serve MAN in all his ills, go out to these far places. There each of you must be what he is, without PRETENCE, standing before everyone in all his VIRTUES and his faults, and open to the call of every victim of the violence and the disease of the wilderness. There I think you may discover something of the NATURE of man; there I think is the WORK for me, and for YOU.
>
> Dr. Walter Reed

"Did I say that? How appalling!"

"Yes, you said something like that to our gathering of young doctors on your way west, remember? I took it down. The patients like it."

"They do?" Doctor Reed said, and fell silent awhile. "Seems incredible." A fine smile lifted the man's eyebrows. "But we get humbled down out here, don't we?"

Now EVEN THE WIFE of the patient with smallpox hurried away from the hospital if she could when she saw Morissa come. "They insist you are bringing outlaws to the river again," Rem Smith told the doctor, still mouthing his words a little from the scarring that drew the lips sidewise. Rem was working out his bill for Morissa by helping to care for her little diphtheria patients.

"You mean they think I'm taking up with Ed?" she asked.

"Well, he's hanging around, and he is your husband, for all that they can see you sometimes favor Tris Polk a little."

Morissa nodded. They were right, and she should do something final about this situation. But the time Ed had set for the meeting at Box Butte was just two days off. When he saw she was not going, he would surely give up, leave.

Then that night he rode up to the door instead of passing as he had before. "Remember, day after tomorrow. Better get there!" he warned.

"You'll remember I told you I was no thief," Morissa snapped.

"You'll come!" Eddie replied softly, and in surprise the doctor saw the gun out of its holster, the small black hole of it pointed squarely upon her, and for a moment it seemed a symbolic gesture from the man who was never quite one. She slammed the door upon him and stood with her back against it, suddenly shaken with pity.

A FEW NIGHTS LATER Blaze seemed restless and Morissa got up to look out, but there was nothing in the windy darkness. She slipped out of her dark dressing gown into a hospital coverall and made one more round through the hospital rooms to look in on the cowboy with a broken hip and then the diphtheria children with Rem Smith beside them in his white cotton uniform. He turned up the shaded lamp a little and gave the doctor a crooked, one-sided smile and a nod. So she went to the disinfecting room and then back to her dressing gown and her bed.

It seemed she was hardly asleep when a shot awoke her. There was a running outside, and then another shot through a red light that flared up suddenly all along the front of the building. Morissa jerked the door open into a wall of flame blazing along the foundation and up in the shingles, too, the strong south wind blowing the fire hard against the house, the smoke stinking of kerosene. She flung a bucket of water against the burning door so it smoldered, and went through it to pull out the hose. But when she turned the pressure on, the water squirted from a dozen places, holes hacked with a knife. The whole building seemed afire as Rem Smith burst through the door with the two sick children bundled in their blankets, shouting, "Too late, Doc! Get everybody out an' let 'er go!"

Choked by a sob, Morissa ran for the rifle and fired three rapid distress shots into the air. By this time the door at the other end was burning, too, so the doctor helped carry the cowboy's cot away and sent the smallpox patient off by himself, to roll up in a buffalo robe. They carried out the surgical instruments and the new microscope, the hospital records and the drug cabinets.

By now Rem was throwing things out the back of the center building. Morissa lugged the piles away, helped by the men who came running from the bridge and the roadhouses into the red light. Finally the smoke boiled through around Rem and they had to drag him out, his arms full of Morissa's dresses.

When the doctor got some of the smoke out of Rem's lungs, they stood back and watched the roof flame up very bright the full length and then fall in, the children crying a little in fright. Morissa had moved off to the side to be alone in her loss, the dressing gown blowing about her as she watched the sturdy log walls stand against the fire inside and then finally begin to go, too, crashing inward.

Then, as the last of the front walls went in under the push of the wind, Rem remembered something. Calling it out loud to the others, he said he had seen a man set the fire along the foundation and shot at him twice, the last time as he dodged off almost to the trees.

With a lantern Etty and a dozen others went to search the ground in the direction Rem motioned, moving the light back and forth over the dead lawn and flower beds. Then they stopped, gathering in a dark little knot about the lantern. Someone called Morissa, and slowly she moved that way, looking back at her smoking hospital as though she could not leave. When she stopped to examine the man who had set the fire she saw it was Eddie Ellis, already stiff and cold.

SOON AFTER DAWN Morissa went to Clarke's to telegraph the sheriff, Ed's father, and Robin and Jack. She wanted to send a message to Tris, but there was nothing that could be said. So she hurried back to help prepare a place for her patients, still out in the cold morning air. Charley was in from his homestead, so she had him whitewash the sod-house used for provisions, with the old wagon heater set up to warm the two diphtheria children. The other patients would have to get along in tents for now, as would Morissa and the rest. By night everybody seemed comfortable enough.

The next day Jack rode in on a hired horse from Sidney. He was a fine, tall young man now, very serious in his new profession and his new position as protector of his sister. "I've come to take you with me," he said. "We need you as head of our hospital."

So Morissa hid her face against his dark coat a moment while he looked angrily at the ashes blowing around, and at all the people come to stand and stare.

"Jacobs at Sidney has agreed to take over your patients," Jack added.

It was fine to hear words like this, to see so many people wanting to help. The next morning an offer to help came from Dr. Reed up at Fort Robinson, too, and in her gratitude all Morissa could do was flee to the errands with her patients. Roadhouse crowds, settlers, travelers, cowboys, and Sidneyites came, all wanting to look at the ashes. They also wanted to see this Jack who had taken over the dispensary, measuring out Epsom salts, calomel, cough syrup, and a dozen other pharmaceuticals, everybody suddenly in need of dosing. And with their small packets in their hands many still lingered, finally daring to ask Charley or Ruth or even Rem what Morissa planned to do. No one knew, although it was plain that Jack had come to take her east.

Then someone noticed that a buggy drawing up carried a man from the Sidney bank. With a blue-backed paper in his hand he went into Morissa's tent and then came out with her, driving up past the grove to a ridge where they could see all her stock and land. When they returned, the banker was gesturing, the sweep of his hand including all the place.

There, with everybody watching and Jack as witness, Morissa started to sign the papers, the people standing away, but Robin Thomas was suddenly there too. Once more his shoulder was the refuge of his stepdaughter. He had brought a letter from Sidney, from Tris, waiting and very anxious but unwilling to cause Morissa more embarrassment just now. "You must know in your heart that I am ready to do anything that is within the power of a man, as though I already stood proudly beside you as your husband. . . ."

Husband, Morissa thought, all the things around her here suddenly like the shimmering heat dance of the midsummer prairies. Husband. Not a father oversolicitous of his good name, or a warped and pitiful son seeking a mother, but a husband to stand beside her, a wife. For a moment it seemed to Morissa that she must cry right there before them all, cry out of the flooding of all her being.

But even in this moment there was no privacy—with the papers in her hand still to be completed. And as Morissa signed the last, once more a man on horseback came galloping, this time John Callwin, his plow mare heaving from the run. "Miss Morissa!" he shouted, sliding off beside her, embarrassed by his need to interrupt, but dogged in his determination to have his say. "Miss Morissa, we are sorry that everything you built here is gone, all your work and your grief for nothing. So we got up a petition asking you to stay. We want you to build a good new hospital, brick, so it won't burn easy. There will be a railroad sometime, and a town, but now"—he rubbed at the plate under his scalp without noticing it—"for now we want to help start the new building right away."

Because there was no comment from Morissa Kirk, no reply, he looked uneasily at the banker still holding the blue-backed documents. But John Callwin was a stubborn man. Firmly, if futilely, he undid the roll of paper he carried. "Over two hundred names," he said, "and we could get you a thousand more if we had time. And every man pledging you something, maybe only a few days' work, or five dollars—all we got. But some's gone as high as a hundred dollars, a couple five hundred, and Sid Martin's put himself down for a thousand."

"Oh!" Morissa exclaimed, "I—"

"Well, Doctor," the banker interrupted cheerfully, "seems I got to you just in time!"

John Callwin's face went dark at this show of triumph, and other settlers moved in closer. "You ain't sold out to this land-grabbin' interest hog," one of them demanded, "leavin' us flat?"

"Oh, no, no!" the doctor cried, with blurring eyes. "The papers I signed weren't a deed but a mortgage. I was just borrowing money to rebuild the hospital." For a moment Morissa Kirk looked around into the earnest, browned faces, from the farthest and the smallest to big John Callwin before her, and in all the crowd she missed only one.

"You can't know how proud I am, how very proud that you—you . . ." Then her voice broke and she turned her face away, for it was not fitting that all these people see their doctor cry.

GIANTS
IN THE EARTH

GIANTS
IN
THE EARTH

A CONDENSATION OF THE NOVEL BY

O. E. Rölvaag

ILLUSTRATED BY HERB TAUSS

Per Hansa left his native Norway
to stake a claim on America's Great Plains,
bringing with him his wife Beret
and their three young children.
For Per and the children, their new home
offered adventure and abundance.
But for Beret, pregnant with a fourth
child, the vast empty prairie
seemed, in the fullest sense of the words,
God forsaken. Could body or soul
survive in such desolation?

O. E. Rölvaag, like Per Hansa,
came from Norway to America
as a young man. His masterpiece
Giants in the Earth has won acclaim on both
sides of the Atlantic for its
psychological insight into
pioneer life.

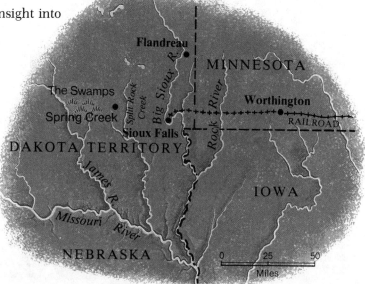

Chapter 1

BRIGHT, CLEAR SKY over a plain so wide that the rim of the heavens cut down on it around the entire horizon. . . . Bright, clear sky, today, tomorrow, and for all time to come.

And sun! And still more sun! It set the heavens afire every morning; it grew with the day to quivering golden light—then softened into all the shades of red and purple as evening fell. Pure color everywhere. A gust of wind, sweeping across the plain, threw into life waves of yellow, blue, and green. Now and then a dead black wave would race over the scene, a cloud's gliding shadow.

It was late afternoon. A small caravan was pushing its way through the tall grass. The track that it left behind was like the wake of a boat—except that instead of widening out astern it closed in again. "Tish-ah!" said the grass. "Tish-ah, tish-ah!" Nothing like this had ever happened to it before. "Tish-ah, tish-ah!" it cried.

A stocky, broad-shouldered man walked at the head of the caravan. He seemed shorter than he really was, because of the tall grass around him and the broad-brimmed hat of straw which he wore. A few steps behind him followed a blond, sunburned boy of about nine. From the looks of these two, and still more from their gait, it was easy to guess that here walked father and son.

Behind them a team of oxen jogged along, drawing a vehicle which once might have been a wagon, but which by now, on account of its many and grave infirmities, should have been consigned to the scrap heap. Over the wagon box long willow saplings had been bent in the form of arches, six of them in all. On these arches, and tied down to the body on each side, were spread two handwoven blankets; on top of the blankets were thrown two sheepskin robes, which were used for bed-coverings at night. The rear of the wagon was stowed full of articles, all the way up to the top. A large immigrant chest at the bottom devoured much of the space; around and above it were piled household utensils, tools, and clothing.

Hitched to this wagon and trailing behind was another vehicle, home-made and quaintly constructed. Considerably wider than the first wagon, it was also loaded full of provisions and household gear, covered with canvas and lashed down. Both wagons creaked and groaned loudly as they moved, breaking the silence of centuries.

A short distance behind them followed a brindle cow. The caravan moved so slowly that she occasionally had time to stop and snatch a few mouthfuls. What little she got in this way she sorely needed. Soon it would be night, and then she would have to furnish milk for the evening porridge, for all the company up ahead.

Across the front end of the first wagon lay a rough piece of plank. On it sat a woman with a white kerchief over her head, driving the oxen. Against her thigh rested the blond head of a little girl, stretched out on the plank, sleeping sweetly. Now and then the hand of the mother moved across the child's face to chase away the mosquitoes. Beyond the girl sat a boy about seven—a well-grown lad, his skin deeply tanned, a certain clever, watchful gleam in his eyes. With hands folded over one knee, he looked straight ahead.

This was the caravan of Per Hansa, who with his family and all his earthly possessions was moving west from Fillmore County, Minnesota, to Dakoka Territory. There he intended to take up land and build himself a home; he was going to do something remarkable out there which should become known far and wide. No lack of opportunity in that country, he had been told!

Per Hansa himself strode ahead and laid out the course; the boy Ole followed closely after and explored it. Beret, the wife, drove the oxen and took care of little Anna Marie, nicknamed And-Ongen (The Duckling), who was usually bubbling over with happiness. Hans Kristian, whose everyday name was Store-Hans (meaning Big Hans, to distinguish him from his godfather, who was also named Hans, but who, of course, was three times his size), sat there on the wagon and saw to it that everyone attended to business. The cow Rosie trailed behind, switching her tail, following the caravan into the endless vista of the plain.

"Tish-ah, tish-ah!" cried the grass. "Tish-ah, tish-ah! . . ."

THE CARAVAN SEEMED miserably frail, unspeakably forlorn, as it crept along at a snail's pace over the boundless prairie. Of road or trail there lay not a trace ahead; the course was always the same—straight west. For more than three weeks now the caravan had been crawling across the plain. Early in the journey it had passed through Blue Earth; it had left Chain Lakes behind; and one fine day it had crept into Jackson, on the Des Moines River. But that seemed ages ago. West of Worthington, Per Hansa had lost the trail completely. At this moment he did not know where he was, nor how to get to the place he had to reach. But Split Rock Creek, which was meant to be his next landmark, must lie out there somewhere; if he could only find it, he could pick his way farther without much trouble. According to his directions he should have been there two or three days ago. Oh, my God! If something didn't turn up soon!

Every now and then Per Hansa's bearded face bent forward and he glanced at an old silver watch he carried in his left hand. It was now nearing six o'clock. He turned and spoke to the boy walking behind. "Go back and drive for a while, Ole. Talk to Mother, too, so that it won't be so lonesome for her."

"I'm not tired yet!" said the boy, loath to leave the vanguard.

"Go back, anyway!"

"Do you think we'll catch up with them tonight, Dad?"

"Good lord, no! They've got too long a start on us. Look sharp, now. If you see anything suspicious, sing out!"

Per Hansa strode onward, and Ole waited till the train came up. Then Store-Hans jumped down nimbly, while the other climbed up and took his seat.

"Have you seen anything?" the mother asked Ole in an anxious voice.

"Why, no . . . not yet," answered the boy evasively.

"I wonder if we shall ever see them again," she said, as if speaking to herself. "This seems to be taking us to the end of the world!"

Store-Hans looked up at her from beside the wagon. Too bad that Mother should be so scared! "Yes, Mother, but since we're both steering for the sun, we'll both land in the same place, won't we? The sun is a sure guide, you know." These were the very words which he had heard his father use the night before. To Store-Hans the truth of them seemed as clear as the sun itelf. He hurried up alongside his father and laid a hand in his—he always felt safer thus. The two walked on side by side.

On and on they went toward the sunset. Ole drove, and the mother took little And-Ongen up in her lap and leaned backward to give relief to her tired muscles. The child's lively chatter made her forget anxiety for a moment. Ole was driving like a full-grown man, getting more speed out of the oxen than she had done.

Out on the skyline the huge plain now began to swell and rise. Although this elevation lay somewhat out of his course, Per Hansa swung over and held toward it.

The sun's golden luster had faded now into a reddish hue. The great ball retreated farther and farther into the western sky; then it sank suddenly. The spell of evening quickly crowded in and laid hold of them all; Rosie lifted her voice in a long moo, which died out slowly in the great stillness. Suddenly the plain had grown desolate. Low down above the little hill a few fleecy clouds hovered, glowing with a mellow light.

The mother drew herself upright. "Per," she called wearily, "aren't we going to stop soon?"

"Pretty soon." He did not slacken his pace.

She shifted the child on her lap and began to weep silently. Ole pretended not to notice; he kept his eyes resolutely fixed on the scene ahead. "Dad," he shouted after a while, "I see a wood over there to the west!"

"Are there any people there, do you think?" Store-Hans asked his father.

"People? Lord, no! There isn't a soul in these parts."

The somber blue haze was now closing rapidly in on the caravan. At last Per Hansa halted. He faced the oxen, held his arms out, shouted "Whoa!"—and the creaking stopped for that day.

Preparations for the night were soon made; each had his own task and was now well used to it. Store-Hans brought firewood from the hind wagon. Ole got the fireplace ready and saw that there was water enough in the keg. The father unyoked the oxen and turned them loose; then he milked Rosie. After that he made up a bed for the whole family under the wagon. The mother placed the pot to boil and set the table: that is, she spread a blanket on the ground, laid spoons on it, and placed bowls for the milk and porridge. Meanwhile she had to keep an eye on And-

Ongen, toddling about in the grass nearby, laughing and prattling.

Finally the mother called to the others that supper was ready. The evening milk was divided between two bowls and set before them; Rosie, poor thing, was not giving much these days. The father said that he didn't care for milk this evening; it had a tangy taste, he thought. But when Ole also began to complain of the taste and asked for water, the father grew stern and ordered him to get that milk down quick! There was nothing on the table but milk and porridge.

They sat around in silence after they were done. Then little And-Ongen repeated the evening prayer in a tiny voice: "Thanks to Thee, our Lord and Maker. . . ." After the amen she climbed up into her mother's lap and threw her arms around her neck.

"Oh, how quickly it grows dark out here!" the mother murmured.

"Well," Per Hansa said dryly, "the sooner the day's over, the sooner the next day comes!" He sat on the tongue of the wagon, smoking his pipe.

Now up from the horizon whence they had come swelled a supernatural light—a glow of pale yellow and green, mingled with strange touches of red and gold. It spread upward as they watched; the glow grew stronger, like the witching light of a fen fire. All sat silently gazing. It was And-Ongen, hanging around her mother's neck, who first found her voice. "Look! She is coming up again!"

In solemn grandeur the moon swung up above the plain. A hush fell on their spirits as they watched her rise. The silvery beams grew stronger; slowly the light mellowed into a mist of green and yellow and blue. Per Hansa at last got up, knocked out his pipe, and wound his watch. These duties done, he gave the order to turn in for the night.

A little while later they all lay under the quilts, gazing off into the opalescent glow of the moonlight. When the mother thought that the children had gone to sleep she asked soberly, "Do you suppose we'll ever find the others again?"

"Oh yes, I'm sure of it—if they haven't sunk through the ground!"

This was all Per Hansa said. He yawned, long and heavily, as if he were very sleepy, and turned away from her.

TRUTH TO TELL, Per Hansa was not a bit sleepy. For a long while he lay staring into the night. Although the evening had grown cool, from time to time sweat started out on his body as thoughts which he could not banish persisted in his mind. It had been just the same last night, too, and the night before. And now, the moment he had lain down, these heavy thoughts had seized upon him with renewed strength. He recalled keenly all the scruples and misgivings that had obsessed his wife before they had started out on this long journey. And that wife of his had more sense than most people. . . . No, it wasn't a pleasant situation for Per Hansa, by any means. He had not seen a happy moment, day or night, since the mishap had struck them on the second afternoon this side of Jackson. There the first wagon had got stuck in a mudhole; in pulling it out they had wrecked it so hopelessly that he had been forced to put back to Jackson for repairs. Under the circumstances it had seemed to him senseless to hold up the rest of the company four days; they must go on without him; he'd come along all right, in his own good time.

So they had given him full instructions about the course he was to follow and the halting places where he was to stop for the night; it had all seemed so simple to him. Then they had started on together—Tönseten, who knew the way, and Hans Olsa, and the two Solum boys, Henry and Sam. They all had horses and strong new wagons. They traveled fast, those fellows!

If he only had paid some attention to Hans Olsa, who for a long while had insisted on waiting for him. It was entirely his own doing that Hans Olsa and the others had gone on, leaving him behind. He soon had learned that it wasn't so easy going alone; hadn't he lost his way altogether the other day, in the midst of a fog and drizzling rain? Until late afternoon he hadn't the faintest idea what direction he was taking. It was after this that he had formed the habit of keeping far ahead of the caravan. He simply couldn't endure listening to Beret's constant questions—questions which he found himself unable to answer.

The only thing he felt sure of was that he wasn't on the right track; otherwise he would have come across traces of their camps. It was getting to be a matter of life and death for him to find the trail—and find it soon. Oh yes, he realized it all too well—a matter of life and death. There weren't many supplies left in the wagon. He had depended on his old comrade and fellow fisherman from Norway, Hans Olsa, for everything.

Per Hansa heaved a deep sigh. It was easy enough for Hans Olsa! He had ample means, and he had a wife in whose heart there wasn't a speck of fear. And they had Tönseten, too, and his wife, Kjersti, both of them used to America. Why, they could talk the language and everything. And then there were the Solum boys, who had actually been born in this country. But here was he, the newcomer, who owned nothing and knew nothing, groping about with his dear ones in the endless wilderness!

He wondered why he had ever left Minnesota. He could easily have found a job there and stayed until Beret got up from childbed; then he could have moved west next spring. This had been what she had wanted, though she had never said it in so many words.

Surely it would be another tough day tomorrow. If only that confounded wagon didn't go to pieces again!

The night wore on. The children slept quietly and peacefully. The mother also seemed to have found rest at last. Little by little Per Hansa slipped the quilt off, crept out of bed, and pulled on his trousers and shoes.

Outside the moonlight shimmered. Per Hansa looked for the North Star, turned about until he had it over his right shoulder, then glanced at his watch and looked back as if taking a bearing on the wagons and the star. The next moment he faced about resolutely and hurried off westward, setting his course toward the point where he thought the crest of the hill must lie.

It was farther off than he had thought. He had walked for a solid hour before he finally reached what he felt to be the highest point. There he looked at his watch again, and then at the North Star, trying to fix his bearings.

On the other side of the ridge the slope was steeper; underbrush covered it. First Per Hansa searched the northerly slope, beyond the edge of the thicket. He stooped as he went, his eyes scanning every foot of ground. When he found no trace of what he was looking for, he searched in the opposite direction; but he discovered nothing on this tack, either.

Now he began to walk along the edge of the thicket, in and out, crisscrossing the line in every direction, searching frantically. Sweat ran off him in streams. All at once, right at the edge of the woods, he struck a piece of level ground with a large clearing on it; in the middle of this clearing lay a round patch in the grass. Per Hansa threw himself on his knees; he bent and sniffed the ground. His hands shook as he dug. . . . Yes—here there had been a fire! The smell of the ashes was still fresh. His eyes had grown so moist and dim that he had to wipe them. But he wasn't crying—no, not yet!

He began to crawl around on all fours, farther and farther down the slope. Suddenly he stopped, sat up on his haunches, and held something in his hand. Crumbling it, he sniffed at it. "If it isn't fresh horse dung!" His voice rang with joy. He got up, walking confidently. The underbrush thickened as he made his way down the slope, and now he heard a stream. Here, then, was Split Rock Creek; and here they had camped, as Tönseten had said they would.

Once he had reached the creek it did not take him long to find the ford the others had used; the ruts were as fresh and deep as if they had been made that very day. For a while he paused and looked about him. Had they chosen the best crossing after all? The bank of the creek on the other side looked pretty steep. At last he waded out into the water. Then, stepping out on the opposite shore, he stood as if rooted to the ground. What in the devil!

Per Hansa bent and picked up the object that lay before him in the moonlight. He turned it over and over in his hands, then smelled it. If it isn't one of Hans Olsa's dried mutton legs! He gazed with deep thankfulness into the moonlight. Yes, that's the way it goes, when people have more than they can take care of! He stuck the mutton leg under his arm, and whistling a Nordland ballad, he crossed the creek again.

On the way back he took his own time. The night was fair and mild. His aching weariness was gone. His wife and children were sleeping safe and sound; they still had food for a couple of weeks; and now he had found the trail again and could be certain of it to Sioux Falls.

When he drew near enough to the wagons to make them out clearly in the moonlight, a shiver passed over him. Wasn't that someone sitting there on the wagon tongue? Surely that was a human form? In growing apprehension he hurried on.

"Good heavens, Beret! What are you doing out here in the middle of the night?" His voice was full of alarm, yet softened by concern.

"It felt awful to lie there alone, after you had gone." Her voice was hoarse with weeping.

"You shouldn't lie awake that way in the night!" he said reproachfully.

"How can I sleep? You might have told me! I know very well what's the matter!" Suddenly she ran over to him and flung her arms around his neck. Her tears broke in a flood of emotion; she wept long and bitterly.

"Now calm yourself, dear. You *must* calm yourself, Beret-girl!" He had put his arm lovingly around her, but found it hard to speak. "Don't you see that I've got one of Hans Olsa's dried mutton legs under my arm?"

That night Per Hansa was good to his wife.

Chapter 2

ON THE SIDE OF A HILL which sloped gently southeast down to a creek on the prairie, Hans Olsa stood, laying turf. He was a man with a huge frame, and his strength was in proportion to his bulk. At this moment he was building a sod-house.

For a man of his massive build, Hans Olsa's motions were unusually quick and agile; but he worked by fits and starts today. His large, rugged features were drawn and furrowed with anxiety. At times he stopped altogether and gazed to the east. No—nothing in sight yet. God Almighty! What can have become of Per Hansa?

Beyond the sod walls a tent had been pitched; a wagon was drawn up beside it. On the ground outside of the tent stood a stove and other articles of furniture. A stout, healthy-looking woman, whose face radiated kindliness, was busy preparing the midday meal. She sang to herself as she worked. A ten-year-old girl she called Sofie was helping her.

Less than a quarter of a mile away, to the southeast, a finished sod-house rose on the slope. Smoke was winding up from it at this moment. This house, which had been built the previous fall, belonged to Syvert Tönseten. Some distance north, though out of sight beyond a hillock, another sod-house was also under construction. There the two Solum boys had driven down their claim stakes. Tönseten's completed house and the half-finished ones marked the beginning of the settlement on Spring Creek.

The woman, who had been bustling about, now turned to watch her husband. At last she went over to him. "Hans," she said, "I think you ought to go look for them."

He put a strip of sod in place. "We haven't the faintest idea of where to look."

"I know. But it would make us all feel better . . . as if we were doing something."

Hans Olsa let his hands fall to his sides. "I know this much—you don't often find a smarter fellow than Per Hansa. That's what makes it so queer! I begin to fear that he's gone on west of us somewhere."

Hans Olsa slumped down on the wall, the picture of dejection. His wife found a place beside him. Together they sat there in silence. The same fear that he felt had long since gripped her heart also.

"I feel so sorry for Beret, poor thing, and the children. I think she is with child again." She paused. "I dreamed about them last night . . . a bad dream."

Her husband glanced at her. "I suppose I'll never forgive myself for not waiting for him." He got up heavily and laid another strip of turf. "He's always been like that, Per Hansa; he never would take help from any man. But this time he's carried it too far!"

His wife made no answer to this. She was watching a short, stout man with a reddish beard who had started up the slope from the house to the south of them. He had cheeks like two rosy apples, a quick step, and eyes that flitted all about; he was noted among them for his glib tongue.

"Here comes Tönseten," said the woman.

"Seen anything of them yet, Hans Olsa?" asked the man.

Hans Olsa wheeled on him. "You haven't caught sight of them yourself, Syvert, have you?"

"Caught sight of them? Why, man alive, that's just what I've come up here to tell you! I've had them in sight for over an hour. Good lord! It won't be long before they arrive here, at the rate they're coming!"

"What's that you say?" the others burst out. "Where are they?"

"I reckon Per Hansa must have got off his course a little. Look westward."

Sure enough, out of the west a little caravan was crawling toward them. "Can that be them? I really believe it is!" said Hans Olsa, hardly daring to give vent to his joy.

"Of *course* it is!" cried his wife excitedly. "Thank God!"

"You might as well go and put your coffeepot on the stove, Mother Sörine!" Tönseten said. "That Kjersti of mine is coming over soon. In half an hour we'll have the lost sheep back in the fold!"

"Yes!" cried Hans Olsa. "Heavens and earth, Sörine, fetch out the best you've got! Per, Per, is it really you, old boy?"

Tönseten coughed, and gave the woman a sly wink.

"Look here, Mother Sörine," he said, "won't you be good enough, please, to take a peek at Hans Olsa's Sunday bottle? Not that I want anything to drink. But think of that poor woman out there all this time without a drop! And I'd be willing to bet that Per Hansa wouldn't object to having his stomach warmed up a little, too!" At that they burst out laughing. Work was resumed on the house, and Mother Sörine went off to make preparations for the reception of the wanderers.

Before a half hour had passed, the caravan came crawling up the slope. Both families stood ready to receive the new arrivals; Hans Olsa and Sörine, Tönseten and his Kjersti, all watched intently the approaching company; but the girl Sofie couldn't possess her patience any longer and ran down to meet them. She took Store-Hans by the hand and fell in beside him; the first question she asked was whether he hadn't been terribly scared at night.

As the slope of the hill grew steeper, the oxen had to bend to the yoke. Per Hansa shouted boisterously, "Hey there, folks! Don't be standing around loafing, now! It's only the middle of the afternoon. Haven't you anything to do around here?"

"Coffee time, Per Hansa." Tönseten bubbled with good spirits.

"You've found us at last!" said Hans Olsa with a deep, happy chuckle. He didn't seem able to let go of Per Hansa's hand.

"Found you? Why, devil take it, it's no trick to follow a course out here, though I guess we stood a little too far to the westward, between Sioux Falls and here. So *this* is the place, is it? The pastures of Goshen in the land of Egypt, eh?"

"Just so, just so!" cried Tönseten, nodding and laughing.

Beret and the child had now got down from the wagon; the other two women hovered around her, drawing her toward the tent. But she hung back for a moment; she wanted to look around.

Was this the place? *Here!* Could it be possible? She stole a glance at the others, at the half-completed hut, and suddenly it struck her that *here something was about to go wrong.* A great lump came up in her throat; she swallowed hard to keep it back and forced herself to look calm. She mustn't give way to tears now, in the midst of all this joy.

Then she followed the other two women into the tent. Sörine patted her on the shoulder. "Come, get your things off, Beret; loosen your clothes. Here's water for washing. Let down your hair, and take your time about it."

The moment they had left her she crossed the tent to look out of the door. How will human beings be able to endure this place? she thought. Why, there isn't even a thing that one can *hide behind!* Her sensitive, rather beautiful face was full of blank dismay; she turned away from the door and began to loosen her dress.

Outside the tent Ole stood with his hand resting on one of the oxen. He was disgusted; the older people never would get done talking—when he, too, might have had a word to put in!

"Hadn't we better unhitch the oxen, Dad?"

"Yes, yes—that's right, Ole. We might as well camp here for the night, since we've run across some folks we used to know. How about it, you fellows?" He turned to the other men. "I suppose there's a little more land left around here, isn't there, after you've got through?"

"Land? " said Tönseten. "Per Hansa, take whatever you please, from here to the Pacific Ocean!"

"You must take a look around as soon as you can," Hans Olsa said. "In the meanwhile I've put down a stake for you on the quarter section that lies north of mine. You would be next to the creek there; and then you and I would be the nearest neighbors, just as we've always planned."

Per Hansa drew a deep breath, as if filling himself with life's great goodness. "Well, well, we'll have to settle all that later, Hans Olsa. For the present I can only say that I'm deeply thankful to you. Unhitch the beasts there, Ole! And now, if you folks have got anything handy to either eat or drink, I'll accept it with pleasure."

"Or *both*, Per Hansa!" put in Tönseten.

"Yes, both, Syvert. I won't refuse!"

Soon they were all gathered around a white cloth which Mother Sörine had spread on the ground. On one side of it lay a whole leg of dried mutton; on the other a heap of *flatbröd*, with cheese, bread, and butter; in the center of the cloth stood a large bowl of milk, and from the direction of the stove the breeze wafted to them a pleasant odor of bacon and coffee. Mother Sörine urged them all to sit down. The stocky figure of Per Hansa, squatting next to his wife, rocked back and forth in delight.

"Come, Sörine, you sit down, too!" he cried. "I guess we've fallen in with gentlefolks, by the looks of things around here."

By this time they were all laughing together. In the midst of the jollification came Sörine, carrying a plate with a large bottle and a dram glass on it. "Here, take this off my hands, Hans Olsa. You will know what to do with it!"

Tönseten bubbled over in his admiration for her. "Sweet Sörine! What a blessing it must be to have a wife like you!"

"Stop your foolishness!" said Tönseten's own wife, Kjersti, but her voice didn't sound too severe.

For a long while they continued to sit around the cloth, eating, drinking, and thoroughly enjoying themselves. Hans Olsa's loud voice led the cheerful talk; his ponderous bulk was the center of the merriment; it seemed as if he would never tire of gazing into that bearded, roguish face of Per Hansa's. They sat on until the first blue haze of evening began to spread eastward over the plain. The talk now drifted to questions of a more serious nature; of their immediate prospects; of what the future might hold in store for them; of land and crops, and of the new kingdom which they were about to found.

As the evening shadows deepened, the conversation gradually died into silence. A peculiar mood came drifting in with the dusk. It seemed to lurk in the vastness and endlessness surrounding them. It brought vague premonitions to them, difficult to interpret. . . . No telling what might happen out here. They were so far from the world . . . cut off from the haunts of their fellow beings . . . so terribly far!

Per Hansa was the first to rouse himself and throw off the spell. He jumped up; a shiver passed over him. "I believe we've all lost our senses, every last one of us!" he burst out. "Here we sit around celebrating in the middle of summer, as if it were the Christmas holidays! Come on, let's go over to see our new home! Ole, hitch up the oxen again and bring the wagons."

With these commands he walked rapidly away; the others had almost to run in order to keep up with him.

"It lies high," he observed after a while, when they had looked over all the plowland. "There must be a fine view from the top of that hill."

Soon the three men reached the highest point. It was so spacious and beautiful to stand high above the prairie. Suddenly, Per Hansa began to step more cautiously; he sniffed the air like an animal; in a moment he stopped beside a small depression in the ground and stood gazing at it intently.

"There are people buried here," he said quietly. "That is a grave!"

"Oh no, Per Hansa! It can't be." Hans Olsa bent over and picked up a small stone. "That's a queer-looking piece of stone! I almost believe people have shaped it for some use. Here, see what you make of it, Syvert."

Tönseten's ruddy face grew thoughtful as he examined the object. "By thunder! It certainly looks as if the Indians had been here. Now isn't that rotten luck?"

"I'm afraid so," said Per Hansa. Then he added sharply, "But we needn't shout the fact from the housetops, you know! It takes very little to scare some folks around here."

He walked hastily down the hill; at the foot he called to Ole, telling him not to drive any farther. "No use in building farther away from you than is absolutely necessary," he said to Hans Olsa. "It's going to be lonesome for the womenfolk at times."

A while later Tönseten made his way homeward, and Per Hansa returned with Hans Olsa to the wagons, where Beret and the children were waiting. He asked Hans Olsa about the line between their two quarter sections; then he asked Beret and Hans Olsa to help pick the best building site. His words had in them a ring of determination. This vast stretch of beautiful land was to be his—yes, *his*—and no ghost of a dead Indian would drive him away! His heart began to expand with a mighty exaltation.

EARLY THE NEXT MORNING Per Hansa set out on the fifty-two-mile journey to Sioux Falls. He took along one of the Solum boys to do his talking for him. Once there, he filed an application for the quarter section of land which lay north of Hans Olsa's. To confirm the application, he received a temporary deed which contained a description of the land, the conditions which he agreed to fulfill in order to become the owner, and the date, June 6, 1873.

Sörine wanted Beret and the children to stay with her during the two days that her husband would be away; but Beret refused the offer with thanks. If they were to get a home ready for the summer, she said, she would have to take hold of matters right away.

"For the summer?" exclaimed the other woman, showing her astonishment. "What about the winter, then?"

Beret evaded the question.

During the first day she and the boys unloaded both wagons, set up the stove, and carried out the table. Then Beret arranged a bedroom in the larger wagon. With all the things taken out, it was quite roomy in there. The boys thought this work great fun, and she herself found some relief in it for her troubled mind. But something vague and intangible hovering in the air would not allow her to be wholly at ease; she had to stop often and look about, or stand erect and listen. Was that a sound she heard? All the while, the thought that had struck her yesterday when she had first got down from the wagon stood vividly before her mind. Here there was nothing even to hide behind!

After they had milked the cow and eaten their evening porridge, she took the boys and And-Ongen and strolled away from camp toward the hill. When they had reached the summit, Beret sat down and let her gaze wander. In a certain sense, she had to admit to herself, it was lovely up here. The broad expanse stretching away endlessly seemed almost like the ocean—especially now, when darkness was falling. And yet it was very different; this formless prairie had no heart that beat, no waves that sang, no soul that could be touched . . . or cared.

The infinitude surrounding her might not have been so oppressive had it not been for the deep silence, which lay heavier here than in a church. Here no warbling of birds rose on the air, no buzzing of insects sounded; even the wind had died away; the waving blades of grass now stood erect and quiet, as if listening, in the great hush of evening.

While the children were playing boisterously a little way off, she sat perfectly quiet, thinking of the interminably long march that they would have to make, back to the place where human beings dwelt. It would be small hardship for her, of course, sitting in the wagon; but she pitied Per Hansa and the boys—and then the poor oxen! He certainly would soon find out for himself that a home for men and women and children could never be established in this wilderness. . . . And how could she bring new life into the world out here?

The purple dimness steadily closed in, and a profound sense of desolation settled upon her. She threw herself back in the grass and looked up into the heavens. Suddenly, for the first time, she realized the full extent of her loneliness, the dreadful nature of the fate that had overtaken her. Lying there on her back and staring up into the quiet sky, she went over in her mind every step of their wanderings, every mile of the distance they had traveled since they had left home.

In Namsos, in Norway, there had been a large ship with white sails that had carried them away from the land they knew. For weeks they had seemed to be crossing an ocean which had no end. At last they had landed in Quebec. There she had walked about the streets, confused. Was this the Promised Land? Ah no—it was only the beginning of the real journey!

They had kept on—had pushed steadily westward, over plains, deserts, into towns and out again. One fine day they had stood in Detroit, Michigan. This wasn't the place, either, it seemed. Move on! . . . It had been as if a flood had torn them loose from their foundations and was carrying them helplessly along on its current—always west. For a brief while they had traveled on water once more, and she could hear the familiar splash of waves against the ship's side. Finally the day had arrived when they landed in Milwaukee. But here they were only to make a new start—to take another plunge into the unknown. Farther, and always farther, the current kept whirling them. Did it have no end?

In the course of time they had come jogging into a place called Prairie du Chien. Had that been in Wisconsin? It made no difference—they had gone on. Finally they had reached Fillmore County, in Minnesota. But even that wasn't the place! It seemed to her that she had lived many lives already, in each one of which she had done nothing but wander farther and farther away from the home that was dear to her.

She sat up at last, heaved a deep sigh, and glanced around as if waking from a dream. The two boys and their little sister were having great fun up here. Store-Hans came running, and brought a handful of little flat, reddish chips of stone; they were pointed at one end like the head of a spear. The mother sat for a while with the stones in her lap; at last, one by one, she examined them. These must have been formed by human hands, she thought. She got up hastily.

"Where are you finding these things?"

The boys took her to the place; in a moment she, too, was standing beside the little hollow which the men had discovered the night before.

"Ole says that the Indians made them!" cried Store-Hans excitedly. "Is it true, Mother?"

"Yes." As she stood there, the same thought possessed her that had seized hold of her husband when he had first found the spot—here a human being lay buried. Strangely enough it did not frighten her; it only showed her, in a stronger light, how unspeakably lonesome this place was.

Beret could not sleep for a long time that night. Her head kept rising up from the pillow to listen, but there was nothing to hear—nothing except the night wind, which now had begun to stir. It stirred with so many unknown things!

PER HANSA CAME HOME LATE the following afternoon; he had many words of praise for what Beret and the boys had accomplished. Now it had taken possession of him again—that indomitable, conquering mood

216

which seemed to give him the right of way wherever he went, whatever he did. Outwardly, at such times, he showed only a buoyant recklessness; but down beneath all this lay stern purpose, a driving force so strong that she shrank from it.

Today he was talking in a steady stream.

"Here is the deed to our kingdom, Beret-girl! Isn't it stranger than a fairy tale, that a man can have such things here just for the taking?" He cocked his head on one side. "What do you say, my Beret-girl?"

Beret stood smiling at him, tears in her eyes, beside the improvised house. What would be the use of speaking now? He was so wrapped up in his own plans that he would not listen nor understand.

"What are you thinking about it all, my Beret-girl?" He whirled her off her feet and drew her toward him.

"Oh, Per—I'm so afraid out here!" She snuggled up against him, as if trying to hide herself. "It's all so big and empty; not another human being from here to the end of the world!"

Per Hansa laughed. "There'll soon be more people, girl, never you fear." Suddenly another idea took hold of him. He made her sit down on the large chest and stood in front of her. "Now let me tell you what came into my mind yesterday, after I had got the papers. I went right out and bought ten sacks of potatoes. You know how we men from Nordland like potatoes! I'm going to borrow Hans Olsa's plow, and tomorrow morning I shall start breaking my ground. If the soil here is half as good as it's cracked up to be, we'll have a fine crop the very first fall! And maybe I can start to build the house. Just wait, my girl. You'll see how wonderful I can make it for you, this kingdom of ours!" He laughed until his eyes were drawn out in two narrow slits.

He explained to her at great length how he intended to arrange everything, while all about them descended the grandeur of the evening.

"Do you know," she said quietly, "I believe there is a grave over there on the hill?"

"Why, Beret! Did you find it? Don't worry, girl. He'll bring us nothing but good luck, the fellow who lies up there."

"Perhaps." She sighed and moved away. Then, holding each other's hands, they climbed the hill together to fetch the children, who were playing up there. There was something in that sad resignation of hers which he was powerless against. She was so dear, so dear to him. Why could he never make her understand it fully? Perhaps she was not built to wrestle with fortune; she was too fine-grained. Oh, well—he knew one person, at any rate, who stood ready to do the fighting for her!

Per Hansa had so much to think about that night that a long time passed before he slept. Thirty dollars was all the money he had in the world, and there seemed to be no end to the things he needed. First of all, for the house, doors and windows. Then food and tobacco, shoes and clothing, and farming implements. If he only had horses and the necessary implements, the whole quarter section would soon blossom like a garden. He ought to get at least one more cow before fall came—no dodging that fact. And pigs—he absolutely had to have some pigs! And chickens—they would be pleasant diversions for Beret.

But now came the main hitch in his calculations. Beret was going to have a baby again. Only a blessing, of course—but what a lot of their time it would take up, just now! Oh, well, she would have to bear the brunt of it herself, as the woman usually did. A remarkably brave and clever wife, that she was . . . a woman of tender kindness, of deep, fine fancies.

How hard he would strive to make life pleasant for her out here! A vision of the whole farm lay there before him as it would be, under cultivation, yielding its fruitful harvests. And over where he was about to build the sod hut should stand a large dwelling, a *white* house, it would be. It would gleam beautifully in the sun—and the cornices should be bright green. Oh yes, that Beret-girl of his should have a royal mansion!

PER HANSA'S WAKING DREAMS passed unconsciously into those of sleep. When he opened his eyelids, morning was there to greet him—the morning of a glorious new day. Heavens, he might have overslept! He jumped into his clothes, and found some cold porridge to quiet his hunger for the time being. Then he hurried out, yoked the oxen, and went to Hans Olsa's to fetch the plow.

Dragging the plow, he drove out for some distance toward the hillock, planted the share firmly in the ground, and spoke to the oxen, "Come now, move along, you lazy rascals!" And a thrill of joy surged over him as he sank the plow in his own land for the first time.

The oxen stretched their muscles, the plow sank deeper, the first furrow was lengthening. When he thought he had gone far enough, he drove the oxen back in the opposite direction, and laid another furrow up against the one he had already struck. Then he let the oxen stand

awhile; taking a spade, he began to cut the sod beside the furrow into strips. This was to be his building material. . . . Field for planting on the one hand, sods for a house on the other—leave it to Per Hansa, he had everything figured out beforehand!

By breakfast time he had made a fine start. No sooner had he swallowed the last morsel than he ordered both the boys to turn to, hitched the oxen to the old homemade wagon, and off they all went to the field. Now Per Hansa began working in real earnest. He and Store-Hans broke up the land; Ole used the hoe. The sod was a dark brownish color on the underside—a rich mold that gave promise of wonderful fertility; it actually gleamed and glistened under the rays of the morning sun, where the plow had carved and polished its upturned face.

When they quit work at noon a good many furrows lay stretched out on the slope. And by the end of the day they had brought home four full wagonloads of building material.

Per Hansa began building the house that same evening.

"You ought to rest, Per Hansa," Beret pleaded.

"Rest—of course! That's just what I propose to do! Come along, now, all hands of you; you can't imagine what fun this is going to be. I don't mean you have to work, you know; but come along and watch the royal mansion rise!"

They all joined in—they couldn't have kept their hands off. They worked until they could no longer see to place the strips of sod. And from then on Per Hansa worked on the house every morning before breakfast and every evening as soon as he finished supper. The whole family joined him; it seemed like a fascinating game.

Per Hansa had such a zest for everything that he could hardly bear to waste a moment in stupid sleep. One morning, as he threw off the blanket at dawn, Beret put her arms lovingly around him and told him that he must stay in bed a while longer. He ought to remember that he was only a human being. She begged him so gently that he gave in at last.

Yes, she was an exceptional woman, this Beret. During the last two days, taking And-Ongen by the hand, she had come out in the field with them and pitched in beside them like any man. And he thought of other things that she had done. When they had harrowed and hoed, Beret looked over her bundles and produced all kinds of seeds. He couldn't imagine where she had got them—turnips, carrots, onions, tomatoes, even melons! What a fine wife she was!

On Per Hansa's estate they had a field all harrowed and seeded down, and a large house ready for thatching by the time that Hans Olsa and the Solum boys had barely finished thatching their houses and started the plowing. Syvert Tönseten, though, was ahead of him with the breaking. Per Hansa had to accept that. But Syvert had been here the previous fall; his house had been all ready to move into when they had arrived. And Syvert had horses, too. Such things gave him a big advantage.

They finished planting the big field at Per Hansa's late one afternoon; all the potatoes, cut in small pieces, were in the ground; so was the seed which Beret had provided. The field looked larger than it really was. It stood out clearly against the hillside; from a distance it appeared as if someone had sewn a dark brown patch on a huge green cloth. That patch looked mighty good to Per Hansa as he surveyed the scene. Here he had barely arrived in a new country; yet already he had got seed into the ground. Just wait! What couldn't he do another year!

"Well, Beret-girl," he said, "tonight we ought to have an extra-fine dish of porridge to bless what has been put into the ground." He stood there admiring his wonderful field.

Beret's back ached as if it would break. She, too, was looking at the field, but the joy he felt found no response in her.

I'm glad that he is happy, she thought sadly. Perhaps in time I will learn to like it, too. But she did not utter the thought; she merely took And-Ongen by the hand, turned away, and went back to their wagon home. There she prepared the porridge for their evening meal.

They all worked at the house-building that night as long as they could see.

Per Hansa's house certainly looked as if it were intended for a royal mansion. When Tönseten saw it close at hand for the first time he exclaimed, "Per Hansa, what the devil do you think you're building? Is it a house or a church? Why, you won't be able to get a roof over this thing! Where will you get roof poles long enough? And there aren't enough willows in this whole region to thatch a half of it! You might just as well tear it down again, for all the good it will do."

As a matter of fact, it was hardly to be wondered at that Tönseten grew excited when he saw this structure; it differed radically from all the others that he had ever seen. His own hut measured fourteen by sixteen feet; the one that the Solum boys were building was only fourteen feet each way; Hans Olsa had been reckless and had laid his out eighteen feet by sixteen. But look at this house of Per Hansa's—*twenty-eight* feet long by *eighteen* feet wide! Moreover, it had *two* rooms, and each had a door. Two doors in a sod hut! Tönseten shook his head solemnly. What folly, what sheer folly!

Per Hansa had put a great deal of thought into this matter of building a house. On the day that he was coming home from Sioux Falls a brilliant idea had struck him. How would it do to build a house and barn under one roof? Didn't people do that in the olden days? It was to be only a temporary shelter, anyway, until he could begin on his real mansion. This plan would save time and labor and both the house and the barn would be warmer for being together. Beret won't like it, he thought. But after a while he picked up courage to mention his plan to her.

House and barn under the same roof? At first it seemed utterly impossible to her; but then she thought what a comfortable companion Rosie might be during the long winter nights. She shuddered, and answered her husband that it made no difference to her whichever way he built, so long as it was snug and warm.

This answer made Per Hansa very happy. "Beret, girl, you are the most sensible woman I know!"

Now he would get ahead of both Hans Olsa and the Solum boys! None of them had even begun to think of building a barn yet, while his barn would be finished when his house was done.

One evening Per Hansa went over with his oxen to Hans Olsa's to borrow his new wagon; the time had come to get his poles for the thatching. The others had been able to gather what they needed along a creek some ten miles south where a fringe of willows grew; but Per Hansa would have to find something besides willow poles for rafters in that house of his. He had been told that the Sioux River was only twenty-five or thirty miles away; big stands of timber were reported to lie in that direction, and there were also several settlements of Norwegians who had lived there for a number of years. Many other interesting things would turn up, of course—things that he hadn't heard about; he wanted to see it all and get an idea of the whole locality.

He brought the wagon home that evening, merely explaining to Beret that he and Store-Hans were going out to gather wood. Ole would have to look after the farm while they were away. Store-Hans was overjoyed that he had been chosen to go on the trip, but his brother was nearly reduced to tears at such an injustice. The idea of taking that *boy* along! For the first time his faith in his father's judgment was shattered. And the situation grew worse and worse as Ole watched the preparations for the trip; it looked for all the world as if they intended to move out west! Why, his father was taking along a kettle, and measuring out flour and coffee. Heaviest blow of all, the rifle—Old Maria—was brought out from the big chest. Ole wept in sheer anger.

Beret, her face sad, got the food ready for the journey. Yes, of course, the house must have a roof; she knew that perfectly well. But he was going to be away for two whole days and a night!

"You'd better take the children over to Sörine's house tomorrow evening," Per Hansa advised her cheerfully. "You can spend the whole evening there, you know, visiting. Do that, Beret!"

To this suggestion she answered neither yes nor no.

PER HANSA HAD TOLD BERET not to begin looking for them before they came in sight. Nevertheless, she had found herself doing it shortly after dinner on the very first day. She knew they hadn't even got there yet, but she couldn't refrain from scanning the skyline in the quarter where they had disappeared.

The following evening she took Ole and And-Ongen up on the hill; they sat there silently, gazing eastward over the plain into the purple dusk; but neither wagon nor oxen crossed the line of their vision. When the day was well-nigh done, Beret suddenly felt that she must talk to someone tonight. Almost in spite of herself, she directed her steps toward Hans Olsa's.

—Hadn't Per Hansa returned yet?

—No. She couldn't imagine what had become of him!

—Oh, well, she mustn't worry; no doubt besides looking for roof poles he would also be looking for winter fuel.

—Winter fuel? She had never given a thought to that before. It suddenly occurred to her how much there was for Per Hansa to worry over; but she also felt a twinge of jealousy because he had not confided in her.

Hans Olsa's wife, Sörine, was well aware that her neighbor did not have any courage to spare. As the visitors were leaving she got up, called her daughter, Sofie, and insisted on accompanying them back to the wagon. They chatted gaily all the way, and that night Beret slept better.

Sometime after noon on the third day Per Hansa and Store-Hans came home. They brought a load so big that the oxen were just barely able to sag up the slope with it. There was a stout timber for the ridgepole; there were crossbeams, scantlings, and rafters for the roof. Farther down in the load lay six bundles of young trees with their roots carefully wrapped in bark. "Those are to be planted around the house," Store-Hans explained. "Would you believe it, Mother—in this bundle there are twelve plum trees! They grow great big plums! We met a man who told us all about them." Store-Hans caught his breath from sheer excitement. And in the back of the wagon, as Per Hansa unloaded, two great bags were gradually revealed. One evidently contained fish; the other seemed to hold the flayed carcass of a calf—at least, Ole thought so, and wanted to know where it had come from.

"*Calf!*"exclaimed Store-Hans. "*Antelope!*"

Beret watched the unloading with speechless admiration. She was so overjoyed to have her dear ones with her again that she could have burst into tears. As she stood beside the oxen she stroked their necks fondly, murmuring to them that they were nice fellows to have hauled home such a heavy load.

"Well, there!" said Per Hansa at last, when he had cleared the wagon. "Now, this is the idea: Store-Hans and I have figured on having fresh fish today, cooked in regular Nordland fashion, with soup and everything. We nearly killed ourselves, and the beasts, too, to get here in time. Beret, what the devil have we got to put all this meat and fish into?"

Store-Hans ate that day as if he could never get enough; there seemed to be no bottom to the boy. When he had finished, the father chased him off to bed at once; and strange to say, he wasn't at all unwilling though it was only the latter part of the afternoon. When evening came the mother tried to shake life into him again, but without success; once he roused enough to sit up in bed, but couldn't get so far as to take off his clothes; the next moment he had thrown himself flat once more and was sleeping like a log.

As TIME WENT ON, this first expedition of Per Hansa's came to be of great consequence to the new settlement on Spring Creek. In the first place there were all the trees that he had brought home and planted. This alone excited Tönseten's enthusiasm to such a pitch that he was for leaving at once to get a supply of his own; but Hans Olsa and the Solum boys advised him to wait until the coming fall. Then when fall came, there were other things to do, and several years went by before the others followed Per Hansa's lead. This is the reason why, in the course of time, a stout grove of trees began to grow up around Per Hansa's house before anything larger than a bush was to be seen elsewhere in the whole neighborhood.

But the most important result of all, perhaps, was the acquaintance with the Norwegians eastward on the Sioux River, which sprang out of this journey. Amid these strange surroundings, confronted by new problems, the two tribes of Norwegians met in a quite different relationship than on the Lofoten fishing grounds. Here they were glad enough to join forces in their common fight against the unknown wilderness.

The great plain watched them breathlessly.

Chapter 3

THE FOOD SUPPLY was steadily vanishing. The settlers shared freely with one another, but even at Hans Olsa's, where plenty usually reigned, bags and sacks yawned empty, and tobacco was rare as gold. No two ways about it—they must make a trip to town.

All the men, accordingly, met together one Sunday to discuss the matter. The seventy- or eighty-mile trip to town was in itself a serious affair; even with horses one couldn't expect to be back in less than four days. And under pressure of time, it was hard to accomplish everything that one wanted to do. Provisions of all sorts must be replenished, as far as their money would go.

They at once agreed that some of the menfolk would have to stay at home in case anything untoward happened. It was a singular thing, not a soul in this little colony ever felt wholly at ease, though no one ever referred to the fact. All of a sudden a vague, nameless dread would seize hold of them and fill them with restless apprehension. None of them would have admitted that this strange feeling was fear. Yes, God defend them! Man's strength availed but little out here. Terrible storms would come up—so suddenly, with such appalling violence! Less than a week ago Hans Olsa's tent had been carried away in a storm; Sörine, trapped inside and half choked, had been swept along with the canvas. Hans Olsa had laid the tent rope across his shoulder and summoned all his giant strength; but despite his size he had been whirled away like a tuft of wool. No one was seriously hurt, however . . . this time.

And then, the Indians! Kjersti, Tönseten's wife, didn't mind the storms so much; they weren't out for your scalp, at any rate! But not a day passed that she didn't search the skyline many times. Truth to tell, her fear of the Indians was very natural. When she and Syvert were living in Fillmore County, Minnesota, two refugees from the Norway Lake massacre of 1862 had drifted into the place; and Kjersti well remembered the story of the horrors they had undergone.

The men never spoke of the Indians while the womenfolk were around. But at other times, whenever the subject came up for discussion, Ole and Store-Hans stood listening with open mouths. The grave where they found the stones had now begun to strike a chill into their hearts; but it also exerted a strange and irresistible fascination.

So here they all were, afraid of something or other. But the women were the worst off: Kjersti feared the Indians, Sörine the storms, and Beret, poor thing, feared the very air.

The outcome of their deliberations that Sunday was only what might have been expected; it seemed the logical thing for Hans Olsa and Tönseten and Henry Solum, each of whom owned horses and wagon, to make up the party for the journey. Three men and three teams; such a caravan ought to be able to haul home whatever the settlement could afford to buy.

Per Hansa sat morose and silent most of that day. He and Sam Solum were to stay and look after the settlement; that was the plan. By God! It was disgusting to have to lie around the house with the womenfolk while the others were off on such a fine expedition! The thirst for adventure was burning in his blood.

When the party left on Monday morning, Per Hansa was in a towering ill humor; he rose with the others at dawn, woke Ole, and hitched the oxen to the plow. On that day he broke up an acre and a half of prairie, with only the crude implements at hand—a record that stood for many years in that part of the country.

But at quitting time that night he felt so elated at what an enormous day's work he had done that he began to whistle an old ballad. If they didn't hurry back, he'd have the whole farm broken up before they arrived. He'd give them a chance to see for themselves who was the better man!

THE NEXT AFTERNOON PER HANSA and Ole were sauntering home from the field when Store-Hans, all out of breath, came running to meet them. "Dad . . . quick . . . people are coming! Look! *Look there!*" He pointed toward the southwest. "Mother thinks they may be Indians!"

Per Hansa took in the whole western horizon in one swift glance and immediately began to walk faster. He found Beret by the wagon, holding And-Ongen in her arms. "They have come," she said, her face pale and drawn.

"Go look after the cooking as if nothing had happened," said Per Hansa. In an instant he was over at the sod-house. The boys followed; he spoke to them in quick, low tones.

"Hans, run over to Sam's and tell him what's up."

"Yes, sir!" Store-Hans was off like lightning.

Per Hansa turned to Ole. "Go get Old Maria from the big chest. Stand her just inside the door here. When I whistle, I want her—but not before. Are you afraid?"

"N-n-no." Ole ran to execute the order.

Per Hansa began to work at thatching the roof, but his eyes were steadily fixed on the approaching train. Little by little the look of anxiety faded from his features. No war party this—nothing but harmless families roaming over the plain! Just then Ole arrived with the rifle.

"Never mind," said Per Hansa, laughing now. "Go back and hide it again."

When the boy returned, Per Hansa gave him his orders: "Run and tell Sörine that the Indians are coming, but don't frighten her. Tell her it's only a wandering tribe—just peaceful people. They are likely to camp for the night over on the hill near the grave; if she is afraid, she can stay with us."

The band of Indians crawled slowly out of the west. Per Hansa counted the teams—fourteen in all. They were headed straight for the settlement. No doubt about it—he had guessed it from the hollow on the hill—here lay an old Indian trail!

He was kneeling on the roof, trying to fit a strip of sod in place, when suddenly Sam Solum appeared below him, frightened and excited, gun in hand. Store-Hans was behind him.

"You must be going hunting," Per Hansa observed dryly.

"Haven't you seen 'em?" Sam had to stop to catch his breath. "Indians! They're right on top of us!"

"I see you look like a scared fool, all right! Put that gun out of sight as quick as you can. Then come here and help me with the thatching. Store-Hans, you'd better go and stay with Mother."

Sam did as he was bid, without half understanding.

"I suppose we ought to warn Kjersti," Per Hansa said. "Why don't you go tell her that our red neighbors are coming?"

But Kjersti herself had seen the enemy. She must have been on the lookout, as usual. At that moment she hove into sight on the slope, leading her cow. At the same time Ole arrived, with Sörine and the girl Sofie close behind him. Sörine, unfortunately, hadn't thought of her cow, which was grazing off on the prairie. Soon they were all gathered in a little knot—the three women, Ole, Store-Hans, and Sam Solum. Per Hansa took a quick slide down from the roof and went over to the agitated group.

"What have we here—a sewing circle? By George! It seems to me that three nice, modest girls like you oughtn't to be standing around making eyes at strange menfolk! They've got their own women with 'em, too."

Per Hansa's sally broke the tension; Beret immediately resumed her preparations for supper; Kjersti milked her cow; and Per Hansa himself went back to his roof.

Supper was ready, and they were waiting for the porridge to cool, when the Indian band finally crept up the hill toward the grave. The settlers watched with anxious attention. The foremost team reached the summit, passed some distance beyond it, and came to a halt, along with the whole train. One by one the horses were unhitched from the rickety wagons and turned loose. Per Hansa's face brightened. People who did a thing like that could have no evil intentions!

Just then, however, Sörine's cow, which was still grazing some distance off, suddenly seemed to go crazy. She bellowed loud and long, lifted her head and tail high in the air, and galloped toward the wagons of the newcomers.

In an instant all the rest of their cattle were smitten by the same craze. At the first bellow of Sörine's cow they had looked up inquiringly, had caught sight of the new arrivals, and at once had started off behind their leader—Rosie first, then Kjersti's Brindlesides, then the Solum boys' Daisy—galloping straight toward the camp of the Indians.

"Damn the luck!" muttered Per Hansa. "The devil salt and burn their blasted tails!"

Kjersti wept and took on; Sörine's eyes were moist; but Beret remained quite calm; she seemed more annoyed than frightened. Why didn't one of the men go after the cows? When they made no move, she rose and laid her spoon aside.

"We must get them at once," she announced firmly. "If the Indians were to leave tonight, the cows would follow." She started for the hill.

"Good heavens, Beret," cried Kjersti. "You must be crazy!"

Per Hansa gazed fondly at his wife; across his face came a light. *There* was a woman for you! He got up and ran after her. "Go back and eat, Beret-girl! Leave the cows to me. It can wait till after we've eaten."

As they sat over the last of their porridge, Per Hansa drew ghastly pictures to Sam of the cruelty with which the Indians would probably treat the cows. The women shuddered at his words. "I've often heard that Indians would rather take the scalp of a cow any day, than of a man. They're just crazy for cow scalps. They use them for winter caps!"

Beret looked at him reproachfully. It seemed to her that the words sounded coarse in his mouth. "Can't you shut up with that talk!" she said in her quiet, cutting way. "It isn't such a brave and manly thing to terrorize poor womenfolk who are frightened already."

Per Hansa fell silent; his face grew red. In all their years together she had never shamed him before others. He ate his porridge slowly. What she had said kept repeating itself in his mind, and cut deeper each time.

At last he laid his spoon aside and got to his feet; he stuck his pipe in his mouth and began sucking the stem. "I suppose in all fairness, Sam, you ought to go chasing your own damned beast—you're such a sharper in both the American and Indian languages!" he snapped. "But—oh, well, I guess I'd better go myself and make it a good job."

Store-Hans jumped up like a flash and put his hand in his father's. Per Hansa glanced down into his ruddy face.

"Come along, then," said the father, and began to walk away.

"Hans, come here!" his mother cried out with wild anxiety.

"No," said Per Hansa shortly. "Hans is going with me." He grasped the boy's hand firmly and started off.

As THEY WENT ALONG, Store-Hans took long, manly strides. He had been too excited to notice the clash between his parents. Besides, they were drawing so near to the Indian camp now that his eyes kept him fully occupied.

There was a good deal to see, up there on the hill. A big tent, or wigwam, constructed of poles and hides, had been pitched, with four smaller ones on each side, forming a crescent. A troop of brown, half-naked children were running around among the tents. They seemed to be playing games, thought Store-Hans, and he picked up courage. There couldn't be any real danger here!

A group of dusky squaws were busy at a fire; around the fire several bronzed men were sitting motionless, with their legs crossed under them. These men were smoking—that was the first thing that caught Per Hansa's eye. The flames of the campfire threw a lurid glare over their copper-colored faces. They smoked in silence, watching the two visitors impassively.

Per Hansa stepped forward and greeted the braves in English—he had picked up enough words for that. The greeting was returned in the same language. Per Hansa stood helpless; he could not understand a word. But in this crisis Store-Hans came to his aid; he whispered, "They want to know if we live here."

"Tell them there isn't any doubt of it—but say it *nicely*, now!"

Store-Hans faced the seated redskins and tried his best to make them understand, using what little English he had learned.

The visit was soon over; after it there seemed to be nothing else for Per Hansa to say or do. The stray cows, all four of them, had finally lain down beside the Indian wagons; he would only need to round them up and drive them home. Yet the tobacco odor from the pipes enthralled and held him captive. He hadn't had a decent smoke for two weeks. At last the temptation grew altogether too powerful. He took his pipe from his mouth and indicated by signs to one Indian that he needed something to fill it with. The man laughed, then pulled a leather pouch from his shirt and held it out with a dignified gesture. Per Hansa gave his pipe a good fill and lit it. "Many thanks, good friend!"

As he stood there enjoying his smoke, he noticed a face on the ground at his side—a face that peered out of the folds of a blanket. The features were distorted in agony.

"Store-Hans!" he called hastily. "Come ask this fellow what's the matter. It looks to me as if he were fighting death itself!"

Again Store-Hans had to try out his meager English. The face moaned and gave answer.

"He says his hand is hurt," Store-Hans reported.

"Is that it? Tell him I'd like to have a look."

But Store-Hans didn't have to repeat the request. The man now got up, unwound a bundle of dirty rags wrapped around his hand, and held out an ugly-looking claw, swollen to the size of a log. The wrist and part of the arm as well were badly swollen from a festering wound in the man's palm. Per Hansa examined the hand. The flesh was hard to the touch, but the wound itself didn't look serious.

"If this doesn't end up with blood poisoning, my name isn't Per!" he observed. "Tell him"—he turned to Store-Hans—"tell him we've got to have some warm water at once—and more rags. But they must be clean—clean white rags, tell him."

That his father wanted warm water, Store-Hans could make them understand; but the request for clean white rags was beyond his English.

The sick Indian meanwhile kept his eyes intently fixed on the man who was examining his hand. Others had now risen and come up to them, one by one, including the women and children; at last the whole camp had gathered in a silent ring around the three.

"I can't see any way out of it, Store-Hans," Per Hansa exclaimed. "You'll have to run home and get Mother. Tell her an old chief has blood poisoning. She must bring the small kettle, and clean white rags, and salt, too. Now run. You aren't afraid, are you?"

Certainly Store-Hans wasn't frightened; this was the greatest experience he had ever had. He had already pressed his way through the throng when his father thought of something else. "Tell Sörine to go home and see if there isn't a drop left in Hans Olsa's bottle. It's a matter of life or death. And Mother must bring some pepper. Let's see, now, how well you can remember everything!"

As soon as the boy had gone, Per Hansa made them understand that he needed water to wash, going through the motion of dipping his hands. They caught his meaning at once, and after he had washed his hands, he motioned for more water. He began to wash the wound, drawing on the great store of experience he had gathered as a fisherman of the Lofoten seas. Next he massaged the flesh around the wound for a long time; then he moved upward to the wrist, and afterward to the arm. He rubbed with the palm of his hand, making circular motions, gently for a while, then more firmly.

At last Store-Hans returned with his mother. Per Hansa noticed that she had put on her Sunday clothes; for some reason this pleased him.

When she stepped within the circle of the campfire, she greeted the strangers quietly and dropped a curtsy.

"What do you think you are doing here?" she asked Per Hansa in a low voice. A wave of bitterness rose again in his heart. What a silly question for a grown woman to ask! Beret continued, "Kjersti is crying her eyes out—and the rest aren't much better off. These people have got to look after themselves. You must come home at once!"

This speech was so unlike the Beret that Per Hansa knew that he glanced up at her quickly. "Give me that kettle!" Then he told Store-Hans, "Tell them that I want *clean* water—yes, clean, that's it. And it must be hot, too!"

After a while he found time to turn to his wife. "If you don't want to stay here to help save a human life, you'd better go home. Here, give me the rest of the things!" Her words of an hour before were still ringing loud in his ears; his own voice had taken on an added harshness; he knew it and felt glad.

Beret stood looking silently at him, flushed and confused.

The kettle had now been placed on the fire.

"Where is the salt? We need salt in the water."

He took the half-full whiskey bottle that Sörine had sent, and the pepper, brought over in a cup. Then Per Hansa concocted for the sick Indian that "horse cure" which is famous among all the inhabitants of Nordland. A goodly tablespoonful of pepper lay in the cup; he filled it up with whiskey, stirred it, put the bottle on the ground, and motioned to the Indian to drink.

The man sniffed at the cup and smiled; then he took a draft, smacking his lips and making a grimace.

"Tell him to drain it off at once, Store-Hans!"

As Per Hansa had set the whiskey bottle down, a couple of the other Indians rose to their feet and sauntered over to it.

"They're taking the bottle!" whispered Beret.

Per Hansa whirled, grasped a brown arm, and gave it a twist. A howl of pain echoed through the camp. "What the hell are you doing?" cried Per Hansa, wrenching loose the bottle. He looked so fiercely at the pair that they slunk off, afraid.

"Now come here and help me, woman! Hold this bottle, and let the liquor drip down on the wound while I rub it in."

Beret did as she was told, though her hand was shaking. He looked at her closely; tears hung in her eyes. And all at once the loud ringing of bitter words died away in his ears.

He massaged the hand of the Indian for a long while, pouring the whiskey on freely. Then he dipped rags in the kettle where the water was now boiling; he wrung them out and began swathing them around the hand. The man gasped and moaned.

"Now, Beret, we ought to have a clean, dry cloth to wrap around the whole business."

She hesitated, and then untied her apron. He knew that it was her very best. "That's just it, Beret-girl—the very thing! . . . Now, Store-Hans, take Mother with you and go home. You can see there's nothing to be afraid of here. I'll bring the cows back with me when I come."

"But when will you come?" Beret asked, a tremor in her voice.

"Oh, I shall have to stay here part of the night, at least. If we can't make the swelling go down, there's nothing under God's heaven that can save him! I'll have to change the rags every half hour. You go right along, now, and don't worry!"

Without a word Beret took Store-Hans's hand and walked away.

During the first part of the night Per Hansa kept constant vigil over the sick man, frequently changing the bandages; every time the hand was exposed he rubbed in a few more drops from Hans Olsa's bottle. It was evident that the man's pain was growing no worse; he even slept at intervals.

Midnight passed. The whole camp was now asleep; the men lay like mummies, wrapped in blankets, their feet toward the fire. Occasionally one would rise and throw on more wood. The night was vast and still; beyond the glow of the fire hovered impenetrable darkness.

Per Hansa felt drowsy; he would have to pull himself together to keep going. Suddenly he pricked up his ears. He had heard a sound like steps in the grass, off to one side—steps that seemed to be hesitating. All the Indians were sleeping. Who could it be, reconnoitering out there? He got up abruptly, standing fully revealed against the glare of the fire. The next moment Beret stood within the campfire circle, silently looking at him.

A great glow of love and tenderness surged through Per Hansa. "Beret-girl, come here," he called in a low voice. "Don't be frightened; the whole crew is asleep."

She advanced slowly to the fire. Her face was flushed and swollen with weeping. He went up to her and took her hand. "Beret, you ought to be sleeping. Have you been frightened again?"

Her body shook with sobs. Like a crushed thing she sank to the ground. He threw himself down beside her, put one arm around her waist, and sought her hand. Then she began to weep softly. After a while he tried to say lightly, "I guess the old fellow is going to pull through, all right." She made no response. Then he heard the sick Indian stir, and looked around at him. The man lay awake, staring at them with his beady eyes.

For a while Per Hansa busied himself once more with the injured hand. Beret rose and stood by, watching. "If you had a string to tie around the rags, they would keep the heat longer," she said in a low voice, but calm and clear.

"Oh yes! If only I did!"

She turned away and fumbled at her clothes; then, with a bashful but determined air, she handed him one of her home-braided garters.

"Beret! That's exactly what we need!" He tied the garter around the bandage. "The fellow's better already!" he cried. "I can see it in his eyes—and his hand feels softer. But he isn't over it yet, by any means."

Now the Indian got up, went to one of the wagons, and fetched three heavy blankets; these he gave to Per Hansa, motioning that they should lie down.

"Now, doesn't that show, Beret, what decent people they are?" He wrapped one blanket around her, another around himself; then they both lay down with their feet to the fire. Pulling the third blanket over the two of them, he put his arm around her. "Now try to sleep, dear Beret-girl," he whispered. She dropped off almost at once, and slept until dawn.

THE INDIANS REMAINED for another day and night. Per Hansa spent more time with them than he did at home. Store-Hans, and Ole, too, practically lived on the hill. But Sam Solum let the Indians completely alone, as did the women. The Indians, for their part, kept strictly to themselves.

It was noon of the third day before they broke camp. The hand of the sick man still looked bad, but the immediate danger seemed to be over. When the long train of teams had got under way, they saw the sick Indian coming down the hill toward the house, leading a fully saddled pony by the bridle. Per Hansa went to meet him. Beret and the children followed. The man uttered a few unintelligible words and laid the bridle in Per Hansa's hand; then he made a short, stiff bow, turned on his heel, and stalked away.

"Has the old boy gone crazy?" exclaimed Per Hansa. "Can you imagine what he means?"

"He wants to give you the pony!" shouted Store-Hans.

Per Hansa roared out a protest and started after the stranger. "No, no!" he cried. But the Indian only strode to a waiting wagon, climbed in, and rode away.

Per Hansa stood as if dumbfounded, holding the bridle over his arm. "Pony, saddle, and everything!"

Store-Hans gave a leap into the air and turned a somersault. Never had he felt so supremely happy! Then he and his brother ran over to claim the prize.

IN THE EVENING of the following day the loaded wagons arrived from town. Hans Olsa, who had carried fifteen dollars from Per Hansa to buy merchandise with, besides going surety for him for a plow and a horse rake, came first to their house to unload. There was a great mountain of bags and packages; but best of all were the plow and the horse rake. The latter, especially—painted in red, blue, and green, standing with its seat reared high in the air—like a veritable throne! Nothing would do but Store-Hans must climb up and try it at once. He wondered if they couldn't hitch their new pony to this wonderful rig!

Over at Tönseten's stood a mowing machine, which could cut both hay and wheat; this also had a seat high up in the air; and at the Solum boys' the sights were equally remarkable.

There was a grand celebration at Hans Olsa's house that night. Tönseten and Per Hansa arrived before the others to have a talk together. Everything that had been borrowed during the past season must now be paid back, and that was a complicated affair. Hans Olsa, who during the shortage had had the most to lend, was now left with enough supplies to stock a store.

But the goods were what interested Per Hansa least of all; he wanted to hear every detail of their difficulties and adventures on the way. Had they run across many people? What news had they picked up? And this fellow who had trusted them for the plow and the rake—did he look like a chap who would extend still further credit?

The returned voyagers, however, thought that the folks at home had stranger tales than their own to tell. It seemed a miracle that Per Hansa had been able to bring the Indian chief back to life. By George! It was more exciting than any storybook! Tönseten swore.

"I declare, Per Hansa," said Hans Olsa, looking at him in open admiration, "it's a queer thing about you. No matter how hard you're put to it, you always give a good account of yourself. It was an act of Providence, I say, to leave you home this time!"

Per Hansa accepted their homage very modestly. "Forget it," he said. "I didn't do anything out of the ordinary. But I might as well own up that when I told Ole to get Old Maria I didn't have any courage to spare! There was the band of Indians—thirty strong or more—and here was I, alone with those three crazy women!"

"Sam wasn't much use to you, eh?" asked Tönseten.

"No, Syvert, Sam isn't quite equal to such a job." But then Per Hansa felt that he had been too harsh; he quickly added, "He will have guts someday. The boy has plenty of good qualities."

Meanwhile Beret and Kjersti had arrived; the Solum boys turned up at last, and then they were all gathered. The women went with Sörine into her new sod-house; they were curious to see what her husband had brought. The menfolk remained sitting behind the barn; they had many weighty matters to discuss; and Per Hansa's boys and Hans Olsa's girl were chasing one another around the sod hut, playing Indian. It was a strange thing, however, the number of trips the men had to make into the barn to look at the window and door which Hans Olsa had purchased. Each time they came out they were laughing and talking more glibly. The children grew curious and sneaked close to the walls whenever the men were inside. And such a volley of coughing and clearing of throats came from the interior of the barn, such whispering, such a smacking of lips, such a gurgling—like water running out of a bottle—that the children couldn't help laughing.

Something very strange, indeed, whatever it was. Now they heard Tönseten swear that it was his turn. He had forgotten himself and spoken out loud. "Can't I treat Per Hansa to an honest drink, when he has saved both my wife and my cow from scalping and dire death? Toss it off, Per, old boy, and let the rest of us get a chance!"

Then more jolly laughter and smacking of lips.

"What do you suppose they're doing?" whispered Sofie.

"Drinking, of course!" said Ole, furious because he was not allowed to be in on this. Surely he was grown-up enough for a drink or two!

Then Sörine appeared in the doorway, shouting to them that they must all come in. In a box which her husband had brought she had found two bottles. She felt pretty sure that it wasn't syrup! All five of the menfolk entered in a body and drew up in a group at the door; at sight of the whiskey they had suddenly become bashful. But Sörine treated them all. As soon as they had emptied their glasses, out they trooped in a body again.

When the celebration was over and they finally set out for home that night, it seemed to Kjersti that Syvert walked very queerly. No matter how she adjusted her own steps, he would either range ahead of her or lag behind, struggling hard to keep his balance. Then he would come to a stop and stand there babbling.

"What ails you, Syvert dear? You act as if you were walking and talking in your sleep on the open prairie!"

"Don't know." He sighed. "Feel awright . . . Maybe li'l queer . . . sort o' dizzy." He lurched ahead like a boat scudding down a wave. "You know, I think . . . must be that stuff . . . that stuff of Sörine's!"

Chapter 4

It was two days later that the great misfortune befell them. And it came while everything seemed safe and serene, and even the thought of ill luck was far away. That afternoon Hans Olsa was cutting hay; his new machine hummed lustily over the prairie, shearing the grass so evenly that his heart leaped with joy to behold the sight. Per Hansa was finishing his thatching. Ole and Store-Hans were helping; even Beret came out from time to time to lend a hand. Now and then they laughed so heartily together that little And-Ongen wanted to get up on the roof with them. Tönseten was breaking some new land, with Sam as helper. Henry Solum was digging a well down by the creek. The little frontier settlement hummed with the keen joy of labor.

Then the blow fell upon them—suddenly!

Kjersti noticed it first. At lunchtime she had brought out a bite to eat for the men. As she was about to enter her house again it occurred to her that she hadn't seen Brindlesides, either on the way over or on the way back. She walked a little way beyond the house, then stopped and surveyed the scene. She kept on looking until her eyes watered—until she could hear the heavy pounding of her heart; but her cow was not to be seen on the whole wide prairie . . . and not a single one of the other critters, either!

She ran to Sörine with her news and the two women went together to tell Hans Olsa.

But he was in such high spirits because of the new machine that nothing could worry him today. "Good lord! They must be around somewhere."

"We must go and tell Per Hansa!" said Sörine. She hurried on ahead, Kjersti trailing after.

Per Hansa took the matter calmly; the cows were probably lying down in the tall grass, somewhere along the creek. They would come back when it came milking time. Surely the trolls hadn't taken them under-ground! "Take the pony, Ole, and ride down to the creek. Search first upstream, then turn and go south."

THE EVENING WORE ON; outside of every hut the settlers stood watching, but no cows appeared. A little later the whole colony gathered on top of the Indian hill near Per Hansa's. The evening was deepening into night, and it brought memories to them—memories of tales which people had heard and repeated long, long ago, off in a far country. There it had been known to have actually taken place—both man and beast spirited away by trolls. The folk stood around in gloomy silence.

"In my opinion," Sam Solum announced finally, "it's the doings of the red man. You saw how crazy the cows acted that night when the Indians came!" Sam spoke in a bold, convincing voice; now he had solved the riddle for them and felt very superior.

His idea at once gained general acceptance; it was at least a natural explanation. Tönseten marched straight up to Per Hansa; he spoke in a voice of great determination. "If that's the case, you've got to go and get the cows the first thing in the morning—you who are so friendly with the Indians."

It seemed as if something had suddenly stung Per Hansa. "Come on, wife," he said, "let's go home and get to bed." Then he stalked away; everyone could see that he was thoroughly angry.

AT THE FIRST FAINT STREAKS of day Per Hansa slipped out of bed, made a fire, and put on the coffeepot. Beret was already awake. She got up immediately, dressed herself, and began to prepare him a meal.

All night long Beret had been lying with her eyes wide open, staring up at a picture that would not go away; a picture of a blue-green solitude, flat, endless, with nothing to hide behind. She had lived here for six weeks and more without seeing another civilized face than those of their own company. To get what supplies they needed they must journey four whole days. What would happen if something sudden should befall them . . . attack or sickness or fire . . . yes, *what would they do?* Perhaps, then, it was an act of Providence that the cattle had been lost. It ought to show them that man could not exist in this savage wilderness. Even Per Hansa might see it.

"You aren't going alone?" she asked him now.

He had not mentioned going yet; he gave her a quick look. "I must try to get the cows back somehow."

"No more than the others!" she exclaimed.

"But look here, Beret," he reasoned, trying to calm her. "Hans Olsa hasn't time to do it, because of the haying; and as for the others, I haven't much faith in them."

"Does it seem right to you, then," she burst out wildly, "that I should be left alone here with the children while you are chasing around in the wilderness? Why can't Sam or Henry go? They have no one sitting at home waiting for them!"

Now she has fallen into one of her unreasonable moods, thought Per Hansa; but perhaps she couldn't help it, poor thing! "It's this way, Beret. You see, I don't believe it would be any use for either one of those fellows to go."

"Then Tönseten will have to do it!" Now she was going to cry—he heard it in her voice.

"Then the cows would surely come home," he groaned, not far from tears himself.

She did not answer; she stood by the window, staring out into the drab, dismal dawn.

Per Hansa found his hat and put it on; then he went to the door and stepped outside. . . . No, no—he couldn't leave Beret this way! But what could he do? . . . In a deep quandary, he walked over to the woodpile, saddled and bridled the pony.

PER HANSA HEARD FOOTFALLS behind him and turned toward the house. Here she is coming now; everything will be all right and I can be off at once. I need to hurry!

But it was Hans Olsa rounding the corner of the house. "I wanted to talk to you before you went," he said. "You're going, aren't you?"

"Someone will have to go, I suppose. It seems best for you to keep on with the haying, so that we can get the job done."

"I know that you can ride faster than I can—that is the better reason. . . . Guess what Sörine told me last night?"

Per Hansa wasn't in a mood to solve riddles just now. His thoughts were in the house.

"Well," continued Hans Olsa, raising his eyebrows significantly, "Sörine suspects that that cow of ours was wanting male company!"

Per Hansa came back to reality with a violent jolt.

"What's that you say, Hans Olsa?"

"Those were her very words—'male company'! Do you suppose that old cow of mine could have taken it into her head to ramble all the way back to Fillmore County, just for *that*—and the others followed her?"

"Ha-ha! Ha-ha! . . . She had to have a man, that old dame of yours— and led the others with her into temptation!"

Per Hansa leaned forward and untied the horse; he sprang quickly into the saddle. "I'm going to make the Norwegians at Sioux River a visit. Perhaps you'll keep an eye on things for me here while I am gone?" He paused, glanced toward the house, and added in a low voice, "Be sure and send Sörine over here tonight."

He headed the pony around the house to the side where the door lay; there he drew up, coughed loudly, listened a moment—then rode away.

In the window looking toward the east a woman's tearstained face watched his figure grow less and less in the dim gray light of the breaking day, until at last it had disappeared.

SOON THE WORD was passed around that Per Hansa had set out eastward to the Sioux River to look for the cattle. Tönseten was fully convinced that Sam's solution of the riddle—the Indians—was the right one. When he heard of Per Hansa's intended visit to the Sioux River settlement his anger knew no bounds. So—Per Hansa was not the courageous fellow, then, that he posed as being! Didn't he know that the responsibility for getting the cattle back rested solely on him? For he had taken gifts from that robber brood—and been gloriously fooled into the bargain! And why did he waste his time now in reveling with the Norwegians on the Sioux River?

Evening came, but neither Per Hansa nor the cattle. Folks did not care to go to bed; they sat about staring and waiting. All of them went over to Beret's, but none of them found cheer in this place either. Beret seemed distant and strangely calm.

When they were leaving, she said quietly, as if musing to herself, "Somehow, I can't figure this out. . . . Per Hansa is wandering off there alone in this endless wilderness. And four grown men are sitting here talking the time away. But aren't the cattle just as much theirs as his?"

When the children were asleep, Beret hung some heavy clothes up over the windows to shut out the night. She felt that she could never go to bed, with all the eyes out there staring in upon her. Last of all, she pulled the big chest in front of the door.

THE FOLLOWING DAY the boys climbed up on the roof immediately after breakfast and sat there hour after hour. Noon came; coffee time went by, yet no one in sight. . . .

Then, all of a sudden, eager shouts rang out from the roof; Store-Hans was screaming that now . . . right over there . . . Dad was coming! Ole's voice joined in, "And he has the cattle with him, too!" They jumped down from the roof and the next instant they were gone. The word was carried to Hans Olsa, then to Tönseten, last of all to the Solum boys. In each place the same message: "Dad is coming! And he's got the cows!"

Sure enough, here came Per Hansa riding the pony and driving before him a small herd of cows. As the caravan came in sight, each family proceeded to count the animals. There should be only four cows—now there were *five!*

Soon they discovered that the fifth animal wasn't a cow at all! No cow, indeed—but a yearling bull! Per Hansa himself was barely recognizable; his face was grimy and streaked with sweat, and he carried something strapped to his chest—some sort of a box, it looked like. . . . No—wonder of wonders! It was a birdcage, made of thin slats, and inside lay a rooster and two hens!

At last Beret stepped outside the house, without paying any attention to the others. "Per, what have you brought?" she asked in a low, tender voice, as if she were shy of him.

Per Hansa was unfastening the cage; he seemed wearied to the point of stupor. "Since I had to go so far, I thought I might as well do something worthwhile," he said with an effort. He handed her the cage. "Here are your chickens, Beret. I don't know whether there's any life left in them or not."

Beret took the cage and walked back toward the house.

The others all thronged about him. Tönseten pushed in ahead.

"I say, Per Hansa, who is that fellow you brought with the cows?"

Per Hansa pretended not to hear; he dismounted and threw the bridle to Store-Hans. "Water him now and feed him well! . . . Who is that fellow? I promised a kind woman ten dollars to let me take him for a year; that makes exactly two dollars and a half for your share, Syvert. But that'll be cheaper for you in the long run, you see, than to chase up and down the whole of Dakota Territory looking for your cow!"

Sörine and Kjersti were both very outspoken in their gratitude to Per Hansa. But it seemed to him that the deepest word of wisdom on this occasion was offered by Kjersti. She stood listening patiently until the story of his long ride had come to an end; then she remarked, as if quietly musing, "When lust can be so strong in a dumb brute, what mustn't it be in a human being!"

At that they all laughed heartily.

Chapter 5

THAT SUMMER PER HANSA was carried farther and ever farther away on the wings of a wondrous fairy tale—a romance in which he was both prince and king, the possessor of countless treasures. And ever more beautiful grew the tale. Nothing tired him these days; how could he steal the time to rest? Was he not owner of a hundred and sixty acres of the best land in the world? He gazed at his estate and laughed happily. Such soil! Just to sink the plow into it, to turn over the sod—and there was a field ready for seeding. This was not just ordinary soil, fit for barley and oats and potatoes and hay. It was the soil for wheat, the king of all grains.

His first quarter section was rightly only tillage land; but he wanted the one to the east, too, for it had open water on the creek. These two quarter sections would make an estate more magnificent than that of

many a king of old. And there were many other delectable thoughts: of livestock, for instance—horses and pigs and cattle, chickens and ducks and geese—animals of every kind. There would be quacking and grunting, mooing and neighing from every corner of the farm. And there would be houses for both chickens and pigs, roomy stables, a magnificent storehouse and barn . . . and then the palace itself! The royal mansion would shine in the sun—white with green cornices; the big barn would be red as blood, with cornices white as driven snow; and he and his boys would build it all! As he beheld these visions, his face shone with a glowing light.

And so Per Hansa could not be still for a moment. A divine restlessness ran in his blood. To remain inactive over the Sabbath would drive him into a fit of ill humor. If nothing else turned up, he took a long jaunt over the prairies; on these trips he selected many a pretty spot that would be a fine site for a home. Someday a settler will locate here, he thought. Wherever he went, no matter how far, he found the same kind of soil. Endless it was, and wonderful!

ONE SUNDAY EVENING the boys had come home wild with excitement. They had made a long trip westward to some big swamps with tall grass growing from them, and long stretches of open water in between. They told of thousands upon thousands of ducks so tame that you could almost take them in your hands. Store-Hans described the ducks until the words stuck in his throat and his whole body trembled; his brother raged on even worse.

244

From then on the boys were always talking about the ducks. Was there no way to get them? But they had no shotgun, the father said; Old Maria had not been built for that purpose. So the ducks continued to live there, flying from one pond to the next whenever the boys came too close . . . plague take it!

The boys made a practice of going out to look at the ducks every Sunday. But their father had not yet found time to go with them and behold this wonder.

Then one Sunday afternoon, in the early part of August, Per Hansa went for a stroll westward with Store-Hans. Ole was told to stay at home; it would never do to leave Mother by herself, the father said, so Per Hansa and Store-Hans made the trip alone.

Plenty of ducks there were, no doubt about that. Per Hansa gazed longingly at the birds. By George! There would *have* to be some way to catch a few. Store-Hans thought that if only he wanted to, his father could easily rig up a contrivance for catching the ducks; he could work miracles when he tried. Well then, why didn't he get busy? But no birds were captured on this first trip to the swamps. Store-Hans had to possess his soul in patience a while longer.

It was on the way home that Per Hansa made his startling discovery. Store-Hans went ahead, taking a shortcut. But the father never liked to follow an old path while there was still unexplored land left around him; accordingly he made a long detour to the southward.

He had a pretty good idea of the location of the south border line of Tönseten's property, as well as of the corners on it where his east and west lines began; the southeast corner, in fact, was near Tönseten's house. He cut across country until he judged himself to be about on this south line, and walked east for some distance; then he decided that it would be too far to go all the way in, just to pick up the southeast corner, so he turned west again. About here Tönseten's southwest corner ought to be, he thought; he stopped and took his bearings for the walk north. He had been following this course for perhaps a hundred paces when the toe of his boot struck against a small stake. Per Hansa looked down, and was brought up with a violent start. Here was Tönseten's southwest corner! What, had Syvert been so cautious as to put down stakes here, too? A careful man, Syvert!

Per Hansa knelt down. Yes, it was a corner stake; there stood numbers indicating both section and quarter. But the name below . . . *the name* . . . good God! What was this? He peered at it until the letters danced before his eyes. The name on the stake wasn't S. H. Tönseten at all; it was O'Hara! The letters had been carved on the fire-blackened stake with a knife, and the arrow pointed east, to Tönseten's quarter! Now Per Hansa laid his course northward. The radiant, happy look had vanished from his face. He hurried on until he had reached the vicinity of Hans Olsa's south line, dividing his land from Tönseten's; here he began to search the ground, working slowly forward into the next quarter section.

At last he found it—another stake, Hans Olsa's southwest corner. He looked carefully around; no one was in sight. He fell on his knees and examined it; he didn't bother to glance at the description this time; but the name—the name! It was as he had feared; this stake had Joe Gill carved on it. *Joe Gill!*

Moving mechanically, he strode north until he had reached the line between Hans Olsa's quarter and his own; but though he zigzagged back and forth for a long time, he was unable to locate any other stake. It was unthinkable that this misfortune should have befallen both Tönseten and Hans Olsa and not have struck him at the same time. He searched until it grew so late that he had to give up and go home. A short while before he had been lighthearted as a child; he came home now full of a weariness greater than he had ever known.

PER HANSA DIDN'T KNOW what to do with himself that evening. His discovery had been so utterly disheartening that he could not have mentioned it to anyone for the price of his soul. He would have liked to tell his wife about it and hear her opinion, but that was out of the question; she was disturbed enough already. But Per Hansa had to do something, or he would go mad. At last he sat down on the woodpile; there he remained a long while, staring listlessly at the ground. The trolls must be after him!

The boys were waiting for a chance to talk with their father, now that he had been to the swamps and seen the ducks. They came up and spoke to him, but he only sat there in a silence like a stone wall. At last Store-Hans could restrain himself no longer; he said in a deep joy, "Weren't there a lot of 'em, Dad?"

"What?"

"Did you ever see so many ducks in all your life?"

But the father made no answer; he was already far away and did not hear.

The next morning Per Hansa was up earlier than usual; he left the house without saying a word. The boys were at the table when he returned. He was heated as if from a brisk walk, his wife noticed. She had to look at him a second time; there was something queer about his face; it seemed so hard-set and forbidding. Instinctively she asked, "Is anything wrong with you, Per?"

"No," he replied, but he did not look up.

As soon as he had eaten he left the table, telling the boys to come along and help him; now was a good time to pace out the west line of their land; it had to be done soon. His words sounded cold and distant; he said no more, and went out.

Striking west from the house, Per Hansa counted the paces. When he had reached the western limit of his quarter, he said to the boys, "There ought to be a small black stake in the grass here somewhere, but I can't seem to find it. Let's go south first; look sharp and see if you can't pick it up."

All three of them kept searching the whole forenoon; they made tack after tack, walking abreast. "Look in the grass, boys, look carefully!" the father repeated a thousand times. They combed the ground east and west; they zigzagged, looking everywhere; but with all their labor and painstaking care, no stake could be found. When they finally stopped after covering every possible place, Per Hansa's voice sounded almost joyful. "It must be that the cows have tramped it down! Well, no harm done; it was nothing but an old stick, anyway."

BERET SOON CAME to realize that Per Hansa was absorbed in things of which she was not to know. He kept her at a distance; all his ardor seemed to have disappeared, and with it his childlike joyousness, which she loved so much in him. She was aware, too, of how often now he lay awake at night, or tossed restlessly about in his sleep. In a short while she became fully convinced that something had happened at last which he had to conceal from her; but she could not imagine what it might be.

This mood lasted with him throughout the week. On the morning of the next Monday he was up early. Beret had been lying awake, feeling keenly that he was wrestling with a monster which would not leave him in peace, but after a while she had fallen asleep again. When she finally opened her eyes in the dim gray of dawn, her husband was gone. She got up, dressed hurriedly, and went outdoors. Per Hansa was nowhere in sight. What had happened to him? What was he struggling with that had to be kept from her? It seemed to Beret that she had never felt the awful desolation of the place weigh so heavily upon her.

In the meantime Per Hansa had gone out and hunted up the spade; then he had started off for the southwest corner of Hans Olsa's land, where a black stake stood in the grass.

He looked about in all directions. Not a soul to be seen. "Lord!" he muttered. "Hans Olsa has got himself into a nice mess!" He grasped the stake, pulled it out of the ground, and laid it aside with great care. Then he examined the hole; he had better make it hard to see that a stake had ever been standing there! First, in his spade he brought some loose soil from a distance and filled the hole almost to the top; next he stopped it up with a grassy sod plug, taking good care not to tramp the grass down near the hole. Then he went on to the place where he had found the stake on Tönseten's land; here he repeated the performance.

When he returned home that morning the boys were eating breakfast; Beret saw him come into the yard and throw down the spade, then pause and glance hastily toward the house. Soon after she heard his footfall outside, passing along the wall. He went into the stable and stayed there for some time before he came into the house. As he entered the room he told the boys that today they were going to plow, yes, *plow!* His voice had an unnatural, metallic hardness; it seemed as if sparks flew when he spoke.

The stable was unoccupied as yet; it served as toolroom, carpenter shop, and storehouse; Beret also used it for hanging spare clothes. After they had all gone, she happened to go there looking for some garments that needed mending. Quite by chance, she found the stakes; Per Hansa had hidden them behind the clothes. Burned black to withstand the moisture, they would not have been seen at all against the sod walls except for the carved letters in the natural color of the wood. She picked the two stakes up and stood turning them over in her hands. Here were figures and letters . . . letters that made something like names. . . . Joe Gill, said one; the other, O'Hara. She kept turning the stakes over; the ends tapered to a point, where particles of soil were clinging.

She put them back, found the garments she was looking for, and returned to the house. But she could not dismiss those mysterious stakes from her mind. It suddenly occurred to her that Per Hansa must have put them there recently; it was only last week that she had hung up those clothes. Could he have done it this very morning? When he came home for dinner, she told herself, she would ask him for an explanation. But then he came, still in a forbidding mood; and her thoughts grew so unspeakably dark and ugly that she could not utter them.

After supper that night she heard him go into the stable; then he came out and went across the yard. She stole to the window; there he stood by the block, chopping a stick of wood into kindling; it was burned black and tapered at one end. He took another black stick and did the same with it. Then he gathered the kindling. Now, what in the world—he was bringing it all into the house! He did not look at her as he came in; he took off the lid of the stove and dumped in the kindling.

"Are you making a fire now?"

"Just some rubbish."

A question trembled on her lips, but the words would not come. It was so hideous, the thought which she harbored; God forgive him, he was meddling with other folks' landmarks! How often she had heard it said: a blacker sin than this a man could hardly commit against his fellows!

Terror possessed her as she stood motionless in the corner, watching her husband burn the proof of his guilt.

That night Per Hansa slept the sleep of the righteous; now it was Beret who had a monster to wrestle with.

DURING THE WEEKS that followed, Per Hansa's temper made him seem hard of approach; the man seemed driven by a restless energy, an indomitable will that knew but one course—to break as much new land as possible each day. "Do you intend to break the whole quarter section this fall?" Hans Olsa asked him more than once.

Before his thoughts stood ever the same problem: perhaps these men would never come back. They might just have happened along here the previous fall, before Tönseten arrived, taken a liking to the place and put down their stakes, and then failed to go to the land office until *after* Tönseten's visit there. Or still more likely, they might never have gone to the land office at all, but had allowed their claims to go by default. That *might* have happened.

In all this time it never once occurred to him that if there had been a prior claim on these quarters, Tönseten and Hans Olsa couldn't have filed on them, and that the act of simply putting down claim stakes made no difference.

Beret's thoughts continued to spin a dreadful web. . . . He has done it, he has done it! He has destroyed another man's landmarks. Oh, my God! And now a new terror—the terror of consequences. Per Hansa, poor fellow, could not even speak the language. How would he ever defend himself when the case came up? And here he was, guilty before the law of one of the blackest crimes that it was possible for man to commit.

THEY HAD BEEN here four months now; to Beret it seemed like so many generations. In all this time they had seen no strangers except the Indians. Almost imperceptibly her terror because of the stakes had begun to fade away. People had never dwelt here, people would never come. *They* were the only ones who had been bewitched into straying out here! At that thought, a hopeless depression would take hold of her; she would look around at the circle of the skyline, and although it lay so distant, it seemed threatening to draw in and choke her.

But then the unthinkable took place: someone from outside did break through the magic circle.

It happened one evening. Ole had ridden the Indian pony west to the swamps; on the way home he noticed a large white speck moving through the haze on the eastern horizon. The boy was so startled that he could hear the beating of his own heart; he had to investigate this thing. He rode directly toward the speck. When he had satisfied himself that west-movers were coming, he rushed toward home. On the way he stopped at Tönseten's with the news, then at Hans Olsa's; hastening on to his own house, he shouted loudly for them to come look . . . hurry!

It was a great procession—six teams of horses with wagons. The boys wanted to start out at once to meet the strangers, but Per Hansa told them both they shouldn't be running out as though they had never seen people before! Time enough for them to speak with these newcomers tomorrow. He himself would go now to find out if they needed any potatoes.

Tönseten and Kjersti were standing outside when he arrived there. "You're going to have visitors," Per Hansa greeted his neighbors. They stood gazing at the train of wagons, now less than a hundred yards away. Kjersti was wondering how she could put them all up for the night. The caravan was now so near that they could hear the panting of the horses. But then it swung off and took a more westerly course; the visitors evidently had no intention of camping here for the night.

"Are they going to pass right by an open door?" Tönseten asked. "Surely they can see us?"

The train moved on until it was on the line between Hans Olsa's and Tönseten's; there the wagons stopped and the horses were unhitched. The newcomers had evidently decided to pitch their camp for the night. Tönseten gazed at them openmouthed. "It's the strangest thing I ever saw!" he said. "Can you imagine anyone coming into a neighborhood where there are houses and not even wanting to talk to the folks who live in them? What's the matter—are they afraid of us?"

The three stood there watching and wondering in the deepening dusk. Apparently the strangers were now building a fire.

"You know, Syvert," Per Hansa said, "since those fellows won't come talk to us, we'd better take a trip over and visit them. We might even talk them into buying some potatoes, eh?"

Tönseten didn't take kindly to that at all. It did seem rather humiliating to go shake hands with folks who had refused to say hello to them. But after a moment they started on their way.

The fire burned lustily now on the prairie; four women were placing food on a big green cloth spread on the ground, and some of the men had already gathered around it. As they drew near, Per Hansa counted ten men in all. Tönseten went briskly up to the fire and greeted those who were there; Per Hansa did likewise. The strangers plainly sneered at their greeting.

—Where did they come from? Who were they? Tönseten asked.

—Irishmen from Iowa.

—Were they going far west?

—No!

This much Per Hansa was able to follow; but here he began to lose the meaning. Not that it made any difference—Per Hansa knew all that he needed to know: *They had come at last!*

Of the conversation that followed, he only understood that the men were making sport with Tönseten, who had grown angry and spoke faster and faster. It was unbelievable how Syvert could rattle off the English!

"Huh!" exclaimed Tönseten, turning suddenly to Per Hansa. "Can you imagine what they are saying? They insist that both my quarter and Hans Olsa's belong to them!"

Per Hansa grasped his arm. "What else do they say, Syvert?"

"They say they've taken up all the land between the creek and the swamps over to the westward, a strip two quarter sections wide. And they talk rough and wild; they're threatening murder and fire and prison!"

"Do they say when they were here?"

"Last summer and fall, and early this spring, too."

"What cultivation have they done to meet the law?"

"They claim that they've been granted exemption because they were soldiers in the Civil War."

"Ask to see their papers," Per Hansa said.

"They'll produce them in the morning, they say."

"Then we might as well go home and get to bed." Per Hansa spoke calmly. "But be sure to ask whether they need any potatoes!" he added with a flash of roguishness.

But Tönseten was once more absorbed in wrangling. The men about the fire had now all risen; a close circle had formed around the pair. Per Hansa watched in silence. Then, as Tönseten stopped to catch his breath, he asked, "Have they got stakes down here, too?"

"On both quarters, they say."

Per Hansa saw that if Tönseten kept on much longer, he would go to pieces entirely. "Come on, Syvert, let's go home to bed."

At that he calmly began to elbow his way out of the circle; Tönseten hurried after. Some one of the Irish must have tripped him; he stumbled and nearly lost his balance; this made them all laugh, but one man in particular roared with glee; his jeering voice had a deliberately insulting tone. Per Hansa wheeled and stood glaring at them, searching the crowd until he found the face from which that insolent jeering came. Holding his clenched fist under the man's nose, he said in a dry, rasping voice, in broad Nordland dialect, "Now, by God! You'd better shut up your mouth or I'll wipe that grin off your face for you!"

Then he straightened his shoulders and glanced around at the crowd. Apparently no one was anxious to have anything to do with him; the jeering laughter died. And so there was nothing left for Per Hansa to do but go away.

"I'll take all our papers along tomorrow and show them—they'll see what's what!" Tönseten blubbered.

"Well, you can try your papers on them, if you want to. But let me tell you this, Syvert, these people don't live according to the Scriptures!"

When they parted it was agreed that all the menfolk should meet early next morning to counsel together as to what must be done. "Don't breathe a word to Kjersti about how things are," Per Hansa said. "If the women get hold of this, they'll die of fright! We'll find a way out of this somehow."

As he walked homeward from Tönseten's, Per Hansa was a different man. He walked with a lightsome, buoyant step, very well pleased with the turn events had taken. These fellows were nothing but a pack of scoundrels. They had not filed claims at all; he doubted very much if they were soldiers; if they had had a clear case, they would have produced their papers at once. Next moment he began to whistle, striking up a merry polka. How fine life was, after all! When he went to bed later in the evening he put his arm lovingly around Beret and fell asleep almost immediately.

BEFORE LIGHT OF DAY Per Hansa was up again; he ate some cold porridge, put his deed into his pocket, and went over to the Solum boys' place; there he roused them, and all three continued on to Hans Olsa's. As they walked along, Per Hansa reviewed the situation for them. Then he told them to go on to Tönseten's; he and Hans Olsa would come as soon as they could.

Everything about Hans Olsa was of unusual dimensions; his great body made strangers stop and look; he loomed up like a mountain when he rose to his full height; and his strength was in proportion to his bulk. New ideas found their way behind that big forehead with great difficulty; on the other hand, when an idea had once become well lodged there, it would remain unchanged forever; and right and wrong were eternal verities with him.

When Per Hansa entered his neighbor's house that morning both husband and wife were up. He did not care to speak of their predicament while Sörine was listening, but time was pressing, so he related frankly the whole experience which had befallen him and Tönseten the night before. "Sörine, I know you are a sensible woman and will keep your mouth shut," he added when he was through. "Beret and Kjersti don't know anything about this; there's no need of alarming them. Now we must hurry. Get your deed, Hans Olsa!"

But it was a sheer impossibility for Hans Olsa to hurry in a matter of this kind. Facts were facts. He had gone to the land office in person; Tönseten had put his finger on precisely this quarter section on the map; there had been nothing in the way, not the slightest claim; it was so stated in the document; and he had moved onto his land and had done everything that the law prescribed. If anything was wrong, the government would have to clear it up.

"Why, certainly," said Per Hansa, with shrewd common sense. "But out here this morning, the government is a little too far away; that's where the trouble comes in."

"You don't mean that they actually intend to kick us out?" demanded Hans Olsa in an astonished voice, unconsciously stretching his huge frame.

"That's just what they intend to do, as I understand them. We'll have to show them where we stand, in black and white! Just put the deed in your pocket, and let's get started."

The Solum boys and Tönseten were waiting impatiently at Tönseten's hut when Per Hansa and Hans Olsa arrived. On the way over to the camp, Per Hansa explained the tactics they were to follow: Henry Solum and Tönseten would be the spokesmen, Sam the interpreter. "I think it will be best for you, Henry, to cut loose; then you, Syvert, can put in your oar when you think it's needed. But don't say much; and for heaven's sake, don't talk too fast!"

Although the hour was still very early, all of the strangers were busily at work when the five settlers reached the camp. Two of the wagons had been unloaded; some of the crew were putting up a large tent. "Aha!" observed Per Hansa to his companions. "They're planning to settle here, it seems. Now, first you must ask to see their papers; and then the stakes—insist on the stakes! Talk pleasantly. If they get ugly, just tease them on awhile."

Their friendly greetings were returned churlishly; the strangers went about their tasks without paying the slightest attention to the visitors.

—What were they doing here? Henry Solum demanded in English. This quarter had been taken up long ago.

—Indeed? Two of the men stopped their work.

—Yes, the man who owned the land was standing right there. Henry pointed to Hans Olsa. He had his papers along, too; and now they must show their papers. If the land office had granted the same quarter section to two different men, a bad mistake had been made, but it could be cleared up.

—Well, so they wanted to see the papers—was that the idea? Had they brought their *spectacles*? A roar of laughter from the others greeted this sally; but the man who had spoken wasn't laughing; his whole face was screwed into an ugly leer.

—Yes, Henry continued, they had come to see both their papers and their stakes. Furthermore, there was a court in Sioux Falls to settle such matters. They had been living here all summer, breaking and planting, and hadn't the least thought of moving away.

The leering Irishman now threw down his sledgehammer.

—All right, boys! Since they wouldn't take his word for it, he'd soon show them! The papers had been packed away and couldn't be found just now, but he would show them the stakes. They'd better come right along with him.

The stranger began to walk rapidly westward; Per Hansa was at his heels. As they approached Hans Olsa's southwest corner, the man slackened his pace and began pushing the grass aside with his foot. The rain and the sun had done their work well; not a blade of grass seemed displaced, not a broken stalk could be seen! Per Hansa all but laughed aloud.

The man searched back and forth, around and around. At first he went at it hastily, as if finding the stake were the easiest thing in the world; after a while he looked more slowly and cautiously. He was swearing now. At last he called loudly to the others from the camp. A small man with red hair came over and they began to talk together in low tones, from time to time casting angry glances at Hans Olsa; again they searched the whole region, but found no trace of what they were looking for.

Hans Olsa gazed at these men, hurrying here and there, trying to prove that he was a scoundrel; he heard what Sam translated of their remarks about him; his big childlike eyes blazed with astonishment; he trembled slightly all over, though he was not aware of it.

Suddenly the two men abandoned the search, turned away, and went back to the camp. The five settlers followed.

"If they have no better luck with the papers," said Per Hansa, "things don't look very bright for them!"

When they reached the camp all ten of the Irishmen stood in a group, talking angrily together. The women were not in sight. As the Nord-landers came up, a burly, red-faced man stepped out from the group, carrying a sledgehammer. "Where are the men who claim to have taken up this land?" he snapped.

—Right there. Henry pointed to Tönseten and Hans Olsa.

The Irishman singled out Hans Olsa and looked him up and down, fingering his sledgehammer.

—What was the matter with that fellow who couldn't seem to get his mouth open—was he deaf and dumb?

—Oh no, Hans Olsa just couldn't talk English.

—Well, he could tell this dirty son-of-a- ——— that he was a thief who had destroyed another man's landmarks!

Sam translated, trembling with fear.

The Irishman came closer.

—If the whole damned gang of sneaking swine didn't get off their land right away, he'd give them something to start with! The man swung his sledgehammer.

"Look out, now!" shouted Per Hansa. "Here the trouble starts!"

When Hans Olsa saw the Irishman loom up before him in that threatening attitude, he stared at him blankly for a moment. Then, all of a sudden, the upper part of his body stretched; he stepped aside to evade the blow and his left fist shot out, striking the man below the ear. There was a crashing sound; with a loud groan the man sank in a heap and lay perfectly still. The crowd of Irishmen stood as if dazed. Hans Olsa stared at them wildly, then bent over and grasped with both hands the inert heap of flesh on the ground; the next instant he lifted it high in the air and flung it bodily over the heads of the crowd, where it crashed into a wagon standing behind.

The group scattered and took to their heels across the prairie. From

one of the wagons sounded a scream of terror; four women came tumbling out and followed after the men.

Hans Olsa stood motionless, quivering in every muscle. Per Hansa jumped to his side and slapped him on the shoulder. "That was beautiful, Hans Olsa! Now I think we can safely go home; those folks aren't likely to start any more arguments about land!"

Hans Olsa was slowly regaining his poise; he sighed deeply. "I'm afraid I handled him pretty roughly; you'd better go and look at him, Per Hansa."

Per Hansa laughed confidently. "No, leave him alone. We're going home. Later I'll take a little trip of my own out westward!"

In the latter part of the afternoon Per Hansa returned to the camp of the Irish to find out how they were getting along; he took Store-Hans with him as interpreter. Once there, he found the whole camp moved to one of the two quarter sections lying west of Tönseten's and Hans Olsa's land.

Per Hansa made frequent visits to them during the next few days; before the third day was over he had sold them more than ten dollars' worth of potatoes.

THE IRISH FINALLY SETTLED on the two quarters west of them. For a long time they were the standing topic of discussion in the little settlement. But whenever they were mentioned, Beret kept silent; she took no part in the joy and relief of the others. Per Hansa had destroyed the stakes; and worse than that, he had kept it secret from everyone . . . even from her!

To be sure, she knew now that the stakes had been put down unlawfully. But suppose it had been otherwise—would he have done any differently? Was this the person in whom she had believed no evil could dwell? The explanation was plain; this desolation out here called forth all that was evil in human nature.

One afternoon a few days later, the Irish came over to Per Hansa's to buy more potatoes. They stayed for some time and asked for information on various matters; the boys translated the questions to their father as well as they could.

At both Tönseten's and Hans Olsa's they had noticed the strangers come and go. In the evening they all went to Per Hansa's to learn how the Irish had behaved.

"Finest people in the world!" Per Hansa assured them, pacing the floor in a surge of high spirits. His sallies of humor kept Tönseten in a continual gale of hilarity; even Kjersti and Sörine, who sat on the big bed with their knitting, had to let their work drop at intervals to laugh at Per Hansa's extravagances.

That evening Per Hansa told them all how he had found the stakes, and of the way he had disposed of them. He related the story with boisterous, carefree zest. Many words of praise were bestowed on his wise action.

"I'll have to admit," said Hans Olsa soberly, "that you played a risky game. For if they had been able to show that their stakes had ever been on my land, we'd probably be building a new house now, somewhere out to the westward. All our work this summer would have been for others. My thanks to you, Per Hansa!"

As Beret listened to the tale, she remembered the morning when Per Hansa had brought the stakes home; how he had chopped them up and put them furtively into the stove; and how his temper had taken hold of him at that time. This was an entirely different person! So it had come to this, that he no longer felt ashamed of his sinful deed . . . and that respectable folks sat around rejoicing with him over it! She got up quickly, overcome by a sudden feeling of suffocation; without stopping to think, she said in a level, biting tone, "Where I come from it was always considered a shameful sin to destroy another man's landmarks. But here, I see, people are proud of such doings!"

Her outburst shocked the others into silence—all but Per Hansa. With a loud laugh he reached out clownishly, trying to catch her in his arms. "Oh, Beret, come on, now!"

"You were anything but confident, I noticed, that night when you chopped up the stakes." She turned away from him and seemed to speak to them all. "Remember what the Book says: *Cursed be he that removeth his neighbor's landmark. And all the people shall say, Amen.* Words like these we used to heed. In my opinion, we'd better take care lest we all turn into beasts and savages out here!"

In the midst of a laugh Per Hansa stopped. A wave of anger suddenly surged over him.

"We need a preacher, I hear. Well, now we've got one!"

To this Beret made no reply; instead, she left the room abruptly. Outside it was pitch-dark; she stumbled over the plow standing in the yard and sank inertly on the plow beam. As she sat there the storm

259

within her slowly died away; deep melancholy came instead. Long after the others had gone she remained in the same position. Per Hansa had not come out to look for her. When she went in at last, he had gone to bed. She did not speak to him.

During the days that followed, words were few and distant between Per Hansa and his wife.

Chapter 6

IN OCTOBER A MEMORABLE EVENT stirred the little Spring Creek settlement. It occurred on a day when Per Hansa, his son Ole, Hans Olsa, and Henry Solum had gone east to the Sioux River after wood; Tönseten and Sam Solum had stayed behind. Beret was sitting by the window at home; she was knitting something tiny. Her needles worked rapidly, but her gaze constantly wandered out-of-doors, flitting back and forth over the plain. Her face wore that weary, abandoned expression which had now become habitual to it whenever she was left alone.

Then her eyes fastened on an approaching object out there—and stayed. She sat and stared for a long time. Why, it must be a caravan! She leaned forward, trying to count the wagons. Someone else has gone astray! Poor folks—poor folks. She laid her knitting on the table and went outside. Store-Hans at that moment came riding up on the pony; when he saw his mother standing there he followed the direction of her gaze and immediately discovered the caravan.

"We must tell Syvert!" he cried, wheeling the pony around.

"Syvert?" What possible help could Syvert be to these poor people? "No, just ride over and ask them if you can do anything."

Store-Hans couldn't remember when he had ever heard his mother talk so sensibly; he gave the pony a slap and shouted to her, "You had better go yourself, then, to Syvert!"

But other eyes than hers had wandered across the prairie that day. All at once Sam came running to tell the news; he stopped only an instant, then continued on toward Tönseten's. Beret went into the house and roused little And-Ongen, who was asleep.

Soon she and And-Ongen and all the others were gathered in front of Tönseten's house, gazing at the approaching train.

Tönseten fussed excitedly. Good lord! he thought, were these more Irish? Then Store-Hans came galloping back.

"They are *Norskies!*" he shouted. "A whole shoal of them, and they are coming right here!"

At once Tönseten began to assume a great dignity; he ordered Kjersti indoors to put on the coffeepot, and taking Sam with him, he went out to meet the strangers, entreating them to enter in under his humble roof.

A great event, indeed! The company consisted of five wagons and horse teams. There were twenty men; some had large families back in Minnesota; they intended to go back east for the winter, but would move west permanently next spring. They had been told at Sioux Falls of a settlement out here; so they had thought they'd look the place over; but they were heading farther southwest, making for the James River or thereabouts.

They camped in the yard in front of Tönseten's house. He brought them potatoes and other vegetables, and milk, and would not hear of their sleeping in the open. So the floor of his house was packed with as many of the strangers as it would accommodate, the rest seeking shelter in the barn.

Tönseten himself didn't get much rest that night. How could he sleep, with a whole settlement of Norwegians snoring right in front of his bed? What a responsibility! If he could only persuade them to settle here, the future would be secure for both himself and his neighbors.

Next morning he had no time to eat breakfast; already he was deep in conversation with the west-movers, telling them all about the land around Spring Creek. Hadn't he been the original discoverer of the place? Surely they wouldn't leave without looking at it.

The west-movers had many questions to ask; of course they would consider the Spring Creek locality. Immediately after breakfast they started out to survey the place. Sam Solum went with them, talking volubly; Store-Hans also tagged along, now and then putting in a word that he thought sounded grown-up.

The prospective settlers liked the place; the land seemed good, and Tönseten pictured the future to them with prophetic fervor. His reddish beard glowed as if with fire; his voice shook with emotion; his arms made magnificent sweeping gestures in the air. He told about the schools which they would found, and the church which they would build together; and about the thriving town which would spring up on the spot where they stood, and the railroads that would crisscross the prairie in every direction; for the railroad had already reached Worthington—soon it would be at Sioux Falls! And just look at Sioux Falls. Only a year ago there wasn't a sign of a land office there—did they realize that?

The strangers listened seriously to him. They went back to camp and held council, and the majority were for settling down right there, on the east side of the creek. When Tönseten heard the decision he gave an excited laugh; he ran hurriedly into the house and told Kjersti, who wept over the news. He had brought in twenty neighbors with a single stroke—Norwegians, every last mother's son of them!

THE MEN RETURNED from gathering wood, but they would soon have to make another trip, this time to town to get provisions for the winter. Beret looked forward to it with dread; it meant that Per Hansa would be gone for a whole week. The nights hung heavy over the hut; she had to struggle with so many fearful fancies, though she felt unable to speak to him about them.

Per Hansa watched her worriedly, and then he spoke earnestly to the boys of how they must look after the place during his absence. Ole, who was the bigger, would assume responsibility for everything out-of-doors, including Rosie, the cow, and Injun, the pony, and the two oxen; and then the wood—he must promise to chop up stacks of wood! Store-Hans should serve as handyman to Mother indoors. The boys were far from enthusiastic. The disappointment hit Store-Hans the harder; he would have to go pottering around indoors like a hired girl! At that, the father called him into the stable and talked to him confidentially. "You see, Mother isn't in such a condition that we can both leave her," he explained in a tone of comradeship.

—There wasn't anything the matter with Mother, was there? Store-Hans asked.

"Oh, she's healthy enough, Store-Hans—it isn't that. But"—the father's voice grew low and queer—"but there may be another little Store-Hans coming here, say about Christmastime. You understand, now, we mustn't both leave her."

Deep wonderment rose in the eyes of Store-Hans. How could another come here—another boy? He didn't dare ask; he turned his head away, blushing. Oh yes . . . of course he would take care of Mother!

But here was another thing: couldn't Father get hold of a shotgun when he went to town—a shotgun for the ducks? Well, the father didn't know; he would see; he had thought of another way to catch those ducks, but what it was he wouldn't let on now.

Indeed, Per Hansa's mind was full of busy thoughts. In the cellar were many more potatoes than they could consume during the winter, and it would be strange if he couldn't find people in town who needed food. It was already October; some nights it froze—and potatoes were sensitive to cold. But the people of Nordland had known how to bring potatoes safely all the way up to Lofoten, even in January. Per Hansa pondered the matter; then he got Tönseten's wagon and packed the potatoes into it, surrounded by layers of hay.

Early the next morning he started off; Henry Solum and Hans Olsa went with him.

A COUPLE OF DAYS after the men's departure, Beret sent Store-Hans over to Kjersti's to borrow a darning needle; she had hidden her own so carefully that she could not find it. Such things occurred commonly now; she would put something away, she could not remember where, and would potter around looking for it without really searching; at last she would forget altogether what she was about, and would sit down with a vacant look on her face; at such times she seemed like a stranger.

Store-Hans came running back with the needle and burst out with the strangest news. Tönseten had killed a big animal! Tönseten said it was a bear, and Kjersti had told him that if he would bring a pail, they could have fresh bear meat for supper. Both boys immediately began pleading to go and see the animal; their mother gave them a pail and asked them not to stay long.

The boys came running down the hill just as Kjersti was cutting up the carcass; Tönseten was struggling with the hide, trying to stretch it on the barn door.

"What's that you've got?" asked Ole.

"Bear, my boy—bear!"

"Bear!" snorted Ole scornfully.

"That's no bear!" put in Store-Hans, though less doubtingly.

"There aren't any bears out here!" Ole protested.

"There isn't an animal living that you can't find out here." Tönseten spoke with such certainty that it was difficult for the boys to gainsay him.

"Where did you get him?" Store-Hans asked.

"Out west of the Irish a little way. There were two of 'em; this is the young one; the old mammy went north across the prairie, lickety-split! Here, now—take some of the meat. This will make delicious stew, let me tell you!"

"Is it fit to eat?" asked Store-Hans, still doubting.

"Fit to eat? No finer meat to be found than bear meat—don't you know that?"

The boys followed him over to where Kjersti was still cutting up the animal; it must have been a large carcass, for the cut meat made a sizable heap.

"Is it . . . is it really bear?" asked Ole in a more humble tone.

"He's meaty enough for it! Here, give me the pail; Beret needs some good, strengthening food. Careful—don't spill it now!"

The boys loitered on the way home. So there actually were bears slinking about this country! Suppose they were to get Old Maria, hunt up the she-bear herself, and put a bullet through her head?

They were gone such a long time that their mother grew anxious; when they came at last she was outside watching for them, almost on the point of starting out to search.

"Just think, Mother. There's a big she-bear over there to the west!" Store-Hans cried.

"We're going to take the gun and shoot her!" exclaimed Ole.

The boys were all raging excitement; their mood frightened Beret still more; she grasped them frantically, one hand on the shoulder of each, and gave them a hard shake. They were to go inside this very minute, and take their books! They weren't to go out of this house today! "Go in, do you hear me? Go in!"

But this wasn't fair! Ole used strong words, his eyes flaming. Didn't she realize that there was a real *bear* over there—a *grizzly* bear! Mother . . . *please!*

Beret had to use force to get them indoors. "Go in, I say, and take your books!"

They burst into the house like two mad bull calves; they sat down to read by the table in front of the window in a state of mutinous rebellion. Trouble soon arose. Each wanted the seat immediately in front of the window, where the most light fell. A terrible battle broke out; Ole was the stronger, but his brother the quicker. Ole burst out with words which he had heard in the mouths of men when something went wrong with their work. As soon as Store-Hans heard this, he, too, began to use vile language; he knew those words and plenty more. The boys kept up their scrimmage until they almost upset the table; their books lay scattered about on the floor. And-Ongen watched them openmouthed until she suddenly grew frightened and set up a howl.

Over by the stove the mother was putting the meat into a kettle. She worked in silence, but her face turned ashen gray. When she had finished the task she went out hurriedly; in a moment she came back with a willow switch. Going over to the table, she began to lay about her with the switch, striking out blindly without saying a word. The switch whizzed and struck; shrieks of pain arose. And-Ongen screamed with terror. The boys at once stopped fighting and gazed horror-stricken at their mother; they could not remember her ever laying a hand on them before. And there was such a strange, unnatural look in her eyes!

They gathered up their books, while the blows continued to rain down upon them. Not until the mother struck amiss, breaking the switch against the edge of the table, did she stop. Suddenly she seemed to come to her senses; she left And-Ongen screaming in the middle of the floor, went out of the house, and was gone a long time. When she came back she went over to the stove and fed the fire; then she picked up And-Ongen and lay down on the bed with her. The boys sat quietly reading; neither of them had the courage to look up.

Store-Hans now recalled clearly what his father had confided in him; he thought of his own solemn promise; here he had been away from the house nearly the whole day! He felt burning hot all over his body.

Ole sat there thinking of how shamefully Tönseten must have deceived them. *He* kill a bear? It was nothing but a measly old badger! Now they were going to have this nasty stuff for supper. And Mother was so angry that one would never dare to explain it to her! There sat his younger brother snuffling. Ole closed his book with a bang, got up, and went outdoors to chop more wood; but he did not dare look at the bed as he passed.

Store-Hans sat over his book until it grew so dark that he could no longer distinguish the letters. His mother lay on the bed perfectly still; he could not see her face; And-Ongen was fast alseep with her head high on the pillow. The boy rose quietly, took an empty pail, and went out for water. He brought Rosie and Injun and the two oxen into the stable and tied them up for the night. By then his mother was up again.

No, she hadn't been crying this time! The thought made Store-Hans so happy that he went straight to his brother, who was toiling over the chopping block, and made friends with him again. The boys stayed outside until it was pitch-dark; they talked nervously about a multitude of things; but that which weighed most heavily on their hearts—the way their mother's eyes had looked when she whipped them—they could not mention.

Inside the house the lamp had been lit. And-Ongen toddled about the floor, busy over her own little affairs; the boys came in quietly and sat down to their books again. At last the meat on the stove was ready; the mother put the food on the table; the boys drew up, Ole somewhat reluctantly. "You get that troll stuff down!" he whispered to his brother. Beret had made a thick stew with potatoes and carrots; it looked appetizing enough, but somehow the boys felt in no hurry to start. Store-Hans dipped up a spoonful, closed his eyes, and gulped it down. Ole did the same, but coughed as if he had swallowed the wrong way.

The mother asked quietly how they liked the supper. At that, Ole looked at his mother imploringly and said in a tear-choked voice, "It tastes like dog to me!"

"I have heard it said many times," the mother went on, "that bear meat is all right."

"It isn't bear at all!" Ole blurted out.

"What?" cried the mother in alarm.

"It's only a lousy old badger! I've heard Dad say often that they aren't fit to eat!"

"It's true!" cried Store-Hans. "I could tell by his tail—Syvert forgot to cut it off! Oh, I'm going to be sick!"

Beret got up, trembling; she took the stew, carried it a long way out into the darkness, and emptied it on the ground. The boys sat on at the table, glaring reproachfully at each other.

That night Beret hung still more clothes over the window than she had before. She sat up very late, her thoughts drifting. So it had come to this; they were no longer ashamed to eat troll food; they even sent it from house to house as lordly fare!

Later, as she tossed in bed, bitter revolt raged within her. *They should not stay here through the winter!* As soon as Per Hansa came home they must start on the journey back east; he, too, ought to be able to see by this time that they would all become wild beasts if they remained here much longer. Couldn't he understand that if the Lord had intended these infinities to be peopled, He would not have left them desolate down through all the ages until now?

After a while her thoughts became clear and shrewd, and she tried to reason out the best way of getting back to civilization. That night she did not sleep at all.

THE NEXT MORNING, she got up earlier than usual, kindled the fire, got the breakfast, and waked the children. While they ate their porridge she looked repeatedly at the big chest, trying to recall how everything had been packed when they came out last spring. Where did she keep all the things now? She had better get the packing done at once—then that job would be out of the way when Per Hansa came home.

When there was no more porridge left, Ole walked toward the door, motioning to his brother to follow; but Store-Hans shook his head. Then Ole went out; the other boy sat there looking at his mother, unhappy and heavyhearted; he felt a sudden impulse to throw himself down on the floor and weep aloud.

As soon as the mother had finished her housework she went over to the big chest, opened the lid, sank down on her knees beside it, and began to rearrange the contents. Then she stood up and looked around the room, trying to decide what to pack first. On the shelf above the window lay an old Bible which had been in her family many generations. On top of the Bible lay the hymnbook, in which she had read a little every Sunday.

She put both books in the chest.

Then Beret glanced around the room. She asked Store-Hans to bring the schoolbooks to her so that she could pack them. "We must begin to get ready!"

Not until then did the boy fully take in what his mother was doing. "Get ready? Are . . . we going *away?*" Store-Hans' throat contracted.

"Why, yes, Hansy-boy—we had better be going back where people live before the winter is upon us," she told him sadly.

Store-Hans stared at his mother with his mouth wide open. At last he got out, "What will Dad say?" The words came accusingly, but there were tears in them.

She looked at him but could not utter a word. The sheer impossibility of what she was about to do was written on the face and whole body of the boy. She turned slowly toward the chest, let down the lid, and sank on it in untold weariness. The child stirred within her, kicking and twisting, so that she had to press her hand hard against it.

Store-Hans ran to her, put his arms around her, and whispered hoarsely between sobs, "Mother, are you . . . getting sick now?"

Beret stroked the head that was pressed so hard against her side; then she stooped over and put her arm around the boy. His response to her embrace was so violent that it almost choked her. O God! How sorely she needed someone to be kind to her now! She was weeping; Store-Hans, too, was struggling with wild, tearing sobs. Little And-Ongen, who could not imagine what the two were doing over there by the door, came toddling to them and gazed up into their faces; then she opened her mouth wide and shrieked aloud.

At that moment Ole came running down the hill, his feet flying, and shouted, "They are coming! Get the coffee on!" Then he threw himself on the pony and galloped away to meet the returning caravan.

Beret and Store-Hans had both rushed to the door and stood looking across the prairie. Yes, there they were, off to the southeast! And now Store-Hans glanced imploringly at his mother. "Would it be safe to leave you while I run to meet Dad?"

She smiled down into the eager face—a benign, spreading smile. "Don't worry about me. Just run along."

PER HANSA SAT at the table with And-Ongen on his knee; the boys stood opposite him, listening to the story of his adventures on the trip to town; the mother went to and fro between stove and table. There was a joyousness about Per Hansa today which colored all he said. It had a positively intoxicating effect on the boys, and even Beret was smiling.

At last the boys had to give an account of how they had managed affairs at home. When Per Hansa had finally heard the whole absurd story of the ill-starred badger stew, he laughed until the tears came. The boys, too, began to see the fun of the incident and joined in boisterously. Beret stood by the stove, listening; their infectious merriment carried her away. She was glad that she had remembered to take the books from the chest.

"Come here, Store-Hans," said the father, still laughing. "What's that across the back of your neck?"

The question caught the boy unawares; he ran over and stood beside

his father. "Why, it's a big red welt! Have you been trying to hang yourself, boy?"

Store-Hans turned crimson, remembering the fearful blows of last night.

Ole glanced quickly at his mother. "Oh, pshaw!" he said with a manly air. "That was only Hans and me fighting!"

"Aha!" exclaimed the father, with another laugh. "So that's the way you two have been acting while I was away? Mother couldn't manage you, eh? Well, now you'll soon be dancing to a different tune; we've got so much work on our hands that there won't be any peace here day or night. . . . Thanks for good food, Beret-girl!"

Finally the father got up, and taking the boys with him, began to carry things in from the wagon. The strange things he had brought! Lime, which he said was for whitening the walls! Planks for making furniture! And twine—*net twine!* He had sold his potatoes for good money and bought many things. At length he brought in a small armful of bottles.

"Come here, Beret-girl of mine! You have earned a good drink." He poured out a half cupful of whiskey and offered it to her. She put out her hand as if to push him away. Yes, indeed, she would have to take it, he told her, putting his arm around her waist and lifting the cup to her lips. She took the cup and emptied it in one draft. He was his old irresistible self again. How strong, how precious to her he seemed! She felt a loving impulse to grasp his hair and shake him. . . .

And the net twine! On the way home he had even whittled some shuttles for net knitting, and he had started making a net; he had knitted four fathoms. Now Ole was put to work knitting more of it. The boys grew wild with enthusiasm; were they going to use the net for fishing in the Sioux River? "Just keep your fingers moving, Ole!" The father made a great mystery of it.

Evening fell all too soon on a joyful day. The boys were at last in bed, fast asleep. But Per Hansa had no time for rest; tonight that net simply had to be finished. Beret lay in bed, talking to him and filling the shuttles with twine whenever they were empty. He explained to her how he intended to set the net in the river tomorrow. Unless the cards were stacked against him he would bring back a nice mess of fish. That, however, wasn't his great plan with the net; but she mustn't say a word about this to the boys. It was to be a surprise for them; they were such brave fellows. The fact was, he planned to catch *ducks* with that net, if only the weather would hold for a few days more!

All at once it occurred to Beret that she had forgotten to cover up the windows tonight; she smiled to herself at the discovery. What was the need of it, anyway? Cover the windows . . . what nonsense! She smiled again, feeling a languorous drowsiness creep over her, and she slept the whole night without stirring.

Right after breakfast the next day, Per Hansa left on the expedition to the Sioux River, taking the boys with him. Beret worked industriously throughout the day, while many thoughts came and went. It must be her destiny, this; after all, the One who governed all things knew what was best, and against His will it was useless to struggle.

But that evening, waiting alone in the house, she again covered the windows.

Chapter 7

DURING THE MIDDLE DAYS of October a few white, downy snowflakes hung quivering in the air . . . floated about . . . fell in great oscillating circles . . . finally reached the ground and disappeared.

The air cleared again. There came a drowsy, sun-filled interval . . . nothing but golden haze.

Then one morning—October was nearly past—the sun could not get his eye open at all; the heavens rested close above the plain, gray, dense, and still. The chill of this grayness drove through the air though no wind stirred. People went indoors to put on more clothes. Bleak, gray, godforsaken, the empty desolation stretched on every hand.

Sometime in the afternoon snowflakes began to fall. They came sailing down from the north until the air was a close-packed swarm of grayish white specks, all bound in the same direction. The evening was short-lived that day, and died in a pitch-black night that weighed down the heart.

Again day came, and all that day the snow fell, and all the next night.

At last it grew light once more—but the day had no sun. A cold wind howled about the huts.

Per Hansa and his boys worked like firebrands during the last days before winter set in. Every task that came to their hands delighted them. But Beret could not share their mood; she would watch them absently as they left the house; or when they were due to return, she would wander about with And-Ongen at her side, keeping a hot dish in readiness on the stove. They were sure to be cold, poor fellows! Then when they were seated around the table, talk would jump from one incident to another, and she would find herself unable to follow it. Their liveliness only drove her heavy thoughts into a still deeper darkness.

She had to admit, however, that Per Hansa could accomplish the most marvelous things. There were the walls, for example, of which he himself was especially proud. He had seen whitewashed walls in one house in town, and had found out how to do the job. He had begun work on the walls immediately after he had returned from the fishing trip to the Sioux River. Lime had been mixed and spread over the walls—three coats of it, no less; now the sod hut shone so brightly inside that it dazzled the eyes. Before the snow came, Beret thought it delightful to have such walls; but after there was nothing but whiteness outside—pure whiteness as far as the eye could see—she regretted that he had touched them. Her eyes were blinded wherever she looked, either indoors or out. The black-brown earthen floor was the only object on which she could now rest them comfortably; and so she always looked down now, as she sat in the house.

She was thankful enough, though, for all the fine fish that Per Hansa and the boys had brought home from the Sioux River. They had made a tremendous catch with the help of the net. Heaps of frozen fish now lay outside all along the wall; Per Hansa kept saying what a godsend it was that the snow finally had come. Now with the aid of the snowdrifts they could have fresh fish through the whole winter.

But in the opinion of the boys, the duck hunt had been the crowning adventure. At last the great secret of Per Hansa's net was revealed. If the ducks got the best of him on one tack, he would fool them on another; into the net somehow they must go! For three nights they had stayed out in the swamps to the west, toiling and fighting among the myriads of birds; in the morning they would come home after daylight, wet as crows, numb and blue with cold. But they always brought a catch.

As soon as evening came they would be off again. Each time Beret pleaded sadly for them to stay at home; what could they possibly do with all these fowl? The boys only laughed at this objection. Just imagine such a ridiculous idea—catch no more birds! The father joined in with them and poked mild fun at the mother. How silly it would be not to grab good food when it lay right at their door! And after they had plucked the ducks, there would be fine featherbeds for both herself and Little Per. Per Hansa's voice softened.

But she would not be carried along. "We won't need them," she said dispiritedly.

Dusk settled, the menfolk left—and she was alone with the child again.

BUT AT LAST winter shut down in earnest; the swamps froze up and duck hunting came to an end for that year.

Every person in the little settlement had been rushed with work during the last days before Father Winter came, and few visits had been made. Hans Olsa, Tönseten, and the Solum boys had been east to the Sioux River again for wood; home had seen very little of them lately. But for other reasons than this, visitors came but seldom to Per Hansa's now; there was something queer about the woman in that place; she said so little; at times people felt that they were unwelcome there. She was apt to break out suddenly with some remark that they could only wonder at; they hardly knew whether to be surprised or offended.

But on the day when the boys carried a gift of ducks to all the houses in the neighborhood, relating what sounded like a fairy tale, everyone went over to Per Hansa's to learn how he had caught these birds.

Once inside, they completely forgot their curiosity about the duck hunting; they stood with their mouths open, looking up one wall and down the next.

Why . . . why, what in the wide world was this? Had they plastered *snow* on the walls? What *was* it, anyway? Paint? My stars, how fine it looked! Per Hansa sat there, sucking his pipe and enjoying his little triumph, while Sörine said to Beret, "Now you certainly have got a fine house! You'll thrive all the better for it." But Kjersti said it was a dirty shame that she and Sörine had picked up such poor sticks for husbands! Why couldn't *they* ever hatch up some nice scheme?

Tönseten felt constrained to remind her that he was the fellow who had risen to the occasion and attracted the Norwegian wagon train. "And I don't exactly see what this new notion of Per Hansa's is really good for," he spluttered on. "It's getting to be so damned swell in here that pretty soon a fellow can't even *spit!*" Tönseten looked accusingly at Beret; it was from her that Per Hansa got these stuck-up airs. She was never willing to be like plain folks, that woman!

Hans Olsa sucked his pipe and said but little; his big, rugged features were very sober. Was this like Per Hansa, who had always confided everything to him? When Per Hansa had learned how a black earthen wall could be made shining white at so small a cost, why hadn't he told the others?

A while later, as the two men stood together outside the door, watching the falling snow, Hans Olsa said quietly, "You have made it pretty fine inside, Per Hansa; but He who is now whitening the outside of your walls does fully as well. You shouldn't be vain in your own strength, you know."

"Nonsense, Hans Olsa!" laughed Per Hansa. "What are you prating about? Here, take along a couple more ducks for Sörine."

It was well enough that winter had come at last, thought Per Hansa; he really needed to lay off and rest awhile. After a good square meal of duck or fish, he would light his pipe and stretch himself, saying, "Ha! Now we're really as well off here, my Beret-girl, as anybody could ever wish to be!" Then he would throw himself on the bed and take a good after-dinner nap, often sleeping continuously into the night.

In this manner he spent quite a number of days. It was uncanny—he could never seem to get sleep enough! He slept both day and night; and still he felt the need of more rest. Now and then he would go to the door to look out at the weather, and glance across toward the neighbors. No, nothing to do outside—the weather was too beastly! He would come in again, stretch himself, and yawn.

The days wore on, one exactly like the other. He knew that they were actually growing shorter every passing day; but—weren't they really growing longer?

In the end his idleness began to gall him. The landscape showed a monotonous sameness . . . never the slightest change. Gray sky—icy cold. Snow fell . . . snow flew. He could only guess now where the huts of Hans Olsa lay. There wasn't a thing to do outdoors; it took but a little while to do the chores. . . . Beyond this, everything took care of itself outside.

The boys were almost as badly off; they, too, sat restless and idle; and because they had nothing at all to occupy their minds they often came to blows, so that the father had to interfere,. At length Per Hansa put on his coat and bade the boys do the same; then they went out and attacked the woodpile. They sawed and chopped; they piled wood up in odd corners of the house; then they built a fort of chopped wood out in the yard and piled it full, too. Work on the woodpile lasted exactly four days; when they had chopped up the last stick there was nothing left for them to do outside. Then they sat idle again.

The bad spell of weather held out interminably. No sun . . . no sky. . . . The air was a gray, ashen mist which hung around and above them thick and frozen. . . . In the course of time there was a full moon at night, somewhere behind the veil. Then the mist grew luminous and alive—strange to behold. Per Hansa would gaze at it and think, Now the trolls are surely abroad!

Finally, though it was only the middle of November, it seemed to Per Hansa, as he sat by the table following Beret around with his eyes, that many winters must have gone by already.

During the last two weeks he had discovered many things about Beret which he had never noticed before. Just trifles they were, but so many of them—one thing after another. Sitting here now, he began slowly to piece together what he had observed; the result pleased him less and less as he went on adding.

Did her face seem a good deal more wasted this time—or was he mistaken? She didn't look well at all. Then why didn't she eat more? Good heavens! She wasn't trying to save on the food? Here was everything—quantities of it, meat aplenty, and any amount of flour. She should help herself, this Beret-girl of his, or he would make her dance to another tune!

One day at table he burst out with it, making his voice sound gruff and commanding: Now she must sit up and eat like a grown woman! He took a big piece of fish from the platter and put it on her plate, but she merely picked at it. "It is hard when you have to force every mouthful down," she said wearily.

Lately he had also begun to notice that she lay awake the greater part of the night; he always dropped off to sleep before she did; yet she would be wide-awake in the morning when he first stirred. And if by chance he woke up in the night, he would be almost certain to find her lying awake beside him. One night she had started crying so despairingly he hadn't been able to make any sense of the few words he got out of her. From that time on he had been afraid to show her any tenderness; he had noticed that when he did so the tears were sure to come. And that, certainly, was not good for her!

As he sat through the long, long day observing his wife, he grew more and more worried. She, who had always been so neat and could make whatever clothes she put on look becoming, was now going about shabby and unkempt; she didn't even bother to wash herself. And her hair, her beautiful hair which he admired so greatly and loved to fondle, now hung down in frowsy coils. Wasn't it two days since she had touched her hair? Well—*that* he didn't dare mention! How could he ever speak of cleanliness at all to his Beret—his Beret who had so often nagged him for being careless about his own appearance? But one day as he sat looking at her, he suddenly got up and stood gazing out the window; and then he said, "I really think you ought to go and fix up your hair, Beret-girl. I kind of feel that we're going to have company today."

She gave him a quick glance, blushed, and left the room. When she came in again he did not dare to look at her. Then she began to tidy herself; she took some water and washed, loosened her braids and combed her hair, and afterward coiled it very prettily. He would have liked to say something loving to her now. But she did not glance at him, and so he dared not speak. In a little while he found an excuse to go out; passing close to her, he said in a tender, admiring voice, "Now we've got a fine-looking lady!"

All the rest of that day he felt happier than he had been for a long while. Of course his Beret-girl would be all right. Indeed, she *was* all right! She was so brooding and taciturn only because she was with child. She would be all right again as soon as it was over. And now the event could not be far away!

WINTER WAS EVER tightening its grip. The drifting snow flew wildly under a low sky; it swept the plain like a giant broom, churning up a flurry so thick that people could scarcely open their eyes.

As soon as the weather cleared, icy gusts drove through every chink and cranny, leaving white frost behind; one's breath hung frozen in the air the moment it was out of the mouth.

At intervals a day of bright sunshine came. Then the whole vast plain glittered with the flashing brilliance of diamonds; the glare was so strong that it burned the sight; the eyes saw blackness where there was nothing but shining white.

Evenings . . . magic, still evenings, surpassing in beauty the most fantastic dreams of childhood! Such evenings were dangerous. To the strong they brought reckless laughter—for who had ever seen such moon-nights? To the weak they brought tears, hopeless tears. This was not life, but eternity itself.

Per Hansa sat in his hut, ate, drank, puffed at his pipe, and in vague alarm followed his wife with his eyes; for the life of him he didn't know what to do. Where could he betake himself when things were in such a bad way at home?

He would be seized by a sudden desire to take Beret, hold her on his knee like a naughty child—just *make* her sit there—and talk some sense into her! For this wasn't altogether fair play on her part. Of course it was hard for her these days; but after all, the time would soon come to an end; and *that* was something real to struggle with—something to glory in. But he! . . . Here he was forced to sit in idleness, and just let his eyes wander.

A DAY CAME when Per Hansa flared up in a rage that frightened even himself. It was one of the Solum boys who brought it about. One forenoon Henry came over and sat chatting as if he had nothing in particular on his mind. When the lad finally rose to go he asked if Per Hansa would be willing to keep their cow until the spring; he could have the calf she would drop in January. Henry spoke slowly, without looking up; he seemed almost ashamed to explain his errand.

Per Hansa blinked. This was indeed handsome of Henry. In fact, it was so generous that Per Hansa felt quite overcome. But it would never do to take the milk away from the Solum boys. "I don't very well see how I can take your cow," he answered.

Henry apparently did not know how to go on. Well, that wasn't exactly the idea, he said, looking at the floor. He and his brother had made a sleigh, and now they wanted to try it out. The cow couldn't be left alone after they were gone.

Per Hansa's eyes danced eagerly. The devil you say—going east to the Sioux River, perhaps. He wished he could go along! Couldn't they hold up for a while—until he got ready? He threw a swift glance at his wife.

—No, that wasn't exactly the idea, either, Henry confessed, still more embarrassed. Their parents were alone back in Minnesota; he and Sam had agreed that they had better go celebrate Christmas with the old folks. There seemed to be nothing to do here in the winter; they could come back in the spring. Couldn't he do them the favor of keeping the cow?

All the light seemed to die out of Per Hansa's face; then it suddenly flared up again in a flame of rage. "Take your damned old cow along with you, Henry! We want none of your milk!"

—Well, said Henry calmly—if that was the way Per Hansa felt about it, he certainly didn't want to force the cow on him! If they had to, they could slaughter the beast. Without further words he left the house.

It was then that the storm broke loose in earnest. The boys were sitting at the table, each with a piece of charcoal, drawing ponies with Indians on top; those of Store-Hans were waging war against Ole's; the boys were so taken up with their play that they hardly noticed what was going on in the room. Beret sat by the stove mending a garment; And-Ongen had also been given needle and thread, and was industriously sewing away at a piece of rag. Per Hansa stood at the window, glaring out. All at once Beret remarked in her quiet manner that it didn't seem a bit strange to her that the Solum boys wanted to leave. Why should they lie exiled out here in the wilderness?

As if something had stung him, Per Hansa wheeled and looked at his wife, his eyes hard and glazed. "Hell!" he snapped. "If they were *men*, instead of such damned *worms*, they would find something to do!" Here lay the finest sleighing that one could wish for! If they were not a couple of babies, they would now be hauling home logs for their new house! If *he* didn't have to sit around here like a sick woman, *he* would have had enough lumber on hand for the finest homestead, long ago! Did she actually believe there was nothing to do around here?

His words cut through the little room like the harsh grating of a file on a saw blade. Again there was silence. Beret broke it. Well, why didn't he go to work and do it, then?

—Go to work? he snarled. Was *she* in such a condition that he could ever leave the house?

—Oh, she was in the condition he had brought her to, she said. No, indeed, he didn't have to sit at home on her account!

Per Hansa drove his fist into the table with a terrible crash. The boys jumped up in fright and shrank away—never had they seen their father like this; he looked as if he would strike their mother the next instant. Little And-Ongen threw her rag in her mother's lap and screamed in terror.

"You talk like a fool!" he cried. "That only shows how much sense you've got!" He found the door, and was gone.

Per Hansa stayed outside nearly all of the day. By evening he had made a pair of skis for each of the boys. When finally he entered the house, supper stood ready on the table. Beret had gone to bed.

As soon as he had eaten he told the boys that he would have to go on an errand over to Hans Olsa's; he wasn't sure when he would be back. No, they couldn't go with him! He gave a glance toward the bed as he went out.

He had barely entered Hans Olsa's house and found a chair when another visitor arrived. Tönseten came in, apparently in bad humor. Did they know that the Solum boys were about to leave?

"I guess we know as much as you do," said Per Hansa dryly.

"What I don't understand is, why have you folks let things come to such a pass?" Tönseten asked irritably.

"*We?*" Per Hansa asked.

"We can't very well *tie up* the boys, when they are bent on going," said Hans Olsa.

"I didn't say we could!" Tönseten waved his arms excitedly. "But we can use common sense, can't we?"

"Very well, Syvert, let's hear your common sense," spoke up Per Hansa.

"Well, Per Hansa, here you both sit around and twiddle your thumbs, doing nothing; but you've got cubs; why don't you join forces and hire Henry Solum to teach school for your brats this winter? Henry hasn't had much schooling, but he was raised in this country and can sling the English like a native—that much *I* know. I haven't any brats of my own to send, but I'll gladly chip in a few dollars when my wheat is threshed next fall!"

The other two listened in silence, though Per Hansa's eyes began to sparkle. Hans Olsa sat pondering.

"I see you're still hesitating!" Tönseten exclaimed snappishly. "I can assure you of one thing, fellows: if we let Sam and Henry slip away from us now, it's certainly doubtful we'll ever see them again—single and unhitched as they are. Then won't we be in a fine mess! For what chance would we stand of ever getting such good neighbors again?"

"We might try," Hans Olsa conceded. "What do you think, Per Hansa?"

Per Hansa jumped up. "I'll do whatever you say, friends. We can get no worse than a refusal." Then he remembered how he had spoken to Henry, and hesitated. "But—oh, well! I might as well give Henry a chance to tell me what he thinks of me!"

They held a lengthy conference with the Solum boys that night. Out-

279

side of their hut the sleigh waited in readiness; the boys were on the point of going to bed when the three men entered, and were evidently annoyed to see them.

Hans Olsa announced their errand.

At this point Henry burst out laughing. No, a schoolteacher he could never be, he said; back east in Minnesota somewhere, a girl was straying about, looking for him; if he could only find her, he, too, would be needing a teacher by and by!

Then Tönseten began to talk; there was a note in his voice that put all joking aside.

"Kjersti and I crossed the Red Sea, as it were, when we left last spring. For her and me there is no road leading back! What do you think we're going to do when you are gone? At Hans Olsa's they don't play cards; and Per Hansa, poor devil—well, he has a sick woman on his hands."

Per Hansa had been silent since he came in; now he knocked the ashes out of his pipe and turned to Henry.

"If you and Sam leave us now, it'll be so dull and dreary for the rest of us that we might as well hang ourselves. You saw how I went to pieces today?" Here he paused for a moment and then went on. "What sort of a schoolteacher you'll make I haven't the faintest idea; I only know this, that you and your brother are both fine fellows and that none of us can afford to lose you."

Per Hansa had spoken with forced calmness. The seriousness of the situation bore in upon them all. Everyone in the room had the same thought: this strong man was likely at any minute to burst into tears.

A long silence fell.

At last Henry spoke—his voice was husky and subdued. "It's harder on us than it is on you. We have only each other; but you have wives and children to squabble with!"

"Children!" cried Tönseten, wiping his eyes. "Good God! What are you saying, Henry?"

"Well, all the same," Henry continued earnestly, "if you will undertake to give us supper, one week with each of you, and have our clothes mended, we'll try to hang on a little while. What do you say, Sam?"

THE DAYS WORE ON. . . . sunny days . . . bleak, gloomy days, with cold that congealed all life.

There was one who heeded not the light of the day, whether it might be gray or golden. Beret stared at the earthen floor of the hut and saw only night round about her. She tried hard, but she could not let in the sun.

Ever since she had come out here a grim conviction had been taking stronger and stronger hold of her.

This was her retribution!

At last the Lord God had found her out and she must drink the cup of His wrath. Far away she had fled, but the arm of His might had reached farther still. No, she could not escape—this was her retribution!

She had accepted the hand of Per Hansa because she must; she had been gotten with child by him out of wedlock. Nevertheless, no one had compelled her to marry him—neither father, nor mother, nor anyone in authority. She and he were the only people who had willed it thus. Her parents, in fact, had set themselves against the marriage with all their might, even after the child, Ole, had come. It had mattered nothing at all what they had said; for her there had been no other person in the world but Per Hansa! He had been life itself to her; without him there had been nothing. Therefore she had given herself to him freely, in a spirit of abandoned joy, although she had known it was a sin.

Now she found plenty of time to remember how her parents had begged her to break with him; she recalled all that they had said, turning it over in her mind. Per Hansa was a shiftless fellow, they had told her; he drank; he fought; he was wild and reckless. He probably had affairs with other women, too. All the other accusations she knew to be true; but not the last—no, not the last! Ah, she knew it well enough: for him she was the only princess! The certainty of this fact had been the very sweetness of life to her.

But now she understood clearly all that her parents had done to end it between them, and all the sacrifices they had been willing to make. The child which she and he had begotten in common guilt they had offered to take as their own. They had offered to use their hard-earned savings to send her away from the scene of her shame, so precious had she been to them. But she had only said no, and *no,* to all their offers of sacrifice and love!

Yet how could she ever have broken with him? Where Per Hansa was, there dwelt high summer and there it bloomed for her. Whenever she heard of one of his desperately reckless cruises through stormy seas, her cheeks would glow and her heart would flame. This was the man her heart had chosen! Or when she sat among the heather in the fair summer night and he came to her and laid his head in her lap, then she felt that she was crossing the very threshold of paradise! Though she had had a thousand lives, she would have thrown them all away for one such moment.

No one had ever told her, but she knew full well who it was that had persuaded Hans Olsa to leave the ancient farm that had been in his family for generations, and go to America. There had been only one other person in the world whom Per Hansa loved, and that was Hans Olsa. She had been jealous of Hans Olsa because of this; it had seemed to her that he took something that rightfully belonged to her.

But when Per Hansa had come home from Lofoten that spring and announced in his masterful way that he was off for America—would Beret come now, or wait until later? . . . Well, there hadn't been a no in her mouth then! There she had sat, with three children in a nice little home which, after the manner of simple folk, they had managed to build. But she had risen up, taken the children with her, and left it all as if nothing mattered but him.

How her mother had wept! Time after time her father had come begging to Per Hansa, offering him all that he had—boat and fishing outfit, house and farm—if only he would stay in Norway and not take their daughter from them forever. But Per Hansa had laughed it all aside. No! he had cried. America—that's the country where a poor devil can get ahead! So they had sold off everything, had left it all like a pair of worn-out shoes—parents, home, fatherland, and people. And she had done it gladly, even rejoicingly! Was there ever a sin like hers?

Beyond a doubt, it was Destiny that had brought her here. Now punishment stood here awaiting her—the punishment for having broken God's commandment of filial obedience. Destiny had cast her into the arms of Per Hansa; Destiny had held up America as an enticing will-o'-the-wisp—and they had followed!

No sooner had they reached America than the west-fever had smitten the old settlements like a plague. People were intoxicated by visions; they spoke as though under a spell. "Go west! The farther west, the better the land!" People drifted about in a sort of delirium, like seabirds in mating time; then they flew toward the sunset, in small flocks and large. Now she saw it clearly: here on the trackless plains, the thousand-year-old hunger of the poor after human happiness had been unloosed!

Into this feverish atmosphere they had come. Could Destiny have spun its web more cunningly? She remembered well how the eyes of Per Hansa had immediately begun to gleam and glow! And the strange thing about this spell had been that he had become so very kind under it. How playfully affectionate he had grown toward her during the last winter and spring! It had been even more deliciously sweet to give herself to him then than back in those days when she had first won him. But—then it had happened: this spring she had been gotten with child again. Let no one tell her that this was not Destiny!

She had urged against making this last journey; she had argued that they must tarry where they were until she had borne the child. One year more or less would make no difference, considering all the land there was in the west. Hans Olsa, however, had been ready to start; and so there had been no use in trying to hold back Per Hansa. All her misgivings he had turned to sport and laughter, or playful love; he had embraced her, danced around with her, and become so roguish that she had been forced to laugh with him.

But this was clear to her beyond a doubt: Per Hansa was without blame in what had happened—all the blame was hers. Who could match him—who dared follow where he led? He was like the north wind that sweeps the cloud banks from the heavens! And this, too, was only retribution. She had bound herself inseparably to this man; now she was but a hindrance to him, like chains around his feet; him, whom she loved unto madness, she burdened and impeded . . . she was only in his way!

But that he could not understand it, that he could not fathom the source of her trouble—that seemed wholly incomprehensible to her. Didn't he realize that she could never be like him? No one in all the world was like him! How could she be?

Beret struggled with many thoughts these days, but one fact stood before her constantly: life was drawing to a close. She would never rise again from the bed in which she was soon to lie down. This was the end.

Often, now, she found herself thinking of the churchyard at home. It was enclosed by a massive stone wall; one couldn't imagine anything more reliable than that wall. She had sat on it often in the years when she was still her father's little girl. Her whole family, generation after generation, rested there. Around the churchyard stood a row of venerable trees, looking silently down on the peace and the stillness within. They gave such good shelter, those old trees!

She could not imagine where Per Hansa would bury her out here.

Now, in the dead of winter, the ground frozen hard! If he would only dig deep down . . . the wolves gave such unearthly howls at night! No matter what he thought of it, she would have to speak to him about the grave.

It worried her to know where he would find material for a coffin. She had looked everywhere outside, but had discovered only a few bits of plank and the box in which he had mixed the lime. If he could only spare her the big chest! Beret began looking at it, and grew easier in her mind. She would lift the lid and gaze down inside. Plenty of room in there, if they would only put something under her head and back! One day she began to empty the chest; she got Per Hansa to make a small cupboard out of the mortar box and she put all the things in there; but she took great care not to do this while he was around.

THE DAY BEFORE Christmas Eve snow fell. It fell all that night and the following forenoon. Murk without, and leaden dusk in the huts. People sat oppressed in the somber gloom.

Things were in a bad way over at Per Hansa's now; everyone knew it and feared what might befall both Beret and him.

"Listen, folks," said Tönseten, trying to comfort the others, "Beret can't keep this up forever! I think you had better go over to her again, Kjersti."

Both neighbor women were now taking turns at staying with her, each a day at a time. Christmas was here, too, and the house ought to be made comfortable and cozy.

They all felt very sorry for Per Hansa. He walked about like a ragged stray dog; his eyes burned with a hunted look. Each day the children were sent over to Hans Olsa's to stay. Per Hansa did not realize that it was bad for Beret to be without them so much; she had grown peculiarly quiet and distant. In the shadow of a faint smile which she occasionally gave him there lay a melancholy deeper than the dusk of the Arctic Sea on a rainy, gray fall evening.

About noon of Christmas Eve the air suddenly cleared. The sun shone down with powerful beams and started a slight trickling from the eaves. Toward evening it built a golden fairy castle for itself out yonder, just beyond Indian Hill.

The children were at Hans Olsa's. But Sofie had said that today was Christmas Eve, and when sunset came Store-Hans suddenly wanted to go home. He was almost beside himself when Hans Olsa said that he couldn't; all the children were to stay with Sofie tonight. They had to hold him back by force. This was *Christmas Eve!*

That afternoon Beret was in childbed. The grim struggle marked Per Hansa for life; he had fought his way through many a hard fight, but they had been nothing compared with this. He had ridden the keel of a capsized boat on the Lofoten seas and had seen the huge, combing waves snatch away his comrades one by one; but things of that sort had been mere child's play. *This* was the uttermost darkness. Here was neither beginning nor end—only an awful void in which he groped alone.

Sörine and Kjersti had both arrived a long time since. When they had come he had put on his coat and gone outside, but he hadn't been able to tear himself many steps away from the house.

Now it was evening; he had wandered into the stable to tend to Rosie, Injun, and the oxen, without knowing what he was about. He listened to Beret wailing in the other room, and his heart shriveled.

Just then Kjersti ran out to find him; he must come in at once; Beret was asking for him! He entered the house and took off his outer clothes. Beret sat half dressed on the edge of the bed. He looked at her and thought that he had never seen such terror on any face.

She was fully rational, and asked the neighbor women to leave the room for a moment, as she had something to say to her husband. When the door closed behind them she rose and came over to him. She looked deep into his eyes, then clasped her hands behind his neck and pulled him violently toward her. He lifted her up gently and carried her to the bed. When he had laid her down she spoke brokenly, between gasps.

"Tonight I am leaving you. I know this is the end! The Lord has found me out because of my sins. It is written, 'To fall into the hands of the living God!' . . . Oh, it is terrible! You had better give And-Ongen to Kjersti—she wants a child so badly. You must take the boys with you—and *go away from here!* How lonesome it will be for me . . . to lie here all alone!"

Tears came to her eyes, but she did not weep; between moans she went on collectedly, "But promise me one thing: promise to lay me away in the big chest, Per Hansa! And you must be sure to dig the grave deep! You haven't heard how terribly the wolves howl at night!"

His wife's request cut Per Hansa's heart like sharp ice; he threw himself on his knees beside the bed and wiped the cold perspiration from her face with a shaking hand.

"There now, blessed Beret-girl of mine! Can't you understand that this will soon be over?"

Her terror tore her only the worse. Without heeding his words, she spoke with great force. "I shall die tonight. At first I thought of asking you not to go away when spring came . . . and leave me here alone. But that would be a sin! I tell you, you *must go!* Human beings cannot exist here! They grow into beasts!"

The throes were tearing her so violently now that she could say no more. But when she saw him rise she made a great effort and sat up.

"Oh! Don't leave me! Can't you stay with me tonight and love me? . . . Oh! *There they come for me!*"

She gave a long shriek that rent the night. Then she sobbed violently.

Per Hansa leaped to his feet, and found his voice.

"Satan—now you shall leave her alone!" he shouted, flinging the door open and calling to the women outside. Then he vanished into the darkness.

No one thought of seeking rest that night. All the evening, lights shone from the four huts.

Per Hansa himself walked to and fro outside all night long; when he heard someone coming he would run away into the darkness. Tears were streaming down his face, though he was not aware of it. Every shriek that pierced the walls of the hut drove him off as if a whip had struck him; but at intervals he went to the door and held it ajar. Each time Sörine came to the door; each time she shook her head sadly and told him there was no change yet; it was doubtful if Beret would pull through; no person could endure this much longer; God have mercy on all of them!

The night was well-nigh spent when the wails in there began to weaken—then died out completely. Per Hansa crept up to the door and listened. So now the end had come! His breath seemed to leave him in a great sob. He staggered forward a few steps and threw himself face downward on the snow. A door opened somewhere; a gleam of light flashed. Someone came out of the hut quietly—then stopped.

"Per Hansa!" a low voice called. "Per Hansa, where are you?" He rose and lurched toward Kjersti like a drunken man.

"You must come in at once!" she whispered.

The light was dim in there; nevertheless it blinded him so that he could not see a thing. He stood a moment leaning against the door until his eyes had grown accustomed to it. A snug, cozy warmth enveloped him.

Sörine was tending something on the bed. What was this—the expression on her face? Wasn't it beaming with motherly goodness? "Yes, here's your little fellow! Come and look at him. It's the greatest miracle I ever saw, Per Hansa, that you didn't lose your wife tonight, and the child, too! I pray the Lord *I* never have to suffer so!"

"Is there any hope?" was all Per Hansa could gasp.

"It looks so, now—but you had better christen him at once. We had to handle him roughly, let me tell you."

"Christen him?" Per Hansa repeated, unable to comprehend the words.

"Why, yes, of course. I wouldn't wait, if he were mine."

Now Beret turned her head, and a wave of such warm joy welled up in him that all the ice melted. He found himself crying softly, sobbing like a child. He bent over the bed and gazed down into the pale, weary face. It lay there so white and still; her hair, braided in two thick plaits, flowed over the pillow. All the dread, all the tormenting fear that had so long disfigured her features, had vanished completely. A small bundle lay beside her, from which peeped out a tiny, red, wrinkled face.

At last Per Hansa gathered his wits sufficiently to turn to Sörine and ask, "Tell me, what sort of a fellow is this you have brought me—a boy or a girl?"

"Heavens! Per Hansa, how silly you talk!" But Sörine immediately grew serious once more and said that this was no time for joking; the way they had tugged and pulled at him during the night, you couldn't tell what might happen; Per Hansa must get the child christened right away; if he put it off, she refused to be responsible.

A puzzled expression came over the grinning face. "You'd better do that christening yourself, Sörine!"

—No! She shook her head emphatically. That wasn't a woman's job, he must understand!

Without another word Per Hansa found his cap and went to the door; but there he paused to say, "I know only one person around here who is worthy to perform such an act; since you are unwilling, I must go and get him. In the meanwhile you make ready what we will need."

The kindly eyes of Sörine beamed with joy and pride; she knew very well the one he intended to get; this was really handsome of Per Hansa! But then another thought crossed her mind.

"Wait a minute," she said. "I must tell you that your boy was born with the caul. I think you ought to find a very beautiful name for him!"

Per Hansa drew his sleeve across his face—then turned and walked away. A moisture dimmed his eyes; he could not see. How remarkable—the child had been born with the caul! He quickened his pace; in a moment he was running.

"Peace be upon this house, and a merry Christmas, folks!" he greeted them as he entered Hans Olsa's door. The room was cold; the Solum boys lay asleep in one bed, fully dressed. His own children and Sofie lay in the other bed, Ole by himself down at the foot, the other three on the pillow; Store-Hans held And-Ongen close, as if trying to protect her. Hans Olsa and Tönseten sat hunched up to the stove. Both men jumped up when Per Hansa came in, and stood staring at him. His laugh sounded pleasanter than anything they had heard in many a year.

"How are things going?" asked Tönseten excitedly.

Hans Olsa grasped his hand. "Will she pull through?"

"It looks that way."

"I'm ready to bet both my horses that it's a boy! I can see it in your face!" Tönseten exclaimed.

"All signs point that way, Syvert! But he's in pretty poor condition, Sörine tells me. Now look here, Hans Olsa, it's up to you to come over and christen the boy for me!"

Hans Olsa looked terror-stricken.

"It's all written down in the hymnbook—what to say, and how to go about it," Per Hansa said.

"No, no—I couldn't think of such a thing!" Hans Olsa protested. "A sinner like me!"

Then Per Hansa made a remark that Tönseten thought was extremely well put. "How you stand with the Lord I don't know. But this I do know: that a better man either on land or sea He will have to look a long way to find. And it seems to me that He has got to take that, too, into His reckoning!"

Hans Olsa gazed straight ahead; his helplessness grew so great that he was funny to look at. "If it only won't be blasphemy!" He finally struggled into his big coat. Then he turned to Tönseten. "The book says, 'In an extreme emergency a layman may perform this act'—isn't that so?"

"Yes, yes—just so!"

Through the frosty morning the two men walked silently across the prairie, Per Hansa in the lead. When they had covered half the distance he stopped short and said to his neighbor, "If it had been a girl, you see, she should have been named Beret—I decided that a long while ago. But seeing that it's a boy, we'll have to name him Per like me, after my grandfather; you must say Peder, of course! But the boy must have a second name—so you'd better christen him Peder Victorious."

Hans Olsa could think of nothing to say in answer to all this. They walked on in silence.

When they came into the house they stepped across the threshold reverently. An air of Sabbath had descended on the room. The sun shone brightly through the window, spreading a golden luster over the white walls; only along the north wall, where the bed stood, a half shadow lingered. A fire crackled in the stove; the coffeepot was boiling. The table had been spread with a white cover; upon it lay the open hymnbook, and beside it stood a bowl of water. Kjersti was tending the stove, piling the wood in diligently. Sörine sat in the corner, crooning over a tiny bundle; out of the bundle came faint, wheezy chirrups, like the sounds that rise from a nest of young birds.

An irresistible force drew Per Hansa to the bed. Beret lay sound asleep. Thank God, that awful look of dread had not come back! He glanced around the room; never before had he seen anything that looked so beautiful.

Sörine got up, went to the table, and bared a little rosy human head. The next moment they had all gathered around her. "Here's the book. Just read it out as well as you can, and we'll do whatever the book says," she encouraged her husband. Her confidence gave Hans Olsa the courage he needed. He read the ritual in a trembling voice, with many pauses. And so he christened the child Peder Victorious, pronouncing the name clearly.

"There, now," said Kjersti with great emphasis. "The coffee is ready and we're all going to have a cup."

But Per Hansa was searching over in the corner; at last he produced a bottle. First he treated Sörine, then Kjersti. "If ever two people have earned something good, you two are it! But hurry up about it, please! Hans Olsa and I feel pretty weak in the knees ourselves!"

After a while both food and drink were served. As they sat around the table Per Hansa said with a laugh, "It looks as if we are going to have a *real* Christmas after all!"

Chapter 8

WHEN BERET HAD FINALLY awakened on that Christmas day she lay still, peeping out at her surroundings and asking herself, "Am I still here? Is this me?" Hadn't she finished with this place some time ago?

But here she was, after all. Daylight shone broadly through the window and lit up the room; wood crackled in the stove; the walls Per Hansa had whitewashed rose before her. Neither Per Hansa nor the children were in sight. There was a woman working about the stove, but Beret could not see her face. Perhaps it was Kjersti. Wasn't she wearing Kjersti's plaid Sunday skirt?

She hovered gently on the border line between sleep and waking. For an instant she dropped off into unconsciousness; then she awoke with a start and felt that things were growing clearer. Making a sudden exertion, Beret was now wide-awake.

And there stood And-Ongen leaning over the bed, stroking her mother's cheek with a cool hand and stretching up on tiptoe to get a better view of the little wrinkled face in Beret's arms. Store-Hans was hanging over the foot of the bed, looking at them, while his father was coming in with an armful of wood.

"What have you done with Ole?" she asked in a natural voice, looking about the room.

"He's off with Henry and Sam, hunting wolf tracks," Store-Hans hastened to answer, happy because his mother was awake again. "Won't you let us see Permand?" He used a nickname meaning little Per.

"Please let us see him," begged And-Ongen.

As soon as Per Hansa had brushed the bark from his clothes he came over to Beret, took her hand, and held it silently for a long time. It was difficult for him to speak, but he managed at last to wish her merry Christmas and thank her for her gift.

"Ah, Beret, Beret! You know how to choose your time. Here you are with a great big boy at the very peep of day on Christmas morning! Who ever heard of such a woman?"

His eyes were tiny slits in his face from the great strain he was under, and she knew that his heart was crying. The knowledge brought tears to her own eyes. A sweet, heavenly peace enveloped her. Warmth and stillness. . . . Sunlight. Ah, it was good, after all, to be alive!

Of that day Beret remembered little else except that she was weak and tired, that a mildness like summer seemed to hover about her; everything was as it should be; all the world was good.

During the next few days she slept and slept. Life in the bundle at her side grew stronger, demanding its due; the button-sized nose dug itself into her breast, and then lay still with satisfied little gruntings. The movement gladdened her heart. Life was returning; Beret's body grew warmer and stronger with every day that passed. And the grunts at her side became more and more insistent. Ah, well, she would have to shift him over, then, so that there might be peace for a moment!

BLIZZARDS SWOOPED DOWN and stirred up a grayish white fury, impenetrable to human eyes. "The Lord have mercy! This is awful!" said the folk.

But ah, that newcomer! That winter it was *he*, that tiny, birdlike thing, who saved people from insanity and the grave. For he beguiled the heavy-hearted folk into laughing, and what can avail against folk who dare to laugh in the face of a winter like this one?

It was Beret's idea that on the thirteenth day after Christmas they ought to have all the neighbors over. Hadn't the good neighbors cared for them throughout the holidays, and long before Christmas, too, as if they had been their own kin?

As they sat there chatting through the long evening, they talked of the newcomer—and again of the newcomer—the first newcomer who had found his way to the Spring Creek settlement. Everyone was aware of the many extraordinary things connected with his arrival. Cunningly he had chosen his time—the high and holy Christmas morn! Besides, he had the caul on when he came. And his father had ventured to give him that bold second name . . . Victorious—that was not at all a human name!

Tönseten thought that Per Hansa must remember that he himself was only a human being. Where had he been on Christmas Eve, for instance? That was a thing Tönseten would like to know! He wasn't outside, and he wasn't inside. Tönseten had said a good many things like this to Kjersti when he had first heard about the name.

But that was one time when Tönseten should have kept still. Kjersti had been very angry with him and let him know that it was both right and proper for an unusual child to have an unusual name. So much Tönseten could stand, but what came next was harder to swallow. Kjersti had talked herself into a fit of crying—all about how lonely it was to sit there month after month without ever having anything to give a name to! He was wise enough about other people's children, but she hadn't seen him do much toward getting one himself. What did he think he was made for, anyway? . . . Well, perhaps not, Syvert had said; and he had added, viciously, Did she suppose that *he* could bear children? . . . Oh, he could talk like a fool, she had cried, stamping her foot on the floor. He could do anything but what he ought to! He was good for nothing in the world, the weak-kneed loafer!

But that episode was forgotten. Now they sat there rejoicing over the newcomer. They all felt themselves to be shareholders in him, but they couldn't agree over the division.

The boy undoubtedly belonged to Beret and Per Hansa. But it didn't follow from this that they possessed the sole and only rights to him. Had not Sörine and Kjersti stood by and been sponsors? Did not godmothers have a strong claim on their godchildren? And hadn't Hans Olsa been called to take upon himself the duties of priesthood? All this was beyond dispute, but just the same, protested Tönseten, it was hardly fair play, either to him or to the Solum boys; they, too, had claims. Not one of them had had a moment's peace on Christmas Eve. For his own part, he hadn't tasted a mouthful of food all day, and hadn't taken his trousers off all night!

No, they could not agree over their claims. Nor did they fare any better when it came to determining the newcomer's destiny. Henry wanted the boy to be a schoolmaster. Schoolmaster! As if that were good enough for such a boy! Kjersti lifted up her voice and announced that he should be a minister. "Minister?" said Sam. He made them all laugh with his two suggestions: either a hymn writer or a general.

Tönseten now arose, cleared his throat mightily, and said as if the thing were foreordained and altogether beyond dispute, "The boy will, of course, be President! He is born in the country—everything points in that direction!"

This fancy threw them into gales of laughter. But Hans Olsa did not join in the merriment; he remained grave and sat gazing thoughtfully at the wall. Now he stretched and said, "I think we'll be more in need of a good governor out here, Syvert; these prairies will be a state someday."

And there the discussion ended. All felt that at last Hans Olsa had proposed something that bore the stamp of good sense.

Neither Beret nor Per Hansa had taken part in this discussion. They sat listening to it, full of secret elation.

STILL, DESPITE THE NEWCOMER, no one knows what might have happened to them that winter if they had not had their school to fall back on.

At first it was held in the house of the Solum boys, but then it occurred to Sörine that Henry might just as well conduct his school in her house; in which case both she and Hans Olsa could benefit by the instruction. A little later, when Beret was quite well again, Per Hansa inquired if it mightn't be possible to move the school to *his* house every other week—for Beret's sake. Besides, both of them needed to learn English.

But then Tönseten felt that they weren't being entirely fair to him. So he proposed that they should move the school to *his* house every third week. True enough, he had no children; but they should remember that he had fathered the school itself. So that became the final arrangement.

Since there was little else to do these days, often the menfolk would sit in the school both morning and afternoon. The women made a practice of attending every afternoon. They came with their handiwork, and the men with their pipes. And at last the school became indispensable to all of them.

Never, perhaps, was a school organized along stranger lines. It served as primary school and grammar school, as language school and religious school. In one sense it was a club; in another it was a debating society; on other occasions it turned into a singing school, a coffee party, or a social center; and sometimes, in serious moods, it took on the aspect of a devotional meeting. In these ways the school bound together the few souls who lived out there in the wilderness.

There were no books, and no school materials of any kind, so Henry resorted to the means that lay nearest at hand—storytelling. All the tales that he had heard or read he related in either Norwegian or English, making the children repeat them until they had been memorized. In this way they learned both the story and the language. Then he proposed to set them the task of writing words and sentences. A fine plan, if they only had something to write on. Hans Olsa made a large wooden slate for Sofie and gave her the last remaining stub of a carpenter's pencil which he had brought from Norway. Per Hansa took two thick pieces of log and whittled each into an object intended to be a writing board for his boys. For pencils they used nails and bits of charcoal.

Problems in arithmetic always had to be worked out mentally, on account of the lack of writing materials. One day as they were doing sums, Tönseten arose and informed them that now *he* proposed to try their skill for a minute or two! He struck a dignified pose in front of the table.

"Listen carefully, you numskulls. Now then: five crows were sitting in a tree. A man came by with a gun. He shot one of them. How many were left in the tree?"

"Huh," grunted Ole, the brightest at sums. "You're fooling!"

"*That* is no problem," said Sofie. "There were four crows left, of course."

"Yes, if they were such dumb crows as you! Now, Hans, how many were left?"

"None," answered Hans thoughtfully. "The others flew away."

"Sure they did! Why should they keep on sitting there?" Tönseten gave Store-Hans a fatherly pat on the head. And then he turned to Henry. "*That's* the way to ask questions, Henry!"

DRIFTING SNOW AND COLD . . . gray weather . . . blizzards that lasted for days. The winter's supply of wood was disappearing very fast; by February it was almost gone, and there was no way out of it—the men would have to go east to the Sioux River for a further supply. Since they couldn't leave the women alone, the school served as a good excuse for keeping Henry at home. He would have to be the guardian of the whole settlement while they were gone.

Both Tönseten and Hans Olsa thought it impossible for Per Hansa to make the journey with oxen at this time of the year; they would be driving horses, and they advised him to join them. But before Christmas, Per Hansa had made a sleigh, such as it was. Now he asked the boys to help him after school, and taking the oxen out, he began to train them for halter driving. Heretofore he had used only the yoke, shouting "gee" and "haw," like everyone else in those days.

He had bought his ox team from a Swede in eastern Minnesota the previous winter, and he had named the beasts Old Sören and Perkel. The boys and the oxen had immediately become firm friends. They scratched the oxen's heads, they rode them like horses, and soon the animals would come trotting after whenever they caught sight of the boys. They stood patiently with the children hanging around their necks giving them a good scratching and saying "Old Sören" to one and "Perkel" to the other, and they must somehow have learned to associate this treatment with their new names, for they always responded when their names were called.

When Per Hansa took them out of the stable that cold winter day to teach them the new kind of driving, they were a pair of ragged and ugly-looking beasts. They stood before the sleigh in their new harnesses and gazed dully over the white prairie. Presently they lurched right into a snowdrift and stood there motionless, sticking out their tongues and licking the snow. This would never do! The boys shot forward and began scratching their heads furiously. When the oxen had thought it over long enough, and the commands from Per Hansa had taken on a brittle tone, they threw themselves forward into the harness and yanked the sleigh out like a feather.

Per Hansa and the boys kept on with the training every day, and at last they had progressed so far that one evening, as they unhitched the team, Per Hansa said to the boys, "There, they are working out splendidly! Now, if you two were worth your salt, you would take this outfit and drive to the Pacific for a load of fish for your mother and me!" The boys grinned and said nothing.

Per Hansa had determined to make the trip to the Sioux River with the oxen. That evening he was very high-spirited. As they were going to bed, Beret said, "I suppose you must make this trip, then?"

"Well, yes, I should say I must, if you and the newcomer aren't to freeze stiff!"

Again Beret lay awake far into the night, turning her thoughts over in her mind. This thing was terrible!

FOR SEVERAL DAYS the men waited for the right sort of weather. The wind kept veering; the cold was fearful. At last, late in February, came a clear, sunny morning with a soft breeze blowing like the first breath of spring. Somehow, it didn't seem natural for this time of year. "It has too sweet a face, I think!" Tönseten said. But they had better make a start, counseled Hans Olsa. The spring thaw would soon be setting in.

It was past ten o'clock before they were ready to set out. They had not burdened themselves with provisions, knowing that the Norwegians

near the Sioux River would be hospitable; but to be on the safe side they
all carried a small supply of food in their pockets.

The whole settlement was out-of-doors to see them set forth. The four
teams formed quite a caravan, each with its own sleigh, trailing in single
file across the white plain. Hans Olsa, who had the fastest horses, drove
in the lead; then came Tönseten; then Sam; while Per Hansa's oxen,
shambling along with him and his sleigh, drew up the rear.

All went well with Per Hansa. Once the oxen had started, they kept
the track without difficulty. The snow was soft, and it soon proved heavy
work to break the track. The three teams of horses had to take turns at it.

Sometime after midday the breeze settled down into a mild south
wind; the snow was growing more and more soggy under the runners;
the air seemed as soft as a May day; the sunshine almost blinded them
with its brilliancy. This lasted without change until after three o'clock.

So far everything had gone without a hitch and Per Hansa figured that
in two or three hours they would sight the hills by the Sioux River. But
just then, chancing to glance back toward the western horizon, he
caught sight of a black, billowy outline above the prairie, looming omi-
nously against the sky. He rubbed his eyes; was it a cloud? His heart
pounded; he spoke roughly to the oxen. The apparition came rushing
forward and upward with uncanny speed. A dark, opaque mass, it
writhed and swelled with life, like sooty smoke out of a furnace. Above
his head the heavens were still clear; but under the rim of the onrushing
cloud a bluish black shadow had settled on the prairie.

The south wind suddenly died in fitful gasps, leaving a chill in the air.
A weird silence had fallen. The thing in the west was possessed of
baleful life. It shot outward and upward. In a twinkling the day had been
swallowed in gloom.

Those in the lead had stopped. When Per Hansa reached them, the
three sleighs were all huddled together.

"It's going to strike us in a minute," said Hans Olsa soberly. He was
standing beside his sleigh, clearing the lashing rope.

"Looks like it," Per Hansa answered dryly. He jumped out and followed Hans Olsa's lead, clearing his own rope.

"This is what we must do," said Hans Olsa. "We'll pass a rope from
sleigh to sleigh, so that we won't lose each other in the storm."

"Yes, yes!" Per Hansa's sailor instincts were all alive. "It looks as if
the storm will travel the way we're going. We'll have to watch the wind.

Keep a sharp lookout for the country we know on this side of the river. If we should sail past the settlement, there'll be hell to pay. Hurry!"

Each man tied his lashing rope to his sleigh, and gave the other end to the one behind. Per Hansa ran forward to the Solum boy. "All ready, Sam? I don't believe I'll be able to keep up with you. But listen, don't give a thought to what lies *behind* you! Hold on like hell to Syvert's rope! It's a matter of life and death. Do you understand?"

Both Per Hansa and Hans Olsa—old fishermen that they were—had seen plenty of storms that made up fast; but nothing like this had ever come within their experience. Like lightning, a giant troll had risen up in the west. Now he would empty his great sack of woolly fleece above their heads.

A squall of snow so thick that they could not see an arm's length ahead, a sucking noise, a few angry blasts, howling in fury, then dropping away to uncertain drafts. High overhead a sharp hissing sound mingled with growls like thunder—and then the blizzard broke in all its terror.

The storm howled and whined, driving the snow before it like giant breakers. Per Hansa knitted his brows and squinted. A violent jerk came on his rope. To save himself from being dragged off his sleigh he was forced to let go. "There goes Sam!" he muttered, grinding his teeth.

The oxen floundered along; with every clumsy step they went more slowly; at last, with a great heave, they stood stock-still. Drawing their heads as far as they could into their short necks, they hunched their backs and lowered their heavy rumps into the snow to meet the force of the gale.

There they stood.

"God Almighty!" muttered Per Hansa. He threw himself out of the sleigh and fumbled his way along the traces till he came to the oxen; he caught hold of their necks and began rubbing their foreheads and talking into their ears. "Now, Old Sören . . . now, damn you, Perkel. By God, you'll have to be good boys!" Then he crept back into the sleigh. "Get along now, you devils!" he shouted. The whip lashed and cracked—the first time that he had ever struck them in earnest. The oxen gave a tremendous plunge . . . another . . . and off they careered into the heart of the storm. The sleigh was scudding now with terrific speed.

But what in heaven's name was that? Something had happened very suddenly. Through the murk he glimpsed a black object flying across the bows and disappearing astern. Wasn't that another? And another? Why, he must be passing the other teams! "Whoa!" he bellowed down the wind. "Stop! Stop! Whoa!"

But the oxen paid not the slightest attention. The spirit of the storm had possessed them; they tore along like mad things. Per Hansa could do nothing but cling desperately to the sleigh. This race through the storm lasted a long time; how long he did not know, but it seemed to him as if it had gone on forever.

Finally the oxen slackened their speed; the wild gallop sank to a trot, then to a jog, and then they stopped altogether. He could hear their exhausted puffing through the roar of the storm.

Per Hansa scrambled down from the sleigh again and managed to open a hay sack. The stinging snow drove like icy needles; it was impossible to turn one's face against it; it broke the skin. He tore out hay and began to rub down the oxen; when his strength was gone he struggled back to fetch the hay sack, held it under their noses, and let them eat. "Hurry now, troll-boys! God be praised, you can still wag your jaws!"

At last he got back to the sleigh and wrapped the blanket close around him. He emptied the hay sack and bundled it over his head. Then he shouted to the oxen; now they must show what stuff they were made of!

But the beasts had a different notion. Instead of rushing off as before, they began to saunter slowly with the wind, as if they were drawing the plow on a hot summer day. Per Hansa swore; he coaxed them and used pet names; he lashed them mercilessly, but the oxen continued to saunter unconcernedly through the storm as if they were on their way down to the creek to drink.

It had now grown pitch-dark; the night pressed close about him. Snow was falling less heavily, but the cold had become intense—it cut into his back like a knife; and the wind had risen, so that he had hard work to keep his seat in the sleigh. He sat there, huddled and freezing, and stared out into the blackness. So, this was his last journey!

The thought only made him impatient. God Almighty might have waited a while longer. He was so cold now that his teeth chattered all the time and couldn't stop. Then, after a while, the cold seemed to be letting up; he felt tired and drowsy . . . a good feeling. . . .

He pulled himself furiously together and deliberately chewed his tongue to keep awake. He knew too well what this drowsy feeling meant. It must not happen! To think of Beret alone with four youngsters!

Making a desperate effort, he flung himself out of the sleigh and staggered along beside the oxen, the lines wound securely around his arm.

Struggling through the storm, he felt more and more disgusted with God Almighty. To take him away from Beret now would be a wicked thing. Was this the way God cared for His own? "Beret, Beret," he kept sobbing. "I'm going . . ."

The storm raged around him; the cold bit deeper and stronger. He staggered on, fighting a battle that seemed to be without end. How sweet it would be to rest . . . to sit down here in this snowdrift.

Per Hansa was stumbling a good deal now; each time he fell it was harder to get up. The lines were jammed tightly around his arm; the oxen plowed onward; he had to get up or be dragged through the snow. . . . Rocky Mountains, Rocky Mountains! . . . Rocky Mountains? What a strange fancy; the Rocky Mountains didn't lie in this direction. Was he going mad? But directly behind those mountains lay the Pacific Ocean. They had no winter on that coast. God! If he could only cross the Rocky Mountains!

What had happened now? The oxen had stopped—were standing still. Per Hansa wasn't being dragged forward any longer. His first impulse was to sink down where he stood, to snatch a moment's peace. But deep within him a voice commanded him to keep on standing. He followed the lines, fumbled his way forward to Perkel, flung his arm across the animal's back, and leaned against his thigh. What nonsense was this? Between the heads of the two oxen a yellow eye seemed to be gleaming through the curtain of the driving snow . . . a great yellow eye.

It must be my death signal! thought Per Hansa.

Suddenly, Perkel gave a long-drawn bellow. He put such a powerful effort into that bellow that the noise shook Per Hansa out of his grim reverie. He felt his way along Perkel's back until he had reached the animal's head. It was rammed full-tilt against a log wall! It was the corner . . . the corner of a house!

Per Hansa trembled so violently that he could hardly keep his feet. He saw now that the shining eye was in reality the light from a small window. He found his way around the corner, came to a door, flung it open without ceremony, and stumbled in.

The heat of the room seemed to flow over him in a great wave, deadening all his senses, and the light blinded him. "Give me something to sit on, good folk," he heard his own faint voice saying from far away.

"You'll find . . . two good oxen outside. Get them under cover at once! I'm all right—but the oxen . . ."

Someone shoved forward a chair. He took hold of it and let himself sink down. His frozen clothes crackled like sheets of ice, shedding snow. A hubbub of voices rose around him. He felt there must be a crowd of people in the room, but their faces were a blank; a thick haze seemed to swim before his eyes. Then a palpable figure confronted him, with a voice that sounded strangely familiar. "For the Lord's sake! Is this you, Per Hansa?" it said.

Per Hansa burst into a laugh. "Where the devil did you drop from, Syvert? Is Sam with you?"

"Can't you see the boy? He's right in front of you. Thank God, Per Hansa, you're still alive!"

No wonder that they had failed to recognize him, no wonder that he couldn't see, for his whole face was covered with a mask of hard-caked snow. But little by little as he thawed out, his five senses came back to him; and sure enough, there they all were, his good neighbors. He knew the room well, too, and Simon Baarstad who owned it. He could see Sam plainly enough now, sitting close to the stove, beside a fair young girl. Ah, Sam, Sam! No doubt about it, you'll be a good man someday!

Simon Baarstad's wife, Gurina, gave him a large bowlful of hot milk to which she had added strong, home-brewed beer. He drank and drank, and then he listened in deep contentment while Hans Olsa related how they had driven like demons to save their lives. They had almost given up hope when they had gotten their bearings and had arrived at this very spot. That had been two hours ago; it was now past nine o'clock.

All at once something occurred to Per Hansa. Had any of them seen him drive past them in the storm?

Drive past them! "You're talking wild, Per Hansa," said Tönseten with an anxious look.

Certainly not! "Didn't you see me, Sam?"

Well, Sam remembered that he did see something go by—something black, just after the squall broke; it flew past like the wrath of the storm. "Was that you, Per Hansa?"

"You're damned right! That was my flying oxen passing your good-for-nothing old plugs."

—But where, in heaven's name, had he been in the meanwhile? asked everyone at once.

Per Hansa tipped up the bowl rakishly. "If you want to know, I took a little run up to Flandreau to see if I couldn't find a good-looking bride for Henry. I thought that was the least I could do for him, poor fellow. His brother can handle such matters for himself, it seems. Tell me, Sam, are you still as *cold* as all that?" Sam blushed crimson and hitched his chair away from the girl.

Later a large bowl of porridge was set out on the table for Per Hansa, a mug of hot milk beside it. He ate and ate; it seemed as if he could never get enough. Afterward there was much cozy talk. But at last it came time for them to retire. The members of the family lay down in their beds; the strangers slept on the floor, which had been piled deep with hay and covered with many thicknesses of blankets.

Per Hansa's mind was numb with weariness, yet he could not sleep. Every nerve of his body was twitching. It was very hot in the cabin; the blanket grew so heavy that he had to throw it off. Something remained still frozen, deep down in the center of his being.

A certain picture stood stubbornly before his mind: a sod-house beset by the western storm, a hut with the wind howling around the corners. A woman was moving about there whose sad face was still full of beauty; she carried a child in her arms. It lay wrapped in a blanket—a red blanket with black borders. It must be cold in her hut tonight. If the boys had only managed to bring enough wood in before the storm broke! Surely they must have some heat, or she would not be walking the floor. He turned over heavily many times, trying to blot out the vision; but the woman continued to pace up and down. He felt that he must let her know that all was well—tell her to go to bed now, so that a fellow might have a little peace. . . .

ALONG THE SIOUX RIVER, both above and below Simon Baarstad's place, there was already a considerable settlement, made up almost entirely of Norwegians. Some of these folk thought of themselves as old settlers already; the first had come in '66. Most of them had a good start now, were living in fair-sized frame houses, and possessed a good deal of land under cultivation.

And what adventures they were able to relate about the first few years! How they had had to cross the region that is now the southern part of South Dakota and go still farther southward into Nebraska to have their wheat ground at the mill; how the Indians had come by in large bands, both winter and summer. . . . *Now* there weren't any hardships, they said; now there were people everywhere, and the country was fairly settled.

Per Hansa liked to listen to these stories. Surely the things that Sioux River settlers could do were not impossible for settlers at Spring Creek!

The next day was clear and still, but bitterly cold. Per Hansa, who on his first trip the previous summer had bought an acre of woodland from Baarstad on time payment, remained on his own lot, felling trees and loading his sleigh. The others went around to different places, buying what wood they could find. The four men from Spring Creek stayed in the Sioux River settlement two whole days, and did not leave for home until the morning of the third day. In many months they had seen few strange faces; this visit was too much fun to cut short. And the hospitable folk would not hear of their leaving sooner. The four were easily tempted. The strain of life had relaxed for a moment; and besides there were a thousand things to consult about. Before they left they had ordered all the wheat and oats they would need for spring seeding.

Per Hansa, when he had finished making up his load of wood, wanted to try his luck on the river. He coaxed Baarstad until the latter consented to go with him. The two men went at it with a will, chopping their way through the thick ice, while the sweat rolled from their foreheads.

At night there was fresh fish on the table, and the two fishermen sat eating and rejoicing while they told tales of the old country.

As they sat there chatting, a boy came in to speak with the girl of the family. He seemed to be in hot haste, that boy, almost as if it were a matter of life and death.

—What was going on? asked Baarstad.

—Oh, Tommaas had company at his house, and they were going to have a little fun tonight.

The girl bustled about, got herself ready, and went away with him. Then it occurred to Baarstad that they might as well go, too. He told his wife to get ready. "We'll show you visitors how folk from our part of Norway can dance!"

A while later, as they opened the door of the Tommaas house, sounds of a scraping fiddle, mingled with the loud tramping of feet, poured out into the frosty night. The house was packed full of people, both young and old.

"Well, I'll be—!" The exclamation had jumped out of Per Hansa before

he could stop it. Here came Sam Solum, swinging past him with the Baarstad girl! Then another couple came rocking past. By God! It was Tönseten, tossing along with an apple-round woman!

"Syvert, old man! What would Kjersti think?"

"Shut your mouth, Per Hansa!"

At that Per Hansa completely forgot himself. "By all the frolicking seraphims, there's Hans Olsa dancing the schottische!" He looked around for the Baarstads, saw them close at hand, and grasped Gurina's arm.

"Come, show me how to dance that tune!"

Forgotten now was everything else; and with his arm around Gurina he maneuvered toward the center of the floor until he had reached his neighbor's side. "Get out of the way, Hans Olsa! I want plenty of room to swing in!"

At exactly eleven o'clock the party was over; Tommaas himself commanded them to stop. No one knew how it came about, but strangely enough, it was Sam who brought the Baarstad girl home.

The next morning, long before daylight, the four men left the settlement and were on their way back to Spring Creek.

THE DAYS WERE GROWING longer with every one that passed. March came, and the winter seemed to be letting up a little. Per Hansa worked with a desperate energy. If the day was too short for what he was doing, he simply added a part of the night to it. And in that month he achieved something that is still told about in legends of the settlement.

Every time he had visited the Sioux River, he had heard tales about the colony of Indians at Flandreau. Their whole winter occupation was trapping, and when spring came they would have large stocks of furs, especially muskrat, though they also trapped mink, fox, and wolf. They sold the skins for whatever they could get; but their best prices were no more than a fourth of what the same skins would bring in eastern Minnesota.

Per Hansa had brooded over these facts throughout the winter. Now March had come, there must be a great supply of furs stored up at Flandreau, and prices would be running high in Minnesota. Every day he went about thinking of it. The plan that was slowly forming in his mind was to go alone and trade with the Indians, making what profit he could. God knows, he needed it! And what was to hinder? Flandreau lay only forty miles away; from there to Worthington was perhaps another ninety miles; and there at Worthington stood the train, waiting for him! By taking Hans Olsa into the project there would be plenty of capital. Still, how could he take Hans Olsa and leave out Tönseten? No, he couldn't seem to hit on the right solution. But it was a thundering pity for that money to be lying right at his door—and he in need of another quarter section of land, with numberless things besides!

The first week of March went by.

One morning Per Hansa got up a little earlier than usual and looked out at the weather. Turning to Beret, he said that seeding time would soon be here—and he hadn't a penny in the world to pay for seeds. They needed many other things, too—food and clothes. It was time for him to think of some way of earning a few extra dollars.

As Beret listened, her heart tightened with apprehension, but she made no answer.

Then he told her about the Indian colony at Flandreau and how a fellow could easily earn a few dollars there. Didn't she think it would be a good plan for him to go up and look around? It wasn't far away. Still receiving no answer, he went on hurriedly. Didn't she suppose she could manage with just the boys at home for a little while? The days were getting longer now and things were looking better all around. . . . His voice trailed off.

Beret stared vacantly out the window. She thought, It was true that they needed much; most of all they needed clothes; she had nothing left to patch with. "I suppose we'll have to try to keep alive as long as we can. . . . When are you going?" she asked.

That made him happy. "Well now, Beret, if you think it's all right, I'd better set out today. I'm going to take the pony. The weather looks steady enough."

Half an hour later Per Hansa took his departure.

LATE AT NIGHT he reached Flandreau and found his way into a hut, where he spent the night. As soon as he had fed the pony the next morning, he took it along with him and poked around the village to interview the Indians. The savages watched him curiously, returning his stares. They recognized the pony, and seemed to know who Per Hansa was, too. He noticed this quickly and felt relieved. This scheme is going to work out all right, he thought. Then he followed the plan that he had formed long ago when he had first begun to think about it. Trusting wholly to his instincts, he selected out of the crowd the face that he liked best, beckoned the Indian forward, and uttered the one word, "Fur." As he did this, he gazed inquiringly into the man's face, but kindly, too, as if to inspire confidence in him.

The Indian understood at once. Of course he had plenty of furs! He took Per Hansa into his wigwam and showed him several bundles of fine muskrat skins.

Per Hansa laughed at his success. With the stick he carried in his hand he wrote the number 10 in the snow, and after it the word cents. Then he drew an object which was meant to be a man with a bundle on his back. He pointed first to the drawing, then to the figures, and at last made a vigorous gesture toward the Indian; this amused him very much, and he couldn't help smiling as he went through the motions. But all the honesty of his heart managed to come out in that smile, and the Indian saw it. A long period of bargaining followed, with many gestures, and much drawing and writing to be done in the snow. The upshot of it was that he bought as many furs as he judged he would be able to carry away. He arranged them in four bundles and hung them pack-fashion over the pony's back. Per Hansa was still laughing when he left Flandreau.

"Well now, forward, in God's name!" he said to himself, steering his course toward Minnesota, where he could sell his furs and buy supplies.

He was gone for a whole week on this expedition. When at last he reached home he had with him many of the things they needed—and even so there were forty dollars left! These he gaily counted out for Beret.

He remained at home two days. On the third day he left again.

Altogether, Per Hansa made three such journeys. The last two took him only six days each. When it was all over he was able to lay one hundred and forty dollars on the table for Beret; besides this, he had brought things for the house on each trip.

He had returned from the last journey with two frozen toes. These were giving him a good deal of trouble when he and Hans Olsa made a trip to the Sioux River settlement for seed. It was necessary to get it home while the sleighing lasted; he was not even properly rested when they had to set off.

In all this going and coming Beret had said very little, either when he set out or when he returned. He couldn't help feeling the strangeness of it; she had recovered from her illness long ago, and seemed quite well, as far as he could see. She might at least have told him that now he was getting on like a man! She would act differently if she had known, for instance, how he had ridden one time until he had nearly fallen from his horse with fatigue! And once or twice he had escaped death by a pretty narrow squeak. But then—better not tell her such things. She would probably be in better spirits when spring set in. If she would only say something brave and tender to him!

Chapter 9

PER HANSA AND THE BOYS sat around the table, sifting the seed; the wheat lay in small heaps on the white cloth. This was important work and must be done with the greatest care; every little weed seed and foreign substance had to be gleaned out. If he found a shrunken or damaged kernel, he threw it away. The best only for new soil! "Careful, boys! Don't shirk!"

It was wonderful to be playing with these plump, precious kernels; never before had Per Hansa been so absorbed in a task of this kind; yet it made him thoughtful, too. Here, then, was the start! These few sacks of grain would not only supply him and his family with all the wheat flour they needed for a whole year, but would raise many shiny dollars as well. And more than that, seed for next year, seed again for the year after, and for all the years to come. . . . And always greater and greater abundance of food for the poor, the world over. Wasn't it wonderful? Reverently he lifted handful after handful from the table and emptied it into the sack.

As the mild spring weather set in, a feverish restlessness seized him; the work on the seed was done and he could not stay indoors. The chickens were laying finely now; he was finding as many as five eggs a day. When fall came, they would have at least fifty fowl on the place! Next minute he was over on the prairie, caressing the oxen and feeling of their necks where the yoke would lie. Now if the ground would only dry up! Per Hansa looked at it first thing in the morning and felt of it every night before he went to bed. Today it had made fine progress. If the sun would only shine as warm tomorrow as it had today!

Beret hadn't seen him in such good spirits since last spring. He walked so lightly; everything that had life he touched with a gentle hand; his voice thrilled with energy. She felt a force emanating from him that made her tremble; she tried to keep out of his way.

And now the sun bore down on the prairie the whole livelong day. As the fine weather continued, Per Hansa became even more restless. Suddenly he would be up by the field. Wasn't it dry enough yet? On the morning of the fourteenth of April he went out three times to test the ground; the last time he made his great decision: *Now we will start!*

No sooner had he finished the noon meal than he filled the seed bag, hung it over his shoulder, and went to the field. He was ready. His whole body shook. He paused for an instant and glanced about the settlement. Yes, sir, he was the first, the very first one! There was Hans Olsa hauling manure to his garden patch; southward Tönseten was pottering around his yard. Muttering "So much for *you!*" Per Hansa stuck his hand into the bag.

Just at that moment both boys appeared on a dead run; they had discovered what their father was up to and wanted to watch the show. "Go home!" shouted Per Hansa.

"Why can't we stand here and watch?" The boys were disappointed.

"I don't want you tramping around here, carrying off this precious seed on your shoes!" But he suddenly realized that it was wrong of him to be so harsh, and his voice grew kinder. "Sowing wheat is such a particular job—each kernel has to lie exactly the way it falls. Be good now, boys, and go straight home. Tomorrow morning you can help with the dragging!" With this promise the boys had to be content; they went off homeward.

Per Hansa thrust his hand into the bag again and his fingers closed on the grain. He felt profoundly that the greatest moment of his life had come. Now he was about to sow wheat on his own ground! He was on the point of lifting his hand out again when something queer happened—the kernels were running out between his fingers! He closed his hand still tighter; again the yellow kernels slipped through his fingers like squirming eels. Then Per Hansa threw back his head and laughed. These fellows aren't very anxious to go into the ground after riches for me!

And now the wheat rained down in yellow semicircles from Per Hansa's hand; the warm rays of the sun struck full across it and seemed to wrap it in golden light.

Late in the afternoon Tönseten came running up the hill. "What in hell are you starting here, Per Hansa?" he demanded.

"Can't you see?" Per Hansa laughed.

Tönseten stared. "You're plumb crazy, man! The ground isn't half dry enough yet—the soil is too cold! You're throwing away all that seed!" And having done his duty and delivered his ominous message, Tönseten turned and stalked away.

As long as the daylight lasted, Per Hansa kept on seeding. After supper he sat at the table without moving; he didn't want to get up; a pleasant feeling of languorous exhaustion had settled on him. The next day he again worked like one possessed. The boys helped with the dragging, and when evening fell all the seed had been sown and only the oats were left to drag. He walked home that night in great satisfaction. Now he had turned a fine trick—he would be through seeding and dragging before his neighbors had even thought of beginning the regular spring work!

WHEN PER HANSA left the house the following morning to finish the dragging, the air was raw and heavy; not a trace remained of the mildness and pleasantness of the previous days. Before he had finished covering the oats, the rain began to fall; along with the rain came huge flakes of snow, floating silently down and turning to slush on the ground. After a while the flakes grew firmer. Before long a veritable blizzard was raging over the whole prairie—there had hardly been anything worse that winter.

Throughout that day and night the storm continued with unabated fury. Early the next morning the weather cleared; but the cold was so intense that it nipped the skin as soon as one stuck one's head out-of-doors. Spring seemed a thousand miles off.

That night Per Hansa did not sleep a wink. He was nothing but an old sailor; he didn't know the least thing about farming. Here he had gone to work and wasted all his precious seed—had simply thrown it away because he was foolish and hasty! Out in the field, under the snow, lay all that priceless wheat, frozen hard as flint. He could stand the loss of the oats, perhaps—but the *wheat!* Twenty-five bushels of seed he had sacrificed, and no possible way of getting a fresh supply.

All the forenoon he lay silent on the bed. When noon came and he refused to eat, Beret asked him, did he feel sick? But he only turned his face to the wall, muttering. Leave him alone; he'd be all right again—sometime!

That afternoon he still lay in bed. Per Hansa felt that he was fighting an unseen enemy. No sooner had the last kernel of wheat fallen to the ground than the very powers of heaven had stepped down to defeat him! Powers of heaven . . . ? A certain image came before his eyes and would not go away. One Sunday not very long ago, Store-Hans had sat by the table reading to his mother. He read in a loud voice, throwing great emphasis into the words:

"And the Lord said unto Satan, Whence comest thou? Then Satan answered the Lord, and said, From going to and fro in the earth, and from walking up and down in it."

The words would not go away. Per Hansa fell to repeating them. And that night as he lay awake, tossing restlessly, he thought that he saw a beam just inside the door of the stable; and there was a rope. . . . Well, if *that fellow* was after him, he might as well give up! Sweat broke out on his body. The beam and the rope beckoned him. They seemed to call to him!

The snow melted faster than anyone would have believed; it grew soft toward evening, and the next day's sun took all of it away. And now came days when the warm, bright sunshine filled everything between heaven and earth; the nights grew soft and balmy, and stirred with mysterious life. But all this could not alter the fact that Per Hansa's precious seed grain lay over there in the field, ruined by frost—those marvelous, pregnant kernels, so delicate and sensitive. Damn the luck!

One day as Per Hansa was pottering about out-of-doors, hardly knowing which way to turn, he caught sight of Tönseten, who had commenced his seeding. Like a condemned man about to be executed, Per Hansa walked over. But today Tönseten was too busy even to talk. His arms cut wide semicircles in the air; golden grain flew out of his hand and rained down through the warm sunlight.

This is beautiful! thought Per Hansa. I couldn't sow it as even as that!

"I was a fool for not waiting to get you to do the seeding for me," he observed.

Tönseten spat before he answered. "Well, some people are bound to cut off their nose to spite their face. But then—this is a free country!"

Per Hansa turned abruptly, his head in a whirl, and walked home to his own field. It was a forbidding sight that he saw there, lifeless, black, and bare. Falling on his knees, he dug into the soil, picked up the first kernel he came across, and laid it in the palm of his hand. The seed was black with clammy dirt. Carefully he picked off the particles of soil—and there it lay, a pale little thing, grayish white and dirty, the golden sheen entirely gone, the magic departed, the seed cold and dead. Per Hansa dug in the ground until he found another kernel. This one had the same lifeless color, but it was swollen and seemed about to burst open. "This is the frost!" he mumbled hoarsely. "It's all begun to rot!"

He rose and stood there, gazing out over his dead dream. *Then Satan answered the Lord, and said, From going to and fro in the earth, and from walking up and down in it. . . .* There can't be much doubt that he's found *this* place, all right—salt and pickle his guts!

FOR THE REST OF THAT WEEK Per Hansa and the two boys were busy planting potatoes. When Sunday morning came, Per Hansa ate his breakfast in silence, and then went back to bed. And-Ongen crawled into bed with him and stirred up a terrible commotion; he must tell her a story. Getting no answer, she pulled his hair and tugged at his nose. The carrying-on of the child made a pleasant diversion for him in his dark mood. Beret sat by the table, reading the Bible. To his great relief she said little these days.

As he lay there brooding he was turning over and over in his mind a new idea—mightn't he make another trip to the Sioux River? Perhaps he could yet scare up a couple of sacks of wheat there. But it was too late now to think of such a thing. Perhaps he had better go to Worthington and try to get work for the summer. Beret and the boys could get along without him. All the while And-Ongen was pommeling him because he wouldn't tell her a story.

Suddenly feet sounded outside, running. Ole jerked the door open. He was wild-eyed with excitement. "Per Hansa!" he cried, calling his father by name. "The wheat is up!" He leaped into the room and stood leaning over the bed. "The wheat is up, I say!"

And now Store-Hans came storming in, out of breath. "Father Per Hansa—the wheat is *so high!*" He was measuring on his finger. "And the oats about up to *here!* Don't you suppose we can buy a shotgun?"

Per Hansa said never a word; he got up, trembling in every limb, put And-Ongen aside, and rushed to the field. There he stood spellbound, gazing at the sight spread before him. His whole body shook; tears came to his eyes, so that he found it difficult to see clearly. And well he might be surprised. Over the whole field tiny green shoots were quivering in the warm sunshine.

Store-Hans was standing now by his father's side.

"Are you sick, Father?"

No answer.

"Why, you're crying!"

"You're . . . so . . . foolish, Store-Hans!" Per Hansa was blowing his nose violently. "*So terribly foolish!*" he added softly, and straightened himself up with a new energy.

He was a different man when he walked home again; the spring had come back to his step. Entering the house, he sat down by his wife, who was still reading the Bible, and said abruptly, "You'd better read us a chapter!" Then he cleared his throat and looked around the room. "No more nonsense, boys! Come here and sit down quietly while Mother reads."

THAT SUMMER MANY HAPPENINGS took place in the settlement by Spring Creek. Many new land seekers joined the Irish; they all settled west by the swamps, so as to have access to water for the cattle. The first part of June the Norwegians from the previous summer put into port; they, too, brought many new homesteaders with them. The latter all settled east of the creek, to be nearer to town. Soon one new sod-house after another began to stick its head above the waving grass of the prairie.

Many other land seekers passed through the settlement on their way west that summer. The arrival of a caravan was always an event. The prairie schooners, rigged with canvas tops which gleamed whitely in the shimmering light, first became visible as tiny specks against the eastern sky; but as one watched, the white dots grew; and after long waiting, they gradually floated out of the haze distinct and clear. The wagons would crawl slowly into the settlement and come to anchor; the moment they halted, people would swarm down, stretch themselves, and begin to look after the teams; cattle would bellow; sheep would bleat as they ran about. Many queer races and costumes were to be seen in the different caravans, and a babble of strange tongues shattered the air. The Lord only could tell whence all these people had come and whither they were going!

The caravan usually intended to stop only long enough for the women-folk to boil coffee and get a fresh supply of water; but the starting was always delayed, for the men had so many questions to ask. Once in a while during these halts a fiddler would bring out his fiddle and play a tune or two, and then there would be dancing. Such instances were rare, but good cheer and excitement invariably accompanied these visits.

One late afternoon as Beret sat out in the yard, milking, a wagon crept into sight. Soon the rest of the family ran out to see who it might be. There was only one wagon, with two cows following behind; on the left side walked a brown-whiskered, stooping man; close behind him came a half-grown boy, dragging his feet heavily. The wagon at last crawled up the hill and came to a stop in Per Hansa's yard.

"I don't suppose there are any Norwegians in this settlement?" asked the man in a husky, worn-out voice.

"If you're looking for Norwegians, you have found the right place, all right!" Per Hansa wanted to run on; but he checked himself, observing that the man looked as if he stood on the very brink of the grave.

—Was there any chance of putting up here for the night?

"Certainly! certainly!" cried Per Hansa.

The man walked to the wagon and spoke to someone inside. "Kari, now you must brace up and come down. Here we have found Norwegians at last!"

On top of his words there came out of the wagon first a puny boy with a hungry face, somewhat smaller than the other boy; then a girl of about the same size. She helped down still another boy, about six years old. The man stepped closer to the wagon. "Aren't you coming, Kari?"

A groan sounded within the canvas. The girl grabbed her father's arm. "You've forgotten to untie the rope!" she whispered angrily.

Curiosity took hold of Per Hansa; in two jumps he stood on the tongue of the wagon. The sight that met his eyes sent chills down his spine. Inside sat a woman on a pile of clothes, with her back against a large immigrant chest; around her wrists and leading to the handles of the chest a strong rope was tied; her face was drawn and unnatural. To Per Hansa it looked as though the woman were crucified.

"For God's sake, man!" Per Hansa said.

The stranger was pleading, "Come down now, Kari. Everything's going to be all right." He had untied the rope, and the woman had risen to her knees.

"O God!" she sighed, putting her hands to her head. She came down unsteadily. "Is this the place, Jakob?" she asked in a bewildered way.

But now Beret ran up and put her arm around her; the women looked into each other's eyes and instantly a bond of understanding was established. "Come with me!" urged Beret.

"O God! This isn't the place, either!" wailed the woman; but she followed Beret into the house.

"Well, well!" sighed the man as he began to unhitch the horses. "Life isn't easy—no, it certainly isn't."

Per Hansa watched him anxiously, hardly knowing what to do. Then an idea flashed through his mind. "You boys run over to Hans Olsa's and stay there tonight. Now run along!" Turning to the man, he asked, "Aren't there any more in your party?"

"No, not now. We were five wagons to begin with—five in all—but the others had to go on. Haven't they been by here yet?" The man sounded as if he were half sobbing.

"Where do you come from?" Per Hansa demanded.

The man didn't give a direct answer, but rambled on in a mournful way. They had been wandering over the prairie for nearly six weeks . . . from Houston County, Minnesota. . . . Strange that the others hadn't turned up here. Where could they be? It seemed to him as if he had traveled far enough to reach the ends of the earth! Good God, what a nightmare life was! If he had only—only known! . . .

"Did the others go away and *leave you?*" Per Hansa hadn't intended to ask that question, but it had slipped out before he realized what he was saying.

"They couldn't possibly wait for us—couldn't have been expected to. Everything went wrong, you see, and I didn't know when I would be able to start again. Womenfolk can't bear up. . . ." The man blew his nose.

Per Hansa dreaded what might come next. "Is she—is she *sick,* that woman of yours?"

The man wiped his face with his sleeve. When he spoke again, his voice had grown even more indistinct. "Physically she seems to be as well as ever. But certain things are hard to bear. You see, we had to leave our youngest boy out there on the prairie. . . ."

"*Leave* him?"

"Ya, there he lies, our little boy! I never saw a more promising one—I mean—when he grew up. But now . . ."

Per Hansa felt faint. "Tell me—how did this happen?"

The man continued with great effort. "The boy had been ailing for some time—we knew that, but we had other things to think of. Then he began to fail fast. We were only one day's journey this side of Jackson, so we went back. That was when the others left us. I don't blame them much—it was uncertain when we could go on. The doctor we found spoke only English and I couldn't understand him, but he had no idea what was wrong with the boy—I could see that plainly enough. . . . Ya, well—so we started again, trying to catch our neighbors. . . . Well, that's about all of it. One night he was gone—just as if you had blown out a candle. That was five nights ago. We buried him out there by a big stone—no coffin or anything. Kari wrapped him in the best skirt she had. . . . But," he continued, "Paul cannot lie there! As soon as I find my neighbors, I'll go get him. Otherwise Kari . . ." The man paused between sobs. "I have had to tie her up the last few days. She insisted on getting out and going back to Paul. I don't think she has had a wink of sleep these five nights. Some people can't stand things. . . ."

The eldest boy was standing a little way off, listening; suddenly he threw himself on the ground, sobbing as if in convulsions.

"John!" admonished the father. "Aren't you ashamed of yourself—a grown-up man like you!"

Per Hansa pulled himself together. "We'd better all go in. There's shelter here, and plenty to eat."

Beret was bustling around the room when they entered; she had put the woman to bed, and now was tending her. Per Hansa told her he had sent the boys to Hans Olsa's for the night.

The man had paused at the door. Now he came over to the bed, took his wife's limp hand, and muttered, "Poor soul! Why, I believe she's asleep already!"

Beret came up and pushed him gently aside. "Be careful!" she said. "Don't wake her. She needs the rest."

After supper Beret fixed up sleeping quarters in the barn for the man and his children. She carried in fresh hay and brought out all the bedding she had. She went about these arrangements with a firmness and confidence that surprised her husband.

Per Hansa came in from the barn after helping the strangers settle; Beret was sitting on the edge of their bed dressing the baby for the night; she had put And-Ongen to bed beside the woman.

"Did she tell you much?" Per Hansa asked in a low voice.

Beret glanced toward the other bed before she answered. "Only that she had had to leave one of her children on the way. She wasn't able to talk connectedly."

"It's a terrible thing!" he said, looking away from his wife. "I'm going over to Hans Olsa's to talk for a minute. These people have got to be helped, and we can't do it alone."

When he returned an hour later, Beret was still sitting on the edge of the bed. She waited until he was in bed, then turned the lamp low and lay down herself. It was so quiet in the room that one could hear the breathing of all the others. Beret lay there listening; though the room was still, it seemed alive to her with strange movements. Finally in a low voice she asked Per Hansa, "You told them everything, at Hans Olsa's?"

"Yes." Per Hansa raised himself on an elbow and glanced at the broken creature lying in the bed back of theirs. "It's a bad business," he said. "We decided to try to get together a coffin and find the boy. We can't let him lie out there—that way."

At first Beret made no answer. Then in a bitter tone she suddenly burst out, "Now you can see that this kind of a life is impossible! It's beyond human endurance."

Every nerve in Per Hansa's body went taut with dismay. But he tried to say, reassuringly, "Hans Olsa and I will both go with the man, as soon as the day breaks. If only we had more board for making the coffin!"

He turned over resolutely, as if determined to sleep; but she noticed that he was a long time doing it. She was glad to have him awake, just the same; tonight there were strange things abroad in the room.

THE SLEEPING WOMAN remained in the same position until three o'clock in the morning. But then her senses slowly began to revive; she realized that she was lying in a strange room, where a lamp burned with a dim light. Suddenly she remembered that she had arrived here last night— but Paul was not with her. . . . I must hurry now before Jakob sees me, because there's no way of stopping him—he always wants to go on! And she would have to take a blanket with her, for the nights were chilly and Paul had very little on—only a shirt that was worn thin.

She sat up and buttoned her clothes, then slipped quietly out of bed. For a moment she stood still, listening; then bending suddenly over the bed, she snatched up And-Ongen. She held the child tenderly in her arms and put her cheek against the warm face. With quiet movements she wrapped her skirt about the sleeping child. Glancing around the room to see if all was well, she glided out like a shadow; she did not dare to close the door behind her lest it should make a noise. "Here is our wagon!" she murmured. "I mustn't let Jakob see me now; he only wants to go on!" Clutching the sleeping child to her breast, she started on the run, taking a direction away from the house.

316

Beret was awakened by a voice calling to her from a great distance; it called loudly several times. What a shame they can't let me alone to get a little rest! she thought drowsily. But the voice kept calling so persistently that after a while she sat up in bed, her mind coming back to reality; she remembered the strangers, and she turned her head to see how the other woman was resting.

"Heaven have mercy!"

In a second Beret had reached the side of the other bed, but no one was there. She did not notice that And-Ongen was gone, too. A cold draft rushing through the room told her that the door stood open. Beret went through the door and circled the house; she listened intently, then called; getting no answer, she ran back into the house, crying to her husband, "She's gone! Get up! Hurry!"

In an instant Per Hansa was up and had tumbled into his clothes. When they came out, the first light of day was creeping up the sky. Per Hansa scanned the prairie in every direction. What was *that,* over there? Was it a human being standing on top of the hill? He called to Beret and they both started out on the run.

When Per Hansa had almost reached the woman, he stopped stone dead. What, in God's name, was she carrying in her arms? His face blanched with terror. "Come here!" he shouted. In a moment he had the child in his arms.

And-Ongen was almost awake now and had begun to whimper. Sleepily she cuddled up in her father's arms, her cheek against his heart. She had to sleep some more! But now Mother was here. Hurriedly she was transferred into her mother's arms and squeezed almost to a pancake. Nevertheless she snuggled as closely as she could, for she still felt, oh, so sleepy!

As Beret walked homeward carrying the child, it seemed more precious to her than the very first time when she had held it in her arms. Upon this night the Lord had been with them: His mighty arm had shielded them from a fearful calamity.

The other woman kept on hunting up there on the hill. Wouldn't these people help her to find Paul? She had to find him at once—he would be cold with so little on.

Per Hansa went up and spoke to her. "Today Hans Olsa and I are going to find your boy." Taking her gently by the arm, he led her back to the house.

At breakfast she ate when they bade her, but never spoke. While they were making the coffin she sat looking on, wondering why they didn't work faster. Couldn't they understand that Paul was cold?

As soon as the coffin was ready, Per Hansa and Hans Olsa, along with the stranger and his wife, left the settlement to hunt for the body of the dead boy. They were gone four days on the search; they crisscrossed the prairie for a long way to the east; but when they returned, the coffin was still empty.

AFTER THE RETURN from the search the strangers stayed one more day with them. The morning they were to leave, the sky looked threatening, but toward noon it cleared, and as soon as the noon meal was over they got ready to go. Per Hansa asked the man where he intended to settle.

—Well, he wasn't positive as to the exact place. It was over somewhere toward the James River—his neighbors had told him that.

—Did he know where the James River was?

—Certainly he did! The river lay off there; all he needed to do was steer straight west. After finding the river, of course he'd have to ask. But that part of it would be quite easy. . . .

Per Hansa shuddered, and asked no more questions.

The woman had been quite calm since their return. She kept away from the others, pottering over insignificant things, much like a child at play; but she was docile and did what anyone told her. The man seemed fairly cheerful as they started; he talked a good deal, heaping many blessings upon Per Hansa, and many thanks. And now they must be off.

The family piled into the wagon; the wagon started creaking; the man led the way; the two cows jogged behind. They laid their course due west. Banks of heavy cloud rolled up on the western horizon—huge, fantastic forms that seemed to await them in heaven's derision.

After they had gone, Beret could find no peace. She reproached herself for not having urged these people to stay longer. That's the way I've become, she thought sadly. Here are folk in the deepest distress, and I am glad to send them off into worse calamities! What will they do tonight if a storm comes upon them? He is all broken up—he couldn't have been much of a man at any time. And the poor wife insane from grief! What misery, what an unspeakable tragedy life is for some!

After supper Per Hansa went to talk to Hans Olsa. The boys went with him. Beret, when she had washed the dishes, went outdoors and sat down on the woodpile. The air had grown heavy and sultry; the clouds in the west had taken on a still more threatening aspect. A nameless apprehension would not leave her in peace, and taking the two younger children, she ascended the hill. The spell of the afternoon's sadness was still upon her. Those poor folk were straying somewhere out there, under the towering clouds. Poor souls! The Lord pity them! How could the good God permit creatures made in His image to fall into such tribulations? How could folk establish homes in an endless wilderness? Was it not the Evil One that had struck them with blindness? Beret was gazing at the western sky as the twilight gathered; her eyes were riveted on a certain cloud that had taken on the shape of a face, awful of mien and giantlike in proportions; the face seemed to swell out of the prairie and fill half the heavens.

She gazed a long time; now she could see the monster more clearly. The face was unmistakable! The eyes were deep, dark caves in the cloud; the mouth, if it were to open, would be a yawning abyss. And the terrible creature was spreading everywhere. She trembled so desperately that she had to take hold of the grass.

Here was the simple solution to the whole riddle. She had known in her heart all the time that people were never led into such deep affliction unless an evil power had been turned loose among them. Hadn't she always clearly felt that there were unspeakable things out yonder?

She sat still as death, feeling the supernatural emanations all around her. The face came closer in the dusk—didn't she feel its cold breath upon her? When that mouth opened and began to suck, terrible things would happen! Without daring to look again, she snatched up the children and ran blindly home. As soon as they were inside, she covered all the windows.

After that time, Beret was conscious of the face whenever she was awake, but particularly toward evening, as twilight came on; then it drew closer to her and seemed alive. Even during the day she would often be aware of its presence; the sun might shed a flood of light, but through and behind the light she would see it—huge and horrible. Many times she was on the point of asking her husband if he saw what she did, towering above the prairie. But why mention it? Couldn't he and the others see it for themselves? How could they help it? Every evening now, whether Per Hansa was away or at home, she hung something over the windows—it helped shut out the fear.

At first her husband teased her about it, as if it were a good joke. But as time went on he ceased laughing; the fear that possessed her had begun to affect him, too.

THE MONTH OF JULY wore on. With every day that passed, the wheat filled out more; the heads grew heavy and full of milk. These days Per Hansa was behaving like a good boat in a heavy sea—as long as the keel pointed the right way, he would go on. He watched his wife covering the windows at night, and felt both sad and angry; but when he saw how everything was growing on the farm—meadows and fields, cattle and youngsters—then he was filled with an exultant joy that made him momentarily forget his wife's condition. True enough, she didn't act as a normal person should; yet it was nothing that wouldn't naturally right itself with time. And meanwhile everything he had planted that spring was blooming like a garden. Why, he could just *hear* the potatoes grow! The oats, too, were standing high; but the wheat—best of all was the wheat! The new neighbors to the east, and even the Irish from over to the westward, would come just to look at his wheat field and say that the sight did them good.

By this time Tönseten had lost the last vestige of ill feeling toward Per Hansa for doing his seeding early. Now they would be able to cut and harvest here before the other fields had ripened.

Tönseten's round, fat body bristled with importance, for of course it would fall to him to do the reaping for these greenhorns. The Solum boys would have to teach them how to bind. Damn it, he couldn't be expected to do everything! . . . Yes, Syvert Tönseten was a very busy man these days. There was the reaper to overhaul and the harnesses to be mended; he had to keep a sharp eye on the grain, too, lest they let it stand too long. So he waddled back and forth between the houses of his three neighbors, invariably finding some important matter to discuss wherever he went.

Per Hansa, who was always so impatient, seemed in no hurry to start his harvesting. Every evening he would make a trip up to the field, and with each trip his mind was more at ease. When Tönseten insisted that it was time to start cutting, Per Hansa would argue with him. "No, Syvert brother, let's give the wheat a spell longer to think it over."

But one forenoon Tönseten came over in great excitement, declaring flatly that now they would have to start cutting here—and no use talking! He had just come from Hans Olsa's; there, too, the grain was ripening fast.

"Let's just give her one more night for extra measure!" argued Per Hansa.

Tönseten waved his arms. "You're a stubborn, ignorant fool, Per Hansa—I don't mind telling you so! What will happen to us if all our grain needs reaping at the same time? I've made up my mind," he said. "We start this afternoon. Now go tell Hans Olsa and the Solum boys!"

The moment the noon meal was over, the whole of the little settlement assembled at Per Hansa's wheat field: men, women, and children; Beret brought And-Ongen and even carried the baby in her arms. Tönseten's shouts and commands put everyone but himself in a festive mood; he felt it to be a solemn occasion; but the others laughed and joked as gaily as if they were in a bridal procession. Well, fools will snicker and chatter, Tönseten observed to himself, as he lay on his back under the mowing machine, hammering away with a monkey wrench.

At last he got things so far along that he could hitch the horses to the reaper; taking the lines, he mounted to the throne. "Now, the Lord help us!" he muttered. With a flourish he maneuvered the reaper over to the edge of the field, shouted to the horses—and the first harvest in the Spring Creek settlement had begun. At first Tönseten was too much taken up with his momentous task even to see the others. But when he had finished the fourth round of the field, he stopped the machine and called to Henry Solum—how was *he* getting along? Kjersti had been a smart binder in her day; but as for the others, had he been able to pound sense into those idiots? All were working; all were having a good time. The greenhorns had caught on to the trick of binding; there were so many of them that it went like a jolly game. Even Beret put the baby down and began tying up bundles.

Per Hansa was in a rare mood that afternoon. Now he was binding his own wheat, his hands oily with the sap of the new-cut stems; he rubbed his hands together and felt a sensuous pleasure. How good it was to be alive! Luck had smiled on him! How absurdly lighthearted he felt today!

The men continued working until the dew became so heavy that the reaping machine refused to go; it was long after sundown before they quit. Beret, Kjersti, and Sörine had left early to fix a supper, and in Per Hansa's hut stood a table heaped with many good things. The men seated themselves quickly at the table, while Per Hansa hunted for

321

something or other in the big chest. "Hold on a minute, boys, before you say grace," came from the cavernous depths of the chest. When he finally emerged, he shook a bottle behind Tönseten's ear, asking gaily, "Did you ever hear a sweeter sound, Syvert?"

There was enough for one round, and then a little drop to swallow on, before the meal started. Tönseten cleared his throat after the drink; he was anxious to make a little speech. "What do you plan on doing in the future, Per Hansa, if you're going to get rich on the very first crop? I never in my life saw such wheat! Why, the kernels are like potatoes!"

"How about yourself, then?" inquired Per Hansa in great good humor. "I like to help worthy people who are in trouble; in case you and Kjersti should run short of stockings to keep your money in, you might come to me!"

"We'll all get rich; no doubt about it!" exclaimed Tönseten. "It's going to be hardest on Sam, poor fellow. He'll have to spend it all in getting married to that fine girl over by the Sioux River! Hard luck, I say!"

BY NOON THE NEXT DAY they had finished the wheat field. Today Tönseten was of a different mind—there really was no great hurry; the weather had turned cool, and if this spell should last, the wheat at his own place and at Hans Olsa's would profit by yet another week. It wouldn't do any harm to rest and visit awhile before finishing off Per Hansa's four acres of oats. . . . So Per Hansa and the other men sat in the shade on the north side of the house, with their backs against the wall, spinning yarns and enjoying the cool breeze that had sprung up from the west. What was the use of hurrying?

As they got up at last and returned to reap the oats, the cool northwest breeze struck them full in the face; Tönseten sniffed it approvingly, declaring that never had the Lord sent finer weather for wheat to ripen in! But Per Hansa had suddenly turned silent; he was shading his eyes with his hand and looking into the west; an intent, troubled expression had come over his face. "What in the devil . . . ?" he muttered to himself. Off in the sky he had caught sight of something he couldn't understand. Could that be a storm coming on?

Tönseten had been hitching the horses to the reaper. He had just mounted the seat when Per Hansa ran over, pointing to the west. "What's that, Syvert?"

Tönseten turned to face a sight such as he had never seen before. Within moments, layers of clouds came rolling from out of the west—

thin layers that rose and sank on the breeze. They had none of the look or manner of ordinary clouds; they came in waves, like the surges of the sea, and cast a glittering sheen before them as they came.

The men stared spellbound, watching the oncoming terror. The horses snorted as they, too, caught sight of it. The ominous waves of cloud seemed to advance with terrific speed, breaking now and then like a huge surf, and with the deep, dull roaring sound as of a heavy undertow rolling in caverns. It seemed as if the unseen hand of a giant were shaking an immense iridescent tablecloth!

"For God's sake, what . . . !" Tönseten didn't finish. The next moment the first wave of the weird cloud engulfed them, spewing over them its hideous, unearthly contents. Tönseten could not hold the horses; they bolted across the field, cutting a wide semicircle through the oats; not until he had the stern of the reaper into the wind could he stop them long enough to scramble down and unhitch them.

At that moment the Solum boys came running up, and Ole and Store-Hans, and then the two women—Kjersti with her skirt thrown over her head, and Sörine beating the air with frantic motions. Down by the creek the cows had hoisted their tails straight in the air and run for the nearest shelter; the horses followed suit; man and beast alike were overcome by a nameless fear.

And now from out the sky gushed down with cruel force a living, pulsating stream, striking the backs of the helpless folk like thrown pebbles; but this substance had no sooner fallen than it popped up again, crackling, snapping; it flared and flittered around them like light gone mad; it chirped and buzzed through the air; it hopped along the ground; the whole place was a weltering turmoil of raging little demons; the cloud was made up of innumerable dark brown bodies!

"Father!" shrieked Store-Hans. "They're little birds—they have wings! Look!" The boy had caught one; holding the wings out by their tips, he showed it to his father. The body of the unearthly creature was about an inch in length; on either side of its head sparkled a tiny black eye; underneath it were long, slender legs with rusty bands; the wings were transparent and of a pale, light color.

"For God's sake, child, throw it away!" moaned Kjersti.

The boy dropped it in fright. No sooner had he let it go than there was a twinkling flash, and the creature had merged itself with the countless flickering legions which now filled all space. They whizzed by in the air;

they lit on the heads of grain, on the stubble, on everything in sight—popping and glittering, millions on millions of them. The people watched, stricken with fear and awe. Here was *Another One* speaking!

Kjersti was crying bitterly; Sörine's kind face was deathly pale as she glanced at the men, trying to bolster up her courage; but the big frame of her husband was bent in dismay. He spoke slowly and solemnly. "This must be one of the plagues mentioned in the Bible!"

"Yes, and the devil take it!" muttered Per Hansa darkly.

To Tönseten, Per Hansa's words sounded like blasphemy. He turned to reprove his neighbor. "Now the Lord is taking back what He has given," he said impressively. "I might have guessed that I would never be permitted to harvest such wheat. That was asking too much!"

"Stop your silly gabble!" snarled Per Hansa. "Do you suppose *He* needs to take the bread out of your mouth?"

There was a certain consolation in Per Hansa's outburst of anger. Kjersti ceased weeping. "I believe Per Hansa is right," she said. "The Lord can't have any use for our wheat."

But her open disbelief only confirmed her husband in his position; clearing his throat, Tönseten began to take Kjersti to task. "Isn't it plainly stated in the Bible that this is one of the seven plagues that fell upon Egypt? Look out for your tongue, woman, lest He send us the other six, too!"

Henry Solum interrupted with a practical idea. Turning to his brother, he said, "Go fetch the horses, so we can finish this field; by tomorrow there won't be anything left!"

Per Hansa looked at Henry and nodded approvingly; then he jumped to his feet and walked across to the field. As he saw the fine, ripe grain being ruthlessly destroyed before his eyes, he began to jump up and down and wave his hat, stamping and yelling like one possessed. But the hosts of horrid creatures scarcely noticed him; they whizzed by, alighting wherever they pleased, chirping; even his own body seemed to be a desirable halting place; they lit on his arms, his back, his head—on the very hat he waved. His utter impotence threw Per Hansa into uncontrollable fury. "Ole!" he shouted. "Run home after Old Maria!"

The boy was soon back with the musket. His father snatched the weapon out of his hands.

Hans Olsa caught wind of what he intended to do. "Don't do that, Per Hansa! If the Lord has sent this affliction on us . . ."

Per Hansa glowered at him; then, facing the hurricane of flying bodies, he fired straight into the thickest of the welter. At first, as the sound died away, nothing appeared to have happened; but presently the cloud of glittering demons began to heave, roll, and lift; in a few minutes it had left the ground and was sailing over their heads.

"Do you suppose you've actually driven them off?" cried Henry.

"Yes, from *here!*" said Hans Olsa. "But see *our* fields!"

Per Hansa apparently did not hear what the others were saying. "Let's get the reaper started!" he cried, and without looking again, he hurried off to help Sam with the horses. Silently the others followed his lead; just before sundown that night they finished the oat field at Per Hansa's. All the while fresh clouds of marauders were passing over. As soon as he could get away, each man hurried home to see how much damage had been done. Would it be possible to save *something* out of the wreck?

Ole and Store-Hans went home with Hans Olsa to see whether they could start harvesting his field in the morning. Per Hansa walked home alone in a troubled frame of mind. The thing that had happened that afternoon seemed harsh and inexplicable. To be sure, *he* had saved his whole crop—but how and why? He had saved it—partly because of his own foolish, headstrong acts, and partly because his land chanced to lie so much higher than that of his neighbors that it had been the first to dry out in the spring. Well, great luck for him! But his neighbors—poor devils! Hadn't they struggled just as hard? Why should they have to suffer this terrible calamity while he went scot-free? And there was something else that worried him desperately. Throughout the afternoon vague misgivings of how it was going at home had plagued him; he had found himself constantly watching his own house, and had every moment expected to see Beret come around the corner. But not a soul had he caught sight of in all this time.

As he approached the house his misgivings grew more pronounced. The house lay in deep twilight; there was no sign of life to be seen or heard except for the malign beings that still snapped and flared through the air; the sod hut, surrounded as it was by flowing shapes, looked like a quay thrust out into a turbulent current; in the deepening twilight the pale, shimmering sails of the flying creatures had taken on a still more unearthly sheen; they came, flickered by, and were gone in an instant, only to give place to myriads more.

Can she have gone over to one of the neighbors? he wondered as he came up. No, she hadn't—something was blocking the door on the inside, he realized as he tried to open it. Per Hansa gasped for breath as he knocked on the door of his own house. He rapped harder. "Open the door, Beret," he called, with his voice tearing from his throat.

At length he thought he heard a movement inside, and a great wave of relief swept over him. He waited for the door to be opened, but nothing happened. Didn't she hear him? What in heaven's name had she put in front of the door?

Per Hansa had begun to shove against the panel. "Open the door, I tell you! Beret—where are you?"

Once more he caught a faint sound. With all his strength he shoved against the door—shoved until red streaks flashed before his eyes. The door gave; at last he had pushed it wide enough to slip through.

"*Beret!*" The anguish of his cry cut through the air.

Now he stood in the middle of the room. It was absolutely dark; he could see nothing. "Beret, where are you?"

Then came another sound. "Beret!" he called again, sharply. He heard it now distinctly—a faint whimpering. He rushed to the beds and threw off the bedclothes—no one in this one, no one in that one—it must be over by the door! He staggered back—the big chest was standing in front of the door. Who could have dragged it there? Per Hansa flung the cover open with frantic haste. The sight that met his eyes made his blood run cold. Down in the depths of the great chest lay Beret, huddled up and holding the baby in her arms; And-Ongen was crouching at her feet—the whimpering sound had come from her.

It seemed for a moment as if he would go mad; the room swam in dizzy circles. But things had to be done. First he lifted And-Ongen and carried her to the bed—then the baby. At last he took Beret up in his arms, slammed down the lid of the chest, and set her on it. "Beret, Beret!" he kept whispering. All his strength seemed to leave him as he looked into her tear-swollen face; yet it wasn't her tears that drained his heart dry—the face was that of a stranger, behind which her own face seemed to be hidden.

He gazed at her helplessly, imploringly; she returned the gaze in a fixed stare, and whispered hoarsely, "Hasn't the devil got you yet? He has been all around here today. Put the chest back in front of the door right away! He doesn't dare to take the chest, you see. We must hide in it—all of us!"

"Oh, Beret!" Speechless, undone, Per Hansa sank down before her and buried his head in her lap—as if he were a child needing comfort. The action touched her; she began to run her fingers through his hair. "That's right!" she crooned. "Weep now, weep much and long because of your sin! So I have done every night—not that it helps. Out here nobody pays attention to our tears."

"Oh, Beret, my own girl!"

"Yes, yes, I know," she said, as if to hush him. She grew more loving, caressed him tenderly, bent over to lift him up to her. "Don't be afraid, dear boy of mine! For . . . well . . . it's always worst just before it's over!"

Per Hansa gazed deep into her eyes; a sound of agony came from his throat; he sank down suddenly in a heap and knew nothing more. Outside, the fiendish shapes flickered and danced in the dying glow of the day.

AND NOW HAD BEGUN a seemingly endless struggle between man's fortitude in adversity on the one hand, and the powers of evil in high places on the other. The scourge raged with unabated fury throughout the years '74, '75' '76, '77, and part of '78; then it disappeared as suddenly and mysteriously as it had come. The devastation made beggars of some and drove others insane; still others it sent wandering back to the forest-lands. But the greater number simply hung on where they were. They stayed because poverty, that most supreme of masters, had deprived them of the liberty to rise up and go away. And in the name of heaven, where would they have gone?

In the course of time it came about that fresh inroads of settlers arrived to help them suffer privation and to wait for better times. . . . Beautiful out here on the wide prairie—yes, beautiful! The finest soil you ever dreamed of! One caravan after another came creaking along, one to settle here, another there; for it really looked wonderful, this vast expanse of level, smiling plain.

But the plague of locusts proved as certain as the seasons. All that grew above the ground, with the exception of the wild grass, it would pounce upon and destroy; the grass it left untouched because it had grown here ere time was and without the aid of man's hand. Who would dare affirm that this plague was not of supernatural origin? Throughout the early part of the summer the air would be as pure and clear as if it had been filtered, caressing the body like the finest silk; everything planted in the ground by man would grow as if by magic. And then on a certain bright, sunny day, strange clouds would appear in the western sky, floating through the clear air; and in an instant the air would be filled with nameless, unclean creatures—legions on legions of them, hosts without number! Now pity the fields that the hand of man had planted with so much care!

It would happen for days at a time, during the height of the pest season, that one could not see clear sky. But not always did the scourge choose to descend, often the locust clouds would come drifting across the sun, very much like streamers of snow, floating lazily by for days on end; then, as if overcome by their own neglect, they would swoop down, spreading out like an angry flood, slicing and shearing, cutting with greedy teeth, laying waste every foot of the field they lighted in.

Impossible to outguess them! No creatures ever showed such a lack of method. One field they might entirely lay waste, while they ate only a few rods into the next; a third, lying close, they might not touch at all. Nor were they fastidious: potatoes and vegetables of all kinds they ate, barley and oats, wheat and rye—it made no difference; or a garment might have been laid out on the ground to dry—a swarm would light on it, and in a moment only shreds would be left.

The folk looked on helplessly; the more timid ones among them were oppressed by a growing fear, while the godless swore so that the air smelled of brimstone; the pious would assemble in homes and churches, entreating the Lord to deliver them from famine and pestilence; but the brave did not lose heart, and kept on busily inventing all sorts of devices with which to drive the demons away.

All the while the folk tried to comfort one another. It will be better by and by, you know! This plague can't go on forever! Wasn't it pretty bad in Egypt? And when it turned out to be just as bad the following year, the same folk would be even more confident. Now, see—we've had this thing with us two years already—this is the end! And even when the third summer came, and there was no letup in the awful visitation, some bright head would remember the indisputable fact that *all bad things are three.* So there! We're through with it at last!

On through the fourth summer the plague raged worse than ever; but now it had begun to lose its power over the people. We're getting used to it, they would say with a bitter laugh. And it takes neither man nor beast—let's thank God for *that,* anyway!

Chapter 10

A DAY IN JUNE of quivering, vital sunlight, with shadows of fleecy clouds drifting by. Over the prairie, making toward the settlement by Spring Creek, rattled an old, dilapidated cart that seemed ready to fall apart. The nag in front was in perfect keeping with the vehicle, so lean and lanky that one could have counted every rib. Only a few miserable hanks were left of what probably had once been a flowing mane.

The man on the seat was of uncertain age; he might be forty-five, or just as likely sixty-five. The expression of his face was still youthful, the eyes bright and sparkling with something boyish in their gleam. But the beard clearly suggested a more advanced age; stretching from ear to ear, forming a thick fringe around the chin, it was originally blond in color, but was now streaked with gray.

The horse trudged slowly on; the man in the cart allowed him to dawdle, and hummed tunes to pass the time. After a long while the sod huts by Spring Creek began to lift their heads out of the ground. There were quite a few by now, and also two frame houses; the settlement had been here for a good six years.

"Hm . . . hm. . . . Well, here they are," said the man. "Move along now, King! We must try to get there before the folks go to bed."

The sun had already set when the horse came to a standstill at one of the huts. "Anybody at home here?" the traveler shouted.

A stout, toilworn, red-faced man came hastily out, an equally stout woman rolled after him, both with their mouths full of food.

"I asked if there were people here," repeated the man, unconsciously falling into the idiom of his native tongue. Behind the fringe of his whiskers beamed a broad smile.

"Oh, the devil! Are you Norwegian, then?" shouted the red-faced man jovially.

"So, so! Do you call on *that fellow* around here?"

Rebuked for swearing, the man on the ground stared. Without waiting for an answer, the stranger stepped out of the cart and stretched himself. "My! How stiff one gets from all this shaking! What's your name, my good man?"

"My name is Syvert Tönseten. What kind of a fellow may you be? Are you looking for land?"

The stranger looked straight at them. "I am a minister," he said. "As for you, my good man, you ought not to stand there swearing into the face of strangers! Now let me ask you, may I stop here tonight?"

"Good heavens!" exclaimed Tönseten, as if hit in the stomach.

"Oh, my!" wailed Kjersti, awestricken, yet overwhelmed with joy. "Can he really be a minister? Of course he must stop here, if he can only eat the stuff we have!"

"Don't worry about that, Mother." He turned to her husband. "And now you and I will attend to the horse."

Tönseten trembled with penitent eagerness to help. He cared for the horse wonderfully well, even spreading straw for its bedding. The minister had many questions to ask; they took their time about coming in.

At last Tönseten ushered the minister into the hut and bade him be seated. The table was now laid with a white tablecloth, on which had been placed *römmekolle* and *flatbröd,* fresh milk and boiled eggs; there were coffee and cakes; but even so, Kjersti thought it too little to offer such a distinguished visitor; now she was busy frying pancakes. Thank goodness, there was plenty of what she had! The room looked cozy, and the minister could not refrain from expressing his admiration.

Finally he sat up to the table, praising everything that he tasted and helping himself bountifully. Tönseten remained standing in the middle of the floor, talking with the minister; his manner was humble almost to the point of unction, his voice taking on a tone of great solemnity. He waxed eloquent, however, when he told how the country had looked hereabouts when they had first arrived six years ago.

Kjersti hung in the background by the stove; she was more concerned about what her husband said than to follow the minister's discourse. Syvert was so easily excited, poor fellow, and had so little experience in talking to people of quality! She watched the minister help himself liberally to the food, and felt the blessing of it descend upon her. How kind of him to say the nice things he did about the food she had prepared! And he chatted with them so pleasantly about ordinary everyday things—crops and prospects, the best way to run a farm.

At last the minister had finished his meal. "Now then, my good man, be silent, and we will thank the Lord for this day."

"Yes, yes—of course!" Tönseten blew his nose vigorously; but not knowing what to do with himself next, he stood where he was in the middle of the floor, utterly unnerved. Kjersti sank down on the woodbox and wiped her eyes with her apron.

Placing his folded hands on the table, the minister began in a quiet way, as if addressing someone they could not see who stood very near; he spoke in a low voice and intimately, as to a dear friend who, unexpectedly, had done him a good turn. He thanked Him for the day that now was past, nevermore to return; he prayed long and earnestly for the people out here, and especially for the man standing there who was so prone to swear. He entreated Him not to be too severe with these poor people, for long had they dwelt in the Great Wilderness, without a shepherd. Truly, life had not been easy for them! After saying amen, the minister remained silent for some time with hands folded. From the candle on the table a pale glow was thrown over his face, touching his beard with pure silver. Peace had fallen on the room.

Kjersti sat on the woodbox, weeping with emotion. The minister came over and took her hand. "A fine meal you prepared for me, Mother, and here are my heartfelt thanks!"

"Oh, well—that's nothing!" She shook her head.

Tönseten again blew his nose. He wanted to explain that he wasn't such a bad case as the minister seemed to think; but confusion overcame him again. The minister now opened his satchel and took out a pouch and an ancient pipe, which he filled. "A little incense, I think, will now be blessedly enjoyable. . . . No, just remain seated, Mother."

THE SLEEPING QUARTERS assigned to the minister were the spare sod-house, a structure which was now to be found on every farm. Clothes were hung in it, and food and tools were stored there. At Tönseten's there was a bed, made and ready for use, with a small table at its side, covered with a rose-colored cloth. The room was small and crowded, but seemed cozy and cheerful withal.

"Oh, here it will be sweet to stretch one's weary limbs!" exclaimed the minister.

Tönseten had aged considerably in the last two years; one who had known him before that time would scarcely recognize him now. He had struggled with a bad cough for two consecutive springs; he became easily tired now, and needed a lot of sleep in order to keep going.

But tonight he didn't get much sleep; he lay awake a long while pondering over how he might be able to gain the ear of the minister. Tomorrow morning, he thought, I'll take some wash water over to him. Then, maybe, I'll get a chance to talk with him alone. I'll tell him everything. There's going to be the devil to pay! If he could make such a fuss over that little innocent word I dropped, what will he say about *this*? Cold sweat was standing on Tönseten's forehead. No, it will probably be better to wait till he leaves; then I can go along with him a little way. This decision brought him something like peace, but no sleep.

So there he lay, wide-awake, staring at his great sin. Until last spring he hadn't known how utterly heinous it was; but at that time, when he was lying prostrate and his violent cough was threatening to make an end of him, he had come to a full realization of the enormity of his deed. Had anyone ever committed a sin like the one that lay at his door?

It would be just four years the coming fall since this transgression had taken place; it had even happened on a Sunday afternoon. The whole crowd of east-siders had come walking up toward the hut, with Johannes Mörstad and his girl, Josie, in the center. Halvor Hegg had explained their errand. "You're a justice of the peace, Syvert Tönseten, and that is a very important office." Halvor had emphasized the word important. "Now, Johannes and Josie, they want to get married, and there isn't anyone but you to perform the ceremony. According to law you'll have to do it, too, as near as you can in the Christian manner."

And that Sunday afternoon he had married the couple!

The neighbors had elected him justice of the peace when they had organized the town, but at that time he hadn't dreamed that it would ever call for legal or technical action, least of all for anything like *that*. How could he, an ignorant layman, have dared to do such a sacrilegious thing! The heaviest sin one could commit was that of meddling in sacred matters. The worst of it was that the young people had made merry with him about it, hurrahing for the "parson," and had applauded the whole ceremony as if it were a joke. And Johannes and Josie had moved at once into a house of their own and had lived together as man and wife ever since. What infamy! The minister would simply *have* to do something about it!

Tönseten turned over for the twentieth time. He *must* be absolved of this sin! If that cough should return next winter, there was no telling what might happen!

At breakfast next morning the minister kept asking a host of questions: Who lived in this hut and who in that? Tönseten didn't seem to have any appetite; throughout breakfast he sat in the grip of a silent fear; as soon as the meal was over he found a pretext for leaving the room.

A few moments later the minister, followed by Kjersti, came out into the yard with his satchel in his hand and called to Tönseten.

—Who lived northwest of them?

—Why, that was Hans Olsa.

—And to the north?

—That was Per Hansa.

—Where was the largest house?

—Did he mean the biggest room. Well, that was at Per Hansa's; he had built on a big scale the very spring he arrived; people had thought him crazy for putting up such a sod-house, but it had turned out that he wasn't so crazy, after all.

"Well, now, let's get to work," said the minister. "First of all, my good man, will you hurry around to your neighbors and tell them that today, at two o'clock, I shall conduct divine services at the house of Per Hansa. And you, Mother"—he turned to Kjersti—"I think it would be kind of you if you were to go help Per Hansa's wife get the house ready for the service."

They gazed at the minister in alarm, but for a while said nothing.

"Well—poor Beret!" sighed Kjersti compassionately.

"Beret? Is that her name? What is the matter with the woman? Are they so very poor?"

Suddenly, Tönseten forgot his reserve and spoke up. "I'll tell you about

333

it. This Per Hansa—he has got rich out here; he has done better than anyone else, though he came here without a cent. The first year we settled, for instance, the grasshoppers made a clean sweep of the rest of us; but Per Hansa saved his whole crop! The same year he made a big haul with his potatoes, and nobody knows how much he has made by trading furs with the Indians."

"Well, well! That's fine! But what ails his wife?"

Now it was Kjersti's turn; sadly she related Beret's whole story. The minister's face clouded as he listened. At last he said quietly, "I think we had better arrange it this way, Mother. I will go over there first, and you follow about noontime. As for you, my friend," turning to Tönseten, "remember that they must bring all the children requiring baptism. And tell them to be sure and bring their hymnbooks, too."

The minister was now making his preparations to go to Per Hansa's; as the distance was so short, he had decided to leave his horse. Tönseten fussed about uneasily, delaying his errand; he assured the minister that he needn't worry—he would get the message around to everybody in good season—it would only take a minute or two!

At last the minister took his departure. Tönseten was on hand to go along with him. They walked side by side, the minister absorbed in thought.

"I want to talk to you about something," Tönseten tried to say casually. His voice was so faint that the other could hardly hear it. The minister stopped short and looked at him. Tönseten's eyes fell to the ground.

"Well?"

Too late now! "I just wanted to ask you if . . . well . . . if it's possible to marry a couple who are already married?"

"You mean they are divorced?"

"No, indeed! But maybe it wasn't done just right; you see . . ."

"I am afraid I do not understand you."

Tönseten looked up at the sky. "You see," he began in a desperate voice, "we had to organize the township; so we had to have officials. Well, they went ahead and elected me justice of the peace. And then, you see, there wasn't a minister to be found in all Dakota Territory—there simply wasn't one in sight!"

The minister's face expanded into a broad smile. "And so you had to serve as minister?"

"That's *exactly* what happened! You see, this fellow, Johannes Mörstad, and his wife, they couldn't wait any longer—they should have been married long before, for that matter. And so they pounced upon me! I refused point-blank, of course. I have witnesses to *that*. But then, you see, at last I had to give in." Tönseten could only whisper now.

"And so you married them?" said the minister.

"Well, yes—I pitched in and did the best I could."

The minister's smile suddenly became a loud chuckle. Tönseten listened incredulously. That chuckle descended on him like a warm shower. So great was his thankfulness that the feeling surged through him: for that man he would gladly die!

"Was it long ago?"

"Four years."

"Are there children?"

"Children! There are three already, with a fourth on the way. That part of it," Tönseten observed in all seriousness, "seems to have been done properly enough! But . . . well, you'll just have to do it over again!"

"No," said the minister, still smiling. "That is your job, and I'll have nothing to do with it. But tell them to bring the children with them."

"Do you think the Lord will ever forgive me?"

"That I truly believe He will!"

Tönseten's joy and relief were almost suffocating; he wiped his eyes as he gazed at the minister. What a marvelously sensible man! Then he sped away in great excitement to announce to all his neighbors that a pastor had come to them at last. And they must gather to hear him, he was such a wonderfully able man!

THE MINISTER STOOD in the corner next to the window, arrayed in full canonicals. The gown was threadbare and wrinkled; the ruff might have been whiter, perhaps; but such trifles were not noticed now, for here stood a real Norwegian minister in ruff and robe!

The table, spread with a white cloth, had been placed close to the window; on it stood two homemade candles in homemade candlesticks cut from pieces of sapling and painted white. A Bible and a hymnbook lay between them.

The time for the meeting had come. The people filed slowly in and settled down wherever space was available. The six rough benches which Per Hansa and Hans Olsa had hastily nailed together were soon filled to capacity; on the edge of the beds sat women close together, and behind them sat the children. On the big chest eight in all had taken seats; others stood up, packed like sardines. But not all who had come could gain entrance; quite a crowd had to remain outdoors.

From outside the house came the sound of talk and laughter. The minister glanced up sharply; the youthful look on his face changed to sternness as he rapped on the table. "Let us have silence, good people! We will begin at once." Now deep silence descended. The pastor read the opening prayer. Then he announced a hymn, and he himself led the singing. Before the first stanza was ended every voice had picked up the tune, and the room was soon vibrating to a surge of mighty song. After the hymn the minister chanted, conducting the full service just as if it had been in a real church. . . . How wonderful it seemed!

The minister preached on the coming of the Israelites into the land of Canaan. He began by reminding his hearers of the dangers which the children of Israel had passed through, and of the struggles and tribulations which they had endured. Then he shifted the scene, applying the parable to those who stood before him; they, too, had wandered from their ancient home into a foreign country; here they proposed to strike root again; and here their seed would multiply from generation to generation. True enough, they had no hostile nations to fight against; yet there were other battles, for the powers of darkness never rested. Here was the endless prairie, so rich in its fertility, but also full of great loneliness. Even the bravest would find it hard to face and conquer the strangeness of it all—the chill, the overwhelming might of this great solitude.

The minister was now spinning out his thoughts and holding them forth for the people to see. He grew in greatness and power before their watching eyes as he showed them their own feelings during the lonely hours. . . . Here they were about to build a new kingdom. The Lord God had spread before them an opportunity the equal of which was unknown in human history; did they have sense enough to thank Him for that glorious responsibility? Thank Him in all humility? Oh, they ought to sing like birds in the morning sunrise, for they had found here the fairest promise given to any people!

The minister's words bore in upon them with irresistible power, and the people hung on every word he said. Only a few were competent to climb the ladder of reasoning that he had raised for them. To others it gave a simple satisfaction just to listen; they rejoiced that such a man had come here today.

In the farthest corner by the stove sat a pale, delicate-featured woman. She listened intently to the sermon—at first with a wondering, happy look; but as the sermon progressed, the expression on her face became covert and cunning; her lips moved as if she were making objections, but no sound came. . . . That! No, that shall not happen, was what the face seemed to say. He is playing us false . . . this man.

By her side sat a man with a handsome, fair-skinned little boy in his lap; the boy had sparkling blue eyes which flitted from face to face, laughing mischievously. Now and then the man laid his hand on the woman's shoulder, as if to reassure her; then she smiled strangely; the smile seemed to say, Don't worry, he shall not deceive me. . . . He is *sly*, though, isn't he?

When the hymn following the sermon had been sung, the minister said to them, "We shall now perform the holy act of baptism. First let all unbaptized children come forward; and afterward those who have been christened at home."

At this a considerable disturbance arose in the crowd; some people got up and pushed out the door; at the same time several who had remained outside during the sermon pushed their way in. Sörine came in with a basin of water which she placed on the table, and laid a clean towel beside it.

Those who were to hold the children now brought them forward, and little by little the disorder subsided, so that the ceremony could begin.

Most of the grown people knew the baptismal hymn by heart, and the singing rose with great fervor. There were fourteen children who had not been baptized, one of them only three weeks old. Josie, the one for whom Tönseten had performed the marriage rite, came last of all; she had three children, the youngest in her arms. Tönseten regarded her with a certain fatherly pride as she came forward.

Then came three children who had been privately baptized by laymen. Sörine advanced first, bringing for his second christening the child at whose birth she had been present and for whom she had once before stood sponsor; the boy turned two bright blue eyes toward the minister, asking Sörine who that man was with the whiskers and the long black skirt. "He doesn't have any pants!" he said. Those who stood near enough to overhear doubled up with mirth.

But as Sörine gave the child's name and the pastor repeated it—"Peder Victorious, dost thou renounce"—something extraordinary happened.

337

From the pale face over in the corner came a sound of anguish. Beret rose up and pushed her way violently through the crowd; Per Hansa tried to follow, but found it hard to make a passage through the throng; all at once her voice, shrill and vibrant, pierced the room. "This evil deed shall not be done!" Some blocked her passage; others tried to silence her.

"Oh, let me go!" she cried. "This sin shall not happen! How can a man be *victorious* out here, where the Evil One gets us all! Are you all stark mad?"

Her shrill cries rose with a wild anguish, striking terror into the hearts of those who stood about; some of the weaker-nerved women began to weep hysterically; the doorway was now crowded with curious faces; all wanted to see what was going on.

The minister paused in the service. "Take your wife outside, Per Hansa! The air in here is close and bad for a sick person. I will talk to her afterward. And the rest of you—please keep quiet!"

Per Hansa had finally reached Beret; he lifted her in his arms, but it was difficult to get through the crowd, and all the while Beret was striking out wildly in an effort to escape. She foamed at the mouth. "This is the work of the devil!" she muttered through clenched teeth. "Now he will surely take my little boy! God save us—we perish!"

AFTER THE SERVICE the people remained standing around in groups out in the yard, discussing in low tones the sad thing that had happened that day. A few women, including Sörine, stayed inside the house to put things in order. They talked in subdued, anxious voices and couldn't seem to take hold of the work with any heart.

The minister had seated himself at the table, folded his hands, and laid his head upon them; then, as if noticing the people in the room for the first time, he got up and walked over to the women. "I would suggest," he said gently, "that you all go home. Only let some one of you who is well-acquainted here remain to help. Let me have that fine little boy awhile," he said to Sörine. "Of course, I think it would be better if you all came often to see her, but never more than one at a time. And never ask her how she is feeling; just take it for granted that everything is as it should be. To me, things do not look entirely hopeless here."

Then the minister took little Peder Victorious by the hand and went out into the yard; he approached each group standing there, talked to them quietly, and advised them to go home and think about the Word of

338

God they had heard. Group after group broke up and melted away. Soon there was no one left in the yard; the day had closed and night was coming on.

The minister remained outside for some time, walking about the yard; the boy skipped along beside him, hanging on to the canonical robe as if it were a great joke. At length the minister bent his steps toward the new sod stable, from which seemed to come the sound of voices; he took the boy by the hand and pushed open the door.

Inside Per Hansa and Beret were sitting on a bundle of hay—she with her face pressed close against his, he with one arm about her neck and the other about her waist. And-Ongen clung to her father's shoulder.

"The sweet peace of God be upon you!" said the pastor gently. "The people have all gone. And now, Mother, I should like very much to take supper with you."

The sound of his voice startled Beret. She sat up, brushed her hair back, and looked abashed.

"I want something to eat!" cried the boy, tearing himself from the minister and going to his mother. She seized the child frantically and hugged him close to her, pushing her face down in the hollow of his neck.

"No, Beret—don't be so violent!" begged her husband. "Please!"

She threw back her head, her face flushed and distorted. "Am I not to love my own child?"

The minister came up and laid his hand on her head.

"That's quite right, Mother! Love him all you can; but do not forget to thank Him who has given you this precious gift."

Beret listened to the minister and then rose hurriedly. Without saying a word, she took a child by either hand and walked out of the stable.

Per Hansa remained sitting on the pile of hay resting his head on one hand. His hair and beard were unkempt and quite grizzled now; his face was deeply furrowed; his whole figure seemed ravaged and broken, like a forest maple shattered by a storm. The minister sat down beside him. "Tell me everything from the beginning. Two can carry what one alone cannot lift."

Per Hansa sighed. "I don't understand it myself, you see. I only know that damnation has come down upon us. It can't continue much longer— I'll probably have to *send her away*." Again he sighed and then fell silent.

"But she is not entirely deranged, is she?"

"Partly or entirely—what difference does it make?" Looking down at the hay, Per Hansa continued. "I don't know that I am guilty of any wrong toward her other than that our oldest boy came before we were married; but in that matter we were equally to blame. And then I brought her out here. I suppose that is where the real trouble lies—and for the life of me I can't see any sin in it. Is a man to refuse to go where his whole future calls, only because his wife doesn't like it?"

The question sprang out of Per Hansa's soul, as if he were for the first time opening the door to years of pent-up suffering.

"*Therefore shall a man leave his father and his mother, and shall cleave unto his wife: and they shall be one flesh,*" the minister quoted. "There you have the Lord's decree. But if the law applies to man, it must apply to woman as well. Between you two there has been no real disagreement?"

Per Hansa shook his head; the words came with great difficulty.

"I sometimes wonder if there ever were two people who cared as much for each other as we do. The only disagreement was that she advised waiting another year! And it isn't so much what she has *said* since we came out here. . . . Suppose a husband and wife cannot agree—what, then, is *he* to do?" Per Hansa grasped the minister by the arm, clutching hard in his terrible agitation. "Please tell me, you who are a minister— *what is the man to do?*"

"He shall humble himself before the Lord his God, and shall take up his cross to bear it with patience!" said the minister impressively.

"Ha-ha!" Per Hansa suddenly burst out in a bitter laugh. "That's too scanty a fare for me to live on. I must have an answer that I can understand. Did I do right or did I do wrong when I brought her out here?"

"That time you undoubtedly did right, my good man, but since then you have let yourself sink into the mire of a great sin, as I am told. You grumble—like the Israelites of old—because the Lord is leading you on paths you do not wish to follow. You are not willing to bear your cross with humility!"

"No, I am not; and let me tell you something more." Per Hansa's voice hardened. "We find other things to do out here than to carry crosses!" Then he fell silent. The minister tried to find words with which to reprove him, but in a moment Per Hansa began again—and now it was he who rebuked the minister. "My experience has been that it is mighty easy for one to talk about things he has not tried! Have you ever thought what it means for a man to be in constant fear that his wife may do away

340

with her own children—and that, besides, it may be *his* fault that she has fallen into that state of mind?"

When the minister finally answered, he had become all gentleness again. "No, thanks and praise to God, such affliction He has spared me!" He put one arm over Per Hansa's shoulder. "Tell me how all this came about."

Per Hansa sat for a while without answering; he seemed like a man trying to climb a steep hill, whose strength has given out. All at once he got up and went over to the door and looked out into the night. The minister followed him.

"There isn't much to say about such things," Per Hansa began. "There are some people, I know now, who never should emigrate, because they can't take pleasure in that which is to come—they simply can't see it! And yet, in spite of everything, we got along fairly well up to the time when our last child was born. . . . Yes, the one you baptized today. Then she took a notion that she was going to die—but I didn't understand it at the time. She struggled hard when the child was born, and we all thought she wouldn't survive—or *him*, either. That's why we had to baptize him at once. In my heedless joy after things had turned out all right, I went and gave him that second name. And then everything seemed to go to pieces!"

"That name?"

"Yes, the second name. It was wrong of me. I see that now."

"What are you saying, man? Such a beautiful name!"

Per Hansa looked at him. "Do you really mean it?"

"Of course I mean it! It is the handsomest name I can ever remember giving to any child. *Peder Victorious*—why, it sings like a melody!"

"Please tell me—is it really a human name? Wasn't it a sacrilege on my part?" asked Per Hansa incredulously.

"My dear man, have you worried about that, too?"

"You mean that the name is all right?"

"Yes, indeed," said the minister. "It is beautiful."

Per Hansa gazed at the man. Slowly his eyes began to light with a new courage. He took a deep breath.

"I must ask you again, for I am an ignorant man: is this really true? And won't you please tell her the same thing—as soon as you can?"

"I certainly will. So she does not like the name?"

"No, that's the trouble. She believes it was an idea that the devil himself gave me in order to get us in his power. Now she can't bear to hear the name; that's why the attack came on her this afternoon, when you fastened it on the boy for good."

"How long has she had these attacks?"

"It began with the grasshoppers. However, she's always had the heavy heart to fight against. And then, those fears of hers—utter fancies!"

"You say it began with the grasshoppers?"

"Well, sir, I came home from work one evening to find a crazy woman! She thought the devil himself had cast the plague upon us—and maybe she wasn't far wrong in that, either! Pretty soon she began to see visions of her mother, who by then had been dead for some time, though we hadn't got the news."

"She must have been seriously deranged."

"Yes—may God help us! One night I lay asleep, the first summer after the grasshoppers had come. Suddenly I was awakened by someone talking aloud in the room. And there she was, pacing back and forth and talking to her mother! And the child—she was carrying the child in her arms!" Per Hansa's breath failed him for a moment. " 'It's no use, Mother,' she said. 'The boy can't come to you with a name that Satan has tricked Per into giving him!' Those were the very words she used. I got up, lit a candle, and as I watched her pacing there, with the little fellow in her arms, then, at last, I saw how it was with her. Until that time I had refused to believe it. You see, she had taken the notion that her mother wanted the child with her. . . . Pastor," whispered Per Hansa, "do you know what it means to feel the skin creep up your back?"

"Did she try to harm the child?"

"Not then." He shook his head. "The rest came later." Per Hansa pulled himself together with a strong effort. "It will be two years this summer; it happened toward evening, one day when the grasshoppers came in such numbers that it was hard to see the sky. If Sörine, our neighbor woman, hadn't been making us a visit, it's hard telling . . ."

"The Lord show mercy unto you!"

"That afternoon, when the grasshoppers began to beat against the walls, she remembered that some of the little fellow's clothes were lying outside to dry. She ran out to get them, but when she picked them up there was nothing left but a few tatters. Then the spell came over her. She ran into the house, wailing, 'Now the devil has come for your clothes. . . . He'd better have you, too! Until he gets you we will have no peace!' Then she grabbed for the child." Per Hansa groaned. "But what might have been in her mind I cannot say."

"And how was it afterward?" the minister asked, deeply moved.

"Well, you see," said Per Hansa, wiping his eyes, "I had to do something about it. So I persuaded her to let Sörine take the child during the summer."

"You got her to agree to that?"

"Yes; at first she wouldn't hear of it, but finally she gave in. And now I don't know whether I did right or wrong; I believe it hurt her terribly to have the little fellow gone. One night after the plague came she stole over to Sörine's. Whether she intended to do the boy harm or not, none of us can be sure. She told Sörine that visitors had come from afar to see the boy, and so she must have him."

"Tell me, how is she between these attacks?"

"Well, she may be all right for months; one who had never known her well would hardly suspect that anything was wrong."

"What do you intend to do about it this summer?"

"This summer?" Per Hansa's face was drawn with fear. "If Satan lets his hosts loose upon us again this summer, then I don't know what will happen!"

The minister patted him on the shoulder. "The plague cannot last forever. And remember that the Lord is always near. Now take this advice from me: from now on keep close to her; let your affection warm her into the understanding that it is good to be human; and lighten her burdens in every way. Above everything, do not take her child away from her again. You will simply have to be as watchful as you can. And now I will perhaps stay here tonight; arrange it so that I can be alone with her awhile tomorrow."

The minister gazed before him in deep thought, his heart wrung with pity and compassion. "Perhaps the Lord will allow me to reach her mind with a clarifying idea. His word can move mountains. . . . When I return, you must take her to Communion."

His hand was patting Per Hansa's shoulder. Per Hansa wept, his sobs coming in short gasps. Soon he experienced a blessing descending upon him, and his burden grew lighter. There was much more he wanted to say, but just now he could not speak.

A long pause followed; then the minister spoke again. "Let us not stand here longer talking about sad things; our bodies need nourishment."

They walked across the yard in the quiet prairie evening. Just as they reached the door of the hut, somebody rounded the corner on the run and called in a scared voice, *"Father!"* Both men jumped, so suddenly had the figure come out of the darkness. It was Ole; he grasped Per Hansa by the arm and tried to pull him along. "Father, please come! Hans is sitting up on the Indian mound, crying and taking on! I can't get him to come home!"

"What's the matter with him?"

"He is afraid of Mother . . . you must come right away!"

All the radiance that for a moment had lighted up Per Hansa's soul had suddenly gone out. He gave the minister a look and bade him enter the house. "Tell them that the boys and I will be right along." Then he ran after Ole.

"Where is he, Ole?"

"Over there! By the grave."

"You run home. I can find him."

Ole vanished. "Store-Hans, where are you?" the father called.

A smothered cry came through the darkness. Per Hansa followed the sound and almost stumbled over a form lying on the ground. He bent over and lifted it up in his arms. "Hansy-boy, what's the matter?"

"Is . . . is Mother queer again?"

"No, indeed. Mother is all right."

"Did . . . did she . . . kill Permand?"

Per Hansa set the boy down, and started downhill.

"Did she do it?"

The father spoke harshly. "I don't want to hear any more of such wicked talk! Mother is all right; all of us are. And now she has supper ready." He stopped and began to dry the boy's tearstained face. "You must wash yourself as soon as you get in the house," he said gently.

NOTHING OUT OF THE ORDINARY happened that evening. When the minister came into the hut he greeted them in an even voice, "God's peace upon this house." Then he looked for a chair and sat down quietly. The table was set for supper. Sörine was still in the house, helping with the meal; And-Ongen sat on one of the beds, playing with her little brother; Sörine kept talking and laughing with the children as she worked, and an air of cheerfulness had come over the room. Beret stood by the stove, washing some pots; she glanced once over her shoulder at the minister as he came in. Presently she picked up a shirt she was making, sat down, and began to sew.

When Per Hansa and the boys came in, Sörine announced that supper was ready. They began the meal. The minister looked at Store-Hans; his eyes were red with weeping. At the sight of the boy the minister felt more like crying than eating. Laying down his knife and fork, he asked for a bowl of milk, which he emptied slowly. When he thought the others had finished, he folded his hands on the table and began to pray to the unseen one.

So quickly did he begin that at first Per Hansa didn't realize what was going on, and was on the point of asking the minister what he said. The same thing happened to the others: Ole had just discovered that he wasn't quite satisfied, and was reaching for another piece of bread; Sörine was about to offer them all more coffee. But Beret sat bowed over her sewing, trying to catch every word; then the work dropped to her lap; something compelled her to turn and look at the minister. The light of the candle cast a reddish gleam over his face; his countenance was that of a good child. His voice was gentle and low. He is really a fine man, thought Beret, and kept on listening.

During the summer there are at times dark days on the prairie. But it may happen that toward evening, just as day is nearly done, a curtain is drawn aside, and in the western sky appears a window, all luminous with splendor; out of it shines a radiance more glorious than anything the eye has ever beheld. Thus was the splendor which now pervaded Per Hansa's sod-house. All had folded their hands without knowing it. Over on the bed the play continued; happy laughter arose. Then Permand heard the voice of the man he had been playing with earlier in the evening. Clad in his little nightdress, he ran across to him, put both hands on the knees that rose before him, and looked up merrily into the minister's face. Without interrupting his flow of words, the minister lifted the boy onto his knees, folded the little hands within his own, and went on with the prayer. The words flowed on without a pause, softly and sweetly, like the warm rain of a summer evening. The minister threw his whole soul into the words.

At last he came to the little boy who sat there on his lap—the child he had christened that day. He laid his hand tenderly on the child's head; his eyes seemed closed, but to those who listened, his words seemed a wonderful thing.

"Set him aside, O God," the pastor prayed, "as Thou didst with Thy chosen ones in times of yore! Let him indeed fulfill the promise of his splendid name and become a true *victor* here, both over himself and for the salvation of his people. And now may Thy blessed peace rest on this house, for ever and ever . . . Amen!"

He sat with closed eyes for some time, his hand still resting on the boy's head. Beret was trembling; the others were very still.

Then the minister began to play with the boy in a natural, happy way, and in a little while they both seemed to be having great fun.

The next morning, as they sat at the breakfast table, the minister was both merry and talkative, and helped himself so liberally to the food that it was a pleasure just to see him do it. He asked many questions regarding the life and conditions in that vicinity, and showed himself so well informed about farming that Per Hansa asked whether he had ever been a farmer. Then he suddenly remembered what the minister had told him to do the evening before; he got up hastily, called to the boys, and they left the house together.

The moment they were gone Beret grew uneasy; she found her sewing again and sat down with it in a furtive, embarrassed way. The minister could see nothing unusual about her, except that her face was so singularly childlike; this impression came mostly from the way she used her eyes, for she kept looking down in extreme bashfulness and timidity; nor could he seem to easily draw her into conversation.

He came over and stood beside her chair.

"Well now, Mother, I have a request to make of you. Two weeks from next Sunday I shall return; and then I plan to conduct Communion services here in your house."

Beret was so astonished that she forgot herself and looked straight at him. "Here in our sod-house?"

"Yes, right here in your house."

"Oh no—that would never do—no! It's too filthy here . . . it's *unclean!*" She stopped abruptly, blushing scarlet.

"No doubt there is much sin here," resumed the minister. "But the Lord will sanctify the house for us. And now I want you to plan how nicely we can arrange it." He looked around. "The table had better be taken out—that will give us more room. That big chest we can perhaps use as the altar—that is, if your husband could fix up something for railing. We could probably find some fitting material to cover both that

347

and the chest; perhaps you had better talk to the neighbor women about it." The minister talked on as if everything were decided, with only the responsibility for its execution left in her hands.

She gave him a quick look, her cheeks flushed. "That is my father's chest. It is a nice chest, too."

The voice had grown querulous again; the minister made no reply. He took her hand, thanked her for her hospitality, and hurried out of the room. When he got outside his forehead was damp with perspiration.

When Beret sat down a while later to dress the little boy, she felt that she could sing aloud today—felt that she had to sing, that she could not help it. Words and melody rose in her throat; it was the baptismal hymn. While she sang she handled the boy so gently, as if she were almost afraid to touch him.

THE WEATHER WAS BEAUTIFUL on the Sunday of the Communion service in that summer of 1879. A light breeze was blowing from the southwest; the air swept one's face like a soft, silken veil. The minister had reached the settlement the evening before and had stayed overnight at Per Hansa's. That morning they hurried through breakfast to put the house in order for the service. It had been thoroughly cleaned before he came; all kinds of wild flowers that were to be found on the prairie had been gathered and hung in bouquets under the ceiling, or put into glasses and bowls that stood around in every conceivable place. There was something strange and haphazard about it, as if it had been done by children at play. As the minister looked around, a chill hand seemed to clutch his heart.

The table had been carried outside and the big chest placed diagonally in one corner, just as he had directed. Per Hansa had constructed a long, low bench that ran along in front of the chest and was covered with two rugs; the chest itself was draped with a white cloth. Yesterday the boys had stripped off a whole tubful of willow leaves; these were now brought in and scattered around on the floor.

The result was satisfactory. The minister looked around; he had scarcely spoken since he came. "Now I am going over to the other hut to dress for the service; I shall be there until it is time to begin and would rather not be disturbed." He said to Beret and Per Hansa as he went out, "God grant to both of you a blessed Communion!"

Entering the hut where he had slept the previous night, the minister

348

slowly put on his canonicals. His lips moved in prayer. When he had dressed he sat on the edge of the bed and leaned his head on one hand. His face looked tired; now he felt the need of a strong faith—and when he sought it, he sought in vain!

With a supreme effort he got up and went out. When he reached the other house it was packed full of people. Per Hansa and his wife sat on the very first bench, right in front of the improvised altar. The minister scanned the crowd, then spoke calmly to Per Hansa, "You two will please come forward first to receive Communion."

As the text for the Communion sermon the minister had chosen the phrase *the glory of the Lord;* rather, he had not chosen it—it had suggested itself powerfully to him on the day he had gone away after talking with Beret. And now, today, the fitness of the theme had returned to him with overwhelming force; here sat people who perhaps for many years had had no chance to confess their sins before the Lord and receive His blessed remission. Among them was one soul, sore perplexed, that he must try to reach. He had seen clearly on his last visit that what the woman needed above everything else was the gladness of salvation, the abiding joy that issues out of the faith and the firm conviction that life is good because the Lord himself has ordained it all.

But as he started to preach, the words he wanted would not come; and in those that came there seemed to be no power. He heard himself speak, and it seemed like the voice of another. He could not fathom it; he had a wonderful text; in all ways he was better prepared to conduct services today than he had ever been before. And yet, here he was preaching about the glory of the Lord and stuttering like a child! . . . "The glory of the Lord—what is it? One might suppose it to be too wonderful for us to talk about." Nothing to that remark! he thought, as soon as he had said it. Nothing but empty words about holy things!

Then he began to enumerate all the examples from the Scriptures calculated to show the wonders of the glory of the Lord. "Did not Adam and Eve behold the glory of the Lord as they walked in innocence in paradise? And Jacob, who wrestled with the Lord?" He toiled through the entire Old Testament and pushed his way into the New. But every time he drew another word picture the idea came to him more and more forcibly: these people, sitting here in front of me, are fisherfolk from Nordland. How can they understand the things that happened to an alien people, living ages ago, in a distant land?

349

His eyes roamed helplessly over the rows of faces and fixed on a fly buzzing around the room, following it while he talked. A little to one side sat a young woman with three small children; she was a fine, bright-looking woman, tanned by the sun—the girl that Tönseten had married. She had the youngest child in her lap. The child had been restless for a long time, and the mother had unbuttoned her clothes to nurse him. The fly made a turn in the air and settled on the nose of the nursing child; the mother raised her hand and swept it away, and as she did so she drew the hand caressingly over the child's face.

Now, taking a sudden shift, the minister began to address the little family directly before him; he commenced to speak of the love of mother and child. And all at once he did something that he had never done before in a Communion sermon—he told a story.

"Once upon a time," he said, "a Norwegian immigrant woman landed in New York City; her name was Kari; she was widowed and had nine children. When she landed and saw the great throngs of people, she got terribly frightened, for she could neither speak nor understand the language. She had been told that in this metropolis almost anything might happen to a mother alone with nine children; and so she had prepared herself in her own way. Around her waist was wound a long rope; she now tied all nine children to it in single file, keeping the end fastened around her waist. In this fashion Kari plodded through the streets of the city, a laughingstock to all passersby. But just the same, she reached her destination with all her children safe and sound! Wasn't that rope a fine illustration of a mother's love?"

It occurred to the minister that he had come down to very common-place things—yet he spoke straight out, from the fullness of his heart. The people were listening intently; the woman with the child had stopped chasing the fly. His words came faster, pouring forth without effort. "But when such love exists between a poor pioneer woman and her children, what must it not be when it rises to divinity—the love of Him who is the source of love itself—of Him who cares for all life, yea, even for the worm crawling in the dust? The love of mother and child can be only an infinitesimal part of that other love; yet it still carries a breath of the divine. If you, pioneer mothers, have not seen the glory of the Lord, then no preacher of the Gospel will ever be able to show it to you! . . . And now come forward to the altar of God and bring Him your trials and your grief! Love itself, eternal and boundless, is present here. God is ready to lighten your burdens. Come and *behold the glory of the Lord!*"

The minister ended his sermon. The people came forward, knelt down before the big chest, and received an assurance so gracious and benign that they could hardly credit its reality. Many eyes filled with tears. . . .

And so the minister brought the service to a close, and ended with a fervent admonition to the communicants to go directly home and remain quiet for the rest of the day. He would return at the end of four weeks, at which time he would take up the question of organizing a congregation.

Having hastily drunk a bowl of milk, he got into his cart at once and drove off. The old nag ambled along; the minister sat immersed in deep gloom. Never before, he thought, have I failed so miserably in any service!

IT RAINED ON THE TWO DAYS following the Communion service, but not so hard that Hans Olsa had to stop building. With two carpenters to help him, he made such good progress that the day was gone before it had begun—or so it seemed to him. Yes, now Hans Olsa was building himself a real house, and he sang all day at his work. And why shouldn't he sing? This was going to be a beautiful house, larger—very much larger, in fact—than he had originally planned; it was to have a roomy kitchen, a dining room, a parlor, and three bedrooms upstairs and two downstairs.

Concerning the matter of bedrooms on the ground floor, there had been a lengthy argument between him and Sörine. Hans Olsa was never in the habit of saying unkind things to his wife; and Sörine always smiled, even when she was upset; so a real quarrel between the two was hard to provoke. But in this instance she held tenaciously to her idea that there must be a bedroom downstairs, and that plan called for an addition to the house. It was so unlike her; she was never known to be extravagant! So he had tried to reason the idea out of her head; but he finally had had to give it up as a bad job. Thus it had come about that there were to be two extra bedrooms downstairs, since while he was about it, he thought, he might as well extend the addition clear across the house. . . . Very unwise, a needless expense; but there stood the framework, all complete. Nothing to do about it now.

That Sörine was a real gift from on high no one knew better than Hans Olsa himself; and now, this particular summer, there was nothing that he would not gladly have done for her. Ever since last spring, when she had confided to him that she was with child, he had been in a state of blissful anticipation. As soon as she had told him the news, he had come to the decision that *that* event should never take place in the old sod-house; and if it meant such a lot to her to get that room downstairs, she certainly should have it.

That summer of '79 Hans Olsa walked about in a state of contentment and thankfulness. After the first grasshopper plague he had gone into stock raising; his cattle had steadily increased from year to year, and he had by now a very large, prosperous herd. And he had neighbors—here, where once there was not a human being to be seen, large settlements had sprung up. And, as the most memorable event that had yet happened in these parts, last summer the railway had come winding its way across the prairie from Worthington to Luverne. It wouldn't be long before it came all the way to Sioux Falls. Good neighbors, schools, fine land, a railroad and everything—what more could anyone wish? And now he was building a mansion for him who was coming. . . . He felt sure it would be a boy. How marvelous it all was!

Hans Olsa had been present at the service last Sunday, and the longer the service had lasted, the stronger and deeper had grown his felicity. He was only a common, uneducated man; yet this he knew for certain, that nothing so glorious as that Communion service had he ever before experienced. As Per Hansa and Beret had knelt before the chest, he had looked at them, thinking of many things. Beret's sad condition could easily be seen in her face. Ah no, when reason once leaves a person, it seldom returns! And Per Hansa himself had become an old man long before his time: his hair and beard were gray; his face was thin and worn; not till then had Hans Olsa fully realized the terrible struggle his lifelong friend was going through.

Coming home from the service that day he pondered over an idea, and on Monday he broached the subject to Sörine: shouldn't they offer to take Per Hansa's youngest child? Did she suppose that would be too much for her?

Sörine now confided that for a long time she had been thinking about this very same thing herself. But she hadn't mentioned it to Per Hansa because he knew that she was only too willing; had he wanted to bring it about, he would only have had to ask her.

They couldn't be sure of that, her husband objected; Per Hansa knew that Sörine was soon going to have one of her own, and he was not the kind of a man to impose on others. He doubted very much, as a matter of fact, if Per Hansa fully realized the seriousness of Beret's condition. "Isn't it really up to us, who can see the true state of affairs?"

Sörine gave an unexpected answer. "I believe that Beret is jealous of me because I'm so fond of her little boy."

Hans Olsa pondered this. Perhaps his wife was right; and there were other difficulties, too. Would it be fair to the parents even to suggest such a thing? And just now, wouldn't it be too great a burden for Sörine?

But Sörine only laughed at him. Certainly she would undertake to be a mother to that dear little boy if it ever seemed necessary. But she doubted very much if Per Hansa would consent to the plan; he thought more of that boy than of any of the other children, unless she was much mistaken.

WEDNESDAY AFTERNOON of the same week a faint mist floated before the sun. A light, warm rain fell at intervals. Between showers the sun peeped through the clouds to see what was going on down on the prairie; he set a rainbow here and there as a sign that he was well pleased.

Beret sat in the old sod barn, sewing a shirt for little Permand. The door was open and she sat where she could look out. She had sent And-Ongen to the field with water for the boys, who were hoeing potatoes. Per Hansa was repairing the roof of the new barn, which had been leaking since last spring. She could not see him from where she sat, but she could hear him working.

Beret's face carried the same childlike expression that the minister had noticed. She felt perfectly happy, but so tired and drowsy; it had been this way every day now since that remarkable man had placed his hand on her and in his prophetic voice had assured her that from this time forth she was released from the bonds of Satan. She knew positively now that he hadn't been deceiving her, because burden after burden had been lifted from her soul; she felt so light that she could almost float on air. But after a while this drowsiness had come on. She slept well at night, and yet during the day it was a constant struggle to keep awake.

A blessed man he was, indeed. . . . And the way he had got them to sing! Just imagine! Melodies were yet wafting throughout the room; yesterday while at work she had heard them everywhere. She had even caught one up and followed it—had sung until Per Hansa came rushing in to ask her what was the matter. He ought not to get frightened just because she sang!

Snatches of the song came back to her again, and she began humming. . . . No, no—this would never do! She might scare someone again—people seemed so easily frightened here. Surely, now, Mother will stop asking for the boy when she hears he is going to be a minister! The smile on her childlike face broadened and lit up. . . . When Mother comes—and she can be expected at any time now—I shall tell her all that has happened here lately. And then I shall say, "You would never have become the grandmother of a minister if I had remained in Norway. Such miracles do not happen there." Then I must tell her that now we have a church, right here in our house. At that she'll probably say, "Now, Beret, you don't know what you are talking about!" But I will answer, "Now, Mother, listen to me. We have a real church. There is an altar with candles on it, and the altar is Father's *big chest!*" That will astonish her still more!

For some time Beret sat deeply absorbed in her thoughts, her sewing on her lap. . . . Mother will sit by the stove, just as she always has done when she is here. "Well," she'll ask, "are you sure now, Beret, that he is going to be a minister?" Then I must answer, "Yes, Mother, for I myself sat here and heard how this wonderful man argued about it with the Lord!" And at last Mother will say, "Well, if God can use him, it certainly isn't proper for me to want him. But now you must take good care of him, my child!"

The sound of steps in the yard brought Beret out of her reveries. Someone stopped at the barn, and then went in; in a moment she heard the voice of Per Hansa. What can they want of him now? First one comes and takes him away, then another—can't they understand that I need him at home?

Beret stepped out of the door, stealthily crossed to the side of the new barn, and pressed herself to the wall. Oh, it was only Hans Olsa! She was straightening up to return, when something arrested her—kind words spoken slowly in Hans Olsa's deep voice. . . . Hush! They ought not to talk about her when she was listening!

"Should Beret get another spell, you know what might happen—a calamity none of us could get over. Now, we will take the boy and care for him as though he were our own. . . . Sörine and I have talked it over."

Beret's childlike features suddenly took on a peculiarly covert expression. Aha! So that's his errand? Hush! There is Per Hansa speaking! "That's more than good of you and Sörine—I realize it all. But she is the mother, and I've decided that she shall keep the child with her. If she doesn't get well by having him at home, it certainly won't make things any easier for her to have him away—that I know. She risked her life for him once, and she shall not be bereft of the happiness of having him with her now, no matter what happens."

"Remember what might have happened when she had the spell last summer," said the other voice slowly.

Beret's features grew tense. Bending over with a quick, fierce movement, she snatched up a piece of stake.

"No," came Per Hansa's voice in meditative tones, "that's just what none of us can say for certain. She might have escaped the attack altogether if the child had been at home. I remember how pitiably she seemed to miss him. Perhaps that burden, added to everything else, became too much for her. And even if the spell had come on with him here at home, she might not have harmed him—I doubt it very much. . . ."

As Beret drank in these words the tension left her; the weapon she had seized dropped from her hand; she looked about in wide-eyed wonder. Were those church bells she heard? . . . But the voices were beginning again on the other side of the wall. . . . Hush! Hush!

"Do you really think so?" asked Hans Olsa.

"Well, I tell you, Hans Olsa, there's hardly an angle to this affair that I haven't considered; I think of nothing else, asleep or awake. And this I do know," Per Hansa added with great certainty, "that a kinder person than Beret the Lord never made. I've come to the conclusion that even in her beclouded moments she has meant no harm to the child—no matter how things may have looked to us. When all is said and done, it's my own fault from beginning to end."

O God! How beautifully these bells ring! thought Beret.

"Because," Per Hansa went on sadly, "I should not have coaxed her to come with me out here. For you and me life out here is nothing; but others may be so constructed that they don't fit in at all; yet they are finer and better souls than either one of us."

"We were playmates, Beret and I," Hans Olsa remarked. "I certainly ought to know her—"

"I doubt that very much," interrupted Per Hansa. "I have lived with her all these years, yet I must confess that I don't know her. She is a better soul than any I've ever met. It's only lately that I have begun to realize all she has suffered since we came out here. I reasoned that where I found happiness others must find it as well. And you see how things have turned out! . . . But this I've decided, that she shall keep the child—though I thank you for the offer."

Beret listened no more; she walked away like one in a dream of happiness. In the southern sky floated transparent little clouds; rainbow ribbons hung down from them. Are there signs for us in the sky? That is the glory of the Lord now. . . . *See!* The heavens are full of it! There—and there—everywhere!

She reached the house. Inside, a child was crying loudly. Beret passed her hand across her face, as if trying to wake herself from a dream; then she went quickly into the house. Over on the bed sat Permand, crying as though his heart would break. Beret threw herself down on the bed, took the boy in her arms, and hugged him close; she felt as if she had got back a child that had been irretrievably lost; she wept as she fondled him, while wave upon wave of gratitude welled up within her.

The boy was so astonished at his mother's strange behavior that he stopped crying; then he threw himself on the pillow. A sudden surge of playfulness swept over her and she lay down beside him. He gave her his very biggest smile, letting a finger that had been hovering in the air fall on her face. At that they both burst out laughing—she so boisterously that he withdrew the finger and gave her a frown. She stopped laughing at once, petting and fondling him until she had won him completely.

As BERET LAY THERE playing with the child she was suddenly overcome with drowsiness; it seemed to her that she simply could not resist snatching a little sleep; it would feel so delicious!

In a moment she had dozed off and was carried away into an infinite, glittering blue space with rainbows hung all around it. The air felt soft and warm, and a beautiful voice was speaking through the sky. She could not have slept long, for when she awoke, there sat the boy close by her side, poking a wet finger into her eyelid. She rubbed her eyes and gazed at the child beside her, but could not seem to connect things in her mind. "Why, what am I thinking about?" she said, half amused. "This is my own little Permand!" She sat up on the edge of the bed and lifted the boy tenderly. To her surprise she was trembling in every limb.

"I want something to eat now!" murmured the boy in a voice full of well-being. He wriggled out of her arms and slid to the floor. She hastily left the bed and started to find something for the child to eat. It was in her mind to get some milk from a shelf in the corner; but instead of going there she remained standing in the middle of the floor, looking about the room, her eyes still large with wonder. What could have happened? Everything looked so strange in here today—as if she hadn't been here for a long time. But the feeling of homecoming filled her with such joy that she could only laugh at her bewilderment. . . . She found one thing here, another there; at last the boy had eaten his fill and was satisfied.

All at once another thought struck her. Where were the rest of the family today? Here they had all been with her only a moment ago, and now she couldn't recall the least little thing! Was she walking in her sleep? Thinking vaguely that she must try to get things cleared up, she went out of the door and looked around.

The mildness of the afternoon greeted her like a friend. What fine weather these days! The trees around the yard caught her eye; again she had the feeling of having just returned from a long journey. The idea! Look how big that grove is getting to be! . . . But who was that tall, stooping man coming out of the barn? Now he had greeted her and walked on. Wasn't that Hans Olsa? Didn't she know her own neighbor? Hearing someone still in the barn, she hurried across the yard and peered in.

"Are you in there?" she called.

A stocky, broad-shouldered man appeared in the barn door; his face was deeply furrowed; his hair and beard, sprinkled with gray, were now full of dust and straw. As she looked at him she felt strangely uneasy, but she couldn't help giving him a bright smile.

"What in the world has happened to you, Per Hansa?"

He stood staring fixedly at her, unable to stir. No power on earth could have taken his eyes away from her face at that moment. God in heaven! What had happened?

Beret saw his agitation. Now her concern over him grew genuine. "Are you sick, Per Hansa?" she asked in tones of sympathy. "You mustn't keep on with this work when you aren't feeling well."

Per Hansa could only look at her.

Her anxiety grew insistent. "You've got to quit right now! I'll run in and boil some milk for you!" She hurried off to the house.

In the open door Per Hansa stood gazing at her as she went; he longed to follow her, to touch her, to talk to her, but he dared not do it. He was shaking violently from head to foot; he had to lean up against the wall. "God be merciful! I haven't seen her like this for many years!" Then he sighed wearily. "But I don't suppose it means anything."

Beret came into the house, moving with purpose and confidence now, and lit the fire. The boy was still sitting at the table; no sooner did he see her than he wanted more to eat. But she had no time to bother with him; she put a pan on the stove and filled it with milk. Poor fellow, he must have caught a cold, she thought. I'd better mix some pepper with the milk. If I could only persuade him to lie down.

As she was tidying up she chanced to get a glimpse of herself in the mirror. Good gracious! What a sight I am today! No wonder he looked worried. While she was waiting for the milk to simmer, she washed her face and combed her hair; that done, she found her best Sunday garments and put them on. The milk boiled; she lifted it off the stove, went to the door, and called Per Hansa.

As a timid child enters a stranger's house, so now Per Hansa stepped across his own threshold. Walking over to the table, he picked Permand up and sat down in his stead; then he put him on his lap and gently stroked his hair. His voice was gone—it would not come; big beads of sweat stood on his forehead. Beret brought him a bowl of the steaming milk. "I put pepper in it; now you must get it down while it's hot. Then you shall go right to bed!"

Without protest he did as she bade him, sipping the strong, hot mixture. He couldn't keep his eyes off her face, but whenever he tried to speak, his throat closed. She came and sat down by his side, telling him innocently how topsy-turvy things had seemed to her today. Why, she had just lain down for a moment with the child, and when she woke up it had seemed as though she had been gone for years and a day! She laughed merrily as she told him about it.

Per Hansa listened in silence, and drank of the hot mixture until the tears rolled down his cheeks. As he gazed at her, he saw in her face only intelligent concern—only loving solicitude—exactly like the dear Beret-girl he used to know! When he found it impossible to swallow another drop of milk, she insisted that he lie down at once; if he would only take a good sweat, this cold would soon pass off. Per Hansa obeyed like a docile child, while she herself came and tucked the quilt around him. "Now try to sleep. . . ."

He turned his face to the wall, crying silently; he had clasped his hands together with a grip of iron, but soon he had to break the grip to wipe the tears away. He lay thus until the paroxysm had passed and he felt that he could master himself. Then he flung the covers aside, sat up on the edge of the bed, and looked intently at Beret. He began to believe . . . and as he looked, he felt his old self returning.

"Are you getting up already?" she asked, surprised.

He laughed boisterously and rose to his feet. "I guess I'd better hurry and get that rickety roof fixed. We must begin building here as soon as Hans Olsa can find time to help with the hauling! We're not going to live like moles in this sod-house all our days!" He came forward, caught Permand in his arms, and flung him up to the ceiling again and again, until the boy shrieked with delight.

"My, my, how funny we all are today!" said Beret with a smile, as she stood there with the bowl in her hands, waiting for them to come to their senses.

Chapter 11

MANY AND INCREDIBLE are the tales the grandfathers tell from those days when the wilderness was yet untamed, and when they, unwittingly, founded the kingdom.

It was as if nothing affected people in those days. They threw themselves blindly into the impossible, and accomplished the unbelievable. If anyone succumbed in the struggle—and that happened often—another would come and take his place. The unknown, the untried, the unheard-of, was in the air; people caught it, were intoxicated by it, threw themselves away, and laughed at the cost. The human race has not known such faith and such self-confidence since history began.

They say it rained forty days and forty nights once in the old days, and that was terrible; but during the winter of 1880–81 it snowed twice forty days; that was more terrible. Day and night the snow fell. From the fifteenth of October, when it began, until after the middle of April, it seldom ceased. Morning after morning one would wake up in the dead, heavy cold, dress himself hurriedly, and start to go out, only to find that someone was holding the door. It wouldn't budge. An immovable monster lay outside. Against this monster one pushed and pushed, until finally one was able to force an opening large enough for a man to work himself out and flounder up to the air. Once outside, he would find himself standing in an immense flour bin, out of which whirled the whiteness, a solid cloud. Then he had to dig his way down to the house again. And tunnels had to be burrowed from house to barn, and from neighbor to neighbor.

The suffering was great that winter. Famine came; supplies of all kinds gave out; for who had ever heard of winter setting in in October?

It was impossible, of course, for anyone to get through to town to fetch what might be needed, and in the houses round about folks began grinding away at their own wheat; for little by little the flour had given out, and then they had to resort to the coffee mill. Everyone came to it—rich and poor alike. Those who had no coffee mill of their own were forced to borrow; in some neighborhoods there were as many as four families using one mill.

But the greatest hardship of all for the settlers was the scarcity of fuel—no wood, no coal. In every home people sat twisting fagots of hay with which to feed the fire.

Whole herds of cattle were smothered in the snow. They disappeared during the great early storm in October and were never seen again; when the snow was gone in the spring, they would reappear low on some hillside. After lying there for six months, they would be a horrible sight. And the same thing happened to people: some disappeared like the cattle; others fell ill with the cough; people died needlessly, for want of a doctor's care; they did not even have the old household remedies—nothing of any kind. And when someone died, he was laid out in what the family could spare, and put away in a snowbank until some later day. There would be many burials in the settlement next spring.

THE THIRD QUARTER SECTION which Hans Olsa owned lay near the creek, north of the Solums'. This he had fenced in and was using as a pasture for his large herd. During the summer he did not need to look after the cattle at all, except to give them salt; the grass was plentiful up north. The preceding year the herd had pastured there until late in the fall. This year he had hauled over a great deal of straw; then he had built a shed of poles and banked it in with the straw, with the intention of wintering the cattle on that quarter. He had finished the shed before winter set in; and now that he had managed to keep the cattle there until

February he felt fairly safe; surely the winter would be over soon. . . . But the winter had only begun!

The seventh of February dawned bleak and cold. Large, tousled snow-flakes came flying out of the west, filling the sky with a gray, woolly blanket. The wind stiffened steadily throughout the morning, and by noon heaven and earth were a swirl of drifting snow. As the afternoon wore on, the west wind cut in more and more savagely, and the weather became so bad that Hans Olsa thought it best to go over north and look after the cattle.

Things were in pretty bad shape there. Most of the straw had been blown away from the west side of the shed. The cattle had left the enclosure, and had sought what shelter they could find to leeward of the strawstacks on the north side. At a glance he saw that unless he could repair the shed at once and get the animals under some sort of protec-tion, he would find himself a considerably poorer man on the morrow. So he set to work putting straw between the poles in order to shut out the wind; that done, he spread more straw over the floor.

It was dark by the time he had got the shed into fit condition to drive the cattle in again. But the moment he drove the beasts far enough away from their shelter to feel the full force of the wind, they wheeled sharply and headed back for the stacks. He waited until they were quiet again, and then he led them over one by one; the smaller animals he literally picked up and carried. These had burrowed themselves so far into the stack that it was difficult even to get them out. With the snow and the wind beating on him, he found this a tough job; but he kept at it without pause, though the sweat was pouring from him in streams.

The evening was gone when he had finished. Round about him lay the night, full of a whirling menace. Hans Olsa stood at the door of the shed, looking out at the storm; he was so weary that every limb trembled. At last he started out mechanically, walked a few steps, but had to stop. Then he began to realize that in this darkness, with such a blizzard raging, he would never be able to steer a straight course home.

He felt his way back to the shed and stood again in the door. After a short while a succession of slight shivers began to run through his body. He wasn't exactly cold—it was only that his muscles wouldn't keep quiet. Now they cramped convulsively; now they arched and slacked up like steel springs. If I lie down close to the animals, I'll be able to keep warm, he thought. Day will soon come, and then I can go home to Sörine and the children. I suppose she'll have sense enough to go to bed and not sit up and wait for me all night.

He felt his way over to where the herd had snuggled together and lay down with his back close up against a large bull. His underclothes were so wet that they stuck to his body; but the warmth of the bull soon penetrated to him, and then he felt better. He lay there thinking how fine it was that he had saved the herd. About hurrying home he needn't worry, for all was well there. . . . Really, now, he was as comfortable as a man could expect to be on such a night—anywhere but at home.

Gusts of wind shook and tore at the frail shelter. The night had turned bitterly cold, and through every crack in the shed the snow came whirling; it settled everywhere, piling itself up in little mounds. Hans Olsa began to twitch violently; he thought he felt someone pricking his arms and legs. With great difficulty he heaved himself up to a kneeling position; a heavy mantle of snow slipped off him, shedding an icy shower which struck him full in the face. What was this—had he lost his feet? And where were his hands? With infinite pains he raised himself and stood unsteadily on his legs. He tried to go to the door to look at the weather, but in a moment he was down again; he had stumbled against a living mound under the snow, which reared up wildly and then was gone in the impenetrable darkness.

He could not understand it. What had happened to him? He knew that he wasn't drunk, but his legs would not carry him. And one of his arms was gone. . . . Well, here was the wall. He leaned against it, panting. Was his hand frozen? . . . He pulled the mitten off his good hand, took hold of the fingers of the other and bent them; yet he could not feel them move. This would have to be attended to at once! He let himself sink down and began to rub the hand. Now he began to feel himself frozen through and through; his teeth were chattering; his whole body was shaking violently.

Even now he was trying to make the best of it. As soon as this hand is all right I'll have to get my feet thawed out. If I don't get that done, I'll be a cripple for life. In his usual levelheaded way he tried to pull his boots off, but couldn't accomplish it. Then he took out his pocketknife, ripped them open, and placed them against the wall. The socks came off easily enough, and these he stuck in the bosom of his shirt.

He got up and started to run in his bare feet, holding to the wall; he stumbled a good deal, but kept on. After a spell of this, he sat down and chafed his feet. He rubbed a long while, then got up again and ran—ran as hard as he could, and then sat down again to rub anew. His mind was calm, but it worked very slowly; his thoughts seemed to be far away; he saw them in bright letters against the darkness: I had better be careful. I've often seen people rub the skin from a frozen limb. If I only had some cold water, this would be easy!

He pulled his socks on again, and his boots. In a corner of the shed he found some steel wire, which he wound around the bootlegs. Then he began to stamp along the wall . . . to beat his arms. The pricking seemed to be going away, he thought; everything seemed better; yet he wasn't certain of anything at all.

"If you stay here tonight, you're done for," said something away there in the dark; "but if the wind continues steady, you ought to be able to find Henry's fence; follow it from there on, and then you come to your own—that runs right to the cattle barn at home. You might as well freeze to death out there as here." Pulling himself together, he went out of the shed and started off before the wind.

Sörine had been up waiting for Hans Olsa all night, well-nigh crazed with fear; twice she had started to go to Per Hansa's for help, but the storm had driven her back each time; then she had lighted a candle and placed it in the window and fed the fire with desperate resolution.

Hans Olsa finally stumbled into his house in the small hours of the morning. As soon as she got him in, Sörine began tending him with frantic haste. She made him drink several bowls of hot milk with pepper in it; then she put him to bed, warmed the bedclothes and tucked them around him. But in spite of all she did, he lay there shivering so that the whole bed shook. Later in the day he began to cough—a dry, rasping cough it was, that seemed to grate on something hard as iron down in the bottom of his chest. During the night that followed he was delirious; he wanted to get up all the time to look after the cattle. Sörine had all she could do to quiet him. The cough that came from deep in his lungs threatened to choke him.

Day came at last, after a long, dismal night; and then he seemed better. Between the coughing spells he talked calmly to his wife, telling her what she and Sofie had to do about the chores. After they had gone out, he tried to get out of bed and put on his clothes, but the chills grew so violent that he could not stand. He fell back on the bed.

For two full days the blizzard raged. On the third day it abated. Hans

Olsa told Sofie to put on her skis and go over to get Per Hansa. "This will never do," he said to his wife. "For three days and nights you haven't been out of your clothes. I may be a long time getting over the cough." He wanted to say more, but the words were lost in a paroxysm of coughing.

Per Hansa and the two older boys were making hay twists in the barn when Sofie brought the first news that her father had been out in the storm and was now very sick. Per Hansa immediately dropped his work and went back with her. Sörine looked worn out and very much worried. She turned her head aside when she spoke to him, saying that things didn't look very good. But Per Hansa's coming cheered her up a little. In a moment she dried her eyes and asked him to follow her into the bedroom.

In a hut on the border of the Irish settlement lived an old woman who was called Crazy Bridget. Tönseten long ago had picked this name up from her countrymen and had translated it into Norwegian—he made it *Kraesi-Brita*. This Bridget had come west with her son, had taken the quarter of land next to his, and had herself put up the hut in which she now lived. Very little was known about her except that she was extremely religious, and that she had a great store of old-fashioned remedies, of which she gave freely, without pay. Most of the Norwegians had consulted her at one time or another, in spite of the fact that they went on saying she was only a fraud. And though they said it, they all had to admit that she had a remarkable way with sick folks.

When Per Hansa saw how seriously ill his neighbor was, he went to fetch Bridget. The old woman came trudging over on snowshoes, carrying an odd-looking bag on her back. After she had looked at the suffering man, she asked for a kettle and opened her bag. First she took out four large onions; these she cut into bits and dumped into the kettle; then she opened a bottle of vile-smelling stuff and poured some of its contents on the onions; at last she set the kettle over the fire and let it boil. From this mixture she made thick poultices, which she put on Hans Olsa's back and chest; but before she put them on she took out of her pocket a small rusty crucifix and stuck it into the poultice which was to lie on his chest. All the while she was muttering strange words in a language they did not understand. These poultices were to be kept on for twelve hours, she explained in broken English, and hot cloths must be put over them to keep them warm. When the twelve hours were gone they must make a

364

fresh poultice. She instructed Sörine how to make it; and they must take good care of the crucifix, she said. Then she wished them God's blessing, put her bag on her back, fastened her snowshoes, and trudged away.

Per Hansa had meanwhile hurried home from Hans Olsa's; he had called the two boys, and had taken them with him to look after Hans Olsa's cattle. Before he left he had asked Beret to go over to Hans Olsa's toward evening and stay there for the night. It might be late before he could get back.

At suppertime Tönseten called at Per Hansa's as he was going by. He just wanted to drop in to see how they were after the storm. When he heard the news about Hans Olsa's cough he decided to go over at once and tell Sörine what to do. If anyone in these parts knew all there was to know about a cough, he was the man!

Out in the bedroom lay the sick man, propped up by pillows; one-year-old Little-Hans sat at the foot of the bed with his playthings; Sörine and Sofie were working in the kitchen; Beret sat in the bedroom, taking care that the poultices were kept hot; she had her knitting and was singing a hymn when Tönseten came in.

On entering the room Tönseten greeted them both cheerily; but instantly he began to feel ill at ease. No need, surely, to begin the funeral before the man was in the coffin! He managed to hold his tongue, however. Since Beret had recovered, he couldn't stand her. She had become so pious that if a fellow made the most innocent remark, she was sure to preach at him. And never a drop of whiskey would she tolerate, either for rheumatism or for cough.

Tonight Tönseten could think only of how serious things looked for Hans Olsa; he went straight to the bedside, and said in a tone of voice that was meant to be cheerful, "I'm surprised at you, Hans Olsa! What do you mean by lying here like this, you slugabed? And here you have the finest ski slide the Lord ever made, clear from your housetop all the way down to my place!"

The sick man's face brightened as he looked into Tönseten's merry eyes; a breath of fresh air wafted from out the red, icicled beard; the whole face bending above him radiated good humor. "I'm glad you came, Syvert," said Hans Olsa in a faint voice.

Tönseten now began to feel that the right atmosphere had been established; he hummed a tune, sat down beside the bed, and started to relate what had happened to him that day. It was simply terrible how much snow there was down his way. Yesterday he had made steps in the snow down to his house; these had packed fairly well, and today they were as solid as ice. And this morning Kjersti had come along carrying a pail of water, and she had been so unfortunate as to slip on the top step—ha-ha! She had thrown the pail into the air, her feet had shot out from under her, and she hadn't stopped until she'd landed on her backside in the middle of the floor! "What in heaven's name are you up to, Kjersti?" he had said, when he saw that she hadn't hurt herself very much; and then he naturally had gone off into a fit of laughing. This had infuriated Kjersti; and when he saw that, he'd tried his damnedest to stop—but for the life of him he couldn't. He'd laughed and laughed until finally she had lost her temper completely and just driven him out of the house.

Well, this is what he had done next; he had put on his skis and gone over to see Johannes Mörstad and his wife, Josie—Josie was about to have her fifth child, you know. So he had sat there gossiping with them until Johannes had hunted up a bottle which he was saving for the coming event, and had given Tönseten a drop or two—perhaps it was three—or four . . . if one must be accurate. . . . All this about the steps, and Kjersti, and about how he had had to take to his heels in order to find peace, he related in epic detail to Hans Olsa—there seemed to be need of something jolly here!

There was something so infectious about Tönseten's good spirits that they almost coaxed Hans Olsa into a brighter mood. But then a spell of coughing came on; he choked it back and asked if Kjersti hadn't hurt herself pretty badly?

"Oh no, never you fear!" hiccupped Tönseten, wiping his eyes with the backs of his hands. "She's all right, except for a few scratches here and there in the bottom, but they'll heal up in a little while," and Tönseten went off into such another gale of laughter that he almost fell out of his chair.

"Well, well!" he said as soon as he could control himself, getting up to leave. "Tomorrow I shall bring Kjersti over here with me. You just wait— we'll get the cough boiled out of that chest of yours! Kjersti knows how to treat a cough, I can tell you!"

BERET HAD STOPPED her singing abruptly when Tönseten came in. As he rambled on, she sat and watched his face—it seemed to her she never had realized before how disgusting his laugh was. His breath smelled of whiskey. At first she wanted to order him out of the house. Didn't the fool know that it was unseemly to talk that way at a deathbed? But instead she took her chair and moved farther off.

When Tönseten had at last gone, the air of the room seemed close and foul to Beret; filth and pollution had entered in where all should have been the serenity and holiness of a Sabbath. Here was one neighbor calling on another at the point of death; if ever there was need of godly speech, it was at this moment; and yet there had been nothing but vileness in his mouth! She felt a physical desire to cleanse the place; folding her hands, she began to sing, soft and low:

> "O Jesus, see
> My misery...."

All that night Beret sat by the bedside. Though the sick man seemed no worse, the specks of rust that he raised from the depths of his chest appeared to her to be larger and more numerous. He slept little, but she didn't wonder at that—he must have solemn things to think about now. Along toward morning the paroxysms of coughing became more frequent and violent; there were times when they almost choked him. Once she grew frightened and got up to hold his head; his face was turning blue as he struggled for breath; then she said slowly, "Now I think you must prepare yourself, Hans Olsa."

He turned his head sharply and looked at her. "Prepare myself?"

"You will hardly be able to stand this very much longer."

The big hulk of Hans Olsa lay very quiet; only his hand was moving nervously over the cover; his eyes had a questioning, startled look. "Well . . . many have got over the cough."

She did not answer him. After a while he added thoughtfully, "It will be worse for those who are left."

"You ought not to say that, Hans Olsa—their time has not yet come. But remember that for you the day of grace is nearly over." She spoke quietly and compassionately, in a tone of confident faith.

For a long time Hans Olsa made no reply; he turned his face to the wall and closed his eyes. Beret stood looking at him. He does not like what I said, she thought. That's how we are, we sinners. But I am glad I said it. I don't believe he will ever get up again.

"Oh, well," murmured Hans Olsa after a while, "He has had mercy on many a sinner before. I suppose there will be a little left for me, too."

A great eagerness suddenly welled up in Beret's soul. "If only you will bring Him a contrite heart! But how can one forgive the erring child who does not repent? . . . Oh, no, we cannot just comfort ourselves with the belief that there is mercy enough—that it is free!" With firm hands she changed the cloths again.

One severe coughing spell after another began to attack him now, and nothing more was said; but after a prolonged struggle he got his breath again; completely exhausted, he turned his face to the wall, and it looked as if he might drop off to sleep.

Beret knit steadily until her hands grew tired. She took the lamp and went into the kitchen. Here she found a great pile of coarse hay stacked against the wall; she set to work at once, making twists of it for the fire. All the while she was thinking about her conversation with Hans Olsa. It will seem strange not to meet Hans Olsa in the hereafter—that it will. In the old country we grew up together. And now he is starting out on his long journey—and will not pass through the heavenly gates! Oh, how can he hope to get in? Not many from the Dakota prairie will ever stand in glory *there*—that I am sure of! For here Earth takes us. What she cannot get easily she wrests by subtle force, and we do not even know it. I see what happens in my own home. It is awful! Here he lay at the point of death, enjoying Tönseten's ribaldry! With thoughts like this he is now to meet his God!

The lamp burned low. The room was growing cold. She got up and threw a couple of sticks of wood into the fire—there were not many left in the box. Then she went into the bedroom again. The sick man was awake; his manner showed that he had been waiting for her.

"How is the weather outside?" he asked slowly. "Would it be possible for a man to travel? Could we try to get the doctor, do you suppose?"

"We shall see when daylight comes. But how about the minister, Hans Olsa?"

"The minister?"

"Yes—when the Lord's hour is at hand, man's help is of no avail; for from His wrath no man can flee! What you need most of all is Communion, Hans Olsa!"

"Communion? Well, . . . yes, I suppose so."

"It is terrible to fall into the hands of the living God," said Beret quietly, and looked into his face with sorrowful despair. "There is nothing but evil in us—yes, nothing! But when He comes to us in Holy

Communion, laying His merciful hands upon us, and assures us from out of eternity that all our sins are forgiven—oh, there is no moment so great as this for the sin-burdened soul! Then we may rest in peace."

Once more he turned his face away and looked fixedly at the wall. He lay still awhile, and then he said wearily, "All my life I have thought it would be blessed to come home."

Tears came to Beret's eyes. "But are you ready to journey on? Do you dare now to meet Him as you are? Here you have lived all these years in error and sin, and have not taken time to give Him any thoughts at all."

"Oh no," he sighed heavily. "But that isn't so very strange, is it?"

She felt uplifted by what she had been able to say; it gave her greater courage to go on. "That's why you must seek Him here, before you meet Him face-to-face yonder!" she cried exultantly. "Now I will pray for you." Without waiting for his consent, she knelt beside the bed and began to pray earnestly that he who now lay here might be given the grace to see his sin and to repent before the door had closed.

But she had hardly begun when something stopped the prayer. Hans Olsa had reared himself up on his elbows, staring at her wide-eyed. As he heard how she pleaded for him he was seized with a sudden convulsion of coughing; he sat up frantically in bed, gasping for breath. The bedclothes fell off him, the poultices slipped down, and Beret had to leave her praying to attend to him. When he was quiet again he asked to have his milk warmed; then he had to get up; from that he got an attack of chills, and Beret had to call Sörine to help her warm the cloths once more and tuck him in.

With the first light of dawn Johannes Mörstad arrived, begging that Beret go with him—Josie was going into labor; he had tried to get Kjersti, but she had lamed herself so that it was impossible for her to walk that far. This is certainly the work of the devil! thought Beret. Just now . . . ! But she went out of the house full of the same great exaltation, like one whose sins had been laid bare before the whole congregation.

A little later Per Hansa dropped in to say that he would arrange with the Solum boys to help carry hay and water to the herd up north; then he would help Sörine with the chores. Now he must be gone.

PEOPLE WERE HARD AT WORK throughout the whole settlement that day; the weather continued threatening, and there was much to be done after the storm; hogs and cattle, as well as human beings, had to be safeguarded against another onslaught of winter. Of some of the farmhouses only the roofs could be seen; of the sod huts only the chimneys; down at Tönseten's the smoke came right out of a hole in the snowbank. If one wanted to go to his neighbor's, he had to put on skis or snowshoes. There were homes where no food was left other than dry corn and the little milk that the cows gave. But folks were cheerful about helping one another in those days.

When Per Hansa came back after supper, Tönseten was sitting in the bedroom at Hans Olsa's. He was downhearted and quiet today. Kjersti had been in bed because of the soreness from her fall; and she was so cross, he explained, that if a fellow as much as looked at her she would bite his head off. As he noticed how Hans Olsa struggled for breath, he wondered if his own cough had ever been as bad as this. If this was *worse* than he had had it three years ago, the man would never be able to throw it off. But he kept the thought to himself.

Things had been in a bad way with Hans Olsa all that day; the coughing spells had come oftener; he had been restless and fretful. Now he began to talk with his two neighbors about the inevitable. He asked them to advise Sörine about running the farm when he was gone, just as he would have done for them, if either of them had been in his place. "Per Hansa, stay with me tonight! Sörine must have some sleep. It may take a long time with me yet—perhaps we shall need help from all of you!"

Thus it came about that Per Hansa watched with him that night. Sörine lay down in the other room, fully dressed. She intended to doze only a minute and not lose herself completely; but she had tramped about working in the snow nearly all day, and was so worn out that she soon dropped off into a sound sleep.

After all had been quiet in the house for some time, Hans Olsa looked up and asked if his wife was asleep. When no answer came from the other room, he lay still for a while, gazing into space; then he began in a calm, matter-of-fact way to tell Per Hansa how he thought everything ought to be arranged after he was gone. He mentioned first a couple of little debts which he had in Sioux Falls; then he spoke of several new settlers who owed him for seed and cattle. Sörine ought to hold the farm and keep on living here. If Per Hansa could hire an honest and capable manager for her, she and the children would get along all right. And then there was Little-Hans—it was hard to go away and not see what this

371

seedling of manhood would grow up into. If he showed any aptitude for his books, they should send him to Saint Olaf College.

Per Hansa nodded his replies; all he could think of to say was, "Don't worry, I will take care of everything." Little by little he got the feeling that his friend had something more on his mind. Every time a pause came in the sick man's talk, he expected to hear what it was. But at last Hans Olsa fell silent. A violent fit of coughing shook his frame. From out of that great chest of his came a dreadful wheezing, grating sound, as from an old pair of leaky bellows.

When the cough had eased itself, Hans Olsa began to talk again. It was hardly what Per Hansa had expected to hear. He merely raised his eyes and asked in a low voice, "Is the snow very deep?"

"Between our farms," said Per Hansa, "it doesn't lie less than four feet anywhere; and it's as deep as that on the level all over the prairie. Down near the creek it must be twenty feet deep."

"So—it is as bad as that?" The sick man sighed heavily.

"Was there something on your mind?"

"Then it isn't possible to get anywhere!" Drops of sweat stood out on the great, shiny face.

Per Hansa's heart stirred with a nameless dread; he felt himself grow dizzy, but he cleared his throat and said firmly, "What is it that you want, Hans Olsa? Do you want the doctor?"

The sick man turned toward him. "Oh—it's the minister I need!" Then, after a moment, he added, "But don't you think the weather will be better in a day or two?"

He got no answer. Finally he looked up and repeated imploringly, "Don't you think so?"

Per Hansa rose to his feet and began pacing back and forth. Thinking of how it was outdoors, he suddenly found himself bathed in perspiration. God pity him who had to travel the prairie these days!

He came back to the bed. "You feel that you must have him?"

"It is terrible to fall into the hands of the living God!" The large, kindly features were drawn and trembling with fear of the unknown. Per Hansa could scarcely endure it to look at him; he had to lean against a chair for support. In broken words his friend repeated, "It is terrible . . . terrible . . . to fall . . . into His hands!"

"Hush, now! Hush, now, man! Don't talk blasphemy!" cried Per Hansa. "Lie down, now. . . . See here, the covers are falling off you!"

The bulky form had reared itself violently up in bed. Through a paroxysm of coughing Hans Olsa whimpered, "Tell Sörine to come here!" It looked for a moment as if he were passing away in the midst of the attack. In wild alarm Per Hansa resorted to pounding the sick man's back. But after a while the spell gradually left him. He settled back, and a little later fell into a deep sleep, which lasted till morning.

The first rays of daylight woke Sörine. Her husband was already awake by that time, and seemed better. Per Hansa put on his coat and prepared to go; he had all his own work to do at home, besides Hans Olsa's cattle up north to look after.

Hans Olsa watched him get ready, following all his movements with a pathetic sadness like that which stands in a dog's eyes when he watches his master go away without him. Then he called him over to the bedside and asked him again what the weather was like. There was an odd little quiver in his voice as he said, almost as though he were ashamed, "I suppose it's still impossible to get anywhere?"

Per Hansa felt like laughing at such childishness; he scarcely knew what to answer. But buttoning his big coat, he said firmly, "You ought to lie still and sleep a while longer, Hans Olsa. During the night you slept like a rock—and see how much better you are already! I promise you that I'll be back sometime later in the day."

"You don't think it can be done?"

Nameless dread again seized Per Hansa. He stepped back and said hastily, "Calm yourself now, Hans Olsa! We'll have to see about it—you understand."

The sick man reached out toward him, caught his hand and held it tightly. "Oh, Per Hansa!" he cried. "There never was a man like you!" Then he fell back on the pillow, exhausted.

ALL THROUGH THE LATTER PART of the last summer and early fall Per Hansa had done a full man's work plus a bit more; nor had he spared the boys, either. And he had hired a number of men besides. But he had gone about his duties in a mood that made any task easy for both himself and for those who worked with him. His wife's improved condition had relieved him of whole loads of worry and anxiety. During the years that her mind had been beclouded he had treated her as a father would a delicate, frail child that, by some inexcusable fault on his part, had been reduced to helplessness. So solicitous had been his watchful care of her through all these years that this paternal attitude had become fixed in him. Even now that she was well again, it didn't change. To desire her physically was far from his mind.

Her growing religious concern didn't alarm him; that, too, he took as a notion on the part of a frail child. He either would meet her admonitions with silence, or else laugh kindly at her eagerness, or he might throw himself into his work all the harder. The fact that she now was quite all right again, that he no longer needed to watch over her in constant dread, but that she, on the contrary, could take care of the house in a capable way and even find time to help with the outside work, was a constant source of thankfulness to him.

Shortly before the Christmas holidays they had had a set-to over religion. She had insisted that he as the father of the family should conduct daily devotion. At this demand he had laughed as if at a good joke. He conducting devotion—the idea! But she had entreated him so earnestly that he was touched. And so he had said, as one yields to the unreasonable whim of a dear child, that he would not do it, but he would be glad to have her do it, for she could read so beautifully. From that time on she had been conducting devotion each day, but both of them had studiously avoided a new discussion, with the result that the relation between them grew less frank; each seemed to feel the guardedness of the other.

As time passed, her devotional exercises became less and less pleasing to him. In the prayers she began to offer, there crept in more and more of concern for him; and little by little the prayers got to be almost exclusively for him. As he sat there listening it sounded to him as if he were the most hardened sinner in all Christendom; he would feel ashamed before the children and would find a pretext to steal out of the house. But he couldn't bring himself to speak to her; for how can one reason with a child that is so delicate as she, he thought.

IN THE GRAY LIGHT of dawn Per Hansa returned from the bedside of Hans Olsa, looking like a man who had reached the end of his rope. He hung up his coat and hat and sat down at the table to eat his breakfast. While Beret brought him his food, she asked how things were over at Hans Olsa's. At first he got very little satisfaction; his answers were short, and he seemed engrossed in his own thoughts. He ate slowly and took a long time over his meal; all the while he kept looking out of the window.

At length he got up from the table, crossed to the stove and turned his back to it, as though he still felt cold and needed the warmth of the fire. "Well," he said meditatively, "I suppose he doesn't expect to get over this sickness—and it's more than likely he won't. He just lies there and whimpers about having the minister. I can't understand it at all."

Per Hansa stood looking straight ahead of him, as if thinking aloud. Beret had stopped working when she heard him; her face lighted up as she answered, with a ring of exultation in her voice, "But *I* can understand it! . . . Now may God be near and hear his prayer! Someone must go for the minister at once."

Per Hansa did not move; he was staring off into space. Beret crossed the floor and stopped directly in front of him. "You must persuade someone to go with you. This is terrible weather! Could you try going on horseback?"

"Horseback! How you talk!"

"But it is an awful thing for a soul to be cast into hell when human beings can prevent it!"

Per Hansa seemed amused at this idea. "Well, if Hans Olsa is bound in that direction, there'll be a good many more from here in the same boat! He'll land in the right place, don't worry."

The words sounded so blasphemous to Beret that she could not repress a shudder of horror. She said fiercely, "You know what our life has been: land and houses, and then more land, and cattle! That's been his life, too—his whole concern. Now he is beginning to think about not having laid up treasures in heaven. Can't you understand that a human being can become concerned over his sins and want to be freed from them?"

"I suppose I don't understand anything, do I?" said Per Hansa in a tone of disgust. "Perhaps I don't understand, for instance, that no man could cross the prairie from here to the James River, as things are now, and come out alive. As for Hans Olsa, the Lord will find him good enough, even without a minister—that I truly believe!"

"The God of this world hath blinded the minds of them which believe not! . . . Here lies one who is about to receive his sight, and we will not reach out a hand to help him!"

"Hold your tongue, Beret!" cried Per Hansa sharply, anger at the hopelessness of the argument getting the better of him. "Do you want to drive me out into the jaws of death?"

"What horrible things you say, Per Hansa!"

"Horrible—well! Don't you suppose the good Lord would have provided other weather if He had intended me to make this trip?"

She gave him a quick look. "It's possible to try, isn't it?" she said with cold persistence. "Why can't you get someone to go with you? Henry has a sleigh; and you could turn back at any time if you couldn't make it. The Lord would forgive us then for what we couldn't possibly do—if we had tried!"

"He had better do that right now!" growled Per Hansa, a gust of hot anger nearly choking him. Without another word he went and called Ole and Store-Hans, telling them to get into their clothes right away. Pulling on his coat, he slammed out of the house to do the morning chores.

Beret looked at the door through which he had just disappeared. There he leaves, she thought, in a fit of temper, fuming and cussing! She took up the morning work, her thoughts busy with many things. Before she realized it she was absorbed in what had so often been on her mind lately: what had happened to him, anyway? His warm playfulness, his affectionate tenderness—what had become of it? . . . Oh no, no!—she caught herself—how can I be thinking of such things again! The sweet desires of the flesh are the nets of Satan.

A hundred things were waiting for Per Hansa outside, but he was so angry that he scarcely noticed what he was about. . . . The world seemed upside down today . . . . That grown people couldn't see an inch beyond their noses! Here lay Hans Olsa, driving himself out of his mind because he couldn't have a minister—when there was no better man than himself in all Christendom! And here was Beret, insisting that he leap right into the arms of death—she who had a heart so tender that she couldn't harm a mouse! People could certainly twist things around! All his life he had worked and slaved in order that she and the children might be made comfortable; and now it was flung in his face and he was taunted with being only a blind mole who saw nothing but the hole he had burrowed himself into! If this went on much longer, he would go out of his mind himself—if he wasn't a little crazy already! He dashed from one thing to another in a frenzy, leaving everything half done.

When the boys came out they all put on their skis and started across the snowdrifts to Hans Olsa's north quarter. The day was bleak, but to Store-Hans all these fields of snow were glorious; now he could skim like a bird over the drifts. Little by little Per Hansa forgot his temper as he caught the infection of the boy's exuberant joy.

While they were working over the cattle, Per Hansa talked in a steady stream to the boys. All this snow, he said, promised a bumper crop next summer—you could depend on that! One of his moods of high good humor had come over him now, and he discussed things with the boys as if they had been grown men. He outlined at length how they could manage their place in order to have the very finest of farms. If all went well, they would build a big barn next fall, a real show barn—red with white cornices.

They saw to it meanwhile that the cattle had water and hay enough; they carried in more straw. But at last they had finished everything that needed to be done, and off flew the boys on their skis like two great sea gulls soaring across the fjord. Wasn't it wonderful . . . all this snow!

Just as Per Hansa reached the yard at home, Sörine came out of the kitchen door and began to put on skis. He noticed that she was very thinly clad, wearing only a shawl as an outdoor wrap; he concluded that she must have left home in a hurry, and he feared that the worst had happened. Was anything wrong? he asked. No, Hans Olsa didn't seem much worse. But her face was sad and she looked down as she spoke. Bridget had been to see him again and had said there was no hope.

"And I guess there isn't, either," she went on. "But I had to come over and ask your advice, Per Hansa. He said that you were going after the minister for him. And I suppose that might be a good thing to do; at any rate, he is very happy about it. But now, of course, I see that it's impossible to go anywhere. . . . Still, I was thinking that if you *did* intend to try, it might be better to get the doctor instead." Her voice had a thin, timid sound in the wind.

"You must stay awhile and get warm before you go," he said quietly.

"No, I must hurry home. I shouldn't have come, but—" Her voice suddenly left her. Then in a moment she went on bravely, "It is so hard to see him go, without being able to help! And we all have a feeling that nothing is ever impossible for you—and I thought that perhaps you might find a way out of this, too!" All at once her pleading had taken on a frantic urgency.

"Did he ask you to come to me?"

"No—but he kept wondering if you weren't getting ready—if you wouldn't be starting soon. I could see plainly enough that he wanted someone to come over."

Per Hansa said nothing more, nor did he look at her again. She went away at once. He took off his skis but he did not go indoors immediately. His thoughts followed Sörine across the snow, passed her, entered the house before her, saw his friend lying there, saw the great face staring up at him, the frightened eyes imploring him like those of a kindly dog. Per Hansa stood still a long time, gazing into vacancy, without the will to move.

On the kitchen floor Permand was playing at threshing. When the father came in the boy hailed him, giving orders like a man. "Come here and help me, you; we've got to get this work done before evening!" Seeing that the noonday meal was not yet ready, the father hung up his coat and sat on the floor beside his son. In a moment they were both absorbed in the play.

During the meal the two parents scarcely spoke to each other, and never once did their eyes meet. As soon as they had finished, the boy wanted his father to play with him some more; the father willingly agreed, and soon they were hard at it again, laughing and talking, making a great deal of noise.

As the mother cleared the table she kept looking at them in wonder and dismay. Here he sat and played with the child, just as if there were nothing serious in the world for him. The day was wearing on. Didn't he really intend to try to do anything? She could have cried aloud in her anguish! Had he become stone-blind? When she had finished washing the dishes she went to the window and stood there, looking out; then she crossed to the wall where her outdoor clothes hung, and began to put them on. This attracted Per Hansa's attention.

—Was she going out? he asked.

—Yes. She put on one of his coats over her own wrap, then pulled his big stocking cap over her head.

He looked up a second time. "Are you going far?"

She waited a moment before she answered. "I have to talk to Henry. *Someone* must go on this errand for Hans Olsa!" Her face was flushed with determination.

Per Hansa burst into a laugh and scrambled to his feet.

"You'll have to behave yourself now, woman," he said, like a man trying to talk reason into a naughty child. "You ought to know that this is no weather for a woman to be out in."

"It's no weather for men to be out in, either, by the way it looks in here!"

He whirled on her suddenly, his face white with passion; the eyes that stared at her fiercely burned with a lambent flame.

God help me! she thought. Now he's going to lay hands on me! But I only spoke the truth!

"I want no more damned nonsense about this!" he burst out hoarsely. "If you . . . if you have something to say to Henry, you'll have to say it here in this house. You can't go chasing from farm to farm today!"

Before she knew it he had gone out of the kitchen.

IN THE EAST PART of the settlement lived two boys who had come over from Norway a couple of years before. They were skilled skismiths; last winter each one had made himself a pair with straps and staffs, the finest ever seen in this part of the country. It was to these boys that Per Hansa now went. In about an hour he returned with one pair of skis on his shoulders and another on his feet. Neither pair was his own.

Beret, greatly agitated by her husband's hasty departure, walked back and forth across the kitchen floor. Now I have brought things to a sorry pass! she thought. I know I said too much—but what could I do? Someone has to go, and I had no one else to ask. When she saw him returning with the skis she felt relieved. It's sensible of him to go on skis; it's the only way he can possibly get along. I wonder who he intends to take with him? He ought to have thought of a plan more seriously this morning. I must make him a cup of coffee; he must have something hot to drink before he leaves. . . . She put the coffeepot on the stove and began to set the table. . . . He mustn't think that I hold any hard feelings.

The two older boys were busy digging a tunnel from the cow barn to the pigsty. Per Hansa went over there first; he talked to them as if he were in no hurry, and when it seemed to him that they were losing interest, he went down into the tunnel where they were. He said that now he was going away, and that it was uncertain when he would return. Could he depend on them to look after things while he was gone? The boys were absorbed in their task and didn't pay much attention to what he said. Certainly he could go. They would look after everything. They went on with their work, and soon fell into a quarrel about how long it would take them to reach the pigsty. . . . He left the boys, took his skis, and went into the granary; there he rubbed the skis with some tallow and adjusted the straps.

While he was doing this Peder Victorious came trudging in and an-

nounced that Mother had made coffee. She said Father must come in
before it got cold.

"What?" Per Hansa's face brightened. "Did Mother really say that?"

"She said coffee was ready."

"Oh!"

Per Hansa now stood looking around for a rope with which to strap the
second pair of skis on his back. "Did she send you out and tell you to say
that?"

"She said—she said—coffee was ready, she said!"

The father looked at his son. "You haven't got enough on, Permand,"
he said in a tender voice, stroking the boy's cheek with his hand and
running his finger down into the soft warm neck. The boy screamed
when it tickled. Per Hansa laughed. "Hm—cold as an icicle! Pack yourself in this minute! So Mother has the coffee ready, you say?"

He carried the boy out lovingly, and went back after his skis. One pair
he tied to his back; the other he put on.

The boy waited, watching him. "Aren't you coming, Father?"

"Get into the house with you!" the father said with mock severity.
"I'll probably be along in a little while." Then, as he put on his mittens,
he suddenly remembered something. "Permand, there's a ball of nice
twine in the bedroom. Ask Mother to give it to you to play with. And now
be a good boy, and get a lot of threshing done before I come back!"

"Yes, Father," said the boy as he trotted away.

Per Hansa stood motionless, watching him until he had passed from
sight inside the house. Then, with a staff in either hand, he started
off. . . . Was that a face that he saw at the window?

He did not look at the house again. In a moment he had passed the
place where the boys were digging the tunnel; he longed to talk with
them once more, but crushed the feeling down. He struck out westward.
Something tugged and pulled at his heart, trying to make him turn back.
He had to bend his head forward against this unseen force in order to
hold his direction.

"No—not now—not now," he murmured bitterly, wiping his mitten
across his eyes.

In the kitchen window Beret stood watching him; her soft, kindly eyes
grew large and questioning. Wasn't he coming in? Had Permand forgotten to tell him? Surely, surely he would come. She had fixed things
so nicely for him. Oh, this would never do! She must find out at once

who was going with him. She hurried to the door, flung it open, and tried to call him—he simply mustn't leave this way! But the westerly gusts, driving full against her, snatched her words away. Her eyes filled with tears, so that she could scarcely see him now. Furious blasts came swirling out of the gray, boundless dusk, sweeping the snow in stinging clouds, whirling it round and round. Per Hansa soon disappeared in the whirling waste.

A little later he turned in at Hans Olsa's; he sat and talked awhile in the bedroom. Their words were few and far between. At length he got up and said that now he was going—what sort of a trip he would have he did not know. If luck were with him, he would bring back the minister. In the meantime Hans Olsa must behave himself and rest as much as possible. The sick man groped for Per Hansa's hand, and did not seem to want to let it go. He acted like a child who has teased and teased until it has finally got its way.

"I didn't dare to ask you right out," he said, as if in explanation. "But I knew you would go as soon as it was possible—that's always been the way with you. Now I can sleep in comfort."

Out in the kitchen Sörine sat waiting at the table; she hurried to pour the coffee, intending to make Per Hansa have a cup before he left. "No, no," he said, jerking up his head. "I've had enough for today!"

With these words he went out.

He put on his skis and remained standing there for some time; as he pulled on his mittens he took one glance homeward. He could just make out the house in the dim distance. Then the whiteness all around rose up in a cloud. Whirls of snow flew high over the housetop—the house itself disappeared. He sighed deeply, brushed his eyes with his mitts, and started on his way.

He took his bearings from familiar outlines of the landscape and laid the course he thought he ought to follow. Perhaps it wasn't so dangerous after all. The wind had been steady all day, had held in the same quarter, and would probably keep on. . . . Oh, well—here goes!

He thought no more about his course for a while; but instead he began to wonder if he had done wrong in not going in to drink the coffee, when Beret had taken all the trouble to make it. Now she'll go around feeling unhappy, just because I am so touchy; and she'll be so melancholy that she'll have little patience with the boys. Such high-spirited colts need to be managed with a careful hand. She doesn't understand that at all!

Thoughts of home continued to come, warm and tender; he laughed softly at them. . . . You may be sure she'll get Permand to remember me in his prayers tonight, if he doesn't think of it himself. It would be fun to listen to them.

He moved slowly on with steady strokes, taking note of the wind at times. The picture would not leave him. It would be fun just to look in on them. Oh, Permand, Permand! Something great must come of you—you who are so tenderly watched over!

The swirling dusk grew deeper. Darkness gathered fast. More snow began to fall. Whirls of it came off the tops of the drifts and struck him full in the face. No danger—the wind held steady. Move on! Move on!

About halfway across the stretch from Colton to the James River a cluster of low hills rear themselves out of the prairie. Here and there among them a few stray settlers had already begun to dig in.

On one of the hillsides stood an old haystack which a settler had left there when he found out that the coarse bottom hay wasn't much good for fodder. One day during the spring after Hans Olsa had died, a troop of young boys were ranging the prairies in search of some yearling cattle that had gone astray. They came upon the haystack, and stood transfixed. On the west side of the stack sat a man with his back to the moldering hay. This was in the middle of a warm day in May, yet the man had two pairs of skis along with him; one pair lay beside him on the ground, the other was tied to his back. He had a heavy stocking cap pulled well down over his forehead, and large mittens on his hands; in each hand he clutched a staff. To the boys it looked as though the man were sitting there resting while he waited for better skiing.

His face was ashen and drawn. His eyes were set toward the west.

IN THE HANDS OF
THE SENECAS

IN THE
HANDS OF THE
SENECAS

A CONDENSATION OF THE NOVEL BY
Walter D. Edmonds

ILLUSTRATED BY JOHN THOMPSON

For centuries the Seneca Indians,
one of the Iroquois Five Nations, ruled
what is now western New York State.
But by the time of the American Revolution,
white settlements were flourishing
there, despite occasional raids
by the Indians. The novel
In the Hands of the Senecas explores
what might have happened to some
women and children captured in such a raid.

Walter D. Edmonds set much of
his fiction in upper New York State,
including *Drums Along the Mohawk* and
The Matchlock Gun. He was a
master of combining exciting plots
with authentic historical detail.

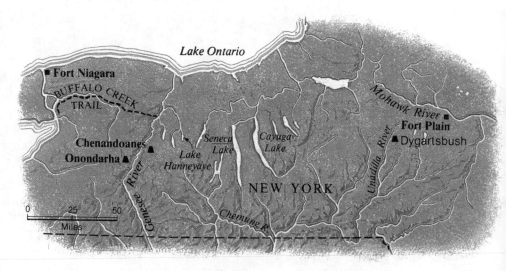

THE CAPTIVES

DYGARTSBUSH was the last settlement on the west of the Little Lakes District, but there was not a spot in it from which two cabins could be seen at the same time. It was too new for that. Most of the people had come in just before 1776, and their cabins stood in isolated clearings connected only by footpaths to the narrow track that led northeastward twenty miles to Fort Plain on the Mohawk River.

Altogether there were fifteen families. Though most were Scotch-Irish, there were also a few Germans, like Nicholas Dygart from whom the settlement took its name. Most were young married couples, like John Borst and his wife, Delia.

Westward the wilderness was mostly unbroken Indian country. Dygartsbush was so hidden away that the first year of the Revolutionary War affected it almost not at all. A few of the young men joined the militia; one of the Kelly boys was killed at Oriskany.

But when the other young men returned at the end of the campaign with news of the defeat of Burgoyne at Saratoga, the settlement was so reassured that the people gave up all notion of building a stockade until the spring planting of 1778 should be completed. They did not get word of the early spring raids on Fairfield and Ephratah. There was no possibility of defense therefore, when, on the third of June, 1778, Dygartsbush was attacked by more than seventy Indians.

The Indians surrounded the clearings individually just before supper-time, while most of the men were still hoeing corn in the stump lots. A light spring rain was falling. A few people did manage to break into the woods. Whether these had escaped or been killed, the survivors who were taken prisoner had no way of telling except for the rain-soaked scalps their captors carried at their belts. They could not even tell how many had been captured, for, as they retired, the Indians broke up their band into several parties.

The Indians were in a hurry. At the edge of the woods they divided their loot by the light of a burning cabin and made it into bundles for the prisoners to carry. There were only two males in this particular lot, Honus Kelly and his thirteen-year-old brother, Pete. The rest were women and girls, from old Mrs. Staats, the mother of Nicholas Dygart's first wife, down to young Ellen Mitchel.

Every one of them had a load to carry. The old Indian who had taken Delia Borst in the doorway of the cabin half an hour before loaded her with her own blankets, her copper kettle, and her little mirror, that had been her wedding present from her mother. She accepted them dully, standing a bit apart from the rest, a straight tall girl with brown hair that reached to her hips.

She had come to Dygartsbush only three weeks before, having been married less than a month. She felt like a stranger in the community; people still spoke of her as Borst's young bride. John had gone away the night before to Fort Plain after flour, and she had expected him back for supper this day. Her whole being had been tensely alert for the sound of his return.

When she had heard a stick break and had gone to the door, she had seen the head of the Indian in the dim white of the chokecherry bloom on the edge of the stump lot. His little eyes fastened upon her and at the first ascending quaver of his yell she had tried to bolt around the cabin.

He came after her, lumbering like a bear with his big stomach, catching her by her hair. Two younger Indians ran down the slope behind the cabin. The three of them crowded close, surrounding her with the rank smell of their deerskins.

Now the load of the bundle weighted her shoulders. The old Indian, the only one who seemed to have any words of English, said, "You come. Walk fast." Another Indian prodded her with the barrel of his musket.

Delia was remembering John's last words to her. "I'll be back right on time," he had said, laughing. "Have a big meal for me, I'll be hungry." She prayed now that he might have been delayed.

Her feet were bruised by unseen stones and roots. Her back ached from the load and her legs became stiff, so that she walked clumsily. She came down on her knees in her first fall and struggled up desperately, snatching at the branches. When they went on again, she found herself silently repeating, "My name is Mrs. John Borst. My name is Mrs. John Borst."

They continued for hours through the dark. None of the captives had any idea of where the Indians were taking them and Delia wondered dully why they hurried. There was no one to follow them, unless—John might have escaped the raid altogether, had he been compelled to wait longer than usual at the mill. Yet even if he had escaped, how would he have found out which party she had been taken with? And suppose John discovered that? He would have to return to Fort Plain for help, twenty miles each way, and if people there took up the pursuit they must start days behind the Indians.

The Indians halted them. "Stop now. Build fire," the leader shouted.

The prisoners instinctively huddled close to the only man in the party. Honus Kelly tossed his pack off and sat down on a wet log. Before this, not one woman among them would have had a decent word for any Kelly. The Kelly boys were perpetually skirting the edge of trouble, either running the woods like Indians, or drinking their father into a stupor. But now the women's voices broke out in questions. "Do you know where we're going? . . . What are they going to do with us?"

"I don't know," Honus said. "Pete, you all right?"

Young Pete Kelly moved up. "They didn't give me much to tote," he said, staring at his brother. "They sure loaded you down, though."

"Where's Jinny?" Mrs. Empie spoke suddenly. "Where's my Jinny?" Toil-bowed, middle-aged, she moved all around the group. "Who was walking ahead of me all the time?"

Presently a timid voice answered, "It was me, I think."

Mrs. Empie stared. "You, Caty Breen! I thought you was Jinny." Suddenly she seemed to lose strength and sat down on the wet earth, leaving the girl alone.

Caty Breen was hired help at the Kelly house, a timid, mouse-haired girl, conscious of the gossip about the way old man Kelly and the boys misused her.

Martha Dygart came up to Honus. "Mr. Kelly," she said, "did you hear anything of my two children?"

He looked at her kindly. Martha was a gaunt-faced, homely woman, the second wife of Nicholas Dygart, whose first had been Mrs. Staats' daughter. People felt that she did not lead an easy life.

"I didn't see them," he said. "Where was they?"

"They'd gone after the cow. Just before the Indians came. They killed Nick but I thought they wouldn't find the children. Mother Staats wanted me to call for them, but I thought they might get away." The tears rose in Martha's plain eyes. "I wanted them to get away."

Mrs. Staats said, "Now they'll never get found probably. The Indians killed everybody else."

Delia Borst fought to speak calmly. "Did anybody see my husband?" A small light entered Honus Kelly's eyes as he studied her round chin and the tenseness of her full lips. "He'd gone to Fort Plain," she said. "He went yesterday. He wasn't due back till just about the time."

Honus nodded. "You mean maybe he didn't get back in time to get caught?"

Suddenly he leaned forward to whisper to Mrs. Staats.

"Ask her, Honus," said Mrs. Staats. "She's got grit."

"It would be worth knowing if he was alive, Mrs. Borst," Honus said. "Would you be able to tell his hair?"

"His hair?"

"Yes, ma'am. These Indians has only a few scalps, but I reckon our bunch will meet up with the rest in a couple of days' time. You'd have to look at the scalps."

Delia gulped down a wave of nausea. "I'll look at them," she promised.

"We've got a chance of somebody coming after us if he's alive," Honus said. "John Borst was a smart man."

ALL BUT TWO INDIANS squatted around the huge fire they had built. The two came up to Honus and threw him suddenly. He made no resistance though he looked big enough to handle them both. They lashed his wrists and ankles to a six-foot pole and left him lying on his back. Then one of them remained as sentry and the second joined the circle around the fire.

They looked more like queer birds than men, squatting around the fire, with the bedraggled feathers leaning damply over their ears. The old one who had captured Delia was wearing John's best hat, which rode down low on his ears. All the others had the elaborate unself-consciousness

390

of young men on their first expedition, paying no heed to the women and leisurely eating boiled beef from a cow slaughtered during the raid.

When they had finished they motioned to the stewpots, and the women, following Mrs. Staats' example, helped themselves. Since they had no spoons, they tried to fish the meat from the pots with sticks picked up off the ground, blistering their fingers.

Delia did not feel hungry. All the time she kept looking at the scalps hanging from the Indians' belts. Again and again she had to force her eyes back to them in an effort to judge the color of the hair. Where it was long she knew it for a woman's. But those with shorter hair did not show their color plainly by firelight. Still she felt a growing hope. She ought to know John's if it were there. She moved around the Indians, and they, understanding what she was after, with half-amused glances lifted up the scalps like peddlers showing calico.

Soon she saw that she had walked near to Honus Kelly.

"You going to eat that meat?" he asked.

She found that she had come away with her piece in her hand. "No. You haven't had any food, have you?"

"No," he said. "I could stand some."

She sat beside him and held the tough beef to his mouth. She hardly had strength to hold it against the wrenching of his teeth. But it comforted her to be helping him; if John had been caught, he would be tied the same way.

"I saw you looking," he said after a time. "It weren't there?"

"No."

"I'll bet he did get off," he said.

She looked at him earnestly. Of all the talk she had heard about the Kellys, no one had told her they were kind. "What happened at your place?" she asked him.

"I guess they got the other boys," he said. "Pa was kilt in his bunk. Drunk and asleep. I was fetching in the wood for Caty." He met her eyes and colored slightly. "Caty's a good girl," he said.

"What will they do with us?" she asked after a while.

He thought it over. "They can do different things. They're Senecas, and I can't understand but a little of their talk. I think they come from a town called Onondarha." He heaved his shoulders. "Ma'am, I got to get away. I'll have to have some help," he said.

"I'll help if you'll tell me how."

"I don't know yet. Pete ought to help some. He's making friends with them, him and that little Mitchel girl, Ellen. See?"

The two children were sitting among the Indians, and the girl was staring at the painting on the naked chest of the Indian beside her. He turned ostentatiously to let the firelight shine on the place.

"He took both the kids," said Honus. "Name's Skanasunk—means Fox. He's real pleased with himself."

"What'll they do with us women?" asked Delia after a time.

"I guess some of you'll get took to the villages. They'll keep you there to work, maybe. They may sell some of you. The old man that took you, his name's Gasotena; it means High-Grass; he's been talking about you."

"Do you know what he says?"

Honus shifted his eyes. "I couldn't make out."

She said, "I wouldn't be afraid if John knew I was alive." She hesitated. "If you could get away, would you tell him that for me?"

"I surely would." His face was in dead earnest. But he was obviously disinclined for further talk. He had closed his eyes.

Delia kept still at his side. She felt a kind of faith in Kelly. She knew rascality was in his blood, however kind he was to her, and surely he would think of some way of escaping. Let him think. She tried impotently to steer Mrs. Staats away with her eyes. But the old woman was white with anger.

"Honus Kelly," she called. "Just look at where your brother's got that little girl. Right in among those savages! Tell him to come over here."

"I can't make him. Try yourself if you like."

At the sound of raised voices the Indians surrounded the prisoners and began binding their hands and ankles. The boy and girl were allowed to remain at the fire.

Delia lay down on the wet leaves. The rain had stopped; there was only the drip from the trees. As the burning logs sank into coals, the darkness came closer. A barred owl passed over the prone figures of Indians and captives with a silent ruffle of his feathers.

THE WEATHER CHANGED with their marching. Even the nights grew warm. The Indians were in no hurry, now, and as long as their captives kept moving at all, they left them alone. At night Honus was the only person they thought fit to bind. It was fortunate for the women, as they were tormented by the flies.

The Indians had washed off their war paint, emerging as rather harmless-looking brown men. They did not, however, relax their watchfulness. Only the two youngsters were allowed to come and go as they pleased around the nightly camps.

One day the Indians halted their journey while a party of them hunted. Pete borrowed a line and fishhook from Skanasunk and went off down a brook with Ellen.

Delia sought out Honus, asking him, "Do you think he'll get away?"

"He won't try to. He knows they're watching him."

It was as Honus said. That evening Pete and the girl returned with a string of trout, which they turned over to Skanasunk. The Indian, who had lain up in the woods all day watching them, manifested a pleased surprise. To Delia, Skanasunk's behavior was the first really human action she had observed in an Indian. . . .

The next evening, just after sunset, another party of Indians joined them. They had only three prisoners. Delia began a search of the scalps carried by the new party. But the Indians were holding a council and made it plain that they did not want her around. She moved away, sitting by herself. When darkness had come, Pete came up to her.

"I been looking for you," he said unexpectedly. "John Borst ain't with them. Honus told me to look. But they say they chased a big white man clear back to Otsquago Crick. They said he dropped a bag of gristing. I guess that was him all right. Weren't no other man after grist that day. . . . Something else," he added suddenly. "Honus wants to talk with you."

Until nightfall, now, the Indians tied Honus to a tree by cords around his waist. He was still sitting so when Delia approached, his big body thrust forward against the cords. "It ain't so bad," he said, "once I can work up some slack." Then he added quietly, "We mustn't talk too loud. Pete thinks one of them new Indians knows English." Delia felt her hands turn cold. "I been waiting for this time," he said.

"Tonight?" She thought, Why now, with all these new Indians?

He nodded. "I know what you think. But there's something else. Pete took a knife to clean them fish with. It ain't been missed yet. I got it in my pocket here. Will you set down?"

"What do you want me to do?" she whispered.

"Don't whisper. Talk low, but so anyone can see you're talking. You got that knife all right? Good girl. Hide it in your dress. When they throw me tonight it would fall out. Will you sleep close by and pass it over?"

"I will." She could not help her whispering now.

He grinned a wide grin, showing his big stained teeth through his beard. "Hain't nothing to get rattled over. Just move around natural and ask Mrs. Staats and Caty will they come and see me."

Delia hunted up Caty first and said that Honus wished to talk to her. The girl started to her feet, looked once in Delia's face to make sure she wasn't being fooled, and crossed the camp.

Delia saw them side by side, Caty sitting like someone entranced, a slow blush coming and going in her face. Honus kept looking at his hands, but he appeared to be speaking earnestly. When he was through, she stood irresolutely for an instant before resuming her former place.

Delia waited awhile before moving on to Mrs. Staats. The old woman had got back a lot of dander from the one day's rest.

"Honus Kelly! Wants to speak to me? Why don't he come over here?"

"How can he?" Delia said. "I'd go if I were you, Mrs. Staats."

Mrs. Staats stared coldly up at her. "Hurrrmph!"

Honus Kelly didn't give her a chance to speak. "Set down," he said. "We ain't got much time for talk." She was too surprised to refuse.

"You've never had much use for me, Mrs. Staats. I ain't thought much of you either. You've done a lot of damage with your talk about Caty. But you've got more nerve than all the rest of these women put together."

"Me, nerve!" the old woman ejaculated.

"Yes." He looked almost friendly. "That's why I want to ask you something. I'm going to get away tonight. But I can't manage it alone."

"And you think I'd help, hey? Why?"

"When this business ends, you'll want someone to know where you've been took to."

Mrs. Staats looked down at her hard-veined hands. "What do you want me to do?"

"I want you to have some bowel trouble," Honus said. "After the logs break down in the fire. There's been only one Injun watching."

Mrs. Staats looked sharply up. "That all?"

"Yes," said Honus.

Suddenly she smiled.

"Give me three minutes, ma'am."

"Oh, more than that. The trouble I've had," said Mrs. Staats. Her face was almost pert.

DELIA LAY CLOSE TO HONUS. Ever since the fire had started giving out, her hands had been like ice. The Indians had poled him, and she knew that she would have to cut him free. His chest swelled and sank with a regular heavy snore. The Indians slept like logs under their blankets. Only one sat upright, his thin face watching the coals.

Delia could not see Honus' face, close as it was to hers, but on the ending of a snore he said, "Keep your eye on Mrs. Staats." A breath. "You'll have to saw my hands free."

She moved with infinite precision, fishing the knife out of her dress. Kelly's snoring went on undisturbed. She began to fumble for his hands, finding the cords.

"Oh," she whispered, feeling a flow of blood from his wrist.

"Hush up and go ahead," he said.

Out of the tail of her eye she saw Mrs. Staats lean up on her elbow, heard her moan. The Indian's head cocked like a buck deer's.

"Quick," said Honus.

Delia bore down with all her strength. Then his huge paw jumped away and took the knife out of her hand. He twisted down and cut the ankle cords with two quick slashes. It made a little sound and the Indian swung toward them. But Honus was lying stiffly again.

Mrs. Staats, mumbling to herself, was walking quietly away. The Indian moved after her phlegmatically.

They could hear only the faintest rustling where Mrs. Staats was. The Indian stepped out of the circle of firelight.

"Good girl," said Honus. "I'll tell John Borst."

In an instant Honus was on his feet, then Delia heard the thresh of underbrush. The watcher's musket exploded and he started after Honus. There was a wild screech from beside the Indian, and a desperate scuffling.

"Go on, Honus. I've got him!" Mrs. Staats' voice, vociferous, triumphant, rose in the night. Delia saw the Indians springing up around their fire. The watcher came blundering back, dragging the old woman by one arm. He pointed the direction Honus took and led six men in pursuit. The other Indians leaped on the women and even the two youngsters, knocking them back to the ground and binding them.

All night Delia thought she heard returning footsteps, but they never came till dawn. She had to take only one look at the Indians to see that Honus had escaped.

Mrs. Statts died during the night. She made no complaints. She lay with a gash in her head and a broken shoulder, staring at the leaves above her face. Her scalp was taken by the Indian who had captured her.

Next morning, early, the Indians took up their march, passing west across the southern edge of the Cayuga lands. They were hard on the prisoners now, dealing out frequent blows. Honus' load was shared among half a dozen, giving them all they could stagger under.

Six days later, just after dawn, a couple of the Indians dropped out of the group and headed north. They took Caty Breen. Delia said good-bye, but Caty could hardly speak.

It was while the other women were looking after Caty that Pete edged up to Delia. "They're splitting up," he murmured. "Me and Ellen is going with Skanasunk. Going to adopt us, he says. You're going on with the main bunch. Old High-Grass figures he's going to make a squaw of you. . . . Honus knew, but he didn't have the guts to tell you." Then he moved away.

Delia stood still, staring after him. She had acquired an apathy from the long days of marching. Then, surprisingly, as the old Indian poked her forward with his gun, her head came up.

Honus had got away. By now, perhaps, John would know she was alive. Nothing but that mattered.

CATY BREEN

THE WOMEN were wearied out with eighteen days of plodding through the woods. Their minds were dulled and their courage nearly spent. They scarcely took notice of the dividing up of the war party. As the two braves led Caty Breen northward along a path as narrow and overgrown as a fox's alley, she looked back once, but the trees had shut off her view of the other captives. She knew the women did not like her, but now, as the green summer woods closed over her, she missed their querulous utterances. She did not know that already she had come nearly two hundred miles from Dygartsbush.

The trail led steadily north, following a shallow valley through upland country. The two Indians paid no attention to the captive. Neither of them carried anything beyond his personal equipment: his musket, powder horn, bullet pouch, blanket, skinning knife, and the little medicine bag on his chest. The sun glistened on the oiled planes of their coppery backs as they moved. The braided scalp locks on the crowns of their heads were like bird crests; they made motions with their heads like birds when they looked to one side.

She remembered suddenly what Honus Kelly had said to her. "Don't ever show them you're scared."

They had come to a wide brook with swift water, which the trail crossed at the head of a long run. As the Indians waded through, she saw one of them beckon. She stepped into the water and felt the current take hold of her petticoat. Overweighted by the bulky pack, she struggled for balance. Looking up again timidly she saw the two Indians still impassively watching her. *Don't ever show them you're scared.* They would not want their plunder wet. Her own good blue shortgown was in the pack, but she no longer thought of it as hers. She felt her way, one foot after the other, and finally reached the far side.

They had covered over twenty miles by late afternoon. Her neck and shoulders were sore from her burden and there were long stretches when she seemed to be walking in her sleep. During the march she had learned to fix her soft brown hair in two braids hanging down in front of her like an Indian woman's to keep it out of the way of the pack.

The first narrow trail they had taken had turned into a second, the second into a third, each seeming more traveled than the last. Now the third entered still another path that dipped downward sharply to a lake and followed its margin under tall timber. There was little underbrush here, and she could see the water was unruffled, clear, and glassy.

The two Indians talked to each other; again and again she thought she heard the same word repeated, *Hanneyaye,* as if it might be the name of the lake. Then, after four more miles of traveling, a sound like barking dogs carried over the still water. Almost at the same moment, the Indians swung from the trail, mounted a knoll, and began questing among the trees. Caty, sagging tiredly, saw one of them point to a deep blaze. He pulled out his tomahawk and slashed a new blaze under the first, then trotted away down the far side of the knoll. The other squatted down and, taking a small sack from his belt, began mixing paints. He gestured that she should put the pack down. Beyond him, the distant barking of dogs was suddenly clamorous and unmistakable.

In a little while the Indian who had gone ahead returned and began mixing his own paint. The water of the lake slowly took fire from the setting sun. A flock of pigeons passed from the far shore, their wings making a whisper overhead. With laborious care the Indians painted their faces. The black and white war paint turned them into masks, and in an instant the horror of the raid that had been dulled by the long days of travel returned to her. She saw again the sudden appearance of the Indians beyond the corn piece fence; the boys running for their guns; Honus felled by a glancing tomahawk in the doorway of the cabin.

The Indians had scarcely finished rebraiding each other's scalp locks when they heard people approaching along the shore of the lake. They rose silently, taking positions behind trees. Caty also heard the approaching footfalls. Looking down toward the water she saw two Indian women carrying bundles in their hands.

The two squaws set down the bundles and retreated. As soon as they were gone, the braves went down to the shore, picked up the bundles, and stepped off into the woods. Caty sat alone in the fading light. *Don't ever show them you're scared.* There was no one to see her now. The tears came unchecked to her eyes and rolled out upon her cheeks.

Then she heard the Indians returning. They were dressed in fresh clothes; the beading on the leggings shone faintly white and red and yellow. Their heads were covered with bright cloths mounted on hoops, an eagle feather slanting backward from each.

They gave Caty their blankets to add to her pack. She knelt with her back to the pack, drawing the burden strap to her forehead. The weight dragged against her neck; she gasped and struggled upward. The Indian prodded her with his musket, sending her forward. Within half a mile the path stepped down into a deep worn slot running east and west. She did not know that this was the great central trail of the Iroquois, but its hard-beaten earth was smooth under her feet as she and the two Indians moved into the dusk.

She heard the clamor of the dogs far below and saw the glow of fires from the house doorways. The houses, built of logs or bark, narrow and long, were scattered among apple trees, and the inhabitants thronged toward the edge of the town, preceded by a mass of dogs. The two Indians in their fanciful clothes looked straight ahead into the town, between two lines formed by the squaws and children, to a central fire burning before the council house. and a bare post beside it.

The dogs were all around them now; one snapped at the hem of her raveled petticoat and another clicked his jaws on her ankle. She was in the midst of the Indians, and it seemed to her as if every last one of them was yelling. The women struck at her and the children poked sticks at her unsteady feet. The instinct to run came over her, but she was hemmed in and her two captors would not let her through the bedlam until the heat of the central fire struck her eyes. She looked up to see them driving their tomahawks into the post. Then, in the midst of silence, an old man, standing solitary and erect before the council house, began to speak. She stood wavering while his voice rose and fell like that of a preacher.

The old man ended his speech at last. As the silence swept in from the surrounding night, Caty was seized by the women. The pack was yanked off her shoulders and she was dragged out of the circle. Behind her one war whoop was echoed by the crowd; it was succeeded by a single voice singing a war song, accompanied by a drum. She could still hear it as she was pushed through the doorway of a narrow cabin. She stumbled forward into pitch blackness and sat down without a sound on the dirt floor.

Beyond the log walls, the singer's voice went on to a wild climax. She tried to shut it out, holding her head in her hands.

Then, all at once, she rose on her knees and listened. Somewhere in the dark she heard another person's breathing.

"Who are you?" It was a man's voice.

"Caty Breen."

The man cursed. "Why do they have to keep on hollering and yelling like that? They'll keep it up all night." His voice sounded muffled; she thought he must be lying on his face. His breathing seemed heavier than was natural.

Suddenly the man asked, "Did they treat you bad?"

"Not awful bad," she replied. "They made me carry a pack a long way. When we got here some of the women hit me with sticks."

"I guess it ain't bad if you ain't a man," he said with bitterness and self-pity. Then he asked her where she came from.

"Dygartsbush," she said simply.

"I never heard of that place," he said. "Where is it?"

"It's a settlement over in the Little Lakes country. Where did you live?" she asked. She was too shy to ask for his name.

"I settled in Kingsland, me and my brother and his wife. They raided

399

there this spring, but we'd moved into Little Falls. I went back to the farm two weeks ago. . . . Where are you? I can't see."

"Here."

"Can't you come closer?"

She crept forward, feeling with her hands. He was lying on a kind of low platform. She touched his bare arm. He put his hand out and groped for hers. "My name's Henry Shoe." He withdrew his hand and said, "Damn them Indians," and then as the yelling was followed again by the drumbeats and the single singing voice, "I had to go back to our place. They told me I was a fool, but I couldn't get out of my mind my corn piece didn't have no scarecrow, see?" His voice rose. "I didn't even get the thing set up when a bunch of them come at me."

Caty was silent so long that he roused himself.

"Maybe you think I was a fool, too?"

"No, I don't," said Caty.

"I reckon you're a nice girl," he said. "It's nice having someone to talk to. Takes your mind off what's outside. You awful tired?"

"Oh, no. I couldn't sleep."

He asked, "Did they do a lot of damage at your place?"

"They burnt the whole settlement. They killed all the men but Honus Kelly, and Pete, his brother. He's really only a boy. We thought maybe Mr. Borst got away."

"I mean *your* place," he said. "They killed your family?"

"I haven't any family," she said. "I was hired girl to the Kellys." She added, "I've been hired out to people ever since I can remember."

"How old are you?"

"Eighteen," she said.

Suddenly she realized that the noise from the direction of the council house was fading out. She turned her head toward the doorway, seeing the dim glow from the central fire and the figure of a watching Indian and a couple of dogs in front of it. The Indian faced the prisoners' lodge.

Henry Shoe shifted on the platform. "It's wonderful having a person to talk to," he said. "You get more scared when you're alone."

"I know," said Caty softly.

It was some time before she realized that he had dropped off to sleep. His hand, hanging over the edge of the platform, lay against her arm. Careful not to wake him, she stretched out quietly and let his fingers stay, drawing a sense of comradeship from their touch.

THE LIGHT OF SUNRISE, FINDING its sole entry through the doorway, fell first on her. She woke uncertainly, lying still at first to listen to the wakening birds, and letting her eyes move around the log cabin.

It was windowless. There was no fireplace or chimney. Fires had been built upon the floor, and the smoke, allowed to escape through small vents along the rooftree, had blackened the rafters. Down each side ran two platforms, the lower about a foot above the ground, with the upper five feet above it. There was no other furniture, nor any bedding.

As she stirred and sat up, her shoulder brushed the hand of her fellow prisoner. She turned quickly to look at him.

He was a big strong fellow, but she thought that he seemed very young. He lay like a boy, flat on his belly, with his head turned to pillow his cheek on his hand, but as the light gained strength, she understood why he did not lie on his back. One glance at his tattered hunting shirt, the welts and open gashes showing through the rents, and the cloth stuck tight to the clotted blood, told her what he would have to go through when he woke. Her heart turned sick; if only she had some heated water, she thought, she could soak off the rotten cloth.

She moved softly to the door of the cabin and looked out into the village. Smoke was already rising from the chimneys or roofs of a few houses, but some of the women evidently preferred to do their cooking out of doors. Caty saw one of them fetching two kettles up from the brook. As far as she could see no men had come out; there was only the brave left to guard the prisoners, sitting a little way from the door.

Caty watched the squaw hang the two kettles on a cross stick over the flames and turn aside to speak to another woman who was coming out of the woods with a faggot of sticks on her back.

After the woman with the wood had gone her way, the one who had set her kettles over the fire went into her cabin. Perhaps it was her deeply ingrained instinct to serve people that gave Caty courage to do what she would never have dared for herself. She stepped from the door and walked directly to the fire. Her heart fluttered as she lifted the cross stick and slipped the bale of the nearest kettle over the end. Hurrying back to the prisoner's lodge she slipped safely inside.

She heard Henry groan.

"Don't move," she called softly to him and hurried forward, setting the kettle down beside him. She tore a piece of calico from her shortgown to make a wad and moistened it.

"I'm afraid it'll hurt you," she said, "but it won't be so bad as if I didn't soak the cloth and blood off."

He winced from time to time, and she said, "I'm sorry. I can't help it. I'm going as easy as I can."

"Where'd you get the kettle?"

"I found it on a fire," she said. He mustn't fret, she thought, and she lied. "They let me take it."

He didn't say anything to that; he didn't speak at all but lay with his face on his forearms and bit his wrist.

"Poor boy," she said as she finished, and blushed, realizing what she had said. But her heart swelled. She had never done anything like this for anyone before. It was not like cooking for a man or fixing his shirt, in which you were just hired help. It was a different thing altogether.

Henry moved to draw the shirt off over his head and Caty said, "I wish I had some salve to put on it, but I'd like to wash off the cuts anyway."

"It feels all right this way. Leave them alone." He started to roll over. But Caty pushed the shoulder down gently and firmly, saying, "Please let me fix them. It would be better."

He gave way sulkily. It occurred to her that she had never before told a person what he must do.

"What did they do to you?" she asked quietly.

His voice was muffled. "I had to run the gauntlet. At the town before we got to this one. There was almost two hundred of them lined up."

Caty said nothing, but he went on talking just the same, in a thickened, almost desperate voice.

"Squaws and children and the men, too. They had clubs and hickory sticks and knives." He twisted his head around to look at her, and the sight of her mild face with its soft brown braids framing the cheeks seemed to rouse his bitterness. "You're just a girl. They say they don't make women run it, generally. I was the only prisoner they had. One of the Indians could talk some English. He told me to run through them lines fast and touch the post in the middle of the town. But I was scared. I said I didn't want to."

"It must have been terrible," Caty said. It was all she could think of to say. She wished she could soothe him.

"When he told me to go, I couldn't move. The Indian said if I ran fast I wouldn't get hurt bad. But I didn't believe him. Then they took me by the arms and dragged me to the line and pushed me, but I hung back. And then one hit me on the shoulder with his tomahawk. I tried to run then. I ran as fast as I could, but a little girl stuck a stick between my legs and I fell down. I thought they'd kill me before I could get up. I couldn't even think, the way they was yelling and laughing, too—"

He broke off suddenly and put his face on his arms.

"Honest, you mustn't show them you're scared," Caty said. "I've got your back fixed now, pretty well." She set aside the kettle.

"Thanks," he said, "it feels some better." He sat up.

She said, "I wonder how we get anything to eat."

"Oh, they'll bring in a mess of something. Where you going?"

"I'm going to take the kettle back. She may want it."

"So she didn't let you take it. You just stole it."

Caty lowered her eyes before his. "Well, I did."

"I reckon she'll act mean. They're meaner than weasels, some of them women. You better not go out."

Caty hesitated. Then it came to her that if she went out, and showed him she was not afraid, maybe he would conquer his own fear.

The woman whose kettle she had was arguing loudly with a couple of others, pointing to the solitary kettle over the fire. The watching brave had got up under his blanket and walked over toward them, as if to listen. Caty lifted her head and walked out of the cabin.

They saw her instantly. The squaw to whom the kettle belonged came up to her with blazing eyes, snatching the kettle with one hand and striking Caty across the face with her free hand. Caty felt the blood on her lips, and instantly the other two squaws rushed up. Caty tried to smile. "I had to have water," she said.

Her voice seemed only to rouse them further. They put out their hands at her and the one with the kettle swung it suddenly. Caty could not have dodged if the brave had not quickly drawn her away. He turned Caty around toward the cabin.

"Stay inside," he said. "Bring meat soon."

He walked behind her to the door and thrust her in.

Henry sat where he had when she went out. But he looked at her curiously. "I heard them hollering. Did they hurt you?"

Caty shook her head.

"They must've. They hit you on the mouth, I can see."

Caty wiped her lips with her bare arm. "No, no. It ain't bad. Honest. One of the men brought me away. He said we'd get food pretty soon."

"Did he tell you anything else? About me, I mean. What they're going to do with me?"

She shook her head. "Don't think of that," she said.

"How can I help thinking of it?" he cried and turned away from her.

She sat down miserably, wiping her mouth from time to time and rubbing her arms clean on her petticoat.

Neither of them spoke until, later, a woman brought them a small bark dish of stew. Then Henry relented enough to say to her, "Have some?"

Even as they ate she felt his mounting nervousness. He was like an animal, the way his head kept rising to each fresh note of sound. He got up finally and began walking up and down the open space between the sleeping platforms and she saw then how big he really was—a great heavy powerful fellow.

Now and then he would survey what was going on outside. He was tense; it was some time before he noticed how quiet she had become.

"Say, Caty, you ain't mad at me, are you?"

"No."

"I'd hate for you to feel mad at me." He sounded pathetically anxious. "You been nice to me. I don't think I ever met a nicer girl than you."

She raised her eyes. "I'm glad, Henry."

His eyes were simple and honest. She saw once more how decent he really was.

Then, like a wave of light, Caty understood what the feeling in her breast had been about. He depended on her not for the work she could do for him, but for herself. Herself, who had been a hired girl all her life.

A sort of peacefulness came between them that had nothing to do with the steady noises of the Indian village, or the warm clear sun beyond the door. The man sat down again and quite easily began to talk to her about the farm he and his brother had started. He told her about his sister-in-law, a steady girl, but not a first-rate cook.

"I'll bet you're a good cook," he said.

And she said shyly, "I can cook pretty well."

It was as if they had re-created a small white corner of the world inside the prisoners' lodge, and yet both knew it could not last.

TOWARD NOON THEY HEARD shouting, and a short time after that the Indian dogs began their barking and went rushing out of the town. Henry rose quickly and went to the door.

When he spoke his voice had become taut and high. "There's half a hundred of them coming in. It looks like a whole town coming visiting."

She heard laughter and greetings going back and forth between the parties. Presently they were passing the door of the cabin on their way toward the council house.

"Do you think they're getting up a gauntlet for me?" he asked.

"No." Her voice was steady, but she did not feel assured.

"I bet they've sent for them so they can see me."

"You mustn't think that way. I don't want the Indians to think a man as strong as you is scared of anything they can do. I don't think so."

Their eyes met in the shadowed cabin and Caty felt brave in her heart. He came over to where she was and sat beside her. His hand reached clumsily for hers and held to it. Then they saw the Indians streaming out toward the open grassland by the stream.

His voice had tightened but his eyes stayed with hers. "When they take me out, you better stay inside."

Her own voice trembled now. "I'll stand out there where you can see me." She hesitated. "Maybe if you could look at me it would be easier than just seeing them."

"It won't be fun to watch. Maybe I can't do it."

She squeezed his hand. Then a shadow came through the door and they saw two Indians standing there.

One of them, pointing to Henry, said, "Come now."

He got up slowly. He did not look back at Caty as he walked out with them.

She would not have supposed there were so many Indians. They were drawn up in two long lines, extending nearly two hundred yards from the stream to the beginning of the town. They stood wide enough apart to have free play for their clubs, tomahawks, and knives.

Caty saw it all clearly, though the start of the line seemed far away. She saw Henry Shoe at the far end. They had stripped him. She saw him lift his arm, and she lifted her own hand as high as she could. Maybe he couldn't see it, she thought, and tore a piece from her shortgown and waved it.

But he had already started running. She heard the men's whooping and the screeches of the squaws. Each succeeding blow marked plainly where he was. The sticks quivered, poised, and struck.

She saw him now, running with a blind fury. He stumbled over a stick but caught himself and hit out with his fist. The squaw screeched and fell backward, and those beside her laughed.

He was not a real runner, but he was strong as she had seen, and the men running along the outside of the lines to see him finish did not overtake him. He burst out of the line, came toward the war post by the council house and stood there, holding it, his thick chest heaving.

Then he looked for her, finding her still in the cabin door, holding the torn piece from her shortgown. He grinned.

The two who had taken him out to the gauntlet were laughing now, and patting him with their hands. When they had let him inside the cabin they handed in his clothes. A little later they brought a kettle of stew and the brave who had captured him came in and asked, "You like to go to Niagara?"

"Sure," said Henry. Then he looked at Caty. "How about her?"

"She go, too. Fetch eight dollars." The Indian was solemn with satisfaction. "Maybe you fetch ten."

Henry laughed. "We'll be prisoners, but I've heard sometimes they'll let you hire out to work. They ought to be glad to get a hired girl like you. Maybe we could get a place together, in Canada, until the war's over. Then we'll go back home."

She glanced timidly along his shoulder, and he turned quickly and met her eyes.

"Would that be all right with you?"

"Yes," she said.

"I couldn't get along without you anymore, you know."

Caty was quiet. She was satisfied to let him talk. He no longer depended on her as he had for that short time before; he might never again; but she took comfort in the thought of other ways she knew of being useful.

DELIA BORST

THE MEMBERS of the Seneca war party that had raided Dygartsbush belonged for the most part to the small towns on the upper Genesee River. They were three weeks making the return journey. Only women were left now in the string of burdened captives, and there were fewer of them than had started the long march from their blazing cabins. Old

Mrs. Staats had been killed; Caty Breen had been taken off to the north; the two children, Ellen Mitchel and Peter Kelly, had left with the young brave to whom they belonged.

The remaining women were too wearied from their long, heavy journey even to think about what would happen to them. They seemed unaware of the clear sky and the south wind drawing down the steep valley. They did not even see the river, a deep blue sinuous cord half hidden by its banks of high natural grass. Only one among them had spirit to lift her eyes and see how beautiful it was.

Delia Borst saw it all before her. The grass seemed a green river in itself, and the trail they were following through it was like a ford—or, she thought, like the crossing of the Red Sea in the Bible, dividing waters of grass. Only, unlike the Israelites, she was entering her bondage, not escaping from it. Her eyes turned to the old brave, Gasotena, at the head of the line. She knew that he had spoken of making her his squaw.

He stopped and raised his arm to point over the valley. His seamed face was impassive as old wood beneath her husband's hat. She followed the direction of his finger and saw, in a bend of the river, a haze of smoke against the sky, and the bark roofs of Indian cabins.

Her head raised with a little jerk. She was a tall girl, as tall as the old Indian, with strong square shoulders and a thick brown rope of hair. Of all the women she alone stood with a straight back under her load.

This was the town, she thought, which they had been heading for through the endless wilderness. An imperceptible shiver passed over her.

The Indians were suddenly full of talk; she heard again and again the name *Onondarha*. Then she saw that Gasotena was watching her with his small dark eyes. She forced her own not to waver. He swung away abruptly down the steep slope, and for those last few moments, while she followed with the other captives, she said over and over to herself, "My name is Mrs. John Borst. My name is Mrs. John Borst."

TIMES CAME LATER when the memory of that clear day of her entering into the Indian town brought a deeper aching to her heart than the thought of her burned cabin. It was the last moment in which she could remember the girl who had been Delia Borst. Now she could not imagine herself as the same person. Not even one day when she slipped away from the cornfield belonging to her lodge and went to the river. Crouching down, she stared for a long time at the face in the water. She could see the same slight arching of the brows that had been hers, the same roundness of the chin, brown of the eyes, and curved meeting of the lips.

It was the kind of face John Borst had said a man could not keep himself away from. The recollection of the words, said in the first days of their meeting, overwhelmed her.

How long she crouched there she never knew. Her mind retraced the night of their arrival in the Indian town. Sitting with Martha Dygart, Mrs. Empie, and the other women in a small unlighted cabin, she listened to the singing and powwow from the council house. They talked about what the Indians would do with them. Mrs. Empie seemed to be the only one who had done any thinking about Indians.

"Do they ever . . ." one woman's voice shook and dropped. "Do they ever—kill women prisoners?"

Mrs. Empie's hard, common-sense voice was easy to believe. Nobody thought to question her knowledge. "If you get sick so you ain't worth nothing to them, maybe, they'll kill you. But it ain't usual."

Delia found herself also questioning. "Do they ever marry white women?"

"You're the good-looker, ain't you?" Mrs. Empie said. "I don't know, it ain't usual. My husband told me that."

"Pete Kelly told me the old Indian talked about marrying me," said Delia.

"I don't know nothing about that."

"I'd die first," said another voice, hushed and full of terror.

"Would you?" said Mrs. Empie. "How'd you stop it, I'd like to know."

"I don't know." The voice broke. "But I would."

"Well," said Mrs. Empie, "I don't calculate there's nothing left for me to get back for. But if there was, I'd see to it I managed to get back if it took me half my life; and I'd keep my mouth shut how I did it, too."

Thinking back, Delia remembered the dry, sane voice. She had not seen Mrs. Empie again. The other women had been taken to other towns.

Lying in the grass beside the river, Delia remembered how she had been adopted. She did not know what it was that was happening. Gasotena made a speech in front of her, and then the head woman of the house stepped out from the crowd, smiling, and led Delia away to a large log house. A double row of cubicles ran down its two sides.

The other women of the Indian household joined them. They examined her tattered clothes, and then picked out many of their own best things to dress her in. It was hard to find anything wide enough to cover

her shoulders, but they gave her one of her own white blankets, and with her shortgown, the blue Indian skirt and quilled moccasins she looked like a tall, straight-standing Indian girl. Her warm heart swelled; they seemed so kind. She said thank you to them one by one, until the youngest, understanding her, said, *"Hi-ne-a-weh,"* whereupon they all beamed, pointing to her lips, until she said stumblingly, *"Hi-ne-a-weh."*

When the head woman took her hand and led her to one of the fires burning on the earthen floor, her anxiousness to please them made her almost tremulous. She quickly comprehended what they wanted of her, mixing cornmeal and water under their direction and baking the unleavened cake on a flat, heated stone. As soon as it was done, the head woman signified that Delia was to carry it to an old woman who, in spite of the heat, sat huddled in furs and blankets, with only her bright eyes alive. The old woman accepted the cake with her twiglike fingers. She stirred, but her voice was low and rather hoarse, like a croaking bird's. *"Go-ah-wuk."* Delia did not know then that it meant "daughter." Even when the head woman led Delia to the central south side cubicle and spread a deerskin for her on the low platform, she did not realize that she had just been married.

When night came and she discovered what had happened to her, there was no turning back. In the cubicles of the log house, with the acrid smoke-smell lading the dark air and the fires buried, people were lying all around her. There were eight families—men and squaws and children—and the ancient woman who seemed not to sleep, but sat upright, her eyes reflecting the one faint spot of red.

During the dark succeeding hours she lay unstirring except for the heavy slow beating of her heart. She was conscious only of the Indians breathing around her, of the night sky and the limitless woods through which she had traveled step by step to that one helpless moment of her life.

Delia was brought out of her recollections by the sound of stealthy approach through the high grass. One of the dogs from her own house had sniffed out her trail. She lifted herself slowly to her feet and moved along the little footpath, hearing the dry pat of the dog's feet behind her own.

As she emerged from the grass she could see the squaws still weeding the long rows of hilled young corn and squash. But she had no heart left for longer working under the hot sun. A fit of weeping had exhausted her, and she still had pride enough never to let any of the Indian women see her own humiliation. She thought of the house, now, as a refuge. At this hour of the afternoon it would be empty. Even the papooses would be in their baby frames, hanging from branches near where their mothers worked.

The winter months and the succeeding spring had made the house familiar, comforting with its feeling of four solid barriers against the wilderness. She pushed open the swinging door and stepped in.

"Daughter." The voice was low and slightly hoarse. Delia had forgotten the ancient woman who never stirred from the house.

"Ucsote." Delia gave her the title of Grandmother. She went dutifully to wait on her, for during the winter the old woman had become almost entirely helpless.

The old woman watched her with upturned eyes, and after a moment of collecting her energies for a new word, she said, "Sit down by me." Delia obeyed, sitting close.

"Why do you grieve?" the old woman asked.

It was the first personal remark Delia had ever heard her make. She was too surprised to answer. But the old woman parted her thin lips and said, "You are young and warm. You should not grieve."

"I am not grieving," Delia said. Though she could see only the profile, it suddenly occurred to her that the old woman's features did not have the tribal resemblance found in the other inhabitants of the town.

"A woman cannot help the things of God." For God, she used the name Ataentsic, and Delia knew enough of the language to be surprised; for Ataentsic, the oldest god, was a woman, the Moon; and in the village all other Indians addressed Areskoui, the Sun.

"No, *Ucsote,*" Delia said. "But you must not tire yourself with talking to me."

The old woman, however, seemed to gain strength as she talked. "I am tired of being still. You grieve because you have married my son." A shadow of irritation crossed her face. "My grandson," she corrected herself. "It is so long since he was born."

Delia bowed her head, looking at her hands. The quality of the old woman's voice did not change, but her eyes were gentle.

"I was brought to this town when I was young. I belonged to the Cherokee nation, more than a lifetime ago." Haltingly she went on to tell how she had been captured when she was fourteen in a raid and brought to Onondarha.

Delia was barely able to follow the dry patter of her words. "I was the wife of a Cherokee chief," the old woman said. "They took him to another town. Then Gasotena, the chief of this place, wished to have a squaw. He would take me, but I said I was married. They then sent to the other town and my husband was burned. So I married Gasotena. I grieved like you."

The silence was broken by the distant shrilling of the children at play.

"My son was born after my fifteenth spring. I named him Little Otter. When his father died he took his name, High-Grass, Gasotena. He was a good man. I have not been sorry. I can sit here now and see my children."

During a long pause she seemed to struggle with herself, and mechanically Delia leaned forward to help her shift the blankets. The hand came forth slowly and took Delia's in the stiff fingers.

"It is a warm hand," the old woman said.

Delia choked a sob. "It is white, *Ucsote*. And I was married, too."

"You should have said so, daughter."

"I did not know."

"Perhaps it was better. If Gasotena knew, he would have to journey back and kill your husband to make it right. Perhaps you will not be like me but go back some time."

"*Ucsote,* I cannot." The eyes suddenly grew moist. "I can't go back—now," Delia said.

"Why not, daughter?"

"Could you have left your son?"

"Why are you ashamed? Because you are white?" There was a faint reproof in the ancient voice. "If you stayed when the time came to go, you would still be white." The hand slowly withdrew and Delia closed the blankets over the old woman.

Far away the dogs began barking. The old woman spoke for the last time, with quiet pride. "All the men of this house are good hunters. My grandson has killed a deer."

GASOTENA, PUFFING, brought in a young dry doe. Delia, standing in the door, watched as he set about the skinning of it. She would have to work the skin tomorrow; she would have to rub it with the brains tonight.

As Gasotena's knife skillfully laid back the hide, he announced to the men gathered together on the ground nearby that he had met a Toryohne man on the beech ridge. The man had told him the Wolf house of his village, Owaiski, were planning a war party within a week, if any of the Onondarha young men wished to join them.

There was a long silence after he had spoken, all looking to see whether he had made up his own mind. But he kept silence, finished the skinning and cutting up of the carcass, and handed out the sections to members of his own house while the women of the other houses looked on enviously—wishing that their own men were as good providers.

Gasotena finished his work and sat down on the edge of the cubicle. When Delia set food before him, he thanked her gravely. He had drawn his blanket over his naked back, but he still wore the hat, which for Delia had long since lost its identity with John Borst. The brim sagged from a winter of snow and there were two slits in the crown through which the quill of a feather could be passed. But it was the best hat that had ever come into the town, and Gasotena never took it off unless to lie down.

That evening he kept it on after his meal, and walked toward the council house. One of his nieces, Deowuhyeh, who had married an ambitious brave from Owaiski, came to help Delia work the hide. She said, "Now there will be a council."

Delia nodded. For a little while the two worked together without speaking. Soon, however, Deowuhyeh's eyes turned toward the council house, from which a single voice issued in a long, rhythmic exposition.

"It is a war council," the girl whispered. "There are no women." As Delia said nothing, she asked, "Do you not hope they go?"

"No," said Delia.

"Gasotena will want to go now," said the girl. "He talked with Ganowauges, my husband, in our house. I wish him to go. We need money. The man from Owaiski said the British are paying eight dollars for a scalp as they did last year. Gasotena is pleased. He said he would need a better musket now to teach his son to shoot." She smiled once more. "Many men will go if Gasotena does. He knows the trails to the white settlements. He is a great chief."

DURING THE ENSUING DAYS, Delia became conscious of a growing excitement in the town. Hardly anyone went into the woods. They stayed near the houses all day long: the older men holding conferences in the sunshine, talking slowly; the impatient younger men going to the river where they practiced throwing their tomahawks at a stake.

The women, upon finding themselves alone at their work in the cornfields, would begin an excited chattering speculation about the number of men the war party would make up to and where they would head for. A few of the older women mentioned names they had heard—Fort Herkimer, Honoagoneh, Dayaogeh, Schenectady—but with no notion of where they were or what they stood for. Their main concern was with the wealth that might be brought back in salable scalps or plunder.

As Delia felt the intensified excitement, her thoughts moved irrationally. She would awaken in the middle of the night and listen to Gasotena's heavy breath on the far wall of the cubicle, experiencing an almost hysterical conviction that he would be killed and she herself consequently released. Again, she passed long waking hours entirely concerned in a kind of dreamy awareness of the growing life she carried. At other times, a vision of her own burnt cabin back in Dygartsbush would rise before her, with John Borst standing by himself and Gasotena stalking him through the high weeds.

But other news broke unexpectedly over the whole Genesee Valley, reaching Onondarha on the fourth of July. Runners came in the third hour before noon. At first two specks appeared in the high grass, shaven heads and braided locks unfeathered, then two pairs of shoulders, glistening with sweat, and at last all the town could see them plainly following the river trail, holding themselves together, keeping their even pace. They went straight to the council house.

The older men, followed by the young, crowded in behind the runners, and the women pushed through after. Delia was left alone in the open space with the yapping dogs about her and the children watching the council house from the grass. A queer feeling of disaster assailed her. One of the runners began his message, and suddenly what he was saying became understandable to Delia. They brought a message from the British Colonel Butler at Canadasaga. The American rebels had collected a great army far down the Susquehanna. They had another army in the Mohawk Valley. There could be no doubt that the rebels were coming from the east to destroy the Indian country. Colonel Butler's army was ready to move down against them when the time came—he now sent runners to all the Seneca towns to call for men to fight.

Gasotena asked how many men the rebels had. The runner said he was not sure, but there were many men in the army, twice as many as all the men of fighting age in the whole Long House, the League of the Six Nations. They were also bringing cannon.

Delia saw dismay and fear on the faces of the women. In the ensuing quiet, she became aware of the hard beating of her heart. A profound conviction of the army's coming even to Onondarha overwhelmed her for an instant and she forgot everything in the belief that she would soon be home.

Then she heard Gasotena's voice uplifted in the council house. He spoke briefly of the founding of the Long House, the League. He told how the Seneca nation were made the keepers of the western door of the Long House and how it had never been invaded through their precinct. Now the enemy were coming to destroy their country, the land their ancestors found for them. This was the land of the men, those who had hunted over it. This was the land of the women, this was the land they planted. This was the land of the children, who were learning the axe

414

and the arrow, who crawled on the floors of the lodges. This was the land where they lived. Let them defend it. . . .

When Gasotena ceased, one after another the old men spoke, asking that the young men go forth, speaking of the love of war that completed a man's soul, and of the strength of the British who would help them. The army of the rebels came from a far distance; they would be lost in the woods.

Delia went into the woods as though to gather a faggot, but really to be solitary. Her one thought was of when the army would come. Would they trouble to look for the white women held by Indians?

When she came out on a slope above the town, looking down on the gray bark roofs and the congregated heads of the Indians, Gasotena was beginning the steps of the war dance. Then came the war whoop, and with full force he buried his tomahawk in the red war post. He went into his dance around the post, and a young man whooped and sprang in behind him while the women applauded.

Suddenly, to Delia, they looked pathetic with their painted faces and outlandish clothes. What could they do against an army? She shouldered her faggot and made her way slowly back to her own house.

THE TOWN WITHOUT THE MEN became still as a forgotten town. After the first week, the women went about their tasks without much talk. The few old men remaining fished, and the oldest of the boys hunted for deer. But they got little meat. No word came from the east, until toward the middle of the month a band of Indians suddenly appeared. There were men, women, and children, even dogs, in the party. They were footsore and hungry. They came from an Indian town on the Allegheny. Looking at them, Delia saw in their dark faces the same dismay and hopelessness that she remembered on the faces of her women neighbors captured in Dygartsbush. They told a similar story—the sudden appearance of the white troops; the ineffectual stand of the men down the river; the burning of their houses and fields.

Onondarha was hard put to feed them all, but no one complained. They were like one family, waiting for news. Early in September, some men of the town came back. All the town packed into the council house to hear of the terrible battle on the Chemung River where the Indians were routed by cannon and an army of men four times as great as the British and Indians combined.

A moan like the wind passing over a hemlock wood rose from the Indian women. The men were still. "Are we to go?" a woman asked.

The speaker shook his head. "Gasotena tells us to wait." The rebels had turned north from Catherinestown; the fall was coming; they might not find the six towns on the Genesee.

Delia forced her way out through the door. Not since that day by the river had she felt so shaken. During those two months she had sustained herself with her belief that the army would surely come. Now a conviction that Gasotena was right made her hopeless.

She entered the deserted house to find, as she had before, the old eyes of the ancient woman watching her. She felt a genuine affection for the *Ucsote,* and now she cried unashamedly before her.

The old woman looked down on her bowed head. This storm of weeping made her uneasy. Indian women concealed grief unless they wept for a departed one. She whispered finally, "He is not dead." As Delia lifted her face, she went on, "It is better for you that he is not dead. If he died, you would have no rights in this house anymore. All your things would belong to the house again."

"I do not care about *things.*"

"Yet if you went back now your child would be born in a white place and it would still be part Indian. Are the white people kinder to part-Indian children than we are? Would they give it rights in property? Here it belongs to the house it is born in."

There was no answer for Delia to make. She knew that if the child were born, the sight of its face would always make her unhappy.

The old woman continued, "My daughter, there are things to consider. With the child in you, you are part Indian, in the part that he is. Would your white husband relish the wife that is part Indian?" Her whispering voice was kind. "You have been good to me. You have been good to these poor people who are our kin. Let your heart be good, daughter. This is the purpose of a woman. You are yet warm and young. There is time."

She never spoke to Delia again. When, at the end of the month, Gasotena led home the half-starved, half-mad warriors, she spoke one more sentence: "Now the Long House is broken." That night she died.

WITH THE PASSAGE of days the extent of the disaster gradually was made apparent. Except for the few small towns on the upper Genesee, and a few west of the river, the American army under General Sullivan had destroyed the Seneca country—not only the towns, not only the orchards and fields, but the caches of dried corn laid down to last two years.

At Onondarha and the neighboring villages, the inhabitants saw a good half of their corn crop used up by refugees as soon as it was harvested. And though these people soon went on to the northwest to Niagara, until late into the winter lone families straggled in from time to time, poorly dressed, starving, and ill.

As her time drew near, it became more and more Delia's concern to look out for the little children of these poor dispossessed folk. She made friends easily, as her heart warmed to them, and they were fascinated by the whiteness of her skin, and the brownness of her hair, and the lowness of her voice.

Sometimes it seemed to Delia the gathering strength of the child's life-spark in her made her, as the old woman had said, actually part Indian. She began to talk more freely with the women of the house, asking their guidance. When Gasotena presented her with choice marten skins for the baby, she took them to cure as her ordinary due, and he was pleased to let her so accept them.

By the turn of the year the food had got so low that the whole town went on rations. In the houses everyone shared alike according to the Indian usage. The dogs became ghostly in their emaciation, what few survived the stewpots for breeding. But Delia kept well and strong. Then in February, during a bitter freeze, Delia's time came. She arose just before dawn and left the house for the cabin set aside for births.

The old woman who had succeeded to the *Ucsote's* name, and the girl, Deowuhyeh, hearing her, rose and came after, the one bringing bear-skins and the other a great faggot of wood. They fought along with her through the snow to the tiny cabin and built a fire on the snow that had sifted in. The head woman took Delia's arm and kept her walking round and round the fire, and even though Delia begged, would not let her rest.

The fire roared high. Deowuhyeh held the robes up before the flames to take the chill from them and then made a place on the platform where Delia might lie when her child was born. . . .

It was snowing heavily then, but the flakes fell without a wind. Delia, her labor over, lay on the bear robes, covered to her eyes against the cold, her gaze following the smoke's seepage through the vent.

The baby that she had wrapped clumsily on his board lay buried under the blankets with her, a shapeless hard small lump.

"He is a fine strong boy, though small," said the head woman.

Deowuhyeh smiled. "Already he has made his war whoop."

In spite of her exhaustion Delia smiled back when she thought of that thin high single crying whine. To call it a war whoop was comical. When the head woman said, "You should think of his baby name while you rest," Delia was not conscious of what she had said for a minute. For it seemed to her that there was a wildness in the baby's cry after all, like something she had once heard at dusk before a snowfall. Gasotena had explained that it was a panther—*Haace*, he called it. She repeated the word more to herself than to the others. But both the women clapped their hands.

"Ha-ace, panther. The little panther. It is a good name."

The head woman's eyes grew brooding and prophetic. "It is a good name for a fighting man. Though his name will be changed in manhood, there will be people who remember that his mother called him Ha-ace. He will remember the time he was born, and he will be a great warrior against the white people."

Then both women looked at Delia, who lay still with her head turned to the hood of the baby frame. Her eyes were closed, but her full lips curved, softening the new lines in her face.

MARTHA DYGART

IT WAS A YEAR and three months since Martha Dygart had been captured, but she did not think of that. She did not even think of where the Indians were going now, or why they had all moved out of Chenandoanes, the great town called the "Seneca Castle." She had never been a quick-witted woman. Even after a year among the Indians she had not learned to understand their language. A few words she knew, like wood, water, dirty, fire, corn, hoe, work, and beat—the words that counted most in a slave's life in an Indian town. Gekeahsawsa, the Wildcat, the head woman of the lodge, would point to the task in hand and speak a word, like a man ordering a dog, and if there was any hesitation, she would set on with the ever-ready hickory club.

Now she could hear the strong steady tread of the woman behind her and could imagine her blocky legs, her thick chest more like a man's than a woman's, and the opaque black eyes with smoke-sore scars about the lids. She always kept just behind, driving her slave as one might drive a pack mare, handling her hickory rod whenever there was a sign of loitering.

Martha herself looked gaunt and ill-fed under her unwieldy pack. Her hands grasping the brow strap beside her face to steady the load showed her bare arms through the torn sleeves of her overdress. Her brown hair, braided like an Indian's, was matted and dull.

She did not see the clear blue autumn sky, or the colors of the turning leaves unless they lay under her feet. Now, after a morning's travel, her one thought was of the end of day when she would be allowed to put down her pack and, after gathering the wood, lie down.

They had started before dawn. The night before, three cannon fired across the Genesee River announced the arrival of the invading Continental Army, and the Indians knew there was no longer hope for Chenandoanes. With the first light they had begun to move out along the Buffalo Creek trail toward Niagara. Maybe the British there would give them enough food to keep alive through the winter.

The long line of women under their heavy loads was here and there punctuated by an old man carrying nothing but his blanket, or a brave with his musket, powderhorn, bullet pouch, and knife and hatchet. A few of the braves, who had been serving with the British all summer trying to stop General Sullivan's overwhelming army, still wore their war paint.

The woman ahead of Martha had a papoose in his baby frame tied to the back of her pack. The smudgy small eyes unwinkingly watched the woman so close to him. He looked like a doll, his face as expressionless as one of the old men's.

Once Martha stopped. Instantly the heavy voice of the squaw behind commanded her to go on and in the same breath the hickory rod swished and struck her legs full force. Martha stepped back, caught her heel on the side of the trail, and fell sideways. As she rolled over to get under her load, the squaw struck again, lashing her full in the face.

Two thick streams of blood burst from her nose. She swayed for an instant, regained her balance, and doggedly took after the squaw ahead. She moved in a daze, unthinking and unreasoning, until in the afternoon they reached a stopping place. There she was allowed to put down her pack and was sent away to gather wood.

A small stream flowed beside the trail through an alder scrub. Lying down on the bank she dipped her face in the water, drinking a little and clumsily trying to wash off the blood.

Behind her among the Indians camped along the trail an excited ruffle of talk broke out. Suddenly from the way they had come appeared a company of men in the green and black dress of the British rangers. They looked worn-out, too; only their guns and bayonets looked clean and ready for service. They passed the woman and made their own camp farther down the trail. But one of them, coming back to the brook to fill his kettles, surprised her still lying there. He looked young, a tall, lanky fellow. As she struggled to get up, he said, "Don't mind me, Grandma," in a good-natured Irish voice.

At the sound of spoken English, she lifted her head with a quick, startled motion and stared at him. He met her eyes.

"You're white!" he said.

She nodded.

"With them?" He tilted his head back toward the Indians.

She nodded again, and finally managed a halting sentence. "I've been with them over a year."

It seemed then that he really saw her—her raggedness, the blood still smeared on her chin, the scars on her legs. "They made you into a slave," he said. "I've heard they do it sometimes. Where'd they get you?"

"Dygartsbush, in June, last year."

"It's September now," he said, feeling suddenly uncomfortable. He thought her voice sounded like a ghost's, as though the most part of her had died already. "What's your name, ma'am?"

"Martha Dygart." She stared at him with widened eyes and suddenly dropped her face to her hands and began to sob.

He looked around nervously. "Hush, hush," he said. "They'll hear. Listen, why don't you clear out and get back and meet the rebel army? They'd take you home."

She shook her head. "*She'd* find me." She lifted her gaunt face. "Can't I go with you? Please," she said. "I can do hard work. I can cook." Her eyes looked pitiful to him.

"I'm just a private," he said. "I can't do nothing."

"I could sew for you. Mend your things." He saw the blood rise painfully in her cheeks. "I used to do fine-sewing when I had my own house." He could hardly hear her voice. "They burned it," she said. "I ain't got anywhere to go."

420

"Did they kill all your family?"

"Yes. Except my little girls. They was hunting the cow. Lucy was seven and Pearl was five. The Indians killed everybody else."

The ranger kept looking around like a man trying to talk his way out of something he hadn't meant to start. "Niagara ain't going to be good this winter. We'll have most of the Seneca nation hanging round eating off us and there's not enough food. I feel sorry for you, ma'am. Honest I do."

Through her torn dress he could see the way her back was scarred. He got up and stood there, trying to think of how he could get away. Then a yell down the trail helped him out.

"Burke! Burke! Where has that ugly dumbhead gone to? Burke!"

"That's Sergeant hollering for me, ma'am." He did feel sorry for her; he remembered what she had said about sewing. Impulsively he reached into his pocket and pulled out a thin fold of black leather which he dropped into her lap.

"It ain't no good to me," he apologized. "But maybe you could use it. Good luck, ma'am."

He went striding off through the gray twilight of the alders, slopping water from both kettles.

Martha heard him going, but she was too tired now even to look after him. She forgot all about the wood she was going to get. Her face hurt her. She knew from other beatings she had had, when Gekeahsawsa had driven her out of the cabin, how the night cold could make its own agony in the hurt places of her body.

Along the trail, fires were beginning to take life from dry bark and sticks. She could smell the smoke, acrid and half sweet, and her eyes smarted, not so much from the smoke itself as from the memory of winter nights when the vent holes in the roof were nearly closed to preserve the warmth, and the smoke became a pall, filling the air. Smoke to Martha Dygart would all her life be an Indian thing.

It was nearly dark under the alders when Martha's hand brushed against the fold of leather the ranger had left in her lap. Her fingers were clumsy, like a child's attempting to open a purse. When she had it open she thought for a moment that there was nothing in it. Still it was nice to have, smelling as it did of white man's leather, a little tobacco-y, a little of sweet oil as if he had spilled a few drops on it once when cleaning his gun, and strangely also a little of green soap. It was the soap smell that reminded her of the clean things of her former life—of washdays and fresh clothes on a line, a whipping wind, a cowbell in the woods. She thought suddenly of her children's dresses. She had made them out of a violet-patterned calico. Violet was a color the Indians did not use. Her breast ached, and her thoughts dizzily mixed in her blurred mind.

The prick on the end of her little finger startled her. It was as though she were learning to sew again. She held the leather up, but she had to turn it until the firelight shone on it before she saw the needle.

The light outlined it with a faint coppery sheen. She could see it, the full length of it, except where it was passed through the linen strap. She saw also that there was a pocket for a card of thread, but that was empty.

For a while she was afraid to try to withdraw the needle, thinking it might become a dream. Then tentatively she touched the eye end. Her fingers were so callused she could hardly feel the slimness of it. But finally, with great precaution against dropping it, she worked it free.

It was a white man's needle, the kind of needle a person could do fine work with. She held it at arm's length so that the eye was barely discernible; then she moved it slowly closer, as though in dim light she were trying to thread it. When she held it very close to her own eye it seemed strange to be able to see so much through so small an aperture. The whole camping group of Indians was encompassed in the needle's eye— the fire, the kettle on the stick, the papoose on the baby frame. A single squaw, thickset, stood on the edge of the trail, looking down into the alder thicket.

Martha recognized her, and now she remembered that the Wildcat had ordered her to bring in wood. She was so full of panic that she almost dropped the needle. For an instant all thought of everything abandoned her except the one idea that she must place the needle safely in the little book. She worked it deliberately into the linen strap.

Then at last, after what seemed like hours, she stood up.

WHEN THE RANGER gave Martha Dygart the needle, he had no idea of the meaning of the gift. Even Martha had no inkling of what the needle might do for her. All she knew was that the needle in this wilderness was far too precious for anyone to lose.

The Wildcat was entering the alders. Martha knew at once that the squaw was coming to find her; she could tell by the way she walked, deliberately soft-footed. As the squaw crossed the firelight, Martha saw that she was carrying a *casse-tête*, or Indian war club. Martha could imagine the Wildcat's fury if she should find out about the needle. She had seen an Indian trade seven beaver pelts for one. The Wildcat would kill Martha half a dozen times to possess it.

She was now not more than sixty or seventy feet away. As the squaw took a few stealthy steps down the creek, Martha stepped carefully into the brook and slid her feet along the bottom, making no splash. The stream itself made a faint sound to cover her wading. When she came to the far side, she lifted her feet carefully onto the bank and stood still.

The squaw also had stopped. Then, whether from some noise she had heard Martha make, from instinct or dead luck, the squaw began to return along the bank of the stream. She came only a short way, however, before stopping once more. Martha quickly bent down. As she crouched there, the squaw stepped into the water and waded over.

They were now on the same bank, with the stream between them and the campfires. Both looked back, watching for a moment the blanketed forms of the Indians quietly settling down for the night.

On the side of the stream on which the two women now stood, scattered alder bushes made some cover, enough to hide them from each other's sight. But beyond these, the woods sloped to a low ridge where several coverts of young hemlock made darker blotches. Martha thought that if she could get into one of these coverts the squaw could never find her in the dark. For the first time, escape seemed possible.

A thin skimming of clouds had stolen over the moon and obscured the stars. The only light in the shallow valley came from the line of campfires. As she glanced back at them, Martha understood why the squaw was heading for the higher ground. It was essential not to let the squaw get far enough ahead to see her against the firelight.

The Wildcat had already started, moving quietly. Once for a moment Martha lost the Indian, then she heard her break a stick, so close that Martha pressed her hands to her breast as if to muffle the sounding of her heart. She waited until the squaw had moved well ahead this time, then struck off at an angle to take cover of the first hemlocks. When she reached them she let herself down under them and lay panting.

She could no longer hear the squaw, but she knew that if the squaw could not find her soon, she would get the men out on a search.

Martha lay still, wondering what she should do. But instead of making plans all her tired brain could think of were the endless miseries the Wildcat had put upon her: the beatings, the overloading on the march, the skimping of her food when other prisoners were allowed to share the best, the inexplicable outbursts of sheer fury.

Martha rose instinctively and, putting aside the hemlock branches with her hands, worked clear of their shelter; then in the silence she moved slowly further into the woods, no longer attempting to move quietly. But whenever her feet encountered a stick on the ground she picked it up. She tried several before she found one of a length and strength that seemed to suit her.

She knew that the Wildcat could hear her footsteps and might call for help. Martha would deal with her before the men could come, for she realized now that her months of heavy labor had strengthened her muscles enough to deal with any other woman.

As Martha reached the top of a ridge, the squaw's voice came abruptly out of the darkness. "Where is the wood?"

Martha stood still, drawing her breath silently, her eyes searching the darkness inch by inch.

"I have seen you coming." The harsh voice sounded almost patient. "I know where you stand, white woman."

That's a lie, Martha thought. She heard a rustle of leaves. Both women listened. Martha moved quickly to face the sound—then realized that the squaw had moved, too. And both of them stood still.

"Go back now," commanded the heavy voice.

I'm not going back. And you aren't either.

"Go back now. If you do not go back I will kill you."

A faint whisper of feathers passed close over their heads. Martha looked quickly up and saw the long wing of an owl float across the cloudy gleam of the moon. His maniacal screech rang over the dark woods. In the appalling hush that followed, Martha caught her breath. *That black lump beside the second beech tree. It had moved.*

"A ranger gave me a needle, Gekeahsawsa," Martha said aloud. "I have it in my hand. A steel needle."

"Give it to me."

Now she could tell where the voice came from. She turned herself with infinite slowness. "You can have it, Gekeahsawsa." She raised her stick, waiting.

The squaw had moved again. Now Martha heard her, a small stick breaking halfway through and leaves pressed down. *I'm not afraid.* She heard the swish of the *casse-tête* and threw herself to one side. The

424

ironwood burl cracked against the tree she had been hugging, glanced, bounced off her left shoulder. She struck out with all her might, and felt the blow hit home. The squaw floundered backward into the brush. Martha hurled her broken stick at the crashing in the bushes and rushed after it herself.

The Wildcat had dropped the club and her hands met Martha's. She yanked her down on top of herself and caught her hair with one hand while the other clawed at Martha's face. Martha threw herself to one side and broke free of the squaw's grip.

They rose unsteadily together. Suddenly Martha threw her arms around the heavy body and they rocked and pitched on the sloping ground. Martha worked around the squaw until she was uphill of her and then put forth all her strength to throw her.

Then without warning the squaw made a frenzied attempt to break away, but lost her balance and went over backward down the slope of the ground with Martha on top. Martha sensed the yell before it was born. She shifted her hands and found the thick neck and pressed her thumbs over the throat with all her might. The first wild screech was shut off in a gasp. Martha could feel the muscles under her thumbs strain with the effort to yell. *Try and yell now!* The squaw was struggling to draw breath as her hands tore at Martha's wrists. *I won't let go.*

A faint wonder came over Martha. There was no motion, no sound. She sat there for a long time.

Finally she rose to her feet and walked a little way back up the slope. She halted suddenly. She had remembered the needle. She knew that it was lost. Her lips quivered. She began to weep. She went for a long roundabout search, but she could not find it.

AFTER SUNRISE MARTHA took the trail back toward Chenandoanes. Several times she dropped flat in the brakes to watch small parties of Indians trotting past. They went by without glancing right or left, as if all they wanted was to overtake the main body of Indians.

Toward noon she noticed a tower of smoke to the east. The smoke rose over the tops of the trees and billowed slightly toward the southeast; fountains of sparks burst upward to immense heights. And suddenly she was on the highland west of the river and had a full view of the valley.

Then she saw the town of Chenandoanes. All the houses were blazing, and the smoke was rusty against the clear sky.

425

Off to the south of the town several small tents were pitched. Before these, from a lance planted in the ground, hung a bright-colored flag. She stared at it and she thought that it was prettier with its red and white stripes than any militia flag she had ever seen.

When she looked down she could see blue-coated men everywhere throughout the town. A great company of them was in the cornfield cutting down the corn and pitching the stalks onto the blaze.

Over the whole scene a continual play of sound was audible, punctuated by the ring of rangers' axes in the apple orchards. At first it sounded strange to Martha, then she realized that it was the sound of thousands of voices speaking English.

Suddenly she was afraid to go among them. She felt naked and dirty and indecent. She sat down, trying to muster courage. She must have sat there nearly an hour before she saw several figures emerge from the tents south of the town. A thin piercing silvery note of a whistle lifted above the roar of destruction and a few moments later some soldiers led horses to the tents.

Martha had not seen a horse for months. As the men mounted she rose with the same motion. They rode directly toward her, making a circuit of the blazing town.

When they were below her, the leader gestured and a man behind him lifted a bugle to his lips. The shining notes rang over all the valley. Other bugles echoed the notes, then a roll of drums beat the muster.

Everywhere platoons formed and marched away toward the tents. The destruction was over. Chenandoanes would never exist again.

Martha moved hesitantly down. A corporal saw her coming and broke out of his platoon. It seemed to her that half the army turned to look at her. The corporal came toward her.

"You're white," he said. "You was a prisoner?"

"Yes, my name's Martha Dygart."

His sunburned face looked kind. "Here, ma'am," he said, and took off his coat and helped her put it on. "The general will want to talk to you." She was led through the entire army. When she came out into an open space, she saw the general standing beside his horse.

He took off his hat to her and smiled briefly.

The corporal saluted. "An Indian captive just come in, sir."

"You just got here in time," the general said. "We are starting our return march in twenty minutes."

426

He pulled out a large silver watch as though to verify himself. Then suddenly he asked her questions. What was her name? Where did she come from? Where had the Indians escaped? How far was it to Niagara?

She tried to answer as well as she could, but she could see that he thought her information worthless.

"Very well, ma'am," he said. "I'll put you under Dr. Minema's care. He's surgeon of the First New York. They come from your section, I believe." He turned. "Doctor, will you look out for this poor woman?"

"Yes, General Sullivan."

That was all. The doctor led her away. He pulled a piece of loaf sugar from his knapsack and gave it to her. "You look as if you need food. We'll be able to give you something more tonight. There's no time now."

Martha said "Thank you" dully. She walked heavily behind the doctor, her gaunt face lost in thought. The rising smoke reminded her of her two children and her own burning cabin. And she thought if only twenty of these five thousand men had been placed under arms at Dygartsbush the Indians never would have dared attack it.

"Why don't you eat the sugar?" the doctor asked.

Dumbly she put it in her mouth, and after that for more than a mile all she could think of was how long it had been since she had tasted sugar.

ELLEN MITCHEL

THE TWO CHILDREN taken captive in the raid on Dygartsbush got over their fear of the Indians almost at once. The boy, Peter Kelly, was thirteen; Ellen Mitchel was a month or two younger. They were of an age to forget what they had seen of the raid, and indeed, in Ellen's case, that was little enough. She had gone out to look for the cow, got twisted in the darkness, and lost her way in the woods. She could hear the shooting, the wild high-pitched yells of the Indians, and see the glow of burning cabins through the trees or against the rainy sky, but instinct had kept her in the woods. She was crouched there on the edge of a clump of bushes when Skanasunk, the Fox, came along hauling Peter Kelly behind him.

He was a great strapping young brave. Often in the years following she was to remember him as he stepped around the bushes, coppery and shining with the rain, the bear on his chest painted in black, the upper part of his face painted red and his cheeks black with white stripes on them. She did not think he looked ugly, just wild and fierce. Later, she liked the feeling that she belonged to him, especially when she saw the way the other Indians abused their captives. She did not know that her own family had been wiped out; she thought that her mother must be with another band of the Indians. She enjoyed the camping at night and the feeling of privilege she and Pete had in not being tied down.

Old Mrs. Staats, before the Indians tomahawked her, had tried to put a stop to Ellen's familiarity with the Indians. It was bad enough, she said, for Ellen to be running around with a good-for-nothing like Peter Kelly. But Ellen was thirteen now, Mrs. Staats pointed out to her uninterested companions; the girl was getting to be womanish.

Ellen had a brief moment of horror the night Mrs. Staats was killed. It made her serious and for several days she stuck so close to Pete that he spoke of her scornfully, calling her a sissy-girl. But she noticed that even Pete was inclined to stay as near to Skanasunk as possible. On the night after, he went so far as to admit that he was glad it was Skanasunk who had taken them both.

It was true; he treated them differently. Skanasunk confirmed this the evening after he left the main band on the headwaters of the Chemung. While they all three hunched around their small fire that evening, he said he would get his wife to adopt them both. Women, he explained, did the adopting in the Indian nations. She was a fine squaw, he said. She had lost one child by her first husband and another child by him, which made her sad. Now that he had two healthy children for her, she would feel better; it made him feel good himself. They would like it in the Indian village. Pete would not have to work and Ellen could learn cooking and making skins soft under his wife's guidance.

"I never was a hand to work," said Pete. "But I'm good at hunting."

"Teach you hunt," said Skanasunk. "I buy you gun maybe. Fine gun like mine."

The name of the village was Tecarnohs. It was a small place of half a dozen houses and perhaps ten families. The council house was no more than a small bark cabin in the open land by the bend of a creek. They came overland to it and looked down at it from one of the steep hills late in the afternoon. The houses for the most part were scattered here and there through the woods.

The creek wound down through the narrow valley. It had the look of good fishing water, and Pete said, "It appears good country to me," as his eyes took in the rough hills and heavy woods.

Skanasunk stretched a bare arm to point out a small house. "My house," he said. He touched Ellen's shoulder. "See Newataquaah."

Looking down, Ellen made out the figure of an Indian woman before the entrance of the house. She was dressed in deerskins and was at the moment bending over a stump mortar to grind corn. It was hard to tell what a person was like, she thought, seeing them from as far as she saw Skanasunk's squaw.

Ellen hardly ever thought of what she herself looked like. She still had the lanky figure of a girl, with long flat legs that were more likely to break out running than to carry her at a nice walk. But there was a suggestion of what Mrs. Staats had called "growing womanish" in the slight rounding under her blue and white shortgown. Except for that shortgown she looked almost a nut brown; brown hair, brown eyes, and a clear, tanned, unfreckled skin.

As he glanced at her, in fact, Pete thought she looked kind of pretty with her curly hair that showed even with the braids. Both started as Skanasunk cupped his mouth in his hands and let out a high-pitched cry.

Instantly the squaw's hands stopped grinding and the barking of dogs broke out here and there along the creek. Skanasunk said, "You come now," and started down the hill at an abrupt trot. The two children were hard put to it to keep pace with him.

Later that summer it seemed odd to Ellen that she had been nervous about meeting Newataquaah. She was a small, neat, birdlike woman ten years older than her husband. As Ellen came to know her better, she even began to think of her as pretty. And though she performed an immense amount of labor in a day, the work never seemed to oppress her and she found time for everything.

With Ellen she showed infinite patience. "You are my own daughter now," she would say. "You must learn beadwork. All men value a fine beadworker, and a woman who tends her house." She had a slight sidelong smile that made her black eyes shine. Ellen, who liked to work, found the life pleasant. She learned that the Indian women did the labor, not because the men made slaves of them as white people supposed, but because they preferred it so. She also learned that hunting was more arduous than it seemed.

The only thing that seemed strange to Ellen was how a man so young as Skanasunk could be happy with an older wife. Newataquaah explained to her. "My first husband was an old man. I married him when I was fourteen years old. He died after a while; he was a wise man. Skanasunk is a young man. From my first husband I learned how to be wise. When I die Skanasunk will have had time to find his wisdom. Then if he likes he will marry a young girl." She gave Ellen her sidelong smile. "And now we have children. We are both very happy now."

Ellen said impulsively, "I am happy, too."

PETER KELLY, OF COURSE, was in his natural element. In Tecarnohs a man was meant to hunt and fish, and trap enough to get a couple of bales of pelts every year or two to trade for beads, an iron kettle, a gun, or a knife. Soon it was evident that Pete was far and away the best shot in the village. Skanasunk went around making boasts of his son's prowess.

"It's a queer thing," Peter said one evening to Ellen. "Old Skanasunk, he really does think I'm his son. It's the same way with Newataquaah—I bet she figures you're her genuine daughter. It's kind of a nuisance."

"What do you mean?"

Pete was at work swabbing out the musket, and when he answered her he used his offhand voice. "Why," he said, "I was talking to Skanasunk about it. I said, 'If you really think we're your own children,' I said, 'how are me and Ellen going to get married?'"

Ellen raised her eyes from the legging seam she was stitching with sinew. "You and me marry!"

"Sure," he said. "I mean, we might have to stay here four, five years. I just thought it'd save you marrying an Indian."

Ellen gasped and stared at him. "I don't think I'd want to marry an Indian."

Pete nodded. "That's it—but how can you and me marry if we're brother and sister this way? That's what I said to Skanasunk. Anyhow he said he'd have to look it up with the Honundeont, whoever she is. Kind of a she-preacher, maybe. But just the same, I wouldn't mind marrying you."

Ellen felt herself flush all over. "I guess I've got something to say about that, Master Smart!"

He just grinned at her. "Oh no, you haven't. You're just a squaw, or you will be when you marry me."

430

He slid off the sleeping platform and strutted out of the house, and all she could think of was that pretty soon his hair would be long enough to braid. Then in his deerskins he would look like an Indian himself.

TECARNOHS WAS a peaceful place. No war parties passed through it. Newataquaah harvested a fair crop of corn and vegetables against the winter and the hunting continued better than usual.

Toward the middle of October, Skanasunk and Peter, with most of the younger men, struck off for the Allegheny and the Ohio lands. A week beforehand, Ellen secretly made Peter a coonskin cap. Shaping it for him made her experience a queer sense of motherliness, and both of them turned red when she presented it the night before he left.

She and Newataquaah had several quiet weeks after the men left. Then the snow began to fall. It mounted quickly in their steep valley and soon the village was snowed in deep. The houses themselves became warm and snug. They were laced together by snowshoe trails.

The men returned from their hunting in early December, just ahead of the first real blizzard. They had had fair luck and got plenty of beaver and had killed three deer on the way back.

At the house of Skanasunk, Newataquaah's eyes sparkled. "Now we will have fresh meat to cook for our two men," she cried to Ellen, and went laughing about her work. It was a happy time. But Ellen was troubled because she could not find Peter's coonskin cap. She asked him about it next day and he explained how it had fallen off when he slipped crossing a brook. The high water had sucked it under. He looked sheepish, though, and she knew he was lying to her. She said nothing. She had noticed when he first came in that he had braided his hair.

The winter passed and spring came with a rush and a white frothing of wild cherry on the hills. In May, Newataquaah took Ellen to the garden patch and planted her corn and beans in regular spaced hills, and in the land between the hills she planted squash. Then every day she visited the patch, watching first the white lobes of the beans, and then the green pencils of the rolled corn leaves pierce the earth.

One night she roused Ellen stealthily and beckoned her out to make with her the woman's circle of the crop. Ellen went from curiosity, but the darkness of a starless night filled her with a sense of magic. A little way from the field Newataquaah stopped and turned. Ellen felt the hands lift her overdress up over her shoulders and unknot the skirt thong. A moment later Newataquaah herself undressed. Then she led the way to the cornfield.

Dragging their clothes along the ground behind them, they made the circuit of the planted ground two or three times, by the power of their garments, yet warm from their bodies, drawing a ring around the field that would keep off the cutworm, the wireworm that ate the corn roots, and the grasshopper, and ensure the fruitfulness of the crop. It was a strange mysterious business to Ellen, who was invaded by a sensation of the power in her body.

When they stole back into the lodge she felt herself mysteriously grown, and she lay awake long after, listening to the creek and hearing Peter's even breathing.

But that summer they became aware of the war. Without warning, the Indians from the Allegheny villages passed by Tecarnohs. They came and went in a day, stopping only to be fed. Skanasunk, with the men of the village, held a long council during the afternoon, and once Peter came back to the house to talk to Ellen.

"There's two armies coming," he said. "One's coming up the Allegheny and the other's coming from Tioga." He stared a moment into Ellen's puzzled face. "Maybe we ought to clear out."

"Clear out?" she echoed.

"Don't you want to go home?"

Ellen looked back at him and suddenly shook her head.

"Me neither," he said. "I like it here. Here I'm as good as anybody."

"Let's stay."

He seemed suddenly relieved. "I'll go back and hang around the council house and see what's going on. But you stay where I can find you."

She promised, and watched him trot away. He did not return till nearly dark. Then he came with Skanasunk.

Skanasunk was serious. "Most people want to go to Niagara," he said to them. "I do not want to go. I do not think the white army will find our little town. Newataquaah does not want to go. In Niagara the British would find our children and make them white again."

For a moment all four were silent. Then Newataquaah's soft voice broke in. "Maybe our children wish to be white again."

Skanasunk turned his eyes solemnly to the children. "They have not said."

Ellen looked down modestly at her moccasins and left it for Pete to answer.

Pete said, "Both of us like it here. But maybe we ought to get out before the other people get mad at us."

Skanasunk said. "They will not hurt you. You are my son." He drew himself up and announced: "We stay here."

The runners coming in during the third week in August reported the American army of six hundred men at Daudehokto, a village on the bend of the Allegheny only a few miles west. Before night half the village had packed up and taken the steep trail to Chenandoanes. The remaining men held another council. Seeing their relatives depart made them less certain of their own wisdom.

But the army did not come. After that the war affected them no more. The women followed their usual occupations and the men hunted. There were too few of them to drive deer, and they killed only half a dozen in four days. Skanasunk predicted a bad winter. The corn harvest was only fair.

The first snow came in November, a light wet slush, and heavy mists hung in the valley. The Indians became silent; there was less laughter when the women visited. During these weeks Pete's uneasiness returned. He spent more time in the house, keeping Ellen company. Once when they were alone he said, "I wish we'd gone back."

Ellen was surprised. "How could we have got back?"

"The army wasn't more than a day's walk for us at Daudehokto. They'd have sent us back through Pennsylvania. Or we could've stayed. I like that westward country."

Ellen was placid. "Skanasunk and Newataquaah are staying here on account of us. We couldn't leave them. Not rightly, Pete."

"I guess that's so." Pete in his Indian dress looked small and unhappy. Ellen moved impulsively toward him, and kissed his lips.

She said, "I'll never marry anybody else but you, Pete."

"You mean that?" he said huskily. She nodded.

They heard Newataquaah returning and moved apart from each other. Newataquaah was coughing. The sound brought back to Pete a queer obsession of approaching death that had been troubling him.

Newataquaah had been up on the hillsides looking for dry wood. She was wet, and she had a chill. As soon as she laid down her faggot, she huddled beside the fire and asked Ellen to brew her some hemlock tea.

She said she felt better after she had drunk it all, and smiled deprecatingly. "We must cook for the men," she said.

But when Ellen put her hand on the woman's forehead she knew there was fever. She said, "The men can wait. Now you are going to bed."

Ellen hung a bearskin and several blankets on the poles nearest the fire, warming them, while Newataquaah changed to dry clothes in the cubicle. She sat on the bed and swayed forward over her knees. Ellen went quickly to her and pushed her back firmly onto the bearskin. "Peter! Peter!"

Peter poked his head in.

"You'd better hunt up Skanasunk," Ellen said. "She's very sick."

"All right," he said. "Don't get scared."

Newataquaah had begun to cough again; the coughs seemed to choke her. She shivered, but her forehead felt hot. Ellen brewed more tea. All at once it came to her that Newataquaah was really the only Indian in the village she knew well. It wasn't the Indian way of living that she liked; it was Newataquaah that made her think she liked it. She longed now for towels to bathe the woman's face with, and above all for the conveniences of a good log cabin. Sitting on the edge of the cubicle she was aware of the Indian's hand reaching out to pat hers. "Don't look so afraid." The same sidelong smile. "I shall get well fast."

Peter came in with Skanasunk, who stalked over and stood beside the cubicle with his arms folded.

"Are you sick?" he asked.

"I am," she said apologetically, "but not very sick."

"I think you are very sick," he replied. "We have no healer now," he said somberly. "She went away when the others did."

He ate a little from the stew Ellen had for him, then got his blanket and hunched himself before the fire. He stayed that way all night. Ellen slept only in spells; whenever she looked up he was still there, looking at the fire. But once he met her eyes and stared long at her. Then as the heavy coughing started again, he dropped his head.

Newataquaah seemed no better two days later. Skanasunk left the house. A high wind cut through the valley from the north. Toward dark he returned carrying a snowbird in a little basket. This he hung at the far end of the house.

The bird made small twittering notes during the night. Ellen heard it over the wind. She would have liked to set it free, but Pete told her not to touch it. "I don't know what he wants it for, but I followed him this afternoon. He's been digging a hole."

"He thinks she's going to die!"

"I guess he does. There's a lot more sick. Half the Indians is sick with the same disease, I guess."

Skanasunk sat beside Newataquaah's cubicle. Ellen got to her feet, walked around Skanasunk, and looked into the cubicle. "She is dead," said Skanasunk. He had not moved.

Ellen burst into a storm of tears, flung herself into her own cubicle and covered herself with her robes, trying to shut out the Indian house.

Pete sneaked up to her and touched the mound of blankets. "Ellen," he whispered.

Her muffled voice answered him. "Leave me alone!"

But he kept his hand on the blankets, as though he were afraid to let go of her. She was glad that he kept his hand there.

Skanasunk took no notice of her or of Pete. He continued to sit by the fire, unmoving. In the morning Pete went to the village and gave the news of Newataquaah's death, and a few Indians came up to the house to condole with the relatives. When they had gone, Skanasunk rose and ordered Ellen to bring a kettle of food uncooked, some tinder, and a little faggot of sticks. He told Pete to carry the snowbird in the little basket. Then he himself picked up Newataquaah and carried her from the house. A cold driving snow had begun to fall. Even in the thick grove of hemlocks, it sifted down with a continual sibilance through the heavy branches.

There was a round hole in the snow, in which Skanasunk placed the body. Beside it he placed the filled kettle. Then he covered the hole with limb wood and piled earth in a mound upon it. He stood still awhile before he took the basket from Pete and opened the cover.

The little snowbird hopped up on the rim. Suddenly, with a soft twitter it flipped up into the branches. As soon as it had disappeared, Skanasunk knelt down and started a small fire. They left while it still crackled brightly, a tiny spot of color in the black and white of woods and snow.

SKANASUNK HAD CHANGED. The whole village had changed. As the snow drifted in it seemed like death made visible. More Indians died. They seemed to have no resistance to the disease, but neither Pete nor Ellen caught it. Once an Indian woman stopped Ellen and said, "We were not sick this way before white people came."

None of the Indians laughed anymore, and Skanasunk had changed more than the others. He would sit by the fire hour after hour following Ellen's motions with his black eyes. He made her nervous. One day she asked Pete to stay nearby.

"Why?" asked Pete.

"He makes me afraid. He does not speak. I know he's thinking about me. But I don't know what."

Pete, studying her, suddenly thought he understood. "We'll leave here when the snow goes," he said. He began turning over plans in his mind. He also made a point of never going out of call while Skanasunk was in the house.

436

Skanasunk began to cough. He lay in his cubicle for days, or dragged himself out to the fire. He hardly ate at all, and the flesh seemed to shrink on his skull. It required all the fortitude she could muster for Ellen to nurse him the three days he was sickest, and at times she felt that Newataquaah was nearby watching. There was one snowbird especially that seemed to hang around the house with no logical persistence.

Skanasunk survived. The sickness left him so weak, however, that Pete felt he could leave the house safely to go out hunting. That day, when Ellen gave him his food, Skanasunk broke his long silence.

"Listen to me."

"Yes, *Hanih*." She gave him the Indian name for "Father."

"Listen to me," he repeated. She had a strange feeling about the intentness in his black eyes. "Newataquaah is dead. Skanasunk has no wife. Skanasunk is not your *Hanih*. You are white."

He paused. "A young girl should marry an old man. It is the ancient law. Skanasunk is not old but he is a good man."

Ellen had no idea what she should do. She could not answer Skanasunk. She caught up her faggot strap as an excuse, ran out of the house. and all that afternoon dawdled on the hillside watching for Pete's return.

She intercepted him on the trail, carrying half a doe, and blurted out her news. He listened with his face intent and white. "We can't go now," he said. "The snow's plain slush. It'll be two weeks before we can travel."

"I want to go now. I can keep up with you."

"Anybody could track us. We've got to wait till we can travel fast." Pete stopped, looking down at the musket. "There's only powder for about four shots left. We can't use it hunting. I'll smoke the other half of this doe. Maybe in ten days we can start."

THE WEATHER HELD. The late March thawing took the snow from the woods but left the brooks so high they made hard crossing. Ellen and Pete had crossed the Genesee on a raft and made the southern circuit of the lakes. At the head of both Lake Seneca and Lake Cayuga they found marks of the Continental Army. The trip had taken longer than they had expected. Their venison had given out and their corn was low. But the Indian towns offered nothing but charred logs. No trees were left standing. Pete refused to build campfires that might attract Indian war parties. At night he cut hemlock boughs and made shelters.

It was the day after they had crossed the headwaters of the Owego

River that they began to feel that they were being followed. By then they were so short of food that the few grains of parched corn Pete doled out were not enough to warm them. A heavy frost had settled, and finally Pete agreed they must have a fire.

They built a small one and huddled over it, luxuriating in the strange sensation of outer warmth. Looking across it at Ellen, Pete was struck by her thinness. He said suddenly, "You're a pretty good girl, Ellen. You ain't made a fuss at all." She only smiled a little and hugged her knees, resting her chin on them.

"If I see a deer tomorrow I'll take a chance and shoot it," he said.

She started to say, "That's wonderful," but suddenly she buried her face in her hands and started crying.

It was then that Pete saw the snowbird and said, "That's queer. That snowbird. It's about dark, and I've hardly ever seen one so late in spring."

She stopped crying to look at the little bird. The sight of it made her remember Newataquaah, and so she thought of Skanasunk. They had slipped out one morning; Pete had gone first, she later, pretending to go for wood, and meeting him on the hill over the village. They had gone down the far side, climbing over rocky places to hide their trail. By dusk, Pete had figured they had a seven-mile start.

After the snowbird was gone, they crept under their hemlock lean-to. They could still feel the fire's warmth against their feet. But Ellen woke Pete several times by talking in her sleep about Newataquaah and Skanasunk. She made him uneasy. In the morning he did what he had not done for days. He scouted around the camp.

He found no tracks that looked human. But he did find a black squirrel dead under a tree. When he picked it up he saw its neck was broken; he had never heard of a squirrel dying of a broken neck. He carried it back to their camp and they roasted it over a small fire.

A little after noon they came on the track of a single Indian and the track was fresh. It was following a small deer run eastward. Pete thought they ought to follow the trail to see where the man was heading. They went very slowly, making no sound, until finally it brought them to a campsite where half a dozen Indians had spent the night.

Pete made Ellen stand still off the run while he rummaged round the tracks. When he returned to her, his face was troubled. "Our man joined up with the others. They broke camp, but he turned back, so he's somewhere back of us now."

The next two days they hurried. But they saw nothing. They began to get desperate for food. Then, on the third day, as they followed another deer path, they found a deer lying dead.

They stopped where they were and made a fire and feasted, too hungry even to question their providence until they had done eating. Peter finally scouted while Ellen hid under a stony hill. Again he found the tracks of one man. They led him due north and then east for nearly a mile and were lost in a shallow river crossing.

Pete studied the river thoughtfully. The trunk of an enormous hemlock lay out into the ford under the water and two huge roots, upended, were joined like praying hands. The queerness of the tree raised an echo of something he had been told. Suddenly he remembered. His brother Honus had said it was the best lower crossing of the Unadilla River.

He lay on the bank for a long time, staring across the smooth slide of brown water without seeing anything. After sunset he went back for Ellen and told her they had reached the Unadilla. They would follow it to the mouth of Butternut Creek. He knew the way, once he found Butternut Creek.

Now they could travel at night, having a moon. They made fair progress, and spotted the Butternut in the gray dawn. They were going to cross when an owl began hooting from the far bank.

Pete stood stock-still. "That ain't no bird," he whispered. "We better wait. It don't sound right to me."

As they waited, a line of men bunched on the bank above them. Then they lined out again over the river. Their shapes were dark shadows against the water, holding guns above their heads. But even in the darkness the children could make out that the arms were bare.

"Indians," Pete breathed into her ear. After an hour of silence they heard an owl hoot again. He said, "That's a natural sounding owl." It came from the far side of the river. "We'll chance crossing."

Next morning on the hills south of German Flats they were only two hours from the forts near Dygartsbush on each side of the Mohawk River. It was a day of bright sunlight. The naked brow of a hill with the dead winter's grass dry underfoot gave them a view of the forts, the burned sites of settlers' houses, and men plowing the ground while a guard surrounded the field they worked in.

Then, as they stepped over the edge of the hill, they saw a feathered arrow stuck in the ground. Beside it was a square of blue calico and on the calico were laid two fox's ears and a little silver brooch of Indian make.

"It's Newataquaah's!" Ellen exclaimed. "What are the fox ears for?"

"It's Skanasunk. So we would know who the brooch was from if you didn't recognize it."

"You mean he left it for us?"

"I guess. I guess it was him, all along."

Pete was lost in thought. Then he set the musket down, the musket he had never fired on all their long journey. "He's hanging round some-where. He'll find it all right. But I guess he means for me to take the arrow. I guess he didn't have nothing else for me."

Long after the war, when she had been Mrs. Peter Kelly for many years, Ellen used to like to wear the brooch. The children often humored her by asking why she wore a queer thing like it, and then she would tell them about how she and Mr. Kelly lived among the Indians.

DYGARTSBUSH

JOHN BORST was the first settler to return to Dygartsbush after the war. When he found that his wife had been taken captive to the Indians' towns, he had joined the army. Now he came home alone in the early fall of 1784, on foot, carrying a rifle, an axe, a brush scythe, a pair of blankets, and a sack of cornmeal. He found the different lots hard to recognize, for only the charred butt logs of the houses remained. The field where he had had his corn was covered with scrub. But near the center of it he found a stunted, slender little group of tiny cornstalks, tasseled out, with ears that looked like buds.

Whenever the work of clearing brush seemed everlasting, he would go over and look at that corn and think how good his first crop seven years ago had looked. It was good land; that was why he had come back to it. Other people were pushing westward; many of them were Yankees from New England who had seen something of the country during the war or heard tell of it from returning soldiers. But the war had taught John Borst to prefer the things he knew and remembered.

John Borst was a methodical man. When he had his land readied again and his house rebuilt, he would think of buying stock and household goods. He needed next to nothing now. He lived on his cornmeal and on pigeons he knocked off a roosting tree at dusk each evening. All his daylight hours he spent in the field, cutting down the brush. He slept in a small lean-to he had set up the first day. But it was at night as he lay in his blankets and watched the fire dying that he felt lonely. He had had no inclination to remarry; he had never got over his feeling that Delia would come back. He felt it more strongly here in Dygartsbush than he had in the past seven years.

At night he would remember her in their one month of married life— cooking his supper for him when he came in; sitting beside him fixing his clothes after the meal; combing her brown hair before the hearth in her nightdress, the light of the red coals showing him the shadow of her body. At night, when she must have felt tired after helping him in the field, she seemed able to renew her vigor, and his with it.

He worked alone all through September. In October, when the dry winds began to parch the ground, he burned his land. That month three men turned up in Dygartsbush. When he first sighted them, he went for his rifle. But as they came nearer he saw that one of them was Honus Kelly.

With Kelly were two New Englanders named Hartley and Phelps who had come to look over the land. Honus explained that he had decided to sell his lot and settle in Fort Plain, and that he had the selling of the Dygarts' lot also. Hartley and Phelps liked the country and suggested to John that the four of them raise three cabins now to move into in the spring.

John spent half that night deciding that he would build his new house exactly on the site of the old one. In 1776 it had seemed to him the best site and he had found no reason to change now. In the back of his mind, however, was the thought of how it would seem to Delia when she came back. With the cabin raised the place would look to her the way it had the day he had brought her in the first time.

They built the cabins in the next three weeks; then the New Englanders left to file their deeds and return east for their families. They would come back, they said, as soon as the roads were passable.

"Ain't you coming out with us, John?" Honus asked.

John said no. He would stay and do finishing work on his cabin and fell some timber over in the hardwood lot. He would put in wheat next fall. The price of wheat was bound to go up with the influx of new settlers.

"You're right," Honus said. Then he added, "They're going to have a treaty with the Indians this month. They're going to ask for all prisoners to get sent back."

"That's good," John said.

"Delia ought to be back next summer," Honus said understandingly. "They wouldn't kill a girl like her. They liked her." He turned to the two New Englanders. "I'd probably have my hair hanging on an Indian post right now if it wasn't for John's wife. Delia's a fine girl; she'll make a good neighbor for your families."

It seemed lonelier to John the day after they left. It would be good to have neighbors, he thought. Delia would like it. She used to say she liked people around.

The rainy weather set in and he spent time in his new cabin chinking the walls. The inside he fixed up with shelves like the old one. He would have to buy boards for a table.

He went out when the snow came, and worked at what he could find around Fort Plain and then trapped a little. In the spring he found he had saved enough money from the work and from trapping to buy a mare, a heifer in calf, three hogs, corn seed, a log chain, and a plough. He hired a man to help him drive in his stock.

It was a bare beginning, but he considered himself well off. He was starting his planting when the Phelpses came in: Phelps, his wife, one child, and Mrs. Cutts, his mother-in-law, a thin-faced woman with a dry way of speaking. John Borst got to like her pretty well.

The Hartleys came later, hardly in time to plant, and John Borst thought he would not make as good a neighbor. He said he was late because he did not like slush traveling; he wanted to have warm weather to settle. He got John and Phelps to lend him a hand with his first field.

Mrs. Hartley was a frightened-acting girl who seemed to take a fancy to John. She was always running over to his place, offering to mend things. He had to admit that the sight of Mrs. Hartley, who was a pretty-looking girl, made him lonely. One day, though he could have put off the trip for another week, he went out to Fort Plain for flour and stopped in to see Honus Kelly. He asked Honus whether any women had been brought in from the Indian towns.

Honus thought quite a few had. "Anyway, when Delia shows up she'll probably come through here. I'll tell her you're back."

"Thanks," said John. He fumbled around for a minute. "Do you think there's any chance of her coming back?"

"Sure I do. I told you the Indian that took her treated her real good." Honus didn't feel it was his business to tell John the old Indian planned to make a squaw of her.

"Yes, you told me that." John Borst looked out the window. "I wonder if it would do any good if I went out looking for her."

"She might turn up just after you left here and then you both would have that much more time waiting."

"I guess that's right." Honus had told him that before, too. Honus knew a lot about the Indian country. A man wouldn't have any chance out there finding out about a particular white woman. He said good-bye to Honus and went over to the store to buy flour and some salt beef. He didn't know quite how it was but when he happened to see a new bolt of dress goods he decided to buy some. Later he realized it was because the brown striping reminded him of the color of Delia's hair.

He started back about two hours before sunset, and it was after dark when he reached the outskirts of Dygartsbush. He could see the light from the Hartleys' cabin; he had a glimpse of Mrs. Hartley crossing the lighted space. She had her hair down her back, as though preparing for the night. The sight brought him a sense of intimacy from which he himself was excluded.

He did not see any light from Phelps'. By the time he reached his own clearing he was alone with the mare under a dark sky. He rode heavily, paying no attention to the trail; and he was entirely unprepared when his mare threw up her head and stopped short, nearly unseating him. He started to kick her sides, jerking her head angrily, when she moved forward again of her own accord but with her head still raised and her ears pointed. Looking up himself, he saw at the far end of the clearing a light in his own window.

He could see no shadow of any person moving in the house, but a spark jumping from the chimney caught his eye and he guessed someone had freshened a fire on the hearth. He dismounted and got his rifle ready. Honus had told him that there were still a few Tories and Indians who had lived along the valley who were trying to get back. Down in Fort Plain they had an organization to deal with them.

He knew how far the light reached when the door was opened. Before he came into the area he let the mare have her head and slapped her flank. She stepped ahead quickly, passing the door to go around to the shed. John lay down in the grass with his rifle pointed.

The door opened, shedding its light over the mare. A woman was standing in the door looking out with large eyes at the mare. The beast stopped, snorting uneasily, then moved on. John could see the woman plainly now. She wore Indian clothes—moccasins and skirt and a loose overdress. He could tell by her height who she was.

He got up slowly, a little uncertain in his arms and legs, walked over to her, and looked into her face to make sure.

But he knew anyway. She stood erect, looking back at him, her hands hanging at her sides. He did not think she had changed, except for the Indian clothes and the way she wore her hair in two braids over her breast. He saw her lips part to say, "I'm back, John," but her voice was the barest whisper. Her face came into the light, showing him again after seven years the curve of her cheek and the tenderness of her mouth. Then he saw that her eyes were wet. Neither of them heard the whip-poorwill calling in the young corn.

AT TIMES, JOHN BORST had the feeling that he and Delia had taken up their lives exactly where they were the night the Indians raided Dygarts-bush. That night also he had been coming home from Fort Plain with flour, almost at the same time. That night might have been a dream—the burning cabins and the rain. He had just come into a clearing when half a dozen Indians spotted him, and he had set out to run for the Fort.

He told Delia about it the day after her return (they had not done any talking that first night). He told her how he had got fifteen men to come back with him and they had found every house in ashes. They had picked up the tracks at the end of his lot, followed them for half a dozen miles. Then they had come back and buried the dead. They had had to camp the night just off the clearing and it was sheer luck that John had waked to hear the crying of a little girl. It was one of Martha Dygart's daughters, being led by the other. Now, he said, they were with their mother, who had been brought back by General Sullivan's army.

As he talked, he watched Delia while she cooked. She had been crouching in front of the fire, like an Indian squaw, and suddenly she got down on her knees, the way she used to do. Now her eyes regarded him with their old searching level glance.

"Did you think I was dead, John?"

He thought awhile. "No. I didn't think so. But I thought I probably wouldn't ever see you again. I joined the army, and I didn't get back for

more'n a year. Then I found out that Caty Breen had got back. She came back married to a man that had got himself exchanged. She's living up in Kingsland now."

Delia said, "I'm glad. She was so scared. They took her off from the rest of us, two Indians did. We went on to the Genesee, the rest of us, except for Peter Kelly and the Mitchel girl."

"They got back four years ago," John told her. "They ran away. Honus told me about it."

"Honus was good to me, John."

"He told me how you helped him get away."

"What else did he tell you?"

John looked at her. "Why, I don't know. Just about how he didn't think

445

the Indians would hurt you any. He said the one that took you thought a lot of you. He had a comic name—High-Grass, I think Honus said."

"Yes, High-Grass. Gasotena."

She drew her breath slowly, and became quite still. He had noticed that about her in the one day she had been home—the way she fell into a stillness. He supposed she felt some kind of strangeness getting back to white people. Maybe, he thought, she felt strange with him.

He said, "It must be queer, coming back to me after so long. Must seem like taking up with a man without getting married, almost." He tried to say it in a light, joking way.

But she whirled suddenly, looking closely into his face. "What makes you say that?" Her lips trembled.

"I didn't mean to make you jump. I thought, maybe, I'd seem like almost a strange man. Like, maybe, there was things you wouldn't remember about me. Things, maybe, you didn't like so well."

He could see her throat fill and empty.

"Did you think that last night?"

He felt himself coloring. "No."

"Are there things about me?"

"No," he said. "God, no." There was visible pain in her eyes. He was a fool, he thought.

She turned back to the cooking, and he looked at her back. She had done up her hair in braids wound around her head, but she still wore her Indian clothing. It was good to work in, she said. Now she was still again for a long time. Then she began to speak. She seemed to have difficulty with her words.

"I used to wonder if you'd got caught. But they never brought in your scalp. I got to believe you were alive, John. Then after I'd been in the Indian town for a while I began to think I'd have to stay there all my life. We knew the army was coming, but it never did come near. It seemed as if I didn't have anything to hope for."

She drew a long breath. "I used to wonder about you, what you were doing, and who you were with, John. Did you wonder about me?"

"Yes."

"When they told me about the treaty and said I could go home, I was afraid. I thought maybe you'd found another woman and married her."

"I saw plenty," he said. "I never had the urge to marry."

"I didn't know that. I wouldn't have blamed you, though. But I had to come back to find out. One of the Indians, named Ganowauges, brought me. He knew the southern way better and he said he'd bring me as far as Fort Plain. I asked him if we could come through here and he said we could. We got here just about dark, John. We came out of the woods—then I saw the house—right in the same place. I was so frightened I could scarcely move. Ganowauges pointed to it and told me to go. I asked him if he would wait. I thought I would go back with him if there was a woman in it. He said he'd wait in the woods. Then I went inside and I saw you'd been living alone. It was so much the same. I just sat down and cried. I forgot all about Ganowauges. I never even thanked him. John, did you build the house right here on purpose?"

He said, "Yes." He saw her eyelids trembling.

After their meal John went out, leaving her looking happy, he thought. More the way she used to be. He took his scythe and went toward the swale to mow grass. But as soon as he entered the woods he made a circuit and picked up Delia's tracks. He found the Indian's plain enough. He had moved along the edge of the woods until he was opposite the door. Probably he had been there when John came home. John stood still thinking what a plain mark he must have made.

He saw Delia come to the door with the bucket she had been washing the dishes in and throw away the water with a swinging motion, making a sparkle of drops through the sunlight. Then she stood staring after the way John had gone. He thought he had never seen her look so pretty as she did in her Indian dress. He thought maybe it was the strangeness of it—as if she were something he didn't really have a right to. After a moment she put up her arm against the jamb of the door and rested her forehead on it. She might have been crying.

Suddenly it came to John that he was spying on his wife. His face reddened, even though he knew himself alone and unobserved, and he went back through the edge of the woods and cut across to the swale.

He whetted the scythe, then mowed with a full sweep. But that afternoon he could not put his heart into the mowing. The image of his wife leaning her head against the doorjamb kept troubling him.

DELIA BECAME SUDDENLY SHY of the idea of calling on the neighbors, and after twice mentioning it, John let her alone. But next day, Mrs. Cutts—Mrs. Phelps' mother—made a point of passing through Borst's clearing on her way home from the berry patch on Dygart's knoll.

With no warning, Delia had no chance of getting out of her way before Mrs. Cutts asked if she could come in. She smiled hesitantly and stood aside from the door.

"It's a good thing for John you've come back, Mrs. Borst," said the old woman, sitting down. "My, the sun's hot. But I got some dandy strawberries. I'll leave you some." Her keen old eyes examined Delia frankly. "You ain't very talkative, are you?" she asked after a moment.

"It's hard to be with people—white people—again."

"It must have been hard," said Mrs. Cutts. "Indians must be awful people. I expect they made a kind of slave out of you. They do that with their own women, I've heard tell."

"Squaws don't think they're slaves. So they didn't treat me bad by their lights. You see I got adopted into a house."

Mrs. Cutts studied her shrewdly.

"You mean you was just like one of them?"

Delia nodded.

"I guess that's why you feel uneasy with white women. Listen, Mrs. Borst," she said, after a moment. "I don't know what happened to you out there. I don't want to know unless you want to tell me. But I like John. You won't make him happy if you keep troubling yourself about what happened."

Delia swung around on the old woman. "What do you think happened to me, Mrs. Cutts?"

"I don't know and I'm not asking. Don't you worry. My tongue's my own and I keep it where it belongs." She gave Delia a hearty smile. "Now, where's a dish?"

She heaped the dish with fresh berries and went out of the door. She was a dozen yards down the path before Delia thought of thanking her and ran after her.

"I meant to thank you for the berries. They're lovely. Let me walk along a way with you."

"That's neighborly." They walked in silence. As they parted at the fork of the path, Mrs. Cutts said, "Delia Borst, just remember that there's some things a man is a lot happier for not knowing."

"The man might find out sometime. Then what would he think?"

"I'd let him take his chance of it."

Delia looked over the top of Mrs. Cutts' bonnet.

"But I love John," she said.

SHE MADE UP HER MIND to tell him that night. But she didn't say anything until she had given him his cornbread and broth, and then she came at it roundabout.

"Mrs. Cutts stopped in this morning, John. She left these berries for us. I didn't like her at first. But after a while I thought she was nice."

"She's a neighborly woman," John said.

"We got talking about what men think. She said it was better for a man not to be told everything by his wife."

John said, "I guess that depends on the wife."

"That's what I said." She finished eating her berries and sat still, leaning slightly toward him, with both hands folded on the table edge.

"You look worried," John said suddenly.

But she did not notice him. Her eyes seemed lost in the darkness gathering beyond the open door. Then Delia shivered and turned her eyes to her husband's.

"John, I've been home most a week, and you've never asked me what happened to me in Onondarha. The town I lived in. You never asked me."

John Borst also had become quiet. His big hands, which he had been resting on the table, he put into his lap. His heavy face with its slow-moving eyes stared back at her. She thought how kind it looked.

"I didn't ask because I figured you'd tell me what you wanted I should know. I've wondered what happened. I got crazy about it sometimes. But now you're back I don't want you to tell me what you don't want to."

"I've got to tell you, John. You can send me away then if you want."

"I won't never send you away."

She put out her hand quickly as though to stop his lips, then let it fall to the table between them. "I won't take that for a promise," she said. "You've got to listen. High-Grass, the Indian that took me, got me adopted into his house. The women dressed me up and showed me how to make a cake and told me to give it to the old woman of the house. I didn't know I was getting married. I didn't know till night."

He didn't say anything. He didn't look at her.

"I couldn't do anything. John, I didn't think I could live."

"You did, though."

"Yes, I did. I wanted to stay alive so I could come back to you." She sounded suddenly calmer. "After a year I had a baby, John. He was the only thing I loved. Yet I didn't love him either. Every time I saw him I thought of you. I thought how you'd hate me."

449

"I don't hate you."

Her lips stayed parted, but she could not speak. After a while John got up. He turned to look out the door.

"Where's the baby?"

"He died."

"You didn't leave him, did you?"

"No, John."

"That would have been a bad thing. Did you have any more children?"

"No." She whispered, leaning forward over the table. "I couldn't have come back, leaving a child, could I? And I couldn't come back with one. I thought when he died it was like Providence telling me I could come back. I knew I had to tell you. But when I got here, I couldn't, John."

"This High-Grass," he said. "What's he doing?"

"He went off on a war party. He didn't come back. They told me he got killed." She rose slowly. "Do you want me to stay?"

He turned on her, his voice heavy with sarcasm.

"Where in hell could you go to this time of night?"

AN OUTSIDER WOULD HAVE SEEN nothing unusual in their relations, and Delia herself was sometimes almost persuaded that John was putting what she had told him from his mind. But in a day or so she would catch him watching her, and at such times she wanted to cry out, "Stop looking at me that way! I didn't do anything bad."

One way he had changed was in laying down the law about their neighbors. He kept after her until she had made a dress from the calico he had brought. He didn't want the neighbors to think he wasn't proud to show her off. One Sunday they visited the Phelps' house.

John was pleased at the way the Phelpses took to Delia and she to them. Mrs. Cutts had said they'd be glad to have Delia visit them the next time he went down to Fort Plain. But the old woman had seen with one look that there was something between the Borsts; she guessed what had happened. She took John aside as they were leaving and said, "John, I want to tell you I think she's one of the best sort of women. You can see she's honest." Then she gave his shoulder a sharp pat and sent him after his wife.

He walked silently until he and Delia were near home. Then he asked, "Did you tell Mrs. Cutts anything about you and that Indian?"

As she turned her head to answer, he could see that she was close to tears. "No. I didn't think anybody but you had any right to know."

Thank God, he thought, Mrs. Cutts wasn't a talkative woman. She was smart, though, and she had probably guessed it. He watched Delia getting their Sunday supper, and then got down his rifle to oil it. He would have to go down to Fort Plain again soon and he thought he might as well go that week. Anything to get out of the house.

Though it was raining, he started next morning, letting the mare take her time so that they reached Fort Plain toward noon. He did his trading before dinnertime. Then he went around to Honus Kelly's to visit, but learned Honus had gone out. He might find Honus down at the tavern.

John went down there in a gloomy state of mind. Nobody was in the place except the tavernkeeper, and John asked about Honus.

"He come in this morning," the tavernkeeper said casually. "He and some others; they went off after an Indian that was in here."

John said, "That's too bad. I wanted to see him. Who was the Indian?"

"Said he was heading south and asked about the settlements. I said there was some people living in Dygartsbush." The tavernkeeper looked up. "Why, that's where you're settled, ain't it?"

John's big face leaned intently toward the tavernkeeper's. "What was the matter with him?"

"He got a couple of rums inside and commenced acting big. I told him to behave himself. I said we killed fresh Indians round here, but he just slammed his hand axe down on the bar and said he'd kill me if I didn't behave myself. I didn't dast move and there wasn't anybody else to send for Honus. So I just waited and pretty soon he said he'd had enough and I told him what he owed me. He paid me in British money, too. I knowed then he was a genuine bad one. He paid and went through that door, clumb the fence and went into the woods. I went right after Honus."

"How long was it before Honus got after him?"

" 'Bout an hour and a half. Honus has got the boys organized pretty well. I figure he'll pick him up before too long a time."

"What did the Indian look like?" John asked.

"Why, looked like any Indian. Looked pretty old."

"Did he say what his name was?"

"Said he was Christian Indian. Called himself Joe Conjocky."

John picked up his rifle and started to leave. But he stopped in the doorway, and the tavernkeeper thought his face was strangely set.

"Did you tell Honus how that Indian asked about Dygartsbush?"

"Why, no. I guess I didn't," the tavernkeeper answered.

"You damn fool."

John went out. He saddled his mare, packed on his flour and beef and salt, and reprimed his rifle.

The wind brought the rain against his face. He swung up on the mare and headed her home. He had a sick feeling in his insides: twenty miles, a wet trail. Even if he pushed the mare hard, he could not expect to reach his cabin before suppertime. Delia would be coming back from the Phelps' house long before that. If the tavernkeeper had only had the sense to tell Honus, Honus would have headed straight for Dygartsbush when the tracking got slow. But Honus would follow his usual plan of getting up with the Indian about dark and taking him by his campfire.

The mare came to the first ford and nearly lost her footing. The creek had risen since morning. The rapids were frothy and beginning to show mud. The rain fell into the gorge without much wind, but John could see the trees swaying on the rim of the rock walls. John settled himself grimly to ride, and managed to keep the mare trotting a good part of the time.

He had told Delia to stay with the Phelpses till he came home, but she wouldn't. She would start out in time to get home well before him. A man ought not to come home from a trip to have to wait for his food, she said.

He seemed to see her kneeling in front of the fireplace, blowing the fire, pink-cheeked. And he could see the Indian trotting along through the woods for the clearing; he'd have plenty of time to get there before dark. Delia wouldn't hear him. She'd only hear the door squeak on its wood hinges, and even then she'd think it was John.

"God help her," John said. He knew then that what had happened to Delia in the Indian country made no difference to him. It was what might happen to her before he could get home.

The ride became a nightmare for him. It was nearly dark in the gorge. He got off and walked at the mare's head, and they came to the turn by the beech tree and climbed the steep ascent to the flat land side by side. Finally he swung onto her again and started her off at a trot. Night came when he was still three miles from home.

When he saw a light it seemed to him that he had already reached Hartleys' farm. Then he knew that the light was too close to the earth to come from Hartleys' window. Someone was camping off the trail.

He cursed himself for not realizing it sooner and brought the mare up hard and tied her to a tree. Then he slid into the underbrush with his rifle and began working his way up to the fire.

He had not gone fifty yards before he saw that there were five men sitting around the fire and he recognized Honus Kelly's black beard. They were hunched close to the flames.

John got to his feet and started for them, shouting Kelly's name. He saw them stop laughing and pick up their guns and roll out of the firelight. When he got into the firelight he couldn't see any more of them than the muzzles of their guns.

"John Borst," roared Kelly, rising up. "What are you doing here?"

"Where'd that Indian get to?" John asked.

"Oh, the Indian. How'd you know about him?"

"I've been down to Fort Plain. I heard about him in the tavern. The damn fool said he didn't tell you the Indian was asking about my place."

Honus let out a laugh. "You didn't think he'd get away from us now, did you?" he asked. He pointed his thumb over his shoulder. Looking upward, John saw moccasined legs hanging from a maple.

Honus Kelly, watching John's face, said, "Sit down. You'd better."

But John shook his head. He could hardly speak for a minute. He was surprised because he still wanted to get home. He said at last, "You boys better come back with me. You can have a dry bed on the floor."

"No thanks," said Honus. He saw that John was anxious to get on, so he walked him back to the mare. "Delia and you won't be wanting a bunch like ourselves cluttering your place tonight," he said.

John shook hands with him.

"You don't need to thank me," said Honus. "I always wanted to get even with that Indian. Him and me had trouble more than once." He watched while John mounted. Then he caught hold of the bridle to say, "You won't tell Delia?"

John shook his head.

"Best not," agreed Honus. "Well, good luck."

He slapped the mare's rump and let her go.

It had stopped raining but the woods smelled of it, fresh and green. The air was light and the mare moved more perkily. When she came into their clearing, John saw a light in the cabin window. He saw it with a quick uplifting of his heart, and he was glad now that Delia was determined about being home before him. He remembered how it used to be before her return, coming home alone and fumbling his way in in the dark.

453

He put the mare in the shed and carried the load around to the door. It squeaked on its hinges as he pushed it open. Delia was kneeling by the fire. She swung around easily, her face apologetic.

"I thought you weren't coming home, John. I let the fire go down. Then I heard the mare."

Her eyes were large and heavy from her effort to keep awake. He warmed himself before the sputtering fire. Suddenly she straightened up. "You're wet. You're hungry."

"I got delayed." He went on awkwardly, "I wanted to get some sausage but beef was so dear I didn't have money left for it."

"Oh John, I don't care." She started to heat water.

"There's a little tea though, and half a dozen loaves of sugar."

"White sugar?"

"Yes. You'd better have tea with me."

"I don't need it."

He felt embarrassed and shy. He didn't know how to tell her what he wanted to. He couldn't say, I thought there was an Indian going to bust in on you and I got scared, but it's all right now. That wouldn't explain it to her at all. She was looking at him, too, in a queer, breathless, tentative way.

"You always used to like tea," he said. "You remember the first tea we had?"

Her gaze was level, but her color had faded. Her voice became slow and her lips worked stiffly.

"You said, 'Will you have some tea?' "

John for a moment became articulate. "No, I didn't say that."

"You did." The look in her face was suddenly pitiful.

But he shook his head at her. "I said, 'Will you have tea with me, Mrs. Borst?' "

She flushed brilliantly.

"Oh yes, John. And I said, 'I'd love to, Mr. Borst.' "

He needn't have worried about her understanding. It all passed between them, plain in their eyes. She didn't ask anything more.

A VERY SMALL
REMNANT

A VERY SMALL REMNANT

A CONDENSATION OF THE NOVEL BY

Michael Straight

ILLUSTRATED BY STEVEN STROUD

The Founding Fathers of the American
nation hoped that a hand of friendship extended
to the Indian inhabitants would ensure
peaceful settlement of the continent from
sea to sea. But by the 1860s, many
officers of the United States Army in the
West viewed Indians as enemies in an endless
war. Still there was a small remnant of
men who held to the original vision.
Michael Straight's novel, based on official
records, tells what happened when a Cheyenne
chief found a white man he could trust.

Michael Straight has an insider's
knowledge of both the military establishment
and government. His earlier novel
Carrington also dealt with
the 19th Century Indian wars.

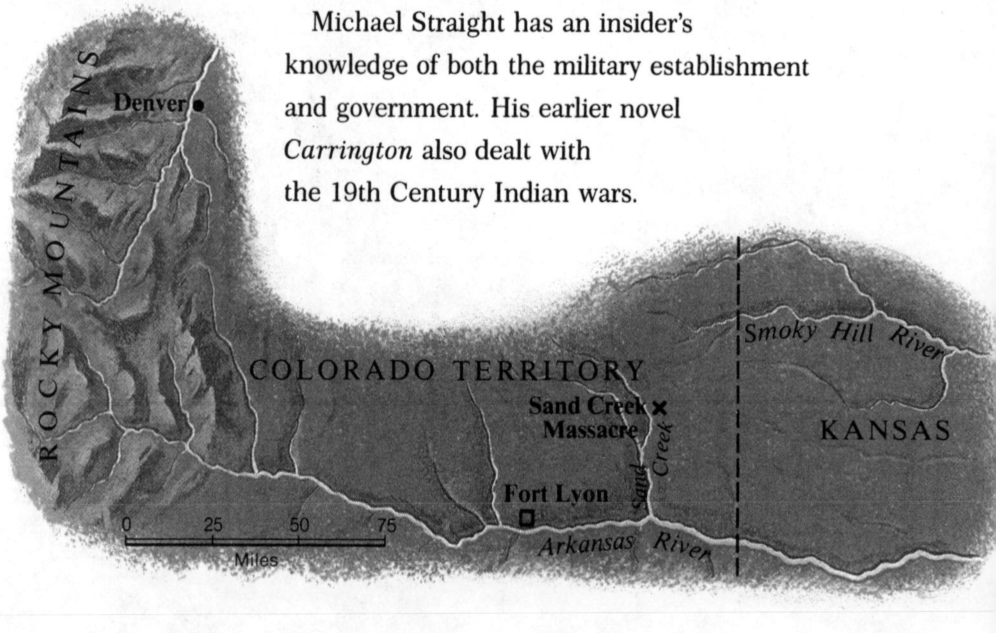

ROCKY MOUNTAINS

Denver

COLORADO TERRITORY

Sand Creek
Massacre ✕

Smoky Hill River

Sand Creek

KANSAS

Fort Lyon
☐

Arkansas River

0   25   50   75
Miles

Chapter 1

THE BLOWS OF DISTANT hammering broke my sleep. I awoke wondering, where am I? I had spent many nights out on the plains, hunting the enemy; I had awaked to many alarms. I felt now the softness of a bed, the heat of the day. I saw the room around me, the rough plaster, the narrow window, and heard Louisa's calm voice as she read to our son.

I am back at Fort Lyon, I told myself, with my family. It is an early afternoon in September, 1864, and following lunch, I must have fallen asleep.

The hammering sounded again, close by, against the door; and a trooper stood in the fierce sunlight. "Indians, sir," he explained. "We struck them five miles out."

"You killed them?"

"No, Major"—he stroked his hat—"we're bringing them in. As prisoners. There are three of them," the trooper said, "a one-eyed man, a squaw, and a boy."

"We take no prisoners, you know that! This fort's in danger; the whole valley is under attack. Why didn't you kill them?"

He said simply, "I didn't have to, Major Wynkoop. I'm not part of your command anymore."

I looked at him. I remembered that he and his companions had completed their army service. They had been on their way to Denver and civilian life when they came upon the Indians. They had acted as I might have acted, had I been free.

"As long as you're in uniform," I told the trooper, "you'll obey orders!"

459

He nodded, staring westward. "Here they come."

I went for my field glasses and made out in the distance four cavalrymen, and with them, on ponies, a woman, a boy, an old man. I watched them in silence.

"We were about to fire on them, Major. Then the one-eyed man held up a paper. It was a message, sir. I'd have brought it to you myself, but he wouldn't let it out of his hands. He said the message is for you."

The troopers rode into the fort and dismounted. The three Indians sat on their ponies, looking around. I assumed that they were spying, and my anger swelled. "Get them off those ponies!" I shouted. "Search them, then bring them to me."

I went to my headquarters and took my place at the commanding officer's desk. There on the top of my papers was the order governing our relations with the Indians of the Arkansas River Valley: *The Cheyennes will have to be soundly whipped before they will be quiet. If any of them are caught in your vicinity, kill them, as that is the only way.*

It was from Colonel John Milton Chivington, the commander of the military district of Colorado. Beneath it was a copy of my reply: *My intention is to kill all Indians I come across. . . .*

I cannot today recapture the spirit in which I wrote those words. I see now that they were contrary to my whole upbringing and to all my inclinations. Yet they were in compliance with army policy, and I was certain then that my highest duty was to carry out that policy.

We were at that moment in a war to save the Union. We thought little of taking the lives of white men who were enemies, and still less of killing Indians. We hunted them down as you would hunt wild beasts. They set out in turn to destroy our scattered settlements. As a soldier, I saw all Indians as one enemy, faceless and nameless, deserving no sympathy, capable of any treachery.

As the captives approached, I laid my papers away in a drawer. John Smith, the post interpreter, stepped into the room, followed by a sergeant leading the three Indians. The squaw crouched by the door; the boy paused in the center of the room; the old man, who I learned was called One Eye, advanced to my desk. His face was one of the saddest faces I had ever seen. I leaned forward. "You understand that you are not prisoners of war. You are enemy captives, entitled to no protection. I should have the three of you taken out and hanged." The old man listened as Smith translated my words; he looked down at me and nodded.

Hanging was a death feared by all Indians, yet the old man showed no anxiety. Either he knows that I cannot kill him in cold blood, I thought, or else he is ready to die. I started over. "Well," I demanded, "why are you here?"

The old man held out his hands; they were bound together. I untied the rope. He reached inside his blanket. He drew out a grubby piece of paper and handed it to me. The message was a reply to the proclamation sent out from Denver by John Evans, the newly appointed governor of the Territory of Colorado, calling upon all friendly Indians to come in and to make peace. Now Black Kettle, the chief of the Southern Cheyennes, answered that his council had met and had accepted the offer. They had never wanted war, so Black Kettle said. They had been driven to it by the whites. I began to lose interest, and then I read, *We have some prisoners of yours which we are willing to give up, providing . . .*

I looked at John Smith. "How many prisoners?"

"They hold four prisoners," Smith said. "A young woman, two boys, and one small girl."

"They admit that they took them captive?"

The old man said, "Black Kettle bought them, with many ponies, to give them back to you." Then he spoke directly to Smith, and Smith turned to me. "One Eye wants me to convince you that his people need peace. He says I should understand, since I am married to a squaw."

"You tell One Eye that he's my captive, and he must speak to me!"

"If you see the village of the Cheyennes, then even you will understand," the old man said. "There is hunger, and there is mourning. The message that I bring is the truth."

I doubted it. "Why didn't you answer the governor's proclamation in the summer, when you do your fighting? Why did you wait until the approach of winter?"

"We tried many times to answer the governor. We sent many messengers. One month ago our messengers tried to reach you. They rode toward the fort and held up the paper. They signaled that they came in peace. Your soldiers fired on them."

I remembered now. Joseph Cramer, one of my officers, had reported an encounter in which the Indians had tried some new trickery and he had responded with a volley of rifle fire.

"The Indians fled," I remarked.

"They were told not to fire back."

461

I nodded. Cramer had reported wounding four of them. I had commended him, and in my report to Chivington had claimed a success.

I looked up at the old man, who stood without stirring. "You knew our orders," I said. "That an Indian coming within range of this post was certain to be killed."

"I knew it."

"Then how did you dare to approach?"

"I have been a warrior," he said. "I was not afraid to die when I was young. Should I be afraid now, when I am old? . . . After the young warriors with this message of peace were driven back by your soldiers, some cried out in the Council that the Cheyennes had no choice but war. But I told the Council, 'Give me true news, such as is written, to carry to the chief at the fort.' " He gestured. "So I am here."

"You did not fear you would be killed trying to reach the fort?"

"I thought I would be killed. I hoped that the paper would be found on my dead body and brought to you, that you might read it."

"And the boy?"

"Min-im-ie?" He turned to the boy and smiled. "He would not let One Eye go alone." The boy nodded as the old man spoke. He stepped forward and took his place at the old man's side.

I looked up at them, bewildered. As I write this, years later, I see the two Indians with unaltered clarity. My own feelings I am still at a loss to describe. I felt as if invisible hands had untied cords that bound me, as I had untied the ropes that bound the wrists of the old man. I asked, "What do you want me to do?"

"If you come to the camp of the Cheyennes, then you may return with the white captives."

"How far away is your camp?"

"Four days on a horse."

"What assurance can you give me that we won't be attacked?"

"The word of the Cheyennes."

"How many warriors are in the camp?"

A fluttering gesture—"As many as the leaves on a tree," Smith translated. He added, "I'd guess there are a thousand or more."

I could take one hundred and thirty men at most. I sent the Indians off to the guardhouse, to be fed and made comfortable. I called for the officers of the post to come to my office in one hour. I sat alone.

After a time I took out my maps and began to mark off distances and days. I wrote out a brief report to Colonel Chivington, to be sent if we failed to return. It was only when my work was done, and I was waiting for the officers to join me, that doubts stole into the darkening room. Had I the right, as a commander of troops, to lead them into the camp of an acknowledged enemy, simply because I accepted the word of one old man? His people were still unknown to me. His Council might not share his longing for peace; his chief, Black Kettle, might repudiate him, finding a small band of whites within his grasp.

I read the message from Black Kettle over many times for reassurance. I took out the copy of the governor's proclamation that I had filed away. It was all that I could ask for. *The Great Father,* Governor Evans declared, *does not want to injure those who remain friendly to the whites. He desires to protect and take care of them.* And then the passage that Black Kettle had noted: *Friendly Arapahoes and Cheyennes belonging on the Arkansas River will go to Major Colley, United States Agent, who will give them provisions and show them a place of safety.*

A place of safety—I repeated those words with a sense of satisfaction on that September afternoon; and with a terrible bitterness in time to come.

THE OFFICERS OF THE POST gathered around my desk. They were men of my own age and inclination—easterners by birth, gold miners by choice, patriots in a crisis, but adventurers at heart. They were ready for any foray, accustomed to unequal odds. But when I told them of my plan to lead a band of volunteers into the stronghold of the Cheyennes, they looked at me in disbelief. I had hoped that all of them would volunteer, but it was plain that my hope was forlorn. So I closed the council, swearing that I would go alone.

It was the idea of going alone that took Captain Silas Soule's fancy. "Provided no one else goes," he said, "I'll keep you company."

Then Lieutenant Cramer, in his dour way, sighed. "The army will need one survivor to write the report," he said. "I'll follow along at a safe distance."

In the last light of the day, the men assembled on the parade ground and I stood before them, with Silas Soule and Joseph Cramer on either side of me. "Word has come today," I shouted, "that the Cheyennes are holding four captives in the Big Timbers. . . . Four white captives: a woman, two boys, and a young girl."

463

The men stood at parade rest, waiting.

"I am going for them tomorrow, to bring them back without a fight, unless we have to fight. I want a hundred and thirty volunteers."

I waited; not one trooper moved. Then Mulkey, the blacksmith, spat on the ground. He stepped forward, and no man dared hold back.

So our column was formed: one hundred and twenty-seven men, all mounted. For hostages we took the three Indians. We rode out before dawn. The sun rose on our right; before long the day was burning. The horizon reached out for miles around us without a landmark; the dust from our column drifted off on a dry wind.

We crossed Sand Creek at noon. We halted for the night in the whitened ruins of a cottonwood grove. The horses fell to grazing; the cooks worked over their cauldrons; the men lit fires and heated coffee. I wandered among them, listening. We had spent many such nights together, surrounded by the war parties of the enemy. Then, no risk or hardship could deaden their good humor. On this night, in contrast, the men were silent, and I knew why. Each believed that we were riding into an ambush.

I walked to where Soule lay, ruddy-faced by his fire. "The men are uneasy," I told him. "In three or four days they may be hard to handle."

His dark eyes glinted. "I told you we should have gone alone!"

And he meant it. He had joined the army as a scout for Kit Carson. Before that he had worked for the Abolitionists in Kansas. It was Soule who led the rescue party for John Brown. Seeing the flask lodged in one of his hip pockets, you would not guess that the other contained a volume of verses inscribed by a friend of his, a poet named Whitman.

We set out again before dawn; we rode through another cloudless day. Buffalo grazed in the far distance; antelope lifted their heads as we passed; the grasshoppers kept up their metallic note all day long.

One Eye had said four days. He rode at the head of the column, his eyes fixed upon some invisible point on the bare horizon. At sunrise on the fourth day, I sent Min-im-ie on ahead to tell Black Kettle we were coming. The boy cantered off to the northeast and we followed. We saw no sign of the Cheyennes during the fiery day. When the sun was low, we moved down a long slope to the Smoky Hill River.

We halted there while the men knelt, filling their canteens. Then One Eye gestured. We looked up and saw the pennons and spears on the horizon, then the horses, and at last, the riders. They paused on the crest of the hill and confronted us: a thousand warriors, drawn up in line of battle, all streaked in white and ocher and vermilion, their war paint.

On the north bank of the river we formed our battle line. The Cheyennes watched us and did not move. I sent One Eye out to tell them that we came in peace. He rode without haste across the half mile separating us. With carbines drawn, we advanced at a walk up the slope.

The center of their line fell back as we approached; their flanks closed in around us. Still moving forward we re-formed as squadrons and, enclosed in a square, we rode the four miles to their village. Outwardly, as Cramer later testified, we kept up an air of "reckless indifference." Inwardly we waited for the shot that would set off a hopeless fight.

At last we sighted the Big Timbers—a grove of ancient trees where the Cheyennes were camped. We rode on past the grove and halted by a stream fringed by green willows. "They want us to camp here," Smith said. The men began to dismount, but I led them on, up to a bare hill where, if need be, we could make a stand. For the first time in two hours, I felt able to breathe.

I had, without authorization, led my troops into hostile territory. I had placed them at the mercy of a people who were believed to be merciless. No worse disaster could overtake me than the one I had been spared. I had never seen Black Kettle, but already I was in his debt.

AT DAYBREAK SMITH stood outside my tent. "Major," he said, "the Indians say you have little chance of getting out of here alive."

I shook my head. "Black Kettle had his opportunity yesterday. He didn't take it."

"I'm not speaking about Black Kettle; I'm speaking about his young men. These young warriors mean to kill you. Their leader is the brother of the chief your soldiers shot down."

Not mine, but white soldiers. For the first time I wondered, are all white men responsible for one white man's folly?

The chiefs were waiting. I left the camp and set out with the men I wanted near me: Soule, Cramer, Smith, one or two more. We crossed the stream and rode into the shade of the cottonwoods where the tepees stood. We passed hanging ribbons of buffalo meat and smoldering fires. In a clearing at the center of the village the chiefs were seated. A crowd of a thousand or more closed behind us as we rode in. We dismounted and took our places on hides that had been set out for us.

The chiefs confronted us unsmiling. Black Kettle was the most inscrutable of them. His forehead was high, his nose prominent, his mouth thin, wide, and drawn down. He regarded us through half-closed eyes.

I scanned the crowd: the silent children, the sullen women, the warriors gripping their weapons. Their hostility was impenetrable. Black Kettle motioned at last; Smith and I stood up. I held out the paper and asked if the chiefs had sent it. They nodded. I explained that because of the paper I had come, in peace. I read aloud the message that One Eye had given me, then said, "You say you are holding four white captives. I have come to take them back."

A murmur started up in the crowd and mounted. I could not say today how great the din was; at the time it seemed deafening.

In a low voice Smith said, "You are talking for your life now; go on."

"You want me to promise peace in return for the captives," I said. "I cannot do that. But if you will give me the captives I . . ." I faltered and the noise billowed again.

The crowd pressed in upon us. In the midst of it all Black Kettle sat. He saw my desperation; his mouth lifted in a faint smile that to me was worth a thousand bayonets. "If you will give me the captives," I cried, "I will take them to our governor in Denver. I will tell him, 'Here is proof that the Cheyennes are friendly.' If you wish, I will take your chiefs to Denver with me. I will pledge my own life to see that they go and return without harm. You have seen the governor's message," I cried. "The one that offers you a place of safety. If you will come in with us, then I will make my post, Fort Lyon, that place."

Close by Black Kettle a young chief stood up. He was Bull Bear, brother of a young chief who had been killed by our troops. He spoke in a voice hoarse with hatred. His followers pushed to the front. Soule and Cramer stood up beside me, gripping their holsters. Black Kettle sat motionless.

From the crowd One Eye broke through. He pointed to Bull Bear and his followers. "Where were they," he demanded, "when I carried the paper to the fort? The white soldier took me in. He trusted the words of the Council. So now the Council must decide if they are dogs or men."

The crowd was hushed; One Eye spoke again. "Bull Bear says we should not give away our captives. He wants to trade them. I say that is shameful. To spare our people the shame, I will trade with him. He may have my horses if he will let the captives go."

466

He waited. After a moment Bull Bear muttered, "I will take the horses." He returned to his place.

Other members of the Council spoke in turn. When they had finished, Black Kettle stood up. He embraced me and led me to the center of the Council. He spoke with his hand on my shoulder. "This white man believed in the word of an Indian although his people brand us unworthy of belief. It was like coming through a fire for a white man to follow an Indian, but he followed our warrior.

"He could not give us peace. If he had promised peace, I would have asked him if he took us for fools. I listened, ready to despise him for lying. I heard only the truth. And I embrace the truth."

He turned to me. "Take your soldiers back on the trail. Make your camp at sunset and stay there until sunset tomorrow. We will spend the night in council, and by tomorrow night you will have some word from us. Whatever it may be, you and your soldiers may return to your fort unharmed."

He embraced me again; the other chiefs came to shake my hand. With Cramer and Soule at my side I stood in the clearing, sustained.

AT SUNDOWN WE MADE camp in a cottonwood grove. The men were jittery. All of them, including Cramer, believed that the Indians meant to attack us. Only Soule was untroubled.

I did what I could to calm the men; I doubled the sentries. It was no use. Our outriders reported that Indian scouts had shadowed us. Wolf calls closed around us in the night; the Cheyennes used the wolf calls as a war signal. The men drew together and argued in low voices. I knew what was coming. There was nothing to do but let it come.

Soule, Cramer, and I waited around my fire. We feigned indifference as the mutiny mounted against us. "They'll try to disarm us," I said.

"No," Cramer said. "They'll try to persuade us."

Toward midnight the men moved off silently into the darkness. "They're going for their rifles," Cramer said. In his detached way he asked, "Are you ready to shoot them?"

"If we don't shoot them," I said, "Chivington will hang them."

"Yes, the Fighting Parson," Cramer said. "Or else he'll hang us for leading them here."

Soule protested. "We did what we had to do."

Cramer shook his head. "We didn't have to come. We could have

467

stayed at Lyon and let the captives die. That would have been the safe course."

"We didn't choose the safe course," Soule said.

Cramer was staring into the darkness. "The men are gathering out there. It won't be long." He squinted down the sights of his revolver and asked, "Will we get out of this place? Will we get to Denver with the chiefs?"

"I think so," I said.

Cramer laid a few dead limbs on the fire and stirred the ashes. The flames were high when he murmured, "Here they come."

A band of men moved into the firelight. Some carried rifles, but surreptitiously. Mulkey and three of his companions stepped forward. "Major," Mulkey began. "We're going back."

I nodded. "When we get the captives."

"At sunrise, Major. We figure the redskins are lying."

"We're staying, Mulkey."

"You can stay, Major. The men are going. If you don't want to lead—"

We moved quickly. Soule and I covered the men; Cramer took their rifles. I called for a wagon and had the four ringleaders bound to the wagon wheels. They hung, spread-eagled, through the night, twisting and groaning as the ropes bit into their wrists. No matter what the men felt or suffered, there was no whisper of mutiny from then on.

I cut Mulkey and his companions loose at sunrise. There was nothing to do but wait. The sun arched over us. We saw dust in the distance, then four or five Indians riding in from the north. Braced around the copper chest of one brave were two pale arms; a white girl was riding behind him.

The Indians came at a walk into our circle of armed men. One of them slid from his pony and lifted the girl to the ground. She stood ashen and mute. An Indian shawl covered her tattered dress. I offered her my jacket, but she clutched the shawl, shivering in the heat of the day.

I led her to a tent and tried to talk to her. It took patience to draw words from this girl. Her name, I learned, was Laura Roper; her parents were settlers on the Little Blue River. One Sunday in August she had walked a mile up the river to visit her neighbors, a family named Eubanks. Since the day was fine they had walked back with her, Mrs. Eubanks carrying her baby, her husband leading their three-year-old, Isabella.

They were picking wild flowers when they heard yelling. They ran into the brush and crouched there. Eubanks stuffed a handkerchief into his daughter's mouth to stifle her cries. The Indians rode past them, but the girl was choking; the father pulled out the handkerchief, too soon. The child screamed; the Indians turned back. They killed Eubanks and scalped him. They tied the women and led them away.

Nearby there lived a simpleminded woman. The Indians caught her ten-year-old son and another boy hiding in a shed. That brought the woman out of her own hiding place, and the Indians took her scalp. The party traveled westward for many days. Before long the baby died. The warriors sold Mrs. Eubanks to a band of north-riding Sioux.

Laura turned from me to the tent wall, plucking at the shreds of her dress. I left her, for the leader of the Cheyennes was waiting with a message from Black Kettle. The Council had accepted my proposal. Black Kettle had guessed that my soldiers would grow restless, so he had sent Laura ahead as evidence of his good faith. Black Kettle himself would deliver Isabella and the two boys to me on the following day. He and six of his chiefs would ride with me to Fort Lyon, and then on to Denver to meet with Governor Evans and to sign a treaty of peace.

I kept Laura's Indian escorts as hostages, just in case. I counted the hours. Some time after noon on the next day, a lone Indian rode into our camp bearing the news that Black Kettle and his party were a few miles away. I went out alone, with the Indian as my guide. I rode with a wildly throbbing heart toward the party. A white boy on a dappled pony broke from its ranks and galloped toward me. He reined in beside me and reached up for my hand. "My name's Dan. Are you the soldier who has come to get me?"

"I am."

"Well, hurray for you!" he cried.

He kicked the pony and galloped off. By then the second boy had joined us. He clung to my side. So we came to the Indians. I should have paused to greet the chiefs, but I rode past them, searching for the child Isabella. She was close to the age of my son. In a squaw's bent arm I saw at last a bundle, wrapped in an Indian blanket; then a tuft of golden hair and blue, imploring eyes. I reached forward, and her arms stretched out to me. I lifted her into my saddle; she pressed her head against my shoulder. Between her sobs she whispered, "I want my mother!" I smoothed her hair, knowing she would never see her mother again.

I rode ahead with her, not wanting the chiefs to see me unmanned. So, alone and bereaved, we led the triumphal procession to the camp. As we rode in, all the men broke into wild cheers.

Chapter 2

WE PAUSED LONG enough at Fort Lyon to rest the children. The boys, to be sure, were healthy; they had been well treated. Laura showed no interest in anything around her, and I realized she would never recover. Isabella clung to my wife, Louisa, and woke each night screaming.

When the time came for leaving for Denver, I packed the captive children in one wagon and the chiefs in another. I set out with Soule and Cramer and thirty men. We traveled light, intending to eat and sleep at ranch houses and stagecoach stations along the way.

Throughout the first day that seemed a sound decision; settlers waved as we approached, and made us welcome. But on the second day all was changed. We rode through the wide and shallow valley of the Arkansas, rich country brightened by the first traces of autumn. Everything wild was fruitful, but where the land had been cleared by settlers, it had failed. The hay that should have been cut was still standing; the corn that should have been harvested was spoiling on the stalk.

We came to a sod house. There was no sign of life. The gate of the corral hung open; a white shirt struggled on a clothesline as if, once freed, it would flap away after its owner. I pushed open the door of the house; the stove was cold in the abandoned room. Four miles up the river we came to a second ranch. Weeds were multiplying where the ground should have been cultivated. The house was deserted.

Throughout the day we passed abandoned settlements. We came at last to the Indian Agency at Point of Rocks. Horses were corralled there; wagons were drawn up in a circle to form battlements; from earthworks dug around the wagons, rifles covered our approach.

I halted the column and rode in alone. A rancher, Haynes, rose from the earthworks with his rifle. "What took you so long?" he called out.

A score of haggard men stood up beside him. One said, "You going to take us back to Lyon, Major, or are we going to make a stand here?"

I looked at the battlements, and beyond them to the agency building. I saw the faces of women and children pressed against the windowpanes. "What's going on?" I asked.

"It's a general war," Haynes said. "Three thousand Indians are ready to strike us—they're going to wipe out every settlement from Denver to Leavenworth."

A settler added, "We may not last long, but we'll take some of the red devils with us." I glanced back at the chiefs, who were sitting impassively in the wagon. They were wearing black hats and shabby cloaks. They looked more like missionaries than devils.

I asked, "What three thousand Indians?"

Haynes was impatient. "Sioux, Cheyennes, Comanches . . ."

"Cheyennes?"

"Satanta, Roman Nose, Black Kettle—they're all out with their war parties."

I nodded toward the wagon. "Black Kettle is here, with me. I'm taking him to Denver to make peace," I said. "He and his chiefs are coming of their own free will."

I waved to the column. The troopers rode up and dismounted; the wagons creaked into the yard. I opened the tailgate, and the chiefs stepped down. The women and children came out of the house, followed by Sam Colley, the Indian Agent, drunk again.

Colley lurched up to the wagon; he upbraided the chiefs for going to a bluecoat when they should have gone to Sam Colley, their tried and trusted friend. The chiefs listened and did not answer. They knew how Colley had swindled them. The settlers knew it too and were ashamed; they came forward and without ceremony led the chiefs indoors.

That night when the children were asleep, I spoke of the meeting in the Big Timbers. I trusted the men and women who sat around me in the lamplight; I knew that they wanted to believe me. When I had finished, Haynes spoke for them. "You say Black Kettle's people will keep the peace while you're in Denver? But we've seen homesteads burned five miles from here. We've seen women and children killed."

"I remember."

"Do you? Or have you forgotten? You were an exterminator when we last saw you, Major. You were one of Chivington's men."

"I still am."

The settlers stared at me for a moment. Their whispers went around and converged upon Haynes, who said, "Major, we're agreed. Our homes are out there, untended; our crops are spoiling. With your permission we'd like to return to our homesteads and save what we can."

"You have my permission."

COLLEY SAT ALONE BEYOND the lamplight. When the last of the settlers had left the room, he came forward. He took a bottle of whiskey from his desk and poured out two drinks. "You despise me," he said.

He was right. To the soldier, there is nothing lower in the white community than an Indian Agent. And Sam Colley was the lowest of his kind. "You despise me," he repeated, "but you don't pity me." He swallowed his whiskey and poured himself a second drink. "I pity you! You're out alone where no man should be."

"I'm acting on orders. Governor Evans sent out orders for the Cheyennes to come in. I've got it in writing." I had carried the governor's proclamation in my pocket since the day I met One Eye. I laid it on the desk.

Colley glanced at the proclamation and shoved it aside. He said, "That was in June, boy; this is late September. Evans talked peace in June. But now . . . " Colley fumbled among his papers. "You've got it in writing; well, so have I!" He thrust a telegram across the desk. "Read it!"

It was from Evans to Edwin Stanton, the Secretary of War. It began: *Extensive depredations with murder of families occurred yesterday thirty miles south of Denver—*

"A lie!" Colley interrupted. "Only one family was killed, the Hungates." He motioned and I read on.

Our lines of communication are cut, and our crops are in exposed localities and cannot be gathered in. Large bodies of Indians are undoubtedly near to Denver and we are in danger of destruction from both attack and starvation. It is impossible to exaggerate our danger.

I looked up. "He'll be glad to see me then."

Colley laughed in an ugly way. "Oh, delighted!"

"Well, Chivington will support me," I said.

Colley looked at me sidelong. He asked, "What makes you so sure?"

"He's a Union soldier as I am; his enemy is the Confederacy. He has no troops to spare, not while the—"

"You've been out of touch, boy." Colley leaned back in his chair. "You don't know what's going on. They've armed the rabble in Denver. . . . Yes," he went on, seeing my chagrin, "they've emptied the saloons, cleaned off the street corners, and put a thousand men into uniform for one hundred days. They call them the Third Regiment."

The taste in my mouth was sour. "They'll join the Union armies in Missouri," I said. "They'll go after the graybacks."

"They'll hunt Indians." Colley laughed. "And they'd better find them! Your friend Chivington is in trouble, boy. His term in the army runs out this autumn. He's heading for the Senate. The pressure is on, boy, and he knows it. He needs a victory."

"I'll give him a victory," I said. "I'll bring in the chiefs, and let him take credit for the peace."

"Ah!" Colley leaned forward. "Don't you see, boy? Evans and your hero Chivington are men of great ambition. They don't want to ship any more boys out of the Territory. So they work up their own war. They hand out a rifle to every tramp in Denver and say, 'Here! Shoot yourself a red man!' Then you come along. You come out of the Big Timbers with Black Kettle! You send the warriors back to their villages and the settlers back to their farms. And you expect Evans to be grateful!"

"I'm carrying out the governor's orders," I said.

"You fool!" He pounded on the desk. "You've made a liar out of Evans, don't you see! You've made a laughingstock out of Chivington. They'll—"

"That's enough!" I said, rising. Colley was an Indian Agent and a thief; they were fine men, my superiors and my friends.

WE RODE ON THROUGH the valley, up the slow rise toward the Rocky Mountains. I paused while the wagon train plodded past me. I remembered the moment, six years before, when I had come to this same place on the trail as one of a party of pioneers sent out to claim the land in the lee of the Rockies.

We moved slowly up the valley, sending the settlers home from each fortified point. At Pueblo we left the Arkansas River and rode north. The ground was stony at the base of the mountains, the soil poor. We met few travelers. Most of the sod houses were boarded up, but there was one place where we were sure of a welcome. The way station two days south of Denver was Charles Coberly's ranch, known as the Half Way House. The creek was clean there, the pasture green, the timber plentiful. The main lodging was warm and dry. The food was spiced with plums and chokecherries gathered by Coberly's two daughters.

I rode on ahead to tell the Coberlys that we were coming. To get to the house, I had to work my way through a barricade. Coberly watched from the door. Recognizing me he laid his rifle aside. "You too?" I said.

He nodded. "My wife's begging me to leave this place," he said. "The girls sleep in their clothes—if they sleep at all."

"I thought you got along with the Indians."

"I thought so too. So did Ward Hungate." He shook his head.

We moved inside. "I'm on my way to Denver," I began.

"You'll see Hungate's ranch then—all that the Indians left of it."

"There are Indians in my party," I told him. "I'm taking them to see the governor. We're planning to stop over here."

Coberly took a moment to reply. "You're welcome to stay, Ned. But keep your Indians out of my house."

The wagon train drew in at the end of the day. We pitched a tent outside for the chiefs and carried supper out to them.

When supper was over, we moved the tables and benches back against the wall in the main cabin and set two chairs out on the floor. Coberly and his son sat down and tuned their fiddles. The elder of the girls joined them and sang an English air. She was nineteen, and a favorite of ours. When she had finished, Soule sang to her in his bantering way. She watched him gravely. If, at the end of the song, he had asked for her hand, she would have chided him for tarrying so long. He took her hand, but only to lead her in a country dance. Other couples joined in. Mulkey came in looking for me and led me outside.

A group of men were crowded around the Indians' tent. The chiefs were seated on the ground. A ranchhand swayed over them, calling on them to stand up and fight. "Just stand up," he cried, "and we'll kill you, same as you killed Hungate."

I grabbed him and spun him around. "Not these Indians," I shouted. "Not these!"

He looked up at me, his face filled with misery. "It was Cheyennes that done it, Major! Same as these here."

I felt, in place of anger, my own uncertainty. I turned to Black Kettle. "Close by here," I told him, "a white family was murdered by Indians. A man and his wife and his two daughters, all killed in cold blood."

The old chief looked at me intently. He shook his head. "They were not Cheyennes," he said.

I stood over him. "Then, damn it, who were they?"

"Arapahoes," he said, "young ones, from far to the north. They did a great wrong." He looked up at me. No one in the crowd could fail to see the pain in his face.

I let the ranchhand go. He and the rest of the men drifted off. I stood by the chiefs, shaking my head.

474

"There is a bad feeling," I said to Black Kettle, "because of the killing." He nodded. "Well?" I asked, "do you still want to go on?"

He looked at me for a moment, then he nodded again.

It was like going through a fire, Black Kettle had said of my journey to the Big Timbers; this, I guessed, was like going through a fire for him.

THE NEXT DAY I turned the column over to Cramer, and Soule and I pressed ahead alone. I wanted to prepare the way with the governor. We came to Denver at dusk. The city had stretched out across the plains; then it had shrunk, leaving its borders dead. No lamps shone in the shacks along the way. We saw nothing stir; yet we were under scrutiny. From the roof of the first brick building a rifle poked out from a narrow battlement, covering us as we passed.

We rode on. The streets were deserted, save for bands of drunken soldiers. The vacant lots were filled with cattle that had been driven into the city. Families who had fled from outlying ranches huddled around low fires. We came at last to a log barrier that blocked the street. From the shadows an officer spoke. "We've been expecting you, Ned."

He was Harry Richmond; before the war we had been amateur actors together. He spoke of the old days and joked about his temporary status as a captain in the Third Regiment.

I gathered in my reins but Richmond held on, fondling the bridle. Casually he asked, "What happened to your red friends?"

"They'll be here tomorrow."

Richmond laid his hand on my arm. "Take the word of an old friend, Ned," he said. "Turn back. This town is crying for blood."

We rode on into the city. Soule headed for the saloons; I walked to the governor's mansion. I rang the bell and stepped inside. The hallway was rich with cigar smoke; from the parlor came the din of voices. I started forward; a servant barred my way. He took my card and vanished, but soon returned bearing regrets. His Excellency was indisposed.

I strode off, and had nowhere to go. The saloons were crowded with my old companions; I could no longer trust them. In the mansions of Denver were many citizens who would listen to my story, but I dared not approach them until I had seen the governor. So I wandered alone, an alien in a city I had helped to found. From the shadows, men I could not see called out my name as if to say, We know you, Wynkoop, and we're watching you.

IN THE MORNING I WAS SUMMONED downstairs at the hotel. There, waiting for me, was Governor Evans. He was an imposing figure in his morning coat and wing collar. He smiled in his cold way and steered me into a back parlor. "Now, Wynkoop," he said, "just what are you up to?"

"Governor, it was your own proclamation that started it. The Cheyennes replied to it and offered to return the captives if we—"

"You should have rescued them, by force of arms."

"The children would have been killed."

"That in itself is proof that the Indians are savages."

I struggled to control myself. "Governor," I said, "I took it to be obedience to your wishes that I should recover the captives, alive."

"I am gratified that you are obedient to my wishes. I wish you now to escort your Indians back where they came from. Now!"

"Governor, they have come four hundred—"

"They are enemies, Wynkoop; we and they are at war."

"They don't want war, sir; that's why they—"

"They don't want to be punished, you mean. And rightly punished for the outrages they have committed. I want them turned back."

"Governor, by now every Indian on the plains knows that Black Kettle is on his way to talk with you. I couldn't turn him back now, even if I wanted to. It was in answer to your proclamation that he set out."

Evans looked at me keenly. For the first time I could see anxiety and doubt in his eyes. "If I could be sure of that," he began. He winced. "Wynkoop—you place me in a most difficult position."

"My own position is not easy, sir." I pointed out that I had pledged my word as an officer that he would see the chiefs. "I think you must see them," I said.

He wavered. "Wynkoop, you cannot conceive of the pressure I am under! When the bodies of the Hungates were brought in, the people blamed me for permitting them to be murdered. And now"—he sank into a chair, shaking his head—"you force me to meet with their murderers!"

"Governor," I said, "Black Kettle and his band did not murder the Hungates!"

"No matter; they kill white men whenever they can. I've tried to make peace with the Indians, Wynkoop; I swear it! But I'm responsible for the lives of every man, woman, and child for hundreds of miles around. I must protect every little farmhouse. And yet," he sighed, "I have been stripped of my troops."

"You have them now."

"That's just it! Now, at last, they have recognized our plight. We've raised the Third Regiment; we're spending thousands of dollars to equip it. . . ." His voice lapsed to a whisper. "What will I do with the Third Regiment if I make peace?"

"Disband it," I said.

"And make a fool of myself?" He stood up, went to a window, and stared out. "The Third Regiment was raised to kill Indians," he said, "and kill Indians it must."

"I ask you, what will Mr. Lincoln think when he learns that you refused even to receive the chiefs, after they came four hundred miles to talk to you?"

He turned on me. "How will Lincoln learn that?"

"I'll tell him, if no one else will."

"Wynkoop," he said, "I pray to God you know what you are doing!" He strode out, slamming the door.

THE NEXT MORNING in Denver men were gathered in knots, leaning against buildings, waiting. Soule and I rode out to meet the chiefs. Three miles south of the city we saw our column approaching. No troops could have looked finer. Cramer led the column; behind him the men rode in close order; the chiefs sat upright in their wagon. From white masts, held by Black Kettle and Bull Bear, there floated two American flags.

We rode on with the column, ready for a mob; instead, at the edge of the city forty carriages were drawn up in line, waiting to escort us into Denver. The men seated in the carriages took off their hats as we passed; the ladies, in white dresses, bowed. I recognized a minister, a surgeon, a federal judge; an Abolitionist or two; a family of Quakers; two ladies who had started the first school in the Territory. Someone, I knew, had organized the welcome. I glanced at Soule; he grinned. We did not pause, and no command was given; the carriages simply fell into line behind us. So we crossed the whole city; we halted in the shadow of the Methodist Church where, two years before, Chivington, the preacher turned soldier, had roared at his congregation about the tortures of hell. There Soule and I turned and stood at attention; the troops clattered by us; in the carriages the ladies and gentlemen smiled.

Camp Weld, outside the city, was the site chosen by Governor Evans for his meeting with the chiefs. It was the training camp of the Third

Regiment, the worst possible place to talk of peace. The next morning we rode through the gates of the camp, halted and looked around. We saw all that you would expect to see in the camp of a regiment that was to exist for just one hundred days. Equipment littered the square; no troops were being drilled; a single squad of cavalrymen stared at us.

These men were the backwash of the Pikes Peak tide: too late to strike gold, too shiftless to work the land, too impoverished to move on west, too stubborn to head home. They were, most of them, bummers and drifters, haunting the fringes of legality.

We were directed to an empty mess hall. Soule, Smith, and I went inside with the chiefs. A bench was set out and, facing it, a table and four chairs. An orderly motioned to us to be seated on the bench. We waited; a carriage creaked outside.

Governor Evans stepped in, pulling off his gloves. For a moment the light from the entrance flooded the room. Then all the doorway was filled by Colonel John Milton Chivington. He was a giant. He wore the largest uniform in the army; his neck, his arms, his wrists, were all immense; he could kill any man in the Territory with his bare hands. He had been a boxer before he turned to the ministry, and he entered the room as he might have entered the ring: his balding head arched back; his bearded chin thrust out; his eyes, small and fierce, appraising us.

After a moment I led the chiefs forward. Evans reached out to shake hands with Black Kettle as if he were offering meat to a fanged animal. Chivington merely nodded. We sat again on the bench.

Evans motioned to Black Kettle to rise and to speak. Instead, the old chief drew from within his blanket a long-stemmed pipe. To light it and pass it around was for him a sacred ceremony, binding all who smoked it to act honorably and to live as friends. Black Kettle stuffed the pipe with tobacco, lit it, and passed it to his left. I took it in turn, as did Evans and Chivington. In time it returned to Black Kettle.

Evans was restless. "Well," he demanded of the chief, "what have you got to say?"

478

Black Kettle rose. He praised the governor's proclamation. He added that he had at once accepted its terms. He spoke with pride of my journey to the Big Timbers. He noted that the chiefs' journey to Denver was for them a risk. "We came with our eyes shut," he said, "following Major Wynkoop.

"You are our father," he told Evans. "All that we ask for is peace."

Evans stood up, shuffling his papers. "So far as making a treaty now is concerned," he said, "we are in no position to do it. Your young men are on the warpath." He granted that the chiefs had always opposed war with the whites. He suggested that they had been unable to control their young warriors.

Chivington wrote a message on a sheet of paper and passed it to the governor, who read it and nodded. "Another reason that I am not in a condition to make a treaty," Evans said, "is that war has begun and the power to make a treaty of peace has passed from me to the great war chief." Evans made it plain that the hostile Indians would not escape punishment for their transgressions. But he knew in his heart that the men who faced him were not guilty and he wanted to be just. He conceded that the chiefs were not at war with the United States. "My advice to you," he told the chiefs, "is to turn on the side of the government, and to show by your acts that friendly disposition you profess."

The chiefs bent forward. "What is meant by being on the side of the government?"

"Keeping close to the soldiers. Having nothing to do with our enemies. Making some arrangement with the soldiers; helping them."

The chiefs asked, "What is meant by helping them?"

"Acting as scouts for them. Keeping them informed; telling them all you know. And fighting beside them, if need be, against their enemies."

The chiefs conferred. Black Kettle spoke. "We cannot answer for all our young men, but I think there will be little difficulty in getting them to help the soldiers."

So the terms of agreement were reached.

The oldest of the chiefs, White Antelope, stood up. He said, "I have called all white men my brothers." He asked, "Who are your enemies?"

"All the Indians who are fighting us," Evans said.

White Antelope nodded. He declared that the Cheyennes and the Arapahoes would never again fight against the whites. But the tribes to the south of the Arkansas River, the Apaches, Comanches, and Kiowas, were all committed to war. So were the undefeated warriors to the north—the Sioux.

Chivington listened intently as White Antelope spoke. I knew that he was agitated. At the mention of the Sioux, his fists closed, his neck tightened; small signals betraying the rage that he kept within himself. He sat in silence through the conference. Then, as it moved to its conclusion, the time approached when he had to speak.

The chiefs answered frankly all of the governor's questions. They offered to fight with the whites, against the Sioux. They added that their decision would expose their wives and their children to great danger of reprisal. They asked for some assurance that we would protect them.

"That," Evans answered, "is a matter for the great war chief to decide."

Chivington stood up and towered over us. He spoke with some difficulty, as if his main effort were to control himself. "I am not a big war chief," he said, "but all the soldiers in this country are at my command. My rule of fighting, white men or Indians, is to fight them until they lay down their arms and submit to military authority. These chiefs are nearer Major Wynkoop than anyone else," he said to Evans, "and they can go to him when they get ready to do that."

The chiefs gestured in assent. They were reassured by what Chivington had said for they were ready to submit, and they trusted wholly in me. They knew that for them safety lay in living close to Lyon. They stood smiling at the close of the conference. They embraced Evans and then myself. They moved to embrace Chivington, but he turned from them and left the room, buckling on his sword.

WE STAYED ON FOR TWO days at Denver. I found good homes for the boys and for Laura Roper. I left Isabella Eubanks with a young couple who had lost their own child.

I went back to the governor's mansion. Evans was preparing to leave for Washington; he promised to give the President a favorable report on all that we had done.

I rode out to Camp Weld to take my leave of Chivington. I felt unsure of him. I was convinced that I had eased his task of safeguarding the Territory by making allies of the Cheyennes, but feared that he had taken the conference as an affront.

As I rode I hardened myself for Chivington's reproaches. To my relief, however, I found him in high spirits, as if his burdens had been lightened. He presented me to George Shoup, the young colonel he had picked to lead the Third Regiment, and to Major Downing, a well-born attorney who had become his principal adviser.

On the parade ground a captain of the Third Regiment was training his company in the use of the saber. We stood watching the cavalrymen charge an invisible enemy, slash the air, and haul their mounts to a halt.

"Well," Chivington said to me, "what do you think of them? For men who have been in service for six weeks."

"They've been in for six weeks? Then they have only eight weeks more to go. When will you take the field?"

Chivington grinned. "When I'm ready."

"Will you follow the Platte route? That's where the Sioux are," I said.

"So I understand."

Chivington issued a few orders that sent his staff officers scurrying off. When we were alone, he turned again to me. "Those Indians of yours," he said. "How many men are there?"

"A thousand or so, when they're all in."

"What have they got for weapons?"

"Bows and arrows; a few old hunting rifles."

He nodded. "And they'll do just as you say?"

"I guarantee it."

"Bring them in close to the fort then. See that they stay there." He glanced at me with a trace of suspicion. "That's an order, Wynkoop!"

"I'll carry it out, Colonel."

"That's the spirit!" He laughed. "You know, you've got Major Downing worried! He can't figure you out! 'Don't worry, Downing!' I tell him.

481

'Wynkoop's my boy! I was the one who promoted him and gave him the command at Lyon. Wynkoop's a good soldier.' "

He laid a heavy hand on my shoulder. "Well, boy," he said, "we've got work to do. Good luck, if I don't see you again."

ALL THE WAY HOME the country was healthy again. The crops were harvested; smoke curled up from the chimney of every sod house; many wagon trains passed us on the road. For the news had traveled before us that the governor and the chiefs had agreed on the terms of peace.

For the chiefs too, our return to Lyon was a homecoming. On the afternoon of our arrival I sought out Black Kettle. "I want you to bring all your people in," I said, "where I can watch over them." He nodded. Taking a blanket and some dried meat, he rode away. One week later, three hundred lodges were standing a mile or so to the west of the fort.

So we lived through the autumn, side by side. The young warriors set out with my permission to hunt buffalo. The women worked, tanning the few hides their men had taken. The old people sat quietly in the autumnal sun. They knew that they were at our mercy; they showed no fear.

They asked for nothing, yet as I rode through their village I could see many signs of distress. The blankets that the women wore were ragged; the pole frames bore few strips of meat. I had no authorization to feed and to clothe the Indians. But twice in the course of October I issued rations for them—bacon, flour, coffee, sugar, a little salt. Say what you will about my rashness—throughout the autumn, from the Arkansas to the Platte rivers, there was not one instance of an Indian attacking a white. A kind of serenity settled on the plains.

In the north, to be sure, the Sioux were gathering. To the south the Kiowas, Comanches, and Apaches had yet to be subdued. But with the Cheyennes and Arapahoes, the holders of the middle ground, as allies, I was certain that we could end the Indian wars.

Only the authorization of the army was lacking. And by a twist of fortune, it was hard to obtain. Fort Lyon was a part of Colorado. Yet it was taken from the military district of Colorado and given to a new district in Kansas, whose commander, General Curtis, was stationed four hundred miles away. On the day after I returned to Lyon, I wrote out a full report for Curtis. In the closing days of October I looked each day for the mail coach that would bring the general's reply.

The reply came on the second of November. The usual crowd gathered at Lyon to greet the coach. It came to a halt; the door opened. The last passenger took his time in appearing. He was a soldier, Scott Anthony, a dandy in peacetime, and now, like myself, a major.

He looked around and saw me; he waited for me to come to him. "What brings you to Lyon?" I began as I approached. "I thought you—"

He cut me short. "Not here."

We walked across the parade ground, talking of inconsequential matters. He talked on in my office. And all the time his eyes were roving over my furnishings. When his appraisal was completed he turned to me. He handed me an army order. "Rough luck, Wynkoop," he said.

The order was from General Curtis. Rumors had reached headquarters that I had issued supplies to hostile Indians, in direct violation of orders. I was, therefore, relieved of my command and ordered to Kansas to explain my unmilitary conduct. Major Scott Anthony was appointed commanding officer of Fort Lyon in my place.

I EMPTIED OUT the desk. I called in the officers of the post. I presented them to their new commander, but I chose not to attend Major Anthony's meeting with them the following morning. Cramer told me Anthony began in a forceful manner. His predecessor, he said, had acted irresponsibly; sound policies would be promptly restored. Indians of all tribes were enemies, and would once more be treated as enemies. They were to be driven from the vicinity of the fort. If they wished to fight, then we would give them the thrashing they deserved. And so on. When he had finished, Anthony asked if there were any questions.

"I have no questions," Soule said. "But I do have one comment: you are committing a breach of faith!"

Anthony demanded a retraction; Soule stood fast. The argument mounted until Anthony threatened to have Soule arrested, but the other officers intervened, saying they'd resign if he pressed charges against Soule. Anthony shifted his ground, dismissing the meeting and busying himself in administrative details.

After two days, Anthony asked me to go with him to meet the chiefs. I requested permission to say a few words to them and he granted my request. "I am no longer chief at Fort Lyon," I told them. "Major Anthony is in command now. There is nothing I can do for you anymore. I ask you now to do as Major Anthony says."

The chiefs conferred; one or two, I think, dissented. But in the end

Black Kettle spoke for all of them. "We trust Major Wynkoop. We will do as he says."

I thanked them.

Anthony had brought along a black book in which he kept his notes. He opened it and began. "First, I wish to know, for what purpose are the Indians camped near the fort?"

"For peace," Black Kettle answered.

"I think not." Anthony glanced at his book. "No body of armed men may camp near an army post. You are forbidden to remain unless it is understood that in all respects you are prisoners of war. All of your weapons must be surrendered at once."

"We will surrender them."

"All of the stock which once belonged to the whites must be given up, forthwith."

"We will give up the stock."

"We shall see!" Anthony shut his book with a snap and returned to the fort.

The next day winter came. The skies lowered; toward dusk snow fell; in the morning it lay heavy on the plains.

At noon, Anthony called the chiefs into the fort. "Many bad reports were given to me about you," he told them. "I came here expecting that we would have a fight. I see now that the reports were wrong and that you are ready to live as prisoners. But I have no authority as yet to give you prisoners' rations. So I want you to leave the fort.

"I want you to go to Sand Creek and stay there. However, your young men may go out hunting buffalo. I will see to it that all the promises made to you by Major Wynkoop are kept."

The chiefs conferred; Black Kettle spoke for them. "Since you wish it, we will go to Sand Creek."

I was reassured. I told Black Kettle, "You can trust Major Anthony."

Black Kettle shook his head. "Major Anthony has red eyes. We do not like his eyes."

For the rest of the day the Indians dismantled their lodges. They set out through the snow; warriors and women, children and old men. I rode beside them a mile or so, then dismounted and gripped Black Kettle in an awkward embrace. I said in his language, "I thank you for all things."

He answered in English: "I cannot appreciate you enough."

On my last night at the fort, a knocking sounded at my door. The officers of the post stood outside. Soule carried a bottle, Cramer an armful of glasses. We celebrated as best we could.

At the end of the evening, as a parting present, Soule handed me two dispatches, neatly bound. The first was a letter signed by the settlers of the Arkansas Valley. They thanked me for preventing bloodshed; they praised me for doing what was "right, politic and just."

The second dispatch was also in the form of a letter. It noted that my course of action had saved the lives of hundreds of men, women, and children, adding that Indians and whites in the valley were now living peaceably side by side. It ended with the hope that I would soon be restored to my command. It was signed Joseph A. Cramer, and undersigned by every officer on the post—with one exception. But Soule held out a third dispatch, saying, "And now a special surprise for General Curtis."

It was an endorsement of the second letter, by Major Scott Anthony. He ended, "I think Major Wynkoop acted for the best in this matter."

As the others left, Cramer said, "Tomorrow is the twenty-sixth of November. The hundred days of the Third Regiment are up."

"They may still be in the field."

"There's been no whisper of them, nothing at all."

Early in the morning the eastbound coach was ready to leave the fort. A crowd of troopers stood in silence as we left. They helped Louisa and our son into the coach. I mounted my horse and an escort of sixteen men lined up behind me; we moved off. I rode in silence, a captive of apathy and bitterness, toward the long, dun-colored horizons of Kansas.

TWO WEEKS LATER I stood before General Curtis. He seemed half as tall as I was, and ten times as fierce. He peppered me with questions. Before long his real reason for depriving me of my command at Lyon became clear. It was that I had taken the chiefs to Chivington and not to him. I cited my reasons, good reasons, and he seemed content.

Curtis read the letters that Cramer had given me and looked up. "You seem to have a great many friends. You say it was Chivington who told Black Kettle to bring his people to Lyon?"

Hope stirred in me. "Yes, sir."

"Who was it who sent them to Sand Creek?"

"Major Anthony, sir." The question struck me as odd, since I had not mentioned Sand Creek.

"So Black Kettle was obedient," Curtis said. "He and his people were reconciled to being prisoners of war."

"They still are, sir."

"They were truly peaceful? They would not have attacked us in the spring?"

"General, if you will give me back my command, I will answer personally for Black Kettle and every member of his band."

I was startled by the air of pity in Curtis' face. "You've been on the road," he said. "You haven't heard." He searched among his papers, found a telegram, and handed it to me. It was headed, *In the field on Big Bend of Sand Creek, Colorado Territory, November 29, 1864.* It read:

> Sir: I have not the time to give you a detailed history of our engagement of today, in one of the most bloody Indian battles ever fought on these plains. We made a forced march of forty miles, and surprised, at break of day, one of the most powerful villages of the Cheyenne nation, killing the celebrated chiefs One Eye, White Antelope, and Black Kettle, with about five hundred of their people, destroying all their lodges and equipage, making almost an annihilation of the entire tribe.
>
> I shall leave here, as soon as I can see our wounded safely to Fort Lyon, for the villages of the Sioux, which are reported about eighty miles from here, and three thousand strong; so look out for more fighting. I will state, for the consideration of gentlemen who are opposed to fighting these red scoundrels, that I was shown the scalp of a white man taken from the lodge of one of the chiefs, which could not have been more than two or three days taken; and I could mention many more things to show how these Indians, who have been drawing government rations at Fort Lyon, are and have been acting.
>
> Very respectfully, your obedient servant,
> J. M. Chivington

Chapter 3

FOR A TIME AFTER MY INTERVIEW with General Curtis, I saw little but the dirt at my feet. Cursing my blindness; cursing my simple faith. Cramer had warned me; Colley had warned me; even Chivington's actions were revealing, if only I had understood. I understood now his confident air when I last saw him at Camp Weld; I had brought the Indians in and laid them like a sacrifice at his feet.

The only purpose left for me was to halt Chivington. Only if the truth were known about Sand Creek could he be weakened. And the truth, I knew, would never be brought out. The War Department and the President would receive only the reports that Chivington wrote. The people would read only the dispatches that he forwarded to the press. Chivington had betrayed me and beaten me; I was beaten as thoroughly as any man he had left lying in the ring.

Then one evening as I lay in my room, a letter arrived. It was from Cramer. He had witnessed all that had happened at Sand Creek and made it plain that Chivington and his men had committed crimes there as terrible as any ever before committed by soldiers wearing the uniform of the United States. He conceded that he himself had obeyed orders and taken part in the fighting, but added that Soule, at the risk of his own life, had defied Chivington and forbidden his men to fight.

It was true, Cramer said, that Black Kettle and the other chiefs had been killed. It was for us to pay the debt owed to them. Speaking for the officers of the Second Battalion, Cramer promised that if I could bring about an investigation into Chivington's conduct, they would testify to the whole story. In his precise way, Cramer told me what to do.

I copied out his letter many times and sent the copies to all the men in high places whose names he had provided.

The mails moved swiftly to Washington; the year had not come to its end when my orders came. I was reassigned as commanding officer to Fort Lyon and instructed to report to the War Department upon conditions among the Indians with particular reference to the recent conduct of Colonel Chivington.

I hurried off with the good news to Louisa. She looked at me, bewildered. I handed her my orders. She read them slowly and looked at me again, trying to smile. I took it for granted at the time that she was glad. Now, as I write, I see that the news came to her as a bitter disappointment. She had shared in my defeat and my humiliation. She had at the same time nourished a secret hope that once my ties to Fort Lyon were broken, I would resign my commission and return to Pennsylvania, to the comfort of my father's house. There she would regain all the things she had grown up with: silver on the table; a bath, a basin even, with soft water to wash her hair in; friends who shared her interests; days without worry and nights without fear. She longed for these things; they were a part of her womanhood and her pride. But no torture would have forced her to confess her longing. She stood for a moment, then turned away, hiding her tears, and began to pack our few belongings.

In the depth of winter we set out. The sky was leaden; the plains were lifeless. The few settlers we met at the way stations were once again oppressed by dread. They knew, as I did, that to the north the Indians were arming for revenge. Once again they spoke of abandoning their homesteads, and this time I could not reassure them.

When we came to Lyon, the troops were waiting, but Soule and Cramer were not among them. Neither was Anthony. Filled with loathing, I went to the office and handed him my orders, as he had handed his to me.

He stared at them, words spilling out of him. He cursed Chivington as a double-crosser and a coward. "Chivington promised me he would go on from Sand Creek to give the Sioux the same treatment," he said, rising. "Then he turned and ran. By God, if I see him again I'll . . ."

"You'll see him," I said, "in court." I moved past him to my desk.

Anthony went on. "You think you'll bring him to court? Well, I hope you do! But I warn you, he'll lie on a stack of Bibles about the so-called Battle of Sand Creek. He'll lie about you and Soule. He'll lie about the Indians. He'll swear that he found fresh scalps of white women in their tepees. All lies. There wasn't a white scalp in all the village; not one."

ONE BY ONE THE MEN who were left at Lyon came to my office to tell their stories. Soule and Cramer, the two men I needed most, were in Denver, but John Smith described the morning of the massacre. "When the troops approached," he said, "I saw Black Kettle hoist the American flag over his lodge as well as a white flag. . . ."

Smith faltered there, and I did not press him. Others were waiting to pick up the story. In no time I was able to reconstruct, hour by hour, all that had taken place after my departure from the fort.

Soule had been the first man to encounter Chivington at that time. On the day after I left Lyon, Soule led a scouting party of twenty men in search of the Sioux, who had sent a challenge to Lyon from their stronghold on the Smoky Hill River. Soule rode through the night. As the moon set, he had still found no trace of the Sioux. Then up from the lowlands came the thousand soldiers of the Third Regiment. At the head of the long column, Chivington rode on a huge black mule, with Downing and Shoup riding beside him. He ordered Soule's men to fall into line; he summoned Soule to his side. Soule took it for granted that Chivington had come to lead a strike against the Sioux.

Chivington did not look at Soule, but he asked many questions. At last he was satisfied that no one at Lyon knew of his approach. "Where are the hostiles?" he said.

"On the Smoky Hill, Colonel; we understand they—"

"I am speaking of the Cheyennes."

"Black Kettle's band? On Sand Creek, where we sent them."

"Where exactly on Sand Creek?"

"On the Big Bend, Colonel; but they are not hostiles, they—"

Chivington had turned to his guide, an old man, Negro by birth and Indian by adoption. "You know the place, Beckwourth?"

The guide nodded. Then Chivington turned back to Soule. "How many are there at this moment?"

"Nine hundred; women and children mostly. The men are out hunting; they went with our—"

"I think you said plundering, Captain. They are out plundering white men's property, are they not?"

"They are hunting buffalo, with our permission," Soule said. "They are our prisoners of war."

"Prisoners, are they?" one of Chivington's officers replied. "They won't be prisoners for long!"

Chivington kicked his mule into motion. He waved for the column to follow.

"You're going to attack the Cheyennes!" Soule shouted to Chivington. "But you can't! They're our prisoners of war, unarmed and . . ."

Chivington turned. "No captain gives orders to Colonel Chivington! No Indian lover tells Chivington what he may do!" Then he called for fifty men. "We're riding ahead," he told Shoup. "You can follow. Hold the captain until you reach the fort. If he tries to escape, place him in irons. Report to me in Major Anthony's office." Lashing his mule, he cantered off toward Lyon.

WHEN SOULE REACHED Fort Lyon it was ringed by a cordon of Chivington's men. No one was allowed out. Soule had been in the saddle for twenty-seven hours. He dismounted and ran to Anthony's quarters.

Anthony was instructing his officers on the expedition to come. Soule's and Cramer's companies and one other would form a battalion under Anthony. Nothing was to be said to the troops about the purpose of the expedition, but the officers could be told. The challenge of the hostiles had been accepted; Colonel Chivington had come to lead a combined force against the Sioux.

"You are lying," Soule told Anthony, "or else you are deceived if you think you're going to the Smoky Hill. You are going to attack Sand Creek!"

Anthony said calmly, "Yes, we shall clean up Sand Creek on the way." An uproar followed.

"First," Cramer said, "Colonel Chivington's term of service has expired. Unless he has reenlisted, he has no authority to command troops."

"He has orders from Leavenworth," Anthony answered.

"Second, Fort Lyon is not in Chivington's district. He has no right to take command here, except with your consent."

"He has my consent."

"To attack Black Kettle? His band are prisoners of war, under your protection."

"They are Indians; they deserve whatever they get."

"One hundred and thirty men in your command," Cramer reminded Anthony, "owe their lives to Black Kettle. In turn, every one of us is bound by the commitment Major Wynkoop made."

Anthony smiled. "I am certainly not responsible for what Wynkoop may have said."

"Oh yes you are! You told the chiefs you would carry on his policy!"

"A pledge given to a savage," Anthony said, "is not the same as one given between civilized men."

"Murder," Soule said. "You are ordering us to murder men who saved our lives."

"We want to talk to Colonel Chivington," Cramer said.

Anthony looked at the officers. He gave in. "Those of you who wish to see Colonel Chivington," he said, "may report here at seven. But you"— he turned to Soule—"stay away!"

At seven, the officers of Lyon returned to Anthony's office. He was working at his desk with Downing seated at his side. Behind them Chivington stood, marking each face as the officers entered the room.

Anthony made certain that all preparations were completed for the expedition. Then his manner shifted. "I now repeat what I first told you. Our objective is to thrash the Sioux at the Smoky Hill."

"Do you mean," Cramer said skeptically, "that we are not going to Sand Creek?"

"We are going by way of Sand Creek," Anthony said. "When we get there we will surround the village. We will call the chiefs out. We will kill a few criminals and hotheads and spare the rest. Our purpose is to save the chiefs from their own enemies. Now, since there are no more questions, this conference—"

"I have one more question," Cramer told Anthony. "When you went with Major Wynkoop to see Black Kettle—"

Chivington interrupted. "Wynkoop is a fool! Bringing red rebels into Denver! Forcing Evans to get down to them on bended knee!"

At that, two other officers spoke up for me.

Chivington looked at them intently. "I see Wynkoop has infected more than one man with his poison. But tomorrow I shall be watching. If any officer hangs back"—he picked up a volume of army regulations from the desk and shook it—"desertion in the face of the enemy; remember that!"

Cramer broke in. "Major Anthony, you're bound in God's name, your oath to Black Kettle—"

"In God's name!" Chivington's roar left every man stunned. "You invoke God's name, for them? They are godless savages. And God Almighty justifies every means the white man can devise for wiping them from the face of the earth! I am in command here. All of you are under my orders. I order you now to assemble your companies!"

THE TROOPS ASSEMBLED in the darkness. Soule and Cramer answered for their companies. They wheeled and followed Anthony out of the fort behind the Third Regiment. Chivington led the column north. The sky was clear and the moon full; the trail was plain that led to Sand Creek.

The men rode in silence, numbed by the wind. At dawn they came to the long descent that ends at the Big Bend of Sand Creek. The creek flows from the northwest into the bend, beneath high bluffs. Black Kettle's village lay within the bend, blind to the approach of the soldiers.

In the village a dog barked. Chivington drew his saber and roared out his command. He ordered his troops to surround the village and destroy it, to fire on everyone who moved within it, and to let no one escape.

The soldiers of the Lyon battalion crossed the creek, dismounted, and stood with rifles ready. Chivington's men massed on both sides of them, firing wildly and without effect. In the village there were sounds of women wailing, and a few warriors chanting their war songs. Black Kettle moved swiftly to raise the American flag and the white flag of surrender above his lodge. Chivington drove his men on. Anthony, in turn, ordered the Lyon battalion to open fire. Cramer passed the order on to his company; Soule defied it, motioning his men back.

The firing from the Third Regiment never slackened. White Antelope strode toward Chivington, holding his arm high in the peace sign, crying in English, "Stop!" An officer shouted an order; the old chief paused. He folded his arms and chanted his death song: "*Nothing lives long except the earth and the mountains. . . .*"

The troopers knelt and fired. "I saw a medal bounce on the old man's chest," one trooper told me; "then he fell on his face."

From then on the women and children moved out of the village and up the creek. The troops shot them down as they fled. It was no battle. There were one hundred men at most in the village—men too young, too old, or too infirm to go buffalo hunting. Some of them climbed up the bluffs and with arrows held a regiment back. Chivington swore they caused all his casualties; again he was lying. The Cheyennes killed four soldiers in all; the rest of Chivington's casualties were caused by his own men firing into one another as they encircled the village.

Anthony ordered Soule to lead his men toward the northwest. There, for four miles along the creek, the killing had continued as the Indians fled, with the troops of the Third Regiment firing upon them. At last the Indians broke up and scattered, a mother going one way, her children another. The troops pursued them over the frozen plain. Soule and his squadron rode beside the Indians, more as escorts than as enemies.

By mid-afternoon the firing had lapsed to occasional shots. Soule returned to the village, where the soldiers had started on a new assignment: they were looting the lodges, bearing off everything of value.

On the bluffs Chivington sat on his mule, flushed with victory. He summoned Soule to his side. "Well?" he cried, waiting for Soule's praise. Soule turned his horse and moved off. Chivington called after him, "We gained a great victory! You are a part of it!"

"You committed a great crime," Soule answered, "and we are no part of it."

Chivington persisted. "You were in the fighting."

Soule shook his head. "I and my men have not fired a shot at the Indians all day, thank God."

ON THE NIGHT OF THE MASSACRE dogs roamed over the battleground. All night they roamed, howling, among the dead. There were no burials. Chivington wanted the Indian dead to lie forever where they had fallen, as proof of the white man's mastery. He and his men slept soundly on the bluffs above the creek. At noon the next day a report reached Chivington that the Sioux were moving against him from the northwest. Then Chivington stirred. He loaded his wagons with plunder; he ordered Cramer to raze the village. He sent Soule and twenty men in pursuit of a band of Arapahoes. At the head of his fighting column, Chivington rode off—to the southeast, back to Lyon.

Chivington stayed on at Lyon for three days, writing his dispatches for the newspapers, while his men drank and his officers sold off the Indian ponies they had stolen. Then on the night before they left for Denver, the officers of the Third Regiment held a victory celebration. At the end of the evening, Major Downing asked for silence. He raised his glass to Chivington. calling him "General" and "Senator . . ."

Chivington bowed. He thanked Almighty God for giving him the strength to crush his country's enemies. He predicted that they, and their friends, would never rise again. He laughed and slapped Downing on the back, saying, "The little man's right! This will put stars on my shoulders! This will take me to the Senate—beyond the Senate! No one can stop Chivington now!"

At noon on the next day the Third Regiment assembled, its plunder loaded, its banners flying, and rode off in triumph to Denver.

ALL THIS WAS TOLD to me by the troopers of Lyon who came to my office to be questioned. I had the testimony copied out for the use of the War Department. I felt as I read it over that nothing remained in doubt.

Then early in January a half-breed slipped into Lyon. He told me that eighty Indian men and one hundred and twenty women and children had died of wounds received at Sand Creek, but he insisted that Black Kettle had escaped and was summoning all the Indian nations to war.

I sent the evidence I had gathered to the War Department, together with my report. My action, I was certain, would make inevitable a full investigation of Sand Creek. Where and when it would take place, I did not know. I waited impatiently, questioning every traveler and seizing from the mail coach every issue of the *Rocky Mountain Daily News*.

The first paper that I read was filled with Chivington's own account of his victory. In later issues I read of the triumphant return of the Third Regiment; the parades and the speeches; the nightlong celebrations. Chivington's domination of the Territory seemed to be assured; his further rise in the nation was foreseen. Petitions were circulated to send him to the Senate—so the newspapers said.

In the midst of all this activity, an item no bigger than a thumb appeared in the *News*. It was from Washington, and it reported that as a result of letters received from certain high officials in Colorado, there would shortly be commenced an investigation into the recent affair near Fort Lyon. A second small item announced that a Military Commission of Inquiry would shortly convene in Denver to investigate Sand Creek, and that its chairman would be Lieutenant Colonel Samuel Tappan.

I remembered Tappan as a journalist and an Abolitionist. He had been cast aside as leader of the First Colorado Cavalry in Chivington's favor and would be filled with hatred of him, as I was, but he could not for a moment stand up against him. I thought of leaving at once for Denver but decided against it. Instead, I wrote to Tappan offering him my assistance; I hung on at Lyon, waiting and scanning the *News*. There, early in February, I read that Tappan had arrived in Denver to organize the Inquiry. A week later I found an item about Soule. "Captain Soule," it said, "is a witness who expects to testify before the Court of Inquiry. Hence he is shot at, at night, in the outskirts of Denver."

I knew then that I could not go on waiting until Tappan summoned me, nor could I count on the men whose affidavits I had taken. The main burden of the testimony would fall on Soule, Cramer, and me. But if I was to be a witness, I would first have to go to Sand Creek.

I set out in the darkness with twenty men. When the day came up at last, there was no color on the plains. A raw wind scraped the ridges. At nightfall we camped above Sand Creek. It was too dark to see beyond the bluffs. But the next morning we could see clearly enough.

I had thought that the Indians would have returned to bury their dead, for the ceremony was sacred to them, and a matter of pride. Certainly they could not have stayed away out of fear. For their own reasons they had chosen, with Chivington, to let the evidence stand. And it stood, preserved by the cold of the winter: the ruins of the village, the dead lying where they had fallen, some with knees or elbows raised, as if to ward off blows. On the edge of the settlement two ponies grazed in the still morning and I saw, moving feebly, the last of the dogs.

I SET OUT FOR DENVER in February with half a dozen men. It was dark when we clattered into the familiar yard of the Half Way House. I walked alone to the door and knocked. At once it was torn open. Coberly's daughter stood there, wild with delight, and then, at the sight of me, crestfallen. "I thought you were Captain Soule," she said.

"He's in Denver."

"I know that—but he's coming back for me. We're to be married!"

"Soule, marrying? I doubt that!"

Coberly had come up behind her. "It's true. Captain Soule's changed," he said. "He came through here a few weeks ago and he seemed like another man." Coberly's daughter had followed Soule to Denver.

"We'd be married by now," the girl said, "but for the Inquiry."

She told me that Tappan had asked Soule to be his first witness, and Soule had agreed. He went to the girl and tried to break off the marriage; she refused. She consented only to postpone the wedding until Soule completed his testimony. In turn, Soule promised that if she would return to the Half Way House and wait there, he would come for her as soon as he was free. "So, when you came to the door, I thought . . ."

"You mean that the Inquiry has been going on?"

Coberly sent his daughter to get our supper. "Who knows if there will be an inquiry?" he said. "Can you see Chivington obeying a summons from Sam Tappan?"

"He'd better," I said. "Tappan may not be much, but he represents the government of the United States."

"The government is two thousand miles away. You may have friends in Washington. But you're on your own in Denver if you testify against Chivington and the Third Regiment. Ten days ago there was a rally to protest the Inquiry, and Chivington told the crowd he believed in action, not speeches. He swore that there was five hundred dollars in his wallet for anyone who would bring in a dead Indian or a dead white man who took the Indian side."

As I left early the next morning, Coberly's daughter was at the front door. "You'll be seeing him! Tell him I'm waiting!" she said. "Oh, why can't you take his place as the chief witness? You started it all!"

"They wouldn't let me. I wasn't at Sand Creek."

"You think he's in danger, don't you?"

"He's been in far greater danger."

"That doesn't mean that he's safe," she said. "A traveler came through from Denver last week. He said that shots were fired from ambush, and that Captain Soule barely escaped."

Beyond her head I could see the troopers waiting. I tried to edge past her. "Tell him," she said, holding me back, "that I can't live apart from him any longer! Tell him that if he cares for me at all he'll—" She broke off. "You're not going to tell him," she said. I shook my head.

WE HURRIED ON and came to Denver at the end of the day. I found Soule in the small boardinghouse where he was staying. I learned from him that the Inquiry was about to begin, and that he would be the first to testify. I mentioned my misgivings about Tappan, and he cut me short. "We were wrong about Tappan," he said.

We sat talking and drinking; it was some time before I remembered I had a message to deliver. "Coberly's daughter wants you to know that she's waiting for you," I said.

Soule looked greatly troubled. "What am I to do?"

"Marry her, of course!" Soule's question sounded foolish.

It seemed less foolish when I learned, from Soule, Tappan, and Cramer, all that had taken place before my arrival in Denver.

It had been late in January when Tappan slipped into Denver. For two days he worked alone. Then he sent word to Soule to visit him, under cover of night. He questioned Soule closely on every aspect of his story. He took notes on the answers and compared them with my transcripts. He showed no feeling until he closed his notebook. Then he said, "Let someone give me a sword, that I may kill this monster."

"We will convene in twelve days," he told Soule. "We will call up our witnesses, and they will testify. Then we will turn them over to Colonel Chivington and his counsel for cross-examination. Afterward he will present his side. He has many witnesses; we have few. That is why the first witness is all-important. If he tells the truth and stands on the truth, it can never be refuted. You are to be the first witness."

"There are dangers—" Soule began.

Tappan interrupted. "Name them."

Soule spoke then of his act of defiance at Sand Creek. "It was desertion in the face of the enemy," he said, "a crime, punishable by death."

Tappan shook his head. "The Cheyennes were prisoners of war," he said. "You committed no crime."

"There are others who would go first," Soule said. "Wynkoop, for instance."

"He was not at Sand Creek."

"Cramer, then."

"He took part in the fighting; he bears some of the guilt."

"If there were a choice . . ." Soule said.

And Tappan answered, "There is none."

Soule said nothing more. He saluted and left the room.

SOULE SPOKE to no man of his meeting with Tappan, but many men were watching him. Two days after this meeting, Soule was summoned to break up a gunfight in a cabin outside of Denver. Being Provost Marshal—for he had been assigned to duty in the city—he had to go. He set out in the dusk and rode to the ragged border of Denver. There he picked his way among the shacks. A group of people told him that the cabin he was seeking was deserted; as for a gunfight, they had heard no shots.

Soule approached the darkened cabin from the rear. As he dismounted, the back door burst open; a man darted out, fired wildly at him, and fled. Soule tried to persuade himself that the man who had waited in the cabin to kill him was not acting for Chivington. But his belief could not last long.

Soule said nothing about the effort to kill him, but the story spread. It reached Cramer, who was stationed at Camp Weld. He went to Tappan and asked to be called as first witness in Soule's place.

Tappan sent for Soule. He questioned Soule on the incident. He was searching for evidence of a master hand, and Soule had evidence. But he still said nothing.

Tappan waited. Then, "Captain," he said, "we need to understand each other. I've placed my faith in you as a witness. But there are others who can testify first and who are not in as much danger. We will build our story slowly around them. And we will come in time to you."

The next day the hotel clerk handed Tappan a note, left early in the morning. It was from Soule; it read: *I choose to be first.*

ON THE MORNING of February 13, 1865, the Military Commission convened to hear the case of Colonel J. M. Chivington. Three hundred men gathered outside the courthouse on that morning. Most of them were veterans of the Third Regiment. Standing closely together they formed a barricade, so that anyone whom they distrusted had some difficulty in entering the courthouse. Only a few of them recognized me, but they knew Soule.

The courtroom was empty when we arrived. The floor was lined with benches. At one end, in place of the judge's chair, two tables were set out for the commissioners and for Chivington. We sat in the jury box and waited. Before long Tappan and his two fellow commissioners entered and took their places. In their dress uniforms they looked imposing enough. But the junior members of the Commission were captains, low in rank and awed by the occasion. Sam Tappan, sitting between them, looked a small man. His uniform was too large for him, his hair too long. His voice was high-pitched and his hands were nervous.

For twenty minutes or more the commissioners waited. Then a shout went up in the street. We heard cheering; Chivington strode into the courtroom, followed by Downing. The crowd flooded in after him—filling up the benches, standing in the empty spaces, blocking doorways and halls. Tappan seized his gavel and pounded upon the table; the crowd laughed. At last Chivington held up his hand; the crowd fell silent.

Tappan stood up and read out the official order defining the purposes of the Commission and its powers. The Commission was directed to determine who were the aggressors at Sand Creek, and whether the campaign was directed by Colonel Chivington in accordance with the recognized rules of civilized warfare.

Chivington listened as Tappan read the order. Then he rose and, speaking in a voice a full octave below Tappan's, warned the commissioners that they were acting illegally. He told them to take no further action until his formal protest had been filed.

Tappan overruled Chivington's objections, and the Commission continued its work. The youngest member, George Stilwell, was appointed recorder for the proceedings. Then Tappan called for the first witness and Soule moved toward the stand. But Chivington barred the way. He challenged the Commission again, on the ground that Tappan was prejudiced. "For a long time Lieutenant Colonel Tappan has been my open and avowed enemy," he said.

At that, all of Chivington's supporters stood up and shouted, hoping to bring the Inquiry to an end. Tappan waited until the shouting died away, then declared that the session was adjourned until the following morning.

The next day was spent in legal wrangling. Tappan replied to Chivington's objections, and the Commissioners dismissed them, one by one. At last the way was cleared for the investigation. Soule was called to the stand without objection and sworn in.

Tappan asked Soule the preliminary questions.

"Your full name, age, and rank in the army?"

"Silas Soule; twenty-six years of age; Captain, Company D, Veteran Battalion, First Colorado Cavalry."

"In September of last year did you accompany Major Wynkoop's command to an Indian camp on the Smoky Hill?"

"I did."

Tappan spoke in a thin monotone. Chivington watched Soule without moving; on the bald dome of his head sweat began to shine.

Tappan led Soule on, through the meeting in the Big Timbers, the journey to Denver, the council at Camp Weld. Soule spoke of the governor's hesitation, and of the conditions which Chivington told the chiefs they must carry out if they wanted peace.

Tappan asked, "Did the Indians in council manifest a desire for peace, and a willingness to comply with the conditions of Colonel Chivington?"

Soule answered, "They did."

"What was the understanding with the Indians?"

"They were to be protected by the troops," Soule answered.

Tappan moved on. "Were you at Fort Lyon on or about the twenty-seventh of November? If so, what happened on that day?"

"I was there," Soule continued. He described the night when he rode out to intercept the Sioux and instead encountered Chivington, leading his column up the road from Denver. He spoke of Chivington's questions concerning the whereabouts of the Cheyennes.

Tappan asked, "What answer did you make?"

Soule spoke slowly. "I said that there were some Indians camped near the fort, but that they were not dangerous, they were considered prisoners. And someone said," Soule added, "that they would not be prisoners for long."

The following morning on the stand Soule spoke of the night ride to Sand Creek; the day of fighting; the dead.

"Have you been at Sand Creek since that day?" Tappan asked.

"I went to Sand Creek on the last of December," Soule testified. "I saw sixty-nine dead Indians."

Chivington shuddered; his neck swelled and darkened. A murmur stirred in the courtroom. In his official reports to the War Department, Chivington had stated that he had left between five hundred and six hundred dead Indians lying on the battlefield.

At the end of the day Tappan asked, "Did any of the Indians advance toward Colonel Chivington's command making signs that they were friends?"

"I saw them advance toward the line," Soule answered. "Some of them were holding their hands up."

Tappan glanced at Chivington. He asked, "Were the women and children shot while trying to escape, by Colonel Chivington's command?"

"They were," Soule answered, but his words were lost. Chivington struck the table before him with his fist. "I've had enough of this!" he cried. "I want it ended, now!"

Tappan waited. When the courtroom was still, he asked if the recorder had heard the last response of the witness. Stilwell was not sure.

"Then let me repeat," Tappan said. "Were the women and children followed while trying to escape, shot down and scalped, and otherwise mutilated, by any of Colonel Chivington's command?"

"They were," Soule said.

Chivington thrust his chair back. He stood, heaving. "You want to destroy me!" he cried.

Tappan was never more calm. He asked Soule, "Were any efforts made by the commanding officers, Colonels Chivington and Shoup, and Major Anthony, to prevent these mutilations?"

Soule waited. "Not that I know of," he said.

Throughout the next morning, Tappan rounded off his questions. At last he declared that he had finished. Soule was turned over to Chivington and Downing for cross-examination.

For three days Chivington questioned Soule. He went over every line of Soule's testimony, probing for inconsistencies. Through his questions Chivington gave his version: that I had acted without authority in going to the Big Timbers, that I had endangered the lives of my men and had presented treacherous enemies as loyal friends. All this Chivington read into the record, but he gained no support from Soule. Chivington moved on to question him about the fighting. Soule held to his story, conceding nothing. At the end of the third day, Chivington motioned to Soule to leave the witness stand. Soule stepped down.

The sheafs of yellow paper—one hundred and seven pages of them— lay stacked on the table: the story of Sand Creek, for the President of the United States and his Cabinet to consider. Whatever happens to us, I thought, the truth is there, intact.

The rest of our testimony was all in support of Soule. I took up the argument in my turn and left the stand, as I thought, unscathed. In the presence of resistance, Chivington seemed at a loss. He insisted that Black Kettle was a merciless enemy; we who had been at Black Kettle's mercy were there in the courtroom to prove him wrong.

It seemed to me that for Soule the danger had passed. Although the Inquiry would continue for weeks, his testimony was taken and could not be erased. No end could be served by harming him, save vengeance. And vengeance would be an act of madness—so I told Soule. He agreed, or he seemed to agree.

Soule and Miss Coberly were married on the first of April. We gathered in the sitting room of one of the few houses in Denver where we were welcome. Soule stood by the fire; I was at his side as his best man. Cramer was there, and Tappan. We turned as Coberly led his daughter down the stairs, dressed in her mother's wedding gown and veil.

At the end of the ceremony Cramer uncorked a bottle of champagne he had brought in from Camp Weld. We gathered in a circle; I said the obvious things. I swore that dragging Soule to the altar was as hard as flogging a mule train into action. I ended with an old line: *May heaven give you many, many merry days.*

Soule, in turn, accepted my comparison of the mule train. "Only," he added, "the mules are smarter than Ned supposes." He turned to his wife. "The halter fits," he said. "I'll settle down. I'll even become a general, if you want to be a general's wife, and I'll sit at a desk. I'll live to be ninety, and die in my bed."

In the weeks that followed, Soule and his wife were busy hanging curtains and papering walls in their home. They went out only once—to the memorial service that was held in mid-April for President Lincoln.

Then a new play was to be presented at the theater. The Soules invited all their friends to a housewarming after the performance. We met at the theater. It was a dull play, but we were in high spirits as we moved with the crowd out into a night that was brilliant with stars.

We heard shots; dim at first, and then close and clear. A block from the theater two men in soldiers' coats staggered into the street as if they were drunk, and fired wildly. Someone shouted, "Soule! Captain Soule!"

Soule started off, but his wife held on to him. He turned and embraced her, speaking softly. Then, calling to the two men to wait, he ran up the street after them. His wife started to follow, but I held her back. Soule walked up to the men and asked for their weapons. One of them held out a revolver, and when Soule reached for it, fired into his chest. Soule pitched forward onto the muddy road. It was only a moment before I reached him and turned him over; he was dead.

I left him and rushed after his killers. The men clambered onto horses saddled and waiting, and pounded off beyond the last streetlight.

Soule lay in the street. The crowd kept its distance; his wife alone clung to him, wiping the mud from his face, trying to keep the warmth in his body. I lifted her from him at last and led her home. A woman, one of the neighbors, came in and took her to the bed she had shared with him.

I went back the next day; the house was crowded. The Coberlys had come to reclaim their daughter; the officers' wives had closed around her to support her, as they always do. The county coroner was also there. Officially he could make no comment on the unfortunate occurrence; unofficially he could tell us that the guilty parties were veterans and that they had escaped, with the aid of persons unknown.

The funeral was held on the following morning. I expected to find a small cluster of mourners at the church; I was mistaken. Around its walls were gathered all of the carriages that had met our column when we led the chiefs into Denver. The church was filled. Tappan was there, of course, with the officers of the First Regiment. I saw many ranchers from the country around the Half Way House. All the good people who had stayed indoors after Sand Creek had come to pay tribute to Soule and to protest his death. I saw Governor Evans, kneeling alone. Only Chivington and his followers had stayed away.

When the service ended, a procession formed outside the church; first the regimental band, then the cavalry of Company D, then the hearse, then the rest of us, riding to the cemetery in a long column. We moved off slowly, to the beat of the drums, a barren wind slicing down upon us from the mountains.

That night at dusk there was a knock on my door. A young officer introduced himself and stepped into the room. "I was at the service today," he said. "I have some information which bears upon the death of Captain Soule.

"I was assigned to Denver in March," he went on. "I was new to the district, and Captain Soule took me in hand. One day we went up to Central City and I asked him a good many questions about himself on the way. He talked freely—as if there was no one else he could talk to."

"Go on," I said.

"He spoke of his defiance of Colonel Chivington, at Sand Creek and on the witness stand. He felt he had placed himself in jeopardy. He said that he was thinking of being married and asked me if he were not doing the girl a great wrong. I replied that I could see nothing wrong in marrying, provided the man loved the girl. And he said, 'Supposing you knew that you were going to be killed?'

"I told him that he must be mistaken," the young soldier continued. "I said to him, 'No one could have any reason for killing you, least of all now.' He shook his head and said: 'They are going to kill me. And after

503

they have killed me they will blacken my character before the Commission of Inquiry. It is the only way to weaken my testimony.' "

So you knew all along, I thought. Even at your wedding you were not deceived. I set a course and never weighed the cost. You knew what the cost would be, and you paid it willingly.

CHIVINGTON WAS APPARENTLY untouched by the killing of Soule. He broke an army tradition by staying away from the funeral. He did not comply with the bare formality of calling on Soule's widow, or sending her a message of condolence. The only feeling he expressed was impatience when the Commission adjourned for two days out of respect for Soule.

Nonetheless, when the Commission reconvened, there were traces of a change in Chivington. There was a gray cast in his face and a lack of vigor in his voice. It was his turn to call his witnesses, but no one moved to the stand. Downing whispered to Chivington and handed him a sheaf of papers. Chivington heaved himself up. "Our first witness," he said, "cannot be present in person to testify. But we have his sworn evidence in a deposition we have taken. We propose to read it into the records of the Inquiry. It contains information vital to our case, bearing upon the character and credibility of a witness who testified against us."

The commissioners agreed that it should be heard. So Chivington read out his questions, and the answers of a man who was invisible, whose name none of us knew.

"State your name, age, and occupation."

"Lipman Meyer; age thirty-four years; freighter."

"Where were you on or about the first day of December 1864?"

"I was on the Arkansas, about thirty miles east of Fort Lyon."

Meyer swore that he had met Soule on the Arkansas, and that he had persuaded Soule to ride to the rescue of his embattled wagon train. Soule led his column south, until he saw smoke rising from the train. Then he turned back—or so Meyer testified.

Why did Soule turn back? Chivington read Meyer's answer. "He was afraid."

At those words I was back listening to the young officer describe the journey to Central City with Soule. "They will kill me," Soule had said, "and after they kill me they will blacken my character." Within two weeks of his death, the second part of Soule's prophecy had come true.

Of all the charges that could be brought against Soule, cowardice was the most unjust. There were murmurs of anger in the courtroom.

Chivington read on: "What was Captain Soule's condition on this expedition, intoxicated or not?"

"I should judge him to be drunk, judging from his actions."

"In what condition was he when his command went into camp that night on the Arkansas?"

"He was drunk."

Most of us in the courtroom were too sickened to stir. Tappan alone covered his pad with furious strokes. Chivington read on in a dull monotone. As if cowardice, drunkenness, and dereliction of duty were not enough, he added a last charge, robbery, against Soule.

"Did you have any blankets on that trip?"

"I had two pair of blankets stolen from me . . . by Captain Soule. . . ."

That was Meyer's story. Chivington held out the transcript to Tappan.

Tappan looked with repugnance at the sheaf of papers. "You propose to place *that* in the record?"

"Of course."

Tappan stood up, reaching the level of Chivington's chest. "Well," he said, "I object! This Commission is charged with searching out the truth. And I object to having our record fouled by lies! First," Tappan said, "this deposition has nothing to do with Sand Creek. It is utterly irrelevant to the investigation. Captain Soule was a brave officer and an honest man! He testified under oath and he submitted himself to cross-examination. And because he testified before this Commission, he was assassinated.

"It is as he said it would be," Tappan added in a low voice. "First he would be killed, because of his testimony. Then his character would be blackened before this Commission."

An uproar followed in the courtroom. Tappan took from his papers and read into the record the affidavit signed by the young officer who had visited me the night of the funeral.

It was a moment I had waited for. I watched Chivington, looking for surprise, or indignation, or guilt, or fear in his face. I saw nothing. Chivington had no conscience, no remorse, no sense of responsibility or of guilt. He had no capacity for sympathy or sorrow. Beyond the narrow realm of his own immediate desires he was without feeling.

Two weeks later the Inquiry came to an end, and the volumes of testimony were sent off to Washington. Chivington had walked out of the courtroom a free man, but broken. In time the Congress and the War

Department would both condemn him. Their words were welcome, but by the time they were published, the issue was settled. Chivington had been defeated on his own ground.

Soule's death was the turning point; from then on, opinion shifted. Doors that had been flung open for Chivington were silently closed to him; men no longer crossed the streets of Denver to shake his hand. He could not rejoin the ministry—his church would not take him. He drifted north to Laramie, then on to Ohio; there, trying in a dim way to vindicate himself, he is running for Congress. And wherever he speaks, men stand up in the audience and shout, "Sand Creek!"

Chapter 4

FROM SAND CREEK, the Indians of Black Kettle's village had stumbled north. Many froze to death or died of wounds on the way. The survivors were taken in and cared for by their hereditary enemies, the Sioux. The young braves of the village, back from their hunting, came upon the ruins of Sand Creek and followed the trails northward. With the Sioux, they plotted a war of revenge.

A thousand warriors rode out in January and sacked Julesburg, a key point on the Platte. They whipped the garrison, butchered the settlers, and fired the town. Then they fanned out, tearing down telegraph wires and burning way stations. From January until October, if an Indian lost his way, he had only to climb the nearest hill. From there he could see the campfires of a dozen war parties; he could hear the throbbing of a hundred drums, beating out the rhythms of the scalp dances.

Only a few coaches ventured across the plains without an escort; one carried three veterans of the Third Regiment. Overtaken by a band of Cheyennes, the passengers pleaded for mercy. A year earlier it might have been granted. But in searching the luggage, one of the braves came upon a small scalp. Entwined in its braids he found a shell that he had woven into his son's hair. Save for this one incident, the innocent died for the guilty. Chivington had punished the Southern Cheyennes for the transgressions of the Northern Arapahoes—for no reason except that they were the same color. So, by his law, white settlers paid with their lives for Chivington's treachery.

In those months no Indian could approach a white settlement and no white man could ride near an Indian camp. But one man was able, at great risk, to cross from one side to the other: Jim Beckwourth. As a one-time chief of the Crows, he was an enemy of the Cheyennes. Yet he was outraged by the killing of women and children at Sand Creek.

In the seclusion of his cabin, Beckwourth brooded over his role in acting as a guide for Chivington that day. He listened as men around him discussed the reports of continuing Indian raids. He was close to seventy; his joints were stiff and his sight was dimming. Still, he saw what he had to do. He picked up his buckskin jacket and rode alone across the frozen plains, to the camp of the Cheyennes.

The Cheyennes knew Beckwourth as an enemy. Yet on his plea, the chiefs called in their Council to hear him. The last to enter the circle was

Black Kettle. "Why do you disturb us?" Black Kettle asked. "Have you not harmed us enough?"

"The harm is done," Beckwourth answered. "Your friends among the whites are sorry."

"We have no friends among the whites. They lied to us."

"Not all of them," Beckwourth said. "Curse Chivington all you want, but leave Wynkoop out."

"He sent us to Sand Creek," Black Kettle said. "He told us we would be safe there. We believed him. We loved him and he betrayed us."

"No," Beckwourth said, "he was betrayed."

The chiefs were silent for some time. Then Black Kettle spoke. "Our wives and our children are lying along Sand Creek," he said. "They cry out to us for revenge."

"You'll get your revenge," Beckwourth said. "The whites killed your women and children, so you'll kill their women and children. . . . And then? Are you going to kill all the whites that come onto the plains? There's no end to them."

After a time Black Kettle spoke again. "We are hunters and we are warriors," he said. "Would you have us live as paupers and as prisoners? Even as prisoners," he added, "we were not protected; we were attacked and slaughtered."

"Do as I do," Beckwourth told the chiefs. "I used to be a slave to whites. I've got cuts on my shoulders and a brand on my hip to prove it. Now I am free and I live with them, in their country, and I get along."

Black Kettle shook his head. "Our land is taken from us," he said. "Our game is gone. Our families are dead. We have nothing left to do but to die well, as our fathers died."

"There's room on the plains—" Beckwourth began.

Black Kettle cut him short. "No peace," he said, and the other chiefs in the circle echoed his words. "No peace."

Beckwourth rode back to Denver, certain that his journey had been useless. His view seemed to be confirmed when news came that war parties were raiding our settlements, and that among the raiders were some young braves of Black Kettle's band. Later we learned that they were renegades. A month or so after Beckwourth's visit, Black Kettle broke away from the Sioux and led his people eastward into Kansas.

The fighting continued, and the Indians won in every encounter; yet when the summer came, new waves of immigrants pressed across the plains and demanded protection. A new commander, General Sanborn, was sent out to Kansas with orders to punish the Indians. It seemed unlikely that Sanborn would distinguish between the warlike and the peaceful; and Black Kettle's band was the nearest to Leavenworth, and the easiest to attack.

Still, other influences were at work through the spring and summer of 1865. The country was weary of war. Within the War Department and the White House, the volumes of our Sand Creek Inquiry were read and understood. Two great men of the West, Kit Carson and William Bent, were persuaded to write to the government pleading for peace. In September the President named a commission to negotiate a new peace.

Carson, Bent, and Sanborn were members of the commission. So was General Harney. All four men were experienced in warfare; yet they possessed qualities that Chivington wholly lacked. Sanborn was trained in conciliation; Bent was a wise man; in Carson gentleness was one aspect of courage, true courage. As for Harney, he was an ardent supporter of Indian rights. A military escort under my command was appointed to lead the commissioners to the camp of the Cheyennes.

THE PLACE CHOSEN for the meeting was east of Larned, where the Little Arkansas flows into the Arkansas. Dr. Taylor, the Indian Agent at Larned, told me how to proceed. "I know these Cheyennes," he said. "They're treacherous, and they hate us. But they're scared. Take three hundred men out there and they won't stay to parley. Take one hundred, and you won't come back. So do as I say, Wynkoop; take two hundred men."

I told him that sixty troopers would make up the escort.

He shook a bony finger in my face and shouted as I walked off, "I'm warning you, Wynkoop! I'm their agent; I ought to know!"

The commissioners rode in from Leavenworth in early October. We set out along the lowlands of the Arkansas. The cottonwoods were still dark green, the days clear and dry, the nights chill. It reminded me of another journey—it was just a year since Soule and Cramer and I had led the chiefs home from Denver.

I set a slow pace in order to reassure Black Kettle, certain that his scouts were watching us. Our runners reported that Cheyennes in great numbers were settled in a grove five miles down the river. I led my column into camp on high ground and posted a heavy guard. Then I told the commissioners to stay in camp while I rode on alone.

Kit Carson reminded me of my part in bringing about Sand Creek. William Bent held that, by the ancient law of the Cheyennes, the young braves would be compelled to take my scalp. I knew the force of those arguments; I set against them my own blind sense of what was right.

It was late in the day and the light was failing when I came to the camp of the Cheyennes. I rode in slowly. I came first upon an old woman, raking the ashes of a smoldering fire. From under a ragged shawl she looked up at me. She recognized me and cried out in a high, thin wail. The sound brought other women hurrying from their lodges; they saw me and took up the cry. So I rode into the camp to the sound of keening; I had raised the dead. I rode among the lodges; the cry cut into me. Young men turned swiftly from me, as if in search of weapons. Old men bowed their heads, as if the sight of me was more than they could bear. I rode on and came to a lodge off by itself. At its entrance Black Kettle stood, waiting.

We did not shake hands. He turned as I dismounted and led the way inside. I had long since prepared my opening lines; I knew them by heart. I spoke each phrase and waited; he did not answer. Soon I had said all that I had to say about the commissioners. We sat in silence.

"We are to trust you?" he said at last. "You come with soldiers."

"Not enough soldiers," I said. "Not enough to fight."

"That is true," he said.

For the first time I felt able to look at him. He was no longer wearing his necklace of eagle bones, and his gray braids were shorn. I remembered Beckwourth's story: that Black Kettle had hacked off his hair after Sand Creek and thrown away all his medals and marks of bravery.

I said: "They claimed they had killed you."

He shook his head. "Not yet."

"But your wife?"

"She was shot, many times. . . . I found her in the creek," he added. "I carried her away."

"And your brother, White Antelope?"

"He was the first to die. He would not fight."

"Soule also," I said. "He refused to fight, and later, because he testified, they killed him."

Black Kettle looked at me steadily. After a time he asked, "Is it true? What Beckwourth said. Is it true that you did not know?"

"I knew nothing. And like a fool, I suspected nothing."

"I believed it," he said. "After Beckwourth came to us I spoke of it in our Council. I told them, 'Not all are guilty.'

"Our young men mutter against me," he said. "They say our ancestors would curse me. They will, if I am wrong again in trusting," he added. Half to himself he said, "What if I am wrong?"

THE COUNCIL MET beneath the cottonwoods. The commissioners took their places on folding chairs; the chiefs in a crescent faced them, some sitting on logs, some on old robes laid on the sandy ground. John Smith, the interpreter for the meeting, stood at one side.

The peace pipe moved without haste, for Bent and Carson were masters of all ceremony. Then Sanborn rose and made his opening speech. "I greet you in the name of the President of the United States. He is filled with sorrow. He has heard that you were attacked by his soldiers while you were at peace with him. The President believes that a great wrong was done. He has sent us to make reparation, and to establish the terms by which we can live in peace.

"We are willing to restore all of the property lost at Sand Creek, or its value. We are willing to give to the chiefs, in their own right, three hundred and twenty acres apiece, to hold forever, and to each of their children and squaws we will give one hundred and sixty acres for their own. We will recognize Black Kettle as chief of the Cheyennes. And we will support him and protect him in everything that he does for the nation.

"We ask him only to take his people away from the lines of travel, so that we may avoid fighting. We ask him to go south of the Arkansas, or north of the North Platte. If he will do that, we will protect and help him and his people, for as long as they live in peace."

The first Indian to speak was Little Raven, chief of the Arapahoes. "It will be hard for us to leave the country of our ancestors on the Arkansas. It will be hard to live where there are no buffalo. Still, we will try to settle and cultivate the land, but we will need time, and help."

"We will give you time, and all the help we can," Sanborn answered.

"Also," Little Raven said, "we will need friends among the whites; honest men."

"We are all your friends."

Little Raven shook his head. "We need them close by us, as our agents. We have been cheated by our agents. Give us a good man, and an honest man, as agent. We will need him in the winter, when our young men will be hungry, and when the whites will trouble us. Give us one such as Major Wynkoop."

There were many more speeches that day and on the following day. Black Kettle, as always, waited until the end. He rose and went to the commissioners, shaking hands with each one of them in turn. "Is it true that you come for peace?" he asked. "I believe it is true. Once before I believed it. I was mistaken, and my people died.

"Now that we are together again," the chief continued, "my shame is as great as the earth. Many wrongs have been done. We have lost our way. We need one who can teach us, and protect us, so that we will not be blamed when others do wrong. Give us one such as Major Wynkoop. He does not cheat us; he speaks the truth."

The conference ended on the afternoon of the second day. The commissioners produced, and signed, a treaty of peace. One by one the chiefs gripped the quill pen and made their marks. Within an hour the supply wagons were driven into the camp, with sacks of coffee, flour, and bacon. For the first time in a year, the Indians had enough to eat.

Early the next day we started back to Larned. Everyone felt that we were once again within reach of peace. As we came to the fort, I saw two of the Indian Agent's men loading barrels of whiskey onto a wagon, to trade with the Cheyennes.

That night when my work was over, I went to the post store for a drink. It was crowded as always; contractors and officers leaned across the bar; a few Indians were there. Someone called my name. I turned and saw General Sanborn at a corner table. "Sit down, Wynkoop," he said. "I've been wanting to talk to you. I've been writing my report for the War Department, saying that the conference was a notable step forward for the United States and that the principal credit belongs to you."

I thanked him. Next to him I saw an Indian woman, stupefied with raw liquor. Her eyes were closed; a baby writhed in her arms.

"You know, Wynkoop," Sanborn said, "you are regarded as a comer in the department. You may not know it, but you—" He broke off, sensing that I was not listening. I was watching the Indian woman; she had slid halfway to the floor. "You have been proposed for a colonelcy in the regular army," Sanborn said. "A full colonelcy, Wynkoop! The President was receptive. The Department is waiting on my report." He gripped my arm. "I have been watching you, Wynkoop, and I like you. I am going to recommend that you be made a colonel."

The woman was flat on the floor—insensible of the crowd. The baby, dislodged by her fall, crawled over her.

"You understand, Wynkoop," Sanborn said, "you'll have a regiment, a major post. In no time you'll be moving up to general rank. Do you hear me, Wynkoop? You seem to be far away."

He was right. I was thinking of Louisa, living in our crowded quarters at Lyon with our boy and our baby. I was wondering how I would explain to her what I had to do.

"LOUISA," I BEGAN while she worked at the sink, "I've been thinking . . . that we've stayed on long enough at Lyon."

"You've been promised a promotion! You've been offered a new post," she said. Eagerly she came toward me.

"It's true," I admitted.

"We'll be moving out at last! But not to Denver?"

"No, never again to Denver."

"To St. Louis then." She turned to a small mirror on the wall and brushed a strand of hair back from her face. Shy, and pleased, she glanced at me. "I'll have to buy new clothes if we're going to be stationed in St. Louis."

"We won't be going to St. Louis."

"To Leavenworth then . . . Omaha? . . . Where?"

"To Larned."

"But—Larned's no bigger than Lyon! Why would we go to Larned, when the regiment is stationed . . . ?"

"I'm leaving the regiment. I'm resigning from the army."

"Resigning?" She was lost, forlorn. "You said we were going to Larned."

"To take Taylor's place, after he's thrown out. And I'll get him thrown out before he ruins every chance of peace with his crooked, drunken . . ."

"He means well, he . . ." She stopped short. "You're going to be an Indian Agent? But agents are despised by everyone; they get almost no pay! They live on what they steal from the Indians."

"I won't."

"Why would you give up all you have for . . . ?"

"Why? Because of Soule. And because of One Eye and White Antelope and all the Indians who were killed because they trusted me. I started it all, and I have to finish it. They need me, and there's no one else."

"What about your family? Doesn't your family need you? We need

513

money, to feed the children, to clothe them! They haven't any warm clothes!"

"It's not that I don't think of you and the children. But I . . ."

"I know. You have to go to Larned. And where you go, we go."

"Louisa . . ." Words welled up in me suddenly that I had never spoken before; never felt. I blurted out that I loved her, because she had come to me when I needed her, and stayed with me; because she had given everything and taken nothing; because she had never demanded more of me than I could give. I stumbled to a halt, and she said nothing. We could not speak; we clung to each other.

Epilogue

I AM AT LARNED NOW, as agent for the Arapahoes and Cheyennes. I have been here with my family for almost three years. I think we will not be here much longer.

It is not that we want to leave. We have a house on the post; we have enough to live on—when I am paid. The climate, of course, is harsh; our children lack warm clothes. Louisa's lace collars are frayed now, her cheeks are hollow. But she has never complained. If we leave, it will not be because of Louisa. It will be because I have done all that I can do.

The control of my territory has passed back to the army. And what influence I once had with the army is gone. To the military, all civilians are suspect if they work for the Department of the Interior. I am no exception to that rule. General Hancock, the new military commander, dismisses me as a special pleader for the Indians. As for George Armstrong Custer—he declared recently that I was enriching myself at the taxpayers' expense. I read the story in a newspaper in the house next to ours—I went there to borrow a can of coffee.

My friends out here who helped me once are scattered now; or else they are dead. I would stay on nonetheless if I could talk to the Indians, but even Black Kettle has moved beyond my reach. The sad truth is, I have lost touch with the people I am supposed to protect.

For a time after we returned from the Little Arkansas, I had great hopes for peace. The treaty that we concluded was ratified by the Senate. I was appointed by the President to take it to the Indians for their final approval, and they approved it. In due course a handsome scroll arrived from Washington: Andrew Johnson, President of the United States, sent greetings, and appointed me agent for the Indians of the upper Arkansas.

I did all I could to justify the President's confidence. I soon found, however, that while the Senate might declare that the Indians were to be clothed and fed in return for taking their lands, the supplies dwindled as each official took his share on the long journey from Washington to Larned. Had we delivered to the Indians the reparations we promised them, we could have held their allegiance and started them on the road toward a settled life. Or, if we had promised them nothing, they would have tried to provide for themselves. We promised them help, and since they believed our promises, they gave up hunting. They waited for supplies that failed to come.

Each winter has been worse than the last, for the buffalo are vanishing. The Indians have had to steal cattle or else starve. The young braves chose to steal. The ranchers, of course, raised a howl, and the government gave in. It turned over the territory to young generals, fresh from victory over the Confederacy. They are impatient, self-confident men who know nothing but war.

In the spring of 1867, when the cattle were stolen, I rode out to meet Black Kettle. I told him that the thieves would have to be delivered up to me for punishment. He promised to do as I asked, but he needed time. The generals, Hancock and Custer, would not wait. They rode into my territory with their troops; they required me to go along with them. I was able to see that no one was killed, but I could not prevent them from burning Black Kettle's village. So the fear of another Sand Creek was revived among the Indians, and their destitution was deepened. When I rode out in January to visit them, I found them close to starvation.

I tried to secure the annuities that were owed to the Indians. The army, of course, opposed me and won. The result was predictable: two months ago, in August, a band of young warriors broke loose from Black Kettle's control. They burned ranches along the Saline and Solomon rivers; they killed ten white settlers.

I set out from Larned an hour after I heard the news. I knew that I had only a short time. I rode southwest. All the country around me, to the farthest horizon, was deserted. On the third day out I came to the campsite where I had last met Black Kettle. The Indians had broken camp and fled. The trail led south, away from any white settlement or road.

For the rest of that day I followed the trail. There's a faint chance, I told myself, that Black Kettle will expect me to follow him, and that he will leave scouts to watch for me. I saw nothing but the tracks beneath me, the hoofprints of the ponies, the marks of the moccasins over the bare earth. The trail then broke up into many trails. They would converge, I guessed, on the banks of the Washita River, a hundred miles on. I could not ride that far alone.

So I AM LEAVING LARNED. I cannot bring in the guilty Indians; I will not stand by here while Custer rides out to punish the innocent. I have written out my letter of resignation to go to Washington by tomorrow's coach. We shall be gone by the time the answer comes.

Where we shall go, and what I shall do, I do not know. Samuel Tappan wants me to tour the States with him, speaking on justice for the Indians. But I am no orator. Instead, I have been writing.

It was Tappan who persuaded me to write this story. He came through Larned three months ago and brought with him a copy of the transcript of our Inquiry. He looked on as I glanced over the testimony taken at so great a cost. "We can be proud of it, Ned," he said, "but it's not the whole story. Soule was our first witness. You should be the last. For you alone know the whole story, from beginning to end."

So I have written out these pages. I have set down each day's events as I remember them. It is on the larger questions that I am unsure.

Thanks to Soule, the plains will not be fashioned in Chivington's image. But have we laid the foundations of a decent civilization here in the West? The test of a civilization, so Tappan says, lies in its treatment of the less civilized. By that standard we have failed.

Was our failure certain from the start? Would it have been better for both sides if we had hoped for nothing and attempted nothing? Would it have been better, for the Cheyennes and for us, if I had never stirred from my sleep on that September afternoon when the trooper came knocking on my door?

CIMARRON

CIMARRON

A CONDENSATION OF THE NOVEL BY
Edna Ferber

ILLUSTRATED BY BART FORBES

"Anything can have happened in Oklahoma. Practically everything has," Edna Ferber wrote in her foreword to *Cimarron*. The state's development from Indian Territory to a land of oil millionaires was marked by events fantastic and improbable, yet true. Those events inspired her novel of Osage, a composite of several Oklahoma towns. Osage was home to strong-minded Sabra Cravat, who believed in its future. And home base to her adventurous husband Yancey— newspaper editor, lawyer, Rough Rider and champion duelist with a six-gun.

Edna Ferber's other works include *Giant, Saratoga Trunk, So Big* and the ever-popular *Show Boat*.

Chapter 1

ALL THE VENABLES sat at Sunday dinner. All those handsome inbred faces were turned, enthralled, toward Yancey Cravat, who was talking. The combined effect was almost blinding, but Yancey Cravat was not bedazzled. A sun surrounded by lesser planets, he gave out a radiance that dimmed the luminous circle about him.

Yancey had a habit of abruptly concluding a meal by throwing down his napkin at the side of his plate, rising, and striding about the room. It was not rudeness. His appetite satisfied, he ceased to eat. But the Venables sat hours at table, shelling almonds, sipping sherry, peeling oranges.

Though the Venables' garb was sober, being characteristic of the time—1889—and the place—Wichita, Kansas—it conveyed an impression as of richly glowing robes. This branch of the family had been transplanted from Mississippi more than two decades before, but the Midwest had failed to set her stamp upon them. There still obtained in that household many of those charming ways, remotely Oriental, that were of the South. The midday meal was, more often than not, a sort of tribal feast—sons and daughters, sons-in-law and daughters-in-law; grandchildren; visiting nieces and nephews and cousins, hosts of impecunious kin, mysteriously sprung up at the sound of the dinner bell. Unwilling émigrés, war ruined, Lewis Venable and his wife Felice had brought their dear customs with them into exile, as well as the superb mahogany oval at which they now sat.

The hot breads of the South still wrought alimentary havoc. The frying pan and the deep-fat kettle still spattered their deadly fusillade in this household. Indeed, the creamy pallor of the Venable women was less a matter of pigment than of liver. Impecunious though the family now was, three or four Negro servants went about the house, soft-footed, charming. "Rest yo' wrap?" they suggested, velvet voiced and hospitable, or "Beat biscuit, Miss Adeline?" as they proffered a fragrant plate.

Even their Kansas garden was of another latitude. Here were passion flower and wisteria and honeysuckle in season. The Kansas sunflower was a thing despised. If one so much as showed its broad face among the scented élégantes of that garden it suffered instant decapitation.

Felice Venable was not very popular with the bustling wives of Wichita. They resented her dimity wrappers, her pointed slippers, her indifference to all that went on outside her own hedge. Sheathed in the velvet of her languor was a sharp-edged wit inherited from her French forebears, the Marcys of St. Louis, fur traders of almost a century earlier.

As the family now sat at its noonday meal it was late May, and unseasonably hot. There had been an early pest of flies this spring. High above the table, on a board suspended by rods from the lofty ceiling, sat perched Isaiah, a little black boy. With one hand he clung to his precarious roost; with the other he wielded a shoofly of feathery asparagus ferns. Its soft susurrus as he swished it back and forth was an obbligato to the music of Yancey Cravat's golden voice. The boy's fuzzed head was cocked at an impish angle the better to hear. His eyes were fixed in entrancement on the great lounging figure. Frequently he forgot altogether his task of stirring the hot moist air above the food-laden table. An impatient glance from Felice Venable's darting black eyes, together with a sharp "*Ah*-saiah!" would set him to swishing vigorously again.

Yancey Cravat had been talking for the better part of an hour. This very morning he had returned from the Oklahoma country—the newly opened Indian Territory where he had made the Run that marked the settling of that vast tract of virgin land known colloquially as the Nation. Now, as he talked, the faces of the others had the rapt look of those who listen to a saga. The men at table leaned forward, their plates pushed away. The women listened, their lips parted. Sometimes a woman's hand reached out possessively and was laid on the arm of the man seated beside her. "I am here," it said. "Your place is with me. I am your wife. I am comfort. I am convention. Don't listen to him like that." But the man would shake off the hand.

Of all the faces, there stood out that of Sabra Cravat. It seemed luminously white as she listened to her husband, their child Cim in her lap. It was plain that in her, as in her mother Felice Venable, the strain of the pioneering Marcys was strong. Her abundant hair was black, and her eyes, and the strong brows arched with a swooping curve. For the rest, there was something more New England than southern in the quick turn of her head, the briskness of her speech and manner. Twenty-one now, married at sixteen, mother of a four-year-old boy, and still in love with her picturesque giant of a husband, there was about Sabra Cravat a bloom sometimes seen at that exquisite and transitory time in a woman's life when her emotional and physical makeup attains its highest point.

It was easy to trace the resemblance between this glowing girl and her mother. But to turn to Lewis Venable, in his armchair at the head of the table, was to find oneself baffled by the mysteries of paternity. He was not old, but aged; a futile, gentle man, somewhat hagridden and rendered more unvital by malaria and a resident bullet somewhere in the ribs, got at Murfreesboro as a member of Stanford's Battery, Heavy Artillery.

Lewis Venable was as spellbound as black Isaiah in his perch. Even the little boy Cim listened as he sat in his mother's lap. Perhaps it was the storyteller's voice, for Yancey Cravat had those gifts of the born orator, a musical and vibrant voice, great charm of manner, a hypnotic eye, and the power of making each listener feel that what was being said was intended for his ear alone.

Yancey was a glamorous figure, a mysterious stranger out of Texas and the Cimarron. No room seemed big enough for his broad-shouldered frame. He seemed actually to loom more than his six feet two. His black hair was overlong, so that it curled a little about his neck. His cheeks and forehead were, in places, deeply pitted, as with the pox. Women found this attractive.

But first of all you noted his huge head, heavy like a buffalo's. Then you remarked about him certain things totally at variance with his appearance of enormous power. His mouth, full and sensual, had still an expression of great sweetness. His eyelashes were long and curling, and when he raised his head to look at you, you saw that his eyes were a deep and unfathomable ocean gray.

Now, in the excitement of telling his story, he sprang to his feet, striding about as he spoke. His step was amazingly graceful for a man of his size. His feet were small and arched like a woman's, and he wore boots of fine soft calf, high heeled and ornamented with cunningly wrought gold stars. He used his slim white hands as he talked, and the eye followed their movements, bewitched. His costume was a Prince Albert of fine black broadcloth; a pleated white shirt; a black string tie; trousers tucked into the boot tops; and outdoors, a white felt hat, broad-brimmed and rolling. His speech was spattered with bits of Latin, Spanish, Shakespeare, the Old Testament. He drank a quart of whiskey a day but was almost never drunk. Yancey Cravat could have been the greatest criminal lawyer of his day, but since he was sentimental, his law practice usually yielded him nothing for his brilliant defense of some Dodge City dance-hall girl or roistering cowboy.

His past was clouded with myths. Rumor floated about his head. They say he has Indian blood in him. They say he has a Cherokee wife somewhere. They say his real name is Cimarron Seven, of the Choctaw Sevens; he was raised in a tepee. It was known he had been one of the early Boomers who followed the splendidly mad David Payne in an earlier wild dash into Indian Territory. He had dwelt, others whispered, in that sinister strip, thirty-four miles wide and almost two hundred miles long, first called No-Man's-Land and later known as the Cimarron, a Spanish word meaning wild. Here, in this strange unowned empire without laws and without a government, a paradise for horse thieves, murderers, desperadoes, it was rumored he had spent at least a year.

They said the evidences of his Indian blood were plain, otherwise why did he protest in his newspaper against the government's treatment of those dirty, good-for-nothing wards of a beneficent country? His newspaper's very name was a scandal: the Wichita *Wigwam*. And its claim: All the News. Any Scandal Not Libelous. Published Once a Week if Convenient. For that matter, who ever heard of a practicing lawyer who ran a newspaper at the same time? Its columns were echoes of his own thundering oratory in the courtroom. He had started his paper in opposition to the established Wichita *Eagle*. His office was a welter of pied type, legal volumes, paste pots, and racing posters. Wichita, professing scorn of the *Wigwam,* read it. Wichita perused his maiden editorial—entitled SHALL THE BLUE BLOOD OF THE DECAYED SOUTH POISON THE RED BLOOD OF THE GREAT MIDDLE WEST?—and saw him, two months later, carry off in triumph as his bride Sabra Venable, daughter of that same decay. Sabra, at sixteen, might have had her pick of the red-blooded lads of Kansas, not to mention more legitimate blue-blooded suitors up from the South. When, over all these, Sabra had chosen the mysterious Cravat, Wichita mothers felt themselves revenged of the Venable airs. But strangely enough, their marriageable daughters seemed more resentful than ever.

During the course of the bountiful meal at the Venable table Yancey Cravat had eaten almost nothing. Here was an audience to his liking, a tale to his taste. His story was of the opening of the Oklahoma country; of a wilderness made populous in an hour; of cities sprung up overnight.

He had been a month absent. Like thousands of others he had gone in search of free land, and a fortune. Here was an empire to be had for the taking. Fantastic as it was, all that he said was true.

"Folks, there's never been anything like it since Creation. It was history made in an hour. Thousands of people from all over our vast commonwealth traveled hundreds of miles to get a bare piece of land for nothing. But what land! Virgin, except when the Indians had roamed it. They came like a crazy procession, scrambling over the ground, pushing to get there for the firing of the shot that would open the promised land. As I got nearer the Border it was like ants swarming on sugar. Over the little hills they came, and out of the scrub-oak woods and across the prairie. They came in prairie schooners and ox carts, in carriages and on horseback. I met one old homesteader by the roadside who told me he had started weeks before, and had made the long trip on foot."

He paused a moment and wrung a breathless, "Oh, Yancey, go on!" from Sabra.

"Well, the Border at last, and it was like a Fourth of July celebration. The militia was lined up at the boundary. No one was allowed on the new land until noon on April twenty-second, at the firing of the guns. These two million acres of free land were going to be made livable territory overnight like a miracle out of the Old Testament. A wilderness one day—except for a few wandering Indians—an empire the next."

"Indians, h'm?" sneered Cousin Dabney Venable, meaningly.

"Oh, Dabney!" exclaimed Sabra. "Why don't you just listen!"

Yancey Cravat raised a pacifying hand, but the great buffalo head was lowered toward Cousin Dabney, as though charging. The sweetest of smiles wreathed his lips. "It's all right, Sabra. Let Cousin Dabney speak."

The time had come for Felice Venable to clear the air. "Well, I must say I call it downright bad manners. Here we all are with our ears just a-flapping to hear the first sound of the militia guns at high noon on the

Border—" She broke off abruptly, cast a lightning glance aloft and called "*Ah*-saiah!"

The black boy's shoofly, hanging limp from his hand, took up its frantic swishing. The figures around the table again turned toward Yancey Cravat. Yancey glanced at Sabra. Her lips formed two words, unseen by the rest of the company. "Please, darling."

"*Cede Deo*," said Yancey, with a little bow to her. Then he was off again, pausing only a moment to toss off three fingers of Spanish brandy. "I've tasted nothing like that in a month, I can tell you. Raw corn whiskey. And as for the water! There wasn't a drink of water to be had in the town after the first twenty-four hours. There we were, thousands of us, milling around like cattle in the dust and burning sun. No place to wash, no place to sleep, nothing to eat. Queer enough, they didn't seem to mind. They laughed and joked all day and all night and until near noon next day. Even the women."

"Women!" echoed Cousin Arminta Greenwood.

"You wouldn't believe, would you, that women would go it alone in a fracas like that. Some were there with their husbands, but there were women who made the Run alone."

"What kind of women?" Felice Venable asked.

"Women with iron in 'em. Pioneer women."

From Aunt Cassandra Venable came the word "Hussies!"

Yancey Cravat spat it back. "Hussies, heh! Behind me in the line was a woman in a calico dress and a sunbonnet and boots caked with mud. She had driven all the way from the north of Arkansas in a springless wagon. A gaunt woman, with rough hair and weather-beaten skin. But it's women like her who've made this country what it is. Good women, with a rigid goodness that comes of work and hardship and self-denial. Their story's never really been told. If ever it is, you'll know it's the sunbonnet and not the sombrero that has settled this country."

"Talking nonsense," drawled Felice Venable.

Yancey whirled to face her. "You're one of them. You came from the South with your husband to make a home in Kansas—"

"I am not!" retorted Felice Venable. "Muddy boots indeed! And I've never worn a sunbonnet in my life. As for my skin and hair, they were the toast of the South, as I can prove by anyone here."

"Oh, Mama, Yancey meant you had the courage to leave your home in the South—he wasn't thinking of—Yancey, do go on."

The prospect of escaping the Venable mind had been one of the reasons for Yancey's dash into the wild melee of the Oklahoma Run in the first place. Now he stood surveying these handsome futile faces, and a great impatience shook him, and a flame of rage shot through him. With these to goad him, and the knowledge of how he had failed, he plunged again into his story to the end.

"I had planned to get on the Santa Fe train that was ready to run into the Nation. But there wasn't room for a flea. People were hanging on the cowcatcher and swarming all over the cars. I decided I'd use my Indian pony. I knew I'd get endurance anyway, if not speed.

"The morning of April twenty-second, thousands began to line up at the Border. Militia all along to keep us back. They had burned the prairie for miles ahead to make the way clearer. To smoke out the Sooners, too, who had sneaked in and were hiding in the scrub oaks ready to shoot those of us who came in the Run. I knew the section I wanted. An old freighters' trail, overgrown and out of use, led almost straight to it. A creek ran through the land, and the prairie rolled a little there, too. Because of the water, I suppose, there were elms and cottonwoods and even a grove of pecans. I had noticed it many a time, riding the range.

"Ten o'clock and the crowd was restless. Hundreds of us had gone as Boomers in the old Payne colonies, and had been driven out, and had come back again. Thousands had waited ten years for this day when the land-hungry would be fed.

"Eleven o'clock and they were fighting for places near the Line. The sound they made wasn't human at all, but like wild animals penned up. The sun blazed down. The dust hung over everything, blinding and choking you. Eleven thirty. The roar grew louder. People fought for an inch of gain. Just next to me was a girl who looked about eighteen—and a beauty she was, too—on a coal-black Thoroughbred."

"Aha!" said Cousin Jouett Goforth. He was the kind of man who says "Aha."

"On the other side was an old fellow with a gray beard and a wooden leg. He was mounted on an Indian pony like mine. We fell to talking, the three of us. We were all headed for the freighters' trail toward the creek land. The girl said she had trained her Thoroughbred for the race. He was from Kentucky and so was she. She was bound to get her hundred and sixty acres, she said. She had to have it. She didn't say why, and I didn't ask her. But she had on a getup that took everyone's attention.

527

The better to cut the wind, she wore a short skirt, black tights, and a skullcap."

Here there was a bombardment of sound as silver spoons and knives were dropped from shocked Venable fingers.

"Five minutes to twelve. The mob had quieted till there wasn't a sound. Listening. The last minute was an eternity. Then up went a roar that drowned the crack of the soldiers' musketry as they fired to signal the start of the Run. Thousands surged over the Line and across the prairie in a cloud of dust. The girl, the plainsman and I swept down the old freight trail that was two wheel ruts worn into the soil. The old man on his pony kept in one rut, the girl on her Thoroughbred in the other, and I on my Whitefoot on the raised place in the middle. That first half mile we raced neck and neck. The old fellow was yelling and hanging on somehow. Then he began to drop behind. Next I heard a terrible scream. I glanced over my shoulder. The old plainsman's pony had stumbled and fallen, and he lay sprawling in the trail. The next instant he was hidden in a welter of pounding hoofs and wagon wheels."

A dramatic pause. The faces around the table swung this way and that as Yancey Cravat paced the room, his coattails billowing. He held the moment of silence like a jewel. Sabra Cravat's voice, sharp with suspense, cut the stillness. "What happened? What happened to the old man?"

Yancey's hands flew up. "Oh, he was trampled to death. The mob couldn't stop for a one-legged old whiskers."

Out of the murmur of horror that now arose there emerged the voice of Felice Venable. "And the girl. The girl with the black—"

"The girl and I—I never did learn her name—were in the lead. We were now beyond the burned area. The prairie was covered with blue stem grass six feet high in places. A horse could only be forced through at a slow pace. That grass kept many a racer from winning his section that day.

"The girl followed close behind me. Her Thoroughbred was built for speed, not distance. I could hear him blowing. My Indian pony was just getting his second wind as her horse slackened into a trot. We had come nearly sixteen miles. She was crouched low over her horse's neck, like a jockey, and I could hear her talking to him, sweet and eager. Then I saw that the prairie ahead was afire. Only the narrow trail down which we were galloping was open. On either side of it was a wall of flame. Some skunk of a Sooner had set the blaze to keep the Boomers off. The dry grass burned like oiled paper. I turned around. The girl was there, her racer stumbling. I saw her motion with her hand. She was coming. I whipped off my hat and clapped it over Whitefoot's eyes, gave him the spurs, crouched low, and down the trail we went into the furnace. I could smell the mustang's singed hair. I could feel the flames licking my legs and back. Another hundred yards and neither of us could have come through it. But we broke out into the open, half suffocated. I looked down the lane of flame. The girl was coming through. I knew that the land I had come through hell for was not more than a mile ahead. I knew that hanging around here would probably get me shot, for the Sooner that started that fire must be lurking about. I began to wonder, too, if that girl wasn't headed for the same section. I made up my mind that, woman or no woman, this was a race. I wheeled and went on.

"Presently I saw a clump of elms ahead. I knew the creek was nearby. But just before I got to it I came to one of those deep gullies you find in the plains—a crack in the dry earth, widened with every rain until it becomes a small canyon. Almost ten feet across this one was. No way around it that I could see. I put Whitefoot to the leap and, by golly, he took it, landing with hardly an inch to spare. I heard a wild scream behind me. I turned. The girl on her racer had tried to make the gulch. He had come down on his knees just on the farther edge, and slid down the gully side into the ditch. The girl had flung herself free. My claim was fifty yards away. So was the girl, with her dying horse. As I raced toward her she scrambled to her knees. I can see her face now, black with soot, her hair all over her shoulders, her cheek bleeding, her tights torn. Then she staggered to her feet and stood there swaying. She pointed down the gully. Her face was streaked with tears.

" 'Shoot him!' she said. 'I can't. His forelegs are broken. I heard them crack.'

"I got off my horse and went down to where the animal lay, his poor legs doubled under him. He was done for, all right. I took out my six-shooter and aimed between his eyes. He kicked once and lay still.

"Then something made me turn around. The girl had mounted my mustang. She was off toward the creek. Before I had moved ten paces she had reached the very piece I had marked for my own in my mind. She leaped from the horse, ripped off her skirt, tied it to her riding whip, planted the butt in the soil—and the land was hers by right of claim."

There was a moment of stricken silence. Sabra Cravat sat staring at her husband with great round eyes. It was Felice Venable who spoke first. And when she did she was every inch the thrifty descendant of French forebears; nothing of the southern belle about her.

"Yancey Cravat, do you mean that you let her have your quarter section! That you had been gone a month for! That you left your wife and child for!"

"Now, Mama!" You saw that all the Venable in Sabra was summoned to keep the tears from her eyes.

"Don't you 'now Mama' me! It was bad enough to think of your going to the Indian Territory, but to—" She paused. Her voice took on a more sinister note. "I don't believe a word of it." She whirled on Yancey. "Why did you let that trollop have your land?"

Yancey regarded this question with deceptive calm. "If it had been a man I could have shot him. A good many had to, to keep the land they'd run for. But you can't shoot a woman."

"Why not?" demanded the erstwhile southern belle.

A shocked titter went around the Venable board. A startled "Felice!" was wrung from Lewis Venable.

Yancey Cravat felt a tide of irritability rising within him. Something about the family's staring faces roused in him an unreasoning rebellion. He suddenly hated them. He wanted to be free of them—of Wichita—of convention—of—no, not of her. He now smiled his brilliant sweet smile which alone should have warned Felice Venable. But that intrepid matriarch was not one to let a tale go unpointed.

"I'm mighty pleased, for one, that it turned out as it did. Do you suppose I'd have allowed a daughter of mine to go traipsing into the wilderness to live among drunken plainsmen and trollops in tights! Perhaps now it's over, Yancey, you'll be content to run that paper of yours and conduct your law practice with no more talk of this Indian Territory."

Yancey was strangely silent. When he spoke it was with utter gentleness. "I'm no rancher. I didn't want a section of farmland, anyway. The town's where I belong. Towns of ten thousand sprang up in a night during the Run. Wagallala—Sperry—Osage. Oklahoma's the last frontier in America. There isn't a newspaper in one of those towns. I want to go back and help build a state out of the prairie."

"That wilderness a state!" sneered Cousin Dabney. "With an Osage Indian buck for governor, I suppose."

"Why not?"

"Ho hum," yawned Cousin Jouett Goforth rising. "This has been very interesting. Now if you'll excuse me, I shall have my siesta."

Lewis Venable also prepared to rise. But Felice Venable's hand darted out and pressed him back.

"Lewis Venable, you heard him!" She turned blazing eyes on her son-in-law. "Do you mean you're going back to that Indian country?"

"I'll be there in two weeks."

Sabra stood up, the boy Cim grasped in her arms. Her eyes were enormous. "Yancey! Yancey, you're not leaving me again!"

"Leaving you!" He strode over to her. "You're going with me."

"I say she's not!" Felice Venable rapped it out. "And neither are you, my fine fellow. You'll stay here with your wife and child."

His voice was dulcet. "I'm going back, and Sabra and Cim with me."

Felice whirled on her husband. "Lewis! You can sit there and see your daughter dragged off. . . ."

Lewis Venable raised his fine white head. "You came with me, Felice, more than twenty years ago, and your mother thought you were going to the wilderness, too. You remember? She made mourning for weeks."

"Sabra's different."

"No, she isn't, Felice. She's more like you this minute than you are yourself. She favors those pioneer women Yancey was telling about. Look at her."

From one end of the table to the other the Venables turned toward the young woman facing them. Seeing her standing there beside her husband, one arm about the child, resolve in her bearing, you saw that what her father said was true. She was her mother, the Felice Venable of two decades ago. She was all the women jolting endless miles in covered wagons, spinning in log cabins, cooking over crude fires. Here was that inner rectitude, that chastity of lip, that clearness of eye, that absence of allure that comes with cold white fire. The pioneer type, as Yancey had said. Potentially a more formidable woman than her mother.

Felice Venable said again, as though to convince herself, "She's not to go. I forbid it."

Sabra stiffened. Perhaps she had not realized until now how she had counted on her husband's return as marking the time when she would be free to break away from the yoke of her mother's dominance. Now all the iron in her fused and hardened. "I *will* go," said Sabra Cravat.

If anyone had been looking at Lewis Venable at that moment he could have seen a ghostly smile irradiating the transparent ivory face. But it was Yancey Cravat who held all eyes. He swung Sabra and the boy Cim high in the air in his great arms, so that Sabra screamed and Cim squealed with delight. It was the kind of horseplay at which Felice Venable always shuddered.

"We'll start a week from tomorrow," announced Yancey, in something like a shout. "Two wagons. One with the printing outfit—you'll drive that, Sabra—and one with the household goods. We ought to make it in nine days. . . . Wichita!" His glance went around the room. "I've had enough of it. Sabra, my girl, we'll leave all this Wichita respectability behind us. We're going to a brand-new, two-fisted, ripsnorting country, full of Injuns and rattlesnakes and desper-*ah*-dos! Whoop-*ee!*"

It was too much for Isaiah high above the table. He had long ago ceased to wield his fan. He had been leaning farther and farther forward, the better to see. Now, at Yancey's cowboy whoop he started violently, and fell into the midst of one of Felice Venable's frosted white cakes.

Shouts, screams. Isaiah plucked, white-bottomed, out of the center of the vast pastry. Felice Venable lifted her hand to cuff him smartly. But with the swiftness of a wild thing Isaiah scuttled across the table to where the Cravats stood, leaped to the floor, and lay there, locked in the safety of Yancey's great knees.

Chapter 2

THERE WAS A LUNATIC WEEK preceding their departure from Wichita. Felice fought their going to the last, and finally took to her bed. From time to time, intrigued by the thumpings, scurryings, shouts, and laughter, she rose and trailed wanly about the house in her white wrapper. She issued orders. Don't take that. It can't be that you're leaving those behind! Aunt Sarah embroidered every inch—

"But, Mama, Yancey says it's all quite rough—"

"That needn't prevent you from remembering you're a lady, I hope."

So Sabra Cravat took to the frontier such elegancies as silverware for a dozen in the DeGrasse pattern; a handsome silver cake dish, upheld by three silver cupids; her fine green challis; her tulle bonnet with the little pink flowers; forty jars of preserves; a lady's rocker, upholstered with bright Brussels carpeting.

There were two canvas-covered wagons. Dishes, trunks, bedding were stowed in one. The printing outfit went in the other—the little hand press, the case rack containing the type, the rollers, a stock of paper, a box of wooden quoins used in locking the type in the forms.

Freighters like these had worn many a track in the Kansas prairie since the day of the old Spanish trail. Yet in this small expedition faring forth there was something particularly poignant. The man, bizarre, impractical; the woman, tight-lipped, determined, her eyes staring with the fixed gaze of one who knows that to blink is to be awash with tears; the child, out of hand with impatience to be gone. From the day of Yancey's recital of the Run, black Isaiah had begged to be taken along. Denied this, he had sulked for a week and now was nowhere to be found.

The wagons stood waiting before the Venable house. Sabra had driven horses all her life; now she climbed to the seat of the wagon containing the printing press and deftly gathered the reins. She wore her second-best gray cheviot, braided with an elaborate pattern of curlicues. Her gray straw bonnet was trimmed with a puff of velvet and a bird. Her feet, in high-buttoned shoes, were found to touch the wagon floor with difficulty, so at the last minute a footstool was snatched from the house so that she might brace herself. This article of furniture, covered with a gay tapestry, was no more at variance with its surroundings than the driver herself. Yancey drove the other wagon.

Cim sat beside Sabra. His dark eyes were huge with excitement. "Why don't we go?" he demanded. He shouted to the horses as he had heard teamsters do. "Giddap in 'ere!" His grandparents, gazing up with sudden agony in their faces, had ceased to exist for Cim.

With a lurch the two wagons were off. Sabra had scarcely time for one final look at her father and mother, at minor massed Venables, at the servants' black faces. She was so filled with a kind of terror-stricken happiness that she forgot to turn and glimpse once more the big white house, the garden. Later she reproached herself for this. And she would say to the boy, in the bare ugliness of the town that became their home, "Cim, do you remember the purple flags that used to come up in the spring in Granny's yard, back home?"

"Nope." It was as though the boy's life had begun with this trip. The four previous years seemed to be sponged from his mind.

They had made an early start but noon came with surprising swiftness. They had brought sufficient food, they thought, to last through most of the trip—salt pork, pies, bread. At midday they stopped and ate in the shade. Sabra prepared the meal while Yancey tended the horses. It was all very comfortable and relaxed.

Short as the morning had been, the afternoon stretched out hot and endless. Sabra became tired, cramped. The boy whimpered. When the brilliant western sunset began to paint the sky at last, Yancey, in the wagon ahead, drew up, tied his team to one of a clump of cottonwoods.

"We'll camp here," he called to Sabra and came toward her wagon to lift her down. She stared at him wearily, then around the landscape.

"Camp?"

"Yes. For the night. Come, Cim."

"You mean sleep here?"

He was matter-of-fact. "Yes. Water and trees. I'll have a fire before you can say Jack Robinson. Where'd you think we'd sleep?"

Somehow she had not thought. To sleep in the open like this, with only a wagon top as roof! All her life she had slept in a four-poster bed with a dotted swiss canopy.

Yancey began to make camp. Cim trotted after his father. Soon meat began to sizzle appetizingly in the pan.

"That roll of carpet," called Sabra to Yancey at the wagon. "Under the seat. I want Cim to sit on it . . . ground may be damp. . . ."

A sudden shout from Yancey. A squeal of terror from the carpeting in his arms—a bundle that suddenly was wriggling. Yancey dropped it with an oath. The bundle lay on the ground, heaving, then it began to unroll itself. A small black hand, a woolly head, a face all open mouth and whites of eyes. Isaiah! He had found a way to come with them after all.

By noon next day they wondered how they had got on without him. He gathered wood. He tended Cim like a nurse. He even helped Sabra to drive her team, change and change about.

Yancey pointed out how the land changed when they left Kansas and came into the Oklahoma country. "Okla-homa," he explained to Cim. "That's Choctaw. Okla—people. Humma—red. Red people. That's what they called it when the Indians came here to live."

Suddenly the land, too, had become red: red clay as far as the eye could see. The little creeks were sanguine with it, and when the trail led through a cleft in a hill the blood red on either side was like a gaping

534

wound. Sabra longed for the green of Kansas. As for the Oklahoma sky, it was not blue but a brazen sheet of steel. Its glare seared the eyeballs.

Cim was by turns unruly and listless. He could not run about, except when they stopped to make camp. Sabra had not the gift of amusing him as Yancey had, or Isaiah. Isaiah told him tales that were Negro folklore, handed down by word of mouth through the years, accounts of the tribulations of a wronged people and their inevitable reward in afterlife.

But when he rode with his father he heard thrilling tales. If it was just before his bedtime, Yancey invariably began with the magic words, "It was on just such a night as this . . ." There would follow a legend of buried treasure. Spanish conquistadores wandered weary miles over prairie and desert, led, perhaps, by the false golden promises of some captured Indian. As in all sparsely settled countries, there were here hundreds of such tales. No bony squatter, wresting a meager living from the barren plains, but had some tale of buried Spanish gold. These stories became as real to Cim as the red clay of Oklahoma.

During the day Yancey told him stories of the Indians. He taught him the names of the Five Civilized Tribes, and Cim repeated the difficult Indian words—Cherokee, Choctaw, Creek, Seminole, and Chickasaw. He heard the Indian story, not in terms of raids and scalpings, but as the saga of a wronged people. Yancey described the Trail of Tears—the story of the Cherokee Nation, driven like cattle from their homes in Georgia across hundreds of miles of prairie to die by the thousands before they reached the Oklahoma land that had been allotted to them, with two thousand troops under General Winfield Scott to urge them on.

"Why did they make the Indians go away?"

"They wanted the land for themselves."

"Why?"

"It had marble, and gold and silver and iron and lead, and great forests. So they took all this away from them and drove them out. They promised them things and then broke their promise."

Sabra was horrified to hear, one afternoon, Cim's secondhand recital of this saga. "Uncle Sam is a mean bad man. He took all the farms and the gold and the buff'loes away from the Indians and made them go away and so they went and they died."

Indians were no novelty in Wichita. Sabra had seen them all her life, and picked up odds and ends of information from family talk about these silent, slothful, yet sinister figures. If she considered them at all, she thought of them as dirty and useless two-footed animals. She had been incredulous at her husband's partisanship of the redskins. He seemed actually to consider them as human beings.

Sabra now undertook to wipe Yancey's version of Indian history from the boy's mind. "Indians are bad people. They take little boys from their mamas. They burn people's houses. They're dirty, lazy, and they steal."

Cim grew enraged. "They're not. You're a liar. I won't ride with you."

He prepared to climb down over the wagon wheel. She clutched at him with one hand. He kicked her. She stopped the team, took him over her knee and spanked him soundly. He announced, through his tears, that he was going to run away and join the Indians and never come back.

"Why can't you talk to him about something besides Indians?" she later protested to Yancey. "Teach him the history of his country. George Washington and Jefferson Davis and Captain John Smith . . ."

"The one who married Pocahontas, you mean?"

But often the days were gay enough. By the second day Sabra's young body had accustomed itself to the jolting of the wagon. By this time she had her hair in a long black braid, and had put on the sunbonnet which one of the Venables had jokingly given her at parting.

As for Yancey, Sabra had never known him so happy. He was tireless, charming, varied.

Once they saw him kill a rattlesnake with his wagon whip. He had unhitched the horses to water them at a muddy stream, Cim leaping and shouting at his side. Yancey had just removed his belt, with his two guns in their holsters, and taken up the whip when Sabra saw the coiled rattler. She screamed, stood transfixed. Cim's face was a mask of fright. Yancey lashed out with his whip, the snake struck out, he lashed again, again, again, until the snake lay in ribbons. Isaiah, though ashen with fear, had to be forcibly restrained from searching for the rattles, which were supposed to be a charm against practically every misfortune known to man. Cim had nightmares all that night.

Once they saw the figure of a solitary horseman against the sunset sky. Inexplicably the figure dismounted, stood a moment, remounted swiftly and vanished.

"What was that?"

"That was an Indian."

"How could you tell?"

"He dismounted on the opposite side from a white man."

That night it was Sabra who did not sleep.

They had two days of rain during which they plodded miserably over roads that had become slithering bogs of greased red dough. Then, at Pawnee, Yancey saw fresh deer tracks. Before this, he had shot prairie chicken and quail, but this was their first promise of big game. He saddled a horse and was off.

Sabra felt no fear at being left alone in midafternoon with the boys. She welcomed this unexpected halt. She and Isaiah carried water from the creek, washed a few clothes, and hung them to dry. She bathed Cim. She heated water for herself and bathed gratefully. Isaiah was gathering fuel for the evening meal, while Cim played in the shade of a clump of scrub oak. She could hear him outside, crooning to himself.

Vaguely she began to wonder if Yancey should not have returned by now. She brushed her hair, braided it, and tied it with a bright red ribbon. She tidied the wagon. She was frankly worried now. Nothing could happen. Of course nothing could happen. And in another part of her mind she thought of a dozen things. Indians. A fall from his horse. Broken bones. He might lose his way. Suppose she had to spend the night alone here on the prairie with the two children?

In a sudden panic she stepped out of the wagon. Cim was not there. He must have gone with Isaiah to gather fuel. Isaiah, his arms full of twigs, was coming toward the wagon now. Cim was not with him.

"Where's Cim?"

He dropped his load, looked around. "I lef' him playin' by hisself right hyah. Might be he crep' in de print wagon."

She ran to peer inside. He was not there.

Together they looked under the wagons, behind the trees. "Cim! Cim! Cimarron Cravat, if you are hiding come out this minute." A shrill note of terror crept into her voice. She began to scream his name, her voice cracking grotesquely. "Cim! Cim!" Dear God, don't let anything happen to him. Help me find him.

Whimpering, she ran this way and that. About a half a mile from camp she came to a little mound. And there he was, seated before a cave in the side of the hill, its front and roof ingeniously timbered to make a log cabin. One might pass within five feet of it and never find it. Four men were seated about the doorstep, their saddled horses nearby. Cim was perched on the knee of one of them, who was cracking nuts for him. They were laughing and having a delightful time. Sabra stumbled as she ran toward him. The men sprang up, their hands at their hips.

"The man is cracking nuts for me," remarked Cim.

The man on whose knee he sat was a slim young fellow with a sandy mustache and a red handkerchief knotted around his throat. He put the boy down gently as Sabra came up, and rose with an easy grace.

"You ran away—you—we hunted every—Cim—" she stammered and burst into tears.

"Why, we was going to bring the boy back safe enough, ma'am. He wandered here lookin' for his pa, he said." He spoke softly, standing with one hand resting tenderly on Cim's head, looking down at Sabra with a smile of utter sweetness.

"Well," she explained a little sheepishly, "I was worried. My husband went off on the track of a deer . . . hours ago. He hasn't come back. Then when Cim was gone, I was so . . ."

She looked very schoolgirlish with her braid and tear-stained cheeks.

One of the men, who had strolled off a way with the appearance of utmost casualness, returned to the group in time to hear this. "He'll be back any minute now," he announced. "He didn't get no deer."

"But how do you know?" Sabra asked.

The soft-spoken young man shot a malignant look at the other, and Sabra's question went unanswered. "Won't you sit and rest yourself, ma'am?" the young man said. The words were hospitable, yet his tone suggested that she and Cim had better be gone. She took Cim's hand.

"I'm ve'y grateful to you-all," she said, using a little southern charm. "You've been mighty kind. If you would just drop around to our camp I'm sure my husband would be delighted to meet you."

The others looked at the young man, an inexplicable glint of humor in their faces. He smiled sweetly. "We're movin' on, my friends and me. Floyd, how about getting a piece of deer meat for the lady, seeing she's been cheated of her supper. Now, if you don't mind sittin' behind, ma'am, I'll take you back."

He mounted so quickly that he seemed to have been drawn to the saddle as a needle flies to the magnet. Cim he drew up to the pommel with one hand; Sabra, perched on the horse's rump, clung with both arms round the lad's slim waist. She noticed his fine Mexican saddle, studded with silver. From the sides of the saddle hung hair-covered pockets whose bulge was the outline of a gun. The horse had a velvet gait, and Sabra found herself wishing that this ride might go on for miles. Suddenly she noticed that the young rider wore gloves. The sight made her vaguely uneasy, as though some memory had been stirred. She had never seen a plainsman wearing gloves. It was absurd, somehow.

A hundred feet or so from the camp he reined in his horse and swung Sabra and Cim to the ground. He was gone before she could thank him. The piece of deer meat, neatly wrapped, lay on the ground at her feet. She stood staring after the galloping figure, dumbly.

Ten minutes later Yancey galloped in, empty-handed. "What a chase! Twice I thought I had him."

Sabra was impatient. She had her own story to tell.

". . . and just when I was ready to die with fright, there Cim was, talking to those four men, and sitting on the knee of one of them eating nuts. Anything might have happened to us while you were off."

Yancey seemed less interested in the adventure than in the four men, and especially the charming young man who had been so gallant.

"Thin faced, was he? About twenty? What else?"

"Oh, a low sweet voice, and his teeth—"

Yancey interrupted. "Long? The two at the side—like a wolf's?"

"Yes. How did you— Do you know him?"

"Sort of." Yancey was thoughtful, then brisk. "Stir that fire, Isaiah. Sabra, get that deer meat a-frizzling, because we're moving on."

"Now? But I thought we were camped for the night."

"I don't just like it here. We'll eat and push on. In another day or so we'll be in Osage, snug and safe."

They ate hurriedly and jolted on. Cim slept in the back of the wagon. Isaiah drowsed beside Sabra, and she herself was half asleep, the reins slack in her hands. The scent of the sun-warmed prairie came up to her, and the pungent smell of the sagebrush.

She must have dozed off, for suddenly the sun's rays were sharply slanted, and she shivered with the cool night air. Voices had awakened her. Three horsemen stood in the path of Yancey's lead wagon. Their hands rested on their guns. Their faces were grim. All three wore the badge of United States marshal. The leader addressed Yancey.

"Where you bound for, pardner?"

"Osage."

"What might your name be?"

"Cravat—Yancey Cravat."

The spokesman smiled like a delighted child. "Yancey Cravat!" he repeated. "I'll be doggoned! I sure am pleased to make your acquaintance. Heard about you till I feel like I know you."

"Why, thanks," replied Yancey, unusually laconic. Sabra knew then that Yancey was playing one of his roles. He would talk as they talked. Be one of them.

"Aimin' to make quite a stay in Osage?"

"Aim to live there."

"Go on! I've a notion to swear you in as deputy marshal right now. Citizens like you is what we need. Lawy'in'?"

"I'm planning to take up my law practice in Osage, yes," Yancey answered, "and start a newspaper as well."

The three glanced at each other, then at Yancey, then away, uncomfortably. "Newspaper, huh?" The marshal spoke without enthusiasm. "Well, we did have a paper in Osage for a little while, 'bout a week."

There was something sinister in this. "What became of it?"

"Well, seems the editor—name of Pegler—died."

"Who killed him?"

A little shadow of pained surprise passed over the marshal's face. "He was just found dead one morning on the banks of the Canadian. Bullet wounds. Might 'a' killed himself, plumb discouraged."

A silence fell. Yancey broke it. "The first edition of the *Oklahoma Wigwam* will be off the press two weeks from tomorrow." He gathered up the reins. "Well, gentlemen, good evening. Glad to have met you."

The three marshals did not budge. "What we stopped to ask you," said the spokesman, "was, did you happen to glimpse four men anywhere on the road? They're nesting somewheres in here, the Kid and his gang. Stole four horses, robbed the bank at Red Fork, shot the cashier, and lit out for the prairie. The Kid is a slim young fella, light hair, red handkerchief, soft-spoken, and rides with gloves on. But then you know what he's like, Cravat, well's I do."

Yancey nodded. "Everybody's heard of the Kid. No, sir, I haven't seen anybody the last three days but a Kaw Indian on a pony."

The three marshals saluted and rode off. Sabra brought her team alongside Yancey's and addressed him in bewildered indignation. "Isn't the person who shields a criminal just as bad as the criminal himself?"

Yancey's smile was mischievous, irresistible. "Don't be righteous, Sabra. It's a terrible trait in a woman." He clucked to his team and was off.

Late next day, just before sunset, he pointed to what looked like a wallow of mud dotted with crazy shanties and tents. He picked Cim up in his arms so that the child, too, might see. But he spoke to Sabra.

"There it is," he said. "That's our future home."

Sabra looked. And she could think only of the green challis trimmed with ruchings of pink which lay so carefully folded in soft paper, in the trunk under the canvas of the wagon.

Chapter 3

ALL ABOUT IN OSAGE were wooden shacks, and Indians and hitching posts and dogs, and wagons like their own. A score of saloons enlivened the broad main street, which stopped abruptly at either end and became suddenly prairie.

"Pawhuska Avenue," said a tipsy sign tacked on the front of a false-front pine shack. Yancey pointed it out to Cim. "That's an Osage Indian name," he shouted. "Pawhu means hair. And scah means white. White Hair. Pawhuska—White Hair—was an old Osage chief."

"Yancey Cravat!" Sabra called. "Will you stop talking Indian history and find us a place to eat and sleep!"

In the eating house labeled ICE CREAM AND OYSTER PARLOR, the greasy food set before them sickened her. At table with them—there was only one, a long board—sat red-faced men shoveling potatoes, canned vegetables, pie into their mouths with knives.

Afterward Sabra took Cim up to the bare but clean little room above a saloon that was to be theirs for the night. From wide-eyed wakefulness Cim had become suddenly limp with sleep. Yancey had gone to see to the horses and get what information he could about renting a house.

"Everything'll look rosy in the morning," he had said. "Don't look so down in the mouth, honey. You're going to like it."

"It's horrible! And those men!"

He had kissed her and gone. Now she could distinguish his beautiful vibrant voice among the raucous speech of the other men below.

The boy was asleep in a rude box bed drawn up beside theirs. Isaiah was bedded down in a little shack outside. Sabra sank down on the doubtful mattress. The walls of the room were mere pine slats with cracks between. From the street beneath the window came women's

shrill laughter, voices raised in jocose greeting. The sound of a piano hammered horribly.

She fell asleep in utter exhaustion, only to be awakened by pistol shots, bloodcurdling yells, the crash and tinkle of broken glass, the clatter of horses galloping. She lay there, cowering. Cim stirred in his bed, sighed deeply, slept again. At last she summoned courage to go to the window. Nothing. No one.

She looked at her little gold watch. It was only nine.

Yancey came in at midnight. She sat up in bed in her high-necked, long-sleeved nightgown. Her black eyes burned in her white face. "What was it? What was it?"

"What was what? Why aren't you asleep, sugar?"

"Those shots. And the screaming and hollering."

"Shots?" He was unstrapping his broad leather belt with its twin six-shooters. He wore it always now, a symbol of the terrors that lay waiting for them in this new existence. "Why, sugar, I don't recollect hearing any—oh—that!" He threw back his great head and laughed. "That was just a cowboy feeling high, shooting out the lights over in Strap Turket's saloon. Scare you, did it?"

He came over to her, put a hand on her shoulder. She shrugged away from him, furious. "I won't bring my boy up in a town like this. I'm going back. I'm going back home, I tell you."

"Wait till morning, anyhow, won't you, honey?" he said, and took her in his arms.

Next morning, magically, the terrors of the night had vanished. The sun was shining. For a moment Sabra had the illusion that she was at home in her own bed at Wichita. Then she realized that this was because she had been awakened by the familiar sound of Isaiah's husky, sweet voice somewhere below in the dusty yard. He was polishing Yancey's boots and singing as he rubbed:

> *"Lis'en to de lambs, all a-cryin'*
> *Lis'en to de lambs, all a-cryin',*
> *Ah wanta go to heab'n when ah die."*

Lugubrious though the words were, Sabra knew he was utterly happy.

There was much to be done—a dwelling to be got, a place to house the newspaper plant. If necessary, Yancey said, they could live in the rear and set up the printing and law office in the front.

"Houses are mighty scarce," he said, snorting and snuffling at the wash bowl. "I heard last night that Doc Nisbett's got a good one. A dozen families are after it, but Doc's as independent as a hog on ice."

Sabra rather welcomed the idea of combining office and home. She would be near him all day. As soon as breakfast was over, she and Yancey fared forth, leaving Cim in Isaiah's care. She had put on her black grosgrain with the three box pleats on each side, somewhat wrinkled from its long stay in the trunk, and her modish hat with ostrich plumes and pink roses. She was nineteen inches around the waist and very proud of it. Her dark eyes, slightly shadowed now, were enormous beneath the brim of the romantic plumed hat.

Yancey struck an attitude of dazzlement. " 'But who is this, what thing of land or sea—female of sex it seems—that so bedeck'd, ornate, and gay, comes this way sailing, like a stately ship of Tarsus . . .' "

"Don't talk nonsense. It's only my second-best black grosgrain."

"You're right, my darling. Even Milton has no words for such beauty."

The little haphazard town lay broiling in the summer sun. The sky hung flat and glaring over the prairie.

"Well, Sabra honey, this isn't so bad!" exclaimed Yancey, and looked about him largely. He seemed enormously elated—jubilant, almost. He stepped high in his fine Texas boots. She tucked her hand in his arm. The air was sweet, and they were young, and it was morning. Perhaps it was not going to be so dreadful after all.

The first thing she noticed, though, as she stepped into the dust of the street, caused her heart to sink. The few women to be seen scuttling about wore sunbonnets and calico. After furtive glances at Sabra in her modish dress and hat, they vanished into this little pine shack or that.

"But the others—the other kind of women . . ." Sabra faltered.

Yancey misunderstood. "Plenty of the other kind, but they aren't stirring this time of day."

"Don't be coarse, Yancey. I mean ladies like myself—that I can talk to—who'll come calling—that is . . ."

He waved a hand about. "Why, you just saw some womenfolks, didn't you? You can't expect them to wear their best to do the housework in. Besides, most of the men came without their women. When they send for them, you'll have plenty of company. It isn't every woman who'd have the courage you showed, roughing it out here. You're the stuff that Rachel was made of, and the mother of the Gracchi."

Sabra was a little hazy about the Gracchi, but basked serene in the knowledge that a compliment was intended.

The street was absurdly wide—surely fifty feet wide—in this little one-street town. A straggling house or so branched off it, but the life of Osage seemed to be concentrated just here. Houses and stores were built of unpainted wood. They stared starkly out into the rutted clay road, with never a tree or bit of green to rest the eye. Tied to the crude hitching posts were all sorts of vehicles: buckboards, dilapidated wagons, here and there a buggy; and everywhere those four-footed kings without which life in this remote place could not have been sustained. Indian ponies, pintos, pack horses, range horses, and occasionally a flashing-eyed creature whose ancestors had known the mesas of Spain.

Crude though the scene was, it had vitality. You sensed that behind those bare boards people were planning and stirring mightily. The very names tacked up over the storefronts had bite. Sam Pack. Mott Bixler. Strap Buckner.

Though they had come to town but the night before, it seemed to Sabra that a surprising number of people knew Yancey and greeted him as they passed down the street. "H'are you, Yancey! Howdy, ma'am." He swaggered a little as a man should in a white sombrero with a pretty woman on his arm; Sabra looked about her interestedly, terrified at what she saw and determined not to show it. Lean rangers in buckboards turned to stare. Loungers in doorways nudged each other. "Hi, Yancey! Howdy, ma'am."

Past the Red Dog Saloon. A group standing about in high-heeled boots greeted Yancey now with a "Howdy, Cim!"

The familiarity astonished Sabra. "They called you Cim!"

Narrowly he watched them as he passed. "Boys are up to something," he explained. "Probably fixing up a little initiation for me."

Sabra, glancing at the group, saw that they were behaving like snickering schoolboys. There was an air of secret mischief afoot.

"But why? Who are they?"

"I suspect they're the boys that did Pegler dirt. Don't get nervous. They won't dare try any monkeyshines while you're with me."

"Pegler? Isn't that the editor who was found dead? Yancey! Do you mean they did it!"

"I don't say they did it—exactly. They know more than is comfortable. I was inquiring around last night, and everybody shut up like a clam. I'm going to find out who killed Pegler and print it in the first number of the *Oklahoma Wigwam*."

"Oh, Yancey! I'm frightened!" She clung tighter to his arm.

"Nothing to be frightened of, honey. I'm no Pegler they can scare. They don't like my white hat, that's the truth of it. Dared me last night down at the Sunny Southwest Saloon to wear it this morning. Just to try me out. They won't have the guts to come out in the open—"

The sentence was never finished. Sabra heard a buzzing sound past her ear. Something sang—zing! Yancey's sombrero went spinning into the road.

"Stay where you are," Yancey ordered, his voice low. She could not have run if she had wanted to—her legs seemed suddenly no part of her. Yancey strolled leisurely over to where the white hat lay in the dust. He stooped carelessly, picked it up, surveyed it, and reached toward his pocket for his handkerchief. At that movement there was a rush and a scramble on the porch. Tilted chairs leaped forward, heels clattered, a door slammed. Of the group only three men remained. One of these leaned insolently against the porch post, the second stood warily behind him, and the third was edging prudently toward the closed door.

Yancey, now half turned toward them, had shaken out the folds of his handkerchief with a gesture of elegant leisure and was flicking the dust from his sombrero. He placed it on his head again with a movement almost languid, tossed the fine handkerchief into the road, and with another motion, so lightning quick that Sabra's eye never followed it, his hand went to his hip. There was the crack of a shot. The man who was edging toward the door clapped his hand to his ear. When he brought it away, it was darkly smeared. Yancey still stood in the road, his hand at his thigh, one slim foot advanced carelessly. His great head was lowered menacingly. His eyes beneath the brim of the sombrero looked as Sabra had never before seen them. They were terrible eyes, merciless, cold.

"A three-cornered piece, you'll find it, Lon. The Cravat sheep brand."

"Can't you take a joke, Yancey?" whined one of the three.

"Joke—hell!" snarled the man who was nicked. "God help you, Cravat."

"He always has," replied Yancey piously.

"If your missus wasn't with you—" Lon began. But suddenly Sabra herself took a hand in the proceedings. Her fright had vanished. These were no longer men to be feared, but mean little boys to be put in their place. She now advanced on them, her fine eyes flashing.

"Don't you 'missus' me, you miserable, good-for-nothing loafers. You leave my husband alone. I declare, I've a notion to—"

For one ridiculous moment it looked as though she meant to slap the leathery cheek of the bad man known as Lon Yountis. Certainly she raised her little hand in its neat black kid. Lon ducked and with a yelp of pure terror fled into the saloon, followed by the others.

Sabra sailed down the steps in triumph to behold a despairing Yancey.

"Sabra! Sabra! What have you done to me! It'll be all over the whole Southwest that Yancey Cravat hid behind a woman's petticoats."

"But they can't say so. You shot him very nicely in the ear, darling." Thus had a scant eighteen hours in Osage twisted her normal viewpoint.

"A woman's got no call to interfere when men are having a dispute."

"Dispute! He shot your hat right off your head!"

"What of it! Little friendly shooting."

Sabra was left speechless with indignation. "Let's be getting on," Yancey continued calmly. "Time to look at Doc Nisbett's house. There are only two or three to be had in the whole town, and his is the pick of them." They resumed their walk.

Doc Nisbett (veterinarian), shirt-sleeved, shrewd, was seated in a chair tipped up against the front of his coveted property. In the rush for town sites at the time of the Opening he had managed to lay his hands on five choice pieces. On these he erected dwellings, tilted his chair up against each in turn, and took his pick of latecomers frantic for shelter.

The dwelling itself looked like one of Cim's childish drawings of a house. It was a box, angular and unlovely, with a spindling little porch. The walls were no more than partitions, the floors, boards laid on dirt.

Taking her cue from Yancey—"Lovely," murmured Sabra, agonized. "Do very nicely."

The tour completed, they stood again on the porch. In the discussion of monthly rental Yancey was a child in the hands of the grasping owner. He clapped his hands together gaily. "There you are! That's all settled."

"Hey, hold on a minute," rasped Doc Nisbett. "How about water?"

"Sabra, honey, you settle these little matters. I've got to see Jesse Rickey about putting up the press and setting up the type racks. Then we've got to buy furniture for the house. Meet you down the street at Hefner's Furniture Store. Ten minutes." He was off.

"Well, now," said Doc Nisbett, "renting this house depends on how much water you going to need. How many barrels, do you think?"

Sabra had always taken water for granted, like air and sunshine. It was simply there. "Barrels," she now repeated. "Well, let—me—see. There's cooking, and cleaning the house, and drinking, and bathing. I should think ten barrels a day would be enough."

"Ten barrels," said Doc Nisbett in a flat voice, "a day."

"I should think that would be ample."

Doc Nisbett regarded Sabra with a look of active dislike. Then he walked across the porch, locked the front door, put the key in his pocket, and went back to his chair.

Sabra stood there, shocked and embarrassed. She did not know what to do. Never had she encountered such abysmal boorishness.

She should, of course, have gone up to him and said, "Do you mean that ten barrels are too much? I'm new to all this. Whatever you say."

But she was young and full of pride. So without another word she turned and marched down the dusty street. On either cheek burned a scarlet patch. Her eyes, in her effort to keep back the tears, were blazing, liquid, enormous.

And then a fearful thing happened. Down the street toward her came a galloping cowboy. Full of her troubles, Sabra was scarcely aware that she had glanced at him. How could she know that he was just up from Texas, that he was already howling drunk as befits a cowboy just off the range, and that never in his life had he seen a creature so gorgeous. Up he galloped; stared, wheeled, flung himself off his horse, and ran toward her in his high-heeled boots. She realized in a flash of terror that he was making straight for her. She stood, petrified. He came to her and threw his arms about her; he kissed her full on the lips, released her, leaped on his horse, and was off with a bloodcurdling yelp.

She thought she was going to be sick. She began to run awkwardly in her flounced silken skirts. Hefner's Furniture Store. Hefner's Furniture Store. She saw it at last. Hefner's Furniture Store and Undertaking Parlor. A crude wooden shack, like the rest. She ran in. Yancey! A man in shirt-sleeves came toward her. Hefner, probably. My husband, Yancey Cravat. No. Sorry, ma'am. Ain't been in. Anything I can do for you?

She blurted it hysterically. "A man—a cowboy—he jumped off his horse—I never saw him b—he kissed me—there on the street—"

"Why, ma'am, don't take on so. Young fella off the range, prob'ly, and never did see a gorgeous critter like yourself, if you'll pardon my mentioning it."

Her voice rose. "He kissed me. He k-k-k-k—"

"Now, now, lady. He was drunk, and you kind of went to his head. He'll ride back to Texas, and you'll be none the worse for it."

At this calloused viewpoint she broke down completely and buried her head on her folded arms atop the object nearest at hand. Her slim body shook with her sobs. Her tears flowed.

A firm note of protest entered Mr. Hefner's voice. "Excuse me, ma'am, but that's velvet you're crying on, and velvet spots terrible. If you'd just lean on something else . . ."

She raised herself and looked down with horror. She had showered her tears on that pride of the establishment, the newly arrived white velvet coffin (child's size) intended for show window purposes alone.

FROM DOC NISBETT, Yancey received the laconic information that his house had been rented by a family whose demands for water were more modest than Sabra's. Sabra was inconsolable, but Yancey did not reproach her for her mistake. "Never mind, sugar. We'll find a house. We're here, that's the main thing. When I think of those years in Wichita . . ."

"Why, Yancey! I thought you were happy there."

"Almost five years in one place—that's the longest stretch I've ever done, honey. Five years, back and forth like a trail horse; walking down to the *Wigwam* office in the morning, walking back to dinner at noon, sitting on the veranda evenings." He groaned with relief at his escape.

Yancey had reverted. Always a romantic figure, he now was remarkable even in this town of fantastic humans. His towering form, his vibrant voice, his dashing dress, his magnetic personality drew attention wherever he went. On the day following their arrival he had taken from his trunk a pair of ivory-handled six-shooters, a belt and holster studded with silver, and a pair of gold-mounted spurs. His white sombrero he had banded with a rattlesnake skin of gold and silver, a treasure also produced from his trunk. Thus bedecked he was by far the most spectacular male in all Oklahoma.

Sabra had never known he possessed such gaudy trappings. She learned many things about her husband in these first few days, some of them terrifying. She learned, for example, that Yancey Cravat was famed as the deadliest shot in the Southwest. He had the gift of being able to point his pistols without sighting, as one would point with a finger. He was one of the few who could draw and fire two six-shooters at once with equal speed and accuracy. He could hit his mark as he walked, as he ran, as he rode his horse. In Osage no man walked without his pistols.

On the very day of her encounter with Doc Nisbett, Sabra had gone with Yancey to see another house owner. He was found in a crude one-room shack which he used as a combination dwelling and land office. He glanced up at them from the rough table at which he was writing. "Howdy, Yancey!"

"Howdy, Cass!"

Yancey performed an introduction and revealed their plight.

"That's plumb terr'ble. Might be I can help you. Just let me step out to the corner and mail this letter. The bag's goin' any minute now."

He rose and took from the table his broad leather belt with its pair of six-shooters, evidently temporarily laid aside for comfort. This he now strapped quickly about his waist as another man would slip into his coat. It was perhaps this simple and sinister act, more than anything she had hitherto witnessed, that impressed Sabra with the utter lawlessness of this new land.

Cass's house turned out to be a four-room dwelling inadequate to their needs. Then Yancey had an idea. He found a two-room cabin made of rough boards. This was hauled to the site of the main house and added to it, providing them with a combination dwelling, newspaper plant, and law office. There was all the splendor of sitting room, dining room, bedroom and kitchen to live in. One room of the small attached cabin was an office. The other served as composing room and print shop. Hefner's store provided them with a large wooden bedstead; a small bed for Cim; tables, chairs—the plainest of everything. Sabra's silver, china, monogrammed linens were as out of place in this roughly furnished cabin as a court lady in a peasant's hovel. But in two days she was a housewife established in her routine as though she had been at it for years. A pan of biscuits in the oven of the wood-burning kitchen stove; a dress pattern of calico, cut out on the table in the sitting room.

Setting up the newspaper plant and law office was not so simple. Yancey was more absorbed in the sign tacked up over the front of the shop than he was in the arrangement of the necessary appliances inside. THE OKLAHOMA WIGWAM, read the sign in block letters two feet high. Beneath, in letters scarcely less impressive: YANCEY CRAVAT, PROP. AND EDITOR. ATTORNEY AT LAW. NOTARY.

The placing of this sign took the better part of a day. While the operation was in progress Yancey crossed the road fifty times, ostensibly to direct Jesse Rickey, his assistant, but really to bask in the dazzling effect of the sign. To Sabra, coming to the door, the attendant clamor seemed out of all proportion to the results.

Yancey, from across the road—"Lift her up a little higher that end!"

"Well, which end, f'r land's sake, right or left?" from Jesse Rickey.

"Right! RIGHT! Don't you know your right from your left?"

"How's that?"

Sabra was beginning to realize that the male might be fallible. Even though a daily witness during her girlhood to the dominance of her matriarchal mother, she had been bred to the tradition that the man was always right. Yancey, still her passionate lover, had always treated her, tenderly, as a charming little fool, and this role she had meekly accepted. But now suspicion began to rear its ugly head. These last few weeks had shown her that the male was often mistaken, as a sex, and that Yancey was almost always wrong as an individual. But these frightening discoveries she would not yet admit even to herself.

"Yancey, this case of type's badly mixed up," she told him. Jesse Rickey, journeyman printer and periodic drunkard, was responsible for this misfortune, having dropped a case in the dust of the road. "It'll have to be sorted before you can get out a paper."

"Rickey'll tend to that. I've got editorials to write, news to get, lot of real estate transfers—and I'm going to find out who killed Pegler and print it in the first issue if it takes the last drop of blood in me."

"Oh, what does it matter? He's dead. Besides, you've got Cim and me to think of. You can't let anything happen to you."

"Let that gang of skunks get away with a thing like that and anything *is* likely to happen to me. No, sir! I'll show them, first crack, that the *Oklahoma Wigwam* prints all the news, all the time."

In the end it was she who sorted the case of type. Five years of Yancey's newspaper ownership in Wichita had familiarized her with many of the mechanical aspects of printing. She even liked the smell of printer's ink, of the metal type, of the paper wet from the press.

The hand press was finally set up, and the little job press, and the case rack containing the type. The rollers were in place, and their stock of paper. Curiously enough, though neither Yancey nor Sabra was conscious of it, it was she who had performed most of this manual work, with Isaiah and Jesse Rickey to help her. Yancey was off and up the street every ten minutes. Returning, he would lose himself in the placing of his law library and his favorite volumes of literature. Glib and showy though he was with his book knowledge, Yancey still had the absorption of the true book lover. He paid close attention to the carpenter who put up crude bookshelves. The books he insisted on placing himself, losing himself now in this page, now in that, so that at the end of the afternoon he had accomplished nothing.

He would call happily in to Sabra as she bent over the case rack, her cheek streaked with ink, her fingers stained, sorting type. "Sabe! Listen to this!" He would clear his throat. " 'Son of Nestor, delight of my heart, mark the flashing of bronze through the echoing halls, and the flashing of gold and of amber and of silver and of ivory.' It's as fine as the Old Testament, Sabra. Finer!"

At last the Cravat family was settled in. The front door, which was the office entrance, faced the main street. The back and the side doors looked out on a stretch of Oklahoma red clay, littered with the empty tin cans that mark any new American settlement, and especially one whose drought is relieved by the coolness of canned tomatoes and peaches. In the midst of this clay and refuse, in a sort of shed, lived little Isaiah; rather, he slept there, for all day long he was about the house and the printing office, tireless, willing, invaluable. He belonged to Sabra, body and soul, as completely as though the Civil War had never been. A servant of twelve, he became as dear to Sabra as a child of her own, despite her southern training and his black skin. He dried the dishes and laid the table; he was playmate and nursemaid for Cim; he ran errands; he was a born reporter, and in the course of his day's scurrying about the town brought into Sabra's kitchen more news and gossip than a whole staff of trained newspapermen could have done. He was so little, so harmless looking, that his presence was more often than not completely overlooked.

Sabra in time taught him to read, write, and figure. He was quick to learn, industrious, lovable. Cim was beginning to learn the alphabet, and as Sabra bent over the child, Isaiah would bring his little stool out of its corner. Perched on it he mastered the curlicues in their proper sequence. He cleared the unsightly backyard of its litter. Together he and Sabra even tried to plant a garden in this barren clay. More than anything else Sabra missed trees and flowers. In this town of almost ten thousand inhabitants there were two trees: stunted jack oaks.

Yancey, from morning until night, was always a little overstimulated by the whiskey he drank. This, together with a natural fearlessness, an enormous vitality, and a devouring interest in everybody and everything, gained him friends and enemies in almost equal proportion.

Already his talents were being sought in defense of murderers, horse thieves, land grabbers. It was known that the average jury was wax in his hands. A tremolo tone—their eyes began to moisten, their mouth muscles to sag with sympathy; a lilt of the golden voice—they guffawed with mirth. Even a horse thief, that blackest of criminals in this country, was said to have a chance for his life if Yancey Cravat could be induced to plead for him.

But in the ten days following their arrival in Osage, his one interest seemed to be tracing the Pegler murder. He asked questions everywhere and watched their effect. Sabra argued with him. "You didn't do anything to help catch the Kid, out there on the prairie, and you knew where he was. He had killed a man, too, and robbed a bank."

"That was different," Yancey answered.

"Different! How? What's this Pegler to you! They'll kill you, too—and then what shall I do? Cim and I here, alone—Yancey, darling—I love you so—if anything should happen to you . . ."

"Honey, hush your crying and listen. The Kid's a bad one. But it isn't his fault. The government at Washington made him an outlaw."

"Yancey Cravat, what are you talking about?"

"The Kid's father rode the range before there were fences or railroads in Kansas, when this part of the country was running wild with longhorn cattle. The railroads began coming in. The settlers came with it, up across Texas, through the Indian Territory to the end of steel at Abilene, Kansas. The Kid was brought up to all that. Freighters, bull whackers, mule skinners, hunters, and cowboys—that's all he knew. I've seen seventy-five thousand cattle at a time waiting shipment to the East, with lads like the Kid in charge. The range was the only life they wanted. Along comes the government. What happens?"

"What?" breathed Sabra, enthralled as always.

"They take the range away from the cattle men—the free range that they had come to think of as theirs. Squatters come in, Sooners, and Nesters, and then the whole rush of the Opening. Overnight the range is cut up into town sites. It must have sickened them to see it."

"But that's progress, Yancey."

"Wilderness one day; town sites the next. And the rangers having no more chance than chips in a flood. They went plumb loco, I tell you. They couldn't fight progress, but they could get revenge on the people who had taken their world away from them."

"You're taking the part of criminals! You're as bad as they are."

"Now, now, Sabra. No dramatics. Leave that for me. I'm better at it. The Kid's bad, yes. But he never kills unless he has to. And he runs a risk. When he robs a bank it's in broad daylight, with a hundred guns against him. He was brought up a reckless, lawless youngster. He's a killer now, and he'll die by the gun, with his boots on. But there's no yellow in the Kid."

Sabra's dark eyes searched her husband's face. "But the men who killed Pegler. Why are they so much worse. . . ."

"Dirty jackals hired by thieving politicians."

"But why? Why?"

"Because Pegler—a decent newspaperman from Denver—had the same idea I have—that here's a chance to start clean, right from scratch. There's never been a chance like it in the world. We can make a model out of this Oklahoma country, with all the mistakes of the other pioneers to profit by. The other settlers of this country—it got away from them, and they fell into the rut. Ugly politics, ugly towns, ugly minds."

"What's that got to do with Pegler?"

"I saw that one copy of his paper. He called it the *New Day*—poor devil. And in it he outlined a belief along the lines I've tried to explain to you. He accused the government of robbing the Indians. He accused the settlers of cheating them. He told just how their monthly allotment was pinched out of their foolish fingers—"

"Indians! Heavens, Yancey! You're always going on about Indians! What good are they? They won't work. They just squat there, rotting."

"White men can't do those things to a helpless—"

"And so they killed him!" Sabra cried irrelevantly. "And they'll kill you, too. Oh, Yancey—please—I don't want to be a pioneer woman. I can't make things different. I liked them as they were. Comfortable and safe. Let them alone. Let's just make a town like Wichita . . . with trees . . . and people being sociable . . . not killing each other all the time . . . church on Sunday . . . a school for Cim. . . ."

The face she adored was a mask, with the look she had seen and dreaded—cold, determined, relentless.

"All right. Go back to your trees and your churches and your whole smug, dead-alive family. But not me! I'm staying here. And when I find the man who killed Pegler I'll face him with it, and I'll publish his name, and I'll see him strung up on a tree."

"Oh, God!" whimpered Sabra, and sank into his arms. But those arms were suddenly no shelter. He put her from him, gently, but with iron firmness, and walked out to the broad red road.

Chapter 4

YANCEY PUT HIS QUESTION wherever he came upon a little group lounging on saloon porch or street corner. "How did Pegler come to die?" The effect of the question was always the same. One minute men were standing sociably, gossiping. Yancey would stroll up and ask his question. As though by magic the group vanished.

He visited Coroner Hefner, of Hefner's Furniture Store and Undertaking Parlor. That gentleman was seated in his combination office and laboratory. "Listen, Louie. How did Pegler come to die?"

Hefner stared at Yancey in dismay. "Yancey, you bought your furniture here, and what's more, you paid cash for it. I want you as a customer, see, but not in the other branch of my business. Don't go round askin' that there question."

"Why not?"

Hefner made a gesture of despair, rose, vanished out his back door.

Yancey strolled out into the glaring sunshine of Pawhuska Avenue. Indians, Mexicans, cowboys, solid citizens lounged along the street. On the corner stood Pete Pitchlyn talking to the Spaniard, Estevan Miro. They were the gossips of the town, these two. News of the whole brilliant burning Southwest sieved through them. Miro sold his knowledge. A quiet man, his movements appeared slow because of their feline grace. Eternally he rolled cigarettes with exquisite deftness between the thumb and first two fingers of his right hand.

Pete Pitchlyn, famous Indian scout of a bygone day, had grown potbellied and flabby, now that the Indians were rotting on their reservations. His wife, a full blood Cherokee, squatted in the shade of a nearby shack. On the ground all around her, like a litter of puppies, were their children.

Late in his career as a scout Pitchlyn had been shot in the left heel by a poisoned Indian arrow. It was thought he would surely die. But a combination of unlimited whiskey and a constitution made of steel somehow allowed him to live. Stubbornly he had refused to have the leg amputated, and by a miracle it had failed to send its poison through the rest of his body. But the leg had withered until now it was twelve inches shorter than the sound limb. He refused to use crutches and got about with astonishing agility. When he stood on the sound leg he was a giant of six feet three. But occasionally the sound leg tired, and he would rest for a moment on the other. He then became a runt five feet high.

These two specimens of the Southwest Yancey now approached, his manner carefree. Almost imperceptibly the pair stiffened.

"Howdy, Pete!"

"Howdy, Yancey!"

Miro eyed Yancey innocently. *"Qué tal?"*

"Bien. Y tú?"

They stood, the three, wary, silent. Yancey balanced from shining boot toe to heel and back again. Then he put the eternal question of the inquiring reporter. "Well, boys, what do you know?"

The two were braced for a query less airy. Their faces relaxed. The Spaniard shrugged. Pete Pitchlyn's eyes were like coals in an ash heap. It was not for him to be seen talking on the street corner with the man who was going about asking a fatal question. He knew Yancey, wished him well. Yet there was little he dared say now before Miro. Yancey continued conversationally.

"I understand there's an element in town bragging that they're going to make Osage the terror of the Southwest, like Dodge City in the old days." Pete Pitchlyn and Estevan Miro maintained an air of nonchalance. "I'm interviewing citizens of note," continued Yancey, "on how they think this town ought to be run."

"Yancey," said Pete, "stick to your lawy'in'. Anybody's got the gift of gab like you have is wastin' their time doin' anything else."

"Oh, I wouldn't say that," Yancey replied. "Running a newspaper keeps me in touch with folks. Besides, it's my way of earning a living. Of course," he continued brightly, "there have been times when running a newspaper has saved the editor the trouble of ever again having to earn a living." The faces of the two were blank as a sponged slate. "Come on, boys. Who killed Pegler?"

Pete Pitchlyn, his squaw, and the litter of babies dispersed. Yancey and the Spaniard were left alone on the sunny street corner.

The face of Miro now became strangely pinched. The eyes were inky slits. "I know something. I have that to tell you," he said in Spanish.

Yancey replied in the same tongue, "Out with it."

The Spaniard did not speak. Yancey knew that Miro must have been well paid by someone to say something to him. He shrugged and sauntered off.

Miro leaped after him in one noiseless bound. He spoke rapidly in Spanish. "I say only that which was told to me. The words are not mine. They say, 'Are you a friend of Yancey Cravat?' I say, 'Yes.' They say then, 'Tell your friend Yancey Cravat that wisdom is better than wealth. If he does not keep his mouth shut he will die.' "

"Thanks," replied Yancey in English. Then he reached out and gave Miro's neckerchief a strong jerk. The gesture was at once an insult and a threat. "Tell them—" Suddenly there issued from his mouth a sound so unearthly as to freeze the blood of any within hearing. It was a sound between the gobble of an angry turkey cock and the howl of a coyote. Throughout the Southwest it was known that when an Indian made this sound, it meant sudden destruction to any or all in his path.

The Spaniard's face went a curious dough gray. With a whimper he ran around the corner of the nearest shack and vanished.

Yancey recounted his triumph to Sabra at noon, but she refused to believe that this Pegler business was as important to him as he made out. It was just one of his whims. Something else would come up to attract his interest or arouse his indignation. The *Oklahoma Wigwam* was due off the press on Thursday. Privately Sabra thought that this would have to be accomplished by a miracle. This was Friday. Less than a week to go, and nothing had been done.

She was overjoyed when, that same day, a solemn deputation of citizens, three in number, called on Yancey with the amazing request that he conduct divine service the following Sunday. The womenfolks, they said, thought it high time that some contact be established between their new town and the Power supposedly gazing on it from above. Sabra warmed toward these women. She made up her mind that once the paper had gone to press she would go calling.

She got out a plaid silk tie for Cim. "Church meeting!" she exclaimed joyously. Here at last was something familiar. Yancey set about making the arrangements for Sunday's meeting. There was no building large enough to hold the thousands who made up this settlement on the prairie. News of the meeting spread. Nesters, homesteaders, rangers, cowboys for miles around somehow got wind of it.

Yancey turned to the one shelter in town adequate to hold the crowd expected. It was the huge gambling tent that stood at the far north end of Pawhuska Avenue, flags waving gaily from its top. For the men it was the social center of Osage. And while faro and stud poker saved them the trouble of counting their ready cash on Saturday night, the great day for gambling was Sunday. Rangers, cowboys, a generous sprinkling of professional bad men and all the town women who were not respectable flocked to the tent for recreation and excitement. It was a question whether the proprietor, Mr. Grat Gotch, would be willing to sacrifice any portion of Sunday's trade for the furtherance of the Lord's business.

Yancey went to confer with him that afternoon. Mr. Gotch was a little plump man with a round and smiling countenance, who looked like an old baby. He was superintending the placing of a work of art just arrived via the Missouri, Kansas & Texas Railroad. His newly acquired treasure was a picture, done in oils, of a robust and very pink lady who, apparently having expended all her energy upon the arrangement of her elaborate coiffure, was unable to proceed further with dressing herself until fortified by refreshment and repose. She had flung herself in a complete state of nature on a couch where she lolled at ease, her lips parted to receive a pair of ripe red cherries which she held dangling between thumb and forefinger. Her eyes were not on the cherries but on the beholder.

This *objet d'art* was being suspended by guy ropes from the tent top so that it dangled just above the bar. Mr. Gotch had pursued his profession in the bonanza days of Denver, San Francisco, and Dodge City. He knew that the eye, as well as the gullet, must have refreshment in hours of ease. "Ain't she," he demanded now of Yancey, "a lalapaloosa?"

Yancey surveyed the bright pink lady. "It's a calumny on nature's fairest achievement."

The word calumny was not in Mr. Gotch's vocabulary. He mistook Yancey's warmth of tone for enthusiasm. "That's right," he agreed. "I was sayin' to the boys only this morning."

Yancey ordered a drink and invited Gotch to have one with him. Over the whiskey he put his case.

"Divine worship! Why, hell yes, Yancey," Gotch said graciously.

They went to work early Sunday. They covered the faro and roulette tables with twenty-two-foot boards. Such of the congregation as came early would use these for seats, along with a few rude benches on which the players usually sat. The remainder must stand.

The meeting was to be from eleven to twelve. As early as nine people began to arrive from lonely cabins, dugouts, tents. It wasn't religion they sought; they were starving for company. They brought picnic baskets, prepared for a holiday. The cowboys were gorgeous in their pink and purple shirts, their gayest neckerchiefs, their most ornate boots. They rode up and down before the big tent, their horses stepping high.

The town seemed alive with Indians. They flocked in by the dozens from their reservations. The men were decked in beads and chains. They rode their mangy horses and brought their entire families—squaw, children of assorted sizes, dogs. Sabra, seeing them, told herself sternly that they were all God's children; that these red men had been converted. She didn't believe a word of it.

She superintended the toilettes of her menfolk from Yancey to Isaiah. She herself had stayed up the night before to iron Yancey's finest shirt. She sprinkled a drop of her cherished cologne on his handkerchief.

He chided her, laughing, "My good woman, is this the way to titivate for delivering the word of God? Sackcloth and ashes is the prescribed costume." He drank down three fingers of whiskey.

Cim cavorted excitedly in his best suit. The boy, Sabra thought, grew more and more like Yancey. "I'm going to church!" he shouted. "Hi, Isaiah! Blessed be the name of the Lawd Amen. . . ."

Yancey's dramatic instinct bade him delay. A dozen times Sabra called to him as he sat in the front office busy with paper and pencil. This was, she decided, his sole preparation for the sermon he would deliver within the hour. Later she found in the pocket of his Prince Albert the piece of paper on which he had made these notes. It was filled with those whorls, crisscrosses and parallel lines with which the hand gives relief to the troubled mind. One word he had written on it: "Yountis."

At last he was ready. Sabra had put on her best black grosgrain and the hat with the plumes. She and Yancey stepped sedately down the street, Cim's fingers in her own. Isaiah had announced that his dressing was not quite completed and urged them to proceed without him.

It occurred neither to Sabra nor to Yancey that there was anything unusual in their thus proceeding toward a gambling saloon which was for one short hour to become a house of God.

559

"Are you nervous, Yancey?"

"No, sugar. Though I'd fifty times rather plead with a jury of Texas cattlemen—" He broke off abruptly. "What's everybody laughing at?"

They turned to look behind them. Down the street, perhaps fifty paces back, came Isaiah. He was strutting in an absurd and yet unmistakable imitation of Yancey's stride. Around his waist was a red calico sash and, over that, a holstered leather belt that hung to his knees. Protruding from the holsters one saw the heads of what turned out to be the household monkey wrench and a screwdriver. He wore a battered sombrero. But this was not the high point of his sartorial triumph. He had found somewhere a pair of Yancey's discarded high-heeled boots. Into these Isaiah had thrust his own bare feet. He teetered and wobbled as the treacherous heels betrayed him. Yet he managed, by the power of his dramatic gift, to give to the appreciative onlooker a complete picture of Yancey Cravat in grotesque miniature.

Yancey gave a great roar of laughter. But Sabra's face went curiously sallow, so that she was suddenly Felice Venable, enraged. She flew toward the small mimic. Isaiah looked up at her, terrorized. She raised her hand in its neat black glove to cuff him smartly. But Yancey was too quick for her. His fingers closed around her wrist in an iron grip.

"If you touch him I swear I'll not set foot inside the tent. Look at him!"

Isaiah's black face gazed up at him. In it was utter devotion. Yancey, himself a born actor, knew that in the boy's grotesque costume there had been only that sincerest of flattery, imitation of that which was adored.

Yancey released Sabra's wrist. He smiled at Isaiah, removed the sombrero, and let his hand rest for a moment on the child's head. Isaiah's fright gave way to injury. "Ah didn't go fo' to fret nobody. I jes' crave to dress myself up Sunday style. . . ."

"That's right, Isaiah. You look fine. Now listen to me. Do you want a real suit of Sunday clothes? Brand-new?"

"Sunday suit fo' me to wear! Fo' true!"

"You'll have one next week if you do something for me. Something big. I don't want you to go to the church meeting." The black boy's expressive face became suddenly doleful. "Isaiah, listen hard. Everybody in town's at the meeting. The newspaper office is left alone. There are people who'd sooner set fire to the house than see the paper come out. I want you to go back and go into the kitchen, where you can see the yard and the side entrance, too. I'm putting you on patrol duty."

"Yes, Mr. Yancey!" agreed Isaiah. "Patrol." His dejected frame stiffened to the new martial role.

"If anybody comes up to the house, you take this—and shoot." He took from beneath the Prince Albert a gun which was not visible as were the two six-shooters that he always carried. It was the deadliest of weapons, a pistol whose hammer, when pulled back by the thumb, would fall again as soon as released. No need for Isaiah to wrestle with a trigger.

"Oh, Yancey!" breathed Sabra in horror. "He's a child!"

"You remember what I told you last week," Yancey went on to Isaiah. "When we were shooting at the tin can in the yard. Do it just as you did it then—draw, aim, and shoot with the one motion."

"Yes, Mr. Yancey! I kill 'em daid." He flashed a smile and was off.

All Sabra's pleasurable anticipation in the church meeting had fled. She turned to Yancey. "How could you give a gun to a child like that!"

"It isn't loaded. Come on, honey. We're late."

For the first time in their married life she doubted his word. "Did you mean it when you said there were people who would set fire to the house? Or was it an excuse to send Isaiah back because of the way he looked?"

"That was it."

Again she doubted him. "I don't believe you. There's something going on. Yancey, tell me."

"Don't be foolish. It occurred to me just now that maybe this meeting was the idea of somebody who isn't altogether inspired by a desire for a closer communion with God. Good joke on me, if it's true."

"I'm going back to the house." She was desperate. Her house was burning up, Isaiah was being murdered. Her linen, the silver . . .

"You're coming with me."

"Yancey! I'm afraid to have you stand up there, before all those people. Tell them you're sick. Tell them . . ."

They had reached the tent. A roar came to them from within. The entrance was packed with lean figures smoking and spitting. "Where's your Bible, Yancey?"

"Right here, boys." And Yancey reached into his Prince Albert to produce in triumph the word of God. With Sabra on his arm he marched through the close-packed tent. "They've saved two seats for you and Cim down front—or should have. Yes, there they are."

Sabra felt faint. She had seen the foxlike face of Lon Yountis in the doorway. "That man Lon," she whispered to Yancey. "He was there. He looked at you as you passed by—he looked at you so . . ."

"That's fine, honey. Better than I hoped for. I like to have members of my flock right under my eye."

RANGED ALONG the rear of the tent were the Indians. Osages, Poncas, Cherokees, Creeks. The Osages—a tall, handsome people—wore striped blankets of orange and purple and scarlet and blue.

Holding Cim's hand tightly, Sabra found the two chairs that had been placed for them. Other fortunate ones sat perched on the bar, on the gambling tables, on the benches, on upturned barrels. The rest of the congregation stood. Sabra glanced shyly about her. Men—hundreds of men. They were strangely alike—young-old, weather-beaten, deeply seamed. The Plains had taken them early, had scorched them with her sun, stung them with her dust. Sabra had grown accustomed to these faces. But she was not prepared for the women. The wives of Osage's citizenry had taken this opportunity to show what they had in the way of finery. Headgear trembled with roses. Cheviot and lady's-cloth graced shoulders that had known only cotton this month past. Near Sabra was a very modish woman who must be, she thought, about her own age; fair, blue-eyed, almost childlike in her girlish slimness. Sabra decided that her nose was the most exquisite she had ever seen; that her fair skin could not long endure this burning climate. The man beside her, who looked old enough to be her father, must be after all her husband. Yancey had pointed him out one day. She remembered his name was Waltz, Evergreen Waltz. He was a gambler and was supposed to be the errant son of the former governor of some state or other. Still, the sight of this lovely face, and of the other feminine faces looking out from decent straw bonnets, gave Sabra a glow of reassurance.

Immediately this was quenched at the showy entrance of a group of women of whom Sabra had been unaware. The leader of this spectacular group had arrived in Osage only the day before, accompanied by six young ladies. They had stepped off the railroad coach at the town of Wahoo, twenty-two miles away, and had mounted a buckboard amid much clamor and a striking display of ankle. Their silks outspread, their parasols unfurled, they had bumped their way over the prairie to Osage.

The leader, a handsome black-haired woman of not more than twenty-three, had taken such rooms as they could get in the town. Within an hour it was known that she claimed the name of Dixie Lee. That she was a descendant of decayed southern aristocracy. That her companions boasted such fancy nomenclature as Cherry de St. Maurice, Carmen Brown, Belle Mansero. That Dixie Lee had driven a shrewd bargain whereby she was to come into possession of the Elite Rooming House and Café, situated at the far end of Pawhuska Avenue, near the gambling tent; and that she contemplated building a house of her own if business warranted. Finally she brought the news that the Missouri, Kansas & Texas was to be extended from Wahoo to Osage and perhaps beyond it.

Dixie Lee had been quick to learn of Sunday's meeting, and quicker still to see the advantage of this opportunity for advertisement. As the six marched in with Dixie Lee at their head, the air of the tent became suffocating with scent. Necks were craned; whispers became a buzz; seats were miraculously found, as for visiting royalty. The tent top, seeming to focus the glare of the Oklahoma sun, cast its revealing spotlight upon painted cheeks and beaded lashes. The nude lady of the cherries in Grat Gotch's art treasure stared down at them with the look of one who is vanquished by an enemy from her own camp.

Yancey, having lifted Cim into the chair next his mother, looked up at the entrance of this splendid procession. "God Almighty!" he said.

"What is it? Yancey! What's wrong?"

"That's the girl. Dixie Lee—she's the girl in the black tights in the Run. . . ." he was whispering.

"Oh, no!" cried Sabra aloud.

So this was the church meeting she had looked to with such hope, such happy assurance. Harlots, Indians, heat, glare, her house probably blazing at this moment, Isaiah weltering in his own gore, Lon Yountis sneering in the tent entrance. And now this unscrupulous woman who had stolen Yancey's land from him by a trick.

Yancey made his way through the crowd, leaped to the top of the roulette table, flung his sombrero dexterously to the base of a suspended oil lamp. Lifting his great head, he swept the congregation with his magnetic eyes. His voice sounded through the tent, stilling its buzz.

"Friends and fellow citizens, I have been called on to conduct this opening meeting of the Osage First Methodist, Episcopal, Lutheran, Presbyterian, Congregational, Baptist, Catholic, Unitarian Church. In my career as a lawyer and an editor I have been required to speak on varied occasions and on many subjects. But this is the first time that I have been required to speak the word of God in His temple." He glanced around the gaudy, glaring tent. "For any shelter, however sordid—no offense, Grat—becomes, while His word is spoken within it, His temple. Suppose, then, that we unite in spirit by uniting in song. We have no hymn books. We will therefore open this auspicious occasion by sing-ing—uh—what do you all know, boys, anyway?"

The faces of the motley congregation stared blankly up at Yancey.

"How about 'Who Were You at Home?' " called out a voice. It was Shanghai Wiley, up from Texas; owner of the vast Rancho Palacios, on Tres Palacios Creek. He was the most famous cattle singer in the South-west. With his high sweet tenor voice he had been known to quiet a whole herd of maddened cattle on the verge of a stampede into the Rio Grande. It was an art he had learned when a cowboy on the range.

Yancey acknowledged his suggestion. "Thanks for speaking up, Shanghai. A good song, though a little secular for the occasion. But you all know it, that's the main thing. Now, then, all together!"

It was a well-known song in an area where so many coming with a checkered past had found it convenient to change their names. The congregation took it up feelingly:

> "Who were you at home?
> Who were you at home?
> God alone remembers
> Ere you first began to roam.
> Jack or Jo or Bill or Pete,
> Anyone you chance to meet,
> Sure to hit it just as neat,
> Oh, who were you at home?"

Somebody in the rear suddenly produced an accordion, and from the crowd up front came the sound of a Jew's harp. The chorus now swelled with fervor. They might have been singing "Onward, Christian Soldiers." Through it all sounded Shanghai Wiley's piercing tenor.

Sabra had joined in the singing. It had seemed, somehow, to relieve her. Perhaps, after all, this new community was about to make a proper beginning. She began to feel prim and good and settled at last.

"Now then," said Yancey, all aglow, "the next thing is to take up the collection before the sermon."

"What for?" yelled Pete De Vargas.

"Because, you Spanish infidel, that's part of the service. Southwest

Davis, you work this side of the house. Ike Bixler, you take that side. The collection, fellow citizens, is for the new church organ."

"We ain't even got a church!" bawled Pete again.

"Once we buy an organ we'll have to build a church to put it in. Stands to reason. So give what you can."

The collection was taken up in two five-gallon sombreros, which were then brought to the roulette table for Yancey's inspection.

"Mr. Grat Gotch will kindly count the proceeds of the collection."

Grat made a swift and accurate count. He muttered the result to Yancey, who announced it. "Fellow citizens, the first collection for the new organ for the Osage church amounts to the gratifying total of one hundred and thirty-three dollars and fifty-five cents."

Yancey's eye swept his flock. Then he took from the rear pocket of his Prince Albert the small and worn little Bible.

"Friends! We've come to the sermon. What I have to say is going to take fifteen minutes. The first five minutes are going to be devoted to a confession by me to you, and I didn't expect to make it when I accepted the job of conducting this meeting. I'll announce my text, and then I'll make my confession. The remaining time will be devoted to the sermon. Anyone wishing to leave the tent, kindly do so now, before the confession, or remain until the conclusion of the service."

Only an earthquake might have moved a worshiper in that hushed and expectant gathering. Yancey waited, Bible in hand. A kind of power seemed to flow from him to the crowd, drawing them, enthralling them. Yet in his eyes there was that which sent a pang of fear through Sabra.

Yancey drew a long breath. "My text is from Proverbs. *'There is a lion in the way; a lion is in the streets.'* Friends, there is a lion in the streets of Osage, our fair city, soon to be Queen of the Great Southwest. And I have been a liar and an avaricious knave. For I pretended not to have knowledge which I have; and I went about asking for information of this lion—though I would change the word lion to jackal—when already I had proof of his guilt. The reason for my deceit I shall now confess to you. I intended to announce today that I had this knowledge, and I meant to announce that I would publish it in the *Oklahoma Wigwam* on Thursday, hoping thereby to gain circulation for my paper, starting it off with a bang!" At the word bang, uttered with much vehemence, the congregation jumped nervously. "Fellow citizens, I repent of my desire for self-advancement at the expense of this community. I no longer intend to withhold the name of the jackal in a lion's skin who has held this town abjectly terrorized. I stand here to announce to you that the name of that cowardly murderer who shot down Jack Pegler when his back was turned"— he was gesturing with his Bible in his hand—"was none other than . . ."

He dropped the Bible to the floor as if by accident. As he stooped for it, there was the crack of a revolver from the rear of the tent. A bullet sang past the spot where Yancey's head had been, and there appeared in the white surface of the tent a tiny circlet of blue sky. But before that dot appeared, Yancey Cravat had raised himself halfway and had fired from the waist without, seemingly, pausing to take aim. The crack of his six-shooter was so close on the heels of that first report that the two seemed almost simultaneous. The congregation was now on its feet, its back to the pulpit. Its eyes were on one figure. That figure—a man—had gripped with his left hand one of the tent ropes, and now, his fingers slipping gently along it, he sank to the floor, sat there a moment, rolled over on one side and lay still.

". . . Lon Yountis," finished Yancey.

Screams. Shouts. A stampede for the door. Then the powerful voice of Yancey Cravat above the roar. "Stop! Stand where you are! Shut that tent flap, Jesse. Louie Hefner, remove the body and do your duty."

"Okay, Yancey. It's self-defense and justifiable homicide."

"I know it, Louie. . . . Fellow citizens! We will forego the sermon this morning, but next Sabbath, if requested, I shall be glad to take the pulpit again. The subject of that sermon will be from Proverbs: '*Whoso diggeth a pit shall fall therein.*' This meeting, brethren and sisters, will now be concluded with prayer." There was a scuffling sound as a heavy, inert burden was carried out through the tent flap. Yancey Cravat bowed his head and sent the thrilling tones of his voice into the crowd.

"Bless this community, O Lord. . . ."

IN ACCORDANCE WITH CUSTOM, Yancey carved a notch in the butt of his six-shooter. It was then that Sabra first noticed that there were five earlier notches in the butts of his two guns.

Aghast, she investigated further. She saw that each weapon was held within the holster by an ingenious steel clip. Sensitive as a watch spring, it gripped the barrel securely and yet so lightly that the least effort would set it free. Yancey could pull his gun and thumb the hammer with one

motion instead of two. The infinitesimal saving of time had saved his life that day.

"Oh, Yancey, you haven't killed six men!"

"I've never killed a man unless I knew he'd kill me if I didn't. Would you have liked to see Yountis get me?"

"Oh, darling, no! But wasn't there some other way? Cim has seen his own father shoot a man and kill him."

"Better than seeing a man shoot and kill his own father."

There was nothing more she could say on the subject. But another question was consuming her. "That Lee woman. I saw you chatting on the street after the meeting. Bad enough if you'd never seen her before. But she stole your land from you in the Run. Yet you stood there, actually talking to her."

"I know. She said she had made up her mind to get a piece of land and raise cattle. She wanted to give up her way of living. She's been at it since she was eighteen. Older than she looks. She was desperate."

"What happened to the land?"

"Before the month was up she saw she couldn't make it go. She sold out for five hundred dollars and went to Denver."

"Why didn't she stay there?"

"It was overcrowded. When she got a tip that the railroad was coming through here, she got together her outfit, and down she came. She's a smart girl. She's a"—he hesitated—"in a way, she's a good girl."

Sabra's voice rose to the pitch of hysteria. "You talk as though you admire that"—Aunt Cassandra Venable's word came to her lips—"that hussy!"

The first issue of the *Wigwam* appeared on Thursday, as scheduled. It was a masterly mixture of reticence and indiscretion. A half column, first page, was devoted to the church meeting. An outsider reading it would have gathered that all had been sweetness and light. On an inside column of the four-page sheet was a brief notice:

It is to be regretted than an annoying shooting affray somewhat marred the otherwise splendid religious service held in the recreation tent last Sunday, kindness of Mr. Grat Gotch. A ruffian, who too long had been terrorizing innocent citizens of our fair city, took this occasion to create a disturbance, during which he shot at the person presiding. It was necessary to reply in kind. The body, unclaimed, was interred in Boot Hill, with only the prowling jackals to mourn him. It is hoped that his nameless grave will serve as a warning to others of his class.

Having thus contained himself, Yancey let himself go on the editorial page in a column entitled LOWER THAN THE RATTLESNAKE:

> The rattlesnake has a bad reputation. Nine times out of ten his bite is fatal, and many homes have been saddened because of his venomous attacks. But the rattlesnake is a gentleman beside some snakes. He always gives warning. It is the snake that takes you unaware that hurts the worst. . . .

Sabra, reading the galley proof, murmured, "It's wonderful! But Yancey, don't you think we ought to have more news items? I don't mean gossip, really, but about people, and what they're doing. Of course men like editorials and important things like that. But women . . ."

Sabra was emerging slowly from her role of charming little fool. By degrees she was to take more and more of a hand in assembling the paper's intimate weekly items. Indeed, had it not been for Sabra and Jesse Rickey, that first issue of the *Oklahoma Wigwam* might never have appeared. While Yancey received congratulatory committees following that eventful Sunday, Sabra—in her checked gingham apron—was selecting fascinating facts from the stock of filler items brought with them from Wichita.

SWIMMING BRIDES
Girls on the island of Himla, near Rhodes, are not allowed to marry until they have brought up a specified number of sponges, each taken from a certain depth. The people of the island earn their living by the sponge fishery.

STRENGTH OF THE THUMB
The thumb is stronger than all the other fingers together.

As the printing plant boasted only a little hand press, the two six-column forms had to be inked with a hand roller. Over this was placed the damp piece of white print paper. Each sheet was done by hand. The first issue of the *Wigwam* numbered four hundred and fifty copies, and before it was run off, Yancey, Jesse Rickey, Sabra, and Isaiah had all taken a turn at the roller.

Yancey made vigorous protest. "See here, honey. This will never do. My sweet southern jasmine working over a miserable roller! I'd rather never get out a paper, I tell you."

"It looks as if you never would anyway." The sweet southern jasmine did not mean to be acid, but the events of the past two weeks were beginning to tell on her nerves.

When the paper came out on that Thursday afternoon, Sabra was astonished to see the occasion treated as an event, with a crowd of cowboys and local citizens in front of the house, pistols fired, whoops and yells; and Yancey himself, aided by Jesse Rickey, handing out copies as if they had cost nothing to print. The paper was considered a triumph, and Yancey was borne away for a toast at the Sunny Southwest Saloon.

It was a man's town. The men rode, gambled, swore, fought, fished, hunted, drank. The saloon was their club, the brothel their social rendezvous, the town women their sweethearts. Literally there were no other girls of marriageable age. But for Sabra Cravat and the other respectable women of the town, there was nothing but their housework, their children, their memories of the homes they had left.

And so, as she began to become better acquainted with them, Sabra set about creating some sort of social order for the good wives of the community. Grimly she (and, in time, the other virtuous women of Osage) set about making this new frontier town like the old as speedily as possible.

Yancey, almost single-handed, tried to make the new as unlike the old as possible. He fought a losing fight from the first. He was muddled; frequently insincere; a brilliant swaggerer. He himself was not very clear as to what he wanted. He only knew that he was impatient of things as they were; that greed, injustice, and dishonesty were everywhere; that here, in this wild land, was a chance for Utopia. But he had no plan. Yancey Cravat, with his unformed dreams, never had a chance against the indomitable materialism of the women.

Most of the women had brought with them some household treasure that in their eyes represented elegance, taste, and background. A chair, a vase, a piece of silver. It was the period of the horrible gimcrack. Women all over the country were painting the backsides of frying pans with gold leaf and daisies and hanging them on the wall. Rolling pins were gilded or sheathed in velvet. Sabra's house became a sort of social center following the discovery that she received copies of *Harper's Bazaar* from home with fair regularity.

With elegancies such as these the women of Osage tried to disguise the crudeness of their wooden shacks. From stark ugliness their interiors were transformed into grotesque ugliness, but the Victorian sense of beauty was satisfied. The fact was, these women were hungry for the feel of soft silken things; their eyes, smarting with the glare, the wind, the dust, ached to rest on that which was rich and soothing; their hands, roughened by alkali water, dwelt lovingly on scraps of silk and velvet snipped from an old wedding dress or bonnet.

Slowly, in Sabra's eyes, the other women of the town began to emerge as personalities. One had been a schoolteacher in Cairo, Illinois. Her husband, Tracy Wyatt, ran the spasmodic bus and dray line between Wahoo and Osage. They had no children. Mrs. Wyatt was a sparse and simpering woman of thirty-nine, who talked a good deal of former trips to Chicago during which she had reveled in the culture of that effete city. Yancey was heard learnedly discoursing to her on the subject of Etruscan pottery, of which he knew nothing.

"You don't know what a privilege it is, Mr. Cravat, to talk to someone whose mind can soar above the sordid life of this horrible town."

Yancey's ardent eyes took on their most melting look. "Madam, it is you who have carried me with you to your heights. 'In youth and beauty wisdom is but rare!' " It was simply his way. He could not help it.

"Ah, Shakespeare!" breathed Mrs. Wyatt.

"Shakespeare!" said Yancey to Sabra later. "She doesn't know Alexander Pope when she hears him. No woman ought to pretend to be intelligent. And if she is she ought to have the intelligence to pretend she isn't."

It was Sabra who started the Philomathean Club. The other women clutched at the idea. After all, a town that boasted a culture club could not be altogether lost.

Sabra had had no experience with this phase of social activity in Wichita. Timidly she approached Mrs. Wyatt with her plan, and Mrs. Wyatt snatched at it with such ferocity as almost to make it appear her own. Each of them would invite four women of the town's elite. Ten, they decided, would be enough as charter members.

"I," began Mrs. Wyatt, "am going to ask Mrs. Louie Hefner, Mrs. Doc Nisbett—"

"Her husband's horrid!" The ten barrels of water still rankled.

"We're not asking husbands," retorted Mrs. Wyatt. "As for Mrs. Nisbett, she was a Krumpf, of Ouachita, Arkansas."

Sabra, descendant of the Marcys and the Venables, lifted her handsome black eyebrows. Privately she decided to select her four from among the more ebullient of Osage's matrons. Culture was all very well, but the thought of mingling once every fortnight with nine versions of the bony Mrs. Wyatt or the pedigreed Mrs. Nisbett was depressing. She made up her mind to call on that pretty and stylish Mrs. Evergreen Waltz the next day. At supper that evening she told Yancey of her plans.

"We're going to take up literature, you know. And maybe early American history." She mentioned her prospective member.

"Waltz's wife!" Surprise and amusement, too, were in his voice. "Why, that's fine, Sabra. That's the spirit!"

"I noticed her at church meeting last Sunday. She's so pretty next to all these—I mean, they're very nice ladies. But even if it is a culture club, someone nearer my own age would be much more fun."

"Oh, much," Yancey agreed. "That's what a town like this should be. No class distinctions, no snobbery."

"I saw her washing hanging on the line. You can tell she's a lady. Such pretty underthings, all trimmed with embroidery, every bit as nice as the ones Cousin Belle made for my trousseau."

"I'm not surprised."

"She looks kind of lonely, sitting there by the window sewing all day. And her husband's so much older. I noticed he limps, too. What's his trouble?"

"Shot in the leg."

"Oh." She had already learned to accept this form of injury as a matter of course. "I thought I'd ask her to prepare a paper for the third meeting on Mrs. Browning's 'Aurora Leigh.' I could lend her yours to read up on, if you don't mind." Yancey did not mind.

Mrs. Wyatt's house was one of the few in Osage used for dwelling purposes alone. She had five rooms and was annoyingly proud of it.

"The first meeting," she said, "will be held at my house, of course. It will be so much nicer."

Sabra's face set itself in a mask of icy stubbornness. "The first meeting of the Philomathean Society will be held at the home of the founder." After all, Mrs. Wyatt's house could not boast a screen door, as Sabra's could. It was the only house in Osage that had one. Yancey had had Hefner order it from Kansas City.

"I'll serve coffee and doughnuts," Sabra added graciously.

The paper on Mrs. Browning's "Aurora Leigh" never was written by the pretty Mrs. Evergreen Waltz. Three days later Sabra, glancing out of her sitting-room window, saw the crippled gambler passing by. In spite of his infirmity he was walking with great speed—running, almost. In his hand was a piece of white paper—a letter, Sabra thought. She hoped it was not bad news. He had looked sort of odd and wild.

Evergreen Waltz, after weeks of watching, had at last intercepted a letter from his young wife's lover. As he now came panting up the street the girl sat at the window, sewing. A single shot went just through the center of the wide white space between her great blue eyes.

"Why didn't you tell me that when she married him she was a girl out of a—out of a—house!" Sabra later demanded of Yancey.

"I thought you knew. All those embroidered underthings on the line. And then 'Aurora Leigh.' "

She was enraged. "What has 'Aurora Leigh' got to do with her?"

He got down the volume. "I thought you'd been reading it yourself." He opened it. " 'Dreams of doing good for good-for-nothing people.' "

Chapter 5

SABRA'S SECOND CHILD, a girl, was born in June, a little more than a year after their coming to Osage. It was not as dreadful an ordeal in those surroundings as one might have thought. She was tended by the best doctor in the county and certainly the most picturesque man of medicine in the whole Southwest, Dr. Don Valliant. He rode to his calls on horseback, wearing a black velveteen coat and velveteen trousers tucked into leather boots. His soft black hat intensified the black of his eyes and hair. It was no secret that he was often called to attend the bandits in their hiding place in the hills when one of their number was wounded in some outlaw raid. Still he was tender and deft with Sabra, though between them he and Yancey consumed an incredible quantity of whiskey during the racking hours of her confinement. At the end he held up a perfect baby girl with an astonishing mop of black hair.

"This is a Spanish beauty you have for a daughter, Yancey. I present to you Señorita Doña Cravat."

And Donna Cravat she remained.

The neighborhood wives showered the household with the customary cakes, pies, and meat loaves. Isaiah was wonderful. He washed dishes, he mopped floors, he actually cooked as though he had inherited the art from Angie, his vast black mother, left behind in Wichita. He was fascinated by the new baby. "Looka dat! She know me!" He danced for her, he sang to her, he rocked her to sleep. He was soon her nursemaid, pushing her baby buggy up and down the dusty street.

When Sabra Cravat arose from that bed something in her had crystallized. Perhaps she realized that she must cut a new pattern in this Oklahoma life of theirs. The boy Cim might surmount it; the girl Donna never. During the hours she had lain in her bed in the stifling wooden shack, mists seemed to have rolled away from before her eyes. She felt light and terribly capable—so much so that she made the mistake of getting up and tottering into the newspaper office where Yancey was shouting choice passages of an editorial into the inattentive ear of Jesse Rickey.

He looked up to see in the doorway a wraith, all eyes and long black braids. "Why, sugar! What's this? You can't get up!"

She smiled rather feebly. "I'm up. I feel so strong. I'm going to do so many things. You'll see. I'm going to paper the whole house. Rosebuds in the bedroom. I'm going to plant two trees in front. I'm going to start another club, one to make this town . . . no saloons . . . women like that Dixie Lee . . . feel so queer . . . Yancey . . ." As she began to topple, Yancey caught the Osage Joan of Arc in his arms.

Incredibly enough, she did paper the entire house, aided by Isaiah and Jesse Rickey, although Jesse's inebriate eye, which so often resulted in scrambled lines in the *Wigwam*, was none too dependable in the matching of patterns. Roses were grafted on leaves and tendrils emerged from petals. Still, the effect was gay. Within a month Louie Hefner was compelled to install a full line of wallpaper to satisfy local demand.

Slowly, slowly, the life of the community, in the beginning so wild, so unrelated in its parts, began to weave in and out, warp and woof, to make a pattern. It was at first faint, but presently the eye could trace here a motif, there a figure, here a motif, there a figure.

"It's almost time for the Jew," Sabra would say, looking up from her sewing. "I need some number forty sewing-machine needles."

And then perhaps next day Cim, playing in the yard, would see a familiar figure, bent almost double against the western sky. It was Sol Levy, the peddler. Cim would run into the house. "Mom, here's the Jew!"

Sol Levy, an immigrant from Alsace, had come over in the hold of some dreadful ship. His hair was blue-black and thick; his face was white and delicate, and his eyes slanted ever so little at the outer corners, so that he had a faintly Oriental look. He came of a race of scholars and traders. He belonged in crowded places, in the color and swift drama of the bazaars. Perhaps in Chicago or Kansas City he had heard of this new country and the rush of thousands for its land. And he had made his way on foot. He had started to peddle with an oilcloth-covered pack on his back. Through the little hot western towns in summer. Through the bitter cold western towns in winter. He was only a boy, disguised with a stubble of black beard. He would enter the yard with a wary eye on the dog. Nice Fido. Nice doggie. Down, down! Pins, sewing-machine needles, rolls of gingham and calico, and last, craftily, Hamburg lace for little girls' petticoats.

He brought news, too. "The bridge is out below Gray Horse. . . . The Kid and his gang held up the Santa Fe near Wetoka and got thirty-five thousand dollars; but one of them will never hold up a train again. A shot in the head. Verdigris Bob, they call him. . . . A country! My forefathers should have lived to see me here!" His beautiful, civilized face, mobile as an actor's, was at once expressive of despair and bitter amusement.

Later he bought a horse—high rumped, like a cloth horse in a pantomime. With the horse and a rickety wagon he now added kitchenware to his stock, and china; bolts of woolen cloth; bright-colored silks and ribbons. Dixie Lee and her girls fell upon these with shrill cries, like children. Sometimes they teased him, these pretty morons, hanging on his meager shoulders.

"Come on, Solly!" they said. "Smile! Don't you never have no fun?"

His deep-sunk eyes looked at them almost sadly. They grew uncomfortable under his gaze, then angry. "Go on, get out of here! You got your money, ain't you?"

In a year or two he opened a little store in Osage, a wooden shack containing two or three rough pine tables on which his wares were spread. But he was a person apart. Sometimes the saloon loungers or the cowboys deviled him. Yancey came to his rescue one day in the spectacular fashion he enjoyed. From the *Wigwam* office Yancey heard hoots, catcalls, and then the rat-a-tat-tat of a fusillade. The porch of the Sunny Southwest Saloon was filled with grinning faces. In the middle of the dusty road stood Sol Levy. They had tried to force him to drink a great glass of whiskey straight. He had succeeded in spitting out the burning stuff. They had got another. And they were shooting at him—at his feet,

575

at his head, expertly, never hitting him, but always careful to come within a fraction of an inch.

"Drink it! You're a dead Jew if you don't. Dance, gol darn you!"

The bullets spat all about him, whipped up the dust about his feet. He stood there facing them, frozen with fear. His face was deathly white.

Yancey rushed out of his office and into the road. It is impossible to say how he escaped being killed by one of the bullets. As he ran he whipped out his own guns, and at that half the crowd on the porch made a dash for the saloon door. Yancey stood beside Sol Levy, his great head thrust forward and down, like a buffalo charging.

"I'll drill the first one that fires another shot. Go on, fire!"

Yancey was by now a person in the community—he was, in fact, the person in the town. The men on the porch looked sheepish. "Aw, Yancey, we was only kiddin'. . . . Lookit—holy doggie, look at him! He's floppin'."

With a little sigh Sol Levy slid to the dust.

Yancey picked the man up, flung him over his shoulder as easily as if he were a sack of meal, and carried him into the house.

Revived, Sol Levy stopped to midday dinner with the Cravats. He sat, very white, very still, and made delicate pretense of eating. Sabra, because Yancey asked her to, had got out her DeGrasse silver and a set of linen. Sol's long fingers dwelt lingeringly on the fine stuff.

"This is the first time that I have sat at such a table in years. My mother's table was like this, in the old country. Here in this country I eat as we would not have allowed a beggar to eat."

"This Oklahoma country's no place for you, Sol," Yancey said.

The melancholy eyes took on a remote—a prophetic look. "It will not always be like this. Wait. Those savages will be myths, like the pictures of monsters you see in books of prehistoric days."

"Don't worry about them, Sol. I'll see they leave you alone from now on."

Sol Levy smiled a little bitter smile. "My ancestors were writing the laws of the civilized world when theirs were swinging from tree to tree."

ONCE ONLY IN three and a half years did Sabra go back to Wichita. At the prospect of the journey she was in a fever of anticipation for days. She was taking Cim and Donna with her. She was so proud of them, so intent on outfitting them with a splendid wardrobe, that she neglected herself and arrived with the very clothes with which she had departed.

"Your skin!" Felice Venable exclaimed at sight of her daughter. "Your hands! Your hair! What have you done to yourself?"

The visit was not a success. Things she had expected to enjoy somehow fell flat. She missed the exhilarating uncertainty of the Oklahoma life. The conversation of her girlhood friends seemed to lack tang and meaning. Their existence was orderly, calm. For herself and the other women of Osage there lay a whole vast Territory to be swept and garnished by an army of sunbonnets. Yet, paradoxically, she was trying to implant in the red clay of Osage the very forms that now bored her in Wichita. She took a perverse delight in shocking the Venables and Marcys that swarmed up from the South to greet the pioneer.

"When it rains we wade up to our ankles in mud. We carry lanterns when we go to the church sociables. . . ."

Then the children. The visiting Venables insisted on calling Cim by his full name—Cimarron. Cousin Dabney Venable said pompously, "And now, Cimarron, my little man, tell us about the red Indians. Did you ever fight Indians, eh, Cimarron?" The boy surveyed him from beneath his long lashes, looking for all the world like his father.

Cim was almost eight now. If it is possible for a boy of eight to be romantic in aspect, Cimarron Cravat was that. His head was long and fine, like Sabra's. His eyes were Sabra's, too, dark and large, but they had the ardent look of Yancey's gray ones, and he had Yancey's long and curling lashes. His mannerisms—the head held down, the rare upward glance, the swing of his walk—all these were Yancey in startling miniature.

His speech was strangely adult. This perhaps because of his close association with his elders. Yancey delighted in talking to the boy; in taking him on rides about the broad burning countryside. His skin was bronzed. He looked like a little patrician Spaniard or perhaps (the Venables thought privately) part Indian. He would probably have seemed a rather priggish little boy if his voice and manner had not been endowed with all the magnetism of his father.

He now surveyed his middle-aged cousin with the gaze of the precocious child. "Indians," he answered with great distinctness, "don't fight white men anymore. They can't. Their—uh—spirit is broken." Cousin Dabney looked slightly apoplectic. "They only fought in the first place because the white men took their buff'loes and their land away."

"Well," exclaimed Cousin Jouett Goforth, "this is quite a little redskin you have here, Cousin Sabra."

577

Cousin Dabney brought malicious eyes to bear on Sabra. "Look out. You may have a Pocahontas for a daughter-in-law some fine day."

Cim sensed that he had not made the desired effect on his listeners. "My father says," he announced suddenly, striding up and down the room in unconscious imitation of his idol, "my father says that someday an Indian will be President of the United States, and then you'll all be sorry you were such dirty skunks to 'em."

The Venables looked from the figure of the boy to the face of the mother.

"My poor child!" came from Felice Venable. She was addressing Sabra.

Sabra took refuge in hauteur. "You wouldn't understand. Yancey's Indian editorials in the *Wigwam* have made a sensation. They were spoken of in the Senate at Washington." Felice dismissed all Yancey's written works with a wave of her hand. "In fact," Sabra went on—she who hated Indians—"he has been in danger of his life from the people who have been cheating the Indians. It has been even more dangerous than when he tracked down the murderer of Pegler."

"Pegler," repeated the Venables disdainfully and without the slightest curiosity in their voices.

Even two-year-old Donna was not much of a success. She was an eerie little elf, as plain as the boy was handsome. She resembled her grandmother without a trace of that redoubtable matron's former beauty. But she wore with undeniable chic the clumsy little garments that Sabra had made for her; and when she was dressed in one of the exquisitely embroidered white frocks that her grandmother had sewn, that gifted needlewoman said tartly, "Well, she's got style at least."

All in all, Sabra found herself returning to barren Osage joyously. She resented her mother's do-this, do-that. That matriarch had lost her crown. Sabra was matriarch now of her own little kingdom.

But she decided that she must take the children more in hand. No more of this talk of Indians, of equality of man. She did not realize that she was, so far as Cim was concerned, years too late. At eight his character was formed. She had taught him the things that Felice Venable had taught her—stand up straight; wash your hands; say how do you do. But Yancey had taught him poetry far beyond his years, and accustomed his ears to the superb cadences of the Bible; Yancey had told him, bit by bit, the saga of the settling of the great Southwest.

Yancey told him why the cowboys wore sombreros—to shield their faces from the rain and sun when they rode the range, and to keep the snow from dripping down their backs. He told him the story of the buffalo; he talked endlessly of the Indians. He even taught him some Comanche, the court language of the Indian. He put him on a horse at the age of six. A sentimentalist and a romantic, he talked to the boy of the wild days of the Cimarron and the empire so nearly founded there. The boy loved his mother dutifully, and as a matter of course. But his father he worshiped.

Sabra had meant, at the last, to find occasion to inform her mother that it was she who ironed Yancey's fine white linen shirts. But she reflected that this might be construed as a criticism of her husband. So gladly, eagerly, Sabra went back to the wilds she once had despised.

BEFORE THE TRAIN pulled in at the Osage station, Sabra's eyes were searching the glaring wooden platform. Len Orson, the accommodating conductor, took Donna in his arms and stood with her at the foot of the car steps as Sabra stepped off the train. Her face wore that look of radiant expectancy characteristic of the returned traveler.

"Well, I guess somebody'll be pretty sorry to see you," Len said archly. He looked about for powerful arms in which to deposit Donna. The engine bell clanged, the whistle tooted. He handed Donna to Sabra and planted one foot onto the car step in the nick of time.

The stark wooden station sat blistering in the sun. Yancey was not there. Not only that, the station platform, usually graced by a score of limp figures, was bare. Even the familiar figure of Pat Leary, the station agent, could not be seen. From within the ticket office came the sound of his telegraph instrument. It chattered unceasingly.

Something was wrong. Sabra left her bags on the platform. Half an hour before their arrival in Osage, she had entrusted the children to the care of a fellow passenger while she had gone to the washroom to put on one of the new dresses bearing the cachet of Kansas City: green, with cream-colored ruchings at the throat and wrists. She had anticipated the look in Yancey's gray eyes at the sight of it. And now he was not there.

With Donna in her arms and Cim at her heels she hurried toward the sound of the clicking. She peered in at the station window. Pat Leary was bent over his telegraph key. A smart little Irishman who had come to the Territory with the railroad section crew. Station agent now, and studying law at night. "Mr. Leary! Have you seen Yancey?"

He looked up at her, his hand still on the key. "Ain't you heard?"

"No," whispered Sabra. Then, in a voice rising to a scream, "No! What? Is he dead?"

The Irishman came over to her then. "Oh, no, ma'am. Yancey ain't hurt to speak of. Just a nick in the arm—"

"Oh, my God! Tell me."

"Yancey got the Kid, you know. Killed him. Battle right there on Pawhuska Avenue in front of the bank, and bodies layin' everywhere. I'm sending it out. Biggest thing that's happened in the history of the Southwest. Shouldn't wonder if they'd make Yancey governor. Seems he was out hunting up in the hills last Thursday—"

"Thursday! But that's the day the paper comes out."

"Well, the *Wigwam* ain't been so regular since you been away." She allowed that to pass without comment. "Up in the hills he stumbles on Doc Valliant, drunk, but not so drunk he don't recognize Yancey. He tells Yancey that he's right in the camp where the Kid and his gang is hiding out. One of them was hurt bad in that last Santa Fe train holdup at Cimarron. Valliant overheard them planning to ride in here to Osage today and hold up the Citizens' National in broad daylight. They was already started. Well, Yancey knows he's got to detour on the way to town or he'll come on the gang. So he cuts across the hills, puts his horse through the gullies and across the scrub oaks. He gets into Osage, dead tired and his horse in a lather, ten minutes before the Kid and his gang sweep down Pawhuska Avenue, their six-shooters barking. But the town is expecting them. Say! Blood!"

Sabra waited for no more. She turned. And as she turned she saw Isaiah coming down the road in a cloud of dust. "Miss Sabra, he ain't hurt—jes' a nip in de arm. Ev'ybody shakin' his other hand caze he shoot the shot dat kill de Kid. An' you know what he do then, Miss Sabra? He kneel down an' he cry like a baby. . . . Le' me tote dis yere valise. Ah kin tote Miss Donna, too. My, she sho' growed!"

The house and newspaper office were packed with people. Mrs. Wyatt was there; Dixie Lee; everyone but Louie Hefner.

"Well, Mis' Cravat, I guess you must be pretty proud of him! . . . You missed the shootin', but you're in time to help celebrate. . . . Say, the Santa Fe alone offered five thousand dollars for the capture of the Kid, dead or alive. Yancey gets it, all right. And the Citizens' National is making up a purse. You'll be ridin' in your own carriage from now on."

Yancey was standing in the *Wigwam* office with his back against his desk, as though he were holding this crowd at bay. His face was white beneath the tan, like silver under lacquer. He looked up as Sabra came in and took a stumbling step toward her. She ran into his arms, but it was her arms that seemed to sustain him.

"Sabra. Sugar. Send them away. I'm so tired. Oh, God, I'm so tired."

Next day they exhibited the body of the Kid in the show window of Hefner's Furniture Store and Undertaking Parlor. All the county came to view him; they rode in from miles around. The Kid. The boy who, in his early twenties, had killed no one knew how many men—whose name was the symbol for terror and mercilessness throughout the Southwest. And now he and Clay McNulty, his lieutenant, lay dead side by side. The crowd was so dense that it threatened Louie Hefner's window. He had to put up rope barriers, and when the mob surged through these he stationed guards with six-shooters. Sabra said it was disgusting. She forbade Cim to go near the place. Isaiah she could not hold. His ebony face was always in the front of the throng gloating before Hefner's window.

"Well, you got to hand it to him," the men said. "He wasn't no piker. No shootin' behind trees in the dark. Nosiree! And ride! Say, you couldn't tell which was him and which was horse. They say he's got half a million in gold cached away up in the hills."

Sabra did a strange, a terrible thing. After denouncing the gaping crowd as scavengers and ghouls, suddenly at the last minute, as the sun was setting across the prairie, she walked out of the house, down the road, and stood before Hefner's window. The crowd made way for her respectfully. This was the wife of Yancey Cravat, the man whose name was appearing in newspaper headlines throughout the United States.

They had dressed the two bandits in new cheap black suits that stood stiffly away from the lean hard bodies. Clay McNulty's face had a faintly surprised look. But the face of the boy was fixed in a sardonic snarl. He looked older in death than he had in life. The eyes, whose lightning glance had pierced you through, now were extinguished forever behind waxen eyelids. It was at the boy that Sabra looked; and having looked she turned and walked back to the house.

They gave them a decent funeral, and when the minister refused to read the service over these two sinners Yancey consented to do it. " 'Whoso sheddeth man's blood, by man shall his blood be shed. . . . His hand will be against every man, and every man's hand against him. . . .' "

They put up two rough wooden slabs marking the graves. But souvenir hunters made short work of those. The two mounds sank lower, lower. Soon nothing marked this spot on the prairie to differentiate it from the red clay that stretched for miles all about it.

They sent to Yancey the substantial money rewards that for almost five years had been offered for the capture of the Kid, dead or alive. Yancey refused every penny of it. "I don't take money for killing a man," he said.

Chapter 6

SABRA NOTICED that Yancey's hand shook before breakfast. Before he ate a morsel he tossed down a glass of whiskey, as one seeking relief from pain takes medicine. When he returned the glass to the table his hand was, miraculously, quite steady.

He was restless, moody. Sabra remembered with a pang something he had said on first coming to Osage. "Those years in Wichita! Almost five years in one place—that's the longest stretch I've ever done."

In the courtroom Yancey sometimes behaved strangely. He would stop in the midst of florid oratory, leaving everyone staring. For when he was defending a case people flocked to hear him. He towered over any jury of frontiersmen—his great head charging menacingly at his opponent. And almost invariably he emerged victorious.

The newspaper was prospering, for Sabra gave it more and more time. But Yancey seemed to have lost interest, as he did in any venture once it got underway. It was now a matter of getting advertisements, taking personal and local items, recording the events in real estate, commercial, and social circles. Mr. and Mrs. Abel Dagley spent Sunday in Chuckmubbee. The Reverend McAlestar Couch is riding the Doakville circuit.

Increasingly Sabra saw to the editing and the actual printing. She got in an Osage Indian girl of fifteen to tend Donna and do the housework. Her name was Arita Red Feather, a quiet gentle girl who had to be told everything over again, daily. Isaiah helped Arita with the heavier work, ran errands, did odd jobs about the printing shop. When Jesse Rickey was too drunk to stand at the type case, Isaiah slowly and painstakingly helped Sabra make possible the weekly issue.

Yancey was often absent now. In a pinch, Sabra even tried her hand at an occasional editorial, though Yancey seldom failed her utterly in this department.

A rival newspaper set up quarters across the street and, for two or three months, kept up a feeble pretense of existence. Yancey's editorials, during this period, were extremely personal.

> The so-called publishers of the organ across the street have again been looking through glasses that reflect their own images. A tree is known by its fruit. The course pursued by the *Dispatch* does not substantiate its claim that it is a Republican paper.

The men readers liked this sort of thing. But it was Sabra who held the women readers with her accounts of the veal loaf, baked beans, and angel food cake served at the church supper, and the costumes worn at the wedding of a county belle.

Sabra, except for Yancey's growing restlessness, was content enough. The children were well; she had her friends; they had added another bedroom, and the house had taken on an aspect of comfort. She was a leader in the crude social life of the community. Church suppers; sewing societies; family picnics.

One thing rankled deep. Yancey had been urged to accept the office of territorial delegate to Congress (without vote), for his oratory and his record in many affairs, including the Pegler murder and the shooting of the Kid, had spread his fame even beyond the Southwest.

"Oh, Yancey!" Sabra thought of the Venables. At last her mate was to be vindicated.

But Yancey had refused. "Dancing to the tune of that gang in Washington! I know the whole dirty lot of them."

Restless. Moody. Irritable. Riding out into the prairies to be gone for days. Coming back to regale Cim with stories of evenings spent on this or that far-off reservation, talking with Chief Big Horse of the Cherokees, or Chief Buffalo Hide of the Chickasaws.

But he was not always like this. There were times when his old fiery spirit took possession. He entered the fight for the statehood of Oklahoma, and here he encountered opposition enough even for him. A year after the Oklahoma Run, the land had been divided into two territories—one owned by the Indian tribes, the other owned by the whites. Week after week, Yancey spoke out in the *Wigwam* for the consolidation of the two halves as one state. Yet, unreasonably enough, he sympathized with the

Five Civilized Tribes in their efforts to retain their tribal laws in place of the United States laws. The thousands who looked upon the Indians as totally unfit for citizenship fought him. Many Indians, too, opposed him, seeking a separate state for the Indians, to be known as Sequoyah, after the great Cherokee leader.

Sabra, who at first had paid little heed to these political problems, discovered that she must know something of them as protection against those times when Yancey was absent and she must get out the paper. She dared not, during these absences, oppose outright his political stand. But she edged as near the line as she could, for her hatred of the Indians was still deep. She even published—slyly—the speeches and arguments of the Double Statehood leaders, stating simply that these were the beliefs of the opposition.

One afternoon at a meeting of the Philomathean Club, Sabra read a paper entitled Whither Oklahoma? But Osage's twenty most exclusive ladies heard scarcely a word of it, their minds being intent on Sabra's new ensemble. Her wealthy cousin Bella French Vian, visiting the World's Fair in Chicago, had sent it from Marshall Field's store. It consisted of a skirt and Eton jacket of blue serge trimmed with black soutache braid; and a garment called a shirtwaist to be worn beneath the jacket. But it was the sleeves of the jacket that caused the eyes of feminine Osage to bulge with envy. Balloon sleeves now appeared for the first time in the Oklahoma Territory. Bouffant, enormous—a yard of material at least had gone into each of them.

Sabra returned home elated. She entered by way of the newspaper office, seeking Yancey's approval. Curtsying, she stood before him.

"Sleeves!" he exclaimed. "Let the squaws see those and there'll be a new fashion for carrying babies."

"Cousin Bella wrote that they'll be even fuller than this by autumn."

"By autumn," echoed Yancey. He held in his hand a telegram—one of the few which the *Wigwam's* somewhat sketchy service received. "Listen, sugar. President Cleveland's just issued a proclamation setting September sixteenth for the opening of the Cherokee Strip."

"Cherokee Strip?"

"Six million, three hundred thousand acres of Oklahoma land to be opened for white settlement. The government has bought it from the Cherokees. It was all to be theirs—all Oklahoma. Now they're pushing them farther and farther out."

"Good thing," snapped Sabra. Indians. Who cared!

Yancey rose from his desk. He turned his rare full gaze on her. "Honey, let's get out of this. Clubs, sleeves, church suppers. Let's get our hundred-and-sixty-acre allotment of Cherokee Strip land and start a ranch—raise cattle—this town life is no good—it's hideous."

Her arms fell, leaden, to her side. "Ranch? Where?"

"You're not listening. There's to be a new Run. Let's go, Sabra. Sell the *Wigwam*, take the children, get our hundred and sixty—"

"Never!" screamed Sabra. "I'd rather die first."

He came to her, tried to take her in his arms. "Sugar, you won't understand. It's the chance of a lifetime. When the Territory's a state we'll own some of the finest land anywhere. I know the section I want."

"You knew the last time, too, and you let that slut steal it. Go and take her with you. You'll never make me go. I'll stay here and run the paper."

She had a rare fit of hysterics after which Yancey, aided clumsily by Arita Red Feather, divested her of the new finery, quieted the now screaming children, and finally restored the household to a semblance of order. The display of temperament was intended, as are all hysterics, to intimidate the beholder. Yancey was solicitous, charming. From the shelter of his arms Sabra looked about the cosy room, bade Arita Red Feather bring on supper. "That," thought Sabra to herself, "settles that."

But it did not. Yancey made ready to go, and Sabra could do nothing to stop him. She even negotiated for a strip of land outside Osage and managed to get Yancey to make a payment on it, in the hope that this would keep him from the Run. "If it's land you want you can farm that."

Yancey took no interest in the farm. It was Sabra who saw to the erection of a crude little farmhouse. The land was very near the Osage Reservation and turned out, surprisingly enough, to be fertile, though the Osage land was barren and flinty.

"Farm! That's a garden patch. D'you think I'm about to dig potatoes!"

September, the month of the opening of the Cherokee Strip, saw him well on his way. Sabra's farewell was intended to be cold. Her heart, she told herself, was breaking.

"You felt the same way when I went off to the first Run," Yancey reminded her. "Remember? And if I hadn't gone you'd still be living in Wichita, with your family smothering you in advice." This was true, she had to admit. She managed a watery smile.

He was making the Run on a brilliant, wild-eyed mare named Cimarron, with a strain of Spanish in her for speed, and a strain of American mustang for endurance. He made a dashing figure as he sat the graceful animal that now was pawing to be off. Though a score of others were starting with him, it was Yancey that the town turned out to see.

An escort rode with the departing adventurers for a distance out on the plains. Sabra had the family horse hitched to the buggy, bundled Cim and Donna in with her, and—Isaiah hanging on behind, somehow—the prim little vehicle bumped its way over the prairie.

At the last Sabra threw the reins to Isaiah and ran to Yancey as he pulled up his horse. He bent far over in his saddle, picked her up and held her close while he kissed her long and hard.

"Sabra, come with me."

"The children!"

"The children, too. All of us. Come on. Now." His eyes were blazing. She saw that he actually meant it. A sudden premonition shook her.

"Where are you going? Where are you going?"

He set her down gently and was off. Five years passed before she saw him again.

Chapter 7

DIXIE LEE'S GIRLS were riding by the office of the *Wigwam* on their daily afternoon parade. Sabra's face darkened as they came into view. Dixie Lee never drove with them, but Sabra knew where she was this afternoon. She was in the back room of the First National Bank talking business to the president, Murch Rankin. The businessmen of the town were negotiating to bring a packing house, a plough works, and a watch factory to Osage. Any one of these industries required a substantial bonus. The spirit of the day was the boom spirit. Dixie Lee was essentially a commercial woman—shrewd, clearheaded. Her business was one of the town's industries, and now she was contributing her share toward coaxing new industries to favor Osage. That way lay prosperity.

Dixie Lee was a personage now. Visitors came to her house from the cities and counties roundabout. She had built the first brick structure in the wooden town: a square and imposing two-story house. She had commissioned Louie Hefner to buy her red velvet and gold furniture and

long gilt-framed mirrors. Dixie herself had gone east for statues and pictures.

This red brick brothel was less sinister than good and innocent women suspected. Dixie Lee ruled it with an iron hand, enforcing rules of conduct so rigid as to be almost prim. In a crude, wild country it occupied a strange place, foreign to its original purpose. It was, in a way, a club, a rendezvous, a salon. For hundreds of men it was all they had ever known of richness, of color, of luxury. The red and gold, the plush and silk, the perfume, the gleaming shoulders sank deep into their starved senses. Here they lolled in comfort while they talked Territory politics, swapped yarns, and played cards. They embraced these women fiercely, thought tenderly of many of them, and frequently married them; and once married, the women settled down contentedly to slavish domesticity.

The week the new house opened, Sabra Cravat, mentioning no names, had had an editorial about it in which the phrase "insult to the fair womanhood of America" figured prominently.

Sabra wrote easily now, with no pretense to style, but concisely and with an excellent sense of news. The *Wigwam* had flourished in these five years of her management. She was thinking of making it a daily instead of a weekly; of using the entire building for the newspaper and building a proper house on one of the residential streets newly sprung up—streets that boasted elm and cottonwood trees in the front yards.

Yancey had told her, tenderly, that she was a charming little fool, and she had believed it. It was not until he left her that she developed her powers. Yancey had ridden gaily away. She had held her head high in spite of hints, innuendoes, gossip.

As the weeks had gone by and he failed to return—failed to write— rumor leaped like prairie fire through the Oklahoma country. All the old stories were revived. They say he is living with a Cherokee squaw. They say he killed a man in the Run and was caught by a posse and hung. They say he was seen lording it around the bar of the Brown Palace Hotel in Denver. They say Dixie Lee is his real wife, and he is the one who has set her up in the brick house. They say. They say. They say.

It is impossible to know how Sabra survived those terrible weeks that lengthened into months that lengthened into years. In spite of it all she still had that virginal look—that chastity of lip, that clearness of eye, that purity of brow. Men come back to the women who look as Sabra Cravat looked, but the tempests of men's love pass them by.

She told herself that he was dead. She told the world that he was dead. She knew, by some deep instinct, that he was alive. Donna had been so young when he left that he now was all but wiped from her memory. But Cim spoke of Yancey as though he were in the next room. "My father says . . ." Sometimes, when Sabra saw the boy coming toward her with that familiar swinging stride, she was wrenched by a pang of agony.

She wrung from the paper a decent livelihood for herself and the two children. When it had no longer been possible to keep Yancey's absence from her parents, Felice Venable had descended upon her deserted child, prepared to bring her home. But Sabra had rejected her mother's plan.

"I intend to stay right here in Osage," she announced quietly, "and run the paper, and bring up my children as their father would have expected them to be brought up."

"Their father!" Felice Venable repeated in withering accents.

Sabra was, without being fully aware of it, a power that shaped the social aspect of this crude southwestern town. The ladies of the new Happy Hour Club, on her declining to become a member, made her an honorary member, resolved to have her name on their club roster somehow. They were paying unconscious tribute to Oklahoma's first feminist. As a woman, Sabra could print statements which for downright effrontery would have earned a male editor a horsewhipping. She publicly scolded the street loafers who lolled on Pawhuska Avenue. Sometimes she borrowed Yancey's picturesque phraseology. She denounced a local politician as being too crooked to sleep in a roundhouse, and the phrase in the end defeated him. Law, order, the sanctity of the home. Though the Osage Hills still were venomous with outlaws; though the six-shooter still was part of the Oklahoma male costume; though the Territory itself had been settled, in thousands of cases, by men who had come to it from cowardice, rapacity, or worse, Sabra Cravat and the other conventional women of the community were working with a quiet ferocity toward a new day.

Slowly, slowly, certain figures began to take on the proportions of personalities, though no one had arisen in the Territory to fill Yancey Cravat's romantic boots. Pat Leary was coming on as a lawyer, and the railroads on which he had worked as section hand were now consulting him on points of territorial law. In his early days he had married an Osage girl named Crook Nose. People said that he regretted it now, that a lawyer could never hope to get on with this millstone around his neck.

There still was very little actual money in the Territory. People traded this for that. Sabra often translated subscriptions to the *Wigwam*—and even advertising space—into terms of fresh vegetables, berries, quail, wild turkey, dress lengths, and shoes for the children.

Sol Levy's store, grown to respectable proportions, provided Sabra with countless necessities in return for the advertisement which urged its readers to trade at Sol Levy's. In a quiet, dreamy way Sol had managed to buy a surprising amount of Osage real estate by now. He owned the lot on which his store stood, the one just south of it, and among other pieces, the building and lot which comprised the site of the *Wigwam* and the Cravat house. In the year following Yancey's departure Sabra's economic survival was made possible only through the generosity of this shy, sad-eyed man.

"I've got it all down in my books," Sabra would say. "You know that it will all be paid back someday."

Sol began in the *Wigwam* a campaign of advertising out of all proportion to his needs, and Sabra's debt to him began to shrink to the vanishing point. She talked to him about her business problems, and he advised her shrewdly. When she was utterly discouraged he would say, as one who states an irrefutable fact: "Someday, Mrs. Cravat, you and I will look back on this and we will laugh—but not very loud."

"How do you mean—laugh?"

"Oh—I will be very rich, and you will be very famous. And Yancey— they will tell stories about him until he grows into a legend. They will remember him when all these mealy-faced governors are dead and forgotten. They will tell their children about him. You will see."

Sabra thought of her own children, who knew so little of their father. Donna, a thin secretive child of almost seven now, with straight black hair and a sallow skin; Cim, twelve, moody, charming, imaginative. Donna was more like her grandmother Felice Venable than her own mother; Cim resembled Yancey so strongly in manner and emotions as to have almost no trace of Sabra. She wondered, with a pang, if she had failed to impress herself on them because of her absorption in the newspaper, in the resolve to succeed. She got out a photograph of Yancey that she had hidden away because to see it was to feel a stab of pain, and hung it on the wall where the children could see it daily.

"Your father—" Sabra would begin, courageously, resolved to make him live again in the minds of the children. Donna was not especially interested. Cim said, "I know it," and capped her story with a tale of his own featuring Yancey in a swashbuckling escapade.

"Oh, but Cim, that's not true!"

"It is true. Isaiah told me. I guess he ought to know." And then the question she dreaded. "When are Isaiah and Father coming back?"

She could answer, somehow, evasively, about Yancey. But at the fate that had overtaken the Negro boy she cowered, afraid even to face the thought of it. For the thing that had happened to Isaiah was so dreadful, so remorseless that when the truth of it came to Sabra she felt all the little world that she had built up about her turning to ashes.

It was in the fourth year of Yancey's absence. Coming suddenly into the kitchen, Sabra saw Arita Red Feather twisted in a contortion at the table. Her face was wet with the agony which only one kind of pain can bring. The Indian girl was in the pangs of childbirth. The loose garment which she always wore and the erect dignity of her carriage had served to keep secret her condition. She had had, too, Sabra now realized in a flash, a way of being out of the room when her mistress was in it; busy in the pantry when Sabra was in the kitchen; in and out like a swift shadow.

"Arita! Come. Lie down. I'll send for your parents." Her father was Big Knee, something of a power in the Osage tribe. He was one of the eight members of the Council and part of the tribe's governing body.

"No! No!" Arita Red Feather broke into a storm of pleading. Sabra had never thought that an Indian would give way to such emotion.

She put the girl to bed and sent Isaiah for Dr. Valliant. He went to work quietly, efficiently, aided by Sabra. The girl made no outcry. Her face was rigid. Sabra, passing from the kitchen to the girl's bedroom, saw Isaiah crouched in a corner by the woodbox. He looked up at her mutely. His face was a curious ash gray. As Sabra looked at him she knew.

The baby was a boy. His hair was coarse and kinky. His skin was black. As Sabra held him in her arms, Doc Valliant said, "This is a bad business."

"I'll send for her parents. I'll speak to Isaiah. They can marry."

"Marry! The Osages don't marry Negroes. It's forbidden."

"Why, lots of them have. You see Negroes who are part Indian every day on the streets."

"Not Osages. Seminoles, yes. And Creeks, and Choctaws, and even Chickasaws. But the Osages, except for intermarriage with whites, have kept the tribe pure."

Purity of the tribe, indeed! She resolved to be matter-of-fact now that the shocking event was at hand. She herself felt guilty. She should have foreseen danger. Isaiah had been a child in her mind, whereas he was in reality a young man.

Dr. Valliant had finished his work. The girl lay on the bed, her black eyes fixed on them; silent, watchful, hopeless. Isaiah lurked in the kitchen. The child lay in Sabra's arms. Donna and Cim were fortunately asleep, for it was now long past midnight. The tense excitement past, the whole affair seemed to Sabra sordid, dreadful.

Doc Valliant came over to her and looked down at the baby. "We must let his father see him." He took the baby from her and turned toward the kitchen. "Let me have some whiskey, will you, Sabra? I'm dead tired."

She went past him into the dining room. As she poured a drink of Yancey's whiskey, almost untouched since he had left, she heard Valliant's voice, very gentle, and then the sound of Isaiah's weeping. Valliant took the child back to Arita and placed it by her side. He stumbled with weariness as he entered the dining room. As he reached for the drink, Sabra saw that his hand shook a little as Yancey's used to do.

"There's no use talking now, Doctor, about what the Osages do or don't do. The baby's born. I shall send for Big Knee. As soon as Arita can be moved he must take her home. As for Isaiah, I've a notion to send him back to Kansas."

Doc Valliant had swallowed the whiskey at a gulp. He poured another glass, drank it. His face seemed less drawn, his hand steadier. "Now listen, Sabra. You don't understand the Osages. This is serious."

He filled his glass again. She wished he would go home. He was repeating rather listlessly what he had said. "This is a bad business."

Her patience was at an end. "What do you mean?"

"They remove any member of the tribe that has had to do with a Negro."

"Remove!"

"Kill. By torture."

She stared at him. He was drunk, of course. "You're talking nonsense," she said crisply. She was very angry.

"Don't let this get around. The Osages might blame you. I'll just go and take another look at her."

The girl was sleeping.

"Go to bed—off with you," said Doc Valliant to Isaiah. The boy's face was wet with tears and sweat. He walked slackly, as though exhausted.

"Wait." Sabra cut him some bread, sliced a piece of meat. "Here. Eat this. Everything will be all right in the morning."

The news got around. Perhaps Doc Valliant talked in drink. Doubtless the new girl who came in to help Sabra. Perhaps Isaiah, who after a night's sleep had suddenly become proudly paternal.

Arita Red Feather was frantic to get up. They had to keep her in bed by force. On the fourth day following the child's birth Sabra came into her room early in the morning and she was not there. The infant was not there. Their beds had been slept in and now were empty. She ran to the yard where Isaiah's little hut stood. He was not there. She questioned the new helper who slept on a couch in the dining room. She had heard nothing, seen nothing. The three had vanished in the night.

Well, Sabra thought philosophically, Isaiah can make out somehow. Perhaps he can even get a job as a printer somewhere. He was handy, bright. He had some money, for she had given him a little weekly wage. Enough, perhaps, to take them by train back to Kansas. Certainly they had not gone to Arita's people, for Big Knee, questioned, denied all knowledge of his daughter, of her child, of Isaiah. He stared with expressionless black eyes and folded his arms.

Chapter 8

"REMEMBER THE *Maine!* To hell with Spain!" Thousands of male children born within the United States in 1898 grew up under the slight handicap of the first name Dewey. The *Oklahoma Wigwam* bristled with new words: Manila Bay—Philippines—Rough Riders. People who had thought of Spain in the romantic terms of the early Southwest explorers—Coronado, De Soto—now were told that they must hate the Spanish.

Rough Riders! That name the Oklahoma country understood—tall, lean, hard young men who had practically been born with a horse under them; daredevils, dead shots. Even their uniforms had dash. And their lieutenant colonel and leader was that energetic young fellow from New York State—Roosevelt, his name was. Theodore Roosevelt.

Osage was shaken by chills and fever; the hot spasms of patriotism, the cold rigors of virtue. A new political group had sprung up, ostensibly on the platform of civic virtue. In reality the founders were tired of seeing all the plums dropping into the laps of the strong-arm politicians who had been the first to shake the territorial tree. In the righteous sunbonnets they saw their chance for a strong ally. Sabra had been urged to help. In the columns of the *Wigwam* she had unwisely conducted a campaign against Wick Mongold's saloon and its particularly lawless back room. With Cim's future in mind she wrote a stirring editorial about shielding criminals and protecting the Flower of our Manhood. Two days later a passerby at seven in the morning saw flames licking the foundations of the *Wigwam* office. The whole had been nicely soaked in coal oil. Alarmed neighbors beat out the fire with wet blankets. It was learned that a town loafer had been hired to do the job for twenty dollars. Mongold skipped out.

Now reform turned its attention to the Scarlet Woman. Almost five years after Yancey's departure it looked very much as though Dixie Lee and her fine brick house would soon be routed by the purity squad.

This was the moment Yancey Cravat chose to come riding home—more dashing, more romantic, more mysterious than on the day he had ridden away.

It was eight o'clock in the morning. The case of Dixie Lee (charged with disorderly conduct) was due to come up at ten in the local court. Sabra had been at her desk since seven. She heard Jesse Rickey in the printing shop just next to the office. "Jesse! Oh, Jesse! The Dixie Lee case will be our news lead. Hold two columns open. . . ."

Horse's hoofs at a gallop, stopping in front of the *Wigwam* office. A quick light step. That step! But it couldn't be. Sabra sprang to her feet, one hand on the desk to steady herself.

He strode into the office. For five years she had pictured him returning to her in dramatic fashion. For five years she had known in what manner she would conduct herself toward this man who had deserted her without a word. But at sight of him, all this left her mind. She was in his arms with an inarticulate cry, she was weeping, her arms were about him, the buttons of his uniform crushed her breasts. His uniform. She realized then, without surprise, that he was in the uniform of the Oklahoma Rough Riders.

It is no use saying to a man who has been gone for five years, "Where have you been?" He took his own return for granted. His manner was nonchalant, his exuberance infectious. He strode magnificently into the room where the children were at breakfast, snatched them up, kissed them. You would have thought he had been gone a week.

Donna was shy of him. "Your daughter's a Venable, Mrs. Cravat," he said, and turned to the boy. Cim, slender, graceful, reached almost to Yancey's broad shoulders. But he had not Yancey's heroic bulk, his vitality. In his narrow Venable face, the mouth was oversensitive, the smile almost girlish in its sweetness.

"Do you want to see my dog?" Cim asked.

"Have you got a pony?"

"Oh, no."

"I'll buy you one this afternoon. A pinto. Here. Look."

He took from his pocket a soft leather pouch and poured the contents onto the table: a little heap of shining yellow. He turned to Sabra. "Gold. It's all I've got to show, honey, for two years and more in Alaska."

"Alaska!" So that was it.

"I'm famished." He reached for a slice of bread from the plate on the table, clapped a strip of bacon on it, and devoured it eagerly. Sabra saw then that he was thinner; there were hollow shadows in his cheeks; there was a scarcely perceptible sag to the massive shoulders. There was something about his hand. The forefinger of the right hand was gone. She felt suddenly faint. She reeled a little. He sprang toward her, his lips against her hair.

"How I've missed you, Sabra, sugar!"

"Yancey! The children!" She had forgotten the pleasant ways of dalliance. A man in the house, touching her hair, her throat with urgent fingers. She was embarrassed almost. Besides, this man had deserted her and his children. She shrugged free. Anger leaped within her.

"Don't touch me. You can't come home like this—after years—after—"

" 'Ah, Penelope! No other woman in the world would harden her heart to stand thus aloof from her husband, who after much travail and sore had come to her . . .' "

"You and your miserable Milton!"

He did not correct her.

One by one, and then in crowds, the townspeople began to come in. They felt proper resentment toward this baffling creature who had ridden carelessly away, leaving his wife and children to fend for themselves, and now had ridden as casually back again. Sabra Cravat would throw him out, likely as not, and serve him right. But at sight of Yancey in his

Rough Rider uniform, they were snared again in the mesh of his enchantment. He became a figure symbolic of the war, of the Southwest—impetuous, romantic, adventuring.

"Well, say, where you been, you old son of a gun!"

"You and this Roosevelt get goin' in this war, I guess the Spaniards'll wish Columbus never been born."

And Yancey, in return, "Howdy, Grat! H'are you, Ike, you old hoss thief!" The fine eyes glowed; the voice worked its magic. The renegade was a hero; the outcast had returned a conqueror.

Alaska. Oklahoma had not been so busy that it had failed to hear of the Gold Rush. "Alaska! Go on! Heard you'd turned Injun."

He got out the leather pouch. As they gathered around he poured out the shining yellow heap. Gold. The hills and the plains had been honeycombed for it; men had hungered and died in the hope of finding it. And here was the precious stuff trickling through Yancey Cravat's fingers.

"Damn it all, Yancey, some folks has all the luck."

"Luck! Call it luck, do you, Mott, to be frozen, starved, lost! One whole winter shut up alone in a one-room cabin with the snow piled to the rooftop. Luck to have your pardner rob you of your gold, all but this handful. I was going to see Sabra covered in gold like an Aztec princess."

As always, Yancey filled his hearers with a longing for the place he described, a nostalgia for something they had never known. Winters at fifty below zero. Two hours of bitter winter sunshine, and then blackness. Long splendid summer days in May and June, with twenty hours of sunshine. Yukon. Chilkoot Pass. Caribou. Huskies. Sledges. Sitka. Snow blindness. Frozen fingers. Cold. Cold. Gold. Gold. To the figures crowded into this little frame house he brought, by the magic of his eloquence, the relentless movement of icy rivers, the vast plains of blinding snow. Two years of this, he said; and looked down at the stump that had been his famous trigger finger.

Two years. Two years, and he had been gone five. That left three unaccounted for. The old stories seeped up in their minds. They saw the indefinable break that had come to the magnificent figure. The massive shoulders did not droop. The rare glance still pierced you like a sword thrust. Yet something had vanished.

"Where'd you join up, Yancey?"

"San Antonio. Colonel Leonard Wood's down there—and Lieutenant Colonel Roosevelt. He's been drilling the boys. We're better equipped than the regulars, thanks to him. Those nincompoops in Washington were all for issuing us winter clothing for a campaign in the tropics—and they'd have done it if it hadn't been for him."

Southwest Davis spoke up from the crowd. "You'll be leaving right soon, won't you? Week or so."

"Week!" echoed Yancey, and looked at Sabra. "I go back to San Antonio tomorrow. The regiment leaves for Tampa next day."

She said nothing, gave no sign. She had outfaced them with her pride for five years; she would give them no satisfaction now. Five years. One day. San Antonio—Tampa—Cuba—war. She gave no sign.

Slowly the crowd began to disperse. Wives linked their arms through those of husbands, and the gesture was one of perhaps not entirely unconscious cruelty, accompanied as it was by a darting glance at Sabra.

"Come on, Yancey!" shouted Strap Buckner. "Over to the Sunny Southwest. Come on, you old longhorn. We got to drink to you because you're back and because you're going away."

"And to the Rough Riders!" yelled Mott Bixler.

They swept the towering figure in its khaki uniform with them. He waved his hat at her. "Back in a minute, honey." They were gone.

Sabra turned to the children, flushed with the unwonted excitement. Her face set itself with that look of quiet resolve. "Half the morning's gone. But I want you to go along to school, anyway. It's no use your staying around here. The paper must be got out. Jesse'll be no good to me the rest of the day. I'll write a note to your teachers. . . . Run along now."

She had made up her mind that she would see the day through as she had started it. The Dixie Lee case was coming to a crisis this very minute. She would not let the work of months go for nothing because this man had seen fit to stride into her life for a day.

She was right about Jesse Rickey. He was even now leaning an elbow on the polished surface of the Sunny Southwest bar. Cliff Means, who at fifteen served as printer's devil, looked up as Sabra entered.

"It's all right, Mis' Cravat. I got the head all set up like you said. 'Reign of Scarlet Woman Ends. Judge Issues Ban.' Even if Jesse don't— why, you and me can set up the story this afternoon."

Suddenly, sharp and clear, Yancey's voice calling her from the doorway. "Sabra! Sabra!" He strode into the back shop. "What's this about Dixie Lee?" His eye leaped to the form. "When's this case come up?"

"Now."

"Who's defending her?"

"Nobody in town would touch the case. They say she got a lawyer from Denver. He didn't show up."

"Prosecuting?"

"Pat Leary."

Without a word he turned. She caught him at the door, gripped his arm. "Where are you going?"

"Court."

"What for?" But she knew. She interposed her body between him and the door. "You can't take the case of that woman."

"Why not?"

"Because I've been fighting her and all that she stands for."

"Why, Sabra, honey, where are you thinking of sending her?"

"Away. Away from Osage."

"Dixie's been stoned in the marketplace for two thousand years and more. Driving her out won't do it. You've got to drive the devil out of—"

"Yancey Cravat, are you preaching to me? You who left your family to starve, for all you cared! And now you take this creature's part against me!"

"I know it. I can't help it, Sabra."

"I'll tell you what I think," cried Sabra. "I think you're crazy! They've all said so. And now I know they are right."

"Maybe so."

"If you dare to think of disgracing me by defending that filth—"

"By God, every citizen's got the legal right to fight for existence!" He put her gently aside.

She became a wildcat. She beat herself against him, like an infuriated sparrow. "I say you won't. I'd kill you first. Why did you come back?"

Her dignity was gone. He lifted her, scratching, kicking, set her gently down in a chair. The screen door slammed. Crumpled, tearstained as she was, she reached for her pencil and wrote a new head. VICE AGAIN TRIUMPHS OVER JUSTICE. Then she sped down the dusty road to the courthouse.

NEWS OF YANCEY'S ABRUPT DEPARTURE from the Sunny Southwest Saloon—and the reason for it—had spread through the town like a forest fire. Mad Yancey Cravat's latest freak. The courtroom, baked by the morning sun, was packed. Judge Sipes was in place, chomping his cud of tobacco. Pat Leary neat, tight, representing law and order; Dixie Lee

all in black, her cheeks unrouged; her girls in full panoply of plumes.

The jury was a hard-faced lot for the most part. Plucked from the plains or the hills; slow of mind, quick on the trigger.

The legal farce had already begun before Yancey made his spectacular entrance.

"Counsel for the Territory of Oklahoma!" Pat Leary stood up. ". . . for the defense." No one. "The defendant having failed to provide herself with counsel, it is my duty, according to the laws of the United States and the Territory of Oklahoma to appoint counsel for her." The judge shifted his quid, while his red-rimmed eyes roved through the crowd seeking the shyster, Gwin Larkin. A stir in the close-packed throng.

"Your Honor!" Towering above the mob, forging his way through, came the romantic Rough Rider.

Faces turned to stare. Here was the kind of situation that the Southwest loved: here was action; here was blood-and-thunder. Here, in a word, was Cimarron.

Yancey stood before the shoddy judge and swept off his hat. "If it please Your Honor, I represent the defendant, Dixie Lee."

No territorial judge, denying Yancey Cravat, would have dared to confront that crowd. He waved the approaching Gwin Larkin back with a feeble gesture and prepared to proceed with the case. The look that he turned on Sabra Cravat as she entered a scant ten minutes later was one of mingled bewilderment and reproach.

Objection on the part of Pat Leary. Overruled, perforce, by the judge. A shout from the crowd. Order! Bang! Another shout. Ten minutes earlier they had been all for the cocky little Leary, erstwhile station agent. Now, with the fickleness of the mob, sympathy flowed to the woman to be tried, to the man who would defend her.

Pat Leary. Irish, ambitious, fiery. His years as section hand had equipped him with a vocabulary well suited to scourge this woman in black who sat quietly before him. Vituperation; adjective on adjective.

". . . all the vicious influences, Your Honor, with which our glorious Territory is infested, can be laid at this woman's leprous door. . . . A refuge for the diseased, for the criminal . . . waxed fat and sleek in her foul trade . . . scavenger . . . disgrace to the fair name of woman. . . ."

A curious embarrassment seized the crowd. There were many who had known the easy hospitality of Dixie's ménage; who had borrowed money from her to save themselves from rough frontier revenge. She had taken the town's money and given it out again with the other merchants of the town. The banker could testify to that; the mayor; this committee; that committee. Put Dixie Lee's name down for a thousand.

A low mutter like a growl sounded its distant thunder. The jurors shifted in their places. Younger than Yancey, less experienced, Leary still should have known better. These men in the courtroom lived in a frontier atmosphere. Women were scarce, and because they were scarce they were precious. No woman was so plain, so undesirable that she did not take on, by the very fact of her sex, a value far beyond her deserts.

Here was Pat Leary, jumping excitedly about, mouthing execrations, when he himself had married an Indian girl out of the scarcity of girls in the Oklahoma country. Out of the corner of his eye, as he harangued, he watched Yancey Cravat. The huge head was sunk on the breast; the eyelids were lowered. Beaten, Pat Leary thought. Defeated, and he knows it. He finished in a burst of oratory so brutal that he had the satisfaction of seeing painful, unaccustomed red surge over Dixie Lee's pale face. He seated himself, chest out, head held high.

The crowd murmured, gabbled. Yancey still sat sunk in his chair as though lost in thought. The gabble rose. He's given it up, thought Sabra. He sees how it is.

Slowly the big head lifted. Yancey rose and walked to Judge Sipes' desk. After a moment he began to speak. His voice, after Leary's shouts, was so low that the crowd held its breath in order to hear.

"Your Honor. Gentlemen of the jury. I am the first to bow to achievement. May I, before I begin the defense of my client, call your attention to a feat which, in my humble opinion, has never before been achieved in the whole of the Southwest. Turn your eye to the person who has so recently and so eloquently addressed you. Regard him well. You will not look upon his like again. For, gentlemen, in my opinion this gifted person, Mr. Patrick Leary, is the only man in the glorious Southwest—I may even go so far as to say the only man in the United States of America—of whom it can be said that he is able to strut sitting down."

The puffed little figure in the chair collapsed, then bounded to its feet. "Your Honor! I object!"

But the rest was lost in the roar of the delighted crowd. "Go it, Yancey!" Here was what they had come for. Doggone, there was nobody like him!

Even today there still are people in Oklahoma who have a copy of the speech he made that day. Yancey Cravat's Plea for a Fallen Woman, it is called; and never was a speech more sentimental, windy, and utterly moving. A quart of whiskey in him; an enthralled audience behind him; a white-faced defendant with hopeless eyes to spur him on; the cry of his wronged and righteous wife still sounding in his ears—Booth himself in his heyday never gave a more brilliant, a more false performance.

"Your Honor! Gentlemen of the jury! A dreadful—a vicious—picture has been painted to you of this woman's life and surroundings. Tell me—do you really think that she willingly embraced a life so horrible? No, gentlemen! A thousand times, no! This girl was bred in such luxury, such refinement, as few of us have known. And just as she was budding into womanhood, cruel fate snatched all this from her, bereft her of her dear ones, took from her with fierce rapidity those upon whom she had come to look for love and support. And then, in that moment of darkest loneliness, came one of our sex, gentlemen. A fiend in the guise of a human. False promises. Lies. Deceit so palpable that it would have deceived no one but an innocent young girl. One of our sex was the author of her ruin. What could be more pathetic than the spectacle she presents? An immortal soul in ruin. A moment ago you heard her reviled for the depths to which she has sunk. You would drive her out. Yet where can she go that her sin does not pursue her? Gentlemen, the very promises of God are denied her. Who was it said, *'Come unto me, all ye that labor and are heavy laden, and I will give you rest'*? She is indeed heavy laden, this trampled flower, but if at this instant she were to kneel down before us all and confess her Redeemer, where is the church that would receive her, where the community that would take her in? Our sex wrecked her once pure life. Her own sex shrinks from her. Only in the shelter of the grave can her betrayed and broken heart ever find the Redeemer's promised rest. . . ."

The beautiful voice went on, the eyes held you in their spell. Dixie Lee became a woman romantic, piteous, appealing.

Sabra Cravat, her pencil flying over her paper, thought grimly, It isn't true. Don't believe him. He is wrong. He has always been wrong. I shall have to print this. How lovely his voice is. I mustn't look at his eyes. His hands—what was that he said? I must keep my mind on . . . oh, my love . . . I ought to hate him . . . I do hate him. . . .

Dixie Lee's head drooped. Even her girls had the wit to languish like crushed lilies and to wipe their eyes with filmy handkerchiefs.

It was finished. Yancey walked to his seat and sat as before. The men of the jury filed solemnly out through the crowd. As solemnly they crossed the dusty road and repaired to a draw at the roadside. Briefly they discussed the case. They stamped back into the courtroom.

". . . find the defendant, Dixie Lee, not guilty."

Chapter 9

IT WAS AS THOUGH Osage and the whole Oklahoma country now stopped and took a deep breath. Ever since the day of the Run, more than fifteen years ago, it had been racing helter-skelter, devil take the hindmost; shooting into the air, prancing and yelping out of sheer vitality and cussedness. A rough roof over its head; coarse food on its table; grab what you need; fight for what you want—the men who had come to the Oklahoma country had expected no more than this. A man's country it seemed to be, ruled by men for men. The women allowed them to think so. The word feminism was unknown to the Sabra Cravats, the Mesdames Wyatt and Hefner and Sipes. Prim, good women and courageous, united in their resolve to tame the wilderness, their power was the more tremendous because they did not know they had it. They never once said, "We women will do this. We women will change that." Quietly, indomitably, secure in their common knowledge of the sentimental American male, they went ahead with their plans.

Yancey had come home from the Spanish-American War a hero. Other men from Osage had been in the Philippines. One had even died there (ptomaine from bad tinned beef). But Yancey was the town's Rough Rider. He had charged up San Juan Hill with Roosevelt. Osage, never having seen Roosevelt, assumed that Yancey Cravat had led the way, a six-shooter in either hand.

He returned a captain, unwounded, but thin and yellow, with the livery look that confirmed the stories of putrid food, dysentery, and mosquitoes more deadly than bullets. Enfeebled though he was, his return seemed to energize the town. He shed the khaki and appeared again in the familiar Prince Albert. Osage breathed a sigh of satisfaction. His dereliction was forgiven, the rumors about him allowed to subside. Again the editorial columns of the *Oklahoma Wigwam* blazed with hyperbole.

Yancey's contributions were brilliant but spasmodic. Sabra still did
most of the work of the paper. A linotype machine, that talented iron
monster, now chattered in the composing room. It was the first of its
kind in the Oklahoma country, and very costly. Sabra was proud of the
machine, for it had been her five years at the head of the *Wigwam* that
had made it possible. It was she who had gone out after job printing
contracts; who had educated the local merchants to the value of advertising. Between them Jesse Rickey and Cliff Means ran the linotype. They
now got out with ease the daily *Wigwam* for the town and the weekly for
county subscribers. In a pinch Sabra herself could run the machine.
Yancey never went near it, and young Cim had a horror of it, as he had of
most things mechanical. For that matter, Cim had little enough taste for
the newspaper. He had no news sense. He had neither his father's gift
for mingling with people and winning their confidence nor his mother's
more orderly materialistic mind. He had much of Yancey Cravat's
charm, and something of the vagueness of his grandfather, old Lewis
Venable (dead these two years).

"Stop dreaming!" Sabra said to him often.

Yancey, hearing her admonish Cim, whirled on her in a rare moment
of rage. "God a'mighty, Sabra! That's what Ann Hathaway said to Shakespeare. Leave the boy alone! Let him dream!"

"One dreamer in a family is enough," Sabra retorted tartly.

Six years had gone by since Yancey's return. Yet Sabra never forgot
what he had said about Wichita. "Almost five years in one place. That's
the longest stretch I've ever done, honey."

He had plunged headfirst into the statehood fight. The anti-Indian
faction still bitterly opposed the plan for combining the Oklahoma Territory and the Indian Territory under the single state of Oklahoma. Their
slogan was The White Man's State for the White Man.

"Who brought the Indians to the Oklahoma country in the first place?"
shouted Yancey in the editorial columns of the *Wigwam*. "White men.
They hounded them from place to place and then herded them into the
piece of barren land on which they now live in misery. It isn't fit for a
white man to live on, or the Indians wouldn't be there now. Give them at
least the right to become citizens of the state of Oklahoma."

He was obsessed by the fight. He traveled to Washington in the hope
of lobbying for statehood, and made quite a stir in that formal capital.
Roosevelt was characteristically cordial to his old campaign comrade.

Washington ladies were captivated by this romantic swaggerer out of the Southwest.

It was rumored that he was to be appointed the next governor of the Oklahoma Territory.

"Oh, Yancey," Sabra said, "governor of the Territory! It would mean so much. It would help Cim in the future. Donna, too. Their father a governor." She thought, Perhaps everything will be all right now. Perhaps all that I've gone through will be worth it. He'll settle down.

At which point Yancey blasted any possibility of his appointment by hurling a red-hot editorial into the *Wigwam*. The gist of it was that the hundreds of thousands of Indians now living on reservations throughout the United States should be allowed to live where they pleased, at liberty. The whites of the Oklahoma and Indian Territories read and ran screaming into the streets, cursing the name of Yancey Cravat.

Sabra had caught the editorial in the wet proof sheet. Her eye leaped down its lines. Then she picked up the proof sheet and walked into Yancey's office. Her face was white, set.

"You're going to run this, Yancey?"

"Yes."

"You'll never be governor of the Territory."

"That's right."

She crushed the proof in her hand. "I've forgiven you many things in the last ten years. But I'll never forgive you for this. Never."

"Yes you will, honey. Not while I'm alive, maybe. But someday you'll be able to turn back to the old files of the *Wigwam* and take this editorial of mine, word for word, and run it as your own."

Curiously enough the editorial, while it maddened the white population of the Territory, gained the paper many readers. The *Wigwam* prospered. Osage blossomed. The town was still rough, crude, wide open. But it was no longer a camp. It began to build schools, churches, halls. Even Grat Gotch's gambling tent had long ago been replaced by a solid wooden structure.

Sol Levy's store—the Levy Mercantile Company—had two waxen ladies in the window, their features only slightly affected by the burning southwest sun. Yancey boomed Sol for mayor of Osage, but, although he was respected, prosperous, the town had never quite absorbed him. A citizen of years' standing, he still was a stranger, mingling little with his fellow townsmen outside business hours. He lived alone. He was shy of the town women though they found him kindly and generous. Occasionally Sabra would say half seriously, "Why don't you get married, Sol? A nice fellow like you. You'd make some girl happy."

Sometimes he thought vaguely of going to Kansas City or even Chicago to meet some nice Jewish girl there, but he never did. It never entered his head to marry a Gentile.

Yancey campaigned for Sol Levy in the mayoralty race—if a thing so one-sided could be called a race. "Why, the very idea!" snorted the redoubtable Mrs. Tracy Wyatt, whose husband was the opposing candidate. "A Jew for mayor of Osage! Mr. Wyatt's folks are real Americans. And I can trace my ancestry back to William Whipple, who was one of the signers of the Declaration of Independence."

Sol did almost nothing to further his election. He seemed to regard the matter with ironic humor. Yancey dropped in to the store to bring him this latest pronouncement of the bristling Mrs. Wyatt.

"Declaration of Independence!" Sol exclaimed. "Tell her one of my ancestors wrote the Ten Commandments. Fella name of Moses."

Yancey, roaring with laughter, used this in the *Wigwam*, and it helped as much as anything to defeat the already defeated candidate.

There was talk of paving Pawhuska Avenue, but this did not come for years. The town actually boasted a waterworks. The *Wigwam* office still stood on Pawhuska, but it now occupied the entire house. Two years after Yancey's return, he and Sabra had decided to build a home on Kihekah Street, where there were trees now almost ten years old.

At first Yancey had said he wanted the house built in native style.

"Native! What in the world!"

"Well, a house in the old Southwest Indian style—almost pueblo, I mean. Or Spanish, sort of, made of Oklahoma red clay. And low, with a patio where you can be out of doors and yet away from the sun. And where you can have privacy."

Sabra made short work of that idea. She built a white frame house in the style of the day, with turrets, towers, cupolas, and a stained glass window in the hall. There were parlor, sitting room, dining room, kitchen on the first floor; four bedrooms on the second floor, and a full-size bathroom. There was a hot air furnace. In the parlor were stuffed chairs and a brown velvet settee. In the sitting room was a lamp with a leaded glass shade in the shape of a strange flower—half water lily, half petunia.

"As long as we're building and furnishing," Sabra said, "it might as well be the best."

By ten every morning she had attended to her household, had planned and ordered the meals, and was at her desk in the *Wigwam* office. She still employed an Indian girl as house servant. There was no other help available. After her hideous experience with Arita Red Feather she had been careful to get girls older, more settled. She preferred Osage girls. They married young, often before they had finished school.

Ruby Big Elk had been with Sabra now for three years. A curious, big, silent girl of about twenty-two—almost handsome—one of six children— a large family for an Osage. Sabra was somewhat taken aback, after the girl had been with her for some months, to learn that she already had been twice married.

"What became of your husbands, Ruby?"

"Died."

She had a manner that bordered on the insolent. Sabra put it down to Indian dignity. When she walked she scuffed her feet ever so little, and this seemed to add insolence to her bearing. "Oh, do lift your feet, Ruby! Don't scuffle when you walk." The girl made no reply. Went on scuffling. Sabra discovered that she was lame; the left leg was slightly shorter than the right. She hid the tendency to limp by sliding. Sabra was terribly embarrassed; apologized to Ruby. The girl only looked at her, her broad face immobile, and said nothing. Sabra repressed a shiver. She had never got accustomed to the Indians.

Still, Ruby was good to the children, never complained about the work. Sometimes she would dig a little pit in the backyard and build a slow smothered fire by some secret Indian process, and there, to the delight of young Cim, she would roast meats skewered with shafts of wood that she herself whittled down. Donna refused to touch the meat, as did Sabra. Donna shared her mother's dislike of the Indians—or perhaps she had early been impressed with her mother's feeling about them. Sometimes Donna, the spoiled, the pampered, the imperious (every inch her grandmother Felice Venable), would feel Ruby Big Elk's eye on her. Back of its utter lack of expression, there seemed to lurk a cold contempt.

"What are you staring at, Ruby?" she would cry. Ruby would walk out of the room, her head regal, her eyes looking straight ahead. She said nothing. "Miserable squaw!" Donna would hiss under her breath. "Gives herself airs because her greasy old father runs the tribe."

Ruby's father, Big Elk, had in fact been chief of the Osage tribe by election for ten years. He had sent his six children and actually his wife to the Indian school, but he himself refused to speak a word of English, though he knew enough of the language. It was a kind of stubborn Indian pride in him. "You have not defeated me."

His pride did not, however, extend to more material things, and Sabra was frequently annoyed by the sight of the entire Big Elk family squatting in her kitchen doorway enjoying juicy bits from the Cravat larder. When Sabra would have put a stop to this, Yancey intervened.

"He's a wise old man. I like to talk with him. Leave him alone."

Often Sabra returned home to find Yancey squatting on the ground with Big Elk, smoking and conversing in Osage. She would come upon them muttering and staring ahead into nothingness or (worse still) shaking with silent laughter, Indian fashion. The sight filled her with fury.

It slowly dawned on Sabra that young Cim was always to be found lolling in the kitchen, talking to Ruby. Ruby, she discovered to her horror, was teaching Cim to speak Osage. One day she found them, their heads close together over the kitchen table, laughing and talking and singing. Rather, Ruby Big Elk was singing a song with a curious pulsating rhythm. Cim was trying to follow the strange slurs and accents, his eyes fixed on Ruby's face, his expression utterly absorbed.

"What are you doing? What is this?"

The Indian girl rose. "Teach um song," she said, which was queer, for she spoke English perfectly.

"Well, I must say, Cimarron Cravat! When you know your father is expecting you down at the office—" She stopped. Her eye had leaped to the table where lay a little round peyote disk—the hashish of the Indian.

She had heard about it, this little buttonlike top of a Mexican cactus plant. The peyote gave the eater a strange feeling of lightness, dispelled pain and fatigue, caused visions of marvelous beauty and grandeur. The use of it had become an Indian religious rite.

Sabra snatched up the little round button. "Peyote!" She whirled on Cim. "What are you doing with this thing?"

Cim's eyes were cast down sullenly. "Ruby was just teaching me one of the peyote ceremony songs. Goes like this." To Sabra's horror he began an eerie song, his eyes half closed.

"Stop it!" screamed Sabra. With the gesture of a tragedy queen she motioned him out of the kitchen. He obeyed with very bad grace.

In the privacy of the sitting room Sabra confronted her son. "So you've come to this! I'm ashamed of you!" She opened her hand to show the peyote crushed in her palm.

"Oh, for heaven's sake, Mom. You'd think you found me drugged in a Chinese opium den. I was just listening to Ruby tell how her father—"

"I should think a man of nineteen could find something better to do than sit talking to an Indian hired girl. Where's your pride!"

He raised his head with the menacing look that she knew so well in his father. "Ruby is the daughter of an Osage chief. She is just as important a person in the Osage Nation as Alice Roosevelt is in Washington."

"I've heard about enough. A lot of dirty Indians! Just you march yourself down to the *Wigwam* office, young man. And if I ever hear that you've eaten a bite of this miserable stuff"—she held out the peyote button—"I'll have your father thrash you within an inch of your life."

But Yancey, on being told the story, only looked thoughtful and a little sad. "It's your own fault, Sabra. You're bound that the boy shall live the life you've planned for him instead of the one he wants. So he's trying to escape into a dream life. Like the Indians. It's all the same thing."

"I don't know what you're talking about."

"The Indians started to eat peyote after the whites had taken their religious and spiritual life away from them. The whites told them that the gods they had worshiped were commonplace things. The stars were lumps of hot metal—the rain a thing that a man in Washington could prophesy by looking at a piece of machinery. Man has got to have dreams, or life is unendurable. So the Indian turned to the peyote. He finds peace and comfort and beauty in his dreams."

A horrible suspicion darted through Sabra. "Yancey Cravat, have you ever . . ."

He nodded his head slowly, sadly. "Many times. Many times."

CIM WAS TWENTY, Donna fifteen. And now Sabra lived alone in the house on Kihekeh Street, except for a colored servant sent from Kansas. She ran the paper alone. She ordered the house as she wished it. She very nearly ran the town of Osage. Yancey was gone, Cim was gone. Donna was gone. Sabra had refused to compromise with life, and life had taken matters out of her hands.

Donna was away at an Eastern finishing school—Miss Dignum's on the Hudson. It had been Sabra's idea.

"East?" Yancey had said. "Kansas City?"

"New York."

"You're crazy."

"Donna's an unusual girl. She's got the ambition and the insight of a woman of twice her age."

"I'm sorry to hear that."

"She doesn't get along with the girls here—Maurine Turket and Jewel Riggs and those others switching up and down Pawhuska Avenue. They'll marry one of the loafers and settle down like vegetables. Well, she won't. I'll see to that."

"Going to marry her off to an Eastern potentate?"

"She knows what she wants. She'll get it, too."

Cim, walking the prairies beyond Osage, said that he wanted to be a geologist. He spoke of the Colorado School of Mines. He worked in the *Wigwam* office and hated it. He could pi a case of type more completely than a drunken tramp printer. Jesse Rickey protested to Yancey: "She can't make a newspaper man out of that kid. Not in a million years. Newspaper men are born, not made."

"I know it," said Yancey wearily. "He'll find a way out."

Osage swarmed with meetings, committees, lodges. The women's clubs began to go in for civic betterment. They planted shrubs about the cinder-strewn railroad depots; they agitated for the immediate paving of Pawhuska Avenue (it wasn't done); and no Osage merchant was safe from cajoling females demanding his name signed to this or that petition (with a contribution).

Sabra was at the head of many of these movements. Also if there could be said to be "society" in Osage, she was the leader. She was the first in the Twentieth Century Club to serve Waldorf salad—that abominable mixture of apple cubes, chopped nuts, whipped cream, and mayonnaise. The ladies fell upon it with little cries and served it until Osage husbands began to roar, "I can't eat this stuff. Fix me some bacon and eggs."

When it again became her turn to act as hostess she planned another culinary triumph: pineapple and marshmallow salad, the recipe for which had been sent her by Donna in the East. Refreshments were to be served at four. Midday dinner was over and Yancey had returned to the office when Sabra was confronted by Ruby Big Elk with the astounding statement that she must go to the Reservation in time for the peyote ceremony.

"You can't go," said Sabra flatly. For answer Ruby turned, walked into her own room, and closed the door.

"Well," shouted Sabra, "if you do go you needn't come back." She marched out to the front porch, where Cim was lying in the hammock.

"This ends it. Ruby has got to leave. Twenty women this afternoon, and she says she's going to the Reservation."

"But she told you a month ago."

"Maybe she did. I can't be expected to remember every time the Indians have one of their powwows. I told her she couldn't go. She's in there getting ready. Well, she needn't come back."

She flounced into the kitchen. There stood a young Indian girl unknown to her. "What do you want?"

"I am here," the girl answered, "to take Ruby Big Elk's place this afternoon. I am Cherokee. She told me to come."

"Well!" gasped Sabra, relieved. Through the kitchen window she saw Cim hitching the two pintos to the racy yellow phaeton that Yancey had bought. She was glad he was clearing out before company was due.

Ruby's door opened. The girl came out. Her appearance was amazing. She wore a dress of white doeskin hanging straight from shoulders to ankles, and as soft and pliable as velvet. The hem was fringed. Front, sleeves, collar were exquisitely beaded. It was the robe of a princess. Her dark Indian eyes were alive. Her skin seemed to glow in contrast with the garment. She was, for the moment, almost beautiful.

"Hello, Theresa Jump. This is Theresa Jump. She will do my work today. She knows about the pineapple and marshmallow salad." For a moment it seemed to Sabra that the faintest shadow of amusement flitted over Ruby's face as she said this. "I will be back in the morning."

She walked out the kitchen door, across the yard. A stab of suspicion cut Sabra. She flew to the back porch, watched Ruby Big Elk walk toward the barn. Cim drove out with the phaeton. He saw Ruby in her white doeskin dress. His eyes shone enormous. At that look in his face Sabra ran across the yard. Ruby had set one foot on the buggy step. Cim held out his free hand.

Sabra reached them, panting. "Where are you going?"

"I'm driving Ruby out to the Reservation."

"No, you're not." She put one hand on the buggy wheel, as though to stop them by force. Yet she knew she must not lose her dignity before this Indian woman—before her son.

Cim gathered up the reins. "I may stay to see some of the peyote ceremony. Father says it's very interesting. Big Elk has invited me."

"Your father knows you're going? Like this?"

"Oh, yes." He cast an oblique glance at her hand on the wheel. Her hand dropped heavily to her side. He spoke to the horses. They were off.

Hot tears blinded Sabra. But her pride spoke, even then. You must not go in by the kitchen. That Indian girl will see you. Go in the front way. Pretend it is nothing. Oh, what shall I do? All those women this afternoon. . . . His face! His face when he saw her in that dress.

Inside, she bathed her eyes, changed, came into the kitchen smiling. "Cut the pineapple into chunks. Snip the marshmallow into it with scissors. Mix whipped cream into your mayonnaise . . . a cherry on top . . ." The door bell rang. "Howdy-do, Mrs. Nisbett."

Theresa Jump proved unteachable. Sabra herself mixed the salad. It proved a great success, but the triumph was spoiled for Sabra. She bundled the girl off as soon as the dishes were done. Wearily she had begun to set the house to rights when Yancey came home.

Sabra poured out upon him all the wrath and anxiety of the past few hours. Ruby. Cim. Peyote. Osages. If his own father allows such things . . .

Yancey, normally so glib, said little. His eyes were bloodshot. He had been drinking even more than was his wont, she knew that at once. By no means drunk (she had never seen him really drunk), he was in one of his fits of moody depression. She felt that he hardly heard what she was saying. She set a place for him at the dining-room table and put before him a dish of the salad.

"What's this?" he said.

"Pineapple and marshmallow salad. With Ruby gone, I didn't get anything for supper—I was so upset—all those women . . ."

He sat looking down at his plate. His beautiful hands were opening and closing convulsively. "Pineapple and marshmallow salad," he repeated. Then he threw back his head and began to laugh. Peal after peal of laughter. "Pineapple and marsh—" Suddenly serious, he stood up, like a tiger about to spring. " 'Actum est de republica.' "

"What?" said Sabra, sharply.

"Latin, Latin, my love. 'It is all over with the Republic.' Pineapple and marshmallow salad!" He walked out of the room, put on his sombrero and went off up the street, arms swinging despondently.

Sabra's eyes burned, her throat was constricted. Men! Cim off with that squaw. Yancey angry because she had given him this feminine dish of leftovers. She allowed herself the luxury of a cleansing storm of tears.

Eight o'clock. She went out on the front porch. A hot September evening. The crickets squeaked away in the weeds. She was conscious of an aching weariness in all her body, but she could not sleep. Nine. Ten. Eleven. Twelve. She undressed, unpinned her thick hair. All the time she was listening. Listening. One o'clock.

Suddenly she dressed again with icy fumbling fingers and walked to Pawhuska Avenue. The *Wigwam* office was dark. Yancey was not there. She unlocked the door, struck a light. With a sudden premonition she ran to Yancey's desk, opened the drawer in which he now kept his six-shooters. They were not there. She knew then that Yancey had gone.

Doc Valliant. She stepped out into the blackness of Pawhuska Avenue. Doc Valliant would go with her. He would drive her to the Reservation. But there was no response at his dwelling. She struck her palms together in a kind of agony of futility. She would go alone if she had a horse and buggy. She could rent one at the livery stable. But then it would be all over Osage. Sabra Cravat driving out into the prairie alone in the middle of the night. Well, she couldn't help that. She had to go.

Toward the livery stable, past Sol Levy's house. A quiet little figure rose from the blackness of the porch. "Sabra! What are you doing out at this hour?"

"Sol! Cim's at the Reservation. Something's happened. I feel it."

He did not scoff at this, as most men would. He seemed to understand her fear and to accept it. "What do you want to do?"

"Hitch up and drive me there. Cim's got the buggy."

He did not ask where Yancey was. "Wait," he said. "I will get my rig."

Sol Levy had two fine horses, but he was a nervous, jerky driver. They left the town behind them, whirled over the prairie. The Reservation was two hours distant. The night air rushed against Sabra's face, cooling it. A half hour passed. "Let me drive, will you, Sol?"

Without a word he entrusted the reins to her accustomed hands. Presently she began to talk disjointedly. He filled in the gaps with his imagination. What she said sounded absurd; he knew it for tragedy.

". . . pineapple and marshmallow salad . . . hates that kind of thing . . . moody . . . drinking . . . Ruby Big Elk . . . Cim . . . his face . . . peyote ceremony . . . white doeskin dress . . ."

"I see," said Sol Levy soothingly. "The boy will be all right. Well,

Yancey—you know how he is. Do you think he has gone away again?"

"I don't know." Then, "Yes."

Three o'clock and after. They came in sight of the Osage Reservation, a scattered settlement of sterile farms and wooden shanties. Dark and still, except for the thud of their horses' hoofs and the whir of the buggy wheels. Then, as Sabra pulled up the horses, they heard the weird wavering cadences of the peyote song, and above it, reverberating, ominous, the beat of the buckskin drum. They sat a moment, listening.

Sabra spoke matter-of-factly to keep her voice from quavering. "He'll be in the large wooden tepee next to Big Elk's house. Yancey showed it to me once, when we drove out here." She gave a cracked laugh that bordered on hysteria. "A drum in the night. It sounds so savage."

Sol took the reins from her. "Nothing to be frightened about. A lot of poor ignorant Indians trying to forget their misery."

Uncertainly, in the blackness, they drove toward the drum beat, into the trampled yard that held the peyote tepee. With difficulty Sol groped his way to a stump that served as hitching post, tied the horses. He took Sabra's arm firmly.

Two great silent blanketed figures stood at the door of the tepee, barring the way. Sol peered up into their faces. Suddenly, "Hello, Joe!" He turned to Sabra. "It's Joe Yellow Eyes. He was in the store only yesterday. Say, Joe, the lady here—Mrs. Cravat—she wants her son should come out and go home." The blanketed figures stood silent.

Sabra loosed her arm and took a step forward. "I am the woman of Yancey Cravat, the one you call Buffalo Head. If my son is in there I want to take him home now. It is time."

"Sure, take um home," replied Joe Yellow Eyes. He stood aside. Blinking and stumbling, Sol and Sabra entered the crowded tepee.

Those within paid no attention to the two white intruders. Blinded by the light of the sacred fire, Sabra could discern nothing except the figure crouched before it. Then gradually her vision cleared.

In the center a crescent of earth about six inches high curved around a fire built of sticks so arranged that as the ashes fell they formed a second crescent inside the other. Within the crescent, upon a little star of sage twigs, lay the peyote, symbol of the rite. Facing them was old Chief Stump Horn, the emblems of office in his hands—the gourd rattle, the wand, the fan of eagle plumes. All about the tepee lay blanketed motionless figures. Some sat with heads bowed, others gazed fixedly upon the

peyote button. And the song went on, the beat-beat of the drum. The room was stifling but scrupulously clean. All about was an atmosphere of reverie, of swooning bliss.

Around the wall, almost level with the dirt floor, were small apertures. A little wooden door was shut upon most of these. As Sabra and Sol watched, they learned the use of the openings. When nausea overcame one of the Indians, he crawled swiftly to one of the doors, thrust head and shoulders out, and relieved his body of the drug's overdose.

Sabra's eyes moved, searching, searching. Then she saw where Cim lay under his gay striped blanket. His face was covered, but she knew well how the slim body curled in its blankets, how it lay at night. They went to him, picking their way over the recumbent forms. She turned back the blanket. His face was smiling, peaceful, lovely. She thought, "This is the way I should look at him if he were dead."

Sabra and Sol tugged and strained at the inert figure of the boy. "Oh, God!" whimpered Sabra. "He's so heavy. What shall we do?"

"We must drag him," Sol said. They took an arm each and struggled with him to the door, past the two towering figures. They dragged him along the earth, through the trampled weeds.

"We can't lift him into the buggy. We can't—" Sabra ran back to the two at the door. She lifted her white, agonized face to Joe Yellow Eyes. "Help me. Help me." Wordless, the Indian walked over to the boy, picked him up easily and swung him into the buggy.

They drove back to Osage. Cim's head lay in Sabra's lap, like a little boy's. One aching arm she held firmly about him to keep him from slipping to the floor of the buggy. The dawn came, and then the sunrise over the prairie. Sabra looked down at the lovely smiling face in her lap. "He wanted to go. I wouldn't let him. Is it too late, Sol?"

"Go? Go where?"

"The Colorado School of Mines. Geology."

"Too late! This is September. It just starts. Sure he'll go."

They drove through the yard right to the edge of the porch steps. Dragging again, they got him in, undressed him; she washed his face.

"Well," said Sol. "I'll go open the store and then have a good cup of coffee."

Her face was distorted with her effort not to cry. But when he would have patted her grimed and trembling hand with his own, in a gesture of comforting, she caught his hand to her lips and kissed it.

The sound of the horses' hoofs died away on the still morning air. She looked down at Cim. She thought, Yancey has gone again. Has left me. I know that. I have had it all, and I have borne it. Nothing more can happen to me now.

Chapter 10

FOR YEARS OKLAHOMA had longed for statehood as a bride awaits her wedding day. At last, "Behold the bridegroom!" said a paternal government, handing her over to the Union. "Meet the family."

Then, at the very altar, the final words spoken, the bride had turned to encounter an unexpected guest embodying all her wildest dreams.

The name of the dazzling stranger was Oil.

Oil. Nothing else mattered. Oklahoma, the dry, the windswept, was a sea of hidden oil. The red prairies, pricked, ran black with it. Every day was like the day of the Opening back in '89. People swarmed to the plains from every state in the Union. Once more shantytowns sprang up where before had been open prairie. Again the gambling tent, the six-shooter, the roaring saloon, the dance hall. Men fought, killed, died for a piece of ground. Every barren sunbaked farm might conceal liquid treasure, rich beyond imagining. Millions of barrels of oil burst through the sand and shale and clay. Drill, pump, blast. Here she comes. Oklahoma went stark raving mad.

Just outside Osage, for miles around, they were drilling. The stuff was elusive, tantalizing. Here might be a gusher vomiting millions. Fifty feet away not so much as a spot of grease could be forced to the surface. There was that piece of farmland Sabra had bought years ago. She had thought herself shrewd to have picked up this fertile little oasis in the midst of the bare plain. She knew now why it had been so prolific. Rich black oil lay under all that surrounding land, rendering it barren. No corroding oil ran beneath the Cravat land, and because of this it lay there now, so green, so lush, like a mirage in the desert.

For years the meandering clay roads that were little more than trails had seen only occasional buggies, farm wagons, rarely an automobile. Now those roads were choked. Frail wooden bridges sagged and splintered with the stream of traffic, but no one took the time to repair them. A torrent of vehicles of every description flowed night and day on their way to the oil fields. Frequently the torrent choked itself with its own volume. Millionaire promoters from the East. Engineers, prospectors, drillers, shooters, roustabouts. Men in oil-soaked overalls that hadn't been changed for days. Men in London-tailored suits. Only the ruthless and the desperate survived.

Tough careless young boys drove the nitroglycerin wagons, a deadly job on those rough roads. It was this stuff that shot the oil up out of the earth. Hard lads in corduroys took their chances and pocketed their high pay, singing as they drove, a red shirttail tied to the back of the load as a warning. Often an expected wagon failed to appear. The workers on the field never took the trouble to trace it. They knew that somewhere along the road was a great gaping hole, with no wood or steel or bone for yards around to tell the tale they already knew.

Mile on mile, as far as the eye could see, were the skeleton frames of oil rigs outlined against the sky, rising from acres once carefully tended. Rawboned farmers and their scrawny wives, grown spectacularly rich overnight, walked away from their houses without troubling to take their furniture or lock the door. Oil smeared itself over the prairies like a plague, killing the grass, blighting the trees, spreading over the surface of the creeks and rivers. Oklahoma—the Red People's Country—lay heaving under the hot summer sun, a scarred and dreadful thing.

Tracy Wyatt, who used to drive the bus and dray line between Wahoo and Osage, was one of the richest men in Oklahoma—in the whole of the United States. The Wyatt Oil Company. In another five years the Wyatt Oil Companies. The big boys from the East came to him, hat in hand. The sum of his daily income was fantastic. The mind simply did not grasp it. Tracy's good-natured face wore the slightly astonished look of a commonplace man who suddenly finds himself a personage.

The new money affected Mrs. Wyatt queerly. She became nervous, full of spleen. The Eastern doctors spoke to her of high blood pressure.

Sabra frankly envied these lucky ones. A letter from Felice Venable was characteristic of that awesome old matriarch.

All this talk of oil and millions! I'll be bound that you and that husband of yours haven't enough to fill a lamp. Trust Yancey Cravat to get hold of the wrong piece of land. Well, at least you can't be disappointed. It has been like that from the day you married him, though you can't say your mother didn't warn you. I hope Donna will show more sense.

Donna, home from Miss Dignum's, seemed indeed to be a grand-daughter after Felice Venable's own heart. She was so unlike the other Oklahoma girls as to make her birth on the prairie almost nineteen years ago seem impossible. She had about her an air of cool disdain very disconcerting to her former intimates, not to speak of her own family. Tall, thin to the point of scrawniness in their opinion; sallow, unrouged, mysterious. She talked with an Eastern accent, said eyether and nyether and altogether made herself poisonously unpopular with the girls. She paid little heed to the clumsy attentions of the open-faced hometown lads. Her school days finished, she now looked about her coolly, calculatingly. Her mother she regarded with a kind of affectionate amusement.

"What a rotten deal you've had, Sabra dear," she would drawl. "Really, I don't see how you've stood it all these years."

Sabra came to her own defense. "Stood what?"

"Oh—you know. This being a pioneer woman and head-held-high in spite of a bum of a husband."

"Donna Cravat, if you ever again dare to speak like that of your father I shall punish you, big as you are. Your father is one of the greatest figures the Southwest has ever produced."

"Mmm. Well, he's picturesque enough, I suppose. But I wish he hadn't worked so hard at it. And Cim! There's a brother! A great help to me in my career, the menfolk of this quaint family."

"I wasn't aware that you were planning a career," Sabra retorted. "Unless slopping around in a kimono most of the day and lying in the hammock reading is called a career by Dignum graduates."

"Darling, I adore you when you get viperish and Venable like that. But this lovely head isn't so empty as you think. I know it's no use counting on Father. What is he doing, anyway? Living with some squaw? . . . Forgive me, Mother. I didn't mean to hurt you. . . . Cim's just as bad and hasn't even Dad's phony ideals. If it weren't for you we'd all be back in Wichita living in genteel poverty. I think you're wonderful, and I ought to try to be like you. But I don't want to be a girl reporter describing the sumptuous sunflowers at one of Cassandra Sipes' parties."

Goaded by a kind of wonder, Sabra put her question. "What do you want to do, then?"

"I want to marry the richest man in Oklahoma, and build a palace that I'll hardly ever live in, and travel like royalty, and clank with emeralds. With my coloring they're my stone."

"Oh, emeralds by all means," Sabra agreed. "And the gentleman—let me see. That would have to be Tracy Wyatt, wouldn't it?"

"Yes," replied Donna calmly.

"You've probably overlooked Mrs. Wyatt. Of course Tracy's only fifty-one. There's plenty of time if you'll just be patient."

"I don't intend to be patient, Mama darling."

Her hard, ruthless tone startled Sabra. "Donna Cravat, don't you start any monkey business. The other day when we went over the Wyatts' new house, I heard you saying some drivel about Tracy's being a man who craved beauty in his life, and sneering politely at the house. Poor fellow, he had been so proud to show it. But I thought you were just talking that New York talk of yours."

"I wasn't. I was talking business."

Sabra was revolted and distressed, all at once. She gained reassurance by telling herself that this was just one of Donna's queer jokes.

As to her own life, she took Sol Levy's advice. "Settle down to running your paper, Sabra, and you won't need any oil wells. You can have the best-paying, most powerful paper in the Southwest. This town will grow and grow. Five years from now it'll look like Chicago."

Just as she had known that Yancey had again left her on that night of the peyote ceremony, so now she sensed that he would come back in the midst of this oil insanity. And come back he did, bringing with him news that overshadowed his return.

He came riding, as always, but it was a sorry enough nag that he bestrode this time. His white sombrero was battered, his whole figure covered with heavy red dust. She thought, Each time he will be a little more broken, older, until at last . . . She only said, "Yancey," quietly.

He entered as he had left, with no word of explanation. He was reeling with laughter as he strode into the *Wigwam* office where she sat at her orderly desk. For a moment she thought that he was drunk or gone mad. He flung his soiled sombrero to the desk top and swept her into his arms. "Sabra! Here's news for you. Jesse! Heh, Jesse! Come in here! I've been laughing so hard I almost rolled off my horse." He was striding up and down as of old, still flashing with fire.

"Oil, my children! More oil than anybody ever thought there was in any one spot in the world. And where? Where? On the Osage Indian Reservation. It came in an hour ago, like the ocean. It makes every other field look like the Sahara. There never was such a joke!"

"Yancey dear, we're used to oil out here. It's an old story. Come now. Come home and have a hot bath and clean clothes."

"Hot bath! Do you realize what this means? Two thousand Osage Indians, squatting in rags in front of their miserable shanties, are now the richest nation in the world. They were given that land, the barest, meanest desert land in the whole of Oklahoma. And our government said, 'There, you red dogs, take that and live on it.' I could die with laughing. There's no stopping that flow. Every buck and squaw on the Osage Reservation is a millionaire. They own that land, and by God I'm going to see that no one takes it away from them!"

He grabbed pencil and paper. "Send this out AP, Sabra, and kill your editorial. I'll write it. Make this your news lead, too. Listen. 'The gaudiest star-spangled cosmic joke that ever was played on a double-dealing government burst into fireworks today when thousands of barrels of oil shot into the air on the miserable desert land known as the Osage Indian Reservation!' "

"We can't use that. That's treason—that's anarchy—"

"It's the truth. They'll be down on those Osages like a pack of wolves. At least I'll let them know they're expected. I'll run the story as I want."

"And I say you won't. I'm editor of this paper."

He turned quietly and looked at her. "Who is?"

"I am."

Without a word he grasped her wrist and led her out into the street. He pointed to the weatherworn sign that he and Jesse had hung there almost twenty years before. She had had it painted and repainted. She had had it repaired. She had never replaced it with another.

THE OKLAHOMA WIGWAM
YANCEY CRAVAT PROPR. AND EDITOR

"When you take that down, Sabra honey, and paint your own name in my place, you'll be editor of this newspaper. Until you do that, I am."

CIM CAME HOME from Colorado for the summer vacation, was caught up in the oil flood, and never went back to school. With his geological knowledge, slight as it was, he was shuttled back and forth, from one end of the state to the other. Cim, like his father, was more an onlooker than a participant in this fantastic spectacle. Both seemed to lack business acumen—or perhaps a certain fastidiousness kept them from taking part. A hint of oil in this corner and thousands were upon it, like pigs in a trough. A hundred times Yancey could have bought an oil lease share for a song. "I don't want the filthy muck," he said. "Let the Indians have it. It's theirs."

His comings and goings had ceased to cause Sabra the keen agony of earlier days. She knew now that their existence, so long as Yancey lived, would always be made up of just such unexplained absences and melodramatic homecomings. She had made up her mind to accept the inevitable.

Yancey spent much of his time on the oil fields. The big boys from the East often sought him out for his company, which they found amusing, and for a certain regional wisdom. He despised them and could be found, for the most part, with the pumpers and roustabouts, tool dressers and shooters—a hard-drinking, hard-talking crew. In his white sombrero and his outdated Prince Albert he was known as a picturesque character.

Yet years of heavy drinking were taking their toll. Local townsmen who once had feared and admired him began to patronize him. Many of them were rich now. They had owned a piece of Oklahoma dirt that suddenly was worth its weight in diamonds. Pat Leary, the Irish lawyer who had once been a section hand on the Santa Fe, now owned such vast oil holdings that his Indian wife, Crook Nose, was considered quaint by the wives of Easterners.

Sabra owned no oil leases, but she still queened it in Osage and had become a power in the state. The paper was read and respected throughout the Southwest. It was said with pride in Osage that no oil was rich enough to stain the pages of the *Oklahoma Wigwam*. Though few realized it, and though Sabra herself never admitted it, it was Yancey who had made this true. He neglected it for years together, but he always turned up in a crisis to hurl his barbed editorials at the heads of offenders. He championed the Indians, he denounced the oil kings, he laughed at the money grabbers, he exposed the land thieves. He was afraid of nothing. He seemed always to sense an important happening from afar and to emerge, growling like an old lion, broken but fighting. He had, on one occasion, come back just in time to learn of Dixie Lee's death.

Dixie had struck oil and had retired, a rich woman. She had gone to Oklahoma City, bought a residence in a decent neighborhood and adopted a baby girl. She had gone to Kansas City for the child. No one knew how she had pulled the wool over the eyes of the Kansas authorities. She never could have done it in Oklahoma. She had had the child almost a year when the women of Osage got wind of it.

Sabra Cravat heard of it. Mrs. Wyatt. Mrs. Doc Nisbett.

They took the child away from her by law. Six months later Dixie Lee died; the sentimental said of a broken heart. It was Yancey Cravat who wrote her obituary:

> Dixie Lee, for years one of the most prominent citizens of Osage and a pioneer in the early days of Oklahoma, one of the few women who had the courage to enter the historic Run in '89, is dead.
> She was murdered by the good women of Osage. . . .

The story was a nine-days' wonder, even in that melodramatic state. Sabra read it, white-faced. The circulation of the *Wigwam* took another bound upward.

"Someday," said Osage, "somebody is going to shoot old Cimarron if his wife doesn't save them the trouble."

It was a gigantic task to keep up with the changes that were sweeping over Osage and all of Oklahoma. Yet the *Wigwam* recorded them faithfully. The local livery stable was replaced by Fink's Garage—Repairs of All Kinds. Osage began to see the world. Mr. and Mrs. W. Fletcher Busby have left for a trip to Europe, Egypt, and the Holy Land.

Most astounding of all were the Indian items, for now the *Wigwam* regularly ran news about those incredible people who in one short year had leaped from the Neolithic Age to Broadway.

> Long Foot Magpie and wife were week-end visitors of Plenty Horses at Watonga recently.

> Mr. and Mrs. Sampson Lame Bull have returned from Osage after accompanying Mrs. Twin Woman, who is now a patient in the Osage Hospital.

The Osage Indians, a little more than two thousand in number, who but yesterday were a ragged, half-fed band, now benefited from the most lavish oil flow in the state. Yancey Cravat's news story and editorial had been copied and read all over the country. A stunned government tried to bring order out of chaos. The Osages were swept off the Reservation to make way for the flood of oil that was transmuted into a flood of gold. They were transported to a new section called Wazhazhe, which is the ancient Indian word for Osage.

Agents appointed. Offices established. Millions of barrels of oil. Millions of dollars yearly to be divided somehow among two thousand Osage Indians. Every full blood, half blood, or quarter blood Osage was put on the Indian roll; each was entitled to a head right, which meant a share in the millions. Five in a family—five head rights.

The Indian Agent's office was full of typewriters, files, ledgers, neat young clerks all occupied with documents that read like some fantastic nightmare, with their storybook Indian names and their cold, matter-of-fact figures.

Clint Tall Meat	$523,000
Benny Warrior	$265,887
Short Tooth	$387,942

The government bought them farms with their oil money, built brick houses and furnished them in plush and linoleum and gas ranges. You saw powerful cars whirling up and down the roads, inexpert hands grasping the wheel. The white man gave these Indian cars a wide berth, for these vehicles stopped for no one, kept the middle of the road, flew over bridges and ditches like mad things.

The Osages were *Wigwam* subscribers. Sabra grew accustomed to seeing the *Wigwam* doorway suddenly darkened by a huge blanketed form.

"Want um paper."

"All right. Five dollars."

The blanketed figure would produce a wallet bursting with silver dollars, for the Osage loved the bright metal disks. Down on the desk they clinked.

"Me want see iron man. Make um name."

Sabra would conduct the visitor into the composing room where three linotype machines now clanked away. Once Yancey had taken old Big Elk, Ruby's father, back there to see how the linotype turned liquid lead into printed words. He had had Jesse Rickey turn out Big Elk's name in the form of a neat metal bar and print it on paper.

The story of the iron monster that could write spread like a prairie fire through Wazhazhe. Whole families subscribed separately for the *Wigwam*. It was useless to explain that they need not take out a subscription in order to own one of the coveted metal bars. It had been done that way once. They always would do it that way.

The merchants of Osage liked to see the Indians in town. It meant money freely spent. The Osage men were broad shouldered, magnificent, the women tall, stately. Now they grew huge with overfeeding. They paced Pawhuska Avenue with slow measured tread; calm, grandly content.

The women walked bareheaded, their brilliant striped blankets enveloping them from neck to heels. But beneath them you saw dresses of silk, American in make and style. On their feet were high-heeled slippers of pale fine kid or patent leather. The men wore the blanket, too, but beneath it they liked a shirt of silk brocade in gorgeous colors, its tail worn outside the trousers. On their heads were huge sombreros trimmed with bands of snakeskin ornamented with silver. They hired white chauffeurs to drive their big cars and sat back grandly after ordering them to drive round and round the main business block.

The Levy Mercantile Company had added a fancy grocery department to its three-story brick store. In its window on the street floor Sol displayed juicy white stalks of asparagus in glass jars, lobster, mushrooms, pork roasts dressed in frills. Dozens of chickens, pounds of pork were piled in the cars of homeward bound Osages. Often, when the food bills mounted too high, the Indian Agent at Wazhazhe threatened to let them go unpaid. He alone had the power to check the outpouring of Indian gold.

"It's disgusting," Sabra Cravat said again and again.

"Keeps money in circulation," Sol Levy replied.

Not only did Yancey agree with Sol, he seemed to find enormous satisfaction in the lavishness with which they spent their oil money.

"Why don't they do some good with it?" Sabra demanded.

"What good's Wyatt doing? Or Nisbett, or old Busby? Blowing it on houses and travel and high-priced cars."

Sometimes Sabra encountered old Big Elk, his squaw and Ruby Big Elk, together with others of the family—one of the wealthiest on the Wazhazhe Reservation. Sabra always greeted them politely. "How do you do, Ruby," she would say. "What a beautiful dress."

Ruby would say nothing, but Sabra fancied that there was something triumphant in her gaze. She wondered if Ruby, the oft-married, had married yet again. Once she asked Cim about her, making her tone casual. "Do you ever see that girl who used to work here—Ruby, wasn't it? Ruby Big Elk?"

Cim's tone was even more casual than hers. "Oh, yes. We were working out Wazhazhe way, you know, on the Choteau field. That's nearby."

"They're terribly rich, aren't they?"

"Oh, rotten. A fleet of cars and a regular flock of houses."

Donna came home from a bridge party one afternoon a week later, her creamy pallor showing a tinge of ocherous rage. She burst in upon Sabra.

"Do you know that Cim spends his time at the Big Elks' when we think he's out in the oil fields?"

Sabra met this calmly. "He's working near there. He told me he had seen them."

"Seen them! That miserable Gazelle Slaughter said he's there all the time. He and Ruby drive around in her car, he eats with them, he—"

"I'll speak to your father. Cim's coming home Saturday. Gazelle is angry at Cim, you know, because he won't notice her and she likes him." Sabra turned her clear appraising gaze upon this strange daughter of hers. "Perhaps it would be better, Donna, if you'd pay less attention to your brother's social lapses and more to your own conduct."

Donna bestowed her rare and brilliant smile upon her forthright mother. "I suppose I say, 'What do you mean?' "

"You know what I mean. If you weren't my own daughter I'd say your conduct with Tracy Wyatt was that of a—a—"

"Harlot," put in Donna sweetly. She came over and put her arms about Sabra. "It's all right, Mama darling. You just don't understand. Life isn't as simple as it was when you were a frontier gal."

Sabra shrugged away from her. "I'm ashamed for you. You press against him like a—like a—" She could not say it. "And that horse you ride. You say he loans it to you. He gave it to you. What for?"

"Yes, he did give it to me. He wants to give me lots of things, but I won't take them, yet. Tracy's in love with me. He thinks I'm young and beautiful and wonderful. He's married to a dried-up, bitter old hag. He's never known what love is. He's insanely rich, and rather sweet. We're going to be married. Tracy will get his divorce. It has taken me a year and a half, but it's going to be worth it. Don't worry, darling. He's making an honest woman of your wayward daughter."

Sabra drew herself up, every inch the daughter of her mother, Felice Venable. "You are disgusting."

"Not really. I shall be happy, and Tracy, too. His wife will be unhappy, I suppose, for a while. But she isn't happy anyway. It'll work out. You'll see. It's Cim that needs looking after. He's got a streak of—of . . ." She did not finish the sentence. "When he comes home Saturday I wish you'd speak to him."

But Cim did not come on Saturday. When Sabra and Yancey drove home from the office in their little car for noonday dinner they saw a great limousine drawn up at the curb. A chauffeur lounged in front.

A vague premonition stabbed at Sabra. "Whose car is that?"

Yancey glanced at it indifferently. "Somebody drove Cim home, I suppose. Got enough dinner for company?"

"Cim!" Sabra called as they entered the house. "Cim!" There was no answer. She went to the parlor, where two massive, silent figures sat. With the Indian sense of ceremony old Big Elk and his squaw had known the proper room to use.

"Why—Big Elk!" Sabra said.

"How!" replied Big Elk, and held up his palm in greeting.

Two pairs of black Indian eyes stared at Sabra. She saw that their dress was elaborate; the formal clothing reserved for great occasions. Suddenly she was moved to nameless terror. "Yancey!" she cried.

He came into the room with his quick light step. At the sight of Big Elk and his wife he smiled his charming smile.

Mrs. Big Elk nodded her greeting. She was younger, perhaps by thirty years, than her husband; his third wife. She spoke English; had even attended an Indian mission school in her girlhood.

Yancey spoke to them in Osage. Big Elk replied with a monosyllable.

"What did he say?"

"I asked them to eat dinner with us. He says he cannot," he explained to Sabra.

"I should hope not. What do they want? Tell her to speak English."

Big Elk turned to his wife. He uttered a brief command in his own tongue. The squaw smiled a strange, embarrassed smile. "Big Elk and me come take you back to Wazhazhe."

"What for?" cried Sabra sharply.

"Four o'clock big dinner, big dance. Your son want um come tell you. Want um know he marry Ruby this morning."

"God A'mighty!" said Yancey Cravat. He came over to Sabra quickly, but she waved him away.

"Don't. I'm not going to—it's all right." But beneath her fine dark eyes you now suddenly saw a smudge of purple, as though a dirty thumb had rubbed there; and a sagging of the muscles of her face.

"Don't look like that, honey. Come. Sit down."

Again the groping wave. "No. I'm all right. We must go there."

Yancey came forward. He shook hands formally with Big Elk and his wife. Sabra realized that he was not displeased. No formal politeness would have prevented him from voicing his anger if this announcement had shattered him as it had her.

"Sugar, shake hands with them, won't you?"

"No. No." She turned woodenly and walked to the door, ignoring the Indians. Across the hall, slowly, like an old woman, down the porch steps, toward the shabby little car next to the big rich one. As she went she heard Yancey's voice at the telephone.

"Jesse! Take this. Ready! . . . Ex-Chief Big Elk, of the Osage Nation, and Mrs. Big Elk announce the marriage of their daughter Ruby Big Elk to Cimarron Cravat, son of—don't interrupt me, I'm in a hurry . . ."

Sabra climbed heavily into the car. Chief Big Elk and his wife came out presently, ushered by Yancey. They heaved themselves into the big car. Yancey got in beside Sabra. She spoke to him once only.

"I think you are glad."

"This is Oklahoma. In a way it's what I wanted it to be when I came here twenty years ago. Cim's like your father, Lewis Venable. Weak, but good stock. Ruby's pure Indian and a magnificent animal. It's hard on you now, my darling. But their children and their grandchildren are going to be such stuff as American dreams are made of. You'll see."

"I hope I shall die before that day."

The shabby little car followed the limousine onto the red clay road.

At Wazhazhe they went into the Indian house and saw Cim sitting beside the Indian woman. He came toward Sabra, his head lowered, his fine eyes hidden by the lids.

"Look at me!" Sabra commanded, in the voice of Felice Venable. The boy raised his eyes. She looked at him, her face stony. Ruby Big Elk came toward her, too. The two women gazed at each other; rather, their looks clashed. They did not shake hands.

Dinner. A long table seating a score or more, and many such tables. Sabra found herself seated beside Mrs. Big Elk. On her other side was Yancey, eating and laughing and talking. Sabra went through the motions of eating. She felt as though she was now a hollow thing, an empty shell that moved and walked and talked.

She went through it and stood it, miraculously.

Chapter 11

OSAGE, OKLAHOMA, was a big city. Where scarcely two decades ago prairie and sky had met the eye you now saw a twenty-story hotel. The Italian headwaiter bent from the waist and murmured in your ear about the veal sauté with mushrooms or the spaghetti Caruso. Sabra Cravat, Congresswoman from Oklahoma, lunching in the Louis XIV room with the members of the Women's State Republican Committee, would say, looking up at him with those intelligent dark eyes, "I'll leave it to you, Nick. Only quickly. We haven't much time." Nick would say yes, he understood. No one had much time in Osage, Oklahoma.

Twenty-five years earlier anybody who was anybody in Oklahoma had dilated on his or her Eastern connections. Iowa, if necessary, was East. Now it was considered the height of chic to be able to say that your parents had come through in a covered wagon. As for the Run of '89— that was Osage's *Mayflower*. At the huge dinner given in Sabra Cravat's honor when she was elected congresswoman, only people who came to Oklahoma in the Run were invited.

The fifteen-story Levy Mercantile Company's building now occupied an entire block. You went to the Salon Moderne to buy little French dresses, and the saleswomen of this department wore black satin and imitation pearls. The Indian women had learned about these little French dresses, and often came in with their stately measured stride. To these, as well as to their other customers, the saleswomen said, "That's dreadfully smart on you, Mrs. Buffalo Hide. It's perfect with your coloring."

Maude Leary, the daughter of Mrs. Pat Leary (née Crook Nose), always caused a flutter when she came in, for accustomed though Osage was to money, the Learys' lavishness was something spectacular. In the matter of gowns it was no good trying to influence Maude or her mother. They wanted beads and spangles on a foundation of loud color. The saleswomen were polite, but they cocked an eyebrow at one another. Squaw stuff. Now that little Cravat girl—Felice Cravat, Cimarron Cravat's daughter—was different. She insisted on plain, smart tailored things. Young though she was, she was Oklahoma Women's Tennis Champion. She had lean, muscular arms, was slim flanked like a boy and practically stomachless. She had a curious trick of holding her head down and looking up at you under her lashes and when she did that you forgot her boyishness, for her lashes were like fern fronds, and her eyes an astounding ocean gray. She didn't seem to mind that her mother wore the blanket and was hatless. Ruby was rather handsome for a squaw, in a big, slow-moving way. Felice Cravat, everyone agreed, was a chip off the old block, and by that they meant Yancey Cravat—her grandfather, who was now something of a legend throughout Oklahoma. Young Cim and his Osage wife had had a second child, a boy—and they had called him Yancey. Young Yancey was a bewilderingly handsome mixture of a dozen types and forebears—Indian, Spanish, French. People said he was the image of his grandmother, Sabra Cravat. Others contended that he was his Indian mother over again—insolence and all. Still others would say, "You're crazy. He's old Yancey, born again. There, look, that's what I mean! They say he's so smart that the Osages believe he's one of their old gods come back to earth."

Donna Cravat, now Mrs. Tracy Wyatt, had tried to adopt one of her brother's children, being herself childless, but Cim and his wife had never consented. She was a case, that Donna. When Tracy Wyatt had divorced his wife to marry this girl, local feeling had been very much against her. Everyone had turned with sympathy to the abandoned middle-aged wife, but she had met their warmth with such vitriol that they finally came to believe the stories of how she had deviled old Tracy all through their marriage. They actually came to feel that he had been justified in taking to wife this young and fascinating girl. Certainly he seemed to take a new lease on life, lost five inches around the waistline, played polo, regained the good spirits of his dray-driving days, and made a great hit in London when Donna was presented at court. Besides, there was no withstanding the Wyatt money. Even in a country blasé of million-aires Tracy Wyatt's fortune was something to marvel about. Motoring through the Southwest you passed miles of Wyatt oil tanks, whole silent cities of monoliths, squatting on the prairies.

As for the Wyatt house—it wasn't a house at all, but a combination of the palace of Versailles and Grand Central Station in New York. A mile-long avenue of great elms, transported from England, led up to the mansion. There were tennis courts, golf links, polo fields, swimming pools. Whole paneled rooms had been brought from France. In the bathrooms were sunken tubs of rare marble. Bathrooms were the size of bedrooms, and bedrooms the size of ballrooms. There was a cooling system that could chill the air of every room in the house, even on the hottest Oklahoma day. When you entered the dining room you felt that here should be seated solemn diplomats in gold braid signing world treaties. Sixty gardeners manned the grounds. The house servants would have peopled a village.

Sabra Cravat came to visit her daughter's house occasionally. She would stand in the great central apartment before the portraits of her son's two children, Felice and Yancey Cravat. Donna had had them painted and hung there, one either side of the enormous fireplace. She had meant them to be a gift to her mother, but Sabra Cravat had refused to take them.

"Don't you like them, Sabra darling? They're the best things Segovia has ever done. I think they look like the kids—don't you?"

"They're just wonderful."

"Well, then?"

"I'd have to build a house for them. How would they look in the sitting room of the house on Kihekah Street! No, let me come here and look at them now and then. That way they're always a fresh surprise to me."

Segovia had got the face of little Felice well enough, but he had made the mistake of painting her in Spanish costume, and somehow her boyish frame had not lent itself to gorgeous lace and satin. The boy, Yancey, had refused to dress up for the occasion—had indeed been impatient of posing at all. Segovia had caught him quickly and brilliantly. He wore a pair of loose, rather grimy white tennis pants, a white sweater with a hole in the elbow. In his right hand—that slim, beautiful, speaking hand—he held a half-smoked cigarette, its dull red eye the only note of color in the picture. Yet the whole portrait was colorful, moving, alive. The boy's pose was insolent, lithe, careless. He was a person.

"Looks like Ruby, don't you think?" Donna had said when first she had shown it to her mother.

"No!" Sabra had replied, with vigor. "Not at all. Your father."

"Well—maybe—a little."

"A little! Look at his eyes. His hands. Of course they're not as beautiful as your father's hands were—are . . . "

It had been five years since Sabra had heard news of her husband. And now, for the first time, she felt that he was dead. She had heard that Yancey had gone to France during the war. The American and English

631

armies had rejected him, so he had dyed his graying hair, lied about his age, thrown back his magnificent shoulders, and somehow hypnotized them into taking him. An unofficial report had listed him among the missing after the carnage on a wooded plateau called the Argonne.

"He isn't dead," Sabra had said almost calmly. "When Yancey Cravat dies he'll be on the front page, and the world will know it."

The *Oklahoma Wigwam* now issued a morning as well as an afternoon edition. Its linotype room was a regiment of iron men, its staff boasted executive editor, editor in chief, managing editor, city editor, editor. When Sabra was in town she made a practice of driving down to the office at eleven every night, looking over the layout, reading the night's news lead, scanning the AP wires. Her entrance was in the nature of the passage of royalty. True, she wasn't there very much, except in the summer, when Congress was not in session.

The sight of a woman on the floor of the House of Representatives was still something of a novelty. Sentimental America had considered American womanhood too exquisite a flower to be subjected to the harsh atmosphere of active politics. But Sabra had stumped the state and developed a surprising gift of oratory.

"If American politics are too dirty for women to take part in, there's something wrong with American politics. . . . We weren't too delicate to cross the prairies in covered wagons and to stand the hardships of frontier life . . . here in this land the women have been the hewers of wood and drawers of water . . . thousands of unnamed heroines with weather-beaten faces and mud-caked boots . . . the sunbonnet as well as the sombrero has helped to settle this glorious land of ours. . . ."

It had been so many years since she had heard this speech that perhaps she actually thought she had originated it. Certainly it was received with tremendous emotional response, and it won her the election.

Perhaps, too, her appearance had something to do with it. A slim, straight, dignified woman, with soft dark eyes. Her white hair was shingled and beautifully waved. Her eyebrows had remained black and thick. Her dress was always becoming, and her silken ankles above the slim slippers with their cut-steel buckles were those of a young girl.

Her speeches were not altogether romantic. She knew her state. Its politics were notoriously rotten. Governor after governor was impeached with musical comedy regularity, and the impeachment proceedings stank to Washington. Sabra had statistics at her tongue's end. Millions of barrels of oil. Millions of tons of zinc. Third in mineral products. Coal. Gypsum. Granite.

In Washington she was quite a belle among the old boys in Congress and even the Senate. The opposition party tried to blackmail her with publicity about certain unproved items in the life of her dead (or missing) husband Yancey Cravat: a two-gun man, a desperado, a killer, a drunkard, a squaw man. Then they started on young Cim and his Osage Indian wife, but Sabra and Donna were too quick for them.

Donna Wyatt leased a handsome Washington house on Dupont Circle, brought Tracy Wyatt's vast wealth and influence to bear, and planned a coup so brilliant that it routed the enemy forever. She brought her handsome brother Cim and his wife Ruby Big Elk, and the youngsters Felice and Yancey, to the house on Dupont Circle, and together she and Sabra gave a reception for them.

Sabra and Donna, exquisitely dressed, stood in line at the head of the magnificent room, and between them stood Ruby Big Elk in an Indian dress of creamy white doeskin. She was an imposing figure; black abundant hair had taken on a mist of gray.

"My son's wife, Ruby Big Elk—Mrs. Cimarron Cravat."

"My sister-in-law, Mrs. Cimarron Cravat. A full blood Osage Indian . . . . Yes, indeed. We think so, too."

"How do you do?" said Ruby, in her calm, insolent way.

Ruby's next public appearance was made in a Paris gown. She became the rage, was considered picturesque, and left Washington in disgust, her work done. No one but her husband, whom she loved with doglike devotion, could have induced her to go through this ceremony.

Donna and Tracy Wyatt then hired a special train in which they took fifty potentates from the eastern United States on a tour of Oklahoma. One vague and not very bright Washington matron voiced her opinion to young Yancey Cravat, seated beside her at a country club luncheon.

"I had no idea Oklahoma was like this. I thought it was all oil and dirty Indians."

"There is quite a lot of oil, but we're not all dirty."

"We?"

"I'm an Indian."

On the roof of the Levy Mercantile Company's building Sol had built a penthouse. It was filled with the rarest rugs, books, hangings. There he lived, alone. At sunset, or in the early morning, he might be seen leaning over the parapet of his sky house like a gargoyle, brooding over the ridiculous city sprawled below; over the oil rigs that encircled it like giant Martian guards.

Money was now the only standard. If Pat Leary had sixty-two million dollars on Tuesday he was Oklahoma's leading citizen. If Tracy Wyatt had seventy-eight million dollars on Wednesday Tracy Wyatt was Oklahoma's leading citizen.

Sabra probably was the only woman of social position who still wore the plain gold wedding band of a long-past day. A slim platinum circlet was much more at ease among its emerald and diamond neighbors. She had not taken off her wedding band in over forty years. It was as much a part of her as the finger itself.

Osage began to rechristen streets, changing the native Indian names to commonplace American ones. Hetoappe Street became the Boston Road. The very nicest people were building out a ways in the new section (formerly Okemah Hill) called River View. The houses themselves were Italian palazzi or French châteaus or English manors; none, perhaps, quite so vast as Tracy Wyatt's, but all provided with such necessities as pipe organs, sunken baths, Greek temples, billiard rooms, and butlers.

Moving-picture palaces, with white-gloved ushers, had all the big films. The Arverne Grand Opera Company came for a whole week every year and performed the best of everything—*Traviata, La Bohème, Carmen*. The display of jewels during that week made the Diamond Horseshoe at the Metropolitan look like the Black Hole of Calcutta.

Still, oil was oil, and Indians were Indians. There was no way in which either of those native forces could quite be molded to fit the New York pattern. The Osages still whirled up and down the Oklahoma roads, crashing into ditches and culverts. They walked back to town and, entering the salesroom in which they had bought the original car, pointed at a new model. " 'Nother," they said succinctly. And drove out with it.

The Indian was considered legitimate prey, and thousands of prairie buzzards fed on his richness.

Sabra Cravat had introduced a bill for the further protection of the Osages, and rather took away the breath of the House by advocating abolition of the Indian reservation system. Her speech, radical though it was, was greeted with favor by some of the more liberal congressmen.

Oklahoma was proud of Sabra Cravat, editor, congresswoman, pioneer. Osage said she embodied the finest spirit of the state and of the Southwest. When ten of Osage's most unctuous millionaires contributed fifty thousand dollars each for a statue that should embody the Oklahoma Pioneer, no one was surprised to hear that the sculptor, Masja Krbecek, wanted to interview Sabra Cravat.

Krbecek turned out to be a quiet little man in eyeglasses, who looked more like a tailor than a sculptor. His eye roamed about Sabra's living room. The old wooden house had been covered with plaster in a deep warm shade much the color of the native clay; the porch and the cupolas had been torn away and a great square veranda and a terrace built at the side, screened by a thick hedge and an iron grille. It was now, in fact, much the house that Yancey had in mind years ago.

"You are very comfortable here in Oklahoma," said Masja Krbecek.

"It is a simple home," Sabra replied, "compared to the other places you have seen hereabouts."

"It is the home of a good woman," said Krbecek. "You are a Congress member, you are editor of a great newspaper, you are well known through the country. You American women, you are really amazing."

Sabra thanked him primly.

"Tell me, will you, my dear lady," he went on, "about your life and that of your husband, this Yancey Cravat who so far preceded his time."

So Sabra told him. Somehow, as she talked, the years rolled back. She showed him the time-yellowed photographs of Yancey, of herself. Krbecek listened. At the end, "It is touching," he said. Then he kissed her hand and went away, taking one or two of the old photographs with him.

The statue of the Spirit of the Oklahoma Pioneer was unveiled a year later. It was a heroic figure of Yancey Cravat stepping forward with that light graceful stride in the high-heeled Texas star boots, the skirts of the Prince Albert billowing behind, the sombrero atop the great buffalo head, one hand resting lightly on the weapon in his holster. Behind him, one hand just touching his shoulder for support, stumbled the weary, blanketed figure of an Indian.

SABRA CRAVAT, Congresswoman from Oklahoma, had started a campaign against the disgraceful condition of the new oil towns. With a party of twenty made up of oil men, senators, congressmen, and news editors, she led the way to Bowlegs, newest of the new oil strikes.

635

Another shantytown had sprung up on the prairie. Dance halls. Brothels. Gunmen. Brawls. Dirt. Crime. The roar of traffic boiling over a road never meant for more than a plodding wagon. Nitroglycerin cars bearing their deadly freight. The human scum of each new oil town was like the scum of the Run, but harder, crueler, more wolfish and degraded.

Sabra's imposing party, in high-powered motorcars, bumped over the terrible roads, creating a red dust barrage.

"It is all due to our rotten Oklahoma politics," Sabra explained to the great senator from Pennsylvania who sat beside her. "Our laws are laughed at. The capitol is rotten with graft. Anything goes. Oklahoma is still a Territory in everything but title. This town of Bowlegs is a throw-back to the frontier days of forty years ago—and worse. It's like the old Cimarron. People in Osage don't know what goes on out here. They don't care. It's more oil, more millions. That's all."

The Pennsylvania senator laughed a plump laugh. "What they need out here is a woman governor."

Arrived at Bowlegs, Sabra showed them everything, pitilessly. The dreadful town lay in the hot June sun, a scarred thing, flies buzzing over it, the oil drooling down its face, a slimy stream.

A red-cheeked young Harvard engineer was their guide: an engaging boy in bone-rimmed glasses and a blue shirt that made his pink cheeks pinker. That is what I wanted Cim to be, Sabra thought with a great wrench at her heart.

The drilling of the oil. The workmen's shanties. The trial, in the stifling one-room shack that served as courtroom, of a dance-hall girl charged with nonpayment of rent. The little room was already crowded. The judge was a yellow-faced fellow with a cud of tobacco in his cheek. The jurors were nine in number, their faces a rogues' gallery, men who had happened to be loafing nearby. The defendant was a tiny rat-faced girl in a soiled green dress. Her friends were there—a dozen or more dance-hall girls in striped overalls or knee-length gingham dresses. Their ages ranged from sixteen to nineteen, perhaps. It was incredible that life, in those few years, could have etched that look on their faces.

The girls were charming, hospitable, to the imposing visitors. "Come on in," they said. "How-do!" Clustered behind the rude bench on which the jury sat, the girls from time to time leaned a sociable elbow on a juryman's shoulder, occasionally speaking in defense of their sister.

"She never done no such thing!"

636

"He's a damn liar, an' I can prove it."

No one, least of all the tobacco-chewing judge, appeared to find these girlish informalities unusual. The jurors filed out and repaired to a draw at the side of the road to make their finding. Almost immediately they filed back. Not guilty.

The dance-hall girls cheered feebly.

Out of that fetid air into the late afternoon blaze. "The dance halls open about nine," Sabra said. "We'll wait for that. In the meantime I'll show you their rooms. Their rooms—" she looked about for the fresh-cheeked Harvard boy. "Why, where—"

"There's some kind of excitement," said a New York newsman. "People have been running to that field we visited a while ago. Here comes our young friend now. Perhaps he'll tell us."

The Harvard boy's color was higher still. He was breathing fast. He had been running. His eyes shone behind the bone-rimmed spectacles.

"Well, folks, we'll never have a narrower squeak than that."

"What?"

"They put fifty quarts in the Gypsy pool but before she got down the oil came up—"

"Quarts of what?" interrupted an editorial voice.

"Oh—excuse me—quarts of nitroglycerin."

"My God!"

"It's in a can, you know. It never had a chance to explode down there. It just shot up with the gas and oil. If it had hit the ground everything for miles around would have been shot to hell and all of us killed. But he caught it. They say he just ran back like an outfielder and gauged it with his eye and ran to where it would fall. He caught it in his two arms, like a baby, right on his chest. It didn't explode. But he's dying. Chest all caved in. They sent for the ambulance."

"Who? Who's he?"

"I don't know his real name. He's an old bum that's been around the field, doing odd jobs. They say he used to be quite a fellow in Oklahoma in his day. Picturesque pioneer or something. Some call him old Yance and I've heard others call him Cim—"

Sabra began to run across the road.

"Mrs. Cravat! You mustn't—where are you going?"

She ran on, across the oil-soaked field and the dirt, in her high-heeled slippers. She did not even know that she was running. The crowd was dense around some central object. They formed a wall, gazing down at something on the ground.

"Let me by! Let me by!" They fell back before this white-faced woman with the white hair.

He lay on the ground, a crumpled, broken figure. She flung herself on the earth beside him and lifted his head gently, so that it lay cushioned by her arm. A little bubble rose to his lips, and she wiped it away with her handkerchief. "Yancey! Yancey!"

He opened his eyes—those ocean-gray eyes with the long lashes. She had thought of them often and often, in an agony of pain. Glazed now, unseeing. Then, dying, they cleared. His lips moved. He knew her. Even then, dying, he must speak in measured verse. " 'Wife and mother—you stainless woman—hide me—hide me in your love!' "

She had never heard a line of it. She did not know that this was Peer Gynt, humbled before Solveig. The eyes glazed, stared; were eyes no longer. She closed them, gently. She forgave him everything. Quite simply, all unknowing, she murmured through her tears the very words of Solveig. "Sleep, my boy, my dearest boy."

ACKNOWLEDGMENTS:

The condensations in this volume have been created by The Reader's Digest Association, Inc., and are used by permission of and special arrangement with the publishers and the holders of the respective copyrights.

Young Pioneers, by Rose Wilder Lane, copyright © 1933, 1961 by Roger MacBride Productions, Inc., and Ed Friendly Productions, Inc.
Miss Morissa, Doctor of the Gold Trail, copyright 1955 by Mari Sandoz, renewed © 1983 by Carolyn Pifer, is used by permission of McIntosh and Otis, Inc., on behalf of the author's estate.
Giants in the Earth, copyright 1929 by O.E. Rölvaag, renewed © 1954 by Jeanne Marie Berdahl Rölvaag, is used by permission of Harper & Row, Publishers, Inc.
In the Hands of the Senecas, copyright 1937 by The Curtis Publishing Company, renewed © 1964, 1965 by Walter D. Edmonds, is used by permission of Harold Ober Associates, Inc.
A Very Small Remnant, copyright © 1963 by Michael Straight, is used by permission of the author.
Cimarron, copyright 1929, 1930, renewed © 1957, 1958 by Edna Ferber, is used by permission of the author's estate.

PICTURE CREDITS:

Pages 2–3: reproduced by permission of The Henry E. Huntington Library and Art Gallery, San Marino, California.
Pages 4–5: reproduced by permission of the Western History Collections, University of Oklahoma Library.
Pages 8, 56, 200, 386, 458, 520: maps by George Buctel.